BRETHREN

ROBYN YOUNG

BRETHREN

HODDER &
STOUGHTON

Copyright © 2006 by Robyn Young

First published in Great Britain in 2006 by Hodder & Stoughton
A division of Hodder Headline

The right of Robyn Young to be identified as the Author
of the Work has been asserted by her in accordance with
the Copyright, Designs and Patents Act 1988.

A Hodder & Stoughton book

1

A CIP catalogue record for this title is available from the British Library

Hardback ISBN 0 340 83969 4
Trade Paperback ISBN 0 340 83970 8

Map © Sandra Oakins

Typeset in Perpetua by Hewer Text UK Ltd, Edinburgh
Printed and bound by Clays Ltd, St Ives plc

Hodder Headline's policy is to use papers that are natural, renewable
and recyclable products and made from wood grown in sustainable forests.
The logging and manufacturing processes are expected to conform
to the environmental regulations of the country of origin.

Hodder & Stoughton Ltd
A division of Hodder Headline
338 Euston Road
London NW1 3BH

ACKNOWLEDGEMENTS

Firstly, thank you, reader, for reading this page when you have no idea who these people are. Just know that without them this book would not be here.

Thanks and love to my mum and dad for all the support over the years. You both made following this dream much easier. Thanks also to the rest of my family, in particular my grandfather, Ken Young, for the stories.

Big thanks to all my friends (you know who you are) for continual encouragement and for helping me to have a life away from my computer, with special thanks to Jo and my second family, Sue and Dave. Much love to fellow writers, Clare, Liz, Niall and Monica, for their invaluable support, emotionally and editorially. Also thanks to my friends and tutors at Sussex University for their excellent guidance and to Sophia for correcting a certain Latin slip.

My gratitude to my agent, Rupert Heath, for the act of faith, tireless, insightful advice, extracting my Yoda-isms and much laughter. Much appreciation to my editor, Nick Sayers, his assistant, Anne Clarke, and the rest of the fantastic team at Hodder & Stoughton for the warm welcome, their enthusiasm and commitment, and Nick's editorial gems. Thanks also to my American editor, Julie Doughty, at Dutton, for coming in at the eleventh hour with some great suggestions.

Thanks to Amal al-Ayoubi at the School of Oriental and African Studies for checking my Arabic and a huge thank you to Mark Philpott of the Centre for Medieval & Renaissance Studies and Keble College, Oxford for checking the manuscript and saving an amateur from looking too histori-cally challenged. Any mistakes within these pages remain, unfortunately, my own.

Lastly, and most of all, my love to Lee, for all the above and everything else.

CONTENTS

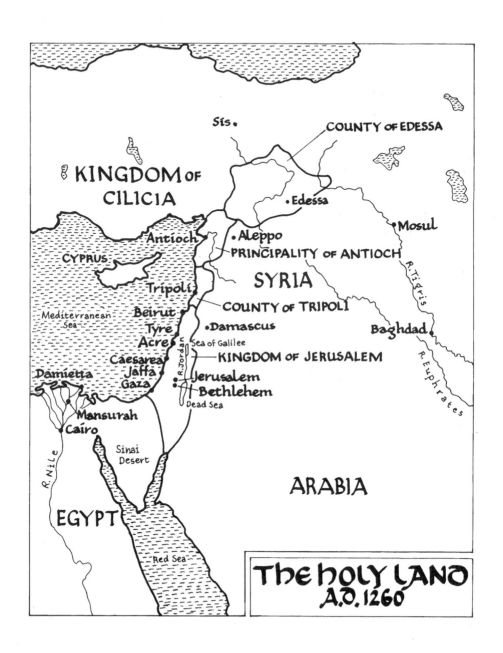

Sis

COUNTY OF EDESSA

KINGDOM OF CILICIA

Edessa

Mosul

Antioch

Aleppo

CYPRUS

PRINCIPALITY OF ANTIOCH

SYRIA

Tripoli

COUNTY OF TRIPOLI

R. Tigris

Mediterranean Sea

Beirut
Tyre
Acre

Damascus

Baghdad

Caesarea
Jaffa
Gaza

Sea of Galilee

KINGDOM OF JERUSALEM

R. Jordan

Damietta

Jerusalem
Bethlehem

R. Euphrates

Dead Sea

Mansurah
Cairo

Sinai Desert

ARABIA

R. Nile

EGYPT

Red Sea

THE HOLY LAND
A.D. 1260

PROLOGUE

From The Book of the Grail

Brighter than the sun this lake,
Boiling as a cauldron deep,
And though no thing alive could stand
This fiery furnace, molten hot,
Perceval glimpsed creatures there,
Most dark and dreadful to behold.
Writhing beneath the seething surface,
Flames of crimson; amber; gold,
Were things of wing and fang and talon,
As though from the abyss had crawled.
But on the shore there stood a knight,
Adorned in mantle, vestal white,
A red cross on his chest emblazoned,
A holy light around him shining.
To Perceval this knight did turn,
He raised his arm towards the lake,
And in a stern, commanding tone
Bade Perceval cast the treasures in.

Perceval stood still as stone,
His heart went cold, his fingers froze,
He felt he couldn't bear to throw
The precious treasures from his hands.
Then the knight did speak once more
His voice an arrow driving deep;
We are brothers, Perceval,
Your Brethren would not lead you wrong.
All that is lost will be restored.

All that is dead will live again.
And Perceval, his faith returned,
Did lean and cast the treasures in.
The cross of bright, unalloyed gold
Yellow as the morning sun;
The candlestick of seven prongs
Of beaten silver, shimmering;
Last the crescent of hammered lead
Its rough-hewn surface shadow-dark.

All at once there rose a song
From many voices joined as one.
Borne on a breeze, sweet and pure,
They filled the sky like breaking dawn.
Now the lake was fire no more
But tranquil blue of water clear,
And from it came a man of gold
With silver eyes and lead-black hair.
Perceval fell upon his knees
And wept and wept for utter joy.
He raised his head and thrice aloud,
Hail to thee O Lord! *he cried.*

PART ONE

I

Ayn Jalut (The Pools of Goliath), the Kingdom of Jerusalem

3 September 1260 AD

T he sun was approaching its zenith, dominating the sky and turning the deep ochre of the desert to a bleached bone-white. Buzzards circled the crowns of the hills that ringed the plain of Ayn Jalut and their abrasive cries hung on the air, caught in the solidity of the heat. On the western edge of the plain, where the hills stretched their bare limbs down to the sands, were two thousand men on armoured horses. Their swords and shields gleamed, the steel too hot to touch, and although their surcoats and turbans did little to protect them from the sun's savagery no one spoke of his discomfort.

Mounted on a black horse at the vanguard of the Bahri regiment, Baybars Bundukdari, their commander, reached for the water skin that was fastened to his belt beside two sabres, the blades of which were notched and pitted with use. After taking a draught he rolled his shoulders to loosen the stiffened joints. The band of his white turban was wet with sweat and the coat of mail that he wore beneath his blue cloak felt unusually heavy. The morning was wearing on, the heat gaining in strength, and although the water soothed Baybars' dry throat it couldn't quench a deeper thirst that blistered within him.

'Amir Baybars,' murmured one of the younger officers mounted beside him. 'Time is passing. The scouting party should have returned by now.'

'They will return soon, Ismail. Have patience.' As Baybars re-tied the water skin to his belt, he studied the silent ranks of the Bahri regiment that lined the sands behind him. The faces of his men all wore the same grim expression he had seen in many front lines before battle. Soon those expressions would change. Baybars had seen the boldest warriors pale when confronted with a line of enemy fighters that mirrored their own. But when the time came they would fight without hesitation, for they were soldiers of the Mamluk army: the slave warriors of Egypt.

'Amir?'

'What is it, Ismail?'

'We've heard no word from the scouts since dawn. What if they've been captured?'

Baybars frowned and Ismail wished he had remained silent.

On the whole, there was nothing particularly striking about Baybars; like most of his men he was tall and sinewy with dark-brown hair and cinnamon skin. But his gaze was exceptional. A defect, which appeared as a white star in the centre of his left pupil, gave his stare a peculiar keenness; one of the attributes that had earned him his sobriquet – the Crossbow. The junior officer Ismail, finding himself the focus of those barbed blue eyes, felt like a fly in the web of a spider.

'As I said, have patience.'

'Yes, Amir.'

Baybars' gaze softened a little as Ismail bowed his head. It wasn't many years ago that Baybars himself had waited in the front line of his first battle. The Mamluks had faced the Franks on a dusty plain near a village called Herbiya. He had led the cavalry in the attack and within hours the enemy was crushed, the blood of the Christians staining the sands. Today, God willing, it would be the same.

In the distance, a faint twisting column of dust rose from the plain. Slowly, it began to take the shape of seven riders, their forms distorted by the rippling heat haze. Baybars kicked his heels into the flanks of his horse and surged out of the ranks, followed by his officers.

As the scouting party approached, riding fast, the leader turned his horse towards Baybars. Pulling sharply on the reins he came to a halt before the commander. The beast's tan coat was stained with sweat, its muzzle flecked with foam. 'Amir Baybars,' panted the rider, saluting. 'The Mongols are coming.'

'How large is the force?'

'One of their toumans, Amir.'

'Ten thousand. And their leader?'

'They are led by the general, Kitbogha, as our information suggested.'

'They saw you?'

'We made certain of it. The advance isn't far behind us and the main army follows them closely.' The patrol leader trotted his horse closer to Baybars and lowered his voice, so that the other officers had to strain to hear him. 'Their might is great, Amir, and they have brought many engines of war, yet our intelligence suggests it is but one third of their army.'

'If you cut off the head of the beast, the body will fall,' replied Baybars.

The strident wail of a Mongol horn sounded in the distance. Others quickly joined it until a shrill, discordant chorus was ringing across the hills. The Mamluk horses, sensing the tension in their riders, began to snort and whinny. Baybars nodded to the leader of the patrol, then turned to his officers. 'On my signal sound the retreat.' He motioned to Ismail. 'You will ride with me.'

'Yes, Amir,' replied Ismail, the pride clear in his face.

For ten, twenty seconds the only sounds that could be heard were the distant horns and the restless sighing of the wind across the plain. A pall of dust cloaked the sky in the east as the first lines of the Mongol force appeared on the ridges of the hills. The riders paused briefly on the summit and then they came, flowing onto the plain like a sea of darkness, the flash of sunlight on steel glittering above the black tide.

Behind the advance came the main army, led by light-horsemen wielding spears and bows, and then Kitbogha himself. Flanking the Mongol leader on all sides were veteran warriors, clad in iron helms and lamellar armour fashioned from sheets of rawhide, bound with strips of leather. Each man had two spare horses and behind this thundering column rolled siege engines and wagons laden with the riches pillaged in the Mongols' raids on towns and cities. The wagons were driven by women who carried great bows upon their backs. The Mongols' founder, Genghis Khan, had died thirty-three years ago, but the might of his warrior empire lived on in the force that now faced the Mamluks.

Baybars had been anticipating this confrontation for months, but his hunger for it had gnawed at him for much longer. Twenty years had passed since the Mongols had invaded his homeland, ravaging his tribe's lands and livestock; twenty years since his people had been forced to flee the attack and request the aid of a neighbouring chieftain who had betrayed them and sold them to the slave traders of Syria. But it wasn't until several months ago, when a Mongol emissary had arrived in Cairo, that an opportunity for Baybars to seek revenge upon the people who had precipitated his delivery into slavery had arisen.

The emissary had come to demand that Kutuz, the Mamluk sultan, submit to Mongol rule and it was this imposition, above and beyond the Mongols' recent devastating assault on the Muslim-ruled city of Baghdad, that had finally spurred the sultan to act. The Mamluks bowed to no one except Allah. Whilst Kutuz and his military governors, Baybars included, had set about planning their reprisal, the Mongol emissary had had a few days to reflect upon his mistake buried up to his neck in sand outside Cairo's walls, before the sun and the buzzards had finished their work. Now Baybars would teach a similar lesson to those who had sent him.

Baybars waited until the front lines of the heavy cavalry were halfway across the plain, then wheeled his horse around to face his men. Drawing one of his sabres from its scabbard he thrust it high above his head. Sunlight caught the curved blade and it shone like a star.

'Warriors of Egypt,' he shouted. 'Our time is now at hand and with this victory we will build of our enemy a pile of corpses that will be higher than these hills and wider than the desert.'

'To victory!' roared the soldiers of the Bahri regiment. 'In the name of Allah!'

As one, they turned from the approaching army and urged their horses towards the hills. The Mongols, thinking their enemy was fleeing in terror, whooped as they gave chase.

The western line of hills that bordered the plain was shallow and broad. A cleft divided them, forming a wide gorge. Baybars and his men plunged through this opening, riding furiously, and the first riders of the Mongol advance came charging through the clouds of dust that choked the air in the wake of the Mamluk horses. The main Mongol army followed, funnelling through into the gorge, causing loose rock and sand to shower down from the hillsides with the tremor of their passing. The Bahri regiment, at a signal from Baybars, reined in their horses and turned, forming a barrier to block the Mongols' approach. Suddenly, the blare of many horns and the cacophonous thudding of kettledrums echoed through the gully.

A figure, dark against the glare of the sun, had appeared on one of the ridges above the gorge. The figure was Kutuz. He was not alone. With him on the ridge, poised above the valley floor, were thousands of Mamluk soldiers. The cavalry, many of them archers, were ranked in sections of colour, marking the various regiments: purple; scarlet; orange; black. It was as if the hills wore a vast, patchwork cloak that was threaded with silver wherever spearheads or helms caught the light. Infantry waited bearing swords, maces and bows, and a small but deadly corps of Bedouin and Kurdish mercenaries flanked the main force in two wings, bristling with seven-foot-long spears.

Now the Mongols were caught in Baybars' trap all he had to do was tighten the noose.

After the sounding of the horns came a war cry from the Mamluks, the roar of their combined voices drowning, momentarily, the kettledrums'

pulse. The Mamluk cavalry charged. Some horses fell on the descent in a
billow of dust, the cries of riders lost in the ground-shuddering thunder of
hooves. Many more hurtled towards their targets as two Mamluk regiments
swept onto the plain of Ayn Jalut to herd the last of the Mongol forces into
the passage. Baybars swung his sabre above his head and yelled as he
charged. The men of the Bahri regiment took up his cry.

'*Allahu akbar! Allahu akbar!*'

The two armies met in a storm of dust and screams and the clang of steel. In
the first seconds, hundreds from both sides went down and the dead clogged
up the ground, making treacherous footing for those left standing. Horses
reared, throwing their riders into the chaos and men shrieked as they died,
spraying the air with blood. The Mongols were renowned for their horse-
manship, but the passage was too narrow for them to manoeuvre effectively.
Whilst the Mamluks drove relentlessly into the main body of the army, a line
of Bedouin cavalry prevented the Mongol advance from outflanking them.
Arrows hissed down from the hillsides and once in a while an orange ball of
flame would explode across the melee as the Mamluk troops hurled clay pots
filled with naphtha. The Mongols hit by these missiles flamed like torches,
screaming hideously as their horses ran wild, spreading fire and confusion
through the ranks.

Baybars swung one of his sabres in a vicious arc as he swept into the fray,
taking a man's head clean from his shoulders with the momentum of the
blow. Another Mongol, face splattered with the blood of his fallen
comrade, took the dead man's place immediately. Baybars lashed out
with his blades as his horse was knocked and jostled beneath him and more
and more men poured into the turmoil. Ismail was at Baybars' side,
drenched in blood and shrieking as he thrust his sword through the visor of a
Mongol's helm. The blade stuck fast for a moment, buried in the man's
skull, before the officer wrenched it free and searched for another target.

Baybars' sabres danced in his hands, two more warriors falling under his
hammering blows.

Kitbogha, the Mongol general, was fighting savagely, swinging his sword
in tremendous haymaker strokes that were cleaving skulls and tearing limbs
and even though he was surrounded no one seemed able to touch him.
Baybars' thoughts were on the bounty that awaited the man who captured
or killed the enemy lord, but a wall of fighting and a hedge of arcing blades
blocked his path. He ducked as a feral youth rushed him, whirling a mace,
and forgot about Kitbogha as he concentrated on staying alive.

After the first lines had fallen or been beaten back, Mongol women and children were fighting alongside the men. Although the Mamluks knew that the wives and daughters of the Mongol men fought in battle, it was a sight, nonetheless, that caused some to falter. The women, with their long, wild hair and snarling faces, fought just as well as and perhaps even more fiercely than the men. A Mamluk commander, fearing the effect on the troops, raised his voice above the din and sent out a rallying cry that was soon taken up by others. The name of Allah filled the air, reverberating off the hills and ringing in the ears of the Mamluks, as their arms found new strength and their swords new purchase. Any compunction was lost in the heat of battle and the Mamluks cut through all those who stood against them. To the slave warriors, the Mongol army had become an anonymous beast, ageless and sexless, that had to be taken piece by piece if it were to perish.

Eventually, the sword strokes grew sluggish. Men, unhorsed and locked together in combat, leaned on one another for support as they parried each blow. Groans and cries were punctuated by screams as swords found slowing targets. The Mongols had led a final storm against the infantry, hoping to break through the barrier and ride in behind the Mamluks, but the foot soldiers held their ground and only a handful of the Mongol cavalry had penetrated the line of spears. They had been met by Mamluk riders and were dispatched instantly. Kitbogha had gone down, his horse pulled over by the sheer press of men around him. Victorious, the Mamluks had severed his head and flaunted it before his broken forces. The Mongols, who had been called the terror of nations, were losing. But, more importantly, they knew it.

Baybars' horse, pierced in the neck by a stray arrow, had thrown him and bolted. He fought on foot, his boots slick with blood. The blood was everywhere. It was in the air and in his mouth, it was dripping through his beard and the hilts of his sabres were slippery with it. He lunged forward and hacked at another man. The Mongol slumped to the sand with a cry that ceased abruptly and when no one took his place Baybars paused.

Dust had obscured the sun and turned the air yellow. A gust of wind scattered the clouds and Baybars saw, flying high above the Mongols' carts and siege engines, the flag of surrender. Looking around him, all he could see were piles of bodies. The reek of blood and opened corpses was thick on the air and already the carrion eaters were shrieking their own triumph in the skies above. The fallen lay sprawled across one another, and among the leather breastplates of the enemy were the bright cloaks of the Mamluks. In one pile, close by, Ismail lay on his back, his chest cleaved by a Mongol sword.

Baybars went over. He bent to close the young man's eyes, then rose as one of his officers hailed him. The warrior was bleeding heavily from a gash at his temple and his eyes were wild, unfocused. 'Amir,' he said hoarsely. 'Your orders?'

Baybars surveyed the devastation. In just a few hours they had destroyed the Mongol army, killing over seven thousand of them. Some Mamluks had fallen to their knees, crying with relief, but more were roaring their triumph as they made their way towards the survivors who had rallied around the discarded carts. Baybars knew that he would have to regain control of his men, or their jubilation might incite them to plunder the enemy's treasure and kill the survivors. The remaining Mongols, especially the women and children, would fetch a considerable sum in the slave markets. He pointed to the Mongol survivors. 'Oversee their submission and see that no one is killed. We want slaves we can sell, not more corpses to burn.'

The officer hurried across the sands to relay the command. Baybars sheathed his sword and looked around for a horse. Finding a riderless beast with bloodstained trappings, he mounted and rode over to his troops. Around him, other Mamluk commanders were addressing their own regiments. Baybars looked out across the weary yet defiant faces of the Bahri and felt the first stirrings of exultation swell within him. 'Brothers,' he shouted, the words sticking in his parched throat. 'Allah has shined upon us this day. We stand triumphant in His glory, our enemy vanquished.' He paused as the cheers rose, then lifted his hand for silence. 'But our celebrations must wait for there is much to be done. Look to your officers.'

The cheers continued, but, already, the troops were forming into some semblance of order. Baybars headed over to his officers and gestured to two of them. 'I want the bodies of our men buried before sundown. Burn the Mongol dead and search the area for any who may have tried to flee. Have the wounded carried to our camp, I'll meet you there when it's done.' Baybars scanned the devastation for Kutuz. 'Where is the sultan?'

'He retired to the camp about an hour ago, Amir,' replied one of the officers. 'He was wounded in the battle.'

'Badly?'

'No, Amir, I believe the injury was a minor one. He is with his physicians.'

Baybars dismissed the officers and rode over to the captives, who were being rounded up. The Mamluks were ransacking the carts and throwing anything of value into a mounting pile on the crimson sands. A scream sounded as two soldiers dragged three children out from their hiding place beneath a wagon. A woman, Baybars guessed to be their mother, leapt up and ran across to them. Even with her hands tied behind her back she was ferocious, spitting like a snake and kicking out with her bare feet. One of the soldiers silenced her with his fists and then hauled her and two of the children by the hair to the swelling group of prisoners. Baybars looked down on the captives and met the terrified gaze of a young boy who was kneeling before him. In the boy's wide, bewildered eyes, he saw himself, twenty years ago, staring back.

Born as a Kipchak Turk on the shores of the Black Sea, Baybars had known nothing of war, or slavery before the Mongols' invasion. After being separated from his family and auctioned in the Syrian markets, he had been enslaved by four masters before an officer in the Egyptian army had purchased him and taken him to Cairo to be trained as a slave warrior. In the Mamluk camp on the Nile, along with many other boys who had been bought for the sultan's military, he was clothed, armed and taught to fight. Now, at thirty-seven, he commanded the formidable Bahris. But even with chests of gold and slaves of his own, the recollections of his first year in servitude were bitter memories that he tasted daily.

Baybars gestured to one of the men presiding over the arrests. 'Make sure all the spoils arrive in camp. Any man who steals from the sultan will regret it. Use the damaged engines as fuel for the pyres and take the rest.'

'As you command, Amir.'

The hooves of his horse churning the red sands, Baybars headed for the Mamluk encampment, where Sultan Kutuz would be waiting for him. His body was leaden, but his heart was light. For the first time since the Mongols had begun their invasion of Syria, the Mamluks had turned the tide. It wouldn't take them long to crush the rest of the horde and once that was done, Kutuz would be free to turn his attention to a more critical matter. Baybars smiled. It was a rare expression that looked foreign on his face.

2

Saint-Martin's Gate, Paris

3 September 1260 AD

The young clerk sprinted down the alley, his breath coming in ragged bursts. His feet skidded in slimy pools of mud and night soil that coated the ground; his nose was clogged with the stink of human waste and rotting food. He slipped, threw out a hand to grab the sharp flint wall of the building beside him, caught his balance and ran on. To his left, between the buildings, he caught a glimpse of the wide blackness of the Seine. The eastern sky was beginning to lighten, the tower of Notre Dame reflecting the faint gleam of dawn, but in the labyrinth of alleyways that crisscrossed between the wharf houses and tenements it was still midnight. His hair plastered to his head with sweat, the clerk headed away from the river and north towards Saint-Martin's Gate. Every so often, he risked a glance over his shoulder. But he saw no one and the only footsteps he heard were his own.

Once he handed over the book he would be free. By the time the bells rang for Prime he would be on his way to Rouen and a new life. He paused in the mouth of an alley and bent forward straining for breath, one hand on his thigh, the other clutching a vellum-bound book. A movement caught his eye. A tall man dressed in a grey cloak had appeared at the other end of the alley and was striding towards him. The young clerk turned and ran.

He zigzagged between buildings, intent on losing those footsteps now echoing after his own. But his pursuer was dogged and the distance between them was closing. The city walls were rising ahead. His hand tightened around the book. It meant a sentence, whether of death or imprisonment he wasn't sure, but without evidence they might not be able to convict. The clerk darted down a narrow passage between two rows of shops. Outside the back door of a wine seller's several casks were stacked in a neat row. The clerk looked over his shoulder. He heard the footsteps, but couldn't see his pursuer yet. Dropping the vellum-bound book behind the casks, he ran on. He could always double back to collect it, if he escaped.

He didn't.

The clerk made it down three more streets before he was caught outside a butcher's, where the ground was stained red with the previous day's slaughter. He yelled as the tall man in the threadbare grey cloak pinned him roughly against the wall.

'Give it to me!' The man's words were masked by a thick accent and even though he wore the cloak's cowl pulled low over his face the dark tone of his skin was apparent.

'Are you mad? Let go of me!' gasped the clerk, struggling vainly.

His attacker drew a dagger. 'I have no time for games. Give me the book.'

'Don't kill me! Please!'

'We know you stole it,' said the man, raising the dagger.

The clerk heaved in a shuddering breath. 'I had to! He said he would . . .! Oh, dear God!' The clerk hung his head and began to cry. 'I don't want to die!'

'Who made you take it?'

But the clerk just continued sobbing.

With a gruff sigh the attacker stepped back and sheathed the dagger. 'I will not harm you, if you tell me what I need to know.'

The young clerk looked up, eyes wide. 'You followed me from the preceptory?'

'Yes.'

'The man I . . . Jean? Is he . . .?' The clerk trailed off, tears streaming down his cheeks.

'He is alive.'

The clerk exhaled sharply.

There was a clatter somewhere behind them. The man in grey turned, his dark eyes scanning the buildings. Seeing nothing, he looked back at the clerk. 'Give me the book and we can return to the preceptory together. I will see you come to no harm if you tell me the truth. Start by telling me who forced you to steal it.'

The clerk paused, then opened his mouth. There was a sharp *click*, followed by a soft whistle. The man in grey ducked instinctively. A second later the bolt from a crossbow had buried itself in the clerk's throat. His eyes widened, but he didn't make a noise as he crumpled to the ground. The man in grey spun round in time to see a shadow move across the dark rooftops above the passage, then vanish. He cursed and dropped down beside the clerk, whose legs were shaking violently. 'Where have you put the book? *Where?*'

The clerk's mouth opened and blood came out. His legs stopped thrashing, his head lolled back. The man in grey cursed again and searched the body, even though it was obvious the young man had nothing on him but the clothes he was wearing. He looked up, hearing voices. Three men were moving through the alley. They were wearing the scarlet cloaks of the city watch.

'Who's down there?' called one, raising the torch he held, the flames quivering in the breeze. 'You there!' shouted the guard, seeing a shadowy figure bent over something on the ground.

Not heeding their commands for him to halt, the man in grey began to run.

'After him!' the guard with the torch ordered his comrades. He went closer and swore as the flames revealed the dead clerk's black tunic with the splayed red cross of the Temple on the chest.

A few streets away, a wine merchant by the name of Antoine de Pont-Evêque was in his shop, sighing over some muddled accounts, when he heard the shouts. Curious, he left his table, opened the back door and peered out. The alley was empty, the sky above the rooftops pale with morning. The shouting was fading. Antoine, yawning deeply, turned to go back inside. He stopped, his eye drawn to something on the ground. It was half hidden by the row of empty wine casks and he doubted he would have noticed it at all if not for the fact that it glinted when the light caught it. With a grunt, Antoine stooped to pick it up. It was a book, fairly thick and neatly bound in polished vellum. The writing on the cover was done in shimmering gold-leaf. Antoine couldn't read the words, but the book was beautifully crafted and he couldn't imagine how anyone could discard, or lose such an expensive-looking item. He had a moment's thought of putting it back, but after a quick, guilty look around, he took it inside his shop and shut the door. Pleased by his find, Antoine put the book on a dusty, cluttered shelf beneath his counter and returned reluctantly to his accounts. He would ask his brother, if the rogue ever visited, to tell him what it was about.

New Temple, London, 3 September 1260 AD

Inside the chapter house of New Temple, a company of knights had gathered for the initiation. They sat in silence on the benches, facing a raised dais upon which was an altar. Kneeling alone on the flagstones, his back to the knights and his head bowed before the altar, was an eighteen-year-old sergeant. His standard black tunic had been discarded and his bare chest was stained amber in the candlelight. The frail flames, spluttering in their sconces on the walls, were unable to dispel the perpetual gloom of the inner chamber and most of the assembly was shrouded in shadows. Aided by two clerics dressed in black, a priest ascended the steps of the dais. He stood before the company, clasping a leatherbound book, as the clerics prepared the altar. After they had arrayed the holy vessels, the clerics stepped back behind the altar where two knights were waiting, clad, as all Templars, in long white surcoats with a splayed red cross emblazoned across their hearts.

The priest cleared his throat and surveyed the company. '*Ecce quam bonum et quam jocundum habitare fratres in unum.*'

'Amen,' replied a chorus of voices.

The priest looked out across them. 'In the name of our Lord, Jesus Christ, and in the name of Mary, most Divine Mother, I welcome you, my brothers. As one we are gathered here for this holy rite and so, as one, let us proceed.' He turned his gaze upon the genuflecting sergeant. 'For what purpose have you come here?'

The sergeant strove to remember the words he was supposed to say, which he had learnt during his night in vigil. 'I come to deliver myself, body and spirit, unto the Temple.'

'In whose name do you deliver yourself?'

'In the name of God and in the name of Hugues de Payns, founder of our holy Order, who, forsaking this life of sin and darkness, cast from him his worldly duties and . . .' The sergeant paused, heart racing. 'And taking up the mantle and the cross journeyed to Outremer, the land beyond the sea, to take sword and fire to the infidel. And who, once there, swore to keep safe all Christian pilgrims on their paths through the Holy Land.'

'Do you now wish to accept the mantle of the Temple, knowing that in doing so you too shall cast away your worldly duties and, following in the footsteps of our founder, become a true and humble servant of Almighty God?' When the sergeant gave his affirmation, the priest took a clay pot from the altar and carefully deposited its contents into a gold censer. The resinous mixture of frankincense and myrrh ignited as it touched the charcoals and a plume of smoke swirled up to engulf him. He coughed and stepped back. Behind him, the two knights came forward.

One of the knights drew his sword from its scabbard and pointed it towards the sergeant. 'See you us now, clad in fine raiment and armed with mighty weapons? Look in wisdom at these things, for you see with eyes that cannot see and heart that cannot comprehend the austerities of our Order. For when you wish to be on this side of the sea you shall be beyond, when you wish to eat you shall go hungry and when you wish to sleep you shall remain awake. Can you accept these things for the glory of God and the safety of your soul?'

'Yes, Sir Knight,' answered the sergeant solemnly.

'Then answer truthfully these questions.'

The knights returned to their places and the priest read from the book, his words echoing out around the chapter house. 'Do you believe in the Christian faith, as decreed by the Church of Rome? Are you the son of a knight, born of legitimate wedlock? Have you made a gift to any in this Order that you may be received as a knight? Are you firm of body and not concealing any ill that may make you unfit to serve the Temple?' The sergeant gave a clear reply to each and the priest inclined his head. 'Very well.' He handed the book to one of the clerics, who descended to the sergeant and held it out before him.

'Behold the Rule of the Temple,' said the cleric, 'written for us with the aid of the blessed saint, Bernard de Clairvaux, who at the founding of our Order supported us and whose spirit lives on within us. Look upon our laws, as they are written here, and swear to uphold them. Swear that you will always be faithful to the Order, obeying without question any command you are given. But only if that command comes directly from an official of the Temple, these officials being first the Grand Master, who governs us in wisdom from his seat in the city of Acre; the Visitor of the Kingdom of France, commander of our Western strongholds; the Marshal; the Seneschal; then the Masters of all kingdoms where we hold sway throughout the East and the West. You will obey, too, your commanders in battle and the Master of any preceptory where you are posted in times of war or peace, and keep civil always with your brothers-in-arms, with whom the bond you now share is thicker than blood. Swear that you will preserve your chastity and live without property, except that bestowed upon you by your Masters. Swear too that you will aid our cause in Outremer, the Holy Land, defending the strongholds and estates we retain in the Kingdom of Jerusalem against all enemies and, in gravest need, giving of your life in this defence. And swear that you will never leave the Order of the Temple, save when permitted by the Masters, for thou art joined to us by this oath and ever shall be in the eyes of God.'

The sergeant put a hand to the book and swore that he would, indeed, do these things.

The cleric ascended the steps and laid the leatherbound book on the altar. As he stepped back, the priest reached down and gently, lovingly, picked up a small black box gilded with gold. He removed the lid and brought out a crystal phial, its many-faceted surface catching the light of the candles.

'Look upon the blood of Christ,' murmured the priest, 'three drops of which, captured within this vessel, were brought to us almost two centuries ago from the Church of the Holy Sepulchre by Hugues de Payns, founder of our Order, in whose name you deliver yourself and in whose footsteps you follow. Look upon it and be received.'

The company sighed and the sergeant watched in awe: he hadn't been told about this part of the ceremony.

'Do you deliver youself, body and spirit?'

'I do.'

'Then bow your head before this altar,' ordered the priest, 'and ask for the blessings of God, the Virgin, and all the saints.'

With his cheek pressed against the wall, Will Campbell watched as the sergeant prostrated himself on the flagstones, arms splayed like the crosses on the knights' mantles. Will, who was tall for thirteen, shifted in his cramped position as his legs began to throb. The tenacious burrowing of mice had eroded an uneven stone at the base of the wall that separated the chapter house from the kitchen's storeroom, forming a tiny cleft. Around him, the storeroom was in relative darkness. Only thin slivers of light sifted through the cracks in the door that led to the kitchen. A musty smell of mice droppings and mouldering grain permeated the air. The two large sacks that he had squeezed between offered some measure of comfort from the cold rising from the stone floor, as well as cover from possible detection.

'You seen enough?'

Will took his cheek from the wall and glanced at the stocky youth huddled behind him, propped against a sack of grain. 'Why? Do you want to look?'

'No,' muttered the youth, stretching out his legs and wincing as the blood found its flow. 'I want to leave.'

Will shook his head. 'How can you not want to see? Not even the . . .' He frowned, trying to think of a good example. 'Not even the *pope* has witnessed a knight's initiation. This is your chance to know the Order's most secret ceremony, Simon.'

'Yes, secret.' Simon cocked his head. 'There's a reason it's secret. It means no one's supposed to see. Only knights and priests are allowed and you're neither.' He stamped his foot on the ground. 'And my leg's gone to sleep.'

Will rolled his eyes. 'Go then, I'll see you later.'

'Through the bars of a prison cell maybe. Listen to your elder for once.'

'Elder?' scoffed Will. 'By one year.'

'One year in age maybe.' Simon tapped his head. 'But at least twenty years in sense.' He sighed, folding his arms across his chest. 'No, I'll stay. Who else is fool enough to watch your back?'

Will returned his eye to the cleft. The priest was stepping down from the dais holding a sword. The bare-chested sergeant rose to his feet, keeping his head bowed.

Will had seen in his mind's eye the priest descending to him a thousand times with the sword and had seen himself sheathe the blade in the scabbard at his side. But most of all, he had imagined the hand of his father, firm on his shoulder, as he was accepted as a Templar Knight; clothed in the white mantle that signified the cleansing of all past sins.

'I've heard they station archers on the rooftops of some preceptories when the ceremony takes place,' continued Simon, prodding a bulge in the sack that was pressing into him. 'If we're caught they'll probably shoot us.'

Will didn't answer.

Simon sat back. 'Or expel us.' He groaned and prodded the sack again, viciously. 'Or send us to Merlan.' He gave an exaggerated shudder at the thought. When he had first arrived at the preceptory a year ago, one of the older sergeants had told him about Merlan. The Templar prison in France had acquired an ominous reputation over the years and the sergeant's description of it had deeply affected Simon.

'Merlan,' murmured Will, not taking his gaze from the priest, 'is for traitors and murderers.'

'And spies.'

The kitchen doors opened with a bang. The shafts of light filtering into the storeroom intensified in their brightness as sunlight filled the chamber beyond. Will ducked down, his back to the wall. Simon scrabbled between the sacks and wedged himself in beside Will as the sound of heavy footsteps drew nearer. There was a clatter and a muttered curse, followed by a scraping sound. The footsteps stopped. Ignoring Simon who was shaking his head, Will inched forwards easing himself out from between the sacks. Padding to the door, he peered through one of the cracks.

The kitchen was a large, rectangular room divided by two long rows of benches where the food was prepared. At one end, near the doors, was a cavernous hearth in which a fire smoked and spat. Shelves lined the walls, crammed with bowls, pots and jars. Stacked on the floor were barrels of ale and baskets filled with vegetables, and suspended on hooks hanging from the rafters were braces of rabbits, joints of salted pork and dried fish. Standing at one of the benches was a brawny man, clad in the brown tunic of a servant. Will groaned inwardly. It was Peter, the kitchen supervisor. Peter hefted a basket of vegetables onto the bench, then took up a knife. Will glanced round as Simon sat up, his scruffy thatch of brown hair appearing over the sacks.

'Who is it?' Simon mouthed.

Will moved back to him and crouched down. 'Peter,' he whispered. 'It looks like he'll be here for a while.'

Simon pulled a face.

Will nodded towards the door. 'We'll have to go.'

'*Go?*'

'We can't stay in here all day. I'm supposed to be polishing Sir Owein's armour.'

'But with him out there?'

Without giving Simon a chance to refuse, Will went to the door and opened it.

Peter started, his knife poised in mid-air. 'God in Heaven!' He recovered quickly, his eyes narrowing as he saw Will. Setting down the knife, he wiped his hands on his tunic, glancing past Will as Simon hastened out and shut the storeroom door. 'What were you two doing in there?'

'We heard a noise,' said Will calmly. 'We went to see what it . . .'

Peter pushed past him and yanked open the door. 'Pilfering rations again?' He scoured the storeroom's shadows, but could see nothing out of place. 'What was it last time? Thieving bread?'

'Cake,' corrected Will. 'And I wasn't thieving, I was . . .'

'And you?' Peter turned on Simon. 'What need has a groom in the kitchens?'

Simon hooked his thumbs in his belt and shrugged, shuffling from one foot to the other.

'The stable broom was broken,' said Will. 'We came to borrow one.'

'Takes two of you to carry it, does it?'

Will stared back at him in silence.

Peter scowled. He had served the preceptory for thirty years and refused to have his intelligence insulted by these upstart adolescents. But he didn't have the authority to force a confession from them. He looked from the storeroom to Will, then ceded with a grunt of annoyance. 'Take your broom and be off then.' Returning to the trestle, he snatched up the knife. 'But if I see either of you in here again, I'll report you to the Master.'

Will hastened through the kitchen, pausing to grab a besom from the wall by the hearth. He headed outside, blinking at the sun's brightness and turned, grinning, as Simon came out behind him. 'Here.'

'How kind,' said Simon, as Will handed him the broom. 'I hope your curiosity is satisfied. If a knight had found us . . .?' He sucked in a breath. 'The next time you want someone to keep watch for you, I'll be in the Holy Land. I expect I'll be safer there.' He shook his head, but gave Will a broad smile that revealed his jagged front tooth, broken when a horse had kicked him. 'Will I see you before Nones?'

Will wrinkled his nose at the mention of the afternoon office. He hadn't even begun his chores and the morning was already drawing to a close. There never seemed to be enough hours in the day for all the things he was expected to do, however fast he tried to work. Between mealtimes, daily training on the field with the sword, and all the menial tasks he had to undertake for his master, there was very little time left for anything else, let alone the seven offices to God. Will's day, as all sergeants', began before dawn with the office of Matins, when the chapel, summer or winter, would be cold and gloomy, after which he would see to his master's horse, then be given his orders. At around six was the office of Prime and following this, Will and his fellow sergeants would break their fast, whilst listening to a reading of the scriptures, then return to the chapel for the offices of Terce and Sext. In the afternoon, between lunch, chores and training, he attended Nones. At dusk there was Vespers, followed by supper, and the whole day ended with Compline. Some Templars might be proud to be known as the warrior monks, but Will resented seeing more of the inside of the chapel than his own bed. He was about to complain of this to Simon, who was already well versed in his objections, when he heard someone shout his name.

A short, red-haired boy was running towards them, scattering the hens that were pecking in the yard. 'Will, I've a message from Sir Owein. He wants to see you in the solar immediately.'

'Did he say why?'

'No,' replied the boy. 'But he didn't look pleased.'

'Do you think he knows what we was doing?' murmured Simon at Will's side.

'Not unless he can see through walls.'

Will grinned, then sprinted off across the yard, the sun warm on his back. Diving down a passage that led past the fragrant-smelling kitchen garden, he came out in a large courtyard surrounded by grey stone buildings. Beyond the buildings to the right rose the chapel, a tall, graceful structure built with a round nave in imitation of the Church of the Holy Sepulchre in Jerusalem. Will made his way towards the knights' quarters, which lay at the far end of the courtyard near the chapel, dodging groups of sergeants, squires leading horses and servants moving purposefully about their various errands. New Temple, the principal English preceptory, was also the largest in the kingdom. As well as extensive domestic and official quarters, the compound contained a training field, armoury, stables and its own private wharf on the Thames. Commonly, up to one hundred knights were in residence, as well as several hundred sergeants and general labourers.

Reaching the doors of the two-storey building that was set around a cloister, Will slipped inside and ran down the vaulted passage, his footsteps echoing. Upstairs, he halted before a heavy oak door, breathing hard, and rapped his knuckles on the wood. Glancing down, he saw that his black tunic was smudged with dust from the storeroom floor. He brushed at it with his sleeve as the door swung inwards, revealing the imposing figure of Owein ap Gwyn.

The knight gestured sharply. 'Inside.'

The solar, a room that some of the more high-ranking Templars shared, was cool and dark. There was an armoire against one wall, several stools in a shadowy corner that was partially concealed by a wooden screen, and a table and bench beneath the window, which looked out over the cloisters onto a square of well-kept grass. A small piece of coloured glass in the trefoil cast a green glow across the piles of scrolls and sheaves of parchment on the table. Will held his head high, keeping his gaze fixed on the view outside the window as the door banged shut behind him. He had no idea why his master had summoned him, but hoped he wouldn't be kept too long. If he managed to polish Owein's armour before Nones, then he might be able to spend an hour on the field before the training session later that afternoon. There wasn't that much time left available in which to practise: the tournament was fast approaching. Owein came to stand before him.

Will saw displeasure etched in the furrows of the knight's brow and his steel-grey eyes. His hope sank. 'I was told you wanted to see me, sir.'

'Do you comprehend how fortunate you are, sergeant?' questioned Owein, the accent of his birthplace, Powys, thick with anger.

'Fortunate, sir?'

'To be in your position? A position denied to so many of your rank that grants you tutelage under a knight-master?'

'Yes, sir.'

'Then why do you disobey my commands, betraying both myself and your eminent station?'

Will said nothing.

'Mute, are you?'

'No, sir. But I cannot reply when I don't know what I've done to displease you.'

'You don't know what you've done to displease me?' Owein's tone roughened further. 'Then perhaps it's your memory and not your mouth that is deficient. What is your first duty after Matins, sergeant?'

'To see to your horse, sir,' replied Will, realising what must have happened.

'Then why, when I passed the stables, did I find the hayrack empty and my horse not groomed?'

Following Matins, the first office, Will had forsaken this chore to investigate the hole he'd discovered in the storeroom wall in readiness for the initiation. Last night, he had asked one of the sergeants with whom he shared quarters to feed Owein's horse for him. The sergeant must have forgotten. 'I am sorry, sir,' said Will in his most contrite voice. 'I overslept.'

Owein's eyes narrowed. He strode around the table and seated himself on the bench behind. Resting his arms on the table, he laced his hands together. 'How many times have I heard that excuse? And countless others? You seem incapable of following the simplest orders. The Rule of the Temple isn't here to be broken and I will not tolerate it any longer!'

Will was slightly surprised: he had done worse than neglect to feed his master's horse before. He began to feel uneasy as Owein continued.

'To be a Templar you must be willing to make many sacrifices and abide by many laws. You are training to be a soldier! A warrior of Christ! One day, sergeant, you will almost certainly be called to arms and if you cannot follow orders now, I cannot see how you hope to maintain order as a knight on the field of battle. Every man in the Temple must obey, to the letter, the commands given to him by his superiors, however trivial they might seem, else our entire Order will fall into chaos. Can you imagine the Visitor in Paris, or Master de Pairaud here in London failing to follow any task appointed to them by Grand Master Bérard? Failing, for instance, to send a requested number of men and horses to help fortify one of our strongholds in Palestine because they overslept on the morning the ship was due to leave?' Owein's grey eyes bored into Will's. 'Well, can you?' When Will didn't answer the knight shook his head irritably. 'The tournament is only a month away. I am considering excluding you from entering.'

Will stared at Owein for a long moment, then breathed a sigh of relief. Owein wouldn't bar him from the contest: his master wanted him to win as much as he did. It was an idle threat and Owein knew it.

Owein studied the tall, wiry boy, whose tunic was dust-stained and whose posture was erect, defiant. Will's dark hair had been cropped raggedly across his forehead and several strands hung in his green eyes giving him a hooded look. There was an adult keenness in the hard angles of his cheeks and his long, hawk-like nose, and Owein was struck by how much like his father the boy was starting to look. It was no use, he knew; anger and threats had never worked. Probably, he thought with some chagrin, because he could never stay furious with the boy for long, or recourse to more brutal punishments employed by other knights.

He glanced at the wooden screen that partitioned the solar, then back at Will. After a moment, Owein rose and looked out of the window to give himself a chance to think.

Will's uneasiness returned as the quiet dragged on. Rarely had he seen Owein so pensive, so ominously silent. Perhaps he was wrong: perhaps his master would bar him from the tournament. Or perhaps this was worse, perhaps . . . The word expulsion flashed in Will's mind. After what seemed an eternity, Owein turned to face him.

'I know what happened in Scotland, William.' Owein watched Will's eyes widen, then narrow to fierce slits as the boy averted his gaze. 'If you want to make amends, this isn't the way. What would your father think of your behaviour? When he returns from the Holy Land I want to be able to commend you. I don't want to have to tell him I'm disappointed.'

Will felt as if he had been punched in the stomach. All his air had gone, leaving him dizzy, sick. 'How . . .? How did you know?'

'Your father told me before he left.'

'He told you?' said Will weakly. He hung his head, then shook it and looked up. 'Can I receive my punishment and be dismissed, sir?'

To Owein, it was as if a mask had come down over Will's face. That fragility was gone almost as soon as it had appeared. He watched a vein in Will's temple pulse as the boy clenched his teeth. The knight recognised that stony resolve. He had seen it in James Campbell's face when he had advised the knight not to pursue a request for transfer to the Temple's preceptory in the city of Acre. James hadn't been called to Crusade and as well as Will in London, he had a young wife and daughters in Scotland, but he had refused to listen to Owein's counsel. Owein wondered whether he was getting through to the boy at all. It was time, he decided, to speak plainly. 'No, Sergeant Campbell, you may not be dismissed. I'm not finished.'

'I do not wish to speak of this, sir,' said Will in a low voice. 'I won't!'

'We won't have to,' said Owein calmly, seating himself on the bench, 'if you start behaving like the sergeant I know you can be.' When Owein saw he had the boy's attention, he continued. 'You have a sharp mind, William, and your enthusiasm and skill on the training field is laudable. But you refuse to apply yourself to the most fundamental obligations of our Order. Do you think our founders wrote the Rule for their own amusement? We must all strive to follow the ideals they prescribed in order to fulfil our role as Christ's warriors on Earth. Being able to fight well is not enough. Bernard de Clairvaux himself tells us that it is useless to attack exterior enemies if we do not first conquer those of the interior. Do you understand that, William?'

'Yes, sir,' said Will quietly. The sentiment touched something deep inside him.

'You cannot continue to jeopardise your position by flouting the Rule whenever you think it dull, or senseless. You must start obeying me, William, in *all* of your duties, not just the ones you enjoy. You must learn discipline else you will have no place in this Order. Is that clear?'

'Yes, Sir Owein.'

Owein sat back, satisfied that Will had listened and understood. 'Good.' He picked up one of the scrolls that was lying on the table. Unrolling the parchment he smoothed it flat with his palm. 'Then your next duty will be to bear my shield at a parley between King Henry and Master de Pairaud.'

'The king? He's coming here, sir?'

'In twelve days.' Owein looked up from the parchment. 'And his visit is a private affair, so you are forbidden from speaking of it.'

'You have my word, sir.'

'Until then, you will be assigned to the stables as punishment for neglecting your responsibilities this morning. This will be in addition to your daily work. That is all, sergeant. You are dismissed.'

Will bowed and headed for the door.

'And William.'

'Sir?'

'My threats may have seemed without substance in the past. But if you test my patience any further, I won't hesitate to have you expelled from the Order. Stay out of trouble. The good Lord knows it follows you around like a stray dog, but the next time you turn and pet it, it may well bite you.'

'Yes, sir.'

When Will had gone, Owein rubbed at his brow wearily.

'You are far too lenient on the boy, brother.' A tall knight with flint-grey hair and a leather patch over his left eye appeared from around the wooden screen, where he had been sitting throughout the meeting. He crossed to Owein, holding a sheaf of parchments. 'To bear the shield of a Templar is a great honour, greater still given the setting. His punishment seems more like a reward.'

Owein studied the scroll before him. 'Perhaps the responsibility will help to temper him, brother.'

'Or lead him to worse abuses of his rank. I fear your affection for the boy has blinded you. You are not his father, Owein.'

Owein looked up, frowning. He opened his mouth to object, but the flint-haired knight continued.

'Boys of his age and breeding are like dogs. They respond better to the whip rather than the word.'

'I disagree.'

The knight gave a tiny shrug and laid the sheaf of parchments he held on the table. 'It's your decision, of course. I merely offer my opinion.'

'Your opinion is noted, Jacques,' said Owein, mildly but firmly. He picked up the parchments. 'Have you read them all?'

'I have.' Jacques walked to the window and surveyed the Temple's grounds. The leaves on the trees were beginning to wither, turning brown and crumpled at the edges. 'What does Master de Pairaud say? Is he confident that Henry will concede to our demands?'

'Fairly. As I have been dealing with this matter for some months, Master de Pairaud has, to some extent, left it in my hands as to how we proceed during the parley. I have talked through my thoughts with him and it has been agreed that we should compile not only the treasury reports of what has been lent to the royal household over the past year, but also exactly where we believe those monies to have been spent. I will need your help with some of the details.'

'You have it.'

Owein nodded his thanks. 'It will all serve to strengthen our case.'

'However strong our case is, the king will not be pleased.'

'No, he will not. But although I believe we should tread with some caution in this matter, Henry does have very little choice but to concede to the Temple's demands. Even if he refuses, we can request that the pope order him to agree.'

'Caution is needed, brother. The Temple may stand beyond the king's authority, but he can still make our lives difficult. He has done it before when he attempted to confiscate several of our estates. And,' added Jacques grimly, 'we currently have more than enough to worry about without having to deal with the petty reactions of jealous monarchs.' He pulled up a stool and sat before Owein. 'You spoke to the Master this morning. Did he say whether he has received any further reports from Outremer?'

'We will discuss it in the next chapter meeting, but, no, he has received nothing since we learnt about the Mongol attacks on Aleppo, Damascus and Baghdad, and the Mamluks' move to confront the horde. And that, for me, is good enough incentive to confront the king sooner rather than later about his debts. We will need all the money we can lay our hands on if we have cause to counter this new threat. If the Mamluks face the Mongols and win we will have their entire army marching triumphant and confident through our territories.' Owein straightened up the neat stack of parchments on the table with the tips of his fingers and shook his head. 'I cannot think of anything more perilous.'

3

Ayn Jalut (The Pools of Goliath), the Kingdom of Jerusalem

3 September 1260 AD

The Mamluk camp was tumultuous; noisy with exultation and preparation as the army celebrated its victory in song and officers shouted their orders, maintaining tight control of what, at first glance, would have appeared to be chaos.

On reaching the sultan's pavilion, Baybars reined in his horse and leapt down. Pausing to tether the beast to a hobbling post he surveyed the gorge, far beneath him. The sun had dipped below the hills, casting shadows across the valley. He could hear the dull echo of axe blades against wood as the Mongols' siege engines were torn down for the pyres of their dead. His eyes moved to the chain of Mamluk wounded which was winding its way slowly up the hillside from the battleground. Those able to walk were being helped by their comrades and the less fortunate were laid out on carts that bounced and rattled over the rocky ground. Come dawn, the physicians would be exhausted, but the gravediggers would be wearier still. Baybars headed for the pavilion. Guarding the entrance were two white-cloaked warriors of the Mu'izziyya regiment, the sultan's Royal Guard. They moved aside and bowed at his approach.

The air inside the pavilion was thick with the scent of sandalwood and the flames filtering through the oil lanterns exuded a soft, buttery light. It took Baybars a moment to become accustomed to the dim interior, but when he did his gaze was drawn first to the throne, which stood on a wooden platform that was covered by a canopy of white silk. The throne was a magnificent item, spread with embroidered cloth, the arms crowned with the heads of two lions sculpted from gold, beasts that snarled down at all those who stood before them. It was empty. Baybars looked around until his eyes came to rest on a low couch that was partially hidden by a mesh screen. Reclining there amidst a panoply of cushions and drapes was Sultan Kutuz, the master of the Mamluks and ruler of Egypt. His brocaded mantle of jade damask was drawn tight against his huge frame and his long black beard was sleek with perfumed oil. As usual, the sultan was not alone. Baybars quickly studied the rest of the men who occupied the pavilion. He had trained himself, on entering any enclosed space, to assess who was there and how many were armed. Invariably, the answers to these questions when in the presence of the sultan, were all those who mattered and everyone but the servants. Baybars had long thought that Kutuz's status was marked less by the slim band of gold that circled his brow, than by the retinue that always surrounded him. Attendants bearing trays of fruit and goblets of hibiscus cordial moved deftly between the royal advisers and the military governors of the various Mamluk regiments, who stood in small groups talking quietly. More of the Mu'izziyya were just visible in the shadows.

A gust of cool air swept into the pavilion with a messenger who hurried over to one of the governors. The draught stirred the incense smoke into fitful clouds. Kutuz looked up. His dark eyes fixed on Baybars.

'Amir.' Kutuz beckoned. 'Come forward.' He waited as Baybars approached the couch. 'My praise to you,' he said, watching Baybars bow. 'Because of your plan, we have won our first victory against the Mongols.' Resting against the cushions, Kutuz took a goblet from one of the proffered trays. 'What do you believe our next move should be?' He shot a glance at a group of men who were standing at the side of the pavilion. 'Some of my advisors have suggested that we fall back.'

Baybars didn't take his eyes from the sultan. 'We should move out to engage the remaining Mongol forces, my lord. The rest have fled east and reports from the borders indicate concern over the throne in Mongolia. It would be good to strike whilst they are in disarray.'

'That may be difficult,' voiced one of the governors. 'It is a long road east and—'

'No,' interrupted Kutuz. 'Baybars is right. We must strike whilst we are able, if we are to complete our success.' He motioned to a scribe, who was seated at a table in one corner of the pavilion. 'I have drafted a letter to the Western rulers of Acre, informing them of our victory and asking for their continued support of our campaign. Have one of your officers take it to the city and place it in the hand of the Grand Master of the Teutonic Knights.'

Baybars took the scroll reluctantly. The act of asking their enemy for permission to enter their territories, *stolen* territories, had affronted him and the brief rest the Mamluks had taken in Acre on their journey through Palestine had only reinforced his hatred. Whilst the army was camped outside Acre's walls, the Teutonic Knights, a military Order from the Kingdom of Germany, had invited Kutuz into their stronghold to feast at their table, where the sultan had asked them for an alliance of arms against the Mongols. Negotiations between the Christian and Muslim forces were not uncommon. There had been many such alliances forged since the first Crusaders had come, at the call of their pope, to redeem the birthplace of their Christ from the unbelievers, spurred by the promise of absolution in the next life and the prospect of land and riches in this. On new shores they had become the infidel themselves and, over time, had learnt to negotiate with their enemy, until, in the midst of conflict, trade and even friendships had flourished. But, on that day, although the Western rulers had permitted the Mamluks to cross their territories, they had bluntly refused the entreaty for a military alliance.

Baybars, seated in silence at the sultan's side for the feast, had watched grimly as Muslim servants had brought the platters to the boards. In Acre, those the Muslims called *al-Firinjah* – the Franks – held the power. It was a term used broadly for the fighting classes of the West whatever their nationality, but the two things the Franks had in common were their Roman Christianity and that they had come to the East uninvited. In the towns and cities ruled by the Franks, native Christians, Jews and Muslims were allowed to work, practise their religions and organise their own administrations. But what the Franks saw as tolerance was insult to Baybars. The Western Christians, who had come to take their Holy Land by force, had enslaved his people and were growing fat and happy on the spoils. Acre's rulers could try to hide behind their adopted refinements, their perfumed hair and flowing silks, but Baybars still saw the filth of the West on them and all the soap in Palestine couldn't wash them clean. He stared at Kutuz. 'I would rather take a war to the Franks than a message, my lord.'

Kutuz drummed his fingers on the arm of the couch. 'For now, we must concentrate our forces on one enemy alone, Amir. The Mongols must pay in full for their insult to my position.'

'And,' interjected Baybars, 'for the eighty thousand Muslims they killed at Baghdad?'

'Indeed,' replied Kutuz, after a pause. He drained the goblet and handed it to an attendant. 'At least the Franks show me courtesy.'

'They show you courtesy, my lord, because they fear to lose territory to the Mongols. Not willing to lift their own swords, they have let us fight their battle for them.'

Baybars held Kutuz's gaze easily. A tense silence descended, broken only by the footfalls of the attendants and the muted sounds of the camp outside. Kutuz was the first to look away. 'You have your orders, Amir.'

Baybars said nothing. There would be time during their campaign to turn Kutuz to his will. 'There is the matter of a reward, my lord.'

Kutuz sat back with a nod and the tension in the pavilion was expelled like a breath. 'The spoils of war will always benefit the soldiers who fight them, Baybars.' He motioned to one of his advisors. 'Have a chest filled with gold for the Amir.'

'It wasn't gold I was seeking, my lord.'

Kutuz frowned. 'No? Then what do you want?'

'The governorship of the city of Aleppo, my lord.'

Kutuz didn't speak for several moments. Behind him, some of the advisers stirred uneasily. The sultan laughed. 'You request a city held by the Mongols?'

'It won't be for much longer, my lord. Not now we have broken a third of their force and prepare to march on their strongholds to finish what we've started.'

Kutuz's smile faded. 'What game are you playing?'

'No game, my lord.'

'Why do you request such a prize? What would you do with Aleppo when your greatest desire is to lead my army to war against the Christians?'

'The position of governor wouldn't deter me from that cause.'

Kutuz folded his arms across his chest. 'Amir,' he said, his soft tone belied by the hardness of his gaze, 'I don't understand why you wish to return to a place so full of memory.'

Baybars stiffened. He knew that Kutuz made it his business to learn everything of his officers, including their histories. But he hadn't thought anyone, Kutuz included, knew of his time in Aleppo.

Seeing that he had struck a nerve, Kutuz smiled slightly.

'I have served you and your predecessors since I was eighteen.' Baybars' deep voice filled the pavilion and advisors and attendants alike stopped what they were doing to listen. 'In that time I have brought fear to the enemies of Islam and triumph to our cause. I led the van at the Battle of Herbiya and killed five thousand Christians. I helped capture the Franks' king, Louis, at Mansurah and killed three hundred of his best knights.'

'I am grateful for all you have done for me, Amir Baybars, but I'm afraid I wouldn't give up such a jewel, even if it became mine to give.'

'Grateful, my lord?' Baybars' voice was light, but his hands were fists at his sides. 'If not for me you wouldn't have a throne to sit on.'

Kutuz rose quickly from the couch, scattering the cushions. 'You forget yourself, *Amir*! In the name of Allah, I should have you whipped!' He strode to the throne and stepped onto the platform. Turning, he seated himself and grasped the heads of the lions.

'I beg your forgiveness, my lord, but I believe I am deserving of this reward.'

'Leave!' spat Kutuz. 'Leave now and do not return until you have considered the position of a sultan and the position of a commander and have a clearer understanding of which is the greater. You will never have Aleppo, Baybars. Do you hear me? *Never!*'

Out of the corner of his eye, Baybars saw that several members of the Mu'izziyya had stepped forward. Their hands were resting on the pommels of their sabres. He forced himself to bow to Kutuz, then swept out of the pavilion, the scroll clutched tightly in his fist.

As he strode through the Mamluk encampment the men fell back at the rage that enveloped him like a cloud. The sun had set and down in the gorge the pyres of the Mongol dead were burning, the flames leaping high into the purple skies. The sounds of laughter and cheering drifted on the chill desert air and, closer, a woman's screams. When he reached his own tent, Baybars wrenched open the flaps. He stopped in the entrance. Standing in the centre of the tent was a Mamluk officer, a lean man with a plain, honest-looking face and a slightly crooked nose.

'Amir! I missed you in the battle, but I've already heard ten tales of your valour.'

Baybars handed his swords to an attendant who was waiting nearby, as the officer came forward and embraced him.

'All I hear when I walk through the camp are men praising your name. They exalt you.' The officer motioned to a low couch, before which was a chest laden with platters of figs and spiced meats. 'Take off your armour and drink with me in celebration.'

'The time for celebration is passed, Omar.'

'Amir?'

Baybars glanced at his attendants. The one who had taken his swords had set about cleaning them. Two others were stoking the charcoals in the braziers and a fourth was pouring water into a silver basin. 'Leave us.'

The attendants looked up in surprise, but seeing their master's expression left their stations hurriedly. Baybars tossed the scroll onto the chest and pulled off his bloodied cloak, letting it fall to the sand. He sat heavily on the couch and seized a goblet of kumiz. He drank deep, the fermented mare's milk soothing his throat.

Omar sat down beside Baybars. 'Sadeek?' he pressed, reverting, now that the attendants had gone, to the more familiar appellation, *friend*. 'In the eighteen years I've known you I've never seen you angered by victory. What is the cause?'

'Kutuz.'

Omar waited for him to continue and remained silent as Baybars spoke of the sultan's denial of his request. When Baybars had finished, Omar sat back and shook his head. 'Kutuz is obviously fearful of you. Your reputation precedes you and he is only too aware of the military's capability in the deposition of a sultan. After all, he too took the throne by force. Kutuz has reigned for only one year and his position isn't fully secured among all in the regiments. I would say he believes you would have too much power should he give you Aleppo. Power that you, in turn, may use against him.' Omar spread his hands. 'I cannot see what you are to do, though. The sultan's word is law.'

'He must die,' said Baybars quietly. So quietly that Omar wasn't sure he had heard correctly.

'Sadeek?'

Baybars glanced at him. 'I will kill him and place a more suitable ruler on the throne. A ruler who rewards his officers. A ruler who will bring them the victories they deserve.'

Omar's eyes moved to the tent entrance. The flaps were open and outside he could see the flickering torchlight and the shadows of men who were hauling the plunder they had taken into the camp. 'You cannot even think such things,' he murmured. 'Get some sleep. Tomorrow is a new day and your anger may diminish with your dreams.'

'You may be one of my highest officers, Omar, and you may be as a brother to me. But if you believe that then perhaps you don't know me at all. You were there when we killed the Ayyubid, Turanshah. It was my hand that wielded the blade that took that sultan's life. I can do it again.'

'Yes,' replied Omar quietly. 'I was there.' He stared into Baybars' eyes and couldn't see one shred of doubt or indecision there. Omar had seen that look before.

On that day, ten years ago, he had been resting with the other officers of the Bahri regiment, following a victory against the Franks at Mansurah, a victory won by Baybars. At the time, the Bahris had been the Royal Guard of Sultan Ayyub, whose predecessors had gathered and raised the Mamluk army. Shortly before the Battle of Mansurah, Ayyub had died and his heir, Turanshah, had ascended the throne. Turanshah had riled the Mamluks by putting his own men in positions of power and Baybars had been ordered by Aibek, the commander of the Bahris, to rectify the situation with the persuasion of cold steel. He had come to Omar and the other officers late that night when Turanshah was holding a banquet. With swords concealed beneath their cloaks, the party had stormed the feasting hall. Turanshah had fled to a tower on the banks of the Nile, but Baybars had followed him doggedly, ordering that the tower be put to the torch. As the flames devoured the wood the sultan had jumped into the river and there, like a half-drowned rat, had begged for his life. Baybars had vaulted down the bank and ended the sultan's cries and the line of the Ayyubids with a single stroke, securing the seat of power for the Mamluks and making the slaves the masters. Omar would never forget the moment when Baybars had plunged his sword into Turanshah's belly, his face twisted beyond recognition by the fervour that consumed him.

Omar shook his head. 'It wouldn't work this time. Kutuz is always guarded. You would be killed.'

A voice from the shadows made them both whip round, Baybars reaching instinctively for the dagger in his boot.

'Oh, it would work. It would! It would!'

A cackle of laughter followed the words and Baybars relaxed. 'Come here.'

A moment later, something crawled out of the shadows. It was an old man with a toothless grin, matted black hair and dark skin that was as wrinkled as old fruit. He wore a threadbare cotton robe and his feet were bare and scarred. The nails on his toes were yellow and his eyes were milky with cataracts. Omar relaxed, slightly, as he recognised Khadir, Baybars' soothsayer. Hanging from a chain around Khadir's waist was a gold-handled dagger, the hilt of which was inlaid with a glossy red ruby. This dagger was the only indication that the wretched figure had once been a warrior in the notorious Order of Assassins, an elite group of radical fighters founded in Persia just prior to the First Crusade. As adherents of the Shi'ah branch of Islam, a Muslim minority who had split from the traditionist Sunnis over Muhammad's succession, the Assassins' mandate was to destroy enemies of their faith and this they did with brutal efficiency. From secret strongholds high in the mountains of Syria they slipped unnoticed to fall like black spiders, silent, deadly, upon their chosen targets, poison or a dagger their preferred methods of murder. Over the years, Arabs, Crusaders, Turks and

Mongols had learnt to fear them, and with good reason. But occasionally they had also used them for their own purposes, at a high price, for there were none better skilled in the art of murder.

Omar didn't know why Khadir had left their ranks. As far as he was aware, the soothsayer had been expelled from the Order, but other than a few unsubstantiated rumours, the reasons for his dismissal were unclear. All Omar knew was that the old man had arrived in Cairo, wearing the same shabby robe he wore now, shortly after Baybars had been handed control of the Bahris, and had offered the commander his allegiance and services.

As Khadir came closer to the braziers' dancing light, Omar noticed that a viper was entwined around the soothsayer's hand.

'Speak,' commanded Baybars.

Khadir crouched in the sand, watching the snake coil around his wrist as if mesmerised, then leapt to his feet. His eyes focused on Baybars. 'Kill Kutuz,' he said coolly, 'you will have the support of the army.'

'You are certain?'

Khadir giggled and dropped to the sand, where he sat cross-legged. Pinching the head of the snake between his thumb and forefinger, he drew it from his wrist and whispered to it, before letting it fall to the ground. The viper slid across the sand, making a thin, waving trail towards the couch. Omar resisted the urge to lift up his legs as it slithered over his boot. It was only young but its venom was still potent.

Khadir clapped his hands as the snake glided closer to Baybars. 'See! It shows you the answer!'

'His sorcery is an affront to Allah,' said Omar quietly. 'You shouldn't allow him to perform it.'

Khadir's hooded gaze swivelled to Omar, who looked away, unable to meet those white eyes.

Baybars was watching the snake slide between his feet seeking the darkness beneath the couch. 'Allah has given him this gift, Omar, and he has never been wrong.' Before the viper could disappear, Baybars lifted his boot and stamped down on its head. He scuffed the dead snake across the sand with his foot and looked at Khadir. The soothsayer was scratching a sore on his leg.

'You say the army would support me in this action, but what of the Mu'izziyya regiment? Surely the Royal Guard would stand with Kutuz?'

Khadir shrugged and rose to his feet. 'Perhaps, but enough of their loyalty can be purchased with gold and *your* men guard today's plunder.'

Walking over to the couch, he picked up the dead snake. After staring sadly at its crushed body, he stowed it in his robes. He looked at Baybars with something akin to fatherly pride. 'I see a great future for you, master. Nations will fall and kings will perish and you will stand above them all on a bridge of skulls that spans a river of blood.' His voice dropped to a whisper as he knelt at Baybars' feet. 'If your hand wields the knife that kills Kutuz, you will be sultan!'

Baybars gave a bark of laughter. 'Sultan? Then Aleppo would be the least of my treasures.' His laughter died as his mind clamped around that thought like a vice.

When Baybars had deposed Turanshah, it had been the privilege of the man who had ordered the killing, the then commander of the Bahris, Aibek, to take the throne. But Baybars hadn't been properly rewarded for his part in it and, refusing to serve the man whose rise he had aided, he had left Cairo. He had returned one year ago, after Kutuz had deposed Aibek's successor, hoping that the new sultan would prove more faithful than the others: to the men and to the cause. He had been sorely disappointed.

Rising from the couch, Baybars moved to the entrance of the tent. Outside, the sky was ruddy from the flames of the pyres and the moon had risen red above the desert. The hills rose and fell in black peaks and troughs, tumbling into darkness as they reached the flat plain that was spread out beneath him. In the south, the Pools of Goliath glinted like steel in the moonlight. The Franks had once come to this plain to challenge the Egyptian sultan, Saladin, with their crosses and swords. Their army had been surrounded, their supply routes cut, but they had survived by fishing the Pools for food, and Saladin, unable to invade their camp, was forced to retreat. For almost two centuries, the Franks had eaten their food, slaughtered their people and defiled their places of worship. Where once Allah had been revered, pigs now rooted in excrement.

But as Baybars stood there, his gaze on the Pools, a sense of anticipation began to replace his rancour. Khadir's words crackled in his mind like fire. He had a destiny, a part to play in the Franks' demise. He could feel it inside. 'If I were sultan,' he murmured, 'I would fight the barbarian Franks so fiercely that not even the buzzards would find a feast of their bones.'

Omar came to stand beside Baybars. 'I know you long for their blood to be spilt, but don't mistake the Franks for mindless savages. They are seasoned warriors and cunning strategists and it won't be easy to destroy them.'

Baybars turned to him. 'You are wrong. They are barbarians. In the

West, the Franks live like swine. Their homes are hovels, their ways uncultured and coarse. They looked to the East and saw the beauty of our cities, the elegance of our people and our great schools of learning. They looked to the East and they wanted it for themselves and so they came on their Crusades. Not for their God, but for the plunder.' Baybars closed his eyes. 'Every day that they have spent in our nation must be avenged.'

'The sultan has given his orders,' said Omar. 'It is the Mongols we go to fight.'

'They won't take long to crush. Once that is done we will make our plans for Kutuz.' Baybars grasped Omar's shoulder. 'Will you stand with me?'

'You have no need to ask that.'

'Take what gold I own,' said Baybars, pointing to a small chest, 'and see that the officers are paid. Pay them well, for if I'm to take this action against Kutuz we must bind as many to our cause as possible.'

'And then?'

'Then?' Baybars looked at Khadir, who was crouching in the sand, eyes gleaming in the braziers' red glow. 'Then we prepare for war.'

4
New Temple, London
14 September 1260 AD

The wooden swords collided with a sharp crack. Will tightened his grip as the concussion rang in his arm. His opponent, a golden-haired sergeant called Garin de Lyons, staggered, feet slipping in the mud. It had rained heavily for the past three days and the field was sodden, pocked with puddles of brown water. To the right, the field stretched down to the banks of the Thames, where a thick fringe of reeds and shrubs concealed the water. To the left and behind, stood the preceptory buildings, half obscured in the misty air. There was a damp chill that the sun wasn't yet strong enough to burn away, but the youths' faces were streaked with sweat. Will's black tunic was stuck to his back and itched uncomfortably. He swept Garin's blade away as it came in at him again. Feinting to the left, he swung in an arc towards the youth.

Garin parried the blow and moved back to drop into a fighting stance, keeping his dark blue eyes on Will. 'I thought you Scots were the war dogs of Britain?'

'I'm just warming up,' responded Will, circling him. 'And I've yet to decide what you are today.'

Garin grinned. 'Well, I've chosen what you are. You're a Saracen.'

Will rolled his eyes. 'Again?' He lifted his sword higher. 'Fine. Then you're a Hospitaller.'

Garin pulled a face and spat on the ground. The Knights of St John, founders of the pilgrim hospitals, were bitter rivals of the Templars. Both military Orders might be formed of noble Christian men who fought for God and for Christendom, but that didn't stop them warring over land and trade and other conflicts of interest.

Will lunged forwards. He just managed to duck and fling up his blade as Garin swung a powerful stroke at his head.

'Halt!'

The two boys moved away from one another, breathing hard, at their instructor's command. The knight strode towards them, the hem of his mantle stained with mud.

'You are supposed to be disarming your opponent, de Lyons. Not trying to kill him.'

'I'm sorry, sir,' said Garin, lowering his head. 'The blow was ill aimed.'

'Yes, it was,' agreed the knight, the hardness of his gaze not diminished by the fact that he only had one eye. The other was covered with a worn leather patch. 'Continue!' he barked, returning to the edge of the field where sixteen boys of Will and Garin's age were standing in a line.

Not all sergeants in the Temple were instructed in the art of combat: many would serve as labourers: cooks; blacksmiths; tailors; grooms, in the numerous preceptories and estates, and would never go to war. But those who were candidates for knighthood were expected to be accomplished warriors by the time they came of age at eighteen. Basic schooling – the trivium of rhetoric, grammar and logic, which most monks in holy orders would be privy to – was considered far less important, although the sergeants were expected to know, by heart, all six hundred clauses of the Rule. So, by the age of fifteen these boys could ride a horse at full tilt carrying lance and shield, but other than a few exceptions, Will and Garin included, they couldn't write their own names.

Will faced Garin, keeping his weapon locked in front of him. The sword was scarred with use, the edges splintered. Garin made the first move, yelling as he charged. Will avoided the first strike, but Garin pressed the attack, forcing him back with a series of short, cutting blows. Will recovered his stance and they crashed together. Swords locked, they pushed against one another, neither willing to give quarter. Their breath steamed on the air and their feet churned the mud to a slick, black slime. Will snarled into Garin's face and shoved his blade forward. Garin's eyes widened as his foot slid sideways in the wet. He fell, his grip loosening. With a quick, stiff-armed strike, Will slapped the sword from his hand, sending it flying and, as Garin sprawled on his back, Will stood over him, pointing the tip of the blade at his throat. A few cheers rose from the sergeants on the sidelines.

The knight silenced them with a brusque wave. 'The battle wasn't worthy of praise.' He gestured to Will and Garin. 'Stand down.'

Will withdrew his sword from Garin's throat and offered his hand. Accepting it, Garin pulled himself up and collected his blade. They jogged to the sidelines, their tunics and hose soaked. Will scowled as the knight began to address the group.

'Campbell's defence was weak. A strong defence could have allowed him to weaken de Lyons, whose opening assault was disorderly and easily anticipated.' The knight turned to the two youths, his eye falling on Will. 'Then you wouldn't have had to resort to such crude methods by which to beat de Lyons. Your final move consisted of brute strength alone and lacked technique. But at least Campbell used the terrain to his advantage.' He turned to Garin. 'Where was your balance, de Lyons?' As Garin opened his mouth to speak, the knight cut him off. 'Brocart. Jay.' He nodded to two of the waiting sergeants. 'Take your places.'

Will flexed his arms, loosening his stiff muscles, as the sergeants headed for the centre of the field. He glanced at Garin, whose gaze was on the knight. 'Your uncle is in his usual good mood then.'

'I think he's concerned about the meeting tomorrow.' Garin turned to Will. 'I hear you will be there.'

Will hesitated. Owein's threat was still fresh in his mind, as were the blisters on his hands from cleaning the stables' stalls, mending tack and polishing saddles.

Garin leaned closer. 'You can tell me,' he said, out of earshot of the other sergeants. 'I'll be at the king's parley also. I'm bearing my uncle's shield.'

'Sorry,' said Will, relaxing. 'Owein forbade me from speaking of it.'

'My uncle did too, but he let slip this morning that you would be there.' Garin gave Will a rueful look. 'I'm afraid the prospect of your presence at such an important event has displeased him.'

Will looked over at the grim-faced knight, who was studying the battling sergeants. Jacques de Lyons, a retired Templar commander, had fought the Muslims at the battles of Herbiya and Mansurah. At the former he lost an eye to a Khorezmian Turk's blade and at the latter he lost three hundred of his fellow knights. At New Temple, his injury and temperament earned him the name given to him by his tutees: Cyclops. This was a name that was only ever whispered as, according to rumour, the last sergeant to use it openly had been permanently consigned to a fly-infested village, six leagues south of Antioch.

'Everything I do displeases your uncle.'

'It wasn't you he slighted just now,' murmured Garin, chewing an already ragged fingernail and watching the two sergeants on the field circle one another. He looked back at Will. 'And can you blame him? You have to be more careful. He says you'll be expelled if you break any more rules. He'll make sure of it, he said.'

The two sergeants came together. Brocart, the smaller of the two, shouted as Jay barrelled into him in an ungainly charge, cracking him on the shinbone with the edge of the blade.

'At least we were better than them,' said Will, as the two sergeants went down in a tangle of limbs.

'Are you even listening?'

Will glanced at Garin. 'What?'

Garin gave him a pained look. 'I was saying you've got to be careful. You neglected a chore for the sake of an hour's sleep and you've spent the last ten days paying for it. I've hardly seen you.'

'It wasn't for sleep. I . . .' Will paused, then dropped his voice to a whisper and told his friend about the initiation he had watched with Simon.

'Are you *mad*?' Garin shook his head, incredulous.

'I had to see.'

'But you'll see it first-hand one day.' Garin's face still showed disbelief and something else now too.

'I couldn't wait five years. We've always talked about it, haven't we? Always wondered what happened?' Will grimaced. 'I would have seen more if that beak-nosed servant hadn't come in.'

'And Simon?' said Garin stiffly. 'Why involve him?'

'I needed someone I could trust to keep watch for me.' Will stopped, noticing Garin's expression. 'I would have asked you,' he said quickly, 'but I knew what the answer would be. I would have rather asked you, you know that.'

Garin shook his head, although Will thought he looked a little placated.

'It wasn't right that you witnessed the initiation, much less a groom. Simon isn't the same as us.'

'He wears the same tunic.'

Garin sighed. 'You know what I mean. Simon is the son of a tanner. We are the sons of knights. Simon will never be a knight, never be noble.'

Will shrugged. 'If kin makes a man noble, then I'm only half high-born. The rest of me is as common as any groom.'

Garin laughed mildly. 'That isn't true.'

'You know it is. My father may be a knight now, but my grandfather wasn't and my mother was a merchant's daughter. We weren't all born with the advantage of your family's heritage.'

'Well, your father is a knight and that is enough to make you noble.' As Garin turned away, his tunic slipped to one side, revealing a livid, scarlet welt just below his collarbone.

Will frowned and pointed to the mark. 'How did you get that?'

Garin followed Will's gaze, then yanked up his tunic. 'You caught me with your blade yesterday.' He forced a smile. 'You don't know your own strength sometimes.'

Out on the field, Brocart disarmed Jay with a sloppy cut to the wrist that caused the boy to drop his sword in pain. The sergeants on the sidelines shuffled nervously as Jacques headed over followed by the two combatants, Jay clutching his hand. At the end of training, the knight would deal out punishment, usually a gruelling ten circuits of the field, to the sergeant who had fared the worst in combat. Will picked at a splinter on his sword, unconcerned. However much Jacques disliked him, he had never been punished after any session. Jacques walked down their line, studying each of them in turn. Will met the knight's gaze, but Garin lowered his head.

Jacques passed them both, then stopped. 'De Lyons. You will run today.'

Garin's head jerked up, his face a mask of disbelief. The other sergeants wore similar expressions. Brocart, whose performance had been pitiful, looked especially bewildered.

'Sir?' Garin fought to keep his voice steady. Like Will, he had never received the punishment before.

'You heard me,' said Jacques gruffly. 'Twenty circuits.'

'Yes, sir,' murmured Garin. 'Thank you.'

As Garin stepped out of the line and the knight turned away, Will touched his friend's arm. 'This isn't fair,' he whispered. 'Jacques is wrong.'

'Campbell!'

Will dropped his hand to his side as the knight rounded on him.

'What did you say?' demanded Jacques.

'Say, sir?'

Jacques' eye narrowed to a slit. 'Do not play with me, boy. What did you say to de Lyons?'

Will glanced at Garin, who gave a tiny shake of his head. 'Nothing, sir. I just . . .' He paused, looking to the other sergeants for support. They all avoided his gaze. Will huffed and turned back to Jacques. 'I just wondered why you picked Garin to run, sir.' He tried to keep his tone light, forming the words as a question. 'I didn't think he was the worst?'

There was a long pause. 'I see,' said Jacques, his voice all the more disquieting for its softness. 'Then who, would you say, deserves the punishment?'

Will glanced down the line at his fellows, then back at Jacques.

'Come now, Campbell,' insisted the knight. 'If you do not think de

Lyons was the worst, then you must have an idea of who was.' As Will
went to speak, Jacques held up his hand. He moved back, gesturing to his
place. 'Step forth, Sir Instructor!'

Will did as he was told. His eyes darted briefly to Brocart and Jay.
Brocart was staring straight ahead, but Jay caught his look and scowled,
knowing what he was thinking.

'Well?' demanded Jacques.

Will remained quiet for a long moment. Finally, he shook his head. 'I
don't know, sir.'

'Speak up!' barked Jacques, his voice lashing out like a whip.

'I don't know who was the worst, sir.'

'Of course,' said Jacques, a humourless smile raising the corners of his
mouth. He turned to the other sergeants and pointed to Will. 'For how
could a boy with no experience of battle, graced with a lineage that
stretches back a mere generation and afforded only the acclaim he gives
himself know anything of such matters?'

Will noticed that Jay was smirking. Garin was staring fixedly at the ground.

'In future, Campbell,' said Jacques, stepping closer to Will, 'keep your
opinions to yourself. It will be less embarrassing.' He bent forward until his
face was level with Will's. 'Don't *ever* question my judgement again,' he
murmured, a fleck of his spittle striking Will's cheek. Jacques straightened.
'De Lyons!' he said, not taking his eyes off Will. 'Campbell has just granted
you an extra ten circuits.'

Will stared at the knight, aghast. Hearing a small, hoarse voice thank the
knight for the punishment, he turned to Garin, trying to communicate an
apology with his eyes and beg forgiveness at the same time. But the boy
didn't meet Will's gaze, or anyone else's as he stepped out of the line and
set off at a run. Will, his face burning, watched Jacques stride towards the
preceptory buildings. His hands were trembling, wanting to curl into fists
and slam that smug smile from Cyclops's face. Around him, the other
sergeants collected their weapons in silence and began to file from the field.
Will caught a few sympathetic glances from some and accusatory glares
from others. Ignoring them all, he watched Garin loping away across the
muddy field, which now seemed much larger than it ever had before. After
a few moments, Will began to run.

Jacques rifled through the scrolls on the table, until he found what he was
looking for. He read the report again slowly, his eye straining in the gloom.
The candle had burned low and the solar was in shadow, apart from a slice

of moonlight that slanted through the window, bleaching the flagstones. Outside, an owl shrieked. Jacques passed his hand across his brow as the words on the parchment blurred into meaningless black lines. Lifting the leather patch, he ran his finger in a slow circle around the deep indent where his eye used to be. The hollow was riddled with ridges of scar tissue. Even though he'd lost the eye sixteen years ago it still seemed to ache whenever he read for too long. He had been closeted in the solar for hours, missing both his meal and the last office. Owein had appeared earlier to suggest that he retire to his bed, saying that if they weren't prepared for tomorrow's meeting by now they never would be. Jacques had declined the advice, wanting to make absolutely certain that Henry wouldn't be able to parley his way out of the situation. But he was tired. Placing the parchment down, he went to the window, welcoming the refreshing breeze. The moonlight turned his skin the colour of ash and the contrasting shadows made knife-edge angles of his cheeks and nose. There was a flash of white as the owl flew out of the cloisters beneath him and disappeared beyond the rooftops. Jacques turned at a rapping on the solar's door.

'Enter,' he called, his voice rough with an evening's disuse.

A servant in a brown tunic appeared in the doorway, looking distressed. 'I'm sorry, sir, I know it's late, but there's someone here wants to see you. He . . . well, sir, he insists it's urgent.'

Jacques frowned, partly at the interruption and partly because he wondered who would need directing by a servant. 'Send him in.'

The servant stepped obligingly to one side and a tall figure in a threadbare grey cloak entered the chamber. The servant shifted his body so that the man wouldn't touch him on the way past. Jacques' eye widened as the man drew back his low-pulled cowl and inclined his head in greeting. 'Hasan,' murmured the knight.

'Is there anything you would be wanting, sir?' came the servant's voice, tentatively from the doorway. 'Perhaps refreshment for your . . .' His gaze flicked dubiously to the man in grey. 'Guest?'

'No,' said Jacques, still staring at the figure, 'leave us.'

The servant bowed gratefully and shut the door. He hastened away down the passage, his hand passing over his chest in the sign of the cross.

Scotland, 9 June 1257 AD

Will stood in the doorway, his hand clutching the frame. The fire in the hearth spat and crackled. On the trestle where the maid prepared the food the evening meal lay unmade, seven white fish, gutted and silvery in the candlelight. James Campbell was seated at the table, back turned, legs outstretched. Will could only see his father's face in shadowed profile: the angular jaw; brow jutting sheer over a long straight nose. His hair was dusted silver at the sides, but his beard was as black as a crow's wing. James's gaze was on the open door through which filtered a warm breeze that smelled of mint and yarrow. In daylight, the view would be of fields and woods stretching from the small estate all the way to the city of Edinburgh, which, on a clear day, was just visible as a patch of grey on the horizon. Now, all was dark. Faint on the wind came the gurgling of the stream that flowed through a rocky gully, leading to a loch that lay several miles in the west.

James had returned that evening from a week spent at Balantrodoch, the Temple's Scottish preceptory, where he kept the accounts for the Master. Over the back of his seat was draped a black mantle. James was a donatus to the Temple and was forbidden from wearing the garments of an initiated knight. Although he spent much of his time at Balantrodoch, working, living and praying with members of the Order, he hadn't taken the vows of chastity and poverty, only the vow of obedience, and was therefore permitted to continue in his duties as a husband and father, dividing his time between the Temple and the estate. His black mantle was the colour of human sin, only the pure being able to don the white of a Templar.

Will lingered by the door, watching his father's chest rise and fall with each breath. He had been concerned when his father had summoned him in an unusually solemn tone. Laughter floated from the adjacent room where Will's elder sisters, Alycie and Ede, were playing with Mary, the youngest.

James Campbell turned at the sound and smiled as he saw Will. 'Come here, William. I have something for you.'

As Will sat at the table, his father planted a large hand over his. James's long fingers were stained brown with the oak gall ink he used to keep the preceptory's ledgers and his palms were soft, unlike the hands of the few knights Will had met, whose skin was coarse with calluses from the regular handling of a sword. During his thirteen years working for the Temple, James had spent several seasons with the knights, learning how to ride their war-chargers and how to fight, but his main obligation had always been to his work. To Will, however, James was as fine a warrior as any man he had ever known; finer, the boy had always thought, as he was also able to read, write, count and speak Latin as well as the pope. Will had even heard him utter a few words in a chanting, musical tongue that James had told him was Arabic, the language of the Saracens.

'Do you remember me speaking of a gift your grandfather left to me when he died?'

Will's first thought was the estate. The spacious yet comfortable dwelling, nestled at the foot of a moor with its outbuildings and barns, had once belonged to his grandfather. Angus Campbell had been a wealthy wine merchant who, tired of family squabbles, had left his clan to set up in business alone. Rich and worldly, he had raised his son as a gentleman, had found him a suitable bride, and, shortly after James's first two children were born, Angus had pledged him to the Templars at Balantrodoch, with whom he had forged close trade links over the years. On his death, Angus had left his gold to the Order and the estate to his son.

'Our home?'

'Not the house. Something else.'

Will shook his head.

'I suppose you were too young then to recall it now.'

James rose and headed to the fire where something was propped against the hearthstones. At first glance, Will thought it was a poker, but as his father picked it up and returned to the table, Will saw that it was a sword, a falchion. The short, curved blade, which widened at the tip, looked, from the scars on its convex edge, to have seen battle. The pommel was disc-shaped and the hilt was crisscrossed with a band of silver wire to enhance the grip. It was a stocky blade designed for an infantryman. Will watched as his father laid it on the table.

'This sword is a birthright. Your grandfather was given it by his father and before he died he passed it to me. It is now yours, William.'

Will stared at his father. 'A real blade?'

'You cannot fight with a stick forever.' James smiled. 'Well, the day you wield it in battle will be far in the future; God willing never. But I believe you're old enough to bear it now. I have spoken with the Master at Balantrodoch and he has agreed to accept you as a sergeant-in-training.'

Will touched the hilt lightly. It was warm from where it had stood by the fire. 'I'm really going?'

'Going?'

'To Balantrodoch.'

James studied his son's face. 'I've trained you the best I can, William. I've taught you your letters and how to ride and to fight, but the skills you've learnt must be sharpened and by better instructors than I. One day, William, you will take the white mantle and be admitted as a Knight of the Temple and when you are, in God's name, I will be at your side.'

Will leaned back as the words sunk in. He was going to be a sergeant in the Order of the Temple. Since he was a toddler that name had filled him with awe. There was no organisation on the Earth, his father had told him, that wielded as much power as the Temple, except, of course, the Church itself. Will would lie in bed in the room he shared with his younger sister and dream he was a knight, one of *the greatest men in all the world, standing tall and dignified like his father: noble in spirit; honourable in battle; generous in heart.*

Will sat up suddenly. 'Can we finish the boat first?'

James laughed and ruffled Will's hair. 'You won't be my sergeant for a year or so yet. We have more than enough time to finish the boat.'

'Would that be your father's sword, James?'

Will looked round as his mother entered, carrying a crock of mint. She was tall in a simple gown of dyed wool, her hair the colour of wild cherries. Her belly pressed against the thin material of her gown, arching with child. Behind her skipped Mary, his eight-year-old sister. Will huffed at the interruption as Mary ran to James.

'That it would, Isabel,' said James, catching hold of Mary and swinging her, squealing, into the air. 'Although it's William's sword now.'

Isabel raised an eyebrow at her husband as she placed the crock on the table. 'I don't care if it is the pope's. What is it doing on my table?'

James let go of Mary and pulled Isabel, protesting, onto his lap.

She swatted him around the head. 'There'll be no food unless you remove that lump of iron and let me be!'

James feigned a shocked expression. 'That is a blade of our clan, woman, not a lump of iron!'

'We don't have a clan, father,' remarked Alycie, the eldest daughter, as she entered with Ede. Like their mother, they both had dark red hair, whereas Mary's was the colour of honey.

'No,' agreed James, 'not since your grandfather left the family, but it's part of our heritage nonetheless.' He let Isabel off his lap and took up the sword. 'Look. This is good Scottish iron.' He gave the air a powerful swipe. The blade caught the crock of mint which shot off the table and smashed in a corner. Will began to laugh.

New Temple, London, 15 September 1260 AD

The hilt was cold beneath his fingers. The sword was slightly rusted around the cross-guard and the bands of silver wire were a little loose. Will glanced round as a snore sounded from the pallet beside his. The flame of the nightlight danced and flickered over the forms of the eight other sergeants with whom he shared the chamber. Like all quarters in the sergeants' building the dormitory was a gloomy, low-ceilinged room. Nine pallets were in a row against one wall, each covered with a rough woollen blanket. Facing the berths were two armoires that held clothes and the sergeants' few belongings, and a table for the candle. A cold wind streamed in through the narrow windows, lifting the sacking that was placed across them and bringing with it the dank, briny smell of the Thames. As sergeants and knights were forbidden from sleeping naked, Will was clad in an undershirt and hose, but the air was cool and he'd wrapped his short winter cloak around his shoulders. Shadows swayed on the walls and hidden cobwebs shone silver as the night candle flared and lit up dark spaces between the beams.

Will placed the sword carefully on the pallet before him and hugged his knees to his chest, wincing as his back twinged. Every time he moved, a new pain would flare in his muscles. His feet were swollen and a blister had formed on the heel where his boot had chafed him. It was gone midnight and he was exhausted, but discomfort and his thoughts kept him from sleep.

When he had caught up with Garin on the field, his friend hadn't said anything for some time and they had run the first few circuits together in silence. Eventually, Garin had spoken.

'Why are you doing this?' he had panted.

Will had shrugged as if it wasn't important. 'I thought you might want the company.'

It was all that needed to be said. In between breaths, their hair hanging in their eyes, they had talked and laughed their way through Jacques' punishment, encouraging each other when the field seemed endless and their limbs were singing with pain. Afterwards, in a small, but satisfying, act of rebellion, Garin had kept watch as Will climbed one of the orchard's trees to pick a handful of plums. Hidden between the curving buttresses at the back of the chapel they had devoured the fruit thirstily as the sun burned away the last of the mist and dried their clothes. For Will, the reminder of how things used to be revealed just how much they had changed.

It was over two years since Will had first met Garin, on the morning after his arrival at New Temple. Will, who had never gone to Balantrodoch like his father had promised, had been led to the training field where he was introduced to the sergeants with whom he would spend the next seven years of his life. Garin had himself recently arrived and Will, making their group an even number, was assigned as his partner-in-training. The other sergeants had been friendly and curious, crowding around him, but Garin had hung back. Will, having answered none of the sergeants' questions, had taken the wooden sword he was handed and had followed Jacques' commands without a word. At mealtimes and in chapel he had sat alone, the rumbling of the priests' voices as they read from the scriptures at dinner and during the offices a constant, dull drone in his ears.

Things had gone on this way for almost a fortnight and the initial interest in Will had waned, his fellows having concluded he was either mute, or arrogant. He might have languished in his silence for much longer had it not been for Garin. Garin had never asked him about his home, or his family. Neither had he questioned why James Campbell was so rarely seen outside the solar where he worked alongside Jacques and Owein as a bookkeeper in place of a sick clerk – the position which had brought James and his son to London.

Several months after their arrival, James had entered the chapter house and had taken his last two vows, those of chastity and poverty. Will had been shocked to see his father dressed in the white mantle of a fully professed knight. The man that had become almost a stranger to him, reserved, formal, was now unreachable, cold and distant in that stark white cloth. Will, in his black tunic, still sinful, still human, had felt as though he had lost him for good. His mother and sisters, his father had told him, had been moved into a nunnery close to Balantrodoch, the estate having been given over to the Order in return for James's acceptance as a knight. There they would be supported by the Temple and would, his father had told him, not want for anything. But that hadn't alleviated Will's grief, or quelled the knowledge that he was responsible for the loss of his father, his family and the one place he had known and loved.

Garin's disinterest in things that Will had neither the strength nor the desire to speak of had put him at ease and when Garin suggested that they practise in their spare time, he had welcomed the boy's incurious company. Haltingly, over the following weeks, Will had begun to talk, about sword moves at first, then asking Garin about the preceptory, then finally speaking of himself. The shadow that had followed him from Scotland never left him, but when they were together it became invisible.

After his father had left for the Holy Land, Will's boldness had grown. Both he and Garin had found the tedium of the daily chores and offices a bind on their freedom and had rebelled against the rigid regime. They weren't the only sergeants to do so, but together, as Owein had often said, they were flint and tinder. Once, last winter, when the marshes outside London's north gate had frozen, the two of them had even dared to slip out of the preceptory in the middle of the night to go skating. Tying blocks of ice to their feet with leather, like they had seen boys from the city do, they had spent several unforgettable, exhilarating hours racing one another across the ice until, half frozen and exhausted, they had made the long trek home, vowing never to tell anyone.

Will couldn't imagine Garin doing anything like that now. He reached for the sword again and placed the length of iron in his lap, tracing the flat of the blade with his fingers. His friend had been absent during the evening meal and when neither Garin nor Jacques had attended chapel for Compline, he'd begun to worry. He wondered what he should do. The answer came back the same as always; there was nothing he could do. Jacques was a knight and he was a sergeant, he had no authority. Will ran his fingertip down the sword's hilt feeling the subtle change between silver and iron. He sometimes thought he knew how Garin felt. And he sometimes wondered whether it was worse to have an uncle who mistreated you, or a father who wouldn't speak with you at all.

5
New Temple, London
15 September 1260 AD

H asan settled his lean frame onto a stool, his dark eyes surveying the solar.

Jacques pushed the parchments on the table aside with a sweep of his arm and sat down. Offering one of the two goblets he held, he smiled when Hasan declined it.

'It is water.'

'Thank you.' Hasan accepted the goblet and returned the smile. 'I am unused to the company of friends. The habit of declining most well-intended offerings is hard to break.' He took a sip, the water clearing the road dust from his throat.

Jacques was listening carefully, struggling with Hasan's accent that rendered some of his clipped speech difficult to comprehend.

'I apologise,' continued Hasan, 'for the surprise and lateness of the hour, but there was no time for notice of my visit. I arrived in London this evening.'

Jacques waved the apology aside. 'What brings you here, Hasan? I haven't heard from Brother Everard in quite some time.'

Hasan placed his drink on the table. 'The Book of the Grail has been stolen.'

Jacques was used to Hasan's plainspoken manner; he usually welcomed it on the infrequent occasions that the two of them met. But if the appearance of the man himself had been a shock it was nothing compared to the abrupt impact of those words. Jacques suppressed the exclamation that almost freed itself from his mouth and remained silent for some moments, letting the words sink in. 'When did this happen?' he said eventually. 'And how?'

'Twelve days ago. It was taken from the preceptory's vaults by a clerk.'

'You know who stole it?' Jacques pushed a hand through his flint-grey hair and checked his impatience with effort.

'Its theft was discovered when the treasurer found the unconscious body of one of the two senior clerks who maintain the coffers. When revived, the clerk said he had gone down into the vaults, hearing a disturbance. He had been attacked by one of his fellows, a young clerk by the name of Daniel Rulli, who had beaten him half senseless with an alms bowl.'

'This Rulli had taken the book?'

Hasan nodded. 'The Visitor ordered a search of the preceptory, but Brother Everard believed Rulli had fled. I was sent into the city to hunt him down. I caught him near Saint-Martin's Gate.' Hasan told Jacques what the clerk had said before he was murdered.

'He was coerced into stealing it?'

'That is what he said, brother.'

Jacques frowned. 'If he was telling the truth, might we assume that the killer and the man who compelled Rulli to steal the Book of the Grail are one and the same, or at least working together?'

'I would think it so. It seems reasonable to guess Rulli was on his way to hand over the book. He might have been killed to stop him revealing where it was, or the identity of his enforcer, or both. Why he did not have it on him I cannot say. He might have hidden it somewhere when he realised I was hunting him.'

'Or the transfer had already taken place.'

'That is also possible. Unfortunately, I could not pursue his killer. The watch arrived and I had to flee. I doubt I would have had the chance to explain why I was standing over a corpse; my appearance alone would have damned me in their eyes. I doubled back to search, but found nothing.'

Jacques made no reply. He took a long drink from his own goblet which was filled with wine.

'When I returned to the preceptory, Everard went to the Visitor and asked to question the treasurer and the two senior clerks who, other than Rulli and the Visitor, have access to the vaults. None of them had any idea why the clerk committed this crime, or who may have forced him to do so. A comrade of Rulli's, a sergeant, we also questioned. This sergeant told us Rulli had seemed troubled for some days, but he had no idea why and denied knowing anything of the theft. Even when threatened with incarceration in Merlan.'

'Does anyone know what was stolen?'

'The clerks and the Visitor know only that it is a valuable document belonging to Brother Everard. They are ignorant of its true importance.'

'That is something at least.' Jacques drained the rest of his wine in one draught.

'When the watch came to the preceptory to inform us of Rulli's murder, the Visitor declared it a theft for monetary gain. A joint investigation by the Temple and the king's Seneschal came to nothing.'

'The king must have taken it seriously then, having his chief minister for justice investigate the matter?'

'The Visitor insisted.'

Jacques rose and poured himself another drink. 'The Paris vaults contain many priceless treasures. In terms of gold, the book is worth very little. Was anything else taken?'

'Nothing at all.' Hasan's dark eyes didn't leave the knight. 'May I speak frankly, brother?'

'Of course.'

'As perilous as this situation is, I have doubts over the ability of whoever may have the book to make sense of it. To a common reader it would appear no more than a Grail Romance, though an unorthodox one.'

'Unorthodox?' countered Jacques, returning to his seat. 'That is too mild a word for sacrificial rites and desecration of the Cross. Anything that goes against the grain of the Church is considered heresy, Hasan. I'm sure you are aware of what happened to the Cathars?'

Hasan nodded. He hadn't been in the West when the Crusade against the Cathars had begun, but he knew of their fate. The Cathars, a religious sect that had flourished in the southern regions of the Kingdom of France, had recognised two gods, one of supreme goodness, the other of absolute evil. In following their own doctrine they had adhered to the Old and New Testaments, but had believed them to be allegorical rather than literal interpretations of the faith. The evil god, they had believed, had created the world and everything in it and that all matter was therefore corrupt. Because of this belief they did not regard Jesus as truly human, denying that the divine, which transcended the polluted Earth, could have ever been a part of it.

Advocating personal experience of the sacred, they had opposed the Church, its priesthood and temporal luxuries. When their teachings had spread and had grown in popularity, the Church had declared them heretics and had gone to war against them. The Crusade had been fought on native soil, had lasted thirty-six years and had seen the extermination of most of their sect. The most devastating blow to the Cathars had come sixteen years ago, with the fall of their last major stronghold and the burning of two hundred men, women and children. To the Church, heresy was a disease that needed to be cut out, severing the limb if necessary, to save the body from infection.

'Besides,' continued Jacques, setting his goblet down, 'I do not believe that the book will be in the hands of any common reader, as you put it. I think we can be certain that whoever coerced the clerk to steal it must know it belongs to the Brethren. Why else would they go to the trouble of forcing the clerk to steal something so seemingly worthless from our treasure-laden vaults?'

'But only a handful within the Temple know, let alone outsiders.'

'There have always been rumours.'

'Rumours, yes, nothing more,' responded Hasan carefully. 'The Soul of the Temple is a legend. In all these years no one has been able to prove your existence.'

'Because there has been no proof to be found, only the testimonies of those involved, who swore oaths on pain of death never to divulge our secrets. And that damn book.' Jacques sat back wearily. 'Not all those who left the circle following our dissolution are dead. Maybe the oaths they swore no longer concern them? Maybe one or more of them has discovered that the Anima Templi is continuing its work without them? That our plans are still in motion? Perhaps the thief means to use the Book of the Grail as evidence against us, or to bribe us with the threat of exposure?' Jacques shook his head. 'Make no mistake, Hasan, we are indeed in grave peril whilst the book remains lost. If our plans were exposed, the Temple could face destruction, the Brethren could face the stake and everything we have worked towards for the last century will have been for nothing. And if the Church was to discover our ultimate plan? Well, I'm not sure a punishment fittingly cruel enough has yet been devised, even by its inquisitors.' Jacques picked up his goblet, put it to his lips, then set it down without drinking. 'Without the Temple's power, without the vast resources of men and money that it unwittingly provides us with we cannot continue our work.'

Hasan was silent, thoughtful for a few moments. 'If the thief knows of the Brethren, perhaps through a former member divulging your secrets, then who might it be? Who would want to destroy us, or the Temple?'

'Over the years we have made many enemies; people envious of our power and our wealth. The Temple answers to the pope alone and stands beyond the laws of kings and courts. As knights we pay no tax or tithe and are given licence to open churches from which to generate donations. We trade in almost every kingdom this side of the sea and have more influence than most beyond it. To annoy us is a crime and to kill or even wound one of us, is punishable by excommunication. Who might it be?' Jacques spread his hands expansively. 'The Hospitallers, the Mamluks, Genoese or Pisan merchants whose trade we have taken, any number of kings or nobles, the Teutonic Knights? The list is long.'

'I shall find the book, brother,' said Hasan quietly, 'if I have to turn over the bed of King Louis himself to do so.'

Jacques stared at the parchments on the table, the contents of which had occupied his waking thoughts for the past two weeks. They now seemed nothing more than a petty annoyance. 'How long can you stay?'

'As long as you need me to, although the sooner I return the better.'

Jacques crossed to the armoire by the window. 'I have business to attend to here. Unfortunately, it isn't something I can abandon. There would be too many questions. But I will return with you to Paris when I am able and aid in the search.'

Opening the double doors, he reached behind a Bible on the bottom shelf and pulled out a small box. Taking a key from the top shelf, he unlocked the box and brought out a pouch. He shook several coins into his palm and handed them to Hasan, before returning the key and the box to their places.

'I will have my horse saddled for you. There is an inn on Friday Street, west of the Walbrook. Look for the sign of the Crescent Moon. Give the gold and my name and you will be welcome there. I will send for you when my business here is done.'

Hasan smiled slightly. 'An aptly named lodging.' He stowed the coins in a pouch at his belt. 'Everard will be glad. He sent me as soon as the Temple's inquiry was ended. I know he hoped you would be free to return with me.'

'I'm sure the priest will be glad. Though he'll not show it.'

Hasan rose from his stool and fished inside the sack bag that he had kept on his lap throughout the meeting. 'There is one last thing, brother.'

Jacques watched as Hasan pulled out a leather scrollcase that was bound with wire to hold it shut. 'What is it?' he asked, taking it.

'The one item of good news I bear.'

Jacques uncoiled the wire and opened the leather sheath. A piece of parchment was rolled inside. As Jacques pulled it out, he could smell the sea, trapped in the thick, yellowed skin. The page was covered with a neat script. He scanned the first few paragraphs, then looked up at Hasan. 'This is good news indeed. I must confess I didn't expect him to have achieved this quite so soon. May I keep hold of it? I should like time to read it properly.'

'Of course.'

Jacques tucked the letter beneath the scrolls on the table and motioned to the door. 'Come. I'll escort you to the stables.'

The River Thames, London, 15 September 1260 AD

Henry III, the King of England, shielded his eyes as the sun appeared from behind a cloud and turned the river a dazzling shade of silver. It was still early, but the sun was surprisingly warm on the heads of the monarch and his large entourage of pages, clerks and guards who sat stiffly on benches, or stood to attention. There was a shout as the captain of the royal barge ordered a rowing boat off the starboard bow to move out of the way. The Thames was busy with fishing boats and merchants' cogs and the crew of the unwieldy, ponderous craft had to negotiate their way carefully upriver, long oars dipping and sweeping.

Henry patted his head where his grey hair was thinnest, checking for the sun's heat on his age-mottled skin. Despite the warmth and his voluminous black velvet robes that were trimmed at the collar and cuffs with the pelt of a wolf, he felt cold. He shifted restlessly on his cushion and tried to catch the eye of his eldest son, who was seated on the bench behind him, but Prince Edward's gaze was fixed on the two men in the offending craft who were rowing frantically out of the barge's path. Henry turned instead to the man dressed in a black cloak and hat who was seated to his left. The man's pale face looked whiter than usual.

'The water bothers you, Lord Chancellor?' enquired Henry.

'No, my liege. It is the motion that unsettles me.'

'It's the quickest way to the Temple from the Tower,' said Henry briskly, as if this might make a difference to the man's discomfort. He waved away a page who attempted to come over with a tray of drinks.

'This way is at least a little more secluded than by horse,' responded the chancellor, 'and for that I'm grateful. The fewer people who see us entering the Temple the better. It is well known that your only dealings with the knights these days lie in their treasury. Your subjects might question why you have need of more gold when you are taking so much of theirs. The new taxes are unpopular enough as it is.'

Henry's frown deepened. 'Those taxes were raised on your counsel, Chancellor.'

'And I assure you, my liege, it was good advice. I merely point out what is in your best interests, and what is in your best interests today is to make our attendance at the Temple as swift and unobserved as possible. It is ill enough that we've agreed to attend their meeting. The Templars grow ever above their station.'

Henry stared out over the water and massaged his jaw, which felt as if it was being slowly clamped shut by a vice. The riverbanks were packed, as always, with the continuous flow of traders and merchants, errand runners and bargain hunters. All along the streets they walked, rode, or clattered past on horsedrawn bronettes and carts pulled by oxen. Beyond, the city was a forest of stone and timber dwellings, wooden wharf houses, shops, mansions and priories, all broken by the lofty spires of chapels and the roof of St Paul's. The sun's glare, the smells from the fish docks and the collective, frantic movement of his citizens made Henry's head throb.

'Their summons was most impertinent, my liege,' continued the chancellor when the king didn't speak. 'No details of their agenda, only a request that myself and the treasury staff attend.' The chancellor's face was subtly turning from white to blanched pink with his rising indignation.

'That should tell you all you need to know, Chancellor,' said Henry dryly, rubbing his brow. 'I would assume it regards our debt.'

'But you spoke with one of them on this matter only recently.'

'Brother Owein. A persistent man indeed. I told him I would pay the debt when I was able and he accepted.'

'If so, my liege, why the summons?'

Henry opened his mouth to respond, but his son spoke before him. 'Perhaps they wish to discuss a new Crusade?'

The chancellor and Henry looked round to see the prince watching them.

Edward's pale grey eyes glinted in the reflected sunlight coming off the water. That one of his eyelids drooped, giving him the look of someone forever deep in thought, didn't detract from his good looks. His voice was soft and he spoke slowly and carefully to disguise the slight stammer that had affected him since childhood. 'It is certainly long past needed. There has been no sustained, effective drive eastward since King Louis' campaign and that ended six years ago. Now we have vague reports that the Mongols have widened their invasion and the Mamluks are preparing to march on Palestine to confront them.'

'For the moment,' responded Henry, 'I need to concentrate on domestic problems rather than foreign troubles that can be dealt with, in the first instance, by the military Orders. That is what they are there for, after all.'

'It's been ten years since you took the Cross, father,' said the prince mildly, but with a challenge to his tone. 'I thought you wanted to go on Crusade? That is what you told the knights when they asked you what the money they were lending you was for.'

'And I will. In time.' Henry turned away, signalling the end of the conversation, but behind him, he could still feel Edward's eyes on him. It made him uncomfortable. Last year, rumours had begun to circulate in the royal household that his son was involved in a plot to overthrow him, masterminded by Henry's brother-in-law, the man he had made the Earl of Leicester, Simon de Montfort. He had confronted the earl and his son, but without proof he had eventually been forced to reconcile himself with them. The incident had, however, left a rift between him and Edward that seemed to broaden a little more each day.

'Well, we will just need to be firm with the knights, my liege,' said the chancellor decisively, 'whatever it is they want from us.'

Henry lapsed into a brooding silence as the barge passed beyond the city walls. In the distance rose the Templars' preceptory.

New Temple, London, 15 September 1260 AD

The chapel doors boomed shut and the last few knights seated themselves as the priest stepped behind the altar. Will darted to his place in the nave with his fellow sergeants and knelt as the priest opened the office of Terce with the usual fervour. Will clasped his hands in prayer, but it wasn't praise for God, or even the impending parley with the king that filled his mind. He had been late for the office and hadn't yet seen Garin. Eyes open a crack, he scanned the nave and breathed a sigh as his gaze fell on his friend. Garin was kneeling several rows in front, head bowed, hair hanging like a curtain across his face.

Will shuffled uncomfortably as the priest launched into a reading of the scriptures. He had sat through seven of these readings every day for two years, and that didn't include Mass, which they heard once a day after the office of Sext, or the vespers and vigils said for the dead each afternoon. Still the readings didn't seem to get any shorter. There were also special services for festivals: the Christ Mass; Epiphany; the Feast of the Annunciation; the Feast of the Assumption; the Feast of St John the Baptist, to name but a few. At least with those, there was always a good meal to look forward to afterwards.

A spider in a crack between the flagstones, disturbed by Will's shuffling, scuttled towards the effigies of knights that were imprisoned in the floor of the nave, solemnity carved into their faces, granite swords at their chests. The nave was a lofty, circular chamber, ringed with the stone heads of sinners and demons that leered from the walls, faces contorted in various expressions of pain and malevolence. It opened out into a choir aisle that led to the altar. Pillars divided the aisle, rising to the vaulted ceiling, and the benches between were filled with knights.

Eventually, the priest raised his hands. 'Arise, brothers. Humble servants of God, defenders of the true faith and upholders of the Divine Law. Arise as we say the Paternoster.'

Will rose, legs tingling, to recite the Lord's Prayer. His voice joined with those of the other two hundred and sixty men in the chapel, their words colliding until they spoke as one in a voice that was as resonant as the surging of the sea.

'*Pax vobiscum!*'

There was a scuffle of feet as the priest shut the breviary, signalling the close of the office.

Will waited impatiently with the other sergeants for the knights to go. When it was the turn of his row to leave, he hastened out, jostling his fellows. After the chapel's gloom the sun seemed overly bright and he shaded his eyes as he stepped through the archway. The sergeants were heading in a line behind the knights, making their way to the Great Hall to break their fast. The buildings around the main courtyard were golden in the autumn morning. The sky was a magnificent, hazy blue, and the smell of ripe apples and plums in the orchards was a sweet perfume masking the general odour of sweat and horse dung that permeated the preceptory. Something in the colour of the morning light, the way it seemed to illuminate everything from within, reminded Will of the day he arrived at New Temple.

Saddle-sore and weary from the fortnight's ride from Edinburgh, he and his father had ridden down out of the Middlesex Forest, through cornfields and vineyards to see London stretched out before them. It had been autumn then too, the leaves russet-red on the branches. They had stopped to water their horses at a stream and Will had stared down over the sprawling city in wonder. Outside the walls, to the right, he had glimpsed several impressive estates stretched along the sweeping riverbanks, one of which he had guessed must be the Temple. Everything had looked so large and grand and hallowed that Will had imagined angels, not men, dwelling within the buildings. He had turned to his father, exalted, and had been met with that same sad blankness in James's face that he had been confronted with for months.

Will pushed the memory aside with effort. Once the shadow took hold it was difficult to shake and he refused to let that darkness in today. Catching sight of Garin in the line of sergeants filing out of the chapel grounds, he ran down the steps, forcing a smile.

Garin looked round as Will ran up beside him. 'Are you coming to the armoury?'

Will caught his arm. 'Where were you last night?'

Garin grimaced. 'In the infirmary with Brother Michael, and the cramps. He said it must have been something I'd eaten. I didn't tell him about the plums.'

'I thought . . .' Will stopped, laughing to cover the near-utterance of what was unspoken between them. 'That'll teach us. Luckily, I've got an armoured stomach.'

'We should collect the shields,' said Garin, moving across the yard. 'This is one meeting I don't want to be late for.'

The two boys headed for the armoury, ignoring the curious glances of the younger sergeants as they broke their ranks.

After collecting their masters' shields they made their way to the inner courtyard, Will hefting Owein's shield higher on his arm as the leather straps pinched his skin. The shields, which were stained white with quicklime and sectioned with a crimson cross, were almost as big as they were. Set in the centre of the knights' quarters, the courtyard lawn was ringed by cloisters where arched doorways led into the lower levels of the buildings. The grass, beaded with dew, glowed with a green phosphor-escence. A large trestle and boards had been placed at the centre and a host of servants were bustling around it in the complex, unfaltering dance of those bred for service, carrying benches, trays of food and wine from the kitchens. Will moved over to Owein, Garin following. The knight was talking intently with one of the Temple's clerks. He looked up. Will opened his mouth to greet his master, but another voice called out before he could speak.

'Brother Owein.'

Will turned to see Jacques heading towards them.

Jacques, ignoring Will and Garin completely, nodded to Owein. 'The royal barge has arrived.'

'Very well, brother. I believe we're ready.' Owein motioned to Will. 'To your place, sergeant, and remember, only speak if spoken to.'

'Yes, sir.'

They headed for the trestle and boards where two other sergeants were bearing the shields of their masters. Garin stood beside Will, holding the shield, one-handed, before him. Will's gaze drifted to Jacques, who was standing with Owein on the edge of the lawn. Cyclops's sour face and stiff, arrogant posture made Will bristle with dislike. A short time later, he heard the sound of voices and many footsteps approaching. The double doors on the far side of the courtyard swung open.

At the head of the company that filed out onto the lawn was Humbert de Pairaud, the Master of England. The Templar Master was a lofty, broad-chested man with a mane of iron-dark hair, whose presence seemed to fill the courtyard. Walking at Humbert's side was King Henry. His ashen hair was curled at the ends in the current fashion, his face pleated with age. At the king's right hand was Prince Edward. The fair-haired youth was almost a head in height above the rest of the company and, at twenty-one, already had the poise of a monarch. A pale-faced man with hollow cheeks dressed in black, and a company of pages, clerks and royal guards followed them.

Owein stepped forward and bowed, first to the Master, then to the king and prince. 'My lords, it is an honour to welcome you to the Temple. Lord Chancellor,' he added, greeting the man in black with a nod.

Henry smiled wanly. 'Sir Owein. How good it is to see you and so soon after our last meeting.'

Will looked at Owein, surprised. He didn't know that his master had met with the king.

'My lord,' Humbert intervened, his voice gruff with age and authority, 'let us sit and discourse in comfort.'

'Indeed,' conceded Henry, with a dubious glance at the seating. Two attendants draped the head chair with a square of scarlet silk. The Temple's servants retreated to the cloisters as Henry sat, his pages fluttering round him like moths. He dismissed them with a wave. 'How you can reside in such barren strongholds is a mystery to me, Master Templar. Surely the wealthiest men in Christendom can afford a little luxury?'

'Our service is to God, my lord,' replied Humbert smoothly, taking the seat to the left of the king. 'Not the comfort of our flesh.'

Will stepped back to allow Owein to sit beside the Master. Edward was at the king's right and three knights, including Jacques and five clerks, two from the palace and three from the Temple, took up the rest of the places around the trestle. There was one space left empty. Will guessed it was for the chancellor who had chosen to remain standing behind the king, like a raven perched on the back of his chair.

Henry looked at the trays of fruit and jars of wine. 'Thankfully, you have been gracious enough to furnish us with more earthly pleasures.'

'Yes, Lord King.' Humbert beckoned a servant to pour the wine. 'The Temple is glad to greet its guests in the custom and manner of their own halls.'

Henry stared at Humbert for a moment, then looked away as the servant poured wine into a goblet and passed it to him with a bow. His gaze swept the company and fell on Will.

'Your soldiers seem to get younger each year. Or perhaps it is I who grows older? How old are you, boy?'

'Thirteen and eight, my lord.' Out of the corner of his eye, Will noticed that Jacques was looking at him.

'Ah!' said Henry, unaware of Will's discomfort. 'A Scotsman unless my ears fail me?'

'Yes, my lord.'

'Then you are privileged to have been a subject of two of these islands' most beautiful ladies. My wife and my daughter, Margaret.'

Will bowed in acquiescence, but said nothing. He had been only four when Henry had married his ten-year-old daughter to the King of Scotland. But he'd grown up with his father's thoughts on the matter and understood that through Margaret, Henry had established a firmer hold over Scotland – a country that the English kings had coveted for centuries.

'It is in the young that old men must place their hopes for the future,' continued Henry, taking a sip of wine. 'Last month I commissioned the best artist in England to recreate the fall of Jerusalem in my private quarters at the Tower. That was the golden age of chivalry, when brotherhoods were Orders of the highest renown and men like Godfrey de Bouillon walked in the footsteps of our Lord Jesus Christ, sacrificing themselves for the glory of God and Christendom. Perhaps,' he added dryly, 'those days may yet come again.'

Humbert raised his brow. 'I was of the belief, my lord, that the monies we lent you were for your planned Crusade in Palestine, not those across the walls of your palace?'

'Do not fret about your gold, de Pairaud, it is well spent. You care too much for such things. The Temple trades in the supply of goods across the lands and sea, charges pilgrims for passage on its ships, takes donations from nobles and kings and, in the service of moneylending, charges almost as much interest as the damn Jews!' The king met Humbert's gaze. 'I think the name Poor Fellow Soldiers of Jesus Christ, by which I've heard you prefer to be known, is somewhat misleading.'

'The Temple must use all means available to generate funds on this side of the sea if we are to continue the fight beyond it. Indeed, we must utilise every facet of our Order to achieve what has been the dream of every man, woman and child in Christendom for the last two centuries: the reclaiming of Jerusalem from the Saracens and the establishment of a Christian Holy Land. As monks we pray for this, as warriors we build arms and send men to fortify our garrisons in Outremer to aid this and as men we produce and sell whatever is in our capacity to do so in order to accomplish this. And if we do not do this,' added Humbert, his eyes boring into Henry's, 'who will, my Lord King? The West may still long for this dream, but few are those who now rush to fulfil it.'

'You hide behind your piety, Master Templar,' snapped Henry, piqued by the barb. 'It is well known that the Temple, with all its properties and assets, is busy building itself an empire in the West. An empire where perhaps even a king is no longer in control of his own kingdom!'

For a moment there was utter silence in the courtyard. It was broken by the soft voice of Prince Edward.

'Has there been any further news from the East, Master Templar? In your last report you informed us that the Mongols had attacked Baghdad and several other cities. Is there any cause to think that they will attack our holdings?'

Henry frowned at his son as Humbert turned his attention to Edward.

'No, we have heard nothing further, my Lord Prince,' replied the Templar Master. 'But I do not believe that we face any immediate danger from the Mongols. It is the Mamluks that concern me.'

Henry scoffed at this. 'Their leader Kutuz is a slave! What power can he wield?'

'A slave warrior,' corrected Humbert, 'and no longer a slave at that. It's my, and my brothers' belief that the Mamluks pose a greater threat than many in the West have reckoned. At present, only the Mongols keep their attention from us.'

'For that we should be glad,' said Henry curtly. 'The Mongols are by far the stronger force and I hear they use Christian women and children as shields in battle. It is good the Saracens occupy their attention.'

'Forgive me, majesty, but you are mistaken. The Mongols are powerful, yes. But, the Church has already converted many of them. At Baghdad it was only the Saracens they killed, the Christians were spared. The last tidings we received from the Holy Land told of the Mamluks preparing to march on Palestine. Our spies in Cairo say they go to war against the

Mongols, following an insult to their sultan. Their vanguard will be under the direction of one of the Mamluk army's ablest commanders, Baybars.'

'Baybars?'

'They call him the Crossbow.' Humbert's expression hardened. 'He was responsible for the slaughter of three hundred of the Temple's best men. Baybars led the massacre of Mansurah, my lord. The battle that ended the Crusade led by your brother-in-law, King Louis.'

Beside him, Will sensed Garin stiffen. He knew the cause. Garin, aged four, had lost his father and two brothers in that campaign. Jacques had been the only one of the de Lyons family to survive the massacre of Mansurah. Will's gaze darted to the knight. Cyclops's brow was furrowed. There was a distant look in the knight's eye, as if his mind was somewhere else entirely. Will looked away as Humbert continued.

'After Louis' forces took the city of Damietta they moved south through Egypt, led by the king's brother, Robert de Artois. They came upon the Mamluk army camped outside the town of Mansurah. Artois conducted a bold assault on the camp in defiance of the king's orders. Many Mamluk soldiers were slaughtered, including the chief of their Royal Guard. Baybars took the place of his dead leader and set a trap in Mansurah, knowing that we would follow his men into the town. In the streets our brothers fell by the hundreds on the swords of Baybars' men. The Mamluks are not to be underestimated, my lord.'

Prince Edward stirred. 'Do we have enough forces to counter this threat, Master Templar?'

'Yes!' said Henry emphatically before Humbert could answer. 'Will those who are sworn to protect Christian citizens in the Holy Land have trouble fulfilling their oath?'

'There is, as with all things, the matter of funding, my lords,' said Owein.

Humbert shot Owein a sharp glance. 'The Mamluks know the lands well from their many campaigns, Lord King. More so than our settlers, who have established livelihoods in one town or another and have been content to remain there. They use pigeons to send messages and their spies are everywhere. At present, they are in a better position to attack than we are to defend.'

'We must act decisively,' said Edward, 'A Crusade would—'

'It's said,' interrupted Henry, patting his son's arm, 'that a hasty decision will incur an even hastier downfall. A Crusade may be necessary, yes, but we must plan carefully for it.'

'Of course, father,' Edward acceded with a polite, slightly stiff nod.

Henry sat back. 'Well, this is very disturbing, Master Templar. But at this time there is little I can do, so why, I ask, have you summoned me here?'

'If it please your majesty,' said Humbert, 'Brother Owein will open the discussion.'

Owein turned to Henry, his hands steepled and resting on the table. 'We have granted you the use of the Temple's treasury, Lord King, for the storing of your goods and the use of our own funds when you require them, as was granted to your father, King John, and his brother, King Richard. While the Temple is pleased to offer monetary assistance to the royal family . . .'

'I should hope so,' interrupted Henry. 'The good Lord knows I allow you enough power in these lands to warrant the meagre bounty you grace me with on rare occasions.'

'The good Lord does know,' said Humbert, 'and you can be assured of a great reward in Heaven for the benevolence you show His soldiers. Please continue, Brother Owein.'

'But while we are pleased to offer this service our funds are not limitless.' Owein held out his hand to one of the Temple's clerks, who passed him a rolled parchment. He pushed it across the table to the king. 'As you can see, my lord, your debts to us have grown considerably over the last year.'

Henry scanned the parchment, the furrows in his brow deepening the further he read. He handed it to the chancellor, who took in the words at a glance before returning it to him. Edward leaned forward to view the scroll as Henry stroked his thin beard and looked at Owein. 'These monies were given to me in good faith. I will repay them when I can, but my situation at present doesn't afford me the opportunity.'

'We have discovered, my Lord King,' said Owein, with a brief glance at Jacques, 'that you recently organised a number of jousts at Cheapside for the pleasure of your French courtiers. Who paid for those?'

Jacques nodded, but said nothing.

Henry glared at both of them.

'Surely, Sir Knight, you can understand my father's position,' said Edward, looking up from the scroll. 'As sovereign of this nation it is his duty to give the people protection in times of war and sport in times of peace.'

'This we understand,' agreed Owein, with a respectful nod to the prince. 'But we cannot afford these debts to go unpaid. We need all the gold we can muster if we are to bolster our forces in the Holy Land.'

'Whatever happened to charity?' said Henry dryly. 'Are the Templars exempt from this Christian duty?'

'If it's charity you seek, Lord King,' said Humbert, 'then, with respect, I would suggest that you petition the Hospitallers.'

Henry's face reddened. 'What insolence you show me!' He threw the parchment to the table. 'You will have your damned money soon enough. I have raised taxes here and in my lands in Gascony, but, I warn you, don't insult me again else you won't see a penny!'

'Taxes take too long to reap, Lord King. The monies must be paid sooner.'

'Christ in Heaven! Would you have me sell the clothes off my back? I cannot pluck gold from the trees, or turn it from lead!'

Owein looked at Humbert, who nodded. 'There is one way to resolve this, Lord King.'

'What is it then, damn you?'

'Pawn the crown jewels to us, my lord. We will hold them until the debts can be repaid.'

'*What?*' thundered the king.

Edward sat up sharply and the chancellor stared at Owein in astonishment. Will fought to keep his expression blank.

'It is the only way, your majesty,' said Humbert.

The king rose swiftly, upending his chair. The scarlet silk slipped off the seat and spilled out across the grass. He slammed his fist on the board, upsetting several goblets of wine.

'The crown jewels are symbols of my line and the adornments of royalty, not of some lick-spit soldiers who seem to place themselves as high as God!' He snatched the scroll from the table, tore it in half and tossed the pieces to the grass.

Humbert rose, his voice even. 'I would remind you that the loyalty of the Temple has always been most beneficial and, some might say, essential for a sovereign of this nation. It would be a great shame, my lord, were you to lose this loyalty.'

'I should have your *head*!' said Henry, his breathing ragged.

At the edges of the lawn the royal guards shuffled uneasily. Two of the knights had risen, their hands on the hilts of their swords.

Edward put a hand on Henry's arm. 'Come, father, I believe this meeting is ended.'

Henry shot Humbert one final look of fury, then, jerking his arm from his son's grip, he strode across the courtyard. With a curt nod to Humbert and Owein, Edward swept out after the king, along with the entourage.

The chancellor remained. He looked at Humbert, his mouth drawn in a thin, flat line. 'You will be formally notified of the king's decision within a month, Master Templar.'

Humbert glanced at the torn pieces of parchment fluttering on the ground. 'I have a copy of those records in my private solar. Will his majesty wish this to be sent to the palace?'

The chancellor shook his head. 'I'll collect them now.'

Humbert glanced around the table. 'De Lyons,' he said, motioning to Garin. 'Escort the Lord Chancellor to my solar. My squire will hand you the relevant scrolls.'

Garin bowed low and headed across the lawn with the chancellor. Will looked round as he heard Owein's voice behind him.

'That didn't go as well as I had hoped. I only hope that the king doesn't decide to retaliate.'

'Barking dogs seldom bite, Brother Owein,' replied Humbert. 'The last time Henry tried to intimidate us he soon backed down when we threatened to depose him.'

6

The Plain of Sharon, the Kingdom of Jerusalem

9 October 1260 AD

'We near the final stretch, Amir.'

Baybars barely caught the sultan's words. The air around them was throbbing with the beating of drums. When the Mamluks returned to Cairo their victory tattoo would sound for seven days. The drums they had taken from the Mongols were cleft and raised on poles. Silent.

'We return home triumphant,' continued Kutuz, raising his voice above the din, 'as I knew we would.'

'The city will sing praises to your name, my Lord Sultan,' said Baybars, the calmness of his voice bearing no relation to his troubled mind.

Kutuz smiled. 'The Mongols will think twice before provoking me again, now that we have tightened our hold on Syria.'

'Yes, my lord,' said Baybars, glancing over his shoulder.

Behind him, the Mamluk army clogged the road for several miles. The flags and banners were lifted high above carts loaded with plunder and wagons crammed with slaves. The sultan's advisors and the officers of the Mu'izziyya were blocking Baybars' view. For a moment, their line broke and he caught sight of Omar some distance behind him at the front of the Bahri regiment, then the ranks pulled tight again.

Baybars turned back to the road. It was almost dusk. The sun was a red-rimmed eye that closed slowly as it met the horizon. In the distance, a broad strip of green cut through the Plain of Sharon, cradling a river that flowed into the sea twenty or so miles to the west. The road crossed the river at its narrowest point and snaked southwards. The army was fast approaching Gaza where they would take a brief rest before making the arduous journey across the Sinai desert and into Egypt.

Baybars studied the sultan out of the corner of his eye. Kutuz was sitting stiffly in his saddle, a frown creasing his brow. The sultan was right, they were returning home in triumph. The Mamluks had done what no one else had been able to, had *dared* to: they had faced the Mongol army and crushed them. But, to Baybars, their victory tasted like dust. He had lost more than Aleppo in this campaign. He had lost the chance for revenge – a revenge he had planned and played out in his dreams for years. Since they began the homeward march he had tried to focus on his plans for Kutuz. Time was running out with every mile that passed and, as yet, he'd been afforded no chance to prepare the details of his removal.

Five days after the battle at Ayn Jalut, the Mamluks had marched into Damascus, the Mongols falling before them. From there they had moved north to Homs and Hamah, where the amirs who had fled the Mongol invasion were restored to their positions and the cities returned to Muslim rule. At Aleppo, the Mongols held out for almost a month, but eventually the Mamluks had shattered their defences and had taken the city. When the fighting had ended, Kutuz had paraded through the streets. The Muslims, who had suffered under the Mongols' yoke, had come cautiously out of their homes to meet their liberator. The Christians, who had prospered, were killed.

By the time the sultan's cortege had arrived in Aleppo's main market square, word had spread and the jubilant Muslim citizens thronged to the square in their hundreds to welcome their new overlord. Baybars had stood in silence at Kutuz's side as the sultan made an elaborate show of handing control of the city to another Mamluk governor. When the ceremony had ended and the governors and officers of the regiments had gathered round Kutuz to congratulate their triumphal leader, Baybars had disappeared into the crowds. After speaking with one of his soldiers, he had headed for the slave platform that loomed up at the centre of the square.

It did not seem so long ago that he had stood in chains on this platform, staring down at the men who eyed him as if he was a beast in a cattle auction. Beyond the market, somewhere south of the city mosque, was the household he had served for six months as a slave.

Baybars had climbed onto the wooden boards, the army's cries ringing in his ears.

'*Allahu akbar!*' God is greatest.

Omar had found him sitting on the edge of the platform, two hours later. 'Amir?'

Baybars looked up, mildly surprised to see how far the sun had moved across the city.

Omar clambered up beside him. 'I've been looking for you,' he said, adjusting his sword belt. 'Have you been here all this time?'

'Yes.'

'I have news. The officers have been paid. You have their support.'

Baybars nodded, but said nothing.

Omar spoke on. 'I can understand why you stayed here rather than return to the camp. Kutuz is drunk on victory and singing praises to the governor he appointed. I think he was disappointed that you weren't there to witness his gloating.'

Baybars stared out across the square, which was golden in the early evening light. The crowds had disappeared, but a squadron of Mamluks had remained to patrol the streets whilst the main force retired to make camp. Kutuz and his retinue had taken over the citadel for their victory feast. Baybars turned to Omar. 'The sultan isn't the reason I didn't retire with the men. Aleppo may not have passed into my hands today, but when Kutuz is dead it won't be praise its new governor will get from me. I shall have the city soon enough.' He looked away. 'And more besides.'

'Then why hide yourself away out here? Come, we'll have a feast of our own.'

'I'm not hiding, Omar, I'm waiting.'

'Waiting?' Omar frowned. 'For what?'

'An old friend.' Baybars rose and gazed at the streets leading off from the square. The dome of the mosque was a great, golden bell suspended above the angular patterns of the flat, white roofs.

Omar stood, following his gaze. 'You didn't tell me you knew anyone in the city. It has been, what? Eighteen years since you were here?'

'Nineteen.' Baybars clasped his hands behind his back. 'Return to the camp. I will join you soon.'

'The officers have been paid, but the time and the place haven't been set. Whilst we are afforded this chance to talk alone we should finalise . . .'

'You disobey my command, officer?' said Baybars, not looking at him.

'Forgive me, Amir,' replied Omar, the hurt surprise clear in his voice. 'I didn't realise it was an order.'

He turned to go, then stopped as Baybars jumped down from the platform. A Mamluk soldier had come riding out of one of the streets nearby. The soldier looked around and trotted his horse over as he spied Baybars.

'Amir.' The soldier dismounted and bowed.

'Did you find the household?'

'Yes, Amir, but the man you sent me to seek out wasn't there.'

'What?'

'The household has been abandoned for some time. I asked in the area, though few knew of the family who lived there. There was a merchant who thought he remembered a Western knight who once owned the estate. He believed the knight to have died, said his family returned to the West ten or more years ago.'

Baybars took a step backwards and gripped the edge of the platform.

'Is that all, Amir?' asked the soldier.

Baybars waved him away.

The soldier bowed. Mounting his horse, he clattered off.

Omar jumped down beside Baybars. 'Who is this knight?'

'Return to camp.'

'Sadeek, talk to me,' pressed Omar, frustrated. 'You've never told me what happened to you in Aleppo, but I've seen how this place haunts you. Was this knight your master here?'

Omar gasped as Baybars grabbed him by the shoulders and spun him round to slam him up against the platform. 'I said *leave!*' Omar stared into his eyes, breathing heavily. Baybars dropped his hands and stepped back. 'We will talk soon, Omar,' he said quietly, 'you have my word. But not today.'

He had walked away, leaving Omar alone in the market square as the call to prayer had sung out in the evening.

Baybars gripped the reins of his horse. Around him, the drums continued their steady thrumming, fast and low like a racing heart. With effort, he forced himself to focus on the matter at hand. He was a commander in the Mamluk army. He had fought the Christians and the Mongols and had won. He had been a slave in life and name, but he would not be a slave to memory. The failure in Aleppo to do what he had planned for so many years had thrown him, but he no longer had time to dwell on the past. The knight was gone, or dead. He would find no retribution.

'You are quiet today, Amir. Is something wrong?' probed Kutuz.

'No, my lord.'

Kutuz studied the commander intently, but Baybars' expression was unreadable. He may as well be looking at a wall, for all the emotion in those eyes. 'You will, of course, be handsomely rewarded for your part in our victory when we reach Cairo.'

'Your generosity is appreciated, my lord.'

'My Lord Sultan!'

A scout rode down the column towards them. He saluted as he swung his horse around and rode in beside Kutuz. 'The road passes close to a village, three miles east, my lord.'

'Another Christian settlement?'

'Yes, my lord, there is a church.'

'I'll send the Mu'izziyya.'

'Your men are weary, my lord,' said Baybars quickly. 'This will be the fourth settlement they have sacked in five days. I feel the need to stretch my legs, let me take the Bahri.'

Kutuz thought for a moment, then acceded with a nod. 'Go then. We'll continue to Gaza. I am sure I have no need to remind you of the proper procedure.'

'No, my Lord Sultan, rest assured that anything of value will be brought to you.'

Baybars kicked his heels into the flanks of his horse. At his command, five hundred men broke off from the main army and followed him. Several wagons pulled off the road after them: the wooden cages on top had room for more slaves.

The village was nestled between two gentle slopes that stretched up from the Plain of Sharon where the olive groves grew thick and tangled. A barricade of bound wooden stakes surrounded the sixty dwellings within; jumbled rows of mud-brick huts clustered around three larger stone buildings and a church. Smoke from the fire pits was coiling into the bruised-pink sky. The farmers who worked the groves had returned for the evening, leading carts pulled by cattle.

Within moments of reaching the village's perimeter, the Mamluks set about tearing down the ineffectual barrier of stakes. Several farmers, who had seen the soldiers ride up from the Plain, had raised the alarm and panic now engulfed the village like a wave, spreading from dwelling to dwelling as the church bell clanged a futile warning. Some men hastened to arm themselves with anything they could find: a stone, a scythe, a broom. Others called for evacuation, for someone to parley with the invaders. But the Mamluks had entered the settlement.

The thin line of farmers who had braced themselves behind a row of carts for the attack scattered as the cavalry charged them, the soldiers on their armoured mounts swinging swords and spiked maces at the bared heads and backs of the fleeing men. Men and boys fell under the sword strokes and were trampled by the horses of the soldiers behind. One farmer, managing to duck a decapitating blow, fled. Three soldiers followed him, whooping as they gave chase, excited by the hunt. A pungent smell of olives rose up as the carts were overturned in the crush of soldiers pouring through the broken defences, the fruit cascading to the ground like beads from a broken rosary.

Baybars rode into the village, the inhabitants fleeing before him, scurrying for the scant shelter of the huts. He scanned the streets ahead as his soldiers dispatched the last of the farmers.

There were scores of such villages scattered across Palestine, once largely inhabited by Coptic, Armenian and Greek Orthodox Christians whose families had worked the land for generations. When the first Crusaders had come out of the West, the relative peace between the native Christians and their Muslim overlords had been swallowed by war. The Frankish dukes and princes had taken Antioch, Jerusalem, Bethlehem and Hebron and had soon commanded a vast tract of southern and central Palestine and northern Syria. This they had divided into four states that together had formed their new empire: Outremer, the land beyond the sea. They had called these states the Kingdom of Jerusalem, the Principality of Antioch and the Counties of Edessa and Tripoli. Powerful houses of the Western nobility governed each province and, over them all, ruled the new Christian King of Jerusalem. Some of the cities, Jerusalem included, and Edessa, one of the four states, the Muslims had since reclaimed, but, for Baybars, those victories were not enough.

He looked over to the church. Its squat, solid greyness was a mark of the West's influence and the infidels' Roman faith.

'Your orders, Amir?' called one of his officers, riding across to him.

Baybars motioned to the mud-brick huts. 'Burn them down. We'll find nothing of value there.' He gestured at the stone buildings around the church. 'Search those.'

The officer galloped away to relay the commands.

Soon, the huts were smouldering as the Mamluks rode through the streets, tossing flaming torches onto the low rooftops. Smoke billowed up, and men, women and children ran choking from their refuge, only to be cut down, or captured in the streets. A heavy thudding came from the centre of the village as the soldiers battered down the doors of the stone houses. The splintering of wood was followed by cries. The ruler of the village, whose ancestors had come from the West, was dragged out into the street along with his wife. Their children were hauled off to the wagons, screaming, as their parents were forced to the ground and beheaded by Mamluk soldiers.

Baybars leapt down from his horse when he saw Omar riding towards

him. With Omar was another Bahri officer, a tall, graceful man called
Kalawun with a handsome, strong-boned face. The two men reined in their
horses and dismounted.

'I was beginning to wonder if you were coming,' said Baybars.

'We must talk, Amir,' said Omar quietly.

'Not here. The sultan has eyes everywhere. He has been keeping a close
watch on me since we left Ayn Jalut. He doesn't trust me.'

'Then,' said Kalawun with a half-smile, 'he is less of a fool than I
thought.'

The three of them turned as a woman ran screaming from a hut opposite.
Part of the roof had collapsed inwards, sending a shower of sparks into the
sky. The woman was clutching a small white bundle to her breast. When a
soldier ran towards her, she darted to one side and tried to go around him.
But he was quicker. His sword plunged into her stomach and back out in a
crimson arc of blood. The bundle slid from the woman's grip as she
collapsed in the dust and the soldier looked down in surprise as he heard a
high mewing sound. He flicked back the white cloth with the point of his
sword and found a baby wrapped within it. The soldier looked about
uncertainly and saw Baybars.

'Amir?' he called, gesturing at the infant which was now screaming.
'What should I do?'

Baybars frowned. 'Were you planning on suckling it yourself?'

Some of the nearby Mamluks laughed.

'No, Amir,' said the soldier, red-faced. He raised his sword.

Omar averted his eyes as the blade stabbed down. It might have been a
mercy to kill the infant, which would have died a much slower death from
exposure or starvation if left, but he didn't have to watch. When Omar
looked back the soldier was walking away and a stain was spreading out
around the baby, turning the white cloth red.

Baybars' gaze fell on the church. The doors were closed; no one had
taken the building yet. 'Come,' he said to Omar and Kalawun, striding
across to it. The church doors squeaked open as he pushed them, then
jammed against something on the other side. Inside, Baybars heard a man's
voice, shaky yet defiant.

'Stay back, you devils!'

Shoving his shoulder against the wood, Baybars forced his way through.
The bench that was blocking the doors screeched on the stone floor as it was
thrust backwards. Drawing his sabre he entered, Omar and Kalawun close
behind him. Baybars took in the chamber at a glance. The church was small

and unadorned save for a rickety altar at one end above which was suspended a carved wooden crucifix. Behind the altar, brandishing a weighty-looking iron candlestick, was an old priest clad in shabby robes. The chamber was crudely lit by the amber glow that came in through two window-slits in the walls. Outside, the village was in flames.

The priest pointed the candlestick at Baybars. 'Stay back, I tell you!' He was a scrawny-looking man, but there was power in his voice. 'You have no right to come in here. This is a house of God!'

'Your church, priest,' replied Baybars, 'is on our land. We have every right.'

'This is God's land!'

'You and your kind are ants, busy building your churches and castles with no thought of where you are, or what you do. You are a pestilence.'

'I was born here. My people too!' cried the priest, waving his hand to the windows where the crackling and spitting of the fires could be heard.

'Sons and daughters of the Franks. There is Western blood in you all. It is a taint you cannot deny.'

'No!' shouted the priest. '*This* is our home!' He stepped out from behind the altar and lashed the air with the candlestick.

Baybars leapt forward, his sabre cutting high. The priest ducked, but the mighty blow wasn't aimed at him. The blade severed the thin rope that held the crucifix, which fell to the floor before the altar with a clatter. Baybars stamped on it, his heavy boot snapping the figure of Christ in two.

The priest stared at him, aghast, as he bent and picked up one of the pieces. 'You may have been born to these lands, but you carry the infection of the West.' Baybars tossed the half-cross aside. 'What we do here, now, we will do all across Palestine.' He strode to the priest and knocked the candlestick from the man's grip with the flat of his blade. The priest went pale and trembled as the tip of the sabre came to rest at his throat. 'Your God, priest, shall weep at the sight of His churches and relics in flames. The ashes of Christendom shall scatter in the winds and its passing will be as a sweet breath across all Muslims.'

'You will die trying,' whispered the priest. 'The warriors of Christ will crush you.'

Baybars thrust forwards, the blade piercing the priest's throat and on, harder through bone and flesh. The priest gave a brief, gagging cough and his body buckled as the blade came out the other side. Baybars twisted the hilt and blood spilled from the priest's mouth. He wrenched the sword back and the priest collapsed sideways, crashing through the altar and onto the floor. Baybars lifted the blade and hacked at the body, the blade falling again and again until the stones were awash with blood. His breaths came short and sharp and his eyes were wild in the flame-light. He would have his retribution! He would take it from them all! Baybars whipped round as he felt a tight grip on his arm and saw Omar. He staggered back, his chest heaving.

'He is dead, Amir,' said Omar.

Turning from the mangled corpse, Baybars reached into the pouch at his side and pulled out a rag. He looked at the questioning faces of Omar and Kalawun as he cleaned the blade. 'Well? Do you want to talk, or not?'

Kalawun stepped forward. 'Omar has told me of your plan, Amir. I will stand with you when the time comes.'

Baybars nodded his thanks. Kalawun had been enlisted in the Bahri regiment two years after himself and Omar. He had followed them through the ranks and proved himself at Damietta when he had helped kill Turanshah. 'Your loyalty will be rewarded.'

'It won't be easy,' said Omar. 'The sultan is rarely without his guards. It may be best for us to wait until we are in Cairo.'

'No,' said Baybars firmly, 'it must happen before we arrive in the city. Kutuz cannot be allowed to reach the safety of the citadel, he will be even more sheltered from attack there.'

'Poison perhaps?' suggested Omar. 'We could pay one of his pages?'

'There is too much risk in that. Besides, I won't pay another for what I can do myself.'

Baybars finished cleaning his sabre and jammed it into its scabbard.

'What do you propose, Amir?' asked Kalawun.

'We will strike when we reach Egypt. After crossing the Sinai we make camp at al-Salihiyya. The town is only one day from Cairo and Kutuz will be less wary so near his city. If we can draw him from the majority of his guards we'll have our chance.'

Omar nodded slowly. 'I agree, but I'm still unclear as to how you will secure the throne once the sultan is dead. Surely one of his governors will . . .?'

'Khadir will attend to it,' Baybars interrupted.

Omar looked concerned at this news. 'Your soothsayer is best kept on a tight leash, Amir. I've heard that the Order of Assassins expelled him because he was too bloodthirsty, even for them. He's a hazard.'

'He will see that the task is done. Are you with me?'

'Yes, Amir,' said Kalawun.

Omar nodded, after a pause. 'We are with you.'

'Amir Baybars.'

The three of them looked round as a soldier appeared in the doorway.

'The village is taken,' said the soldier, bowing. 'We're loading the wagons.'

'Come,' said Baybars to Omar and Kalawun as the soldier disappeared. 'Let's take the sultan his last plunder.'

Together they strode from the church. Flames darted into the sky as the last of the women and children were herded into the cages, encouraged by the swords of the Mamluks.

Kutuz turned in his saddle and stared into the darkness. The hills that rose up from the Plain were crowned with a faint, orange halo. He could just make out the tongues of the fires that signalled that Baybars had taken the settlement. Kutuz swung his gaze back to the road and rubbed at his neck. His shoulders were knotted and not just from the long day's ride.

For several weeks now, uneasiness had been gnawing at him, growing steadily worse since they had left Ayn Jalut. He'd had doubts before then. But Baybars' audacity in asking for the governorship of Aleppo proved beyond question the scale of his ambitions. After Kutuz's refusal of the request, he had expected Baybars to be angry or bitter; the commander's subsequent calm had unsettled him. Kutuz drew a long breath and scanned the ranks until he saw his chief of staff, several rows behind him.

'A word, Aqtai,' he called loudly.

The fleshy, olive-skinned man looked up at the summons and trotted his horse through the ranks. 'My Lord Sultan?'

'I require your advice,' said Kutuz, as his chief of staff drew alongside him.

'How may I be of service, my lord?' asked Aqtai in an oily tone.

'There is a splinter beneath my skin. I want it removed.'

7

New Temple, London

13 October 1260 AD

J acques took a goose quill from the clay pot on the solar table and rolled it absently between his thumb and forefinger as he studied his nephew.

'Did you know that your father and I had won two of these tournaments by the time we were your age? You have been here for two years. It's time for you to win.'

Garin looked up, surprised by the mention of his father. Jacques rarely spoke of his dead brother. 'It will be the first real chance I've had, sir,' he said quietly. 'I was ill last year and the year before I had only just started training.'

'This year will be different, won't it?'

'I will try my best, sir.'

'Make sure you do. I mentioned you to our guests this morning and the masters of our kindred strongholds are expecting great things of my nephew on the field.'

Garin swallowed back the dryness of his mouth. That morning, the Masters of the Scottish and Irish preceptories had arrived with their knight-escorts for the chapter general that would take place in four days. The chapter was convened each year to discuss Temple business in Britain and the day after would see the tournament that was held in honour of the meeting.

'The competition will be fierce, sir. Will is a good fighter and . . .'

'Campbell is a peasant,' snapped Jacques, closing his fist around the quill. 'You are of the family de Lyons. When you stand for the position of commander your record must speak for itself. Campbell will never be a commander. It isn't important for him to win. But, for you, it is imperative.'

'Yes, sir.' Garin went to chew on a fingernail, then clasped his hands tightly behind his back. His uncle hated that habit.

Jacques sighed and sat back, tossing the quill to the table. 'You have a duty to your family. Who else will uphold our name now that your father and brothers are dead? My days of glory are spent. Your mother has seen the demise of her husband and sons and with them the dream of restoring this family to its rightful place in the ranks of the kingdom's nobility. She puts a brave face on it, Garin, but Cecilia told me she cries herself to sleep most nights in that damp hovel. She once had jewels, perfumes, gowns; everything a woman of her status should have. Now she just has memories.'

Garin fought back tears. He had never seen his mother put a brave face on anything. Her expressions had always told him everything she was feeling: anger, misery, bitterness, frustration. It physically hurt him to think of her crying at night in her bedchamber, startled by the scratch of birds in the roof, the shifting and settling of floorboards. On the small estate in Rochester, paid for by the modest pension she received from the Temple, there were three maids to cook and clean for her, but Garin knew they were a poor substitute for the army of servants Cecilia had commanded back in Lyons, where his father had been a wealthy, secular knight, before joining the Temple.

'I will make it better for her, I promise, sir,' he whispered.

Jacques' voice softened a little. 'Your mother and I have spent much time and effort making you fit to carry this burden. Since you were six you've had the best tutors she could afford and now you have the benefit of my tutelage. In my years of service to the Temple I have gained much experience. You can benefit from this, if you're willing to learn.'

'I am willing.'

'Good boy.' Jacques smiled, his eye wrinkling at the corner.

Garin was startled by the expression. He took an involuntary step back as his uncle rose and came around the table towards him.

Jacques put his hands on his nephew's shoulders. 'I know I've been hard on you these past months. But it's for your own good, you understand?'

'Yes, sir.'

'There are considerable prospects available to you here, Garin, greater even than a commandership.'

'Greater, sir?'

Jacques didn't respond. Taking his hands from Garin's shoulders, he stepped back, his smile vanishing. 'Now go. I'll see you on the field at practice.'

Garin bowed. 'Thank you, sir.' He turned to leave, his legs feeling watery.

'Garin.'

'Yes, sir?'

'Make me proud.'

As Garin left the solar and headed to his quarters, he was under no illusion as to what his uncle had meant. Make me proud was just another way of saying do not fail me.

Finding the dormitory empty, Garin shut the door and leaned against it. One of the preceptory's cats was sitting in a patch of sunlight below the window. On the floor beside it was a bird. Its tiny eyes were half lidded and lifeless, entrails hung in purple-blue lines from its stomach. Garin bent down as the cat came towards him and wove around his legs. 'You are supposed to catch rats,' he chided, picking the animal up and walking over to his pallet where he sat down. As Garin lay back, the cat stretched out on his stomach and he stroked its soft, black fur. He was going to be a commander in the Temple, but he envied sergeants who had no such grand destiny. He was tired of living on the knife-edge of his uncle's anger and tired of his name like a stone around his neck.

The cat, still spirited from its kill, swiped at him. Garin sat up with a wince, watching scarlet beads of blood well in a line across the back of his hand. He stared at the blood, surprised by its brightness, as the cat settled down in his lap and began to purr. His uncle said that to be a commander you had to be ruthless. You had to bear pain and hardship and learn how to deal it out to others. Garin bit his lip, but couldn't stop the tears. Burying his face in the cat's warm fur, he surrendered to them.

Taking a shortcut through the chapel grounds on his way to the knights' quarters, Will threaded between the gravestones that jutted like teeth from the grass. Vaulting over the low wall that separated the chapel from the orchard, he had gone only a few paces when he was halted by the sound of a young girl singing. Though he didn't understand the words, he recognised the language of Owein's homeland. The girl was walking between the trees. She paused in a patch of sunlight and crouched down, reaching for an apple in the grass. Will had heard of sister preceptories in the Kingdom of France, but for a woman to enter one of the Order's principal strongholds was strictly forbidden according to the Rule and it was as if this girl had slipped in from another world. Will, staring at her, realised that he had seen her once before. It had been about eighteen months ago, shortly after his father's departure.

James Campbell had not long returned from a brief trip escorting

Humbert de Pairaud to the Temple's preceptory in Paris when he had summoned Will to his chambers and told the boy he would be leaving for Acre. Will had begged to be allowed to go with him, but James hadn't relented. On the morning of his departure, three weeks later, he had held Will's hand, just for a moment, then, without a word, he had climbed the gangplank onto the warship that was moored at the Temple's dock. Will had remained sitting on the dock wall until late that evening, long after the ship had gone and the Thames had turned from grey to black.

The day after, he had begun his apprenticeship under Owein. The knight had been sympathetic to Will's situation, but only a few days later he too had left, suddenly. He had been gone for over a month and Will had been temporarily placed under Jacques' mastery. Will had never known where Jacques' unfathomable dislike of him came from, but during those few weeks and ever since, the knight had made it plain that he thought Will no better than something he might scrape from the bottom of his boot. What had made Jacques' treatment of him worse was that Owein and his father had always seemed to like the knight. It had felt like a betrayal.

Will had been working in the stables when Owein had returned late one evening. He had been surprised to see a girl of about his age perched on the destrier behind his master. The two of them had been met in the stable yard by Humbert de Pairaud. The girl, who had jumped down from the massive horse without aid, was tall and thin, lost in the folds of a travel-stained robe several sizes too large. Her hair hung in a tangled mass down her back and her pale skin was stretched taut over the raised bones of her cheeks. She had seemed to Will to be a cold, wild creature, her large, luminous eyes darting everywhere, even to the Master whom she had studied intently as if it were her right to do so. She had left the next morning. When Will had asked who she was, Owein had said that she was his niece and that she could no longer stay in Powys, but he had refused to be drawn further on the matter.

How different Owein's niece looked now. Willowy rather than gaunt, her cheeks fuller and her skin, defying fashion and modesty, still bronzed from the summer sun. While most girls would wear their hair pinned beneath a cap, hers hung loose around her shoulders, gleaming like copper-gold coins. As Will walked towards her, the girl looked up and paused in her song. She rose to her feet, the skirts of her white dress gathered in her hands, heavy with fruit she had collected.

'Hello.'

Will was silent for a moment, unsure of what to say. 'You are Sir Owein's niece.'

'I am.' Her eyes, a much paler shade of green than his, sparkled. 'Although I prefer to be called Elwen. Who are you?'

'Will Campbell,' he replied, discomfited by her searching gaze.

'My uncle's sergeant,' she said with a slight smile. 'I've heard about you.'

'You have?' said Will, trying to sound nonchalant. He folded his arms across his chest. 'What have you heard?'

'That you come from Scotland and you're always in trouble because your father is in the Holy Land and you miss him.'

'You know *nothing* of me,' spat Will, 'and neither does your uncle!'

Elwen took a step back at the flare of anger from the boy. 'I'm sorry. I didn't mean to upset you.'

Will looked away, fighting back the temper that came on him so suddenly. 'You're just a girl.' He kicked moodily at one of the fallen apples. 'What would you know of anything?'

Elwen straightened. 'More than a boy who spends his days hitting things with a stick!'

They stared at one another in silence. A shout made them both turn. Will swore beneath his breath as he saw the priest who had presided over the morning office striding towards them, black robes skimming the grass.

'In God's name, what is this?' bellowed the priest, glaring at Will.

'We were talking,' said Will. Out of the corner of his eye, he saw that Elwen was staring stonily at him.

'And why, sergeant, are you *talking* when there is work to be done?' The priest scowled. 'There shall be discipline within these walls lest we fall to the ways of the faithless. In indolence and disobedience you will find the Devil. These are his workings and they are an affront to the work of our Lord.'

Elwen stirred. 'We were just . . .'

'Silence, girl!' snapped the priest, spinning round to look at her for the first time. 'It was with great reluctance that we agreed to Sir Owein's request to house you here.'

'My guardian has a sickness. I had nowhere else to go.'

'The Master assured us that you would remain in your quarters. But I see that your presence is . . .' The priest stopped as he noticed the fruit gathered in her skirts and, below, her bared, brown legs.

Will was delighted to see a deep blush bloom on his cheeks.

'And what's this?' seethed the priest, jabbing a finger at the apples. 'Stealing, are you?'

'Stealing?' Elwen feigned a shocked expression. 'Of course not. I was hoping the servants could make something sweet of them for the Master.'

Flustered, the priest opened his mouth, then shut it again.

'It seems a shame to let them rot, doesn't it?' suggested Elwen sweetly, holding out an apple to the priest.

Will had to hide his smile with his hand. As Elwen caught his eye, her face softened slightly.

The priest looked at both of them, his brow drawn in suspicion. 'To your duties, sergeant!' he ordered finally. He turned on Elwen. 'As for you, I'll convey you to your quarters where you'll remain. The Master, God keep him, may see fit to bend the Rule according to his will, but I'll not stand for such flagrant violation of his charity.'

He went to put his hand on her arm and then stopped, inches from her skin, as if afraid to touch her. The priest had no need to usher her. Elwen, skirts still laden with apples, strode off ahead of him.

Will, shaking his head admiringly at the girl's audacity, jumped over the orchard wall and entered the main courtyard. Before the afternoon office there was something he had to do; something he'd been putting off for too long. Write to your mother, his father had said before leaving. It had been the only request made of him and, as yet, Will hadn't acted upon it. The memory of their parting back in Scotland, his mother's lips brushing lightly against his cheek and her thin smile, still haunted him. But time was marching on and at least now he had something good to tell her: that he had borne his master's shield at a parley with the king.

Will knocked on the solar door, hoping it would be Owein and not Jacques who opened it. He waited, then knocked again, harder this time. Still there was no response. After checking the passage, Will opened the door cautiously and looked inside. The solar was empty. He went to pull the door to, then stopped as he saw a stack of parchments on the table. A dove, perched on the window ledge, flew off as he entered.

The sheaves had been placed in three piles. Will picked through them quickly, looking for a clean sheet. All of the skins had been used. Some of the writing, he noticed, was in Owein's flowing hand, some in Jacques' spiky scrawl. He paused, holding one of the parchments, as he saw the king's seal stamped in red wax, at the top of the skin. Will looked to the door, then back to the skin. His eyes moved curiously over it. The letter, addressed to Humbert de Pairaud, was a request that the knights reconsider their demand for the pawning of the crown jewels. Will, disinterested after the first few lines, flicked through the last skins. These were records of

Henry's debts and were a little more interesting. Will let a soft whistle out through his teeth as he saw how much the King of England had borrowed from the Temple over the past few years. After a moment, however, he made himself put the skins down. His gaze fell on the armoire. Padding over and opening the double doors, Will found a small stack of fresh skins on one of the shelves. He reached in to take one and, in doing so, dislodged the pile. As he bent to straighten them, he noticed that one had writing on it. He folded the fresh skin, stuck it down the back of his hose, then pulled out the cracked, yellowed parchment, mildly curious as to what it was doing in the middle of the blank sheets and not in the pile with the other letters. The writing was in Latin, but what caught Will's attention about the neat script was that it didn't look natural, as if the writer had purposefully tried to disguise his or her handwriting. He checked for a seal, but, and again this struck him as odd, there wasn't one, nor was it addressed to anyone. There was, however, a date.

1 April. Anno Domini, 1260

I apologise that I have not sent word before, but there has been little to report until now. Having arrived safely in the autumn of last year, I made contact with our Brethren in Acre. They send greetings to their master and ask that I inform you that the work here is continuing well, albeit more slowly than we would like. One of our brothers passed away during the winter and we have been sorely diminished by his absence. The others wonder when you will return to elect more into our circle.

There are other factors, too, that have made my mission here more difficult to achieve than was reckoned. The year began with war and has continued in the same relentless fashion. In January, the Mongols stormed the city of Aleppo and by March they had swept on to Damascus. Last month we learnt that their general, Kitbogha, ordered his troops to take the city of Nablus and our forces found themselves surrounded. They have made no attempt to engage us, but the threat has spurred Grand Master Bérard to strengthen the Temple's positions. We have attempted to enter into negotiations, but have been met with little success thus far.

Despite these obstacles, I have managed to complete my assignment. The contact I have made in the Mamluk camp has, *already, proved most useful and we have learnt much. The Brethren are optimistic about what this could mean for the future. He is in a high position within one of their regiments – higher than we could have hoped – and will do what he can to aid our work here. I am sure you will hear soon enough through normal means, but the Mamluks are currently preparing to confront the Mongols in . . .*

Will looked up sharply, hearing movement in the passage. He slipped the skin back into the pile and darted behind the wooden screen that partitioned the solar, just as the doors swung open. Will, heart thudding, crouched down, hearing footsteps, then the rustle of parchment. After a few seconds, he risked a glance around the screen and his heart beat even faster as he saw Jacques de Lyons stooping over the skins on the table. The knight picked up one of the piles and turned to leave, then stopped and looked back, frowning, at the armoire's open doors. Slowly, he crossed the room, glancing around. Will froze, but he was far enough below Jacques' line of sight to remain unnoticed. The knight bent down to the shelf where the skins were, then, without any hesitation, pulled the letter from the centre of the pile. Still frowning, he placed it between the sheaves he held, then firmly shut the armoire, pressing it twice with his hand to check that it stayed shut. Will waited for the door to close and the footsteps to fade before he stepped out from behind the screen.

Westminster Palace, London, 13 October 1260 AD

King Henry stared out of the window, the stained glass patterning his face in blue and red diamonds. A low-lying fog had seeped in from the marshes that surrounded the jumbled maze of buildings.

The Romans had founded a settlement on the island that was formed where the two branches of the Tyburn met the Thames. The Island of Thorney had been the home of kings since the time of Edward the Confessor and the multifarious styles of the buildings displayed the different tastes of all of them. Behind the palace, the white walls of Westminster Abbey towered to the sky, the many outbuildings in its grounds huddled around it like small children sitting at the feet of a wise grandfather. Henry favoured the palace above all his residences: it was less austere than the Tower and close to the city.

There was a soft cough behind him. 'You wanted to see me, my liege?'

Henry turned from the window to see the chancellor looking expectantly at him. The man's plain black clothes and white skin contrasted sharply with the vivid colours of the room he stood in. The walls of the chamber, twenty-seven yards long, were decorated with paintings and strung with tapestries. The windows were stained glass and the tiled floor was laid with deep, sumptuous rugs. There were plants in great urns, an oak table with five intricately carved chairs placed around it, cushioned couches and an array of statues and ornaments. A person entering the room for the first time would have been forgiven for thinking that they had set foot in a treasure house. The king had lavished gold on many of his properties, but on the Painted Chamber he had showered a fortune.

Henry crossed to the oak table and picked up a scroll that was lying there. 'This came an hour ago.' He thrust it at the chancellor.

Whilst the chancellor was reading, the door opened and Edward entered. His fair hair was plastered to his head with sweat and his riding hose and boots were mud-spattered. 'Father,' he greeted with a brief bow, closing the door. 'I was about to lead a hunt,' he added, glancing at the chancellor. 'Your summons said it was urgent?'

Henry pointed to the scroll the chancellor held. 'Read that.' He sat heavily on one of the couches. 'They want to take them to their preceptory in Paris! I presume they think the jewels are best kept as far from my sight and influence as possible, damn them to hell!'

Edward took the scroll from the chancellor and scanned it. 'We should ask for another meeting,' he said, looking up at his father. 'Attempt to renegotiate.'

Henry pushed a hand through his thin hair. 'What is the use? I have already asked the Templars to reconsider.' He gestured at the scroll. 'Their reply is to *politely request* the transfer in nine days!'

'What will you do, my liege?' asked the chancellor.

Henry leaned back against the cushions and closed his eyes, feeling his head begin to pound. 'If I defy the knights, Chancellor, what, do you believe, they would do?'

'It is impossible to say for certain, my liege, but I would imagine that they would seek approval from the pope for this order. I expect they would use the current situation in Outremer as a key by which to turn papal consent to their favour. The pope may then make a personal request of you.'

'Then I have no choice but to agree.'

Edward's smooth brow furrowed. 'You are yielding so easily? You must be firmer with the knights. Stand up to them like you did at the Temple. It is you who is king, not them.'

'They may as well be for all the power they hold.'

'The crown jewels are ours, father. *Ours*.'

Henry's eyes snapped open. He glared at his son. 'You think I want to do this? What other option is there? That I wait around for a papal edict, then, ignoring that, excommunication?' Henry rose, one hand pressed to his brow. 'We will repay the money when we are able, then we will see our treasure returned to us. Until that time let the knights take them. At least it will keep them off my back.' He headed for the doors, the hem of his velvet cloak swishing over the tiles. 'Inform the knights, Chancellor. Tell them I accept their terms. I cannot bear to think of it anymore.'

Edward, his face full of protest, went to go after the king, but the chancellor took hold of him before he could follow. Edward looked at the hand on his arm, then up at the man who had hold of him. His pale grey eyes glinted.

The chancellor had only served in the royal household for one year, but he'd seen that look on the prince's face once before. He had been heading through the palace corridors on his way to a meeting with his staff when he had seen a young page, carrying a tureen of soup, trip and accidentally spill the tureen and its contents on the floor. Prince Edward had been walking just ahead of the boy and some of the soup had splattered his robes. The prince, who, up until that point, the chancellor had presumed to be a pleasant, decisive young man of a self-possessed disposition had made the terrified boy lick the soup from the floor, then tongue-clean his boots for good measure.

The chancellor dropped his hand from Edward's arm. 'Forgive me, my Lord Prince. But your father is, I believe, right. He does have no choice but to deliver the jewels to the knights.'

'My father is old and ailing,' said Edward in a glacial tone. 'Who do you think will be responsible for the debt when he is gone? Until it is paid, the knights will keep the jewels that I am supposed to be crowned with. I refuse to let them take what is rightfully mine.'

'I do not want the Templars to take this treasure either,' said the chancellor. 'But there may be a way for you to turn this situation to your advantage without further upsetting, or involving your father. Although I believe it would probably require the aid of your . . .' The

chancellor tried to think of a polite term of address. '. . . manservant.'

'Go on.'

'I found something out at the preceptory, something you might be able
to use.'

8

New Temple, London

15 October 1260 AD

'**P**aris?' said Simon dubiously.

'Owein told me this morning,' said Will, grinning, as he helped the groom haul a large bundle of hay across the yard. 'I'll be escorting the crown jewels.'

'Just you?' said Simon a little sardonically.

'Well, with Owein, nine other knights and their sergeants and Queen Eleanor.' Will nodded in the direction of the docks where the mainmast of a ship was poking up above the treetops. 'We'll be going on *Endurance*.'

'That hulk?' said Simon, wrinkling his nose. 'Doesn't look like it could cross a puddle. Pick up your end a bit.'

Will lifted the bale higher, his feet slipping in the wet ground. It had rained solidly for the last two days and everywhere, including the training field, was waterlogged. There were only three days left until the tournament and Will had spent the last few offices praying for sun. Today, his prayers had been answered with a cold, foggy dawn that had turned into a chill, bright morning. Together, he and Simon hefted the bale through the stables' entrance and set it down. Will sat heavily on it, his nose filled with the stables' warm, animal smell, as Simon disappeared into the storeroom where the tack was kept. The stables were long and shadowy. The destriers were in the stalls at one end and the palfreys, used by sergeants, were at the other. A groom was sweeping the floor at the far end. Dust from the straw swirled up around him and he sneezed.

'You all set for battle then?' came Simon's voice from inside the storeroom.

'As much as I can be.'

'Sir Jacques been pushing you hard?'

'Umm.' Will tugged loose a straw from the bale and twisted it around his finger. For the past two days, his concentration on the field had been a little impaired. Jacques had shouted at him several times.

'*God in Heaven, sergeant, are you deaf, or just plain witless? Stop staring at me and get your damn feet moving! It's not as if you don't need the practice!*'

But Will had found it difficult not to stare at the knight. The letter he'd discovered in the solar, that seemed to belong to Cyclops, had been playing on his mind. Although much of it seemed straightforward there were certain words Will kept coming back to, words that made him wonder about their significance: *our Brethren, their master, our circle.* He knew that the Temple employed spies who worked in hostile territory, but the letter had seemed to suggest something more than this, some kind of link between the Temple and the enemy. And why no seal? He wished he'd had time to finish it.

'You'll win,' said Simon matter-of-factly, coming out of the storeroom with a saddle in his hands, which he hefted onto a bench.

'What?' said Will, looking up. 'Oh. Well, maybe.' He shrugged, but smiled, pleased by his friend's unerring confidence.

'So,' said Simon, picking up a cloth and a jar of beeswax, 'how long will you be in Paris for?'

'A week?' Will wandered over as Simon scooped out a smear of the dark-yellow wax. 'Maybe longer?'

Simon glanced at Will as he rubbed at the saddle. 'I hope you don't forget about me when you're all knightly and noble and off across the seas.'

'Never! You're my . . .' Will shook his head, unable to think of the right words. 'I don't know. Two things that go together.'

'The shit to your shovel?' offered Simon.

They both laughed.

The sound of hoofbeats rang out in the yard. Simon put down his cloth, wiped his hands on his tunic and headed out to greet the rider. Will, who remained inside, heard voices a moment later. The first voice, Simon's, sounded wary and unsure; the second, a man's voice, made Will look round in puzzlement. He headed for the entrance to see Simon taking the reins of a black destrier with a white star on its nose. Will knew the horse: it was Cyclops's, but he didn't recognise the rider, who had spoken with an accent he'd never heard before. The rider wore a grey cloak with the cowl pulled over his face, but as he nodded to Simon and turned to leave, Will caught a glimpse of black beard and skin that was much darker than any Englishman's. He watched the man walk off across the yard in the direction of the knights' quarters. 'Who was that?' he asked, as Simon led the large horse into the stables.

'Don't know. Bit foreign-looking, weren't he?'

'Why did he have Cyclops's horse?'

'I guess he must be the one who took him last month. The stable master said a comrade of Sir Jacques' was being loaned his horse for a few weeks.' Simon hooked the reins over a hobbling post and bent down to loosen the stirrups. 'You going to stay here for a bit? Help me out?'

'No,' said Will, distractedly. 'I can't,' he added, seeing Simon's disappointed look. 'I've got practice.'

'You'll come by soon though? I haven't seen you for weeks.'

'I will.'

Simon watched Will head off, then removed the saddle from the destrier and led the beast into its stall. Moving over to the bale of hay, he began cutting the tether that bound it with his knife. A shadow partially blocked the light at the stable door and Simon looked up to see another stranger standing there, this one clad in a stained russet cloak.

The man, who had long straggly hair and a lantern-jawed, pockmarked face, gave Simon a perfunctory nod. 'Which way to the sergeants' quarters?'

Simon straightened. Sticking the knife in his belt, he headed over. 'Who are you looking for?'

The man smiled, revealing a mouth half full of brown stubs of teeth. He had a curved, wicked-looking dagger hanging from his belt. 'That's my business, boy. Which way?'

Simon paused, but he didn't have the right to question visitors, or deny them access to the preceptory, however foreign, or, in this case, unpleasant the look of them. 'Across the yard,' he said curtly, pointing to the buildings at the far side of the compound. 'The tall one there.'

The Tower, London, 17 October 1260 AD

The public barge glided slowly towards London Bridge, after dropping all but one of its passengers at the Walbrook docks. Garin, huddled by himself on a bench at the stern, watched the wagons shunting past the chapel and the many shops that spanned the bridge's length. As the barge passed beneath the arches, he caught a glimpse of the heads of traitors that were strung like lanterns from the posts. Garin pulled his cloak tighter around him to cover the red cross on his black tunic, terrified that someone on the distant banks, or the bridge above might recognise him. He was out of the preceptory alone, without permission. It made him dizzy to think of it. But beneath his anxiety was a sense of curious anticipation. It was this feeling that had brought him this far, that and the fear of refusing the summons. On any other day, neither would have been enough to spur him to leave the preceptory, but today was the chapter meeting and the knights would be closeted in the chapter house for most of the day. No one would miss him.

Beyond the bridge, the Tower of London dominated the view, its vast, curtained walls sweeping down to a moat that flanked it on three sides. The barge turned inland and docked before reaching the walls: no vessel was allowed through the watergate without prior permission. As the board was thrown across by one of the crewmen, Garin rose from the bench and stepped cautiously across to the banks. Following the instructions that had been given to him, he made his way through a riddle of alleyways until he came to the city-side walls. Here, he found a narrow drawbridge across the moat that led to a small, arched doorway in the otherwise featureless stone. Two royal guards in scarlet liveries were standing to either side of the door. One of them drew his sword as Garin stepped onto the bridge.

'Stay where you are.'

Garin did as he was told and waited as the guard came forward.

'State your business.'

'My name is Garin de Lyons.' He faltered. 'I . . . I think I'm expected?'

'Follow me.'

Garin followed the man across the bridge and the second guard unhooked a set of keys from his belt and unlocked the door. He pushed open the door and Garin saw a great courtyard stretching away to a colossal grey-white fortress of stone and marble, its turrets thrusting to the sky. Around the fortress were tree-lined gardens and several outbuildings, including one long timber structure that dominated the courtyard.

'Go on then,' said the first guard, impatiently.

'Where do I go?' asked Garin, feeling his cheeks redden.

'You'll be met in the yard. That's all we were told.'

Garin stepped through and flinched as the door banged shut behind him. He heard the clunk of the key in the heavy lock and felt the fragile confidence he'd managed to summon to get him this far slip from him like a robe, leaving him naked, insignificant beneath the walls' stern, indomitable towers. Slowly, he began to walk.

After a short distance, he reached the timber structure and moved alongside it, wrinkling his nose at a rank, musky smell that came from within. There were guards moving about in the grounds and a few solitary figures that he guessed to be servants near the fortress, but the courtyard itself was empty. Garin turned as he heard a shuffling sound coming from the building beside him. Curious, he moved closer and squinted through the gaps in the slats. He could see nothing in the darkness inside. Further down, he noticed a square aperture cut into the boards. He headed along and, standing on tiptoe, peered in. The smell was worse here. There was something hanging just in front of the opening. It looked like a sheet of grey, wrinkled leather. Garin grasped the edges of the hole and pulled himself up. The leather sheet moved and suddenly he was looking into a huge, narrowed eye. The eye winked and a colossal head turned to face him. Garin yelled as a giant snake writhed out of the hole. He fell back and staggered into the chest of a figure behind him. Whipping round he found himself staring into the lantern-jawed, pockmarked face of the man who had delivered him the summons two days ago. From the building came a noise like ten trumpets.

'What . . .! What is it?'

'King Henry's pet,' replied the man bluntly. 'Hurry.' Gripping Garin's shoulder with a filthy hand, he steered the shocked boy towards the Tower, his stained russet cloak flapping about him in the cold wind that swept the courtyard. 'He's waiting.'

'But what is it?' asked Garin, looking over his shoulder at the snake that was swinging about through the hole and which he now saw was attached to the beast's face.

The man, who had called himself Rook, scowled, but he seemed at pains to be civil. 'An elephant. It was a gift from King Louis. He brought it back from Egypt.'

Garin, tearing his gaze from the monster, allowed himself to be led away. A smell of dampness and sweat and sour breath came off Rook in thick, repellent waves and Garin had to take tiny sips of air in through his mouth to avoid inhaling it. He felt nauseous enough as it was.

'Did you tell anyone you was coming here?'

Garin shook his head. 'No. I did what you said. I told no one and I wasn't seen leaving.'

Rook studied the boy intently, his calculating gaze unwavering. After a moment, he grunted.

Garin had to almost jog to keep up with Rook, who quickened the pace as they neared the main building and walked alongside it, past several guards who paid them little attention, and round to the back where they entered by a low wooden door. It looked like a servants' entrance; certainly not, Garin noted nervously, the entrance any normal guest would be taken through. Rook kept his hand clamped firmly on

Garin's shoulder as he marched the boy along a dim passage and up through a tight, spiral staircase that was cut into a wall at the far end, more propelling than guiding him. Garin was struggling for breath by the time they reached the top, where a row of arched openings looked down on the bleak courtyard and over the walls to the Thames. Rook, breathing hard, but not slowing his pace, led them to a set of oak doors. He paused to rap twice, then opened them. As the doors swung inwards, Garin was struck by an urge to turn and run. His curiosity had run dry and now his mind was just filled with the question that had plagued him since Rook had sought him out at the preceptory. What on earth could the heir to the throne of England possibly want with him? But Rook was right behind him and there was nowhere to go but forward.

The chamber was large and dark. Heavy black drapes covered the windows, blocking out most of the daylight. At irregular intervals, beams of light filled with swirling dustmotes pierced through the gaps and stabbed down onto wide, smooth flagstones. Other than this frail illumination, there was just a single candle burning on an oak table, to either side of which were two benches. Grain could just make out the humped shape of a large bed against the far wall of the chamber. As his eyes grew used to the gloom, he realised that the walls of the chamber were covered in painted scenes. He strained against the dimness, trying to make them out: buildings; a forest; soldiers on horses; a tall man in black robes. As his eyes fixed on this last picture, Garin almost cried out as the painting detached itself from the wall and came towards him.

'Sergeant de Lyons,' said Prince Edward, smiling. 'I'm glad that you came.'

Still in shock, Garin forgot to bow.

The prince didn't seem to take offence. 'Please sit,' he said, gesturing to the bench in front of the table.

Garin, his legs feeling weak and wobbly, did as he was told, after glancing back at Rook who had taken up position by the closed door.

Edward sat on the bench opposite Garin, his face up-lit by the candle, making his strong jaw and cheekbones appear even more chiselled. He picked up a jug that was placed beside two goblets. 'Would you like a drink?'

Garin swallowed thickly. 'Yes. I mean, yes, my Lord Prince.'

'It's from my father's lands in Gascony,' said Edward, pouring the drinks and handing one to Garin. 'The best wine in Christendom.'

Garin, hardly tasting it, took several greedy gulps, trying to moisten his throat. After a few moments, the warmth and potency of the wine filled him and he relaxed slightly.

Edward refilled the boy's goblet. 'I take it you had no trouble leaving the preceptory?'

'No, my Lord Prince.'

'Good.' Edward sat back, cradling his goblet in his long-fingered hand, on which were several gold rings, studded with jewels. 'I am sorry to have summoned you in such an unaccustomed manner, Garin, but I wanted to speak with you as soon as possible and due to the delicate nature of my request, the secrecy was necessary. I hope I haven't caused you any undue alarm.'

'No, my Lord Prince.' Glancing round, Garin could see the shadowy form of Rook, blocking the door. He didn't say that the summoner had alarmed him far more than the summons. Rook had cornered him in his dormitory, had given him the message that the prince wanted to see him and money for the barge, and hadn't left until Garin had promised to come to the Tower.

'The reason I wanted to see you,' continued the prince, his voice quiet and measured, 'is because I believe that you may be able to help me with a problem. The king has agreed to pawn the crown jewels at the request of Master de Pairaud. In five days they will be taken to Paris where they will be stored until such time as the king's debt to the Temple is repaid.'

Garin nodded. His uncle had told him last night that King Henry had agreed to the Master's request and that he would be in the company escorting the jewels. He was feeling evermore uncertain as to what he was doing here.

Edward paused to take a sip from his goblet and studied the boy carefully. 'I'm going to be very candid with you, Garin. I do not want the jewels to go to your Order. They belong to my father and to his line. We have tried to talk with the knights and have offered other ways whereby the debt may be paid, but they have refused any further dialogue and insist on this course. They have left me no option other than to take this matter into my own hands. The jewels will pass to the knights as my father has agreed, but I will take them back.'

Garin struggled to understand what the prince was saying. 'My lord, I . . .?'

Edward held up his hand for silence. 'I want you to help me achieve this, Garin. My mother, the queen, will be escorting the jewels at the behest of my father, but the knights have kept the details of the journey secret. As the nephew of one of the knights involved in this arrangement, you will, I am sure, have access to these details.'

The realisation of what the prince meant hit Garin like a slap. He rose, his head spinning from the wine and the revelation. 'I . . . I'm sorry. I can't!' He almost stumbled over the bench as he hastened for the door, wanting to be out in the daylight, the air, away from this chamber of shadows and adult intent.

Edward's voice sounded behind him. 'Don't you wish to restore your family name? For the de Lyons to again be the grand and noble household they once were in the Kingdom of France?'

Garin faltered. As he looked back at Edward, he didn't see Rook step forward, unsheathing a curved dagger.

'Isn't that what you told the Lord Chancellor when you escorted him to the Master's solar?' questioned Edward. 'Didn't you say that it was hard to be the nephew of a high-ranking knight? That you felt burdened by the pressure of duty that had been placed upon you to restore the wealth and nobility of your family?'

Garin shook his head. That wasn't what he had said, *exactly*.

'I can do this for you, Garin. I can make you a lord, bestow lands and titles upon you. I can make you rich.'

Garin stayed where he was. Behind him, Rook's dagger glinted.

'You need only tell me what you know of the voyage. That is all. And I will give you anything I can in return.'

'What if someone found out?' whispered Garin, his voice sounding strange in his ears.

'No one would ever know.'

'But how . . .?' Garin fought to meet the prince's eyes. 'How would you take back the jewels?'

Edward finished his wine and set the goblet down. 'You don't need to worry about how it will be done. No one will be hurt.' Rising, he came around the bench to Garin. To the boy, the tall, handsome prince seemed like a warrior from an ancient poem, both terrifying and impressive, more myth than man. 'The jewels belong to my family. I am only doing what I must to safeguard our property, as I'm sure you can understand.' He picked up the candle on the table. 'Walk with me, Garin.'

Garin hesitated, but after a moment, he followed the prince to the large wall at the back of the chamber. As they got closer, the candle flame lit up the paintings, the dark swirls flaring into colour.

'My father had this painted for him,' said Edward, holding the candle up to the pictures, 'in honour of those who gave their lives wresting Jerusalem from the infidel almost two hundred years ago.'

Garin's gaze moved over the scene of a walled city. Jerusalem. White buildings with onion-shaped, gold domes marched up a hillside to a vast, ornate structure on the summit that he guessed was the Dome of the Rock, an important Islamic shrine before the fall of the city, after which it had been converted into a church. The whole scene was one of majestic beauty and gave Garin the feeling that he wanted to stand on the grass that was painted in the foreground and walk through the olive groves up to those high, white walls. But as Edward moved along, the image faded and the candle lit a new scene. This time the city was closer and some of the buildings obscured by plumes of smoke. In front of the walls was an army, a dark, sprawling mass of men and machines of war, horses, wagons, tents and banners.

'When Pope Urban II preached the call to Crusade in the year of Our Lord 1095 many men took up the Cross: knights, nobles, kings and peasants, and set out to claim the Holy City from the hands of the unbelievers. But it wasn't until four years later, after an arduous journey across land, during which many lost their lives, that they saw these walls before them.' Edward pointed to the siege engines that were lined up between the city and the Crusaders' camp. 'They spent almost a month building weapons for the battle. Then, on the thirteenth of July, worn down and weary from the long campaign and the many privations they had suffered, they began their assault.'

The candle moved again and this time the colours were all dark; black and scarlet for the smoke and the tongues of fire that licked around the rooftops of buildings; crimson and purple for blood.

'They took the Holy City by the sword and within just one day their dream, and the dream of all those they had left behind, was realised. Jerusalem was ours. Its streets were cleansed of Saracens and Jews by our knights. The holy sites where Christ chastised the moneylenders, the tomb where He rose from the dead, the place where the Virgin once slept, all were sanctified by our priests. It was a day unlike any other.' Edward's eyes were gleaming in the candlelight, his face animated. 'I only wish I could have seen it.'

Garin looked on in silence as the scene elongated and he saw rivers of blood flowing through the streets, men and women cut down by knights, hauled from mosques and houses, mountains of gold and plunder beside piles of corpses. The victory on the faces of the Crusaders looked gleefully demonic in the ruddy light from the fires that had been painted on their cheeks.

Edward turned to Garin. 'The Saracens took Jerusalem from us sixteen years ago. We must recapture it if the lives of those who ploughed the way eastwards for us are not to have been in vain and if the hope of Christendom is to be once again rekindled. Do you want them to worship their false god in halls that have been blessed by our own priests?'

Garin didn't know what to say. He just shook his head.

'If my great-uncle, Richard the Lionheart, were still alive, do you think he would wait until the enemy had taken all of our strongholds before doing something about it? Of course he wouldn't.' Edward's expression hardened. 'My father will not lead a Crusade in this life. Of that I am certain. But I will. The jewels are rightfully mine and I will be crowned with them when I become king. Neither myself, nor my father can afford to repay the debt we owe to the Temple when we, *all of us*, have need of a new Crusade. I want the same thing as the Templars, but I will do it on my own terms, not theirs. Do you understand that, Garin?'

Garin chewed on a fingernail and nodded.

Edward smiled, then turned from the wall and headed for a chest that was placed at the foot of the bed, leaving the paintings to fade into darkness.

Garin followed cautiously, watching as Edward lifted the lid of the chest and reached inside. He pulled out a velvet drawstring pouch that he handed to Garin. 'Here.'

The velvet bag clinked as it landed, soft and heavy, in Garin's palm. It was filled with money.

'That is just the start,' said Edward, watching the boy, wide-eyed, squeeze the bag in his hand. 'Help me, Garin, and, I promise, I will help you. You will lose nothing. In my service you will only gain.'

Garin thought of his mother in the cramped house in Rochester, weeping in her bedroom at night, her gowns and finery gone, sold off, she had often reminded him, to pay for his tuition. The contents of the bag in his hand could, he guessed, buy her all the gowns she could ever wish for. Garin thought of his uncle, of all his failures and mistakes. Was there, he wondered, any way to make him proud? He had tried. God, he had tried. But it had never been enough. He looked up at Edward.

'You will restore my family name? Make us noble again?'

'In time, yes.'

Garin looked into the prince's face. He saw shrewdness there, ambition and ruthlessness, but he did not see deceit. 'I just want my mother to be happy,' he said in a whisper. 'To make my uncle proud.'

'I know how hard it is to live up to the expectations of family,' said the prince softly.

Garin blinked away the tears that threatened. 'Our ship, the *Endurance*, won't take us all the way to Paris,' he said in a rush. 'She will be loaded with cargo, wool from our London looms, for trade in the Kingdoms of France and Aragon. *Endurance* will put in at Honfleur on the mouth of the Seine, where we will disembark with the jewels, then she'll sail for our base at La Rochelle.'

'You will be in the company?' asked Edward keenly.

'Yes. My uncle has sent word to the preceptory in Paris, asking them to send a smaller vessel to meet us at Honfleur. I think the queen will spend the night in a smallholding we own at the port, then we will sail the next morning.'

'You've done very well, Garin. I'm impressed.'

Garin bit his lip and looked at the floor. He felt sick.

'Now,' said Edward, brusquely, 'you had best return to the preceptory. Go about your daily business as usual. If I need to contact you again before the voyage, I will send Rook. Hide the gold in a safe place where it won't be found.' As Edward reached the door, he turned abruptly and looked down at Garin, placing a firm hand on his shoulder. 'And if you tell anyone about this meeting, I shall deny that it ever took place and I will make sure that you and your family spend the next life staring at the view from London Bridge. Do you understand me?'

Garin nodded quickly, his mind filled with the misshapen, maggoty heads hanging from the posts. His bladder felt full from wine and fear and he was desperate to leave. 'I won't say anything, I swear.'

'Make sure of it.' Edward gestured to the door. 'Wait outside. Rook will take you down.'

Garin reached for the door. For a moment, Rook remained standing there, eyes full of menace, then he gave a contemptuous chuckle and moved out of the way allowing the boy to rush out into the passage.

Rook pushed the door to. 'Do you think we can trust the little rat to keep his mouth shut?' he murmured.

'If I didn't think so, I wouldn't have let him leave this chamber,' responded Edward quietly. 'We had no other choice. This will be the only opportunity we have to take the jewels back. Once they are in the Paris vaults, I doubt we will ever see them again.'

'Do you'll reckon the runt'll co-operate if we have need of him again?'

'I believe so. But find out what you can on his family to make certain of it. Meanwhile, we must set our plans in motion. Five days doesn't give us much time.'

'Don't worry, the jewels will never see those vaults.'

Edward smiled. 'I'm glad my efforts to free you from your sentence weren't wasted, Rook. A man of your talents shouldn't be squandered on the gallows.'

Rook inclined his head. 'My life is yours.'

9
New Temple, London
18 October 1260 AD

W ill flicked his hair out of his eyes with a toss of his head, his attention on the bull-shouldered sergeant in front of him, a boy a year older than him called Brian. He was used to the wooden practice swords and the iron blade was heavy in his hand. He wore a jerkin of stiff rawhide, studded across the chest, and leather greaves and vambraces shielded his shins and forearms. He circled the sergeant, whom he hadn't fought before today. It had taken Will one round to get his measure. Brian was strong, but slow.

Ignoring the scattered calls of encouragement from the sidelines, Will stayed where he was, poised on the balls of his feet. Brian charged. Will parried the first strike, ducked under the second and spun, bringing his sword, two-handed, into the sergeant's back. The swords had been blunted as a precaution against serious injury, but the force of the strike knocked Brian to his knees with a grunt. Lifting the blade, Will brought it, point down, over the boy's neck in a move that would have killed him had it struck. A cheer erupted from the edges of the field, sending several birds flying into the air from a nearby oak, wings clapping. The herald called Will's name and Brian struggled to his feet and embraced his victor briefly before walking from the field.

The cheers died away as Humbert de Pairaud stood. On the bench beside the Master of England, sat the Masters of Scotland and Ireland. On the trestle before them lay the prizes: a sword for the winner of the older group and, for Will's age group, a brass badge displaying two knights astride a single horse – a trophy replica of the seal of the Order. Will bowed to the three masters.

'I declare William Campbell, sergeant to Sir Owein ap Gwyn, master of the field,' Humbert's voice resounded. 'Campbell will fight in the final duel.' He looked to Will. 'You may leave the field, sergeant.'

Will bowed again, then sprinted for the tent that had been erected on the sidelines.

Only an hour before, he had been fifth in the running out of the thirty sergeants in his group. He had come fourth in the rounds at the quintain, almost falling from his horse and missing the ring with his lance three times. But when Garin had won and Will had seen victory slipping from his grasp, he grew dogged, coming first in the foot race and beating his three opponents in the duels. His sword-arm was numb, but triumph was hot in his veins, burning away his exhaustion. He had won through to the last duel and was one fight from possible victory. He wished his father were here.

When Will entered the tent, he saw Garin by the trestle where the weapons were laid. He was testing the weight of a sword, swinging it back and forth. There was an older sergeant in one corner, untying the straps of his jerkin. Outside, the field was being readied for the next duel.

Placing the blade on the trestle, Garin looked round at Will. 'Well done.'

'Thanks,' said Will, not noticing the flatness of his friend's tone. He wiped the sweat from his forehead with the back of his arm. 'My opponent was fierce. I didn't think I could best him.' He grinned. 'If you win your duel, we'll meet in the last battle.'

Garin nodded dully.

'What's wrong?'

'Nothing.' Garin shrugged as Will frowned at him. 'There's no prize for second best.'

'That doesn't matter,' said Will offhand. 'If we fight in the final duel we'll both be the champions of the day, whichever of us wins.' He glanced round as the older sergeant pulled off his jerkin and headed out. 'Where were you yesterday?' Will asked Garin, lowering his voice.

'Nowhere,' said Garin quickly. 'I mean, in the armoury,' he added, moving away to pick up another of the swords on the bench.

'I tried to find you. I've been wanting to ask you something.' Will paused. 'When was your uncle last in the Holy Land?'

'He came back after he was injured at Herbiya, after the Saracens took Jerusalem. Why?'

Will sucked on his lip. 'Has he kept in contact with anyone out there, perhaps someone foreign, someone who might have visited him?'

Garin turned back. 'Why are you asking this?' He gestured at the field. 'I've got to go out there and fight any minute. What is it?'

Will looked round, hearing the heralds call Garin's name. 'It's nothing.

Just a question I had about the Holy Land. I was wondering whether I should ask him. You'd best go.' He put his hand on his friend's shoulder. 'Good luck.'

Garin stood staring at the field beyond the tent flaps for a long moment, then strode out, the sword grasped tightly in his fist.

Garin's opening charge was fierce, his sword cutting in a series of mighty strokes that pushed the other boy back. His opponent recovered, moving in, face set in concentration. The two of them stamped and cut across the centre of the field. The air was hushed, the only sound the ring of the swords. Within a few moments of the opening assault, Garin had slashed the boy's tunic, scoring a red line down his arm. A brief roar sounded from the sidelines. Will had never seen his friend fight so well. Garin was moving gracefully, every blow precise and powerful. His opponent was tiring quickly.

Garin deflected several short thrusts, pivoted lightly on his feet and swept round to the sergeant's left. Two of his lightning-quick lunges were turned aside, the sergeant having to spin awkwardly to counter. Garin feinted right, but his opponent didn't fall for the trick and instead stepped up to meet him. They collided heavily, Garin lost his balance and stumbled to his knees. It wasn't over. Blocking the sergeant's blows, Garin staggered to his feet and hammered at the boy, forcing him back once more. As the sergeant pulled away, Garin glanced briefly to the judges' bench. Jacques was deep in conversation with the Master of Ireland.

The sword now looked awkward in Garin's hand. His wrist was no longer loose, allowing the fluid moves he had made in the earlier round, but locked tight, meaning that every strike was slower, every parry more jarring. Will saw him lose the chance of a side thrust and only just manage to block a low, sweeping cut to his thigh. His opponent had also noticed the change and now stepped up the attack. The sergeants began to cheer, sensing victory. Garin took a half-hearted swing. Will saw his grip slacken. The sword fell from his hand, he made an attempt to retrieve it, but wasn't fast enough. His opponent rushed in to cut a line across his leather jerkin. The sergeant shouted triumphantly, raising his blade as the herald called out. Will watched as Garin, not even bothering to pick up his sword, stood there, staring at Jacques. The knight was on his feet, his expression cold as death. Garin set off towards the tent, his head lowered. Will pushed through the crowd of cheering sergeants to go after him, but was stopped by his name being called for the final duel. He hesitated, then walked onto the field.

As Garin entered the tent, he tore off his jerkin and let it fall to the floor. He planted his palms on the bench, the lump in his throat swelling to constrict him. His vision became blurred and he swiped at his eyes angrily, determined not to let the tears fall. If he started, he didn't think he'd be able to stop.

'Get out.'

Garin started at the voice. Jacques stood in the tent opening, his tall form filling it. The light behind him was too bright for Garin to see his face, but the boy didn't need to know the expression that was there. It was all in the voice. Garin's dread coiled around his gut, a cold snake, winding tight. 'Sir,' he managed to say. 'I'm sorry . . . I . . .'

'Save your excuses,' said Jacques, still speaking in that low, frigid tone that Garin hated. 'Come with me.'

'But the tournament . . .?' Garin drew back, banging into the bench as Jacques came forward.

Jacques gripped his arm, hard, and hauled him from the tent. Garin, half stumbling, half running to keep up with his uncle's long-legged stride, looked back as he was marched towards the preceptory buildings to see Will stamping back and forth on the tournament field, sword wheeling.

The yard was quiet, only a few servants were moving about. Some of them eyed Garin and Jacques curiously. Garin wanted to call to them, beg them to save him. But his throat was locked tight and, anyway, he wouldn't: pride wasn't easily quelled, even by terror. When they reached the knights' quarters, Jacques forced him up the stairs and pushed open the solar door.

'In,' he said, shoving Garin through.

Garin turned, rubbing his arm, as his uncle shut the door. 'Sir, I—' His words were cut off abruptly when Jacques backhanded him viciously across the face, sending him reeling into the table, which rocked back, the quill pot rolling off and smashing on the tiles. Garin banged his hip on the sharp corner of the wood and cried out, the pain from both injuries piercing through the numbing shock of the first blow. The second blow came a moment later as Jacques stepped forward and struck him around the head, fist closed. Garin held up his arms to defend himself. 'Please, uncle!' he begged, shielding himself as much as he could as the punches rained down on him. Even with the force of them and with the blood starting to pour from his nose and lip, he managed to stay standing. It was worse if he fell to the floor. His uncle would use his boot. *'Please!'*

'I told you I wanted you to win!' barked Jacques, his breathing laboured from the exertion. 'What did I tell you?'

'To win,' cried Garin, 'you told me to win. But I couldn't . . . I . . .!'

'I saw you, you insolent whelp! You lost that battle on purpose! To spite me, was it?' Jacques grabbed Garin by the shoulders and shook him roughly. '*Was it?*'

'No!'

Through the windows came a loud cheer from the training field. Jacques dropped his hold on Garin. Within the roar, they heard the name of Campbell being shouted by the heralds. Jacques' face, thunderous red in colour, darkened further. He swore loudly and turned on his nephew. 'Do you hear that? You let that brat win!'

Garin, distracted by the cheer, put his arm up, too late, as his uncle cuffed him brutally across his face. Garin staggered into the corner by the window. He stayed there for a moment, suspended like a frozen image of himself, then slid slowly to the floor, his cheek on fire and the red imprint of a hand already flaring on his skin, over other, more serious injuries that would reveal themselves more slowly. His face was a mess of blood and two ropes of snot were hanging from his nose.

'Get up!'

'You weren't even watching,' said Garin, struggling to speak, his chest heaving.

'What?'

Garin looked up at his uncle, not bothering to wipe away his tears. 'You weren't watching me fight. I saw you! You were talking to the Master of Ireland!'

'I was telling him how impressed I was with you!' responded Jacques, in a scathing tone.

Garin shook his head, sobbing openly now. 'It isn't just today. It's all the time. You want me to do everything for you.' He pushed himself up the wall and stood, shaky but defiant. 'But even when I do it you aren't satisfied. How can I please you? You've never given me any chance!'

'I've given you every chance, boy! All the chances your father and I never had when we were . . .'

'*I'm not you!*' Garin shouted, stepping forward, fists clenched, blue eyes bright with pain and humiliation and fury. 'I'm not you and I'm not my father and I'm not my brothers! I know I'm not good enough to be. I *know* that! But I've always tried my best!'

Jacques stared at his nephew, whom he had never heard speak so plainly and passionately before. And as he saw the blood and the tears and the mark of his own hand on the boy's face an image of his brother, Raoul de Lyons, came into his mind.

On a dusty street in the city of Mansurah, Raoul lay dying, his back broken and his chest pierced with three arrows. His horse had thrown him soon after a group of Mamluk soldiers, under the command of Baybars, had pushed beams of wood down from the rooftops to block the narrow streets, trapping the knights there in a killing zone. Nearby, Raoul's two eldest sons lay dead. The fighting had since moved on, leaving the path littered with corpses, and it was to distant war cries and the faint ring of swords that Jacques had knelt beside his brother and cradled his broken and bloodied body in his arms.

'*Take care of my wife and son, brother,*' were the last words Raoul had said. He was dead before Jacques had been able to answer.

'I'm doing this for you,' said Jacques, quieter now, still staring at Garin. 'You have to understand that.'

Garin was crying too hard to answer.

'Garin.' Jacques moved to the boy and placed two hands on his shoulders. 'Look at me.' Garin tried to turn away, but Jacques took the boy's chin in his hand. 'Do you think I want to punish you like this? You force me to it when you fail to achieve what I know you are capable of achieving.'

Garin stared up at Jacques. His right eye was swelling, beginning to close. 'I will be made a knight, uncle,' he said hoarsely. 'You don't need to do this. I will restore our family honour and make my mother happy. She won't have to live in that place forever. I'll do all this, I *swear!*'

'I don't mean being made a knight,' answered Jacques, frustrated. 'There are other things I want for you. Things you know nothing of.' He went to the window and placed his hands on the ledge. He could still hear the cheers coming from the field, shouting Will's name over and over. Jacques turned back to his nephew. 'There is more to the Temple than you know.' He paused for a long moment. 'I belong to a group of men, *brothers*, within our Order. We are few now, but we are still powerful. Many have aided our cause, knowingly and unknowingly, over the past century since our establishment. King Richard the Lionheart was one of our patrons for a time. But we work in secret and even the Grand Master knows nothing of us. We are called the Anima Templi: the Soul of the Temple.'

Garin shook his head, bewildered. 'I don't understand. What does this group do? How are you involved?'

Jacques held up his hand. 'I cannot tell you everything yet, but in time I will. At the moment, we are all in great danger. Our group has had something precious stolen from it which, in the wrong hands, could prove fatal to us and perhaps even to the Temple itself.'

'What is it?'

Jacques hesitated, uncertainty plain in his face.

'Tell me, uncle,' begged Garin. 'If I don't know what you want from me, I'll never please you.'

Jacques looked back at him. After a long pause, he spoke, his voice quiet. 'It is called the Book of the Grail. It is our code and contains our initiation ceremony and details of our plans for the future, plans no one must know of until we are ready. After I have helped escort the crown jewels to Paris, I will remain in the city to aid in the search for the book.' He crossed to Garin. 'I want you to stay there with me and meet the head of our group, Everard. I have always hoped that you will one day take my place in our circle, but to be a member of the Brethren requires certain attributes and to impress Everard takes a man of great strength and character. I am sorry, Garin. I have not always found teaching to be an easy task. Afraid of showing favouritism, I have perhaps treated you more harshly than the others. But induction into our organisation carries with it grave responsibility, the kind of responsibility that few men can endure. That is why I push you, why I need you to be better than boys like Campbell. That's why I do this,' he murmured, touching his nephew's cheek. He sighed roughly and pulled Garin into his arms.

Garin stared at the floor, hearing his uncle's heartbeat, fast and low against his ear. He closed his eyes and heard Prince Edward's voice. *If you tell anyone about this meeting . . . I will make sure that you and your family spend the next life staring at the view from London Bridge.* Blood from Garin's broken nose trickled down his chin, staining his uncle's white mantle.

New Temple, London, 19 October, 1260 AD

Elwen paced the chamber, arms folded across her chest. She was clad in a tight-sleeved gown of pale green linen girdled with a belt of plaited gold silk. The dress clung to her slender frame and the long skirt made her appear even taller. Her supper stood untouched on the table by the bed. The servant had delivered it an hour ago and a greasy skin had congealed on the surface of the thin stew. Elwen wrinkled her nose. The room, in the annex adjoining the knights' building that held the preceptory's wardrobe, was small and sparsely furnished. Owein had said that it was used as a storehold for the tailor's materials. It smelt of wool and old leather. In the corner by the window was a perch, from which hung several gowns and a dark blue cloak. On the table, beside the tray of food, was a small embroidery frame and a heap of coloured threads. There was a half-finished pattern in the frame: two indigo hills with a blue-thread river running through them.

Elwen went to the window. Clouds were racing across the sky. For a moment, the sun appeared from behind them and she closed her eyes at its brightness. She turned as there was a loud knock at the door.

'Elwen?'

Hearing Owein's voice, muffled through the thick wood, Elwen drew back the bolt and opened the door. 'Uncle,' she greeted him, with a smile.

Owein entered, closing the door behind him. He drew her to him and kissed the top of her head. As he stepped back, his eyes fell on the tray of food. 'You haven't touched your meal.'

'I'm not hungry.'

Owein laid a hand on her brow. 'Are you feeling unwell?'

Elwen moved away. 'No, uncle, I'm just . . .' She sighed heavily. 'How long do I have to stay here? I feel as if I'm in a prison. I wasn't even allowed to watch the tournament yesterday. I heard them calling your sergeant's name. Did he win?'

'You must remain in your quarters,' said Owein gently, but firmly. 'We cannot abuse the Master's charity. If he hadn't agreed to allow you to lodge here I wouldn't have known where to send you.'

'I am grateful for his charity.' Elwen went to the table and pretended to study her embroidery. 'But I'll go mad if I have to stay locked in this room for much longer.'

'That is, in fact, why I have come, Elwen. You will be leaving soon.'

'My guardian? She's better?'

Owein met her hopeful gaze. Taking her hand, he led her to the bed. 'I'm afraid not,' he said, sitting her down. 'Your guardian has died, Elwen. I received word of it this afternoon from the infirmary in the city. A sudden sickness overwhelmed her and the physician could do nothing.' Owein sat on the bed beside Elwen and put his arm around her slim shoulders. 'I'm sorry, my love. I know you were happy there.'

Elwen looked down at her hands. 'Yes.' She was quiet for a time. Taking a breath, she wiped her eyes. 'What will happen to me? Will I stay here?'

Owein gave her shoulders a squeeze. 'These lodgings are only temporary, Elwen. The Temple is no place for a woman.'

'I meant in London.' Elwen turned to him, her large eyes bright and wide. 'I don't want to return to Powys, uncle.'

Owein smiled. 'You won't have to. I sent a message to a comrade of mine in Bath. Charles retired from active service in the Order with an injury several years ago and oversees the running of one of our farmsteads where the Temple's horses are bred. He has an estate outside the city and I'm certain he will admit you into his household.'

'Bath?' Elwen's voice cracked. 'I like it here.'

Owein stroked her hair. 'I'm leaving for Paris in three days. I don't know when I'll return and I'll be afforded no opportunity to hunt the city for suitable lodgings for you in the meantime. You will like Bath. Charles's estate is certainly grander than what you've grown accustomed to here.' He gave her a smile of encouragement. 'He has three daughters, one of your age. In his care, you'll receive the education a young lady should.'

Elwen picked up a corner of her blanket and tugged at a loose thread. 'How long will I stay there?'

'A year at most, until you are of a suitable age.'

'Suitable age?' she said slowly. 'Suitable for what?'

'For marriage, when I've found you a worthy suitor.'

'Uncle!' Elwen tried to laugh. 'I don't want to marry!'

'Not now, of course,' he said reassuringly.

'No!' said Elwen vehemently. 'Not ever!'

'You will grow accustomed to the idea in time,' said Owein firmly.

'Is that my only choice?'

'You can choose either to marry, or be consigned to a sisterhood and live as a nun.'

'I do not want that either,' she said hurriedly. 'At least let me stay in London, until . . .' She drew a breath. 'Until you find me a suitor.'

Owein took his arm from her shoulders. 'I'm sorry, Elwen, but you cannot remain here. The lodgings in Bath are the finest I can offer you with the most opportunities for your future. You haven't had the benefit of a father's guidance and I know you've grown accustomed to your independence, but you are past an age where you can do as you wish and go where you please. You need a firm hand to guide you and the proper instruction in the deportment suitable for a young woman. I promised your mother I would care for you as if you were my own.' Elwen opened her mouth to speak, but Owein cut her off. 'I won't be swayed.' He rose from the bed. 'I expect to hear from Charles within the next few weeks. If all is well, when I return from Paris you will leave for Bath.' He went to the door and opened it. He looked back at her as if to say something, then left without a word, closing the door quietly behind him.

Alone, Elwen wrapped her arms about her and stood in the centre of the tiny room. The walls crowded in around her. When her widowed mother had been forced by encroaching poverty to take permanent employment in the household of a landowner, Owein had pulled Elwen up behind him on his horse and taken her to London. When she had cried, her uncle had thought it was with sadness. But in truth her tears had been born of relief.

In Powys, her mother would leave every dawn, pale faced and silent, for a day's labour as a maid. Elwen would race through her own chores, cleaning the two rooms of the dank, dark hut, feeding the ill-tempered sow and the few scraggy-feathered chickens they kept. As soon as she was done, she would head out into the wide open spaces of the fields, searching for new trees to climb, or children to play with. All those cold afternoons, watching the farmers and their sons come down from the pastures, calling to one another, familiar in manner. As time had gone by, Elwen's mother had grown more withdrawn, until she had faded into a shadowy presence that had lingered on the borders of her child's life. A voice raised, or a burst of laughter seemed to give her pain and Elwen had learnt to live in silence. When she had arrived in London, Elwen had spent the first three days at the door of her guardian's home, just listening to the city.

The years scrubbing floors to put scraps on the table had left her impoverished mother a shell of a woman who could neither give nor receive love, having forgotten how to feel, to dream. Owein didn't understand. He knew only the kind of death that came at the point of a sword.

'Will Campbell!'

Will, carrying buckets of water to the stables to refill the troughs, saw two sergeants from the group below his coming over.

'We watched you fight in the tournament,' said one, a small, freckled boy with a turned-up nose.

'What of it?'

'Can we see the badge?' asked the other.

Will sighed impatiently, but put the buckets down and stuck his hand in the pocket of his tunic. He drew out the brass badge, his prize from the tournament. 'Here,' he said, offering it to the freckled boy.

The boy took it reverently and bent over to study it with his friend. Will saw a door opening in the building opposite him: the infirmary. A sergeant came out.

'How did you do that last move?' the freckled boy asked.

Will didn't answer. The sergeant who had emerged from the infirmary was Garin. Will knew it was him by his hair, but Garin's face was almost unrecognisable. 'Mother of God,' he breathed, disregarding the sergeants' gasps following the blasphemy. Snatching the badge, he ran. His friend's right eye was swollen shut, the lid hideously red and taut. The skin around it was bruised a dark plum-purple, yellow and blotchy at the edges. His lip was also swollen, the skin cracked where it had split, and the whole right side of his face was distended as if he had a wad of cloth stuffed in his cheek. 'Garin? How . . .?'

'Leave me alone,' Garin mumbled, his voice as distorted as his face.

Will put the badge in his tunic pocket and grabbed Garin's shoulder. 'Did Cyclops do this?'

'Don't call him that!' Garin jerked his arm away and sprinted for the passage that led to the preceptory's docks. Will followed.

Endurance, the ship that would take them to Paris, was straining against her moorings and grating on the dock wall. The round galley with its two masts, high-sided hull and spindly-looking castles on the fore and aft decks was a hulk of a ship, built for carrying cargo, unlike the slender warships. Above the decks, rigging crisscrossed like spiders' webs and the Temple's black and white banner – their rallying point in battle – fluttered and snapped from the foremast. The crewmen on the dockside, keeping watch on the ship, looked up briefly as the two sergeants came running down to the dock wall, then went back to their game of draughts.

Garin stood rigid, fists clenched, then he slumped down on the dock wall.

Will sat down beside him. He looked out over the water. The Thames was reflecting the sun like a broken mirror, its surface scattered with a thousand shards of light. Its brilliance made his eyes water. 'How could he do this? You're his own flesh and blood.'

'I lost the tournament. He was angry.'

'When did it happen?'

'Yesterday.'

Will nodded. 'I couldn't find you at supper. I was worried.'

Garin's face was impassive. 'The injuries don't bother me. I deserved them. I failed.'

'Deserved them?' Will shook his head. 'What did the infirmarer say?'

'That I should be able to see again when the eye opens.'

'Christ.'

'Perhaps I can get an eye patch,' said Garin, looking away. He took a cloth pouch from his tunic. It was filled with a pungent-smelling, dark green matter. 'Brother Michael gave me a poultice for the swelling.' Garin studied the pouch for a moment, then drew back his hand to throw it into the river.

Will caught his arm. 'Don't! It will heal you.'

Garin stared at him, then laughed.

The constricted, high-pitched sound unnerved Will and he was glad when it stopped abruptly. 'I could go to Owein. He might talk to your uncle, ask him to stop this.'

'This is a family matter,' said Garin sharply. 'It has nothing to do with Owein . . . or you. Just leave it be.'

'The bastard has gone too far this time,' Will murmured. 'I wish you would stand up to him more.'

'Like you did with your father?' snapped Garin.

'That's different,' said Will tersely. 'My father never beat me.'

'You told me once you wished he would,' responded Garin. 'His fists would be better than his silence, that's what you said.'

Will gritted his teeth and looked away. 'We aren't talking about me.'

'My uncle just wants to teach me how to be a commander. He only wants what's best for our family, as I do. He punished me because I did something wrong. He isn't an evil man. It's my fault I don't do things right.'

'How can you say that? He has changed everything! *You've* changed. We used to have fun, didn't we?'

'I'm almost fourteen, Will, as are you. If Owein wasn't so easy on you, you would have been expelled months ago for all the Rules you've broken just because you think it fun. You need to start acting like a man.'

'If being a man means losing your good humour, I'll stay as I am. And most of the Rules are *pointless*. They tell us how we should cut cheese at the dinner table! That's not what being a knight is about.'

'Sometimes, I don't think you even want to be a knight,' said Garin with a sniff.

'Stop changing the subject,' said Will shortly, annoyed at the turn the conversation had taken. 'Your uncle shouldn't have done this. It goes far beyond punishment, as you put it.'

Garin gave a humourless laugh. 'Do you think he's the first person to beat me? My mother used to hit me with a stick when I did something she didn't like and my tutor . . . he was different. When I got a lesson wrong, he preferred the belt.' Garin's eyes were stormy. 'You don't know what it's like to have a name you have to live up to, what you have to do to make everyone happy.' He looked at Will. 'You don't understand anything, Will. You don't *know*.'

'Listen, Garin,' said Will quietly, 'there may be a way to stop him treating you like this. I think he's up to something. First of all, he loaned his horse to someone, a man who . . .'

'You've never understood why he treats me this way,' Garin interrupted, not listening. 'He just wants me to do well. Maybe if Owein treated you firmer *you'd* be a better sergeant.'

'What?' said Will, taken aback.

'You get away with everything just because you're good with a sword. You don't take anything seriously, but you're not going to be a commander like me. You're really just no one!' Garin's words hung in the air. He sighed roughly. 'I didn't mean that,' he muttered. 'But it's what my uncle thinks. He says you are bad company and that he would forbid me from speaking to you if we weren't training partners. He blames you for a lot of things I do wrong.'

'Oh.' Will sucked his lip. Taking a stone from the ground beside him, he flung it at the hull of the ship. It hit with a soft *plink*, then dropped into the water.

Will stood up. He put his hand in his tunic pocket, his fingers touching the badge, his prize. He had been going to give it to his father; proof, he had thought, that he was worthy of his father's pride; still good enough to be his son. But his father wasn't here. His father hadn't seen him training for hours every morning, hadn't seen him win the tournament, hadn't seen him sitting awake at night, holding that damn sword and staring into the darkness, trying to forget. Will paused for a moment, then drew the badge from his pocket. He ran his fingertip over the two brass knights, before handing it to his friend. 'Here.'

Garin rose and stared at the badge. 'I don't want your prize,' he said stiffly.

'It isn't a prize anymore,' said Will, taking Garin's hand and pressing the badge into his palm. 'It's a gift.'

Garin said nothing for a few moments, then his hand curled around the badge. 'Thank you,' he mumbled.

Will nodded and stuffed his hands back into his tunic. Garin opened his mouth as if to say something, then walked away. Will sat on the wall when his friend had gone and leaned back on his elbows, watching a merchant's cog glide upriver. The Thames here was always crowded. The ships brought spices, glass, cloth and wine from Bruges, Antwerp, Venice, even Acre, for trade across Britain. Last spring, the captain of a Genoese merchant galley had sailed close enough to throw Will two large oranges and a fistful of dates. On that night, he and Garin had feasted like kings.

Will picked another stone from the wall and tossed it into the river. The stone struck the water and disappeared, leaving rings rippling across the surface. Garin was wrong. He didn't break the Rules because it was fun. The endless chores and prayers and meals, all performed in reverent silence, trapped him inside himself, giving him time to think. Only fighting on the field, the thrill of it, the fierce concentration, would banish those thoughts. It was the same whenever he was doing something he shouldn't; the excitement made the shadow disappear, the memories fade.

As evening drew in and the temperature dropped, Will headed slowly down the narrow passage that led into the preceptory. He made his way past the armoury and on towards the chapel. A figure in a dark blue cloak was sitting on the low wall that ringed the cemetery. It was Elwen. She was looking out across the orchard, her long hair whipped by the wind. He made to go past, then changed his mind.

'Elwen?' Even in the gloom, Will could see she had been crying.

'What do you want, Will Campbell?' she said, looking away.

He shrugged and turned to leave.

'Wait!' called Elwen. 'Stay,' she said, as he looked back. 'I'd like the company.'

Will sat on the wall beside her. 'What's wrong?' he asked, studying her downcast expression.

'I'm leaving.' Elwen picked at a speck of dirt beneath her fingernail and told him what Owein had said.

'I'm sorry,' he said awkwardly when she had finished.

She bristled at his tone. 'Why should you be sorry? You aren't going to be married off to some ugly old man!'

'I meant about your guardian. I'm sorry she died.'

Elwen wiped her face with her sleeve and avoided his eyes. 'So am I, but . . .' Her tone softened. 'I don't want to go to Bath.' She laughed bitterly. 'I'll not see the Holy Land now, will I?'

Will was surprised. 'You want to make a pilgrimage?'

'Not a pilgrimage.' She faced him, smoothing the folds of her cloak over her skirts. 'There was a man in the village I lived in who went to the Holy Land. He said there are cities with castles and towers of gold and the sea is so blue it hurts your eyes. He said there are places where it never rains. It always rained in Powys.' Elwen's eyes were shining in the last of the light. 'I want to see it. *All* of it. Everything and everywhere I used to make up stories about. If I had stayed in Powys it wouldn't have been long before my mother gave me to some farmer as a bride. I would have raised pigs and children and seen nothing more than the fields outside whatever hovel I lived in. I had a friend in Powys, the same age as me, who was betrothed to a man twenty years older than she was. I expect she's wed now and scrubbing his floors. And the same fate awaits me here.' Elwen rose to her feet and pulled her cloak around her. 'I want to travel, see different places, not grow old and unhappy and poor like everyone else where I come from. Like my mother. I'd die before I do that,' she added fiercely, 'I really would.' Will opened his mouth to speak, but she cut him off. 'And don't tell me it's only men who can travel. Plenty of women have gone to the Holy Land and girls as well. My guardian told me about the Children's Crusade.'

'The Children's Crusade doesn't count. They only made it as far as Marseilles where they were sold off as slaves. But I wasn't going to say that. I was going to say that I understand. If I could, I would go tomorrow. Believe me, I would,' he added fervently.

'For the war,' she said flatly.

'No.'

'Why do you train if not to fight?'

Will sighed. 'When I go to the Holy Land it will be for war,' he acceded, 'but it isn't why I want to go.'

'Why then?' she asked simply.

'I want to see my father,' he said quietly.

'I was right then, in what I said? You do miss him?'

Will rose. 'You don't know that you won't see the Holy Land. Owein said you would only be in Bath for a year.'

'And do you think my *husband* will let me go? No,' she sighed. 'I think I should be too busy with babies and making bread. That's what wives do, isn't it? That is their duty?'

'Not always,' said Will uncertainly.

'No? Didn't your mother do those things?'

'I'm just saying,' replied Will, 'that you never know what will happen.' He glanced round as a group of sergeants marched past, their boots stamping the ground. A few of them looked inquisitively at Elwen. 'I should go.'

'It was good to meet you again, Will Campbell.'

Will went to walk away, then looked back. 'Owein once told me that a man makes his own destiny. Perhaps it can be the same for a woman?'

'Yes,' said Elwen, with a small smile. 'Perhaps it can.'

10
Honfleur, Normandy
22 October 1260 AD

Endurance cut through the swell, spray misting the bowsprit. The sky was a deep, cloudless azure and the triangular sails billowed from the lateen-yards. The calls of men rang out, relaying orders.

Endurance had a Templar captain and five knight-officers, but the rest of the crew were made up of sergeants and contracted seamen. Will rested his arms on the sides and peered down into the water. He had travelled on barges on the Thames, but those slow, sedate journeys were nothing like this. Every way he turned he could see nothing but the wide expanse of blue. It felt like flying. Nearby, an ashen-faced sergeant was vomiting noisily over the side.

Will turned from the sergeant's retches, his gaze coming to rest on the figure sitting on the quarterdeck above him. The man's long legs were dangling over the edge, his grey cloak pulled tight about him. In the bright daylight, the cloak's cowl offered little concealment of his face. Everything about him was dark: his eyes were charcoal-black; his hair and beard raven; his skin a glossy mahogany. Will wasn't the only one who had been studying him. Earlier, he had overheard two of the older sergeants in the Temple's party talking about the stranger in hushed tones.

'He could be a Genoese,' one of them had whispered to the other, 'or a Pisan. But what he's doing here, I cannot guess. I heard a knight say he's a comrade of Sir Jacques.'

'No,' the other sergeant had murmured, giving the man in grey a grim look. 'He isn't from the Maritime Republics. I believe he is a Saracen.'

The first sergeant had crossed himself and rested his hand on the hilt of his sword.

Will averted his gaze, pretending to study something in the water, as the man locked eyes with him and smiled. When Will looked back he was staring out to sea, a thoughtful expression on his face. Could he be a

Saracen? Will didn't think it was possible: an enemy of God on board a Templar ship? But he thought of the man's strange accent and the letter in the solar and he wondered.

Will glanced over at Garin, keen to share his concerns about the stranger. His friend was sitting alone on one of the benches near the stern. The swelling on his face had gone down slightly, although his right eye was still partially closed. Will took a step towards him, then sank onto the bench beside his sack which held his belongings: a spare tunic and hose and his falchion. Over the past few days, Will had tried talking to Garin, but the boy's withdrawn indifference had just frustrated him. He decided he would let Garin come to him.

Stretching out his legs, Will looked over at the captain's cabin beneath the quarterdeck, the door of which was ajar. The ten knights from the Temple were seated around a table inside, drinking wine with their afternoon meal. On the floor beside Owein's stool, Will could see a large black trunk upon which, gilded in gold, was the king's crest. He guessed that in the trunk lay the crown jewels. Queen Eleanor and her retinue were stationed in the adjacent cabin.

After they had sailed out of the Thames estuary the queen had appeared on deck with two of her handmaidens. Her dark-brown hair was piled beneath a lacy coif, a few escaped strands floating about her delicately-boned face, and her crimson silk gown was embroidered with gold fleur-de-lys, the royal emblem of the Kingdom of France. Eleanor, who had come to Henry as a young bride from Provence, was the sister of Marguerite, wife of King Louis IX.

She had watched the southern skyline anxiously as they sailed round the eastern tip of England and a short while later had disappeared inside her cabin, followed by her attendants. Occasionally the twinkling notes of a softly played harp had drifted out through the scarlet drapes that covered the cabin's window.

Leaning his head against the side, Will closed his eyes.

Some time later, he was woken by the sound of gulls. He yawned, tasting salt on his lips. The sun was low in the sky, the sea mirroring the purple underbellies of the clouds. They were approaching land. The green ribbon slowly unfurled into low, sweeping hills chiselled with sheer, white cliffs. Will was disappointed by the sight. He had thought that the Kingdom of France would offer something more of a revelation, but the green fields and pebbled beaches looked the same as the English coastline. The galley rounded a narrow peninsula that pointed like a finger out to sea and, as it sailed into the wide mouth of a river, Will, listening to the crew's conversation, realised that they had arrived at Honfleur.

The hills fell back to reveal a small port nestled in a sheltered cove on the starboard banks. Beyond the harbour, houses formed a ring around a square, which was packed with people, their faces golden in the evening light. A market had been set up and above the stalls brightly coloured flags were flapping in the breeze. The sounds of laughter, music and the words of a language Will didn't understand floated out over the water. He picked up his sack, steadying himself as the galley grated against the harbour wall. Jacques and the man in grey were standing below the quarterdeck, talking quietly. Will wandered closer to them, but the two men fell silent as Owein's voice called out.

'Hail, brother!'

Will saw a short, portly man with a tonsured head and a bushy, mousy-brown beard hurrying across the docks. He was wearing the black mantle of a Templar priest.

The priest raised a hand at Owein's call. '*Pax tecum*,' he puffed, the sweat gleaming on his bald pate.

Owein stepped down the planks to meet him. '*Et cum spiritu tuo*. I take it you are expecting us?'

'We received the message from Humbert de Pairaud last week. Her majesty's rooms have been readied,' said the priest, pursing his lips, 'though I'm afraid our quarters are most humble, more fit for a commoner than a queen.'

'I'm sure it will suit for one night. Is our boat ready?'

'Yes, brother.' The priest pointed to the other end of the harbour. '*Opinicus* arrived this morning from Paris.'

Will followed the priest's finger and saw a squat, sturdy vessel with one mast and a square sail. There was a picture of an Opinicus on the sail – a heraldic beast composed of a lion, a camel and a dragon.

'Her crew are taking supper with us. Our lodgings aren't far.' The priest motioned up the hillside to a grey stone building surrounded by a crumbling wall. 'Will you be joining us for food and the evening prayer? We are but a simple company here and rarely receive word from our brothers.' He smiled beatifically and clasped his hands together, resting them on his expansive stomach. 'In following in the footsteps of the blessed Bernard de Clairvaux our service to the Order lies solely in spiritual deeds. We, here, prefer to think of ourselves as monks rather than warriors. But,' he added quickly, 'it would be an honour to dine with such grand company.' He looked up at the ship and her large crew doubtfully. 'Though it may be difficult to feed so many mouths.'

'Perhaps later,' replied Owein. He glanced at the sky. 'We'll wait a few hours, then escort the queen to your estate. The less attention we draw to our presence the better. Send *Opinicus*'s crew to meet us at the vessel.'

The priest looked somewhat peeved by Owein's brusque manner. 'As you wish, brother,' he said stiffly, before waddling away, hitching up the girdle around his mantle.

Several hours later, Will found himself on the dockside guarding a mounting pile of chests, crates and casks that the crew and the sergeants were off-loading from *Endurance*. Most of the cargo belonged to the queen, including the harp he had heard being played, but some of the crates and casks, filled with salt and ale, were to be delivered to the Paris preceptory. Will heard a shout and a giggle and turned to see a group of children staring at him curiously. The market was still bustling even though it was almost midnight. Torches had been set up around the area and the smell of roasting meat from the spits made Will's stomach groan. One of the older sergeants had told him that the celebrations were in honour of the last harvest of autumn. Many of the women wore crowns of corn and the men had donned grotesque masks fashioned in the likeness of wolves, hounds and stags. It was an eerie sight; these parodies of beasts that danced and twirled in the torchlight beneath the shadow of the church.

Will turned from the square to see two crewmen lugging a crate down the planks. Behind them, a slender figure in a dark blue cloak, hood pulled low, was struggling with a heavy-looking box. The figure stumbled. Will moved to help, but the two crewmen who had deposited the crate were already there.

'Let me take that, miss,' said one of the men.

The woman hesitated.

'I doubt your mistress would want her handmaiden to injure herself,' said the crewman taking the box from her, 'or her goods,' he added, hefting the box easily onto his shoulder.

Will heard footsteps behind him and saw a tall man he didn't recognise clad in a sergeant's tunic.

'Where's Sir Owein?' asked the man, glancing up at the ship.

'On board,' replied Will.

'Tell him *Opinicus* is ready. I'll send some of my crew to help.'

Will looked back to the ship as the man headed across the docks. *Endurance*'s crewmen had gone to fetch more crates. There was no sign of the queen's handmaiden. Owein disembarked with two sergeants, one of them Garin, who were carrying the black chest, gilded with the king's crest. Will told Owein what the crewman from *Opinicus* had said.

'Good,' said Owein. 'Sir Jacques will oversee the loading.' He turned as three knights and the queen and her entourage stepped down the planks.

'Are you ready, my lady?' Owein asked the queen, as one of her pages helped her down the last few feet. Her guards were scouring the dockside warily.

'Yes,' replied the queen, her voice soft and musical. 'My belongings . . .?' She gestured to the pile Will was guarding.

'Are to be loaded onto *Opinicus* immediately,' assured Owein. 'Come, my lady, we'll escort you to your lodgings.'

Garin and the other sergeant had hefted the black chest over to the rest of the cargo. The queen paused. 'I should prefer it if my husband's jewels remained with me.'

There was a clatter as Garin lost his grip on the chest and it crashed to the ground. 'I assure you, my lady,' said Owein, glowering at Garin, who was bending over, red-faced, to right the chest, 'the jewels will be safe with us.' He glanced at the children who were gawping at the queen and her stately entourage. 'We should go,' he urged, motioning to the three knights who had joined him on the dockside.

The queen and her entourage moved off across the harbour wall, flanked by Owein and the knights. The group of children followed them, chattering excitedly, until one of the knights shouted at them and they ran off.

'That's the last of it,' said Jacques, heading down the planks with the remainder of the knights and sergeants. With them was the man in grey. *Endurance*'s crew hauled in the planks and loosed the mooring ropes. 'Let's move these crates,' barked Jacques, 'quickly.' He ordered two knights and two sergeants to guard the pile, then set off with the others towards *Opinicus*, bearing the chest containing the crown jewels himself.

Will found himself hauling a crate of salt. The grey man, as Will had privately dubbed him, was walking in front, carrying a sack slung over his shoulder and a small cask. The area was shadowy with just a few torches throwing pools of light over the slimy stones. The party passed several members of *Opinicus*'s crew on the way, hastening across the docks to help. When they reached the boat, Will set the crate down where it was loaded with the others. The vessel was much smaller than *Endurance*, with a single cabin beneath the raised deck at the stern.

Jacques passed the black chest up to one of the boat's crew. 'Leave that here, Hasan,' he said, motioning to the cask the man in grey was carrying.

'What did I tell you,' hissed a sergeant behind Will. 'Hasan is an Arab's name!'

'Campbell!'

Will tore his gaze from the grey man to see Jacques glaring at him.

'Help de Lyons with the rest of the crates.'

'Yes, sir,' said Will curtly. He loped back across the docks. But when he reached the pile of cargo his friend was nowhere to be seen. 'Where's Garin?' he asked one of the sergeants.

The sergeant shrugged distractedly. 'With *Opinicus*, I think.' He turned from Will and picked up one of the crates which he handed to another sergeant.

Will scanned the dockside, thinking he must have passed Garin coming back and not seen him. As he glanced over at the market square, his gaze fell on a tall man who was weaving between the stalls. It was Hasan. Will bent down, pretending to adjust his boot as two sergeants passed him, and kept his eyes on the grey man. Hasan was moving around a crowd of men who were singing in loud, drunken tones. After casting a glance in the direction of *Opinicus*, he disappeared in the throng. Will's curiosity overtook his caution. He headed for the square, crouching behind some rotten crates that stank of fish to avoid a knight who was carrying the queen's harp.

After the darkness of the dockside, the light from the fires and the sounds of music and singing were disorientating. A heavy-set woman danced past him laughing, her skirts twirling. Hasan was lingering at a stall some distance ahead, inspecting rows of bread and cakes. Will moved closer, careful to keep out of sight. Nearby, a garishly dressed jongleur was juggling apples. Beside him sprawled a large, mangy dog. The jongleur threw the apples high into the air, turned a cartwheel and caught them to the cheers of the crowd. Will sidestepped the dog that opened one yellow eye and snarled. He stood on his toes to see over the heads of a group of men. Hasan had moved from the stall and was near the tall buildings at the back of the square. Will struggled his way through the press of bodies. By the time he emerged, Hasan had vanished.

The church bell began to clang for midnight. Will couldn't stay here for much longer: Cyclops would soon notice his absence. Near the buildings at the back of the square the crowds were thinner. Will glimpsed a swish of grey as a shadow disappeared through one of the openings that led between the buildings. He ran, not thinking what he would do if he caught up with Hasan, and came to a stop outside the entrance to a narrow passage which stank of urine and rotten vegetables. As he peered into the darkness a wave of noise and a smell of ale washed out from the building beside him. Two men came out carrying flagons. There was a crude sign painted on the door that Will guessed was some kind of guesthouse, or inn. He couldn't quite make it out, but thought it might be a picture of a yellow sheep standing on a blue-green field. The church bell ceased its clanging. Will shouted as someone grabbed him from behind in an iron-like grip. He was dragged roughly down the alley. He struggled, trying to turn, or kick, but whoever held him was too strong. Will was flung against the wall of one of the buildings. He made to run when the hold on him was loosened, then froze as something cold and hard was pressed against his throat. Will stared up at the man holding the dagger. In the faint light coming down the passage, Hasan's eyes gleamed.

Al-Salihiyya, Egypt

23 October 1260 AD

B aybars entered the tent behind two of his attendants, who were carrying a platter of fruit and a jug of kumiz. Sweeping past them, he saw Omar seated on one of the cushions that had been laid on a rug before a chest. Aside from the scant furnishings and a brazier that lit the interior with a ruddy glow the tent was bare.

The army had arrived at al-Salihiyya late in the evening, waking the townsfolk some time before they reached the walls with the thudding echoes of their drums. The town, which lay eighteen or so miles from Cairo, had been built by Sultan Ayyub twelve years ago as a point of rest for the army on the return journey from Palestine. It was inhabited by a small garrison of soldiers and local farmers and their families who, as soon as they heard the drums, had left their beds and busied themselves with the preparation of fresh supplies for the march-weary troops. The Mamluks had made camp beyond the walls across a flat, grassy plain which glowed a translucent silver in the moonlight.

Baybars found the tent's uncluttered interior pleasant in contrast to the bustle of the camp outside: its emptiness seeming to replicate a clarity of thought in his mind. Kutuz and his governors had ordered that their own pavilions be decked out with the usual array of finery, but comfort had been the least of Baybars' concerns. He nodded to Omar as he unbuckled his sword belt. 'Where is Kalawun?'

'He'll join us shortly, Amir. He is . . .' Omar stopped, his eyes on the two attendants.

Baybars followed his gaze. 'Go,' he said to the attendants, motioning to the tent opening.

As the attendants set down the food and left, Baybars laid his sabres on the rug and knelt beside Omar. He stifled a yawn and pushed his hands through his hair, leaving his scalp tingling. Kutuz had kept him busy for the past three hours with the camp preparations and it was gone midnight. The nine-day march across the Sinai beneath the burning sun had been relentless and his skin felt tight, hot.

'You should eat something, sadeek,' said Omar.

Baybars glanced at the figs and glossy segments of orange. 'I'm not hungry. But,' he said, reaching for the kumiz, 'I would welcome a drink.'

Omar watched him drain the contents of the jar. 'Kalawun is meeting with the last of the governors whom he believes can be swayed to support us.' He smiled slightly. 'I think he enjoys his new role.'

'He has a talent for persuasion,' replied Baybars, returning the empty jug to the chest. 'When he speaks men listen. And,' he admitted with an indifferent shrug, 'his tongue is smoother than mine.'

They looked up as the tent flaps opened and Kalawun stepped in. He bowed to Baybars.

'Amir.'

'How did you fare with the governors?'

'The two whom I spoke with will make no move to obstruct your path to the throne once the sultan is dead. They feel that you would be the better candidate.'

Baybars smiled wryly. 'How much did their loyalty cost me?'

'A mere drop in the ocean of the treasury that lies waiting for you in the Citadel.' Kalawun turned and flicked back the tent flaps. 'Whilst I was out I found something of yours, Amir.'

Khadir entered the tent. The soothsayer's robe was damp and muddy and he was holding a dead hare by its ears. He scuttled into the shadows beyond the brazier, where he laid the hare before him and crouched on all fours. With his long, bony limbs splayed out on the sand he gave Omar the disturbing impression of a spider waiting to strike. Omar fought back his discomfort. He didn't understand why Baybars insisted on having the wretch so closely involved in such important affairs. It worried and annoyed him.

'Where have you been?' demanded Baybars.

'Hunting,' replied Khadir petulantly. The gold-handled dagger that hung from the chain around his waist was blood-flecked. He reached out and stroked the hare's ears. 'So soft,' he murmured.

'Did you discover what I need to know?' Baybars asked Khadir, as Kalawun sat himself on one of the cushions and plucked a fig from the platter.

'Yes, master.' Khadir sat back and looked at the three men. 'The key to the throne can be turned.'

'What does he mean?' Omar asked Baybars. 'Key to the throne?'

'Aqtai, the sultan's chief of staff. He has the power to surrender the throne to a successor on the sultan's death.' Baybars looked to Khadir. 'You are certain?'

'I've watched him closely these past weeks, master. The man is a faint-hearted fool. He will fold easily enough if pressed.' Khadir smiled. 'The time is right. The red star of war dominates the sky. It calls for blood.'

'Then blood it shall have.' Baybars turned to Omar and Kalawun. 'Kutuz has decreed that we rest here for the day. No doubt he wishes to rouse the men with a speech boasting of his great triumph before he makes his glorious return to Cairo.

'The royal pavilion has been erected beneath the walls of the town. Following the prayer of morning at sunrise, he will break his fast after which he always sleeps for an hour. This will be the time when he is most vulnerable and away from the majority of his guards. I have discovered, between the pavilion and the wall, a grove of lemon trees where the undergrowth is thick. At first light we'll conceal ourselves there and when Kutuz takes his rest we will cut through the back of the pavilion and enter his private compartment. Kalawun, you will dispatch the two Mu'izziyya who will be guarding him, then take up position at the entrance to the throne area. Omar, you will watch my back and deal with any servants who may attempt to intervene. I will kill Kutuz.'

They both nodded.

'As this doesn't leave us much time,' continued Baybars, 'I need you to go now to Aqtai, Kalawun. He must be there when the deed is done to hand control of the throne to me. Threaten him, or pay him if he can be bought, I don't care how, just get him to agree.'

'As you command, Amir Baybars,' said Kalawun, rising to his feet.

'Aqtai retired an hour ago,' said Baybars, looking up at him. 'You will find him in his pavilion.'

Kalawun slipped out into the night and moved through the camp. As the army would rest at al-Salihiyya for one day only, not all of the tents had been erected and many groups of men had bedded down under the stars, huddled around yellow pockets of fire. The drummers had ceased their relentless pounding and a soft stillness had spread across the army, broken only by the murmuring of soldiers and the strains of a lute. In the shadows on the edges of the camp, the siege engines and wagons made strange contours of the darkness and camels were being herded in a long train through the cotton fields to one of the many streams that cut through the plain. Kalawun made his way past the royal pavilion, behind which he could make out the low walls of the town and the mud-brick houses beyond. The heavy folds of cloth at the front of the pavilion had been pulled back and fastened in two wings, revealing the dais on which was placed the sultan's throne. Several of the Mu'izziyya were standing stiff and silent in the entrance. Kalawun moved past them, his footsteps making no sound on the springy grass, and approached the smaller tent that belonged to the sultan's chief of staff.

'Officer Kalawun.'

Kalawun halted. Turning, he saw one of the governors he had been sent to bribe earlier.

'We must speak,' said the governor, coming to stand before him.

Kalawun nodded respectfully. 'At this moment, Governor, I have an audience with the sultan's chief of staff. I'll be free to meet with you afterwards.'

'If it's an ally you seek,' said the governor, motioning to Aqtai's tent, 'you'll not find one in there.'

'What is this concerning?' asked Kalawun, frowning.

'I have valuable information.'

Kalawun glanced around, then gestured for the governor to follow him. They moved into the darkness, some distance from Aqtai's tent. 'Tell me.'

The governor smiled slightly. 'As I said, it is valuable information.'

'You will be compensated.'

The governor paused, then nodded. 'The sultan, with the aid of his chief of staff, has arranged a hunt after the morning prayer, to which Baybars will be invited. Kutuz plans to kill him.'

Kalawun drew in a breath. 'Why would Kutuz do this? Has he heard word of our plan?'

'No,' replied the governor, 'I believe he has been plotting Baybars' death for some time. The sultan knows that Baybars has much support among the men and not just those within the Bahri regiment. Kutuz fears that, in time, Baybars may try to raise an army and turn it against him.'

'How do you know this?'

'Kutuz believes I'm still loyal to him. He invited me to a meeting he held with Aqtai, during which he finalised these arrangements.'

Kalawun shook his head, digesting this news. 'How many will be in this hunting party?'

'Kutuz, six of the Mu'izziyya and five governors, including myself.'

'Can you speak with any of the other governors before the hunt? Perhaps sway those Baybars hasn't yet paid to support him?'

'One, maybe two,' replied the governor.

'Baybars will see that you are rewarded greatly for your loyalty.'

'I would expect no less.'

Kalawun melted into the shadows and made his way back through the camp. In the tent, he found Baybars and Omar still talking.

'Amir,' he said quietly.

Baybars looked up.

12

Honfleur, Normandy

23 October 1260 AD

H asan pressed the dagger harder against Will's throat. 'Why are you following me?' he repeated, his words viscous with his accent. 'Answer!'

'I wasn't,' breathed Will, forcing his eyes from the dagger to meet the man's stare.

The corner of Hasan's mouth twitched. 'I know when I am being tailed. You have been watching me since we left England. Do not mistake me for a fool.'

'I wanted to see where you were going. I heard some of the others talking. They said you are a Saracen. They don't trust you.'

'I see,' said Hasan thoughtfully. 'So you followed me to see if . . . what? I was taking a moment to kill a few Christians, rape nuns, devour children?' Will saw a flash of white as the man grinned. 'That is what *Saracens* do, is it not?'

Hasan stepped back, removing the dagger, and drew something from his sack. Will didn't dare move.

'There,' he said, holding out a loaf of bread. 'That is what I was doing. Buying a meal.' He stowed the bread in his sack and sheathed the dagger in a short leather scabbard at his hip. 'I suggest you return to the boat.' His smile faded. 'This is not a safe place for children, however bold they might be.'

Will stepped from the wall, keeping his eyes on Hasan, and backed away. Slowly, his heart knocking against his chest, he turned and walked stiffly down the alley. With every step he could feel Hasan's gaze upon him. When he reached the end, he glanced back. Hasan was still standing there watching him. Will sprinted for the dockside, barging past a man in a black robe who swore savagely at him through a white mask that looked like a skull.

Endurance had gone, swallowed by the blackness of the river mouth. Will carried the crate he'd collected from the now diminished pile to *Opinicus*. Twice, he had to stop and set the crate down, waiting until his strength returned and his legs stopped shaking before he picked it up again. Fighting another sergeant with a sword was one thing; being threatened by a man with a dagger brought about an entirely different sensation.

Torches had been set in brackets around *Opinicus*'s sides, casting light across the deck and the dockside below. Garin was there, dragging a chest into the small cabin where the queen's belongings were being stored.

Owein looked down from the deck, as Will approached. 'Sergeant!' The knight held up a sack. 'Is this yours?'

Will recognised the bundle that contained his clothes and sword. 'Yes, sir,' he said, placing the crate on the wall.

'Don't leave it lying around.' Owein tossed the bundle down to him. 'I doubt the queen would want your hose to end up in her possession.'

Will watched his master order two sergeants on the dockside to move a heavy-looking chest up the planks. He wondered if he should tell Owein what had happened. Hasan was armed and clearly dangerous. But if he was a comrade of Jacques, then perhaps Owein already knew that he was a Saracen? Will didn't understand it. And was the letter he had found in the solar connected to Hasan, or was that something else? A movement caught his eye. Someone was creeping alongside the wooden shacks that lined the docks, keeping close to the shadows. The figure dropped suddenly down behind a stack of wicker eel traps. A knight, standing on the prow of *Opinicus*, was staring in the direction of the shacks. As the knight turned away, the figure began to move again. Frowning, Will headed along the wall, past *Opinicus*. Behind him, there was a clatter and a few cries and curses.

'Careful with that, damn it!' Will heard Owein shout.

There was, Will realised, something familiar about the approaching figure; something in the way the cloak's hood was drawn so low over the face. It clicked in his mind: it was the handmaiden he had seen struggling with the box on *Endurance*. Will stepped out of the darkness in front of her and she halted.

'What are you doing here?'

She backed away from him.

'Did the queen send you?' he asked, following.

She kept backing away until she tripped over a knotted heap of nets behind her and stumbled, losing her balance. Her hood slipped from her

head. As she fell, Elwen's hair tumbled free. From the boat, there was
another clatter followed by several loud splashes and a yell. One of the
planks resting on *Opinicus*'s sides had overturned, sending the two sergeants
and the large chest they had been hauling into the water. Owein was
shouting at them to get the chest before it sank. Will stood rooted to the
spot for a moment, then rushed towards Elwen. She was thrashing about,
caught in the fishing nets she had tripped over. As he knelt beside her, she
lay still and gave a frustrated sob. Will dropped his sack and tugged a
section of the net from around her arm. 'Elwen? How did . . .?' He sat
back on his heels as the net came away. 'What the hell are you doing?'

Elwen was white and shaking. Her blue cloak had fallen open and there
was a dark stain on the front of her gown.

'Blood?' he murmured, reaching towards her.

'No,' she said, pushing his hand aside forcibly and pulling her cloak
around her. 'I was sick.' She got to her feet with effort.

Owein was still shouting. The two sergeants who had fallen into the
river were trying to swim for the wall, clutching the chest. One of the crew
had thrown a rope down to them.

'What were you thinking of?' said Will, getting to his feet and staring at
her. 'How did you get on board *Endurance*?'

'I hid in the hold last night when the guards weren't looking.' Elwen's
brow furrowed. 'The smell. It was so cramped and I was so sick, I thought I
was going to die.' She looked down the wall to where Owein was kneeling
over the side, trying to reach the half-submerged chest. 'But I thought if my
uncle saw he couldn't make me go to Bath, he would have to listen to me.'
She shrugged. 'Either that or I would remain at the port, maybe make my
own way to Paris.'

Will stared at her in a mixture of disbelief and respect. 'You are—' He
stopped abruptly as a large company of figures dressed in black robes moved
out of the shadows of the dockside. Their faces were skulls, stark white in
the torchlight. As one, the company ran towards *Opinicus*. There was a
rasping sound as many swords were drawn simultaneously from their
scabbards.

Will shouted a warning, but the knights on the boat were already
drawing their blades. Two of the black-robed figures pulled away from the
pack, making a line for Owein. Will yelled the knight's name as, beside
him, Elwen screamed. Owein spun round, his sword sticking in its scabbard
for one terrible moment then coming free as one of the men flew at him.
The ring of metal meeting metal echoed sharply. The two sergeants who

had fallen into the river had been halfway up the wall when the assault came. They now dropped the chest and struggled over the side. One of them went down immediately under an attacker's blows, falling back into the water with a wail that cut off as he went under.

'The jewels!' roared Owein, slamming his sword into the side of one of the men, sending him spinning to the ground. 'Protect the jewels!' The second man charged Owein and their blades arced in the air, sparking as they collided.

Sixteen of the attackers boarded *Opinicus*, sprinting up the planks, or vaulting over the low sides. Fighting broke out across the deck. Two of *Opinicus*'s crew battled alongside the knights and the three armed sergeants, but the rest, unarmed and untrained, were easy targets; three of them went down in the first wave of the assault. Jacques was fighting two of the men, his sword whirling in his hand, face locked in grim concentration. Garin was pressed against the cabin door, his face a mask of fear, watching his uncle. There was an anguished howl from one of the knights as a blade slashed viciously across his face, opening his cheek to the bone. His attacker shoved into him, sending him overboard. Owein, another knight and the remaining sergeant dispatched the three men on the dockside and jumped on board to aid their fellows.

Will ran forward, then halted, his hands flexing, empty. Elwen gripped his arm, hard.

'What do we do?' Terror had risen the pitch of her voice. 'Will! What do we do?'

Will held his breath as he saw Owein forced back by a series of lunges from a powerfully built man. The knight ducked, pivoted round and thrust his sword into the man's back, but not before he had taken a deep cut across his sword arm. Jacques had dispatched two of the men and was now facing a third. Another knight went down, then two more of the attackers. One of the unarmed crewmen snatched a torch from its bracket on the side of the boat and swept it back and forth to defend himself from the sword strokes. The flames made bright traces in the air. There was a yell from the back of the boat as Garin was shoved aside by a heavy-set man. The man wrenched open the door to the cabin and ducked inside, kicking a barrel into the path of a sergeant who ran at him. Will whipped round, remembering his sack. It was lying on the ground by the nets. He sprinted to it and tore it open. Pulling out the falchion, he ran for the boat.

'*No!*' Elwen screamed behind him. '*Will!*'

Will raced up the plank and vaulted over the side. He ducked as one of the men, who had just killed another sergeant, swung at him. Stepping back, he banged into the side, as the large man came at him, snarling through the skull mask. Will flicked out with the blade to meet the blow and the impact throbbed through the sword and up his arm, loosening his grip. He clenched his teeth and tightened his hold on the hilt as the man came at him again and again, each blow harder, faster than the last. All around him was chaos, but his eyes were fixed on the man that swiped the blade at his chest and stomach. Will dodged out from between the side of the boat and his attacker, spinning round and snapping back his head as the sword whistled over him, missing his scalp by inches.

The deck, slippery with blood and strewn with bodies, wasn't a training field. His opponent didn't halt the blade before striking. The swords weren't made of wood, or blunted. Will felt, suddenly, and with absolute certainty that he was going to die.

His attacker's sword came at him slowly, almost lazily. His own blade had gone too wide to block it. There was nothing between the length of iron that was flying towards him and his chest. Will stepped back, his eyes closing at the last moment, then his foot slipped in a pool of blood and his legs went out from under him, the sword cutting air as he fell to the deck. He heard a shriek from above him and his face was splattered with blood, its hotness startling him. A sword point had come through the large man's stomach. Will rolled to avoid the body as it collapsed and saw Hasan standing behind the man, his sword blood-streaked. Hasan sprinted across the deck. Will struggled to his feet as a girl's scream sounded from the dockside. Whilst he had been fighting, the ten remaining black-robed figures had forced their way to the cabin. Two of them had the chest that contained the crown jewels. The other eight were clearing a path to the side of the boat. Owein had been cornered by two who were fighting him savagely. One man went down under a sharp thrust from Jacques who was battling side by side with Hasan, but the two with the jewels made it to the gangplanks. They charged down onto the dockside, straight into Elwen who, seeing Owein in danger, had run towards the boat.

In the collision, Elwen was sent sprawling to the ground. One of the men dropped his hold on the chest, which crashed to the stones with a splintering sound. Will cried out as the man turned on Elwen, sword raised. There was a blur of motion and the man was knocked flying, his sword sailing from his hand, as Garin barrelled into him. There was a dull crack, followed by a splash. The man had tumbled into the river, hitting his head on the side of the galley on his way down. Will vaulted from the boat.

The second man had let fall his sword and had grabbed the chest. He set off at a run, but Owein and another knight were on his heels in an instant. The man fell, only feet from the boat, at a short thrust of Owein's sword in his back. The chest smashed to the ground beside him, spilling its contents onto the stones. A crown encrusted with precious gems went rolling across the wall and clattered to a stop at the edge. Rings, a heavy gold orb and a glittering sceptre sparkled in the torchlight.

Owein spun round and saw Will and Garin, who had now picked up the sword of the man he had sent into the river. 'Guard the jewels!' he yelled at them. His jaw slackened, his sword swinging loose in his hand as his eyes fell on Elwen standing behind them. Owein turned, distractedly, at a cry from the boat.

Garin let out a shout of his own as he saw his uncle go down, a sword plunging into the knight's side and back out again. The man who delivered the blow fell a moment later under the fierce swings of Hasan. Six of the attackers jumped from the boat. Three ran at Owein, but the sight of the jewels scattered, irretrievable, and the knights leaping down from the sides behind them deterred them. The men turned and fled with the remainder of their company. Four of the knights and two sergeants chased them across the dockside as Garin charged onto the deck, yelling Jacques' name. A small crowd had gathered some distance from the boat, people running from the market square to see what the commotion was. They parted quickly as the black-robed figures rushed them, swords drawn. Women screamed and dragged their children out of harm's way.

Owein turned back to his niece. 'Elwen?'

There was a groan behind him. He glanced round. The man Owein had stabbed in the back was struggling to his knees, his sword grasped weakly in his hand. Owein strode towards him. The man raised his head, his eyes focusing on the knight.

'*Pax!*' he cried, dropping his sword. '*Pax!*'

'Get up!'

The man did so, slowly, head bowed as if in respect. It wasn't until he took his hands from his sides that Will caught sight of the dagger. Will went to cry out, too late, as the man leapt at Owein and thrust the blade into the knight's chest, driving it through his heart. Owein's sword clanged on the stones. He fell back, his hands clutching at the hilt of the dagger. The cry loosed itself from Will's mouth as Owein collapsed on the dockside, flopping and gasping like a fish out of water. The man turned and staggered away. He glanced over his shoulder as footsteps pounded up behind him and his brown eyes, through the skull mask, widened, seeing the falchion in Will's hand come smashing towards him. The blade struck the man in the side of his head with a blunt cracking sound, a gout of dark blood spurting from his temple. He slumped to his knees. Will drew back the sword. As their eyes met, he hesitated for one infinitesimal moment which seemed to last much longer, then he stabbed forward, punching through the man's throat, feeling resistance, then the yielding softness of flesh and tissue.

'*Owein!*'

Will whipped round and saw Elwen bending over Owein. He pulled the falchion free and ran. Elwen was holding Owein's head in her hands, screaming his name over and over. The dagger was protruding from Owein's chest, buried up to the hilt, and a bubble of blood had burst on his lips, staining them like wine. His eyes were open. Will stared at his master, then looked down at the falchion in his hand. There was a wide smear of blood on the short blade. He felt bile rise in his throat as Elwen's screams rang in his ears. He dropped the sword and sank to his knees beside her. Grabbing her shoulders, he tried to pull her back to quiet her. Her hands were covered in blood.

'Come away!'

She carried on screaming.

'*Elwen!*' he shouted, dragging her back.

Her hands slipped from Owein's cheeks. His head rolled back. '*No!*' she shrieked, pounding Will with her fists. '*No!*'

Will took hold of her wrists and drew her to him, enfolding her tightly in his arms, almost crushing her. Over her shoulder, Will stared at Owein's face: his slack mouth, his unseeing eyes.

13

Al-Salihiyya, Egypt

23 October 1260 AD

K utuz sat on his throne, watching the east flush pink with the sun's arrival. It would be a good morning for hares, possibly even boar. The camp was stirring. Men rolled up their blankets, broke their fast and tended to their horses. The five governors and six Mu'izziyya he had summoned for the hunt were waiting at the entrance to the pavilion. Of Baybars, there was no sign.

Kutuz rose from the throne, stepped down from the platform and across the grass to where his pages had spread his prayer mat. He turned towards Mecca as the first rays of sun flamed in the sky. And all the men of his army did the same. The song of their words drifted across the plain.

'*Bismillah arrahman arraheem. Alhamdulillah, rabb al 'alamin. Arrahman arraheem. Malik yawm addeen.*'

When he had finished, Kutuz, kneeling on the ground, touched his forehead to the grass, breathing in the damp, green smell. He sat back and saw three figures heading towards him. Kutuz frowned as he saw Omar and Kalawun at Baybars' side.

'Amir,' he called, standing.

Baybars bowed. 'My lord.'

'The invitation was for you alone, Baybars,' said Kutuz with a quizzical smile at Omar and Kalawun.

Baybars appeared surprised. 'My apologies, Lord Sultan. I didn't realise the hunt was to be a private affair.' He turned to Omar and Kalawun. 'Leave us.'

'Wait!' called Kutuz, holding up his hand. 'There's no need. Your officers are welcome to join us, Amir.' He smiled. 'I'm sure there will be enough quarry for us all.' He gestured to his pages. 'Saddle two more horses.' Kutuz moved over to his white mare. 'Let us ride!' he called to the party. Just before he mounted, the sultan took his light hunting spear from one of the Mu'izziyya and leaned in close. 'Tell the others,' he muttered, 'there will be three deaths today.'

As the hunting party rode out of the camp and headed north, the land turned golden in the morning sun. Their horses leapt over narrow streams and sliced a path through the cotton fields, which had been thinned by the recent harvests. The farmers, who were out gathering the last crops of autumn, looked up and watched as they passed.

Kutuz eased himself into the rhythm of his horse, gripping the flanks of the mare with his knees and feeling the breeze dry the sweat on his skin. They had been away for four months, but it felt much longer. When they had left Egypt, the Nile floods were just beginning: the river rising up to engulf the Delta and swelling the streams and canals. The waters had since receded leaving a land that was flat and green in every direction. He had returned home triumphant and by tomorrow night all Cairo would ring with his name.

The party approached the glittering waters of Lake Manzala, passing reedy lagoons and gnarled copses of trees, sending storks and wildfowl flying up as they crashed through the undergrowth. Down on the shores where the grass was short and spongy, buffalo were grazing. Two of the men shouted as they spotted the first hares vaulting over the grass towards the waters, agile bodies rising and falling, brown against the green. Kutuz took up the cry and the men gave chase, thin spears raised. Three of the governors cantered ahead, to round up the hares and soon the air was filled with whoops and cries as one by one the animals were killed. Kutuz let fly his spear, the tip piercing the last of the hares which flopped to the ground and lay still.

Baybars wheeled his horse around beside Omar and Kalawun as the sultan dismounted and the Mu'izziyya spread out to gather their catch. Baybars slid from his horse. 'Are you ready?' he asked them, his gaze on Kutuz.

'Yes, Amir,' replied Omar, jumping down and closing his hand around the hilt of his sabre.

Kalawun nodded.

Aqtai wandered idly to the platters of food that had been laid out on the board. The tent was hot and stuffy and he fanned himself with his hand as he picked up a piece of meat and popped it into his mouth, sucking the grease from his fingers. His white silk robe clung in limp folds to his fleshy body, and there were two damp circles under his arms. He sighed and closed his eyes as a welcome breeze filtered in behind him, then cried out as he felt something sharp dig into his back. His cry was muffled by a hand that clamped tightly over his mouth.

Aqtai blinked in terror as he heard a voice hiss in his ear. '*Be silent!*' The point in his back dug deeper and he nodded frantically. As the hand was removed, slowly, from his mouth he turned to see Khadir grinning at him. The soothsayer was pointing a gold-handled dagger at him.

'What are you doing?' Aqtai motioned to the tent opening with a shaking finger and tried to puff himself up. 'Get out!' He was dismayed to hear the words come out as more of a squeak than a command.

Khadir twisted the dagger between his fingers, the ruby embedded in the hilt capturing the light in its crimson depths. 'My master sent me.' His voice dropped to a whisper. 'He has a message.'

'What message?'

Khadir darted towards him and brought the blade to a stop inches from Aqtai's stomach. Aqtai stepped back and knocked into the board behind him, upsetting a jar of wine. 'Please,' he begged, 'don't kill me!'

'When my master returns from the hunt, he asks that you meet him in the royal pavilion.'

'What does Amir Baybars want with me?' stammered Aqtai, his eyes locked on the dagger.

'Amir Baybars has gone.' Khadir giggled. 'It isn't him you will be meeting.' He traced the dagger lightly up Aqtai's stomach, the tip nicking the fine silk threads. He stopped it at Aqtai's chest. 'You will meet *Sultan* Baybars.'

'What do you—?' Aqtai stopped, his eyes widening.

'You will greet him at the royal pavilion and bid him sit upon the throne as Sultan of Egypt and ruler of the Mamluk army.'

'*No!*' Aqtai's voice rose. 'I'd see Baybars hang first!' He bolted to the left, the dagger tip scratching a red line through his skin, and made a dive for the entrance.

Khadir was before him in an instant, shoving him to the ground with a strength that startled him. Khadir stood over the sultan's chief of staff and drew back his soiled robe, revealing the dead body of the hare he had caught that morning which was tied by the ears from his waist with a cord.

Khadir yanked the animal from the cord and held it up over Aqtai, who was sprawled on the rug, panting. 'I give a name to this creature. The name of Aqtai.' Khadir lifted the dagger and sliced opened the hare's mouth. 'Aqtai shall speak only what we tell him to speak.' He hacked off one of the hare's ears. 'Aqtai shall tolerate no ill word spoken of Baybars.' He plucked out one of the creature's eyes and dropped down, straddling Aqtai's stomach. 'And Aqtai shall see only the power of the new sultan.' He laid the hare across Aqtai's heaving chest. 'And if Aqtai fails in this . . .' Khadir took the dagger and made a long cut through the hare's stomach. Blood and purple-blue entrails spilled out over his hands, soaking Aqtai's robe. 'He will die.'

Baybars moved across the grass which was littered with hares. The party had dispersed to collect their fallen spears and Omar and Kalawun had fanned out behind the sultan. Baybars headed for Kutuz who was picking up a hare he had killed.

Kutuz lifted the animal up by the ears. 'We'll feast well tonight!' he said, motioning to their catch. He looked round as Baybars approached. 'A good hunt, wasn't it, Amir?'

'Yes,' replied Baybars, 'a good hunt.'

Kutuz looked past Baybars to the two Mu'izziyya who were behind the commander. He nodded to them. Baybars, all his attention on Kutuz, didn't notice the guards drawing their sabres at his back. But Omar did.

'My Lord Sultan!' Omar called, drawing his own blade.

Kutuz turned to him, looking away from Baybars. His smile faded as he saw the sword in Omar's hands.

Omar lifted the blade and glanced at the men. 'Let us pay homage to our lord!' he cried, dropping to his knees before Kutuz.

The governors looked at one another, then followed Omar's example so as not to appear discourteous, as did Kalawun. The Mu'izziyya and Baybars, who was frowning at Omar, remained standing. But after a moment, they too drew their swords in a gesture of fealty and knelt on the grass. Omar's eyes flicked to Baybars who was on the ground, behind the sultan. He smiled faintly.

Kutuz looked down on them all, surprised.

'My lord,' said Omar softly. 'May I swear my loyalty to you?'

Kutuz laughed and offered his hand. 'You may.'

Omar took hold of his hand, firmly, and kissed it.

Kutuz heard a shout, then felt a fierce pain in his back. He staggered to his knees and, looking down, saw a sword tip protruding from his stomach. The sword was withdrawn and blood gushed hotly down his thighs as a terrible pain engulfed him. Around him he heard the ring of steel on steel and, dimly, through the haze of his vision, he saw Omar rise and rush forward, with Kalawun, to attack his guards. He tried to stand but his body wouldn't obey his command and merely sagged forwards uselessly. He coughed weakly and placed his palm on the damp grass, beside one of the hares. He saw a pair of boots walk into his line of sight and he lifted his head, which felt as if it were made of stone. Baybars was standing above him. The sabre in his hand was streaked with blood. Baybars kicked his arm from under him and Kutuz toppled sideways and rolled onto his back. He felt the wet chill of the earth seeping into him and heard a voice that sounded as if it came from far away.

'I am no longer your slave.'

Baybars walked away. Four of the Mu'izziyya were dead, the other two had surrendered. He moved over to Kalawun who was pointing his blade towards the two governors who still held their swords in their hands. 'Drop your weapons,' Baybars barked at them.

One of the governors protested. 'You cannot do this!'

'I just did.'

The two men, powerless, let fall their swords. Kalawun picked up the weapons and nodded to the governor who had informed him of Kutuz's plans.

Baybars headed down to the edge of the lake. Dropping his sabre to the sand, he waded into the shallows to wash the blood from his hands. He rose, shielding his eyes against the sun's glare, and looked out across the waters as a flock of flamingos soared over the lake in a pink cloud. Baybars laughed. This was his. The lake, the plain, the birds; they all belonged to him. He dredged his hand through the clear water. It was his. For the first time in years, perhaps ever, there was nothing that bound him: not the bonds of slavery, not the strings of fealty. He thought himself free.

The depleted party rode into the camp, Omar and Kalawun at the head beside Baybars. They had brought back the sultan's white mare and the horses of the dead guards, but despite the protests of the surviving guards and one of the governors, Baybars had left Kutuz's body, unburied, on the grass beside the lake. The soldiers in the camp stopped what they were doing as the party passed them, their gazes on the riderless mounts. Baybars pulled his horse to a stop before the royal pavilion and jumped down as several governors came hurrying towards him. Ignoring their calls, he strode into the opened pavilion. Aqtai was standing on the platform beside the throne, pale faced and shaking. Khadir was at his side. Baybars nodded to the soothsayer and stepped up onto the platform to face the men who were crowding around the pavilion. More joined them as soldiers came running, roused by the calls of their comrades.

Baybars' deep voice echoed across the camp. 'Sultan Kutuz is dead!'

Aqtai stepped forward at a look from Khadir. 'Amir Baybars,' he called, his voice quivering. 'The throne is yours.'

The murmurs of the crowd, which had begun with the announcement, now rose to a chorus of shocked cries and exultant cheers. Baybars sat on the throne, his hands on the two golden lions at its arms.

Aqtai fell to his knees before him. 'To you I pledge my allegiance, Baybars Bundukdari, Sultan of Egypt!'

The soldiers and officers of the Bahri were the first to copy Aqtai's example, followed by the other regiments and the men of the free-companies. The white-cloaked warriors of the Mu'izziyya stared at one another, stunned, as they realised that they had also been replaced: the Bahri would once again be the Royal Guard. But, one by one, they too bowed down before their new leader.

Kalawun and Omar rose and moved to stand either side of the throne and Kalawun raised his sword. 'Hail to Baybars al-Malik al-Zahir!'

The Mamluk army stood as one to take up his call and Baybars' name was lifted to the sky.

'Hail to Baybars al-Malik al-Zahir!' Hail to Baybars, Victorious King.

Baybars rose from the throne and walked to the edge of the platform. He lifted his hands for silence. 'Kutuz planned to stand here before you tonight to make a speech celebrating our great victory against the Mongols.' A few cheers continued. 'But I'll not speak of our triumphs. I shall speak of our failures.' The cheers died away. 'For we have failed.' Baybars' voice echoed in their silence. 'Too long have we languished under the dominion of rulers without the will to lead us on the path to victory. Too long have we idled in the safety of our strongholds, whilst in Palestine our people live with no choice other than to fight and die. Too long have we allowed the West to creep like a shadow across our lands. For almost two hundred years it has sent its soldiers with their crosses and swords, to defile and destroy us. Will we be slaves to their presence forever?'

'No!' came the scattered cries.

'Will we stand by and do nothing?'

The refusals grew louder, as more men added their voices.

'I'll not stand by!' roared Baybars. He drew his sabre as the voices were drowned by thunderous applause. 'The time of waiting and watching has passed.' His words cracked across them. 'Will you stand with me against the Franks?'

The Mamluk army answered him as one.

Baybars thrust his sabre to the sky. 'I invoke the Jihad!'

14
The Temple, Paris
26 October 1260 AD

A light rain was falling, beading on the bowed heads of the men and clinging to the sail that hung limp from the mast with no wind to fill it. Everything was silent; the oars made no sound as they lifted and fell and no one spoke. The city that rose beyond the bend in the river was veiled by a watery haze; a dark smudge growing larger with every turn of the oars. Up ahead, the river broke in two, sweeping round to either side of an island which housed several grand and imposing structures, the tallest and most magnificent a gleaming white cathedral on the far side. *Opinicus* took the left-hand branch of the river, slicing the water between the island and the bank, gliding past a fortress with gardens that stretched down to the water's edge where the ghosts of trees loomed out of the white air. The fortress fell away to reveal churches, monasteries, stately mansions, then flimsy wooden houses, a marketplace and tightly packed rows of workshops and inns, crisscrossed by narrow streets.

Will watched the people moving on the banks, entering inns, exiting churches, like so many ants in the shadow of their hill. They were all dressed in black. The rain was heavier now, falling soundlessly on the rooftops and spires, falling on the bodies of the nine dead men laid out on the deck, shrouded in their mantles; white for the knights, black for the sergeants and crew. The deluge washed the blood from the corpses, forming red pools that stained the boards. Elwen was kneeling beside Owein, her knuckles pressed to her eyes. Will watched the blood from the deck seep into her gown, soaking the thin material.

'Come away,' he said, his voice muffled.

The crimson stain spread up to her stomach, chest, neck.

'Elwen!' he called, urgently now. 'The blood . . .'

Then she was before him, brushing his cheek with her finger, her green eyes laughing.

'Will Campbell,' she admonished him mockingly, 'your master isn't dead.'

Will turned to Owein's body and saw that she was right.

'To be a Templar you must be willing to make many sacrifices,' said Owein, crossing the deck towards him.

Will's eyes locked on the dagger protruding from his chest.

'You killed me, sergeant.'

'No.'

You killed me.

Will realised that Owein hadn't spoken.

'I didn't kill you,' Will shouted, desperate for Owein to hear him.

But the knight was gone.

Will stood on the banks of a black loch. Someone was screaming. The sound prickled his senses. Nearby, a young girl with honey-blonde hair was dancing, her scarlet skirts flying. She spun towards him, closer and closer, and as she twirled, her skirts became a red mist around her. The girl passed him and when she had gone Will saw a man standing before him. The man's brown eyes stared out from a white nothingness where his face should have been. He slowly raised his hand, reaching for a flap of white skin that Will saw was hanging loose from his temple. He took hold of the flap and pulled. The whiteness ripped away with a sound like parchment being torn. As the mask fell, Will cried out.

'*You killed her!*' said his father, reaching out and grasping his shoulder.

'Is he going to do this every night?'

The voice had come from the adjacent pallet.

The sergeant crouching beside Will turned. 'Quiet, Hugues.' He looked back at Will. 'Your cries woke us.'

Will pushed back his hair which was hanging in his eyes. His blanket was tangled around his shins and his undershirt and hose were sweat-drenched, clinging coldly to his skin. He brushed the sergeant's hand from his shoulder. 'I'm fine.'

The sergeant, who had introduced himself yesterday as Robert de Paris, shrugged and headed across the chamber to his bed.

Will tugged off the blanket and rested his feet on the freezing stones. A loud, erratic snore issued from one of the beds as he rose. The sergeant called Hugues huffed and turned over, yanking his blanket up around his ears. Will moved to the table, on which was placed a ewer of water, a basin and the night candle. The candle had burned low, the molten tallow pooling and hardening around the base. Creamy-yellow drips hung suspended like icicles from the holder. Will cupped his hands in the ewer and lifted them to his face, the water shocking his skin. He went to the chamber's single round window and sat on the ledge, resting against the curve of the stone. The wind was icy. He looked round as another snore sounded and Hugues sighed in annoyance. Will was an outsider here, disturbing their routine, their familiarity. He had told them fragments of the battle at Honfleur, but he hadn't spoken of what it had been like afterwards; chaos on the dockside and days on the boat that had passed in silence.

After the battle, the men who had chased the six fleeing attackers had returned to the docks having killed two, but losing the others. The knights wanted to stay to hunt them down and find out who sent them. But the captain of *Opinicus* had wanted only to leave the port immediately.

'They were mercenaries!' one of the knights, a middle-aged man called John, had shouted. 'We must discover who sent them!'

The attackers had been searched, but their corpses revealed no clue as to who they were, or how they had known about the shipment. The remaining crewmen hauled the bodies on the deck down to the dockside. Two of the skull masks floated in the river, twin white faces bobbing on the surface.

'Three of my crew are dead,' answered the captain, bitterly. '*Opinicus* leaves before there are no hands left to sail her.'

'They won't make another attempt. For the sake of Christ, we killed most of their company! Let's finish it.'

'You don't know that,' insisted the captain, 'there may be more of them.'

'We have to find those responsible,' said John in a low tone.

One of the sergeants drew his sword. 'I think we should ask *him* who's responsible.' He pointed the blade at Hasan, who was on the boat watching the exchange in silence.

Some of the knights and the captain turned to look at Hasan, whose gaze didn't leave the sergeant. 'You have reason to accuse me?' he questioned calmly.

'You are a Saracen,' spat the sergeant. 'What other reason do I need? No one knows why you are here. No one knows you.'

'Sir Jacques knew me. Is the word of a knight not enough for you?'

'Sir Jacques is dead!'

'Enough,' said John, stepping forward and placing a hand on the sergeant's shoulder.

The shouting had gone on for some time, until the captain of *Opinicus* had won his way and a sergeant was sent to the preceptory to wake the queen. The queen had arrived on the dockside with her entourage, the priest and several brothers from the preceptory.

The portly priest wrung his hands, staring about in disbelief as if expecting to awaken at any moment. 'Lord have mercy!' he kept saying. 'Lord have mercy!'

The queen surveyed the carnage with her hands pressed to her cheeks. The crowds, who had come down from the market square during the commotion, were still lingering around the harbour. They gazed at the queen as she passed, whispering to one another.

'The jewels?' Eleanor asked in a papery voice, her eyes on the bodies that littered the deck and the dock wall.

'Are safe, my lady,' said John.

The jewels had been collected from where they had been scattered about the broken chest, and placed in an unadorned box which had been stowed in the cabin.

As the queen and her entourage boarded *Opinicus*, two knights headed over to Owein's body, which had been left on the dockside. So far, no one had seemed willing to disturb Elwen, who had draped herself across her uncle's corpse. Will had tried to move her, but to no avail.

The knights weren't so gentle.

'She is Sir Owein's niece?' one of them asked, striding over to Will. Will nodded.

'What in God's name is she doing here?'

Will saw no point in lying. He told the knight that she had stowed away on board *Endurance*.

The knight cursed and shook his head in disgust. Bending down he grabbed Elwen by her arms. 'On your feet, girl!'

Will stepped forward as Elwen screamed.

'Stand down, sergeant!' the second knight barked, helping his comrade to pull Elwen away. 'Owein is dead. Her weeping won't bring him back.'

Between them the knights half dragged, half carried Elwen onto the *Opinicus*, where they left her slumped on one of the benches. Their brutality shocked away her tears and she sat in an exhausted silence, staring blankly as Owein's body was laid out on the deck and covered with his white mantle.

Three of the knights, along with the priest and the brothers from the preceptory, left to scour the port for any sign of the four surviving attackers. They soon returned. The knights ordered the men from the

Honfleur preceptory to continue the search at daybreak. But no one held out much hope. The priest and his brothers were also given the task of burying the mercenaries.

'Don't put them in consecrated ground,' John had added.

'Brother,' said the priest, shocked, 'surely we cannot consign their souls to Satan without trial or fair judgement?'

'They'll receive judgement in hell.'

Will had climbed on board behind the knights, carrying Owein's sword, which he placed next to his master. It was then that he had seen Garin kneeling beside Jacques' body. Garin had drawn back the mantle from the knight's head and was staring at his face which was frozen in the grimace he had worn at the moment of death. Garin's cheeks were wet and his hands were balled into fists on his knees. He reached out to his uncle's face, then stopped, his hand hovering in the air over Jacques' eye patch. As Will put a hand on his shoulder, Garin started and twisted round, his face contorted with grief. *'Don't touch me!'*

Will stepped back, startled by the vehemence in his voice. Leaving Garin to stare at Jacques' body, he crossed the deck to a bench, where he sat, head in hands.

The chaos following the battle had been hard. But worse had been the silence that descended as *Opinicus* sailed down the Seine: a silence that had closed around the company like a fist. The queen's guards and pages sat on the benches with the knights and sergeants. There was just enough room for the queen and her handmaidens in the cabin, cramped as it was with her belongings. Of them all, only Elwen seemed capable of expressing her sorrow. Her sobs had begun again in the night and continued through till dawn. Even Will, who shared her grief over Owein's death, had wished she would be quiet. Eventually, one of the sergeants had shouted at her, his voice terribly loud in the stillness. The cabin door had banged open a moment later to reveal Queen Eleanor, her pale face framed in the doorway.

'Have you no heart?' she had said to the sergeant, who had stared at her open-mouthed.

The queen had gone to Elwen and helped her to her feet with soft-spoken words of encouragement that reminded Will of the way Simon always soothed the horses in New Temple's stables in a storm. She led Elwen into the cabin, where they remained for most of the journey, which had passed, for Will, in a haze. There had been nothing to do but wait and watch the slow-changing landscape and the flies that buzzed around the bodies on the deck.

When *Opinicus* arrived in Paris, late in the evening, one of the crew went ahead to the preceptory to have carts sent down to the docks for the crates of salt and ale, and the dead. The queen ordered two of her guards to the palace, where her sister, Queen Marguerite, was expecting her. When a wagon and a carriage pulled by four black horses arrived, Elwen was ushered inside with the handmaidens as the queen's belongings, everything except the crown jewels, were loaded onto the wagon.

'I will take her to the palace,' the queen said to the knights, stepping into the cushioned interior. 'Your preceptory is no place for a woman. Certainly not one who is grieving,' she said with a glance at the sergeant who had shouted at Elwen.

As the carriage pulled off, the knights and sergeants had trudged through the winding streets of the Ville, past rows of workshops, the preceptory of the Hospitallers, then on up the Rue du Temple to the preceptory which lay outside the city walls in a pleasant expanse of fields. Will had taken in little of his surroundings. When they reached the preceptory, he had been shown to a dormitory where he had spent most of the following day.

Today was his second day in Paris, the day of Owein's funeral.

When the Matins bell chimed, Will remained sitting on the window ledge as the other sergeants rose from their pallets with a chorus of yawns and muttered conversation. Their accents were strange to Will, but as they spoke Latin he understood them. In the preceptories, with so many knights from different countries living together, Latin had become the communal language.

The sergeants threw their black tunics over their hose and undershirts and took turns at the ewer and basin, splashing their faces. Outside, it was still fully dark. Three of the sergeants had already gone by the time Robert came to the table to cup his hands in the icy water. He patted his face dry with the hem of his tunic, swept back his fine blond hair, and nodded to Will.

'Are you coming to chapel?' he asked, heading to the armoire in the corner of the room and opening the cabinet's double doors.

Will shook his head.

'Let him stay, Robert, if that's what he wants.'

Will looked at Hugues, who was straightening his tunic.

Hugues gave him a pointed look. 'Perhaps you should sleep whilst we are gone. Then we won't have to share your dreams.'

Robert rolled his eyes. He had taken a twig from one of the armoire's shelves and was scraping at his teeth, which were unusually white. 'Don't mind him,' he said to Will, removing the twig from his mouth. 'Hugues just needs his sleep.'

Hugues glared at Robert. 'Don't speak about me as if I weren't here! You always do that!'

Will, watching them, felt the twinge of a smile. The two youths, who were both a year older than he was, couldn't have been more different. Robert was tall and slender, with almost feminine good looks in the delicate angles of his high cheekbones and arched brows. Hugues was short and chubby, with close-set, dark eyes that peered out from beneath a mop of lank black hair to either side of a blunt, turned-up nose.

Hugues turned his back on them both and went to the armoire. He took out a black cloak which he tugged over his shoulders.

'Pay no attention to him,' said Robert quietly to Will. 'He's just wary of anyone he doesn't know.' When Will didn't say anything Robert added. 'Because of his name.'

'His name?' asked Will flatly.

'Hugues de Pairaud. Humbert, the Master of England, is his uncle. The Pairaud family has served the Temple for years and Hugues fears that some sergeants, those of less noble birth, may seek friendship with him for their own advancement.'

'What are you talking about?' demanded Hugues, smoothing his cloak as he crossed the room.

Robert turned. 'I was just telling Will that you are going to be Grand Master some day.'

'That's right,' replied Hugues haughtily. 'Or at least Visitor of the Kingdom of France. It is what I've been groo—'

'If you say groomed again I'll flog you,' Robert cut across him. He tossed the twig onto his pallet and steered Hugues towards the door. 'Come on, Hugues. God gave you a soul, let's see if He can give you a little heart to go with it.' He winked at Will as he left the chamber.

Some time later, the Matins bell ceased its chimes, signalling that the office had begun. Will didn't leave the window ledge. Every day for the last four years, first with his father, then at New Temple, he had risen before dawn for the first office. He wouldn't kneel today. Instead, he watched the sky gradually lighten and listened to the birdsong begin.

The sergeants' quarters were set around a quadrant near the stables. Over the stable roof, he could see fields stretching off, ringed by gnarled oaks and silver birch. Wicker domes were scattered about one of the fields for the bees that provided the preceptory with honey. A stream cut through

the grass to a watermill. Beyond the mill, fishponds reflected the pale dawn
sky and the blurred shapes of outbuildings and barns that Robert had told
him housed the servants' rooms, armoury, wardrobe, bakehouse and
granary. There was even a potter's kiln. If Will leaned out of the window
far enough he could see the tall towers of the donjon. The Paris Temple, the
West's principal preceptory, was much larger and grander than New
Temple, which now seemed, to Will, rather humble by comparison.

When the aching in his back and legs became unbearable, Will slipped
down from the ledge. He stared at the sack he'd placed at the foot of his pallet.
Crouching down, he pulled out his sword and the tunic and hose he'd been
wearing during the fight. The bloodstains had dried into the weave. Will
dipped the clothes in the basin and began to scrub. The water soon turned a
reddish brown. He scrubbed harder. Water sloshed over the basin's rim,
pooling on the table and trickling to the floor. The rancid smell of the blood
permeated the chamber, making Will's stomach churn. He saw the eyes of the
mercenary widen behind the skull mask as the blade in his hand swung in. He
felt again that sickening impact. It shocked him to know how easy it was to kill
another man, to know how frail flesh was. He was glad, at least, that he had
not seen the man's face. He could have; the bodies of the mercenaries,
removed of their disguises, had been piled up on the dockside at Honfleur. He
could have found out which one had been his kill, but he had kept well away. A
man in a mask was inhuman; without family, history, future.

A boy's voice called out in the passage outside the chamber. Footsteps
echoed, then faded away. Will laid the clothes on the window ledge,
wondering if anyone would notice that he wasn't attending chapel, that he
hadn't even left the dormitory. But the only person he really knew here was
Garin and they hadn't met since they had arrived and were shown to
separate quarters.

He set about cleaning the falchion. The blade was no longer a child's toy
to play at soldiers with, or a gift from a loving father. It was an instrument
of death. As he wiped the length of it, the dry blood peeling and flaking
away from the edge, Will tried to imagine his father sitting beside him,
telling him that he had done the right thing; that it was necessary and what
he had been trained to do; that it was his duty. But all Will could hear was
his father, in a flat monotone that betrayed him, saying that it wasn't his
fault and that it was an accident and that he didn't blame his son.

The bell tolled as the knights and sergeants followed the priest, who had led
the Requiem Mass, out of the chapel. Will walked behind Owein's coffin,

which was held aloft by four of the knights from New Temple. The two other knights who had survived the battle, the crew of *Opinicus*, Garin, and a host of knights, priests and sergeants Will didn't recognise carried or walked behind the eight other coffins. Robert and Hugues were both there, but of Elwen, there was no sign. Will resented so many people who did not know Owein being here for his burial. He felt protective of his master and of his own importance as Owein's sergeant.

The priest led the procession into the chapel grounds, which were set within a walled enclosure. Beside him strode the Visitor of the Kingdom of France, Commander of the Western strongholds, the post of which was second only to that of Grand Master. The Visitor was a regal-looking man with a beard shaped like a trident. On the far side of the cemetery, nine graves had been dug in a row. The men formed a circle around the graves as the coffins were lowered into the earth. Will averted his gaze as Owein's coffin disappeared, jerking down on the ropes, inch by torturous inch.

The priest began to chant. '*Requiem aeternam dona eis, domine, et lux perpetua luceat eis.*' Eternal rest give them, O Lord, and let everlasting light shine upon them.

After his prayers, the priest reached down to the earth, picked up a handful of soil and tossed it onto Owein's coffin. He passed to each grave in turn and did the same.

'Dust thou art, and unto dust thou shalt return.'

The Visitor stepped forward and drew his sword. Holding the hilt clasped in both hands he lifted the blade. 'What we sacrifice below shall be rewarded above. As our brothers pass into the Kingdom, may they find peace in the arms of God.' He sheathed the sword and moved back to stand beside the priest as the gravediggers hefted their shovels. The thuds of the clods of earth hitting the coffins had the blunt tone of finality.

Will remained by the graves as the company began to file out of the chapel grounds. Garin left through the arch in the wall. Garin hadn't said a word to him, hadn't even looked at him throughout the ceremony. Will, too exhausted to go after his friend, knelt down, the damp grass soaking his hose. Back at Honfleur he had wanted to tell Garin about the letter he had found in the solar, but it didn't matter now. His concerns over Jacques' allegiances had paled into petty insignificance in the face of what had happened over the past few days. Will saw the Visitor move over to the knights from New Temple.

'We'll leave for London the day after tomorrow, sir,' said John, the knight who had taken command after the battle. 'With the jewels safe in

your vaults and our brothers laid to rest there is little need for us to stay.
The Master of England will need to be informed of what has happened. An
investigation into this matter must be conducted as soon as possible.' He
lowered his voice. 'Although I fear it may prove difficult. No one outside of
the Temple knew the details of our voyage, but King Henry made it plain
that he was giving up the jewels unwillingly. It isn't inconceivable that he
could had attempted to retake them.'

'I will have a boat readied,' replied the Visitor. 'Inform Master de
Pairaud that whatever he requires for the investigation, be it force of arms
or financial aid, is at his disposal. He has full authority in this matter. I'll
send word to Grand Master Bérard in Acre.'

'Yes, sir.'

As the last grave was filled, masons brought slabs of granite to cover the
mounds. Tomorrow, so as not to disturb the passing of the men's souls to
Heaven, the masons would chisel the outlines of the knights' swords onto
the tombstones.

Will looked up as someone touched his shoulder and saw Robert.

'Do you want me to stay?'

'No,' said Will, looking away and wiping his eyes roughly with his
sleeve.

'I have duties in the armoury. I'll be there for the rest of the day, if you
need the company.'

Robert walked away, but Will was still not alone; a priest stood to his
left. The face was partially hidden by the halo of a cowl, but Will could see
that the man was old, older than anyone he had ever met. Strands of hair,
white and fragile as cobwebs, floated about the priest's neck and his beard
was patchy around his chin where an ugly scar twisted his mouth in a
permanent scowl. He was hunched and still like a gnarled black tree,
showing no sign that he had even noticed Will.

Will briefly touched the turned soil around Owein's grave and rose. The
priest's silent proximity made him uncomfortable. 'Wait,' he said, jogging
after Robert. 'I'll join you.'

Robert nodded, but said nothing as Will fell into step beside him. As
they walked down the path, Will looked back at the priest. 'Who is that?'

Robert looked round. 'Father Everard de Troyes.' He gave a half-smile.
'But don't be fooled by his apparent dotage. I'd sooner cross the Devil.'

'What do you mean?'

'Did you see his hand? The one with two fingers missing?'

Will hadn't, but he nodded anyway.

'He lost them in Jerusalem when the Khorezmians retook the Holy City sixteen years ago. He fought off and killed ten warriors single-handed. He was in the Church of the Holy Sepulchre when the attack came and had to hide under the corpses of the dead priests for three days to avoid capture.' Robert's tone was grave, but Will had the impression that he enjoyed telling this story. 'Can you imagine it? Three days in that heat with the flies and the stench? They say he was the only Christian to survive the massacre.'

Just before the two of them entered the arch that lead out of the chapel grounds, Will glanced round to see the old man still standing motionless beside the graves. He thought a strong gust of wind might topple the frail-looking priest who had fought off ten warriors.

The Temple, Paris, 27 October 1260 AD

The next day, his last in Paris, Will returned to Owein's grave after Nones, unsure of where else to go. He was glad to be returning tomorrow to the familiarity of New Temple – and dreading it. As he rounded the corner of the chapel where a moss-clad gargoyle leaned out from a buttress, its toothy, lunatic smile directed at the sky, Will saw Elwen kneeling by Owein's grave, a bunch of lilies clasped in her hands. Her gown was plain and black, edged with white along the hem and her hair was tucked beneath a cap. As he approached she glanced up briefly, then looked back at the grave.

'Do you think he would mind that I wasn't here for his burial?'

'No,' said Will quietly, kneeling beside her.

'No one came to the palace to inform me of the funeral. I am his blood, I should have been there.' Elwen placed the lilies on the tombstone. 'I asked Queen Eleanor if I could come this morning. One of her guards escorted me.' She reached out to straighten one of the lilies. 'What was it like? The ceremony?'

Will shrugged listlessly. 'Like all funerals.'

'I keep wondering if he would have died if I hadn't been there. He might have been more careful. He might have seen that dagger sooner, or . . .'

'You cannot think that,' said Will, watching her run a finger over the tombstone where flecks of quartz glimmered in the granite. Her finger came back white with dust from the chiselled outline of Owein's sword. 'What will you do when you return?'

'I'm not going back to London,' said Elwen, folding her hands in her lap. 'I'm staying here.'

'In the preceptory?' Will was surprised.

'In the palace. When I told Queen Eleanor that I couldn't return to my mother, that I didn't have anywhere to go, she said she didn't want to see any more grief come from this tragedy. She spoke with her sister, Queen Marguerite, who agreed to take me into her employ. I am called a handmaiden.' Elwen turned to Will. 'You should see the palace. It's so big I cannot leave my room without a servant, or I'll get lost. There are gardens on the riverbank, beautiful lawns, hundreds of trees. It feels like home, a proper home filled with people and laughter.' She looked at Owein's grave. 'And I'll be close to him.'

'Owein would have been pleased for you,' said Will dully, feeling the weight of his own purposelessness. He had no master; he had no place. He tried to keep the jealousy from his tone. 'That's a high position.' Will heard footsteps and looked round to see Garin heading towards the graves.

Garin halted on seeing Will and Elwen.

Elwen rose. 'You're Garin de Lyons, aren't you?'

'Yes.' Garin spoke stiffly.

Elwen crossed to him. 'Thank you,' she said earnestly. 'You saved my life. I heard you, too, lost family in the battle,' she added softly. 'An uncle?'

'Yes.' Garin walked away.

'Garin!' Will passed Elwen, who was biting her lip and staring after Garin. He caught up with his friend. 'What's wrong?'

'Nothing.' Garin's eyes flicked briefly to Will. 'I wanted some peace.'

'We can go.' Will glanced at Elwen, who nodded.

'I'll go.' Garin continued walking.

Will moved to block his path. 'Garin, please, you haven't spoken to me since the battle. What is going on?'

Garin's face tightened. 'I don't want to talk to you.'

'Why?'

Garin pushed past him and ran around the graves. 'Just leave me alone.'

Will caught him by Owein's grave. He seized his friend's arm harder than he meant to. 'I lost my master too! I know how it feels!'

'You have no idea how I feel!' shouted Garin. As he pulled himself roughly from Will's grasp, something fell from his hand.

Will bent to pick it up. It was Jacques' eye patch. The leather was creased and warm from Garin's fist.

Garin leapt forward and snatched it from him. 'This is all your fault!' he shouted.

'What?' Will stared at his friend.

'All those times you were in trouble!' Garin's voice was high, his face flushed. 'All those times Owein let you off with nothing but a stern word! What did I get?'

'That isn't my—'

'I got every punishment you should have received!'

Elwen was watching them.

'I didn't punish you, Jacques did. He would have done it anyway, even if I hadn't been there.'

'No! If it weren't for you, my uncle wouldn't have needed to punish me and I wouldn't have needed to—!' Garin stopped, his eyes filling with tears. 'He's dead. My uncle is dead. And it's *your fault!*'

'Why are you blaming me?' demanded Will. 'I've done nothing wrong!'

'You never do anything wrong, do you?' hissed Garin, his bruised face ugly with fury. 'Owein was still proud of you when you disobeyed him. And your father? He still enlisted you in the Temple even after you killed your sister!'

Will felt a rush of anger. He lashed out, catching Garin squarely on the jaw. Elwen shouted as Garin stumbled. His heel caught on the edge of Owein's tombstone and he fell back on the slab, flattening the lilies she had placed there. Will moved forward, fists raised, then he saw the blood coming from Garin's lip. He stepped back. 'Garin. I . . . I didn't . . .'

Will trailed off as Garin straightened and took his hand from his mouth. He stared at the blood, then at Will, then lurched away, Jacques' eye patch in his fist.

Will started as he felt a hand on his arm.

'Why did you hit him?' Elwen murmured. 'What did he mean about your sister?'

Will's brow creased as he saw her lilies, crushed and scattered on Owein's tomb. 'I'm sorry.' Shrugging away from her touch, he ran.

15
The Temple, Paris
27 October 1260 AD

W ill sat on his pallet, his breath over-loud in the empty dormitory. Red marks had already appeared on his knuckles. Garin was the only person he had ever told about his sister, even Simon didn't know. He couldn't believe his friend had used it against him. Garin. Will hung his head in shame as he pictured the blood pouring from the boy's lip. With a shaking hand he reached into his sack and pulled out a folded square of parchment. He had begun the letter to his mother just before they had left for Paris. It was still unfinished. Will sat on his pallet and stared at the words written in his small, blunt hand.

Some hours later, after the bells had rung the ending of Vespers, the door opened and Robert entered.

'I was wondering where you had got to. It's almost time for supper.'

Will was sitting on his bed, shreds of parchment strewn over the blanket. He wiped his face as Robert came over.

'What has happened?' said Robert, glancing at the torn skin.

'I don't want to talk about it.'

Robert shrugged and sat at the foot of the pallet. 'Then we won't.'

Will lifted his head. 'Why is he blaming me?'

'Who?'

'Garin. He says it's my fault his uncle died.'

'My mother died when I was young,' said Robert. 'For a time, my father blamed everyone for her death, but it was no one's fault. It was a sickness. There was nothing he, or anyone could have done.'

'Jacques was murdered. There is someone to blame.' Will lay back, blinking at the ceiling. 'Perhaps it was me.'

Robert turned on his side and rested his elbow on the bed, his head in his hand. 'How could it be?'

'Sometimes, I wished Jacques would pay for hurting Garin. Perhaps, by wishing it, I made it happen.' Will ran a finger slowly across his bruised knuckles.

Robert nodded to the marks. 'Does someone have bruises on their face to match those?'

'Garin.'

'Why did you fight?'

'He said something about my sister,' said Will, sitting up, 'something he shouldn't have.'

Robert waited.

'I killed my sister,' said Will suddenly. The words seemed to take tangible presence in the chamber. He waited for Robert to see their dark, twisted shapes, huddled, breathing in the corner.

Finally, Robert spoke. 'How?'

Will was silent.

'How did she die?' Robert pressed gently.

Will closed his eyes. 'My father called her his angel. He used to bring her ribbons from Edinburgh. He would spend hours watching her play.' Will hugged his knees to his chest. 'But Mary wasn't an angel. She was always stealing bread from the kitchen and blaming me, or letting the chickens out, or smashing the eggs, or sulking because someone asked her to do something.

'I remember wishing that she would disappear, not that she would die, but that somehow she would be lost. I didn't mean it.' Will looked at Robert. 'It happened in the summer before I went to New Temple. My father was away at Balantrodoch. I was going to the loch to finish the boat we had been building. We were going to use it to fish. I wanted to surprise him when he came home. Mary followed me. I said I didn't want her to come because I knew she would get in the way, but she kept following. We got to the loch and I started work on the boat. It was hot. Mary got bored and went to collect shells. I wanted to spend the day there, to get it finished, but Mary started saying that she wanted to leave. I told her to go, but she pretended she didn't know the way. There were woods on the other side of the loch. I went to find some branches I could use for oars and Mary came with me. She kept saying that our father would much rather have the shells she had found than some stupid boat I'd made.' Will put his head in his hands. 'We were on some rocks above the water. Mary said . . . I can't even remember, but she said something and threw the shells at me and I got angry.' He paused. 'So I pushed her. I didn't mean to do it so hard. She fell back off the rocks and into the water. She hit her head on the way down. We were higher than I thought. I jumped in and found her, but . . .'

Will shook his head hard. 'I pulled her out and carried her home. It was miles and she was heavy. I kept talking to her, but she wouldn't wake and her head was all cut up. My father was home. He was walking across the yard carrying a pail of water from the stream for his bath. He smiled and started to wave, then he saw Mary. He dropped the pail and ran to take her from me.' Will swallowed thickly, remembering his father's anguished cries as he cradled his dead daughter and his mother dashing barefoot across the yard towards them. 'Later, he took me outside and asked me how it happened and I told him she fell.' Will hung his head. 'But he kept asking questions and I had to tell him the truth. It was as if he already knew. He just nodded, stood up and went back inside. He wouldn't even look at me.

'When we buried Mary, my mother cried. For months. She had another baby, a girl called Ysenda, but she never smiled, or laughed like she used to. My father was away most of the time. He never took me to Balantrodoch like he said he would. He took me to London when he was asked to stand in for a sick clerk.' Will rose and wrapped his arms about his chest. 'He took me to London to get rid of me. He spent lots of time away and in the solar working with Garin's uncle. I hardly saw him. We could have gone home when the clerk got better, or even stayed in New Temple, but he became a knight and went to the Holy Land and left me. I've heard nothing from him for eighteen months.'

Robert stood before Will. 'You only meant to push her, not to kill her. Your father must have known that.'

'Then why does he hate me?' said Will in a choked voice.

The door opened and Hugues came in. 'What is going on?' he asked, coming to stand beside Robert. He clicked the roof of his mouth with his tongue as he saw the torn parchment. 'What a mess.'

Robert gave him a warning look. 'Hugues.'

Hugues frowned at his friend. 'And why are you here with him when you're supposed to be at supper? He's off back to London tomorrow anyway.'

Before Robert could speak, Will pushed past Hugues and strode out of the chamber.

He ran from the sergeants' quarters, his feet pounding the dust. Several groups of knights were heading for the Great Hall, their mantles making them ghostlike in the twilight. Will passed them without slowing, even when one of them shouted at him to halt. He kept running, past the knights' quarters and beneath the long shadow of the donjon, past the officials' buildings and the armoury, not knowing where he was going, but not wanting to stop. Sweat beaded his skin and his legs began to ache as he entered the graveyard and headed down the path to the chapel.

The chapel was lit dimly by candles that were placed around the altar. There was a tendril of smoke curling from a censer where the incense had burned during Vespers. Will shut the doors behind him and moved slowly down the aisle, trailing his hand across the arms of the benches and the curves of the marble pillars. He walked up to the altar, where a small wooden crucifix stood, the eyes of the figure of Christ downcast, heavy-lidded. There were a few crumbs scattered about the surface of the altar, remnants of the host. Will's hollow stomach growled, reminding him that he hadn't eaten since morning. He dabbed up a few of the crumbs, put them to his mouth, then wandered restlessly over to the sacristy, the door of which was ajar. Inside, a single candle was burning on a table in the corner. The room was filled with a cloying smell of incense. Candles and vellum-bound books were stacked on a bench beneath the small chamber's high window. Will paused in the entrance, his eyes drifting over the jars of wine that were placed on shelves behind the table, upon which was an oak pyx and the Communion chalice.

After a moment, he entered, crossed to the shelves and took down a half-empty jar. The wine inside glowed crimson in the candlelight. Will poured a large measure into the Communion chalice. He then opened the lid of the pyx and brought out a fistful of Communion bread. The blood and the body of Christ. Sitting cross-legged on the floor, he raised the chalice to his lips. 'Our Father,' he said, then laughed. After draining the wine, he stuffed the bread into his mouth and looked to the shadows of the vaulted ceiling, waiting for God to punish him, *daring* Him to. Nothing happened. When he had finished his meal, Will leaned against the table leg, his knees hugged to his chest. He felt exhausted. He would stay here until the last office, then hide in the graveyard. When the others went to bed, he could come back and sleep till morning. And tomorrow? Will curled up on the cold stone floor, resting his head on his arm. He would think about tomorrow then.

'Wake up, I said!'

Will came slowly round, feeling something prodding his leg. He opened his eyes and sat up groggily. The wine had made his head heavy and a sour taste was in his mouth. He didn't know how long he had been asleep, but outside the sacristy's high window it was fully dark. The man standing over him was wearing the black mantle of a priest. It was Everard de Troyes, the old man from the graveyard. His cowl was drawn back and Will could see that the scar that began at his lip ran all the way to his forehead, a pink, sore-looking runnel. The priest's skin was stretched thinly across his cheeks, but hung in folds beneath his eyes as if, like a well-worn garment, it no longer fitted him properly. His hands were gnarled and there were two bony stumps on one where his fingers should have been. He studied Will, his pale, red-rimmed eyes intent. Under that stare, Will felt as if his soul were being scoured.

'Who are you?' Everard's voice was little more than a dry wheeze, yet there was a sharpness behind it that was compelling.

Will struggled to his feet. He glanced at the floor beside him, the empty chalice and crumbs of bread, and he hesitated.

'Answer me!' demanded the priest, his voice hissing like wood in a fire.

'My name is William. I came here on *Opinicus*. My master, Sir Owein, was one of those who died in the attack at Honfleur.'

'What are you doing in here?'

'One of the sergeants told me to fetch a fresh candle for our dormitory,' said Will, adopting the innocent expression that had always fooled Owein.

Everard smiled humourlessly and Will felt uneasy.

The priest leaned closer to him and gave the air a keen sniff. 'Have you been drinking, sergeant?'

'No, sir.'

'No?' Everard gave the air another sniff. 'I'm certain I can smell cheap wine.' He looked at the chalice on the floor. 'Perhaps you were sleeping off the effects of the Eucharist? The blood of Christ makes for a potent concoction. Especially,' he murmured in a dangerous tone, looking back at Will, 'if it is taken as an alehouse spread, rather than a holy act performed in deepest reverence!'

Will opened his mouth to say something in his defence, but the priest put a bony hand on his shoulder and turned him towards the door.

'Where are you taking me?' said Will, trying to sound indignant and dismayed to hear the fear in his voice.

'To the Visitor,' growled Everard. 'I cannot authorise an expulsion myself.'

Will tried to think of something to say to make the priest relent, but his head felt muddled and all he could manage were several stammered apologies on the way to the Visitor's solar, all of which fell on deaf ears.

The Visitor's rooms were set in the officials' buildings beneath the tower of the donjon. The area was busy with knights, who had finished the evening meal and were now completing the day's assignments and meetings before the last office. Will forced himself to hold his head high as they entered the building through a wide porch and headed down an echoing passage to a set of black double doors. Everard rapped smartly on them.

'Enter,' came a deep voice.

Everard opened the doors, propelling Will in front of him.

The chamber was spacious and more opulently decorated than any of the knights' quarters at New Temple. Against the far wall was a polished table with four stools set before it and a throne-like seat behind, cushioned and covered with an embroidered dorsar. The large window was partially draped with a heavy cloth and rugs covered the floor. Candles stuttered in iron sconces and a fire smoked thickly in the hearth, crackling and flaring around a large log that gave off an earthy, woods-smell.

The Visitor was sitting in the throne-like seat behind the table with a book open in front of him. 'Brother Everard?' he said, looking from the priest to Will with an expectant frown. 'What is the matter?'

'This miscreant has defiled the Sacrament. I went in to ready the chapel for Compline and caught him sleeping off the effects of the Eucharist.'

The Visitor's frown deepened and Will lowered his head, unable to meet the man's stern, disapproving gaze. 'Well, that is reprehensible indeed.' The Visitor's eyes moved to Everard. 'But it is also something which, I am sure, can be dealt with in the next chapter.'

Will looked up hopefully. Everard's expression, however, remained resolute.

'Usually, I would have waited until then, brother, but this one is from England. He leaves tomorrow and I will not have him come in here and treat our chapel like a tavern without any punishment for the violation.'

The Visitor paused for a moment, then closed his book and laced his hands together on the table in a way that reminded Will, with a painful stab, of Owein.

'What do you have to say for yourself, sergeant?'

Will opened his mouth, but couldn't speak. He cleared his throat and tried again. 'I went into the chapel and fell asleep, sir. I didn't mean to.'

The Visitor's expression didn't change. 'Your sleeping in the chapel is obviously not the issue. What I want to know is why you defiled the Sacrament?'

Will stared at the floor.

The Visitor tapped his thumbs together. 'You are one of the sergeants from New Temple, yes?'

'Yes, sir,' said Will quietly. 'My master, Owein, died at Honfleur.'

'What is your name?'

'William Campbell, sir.'

'Campbell? You're not James Campbell's son, are you?'

'Yes, sir,' said Will, raising his head.

'I met him a few times when he visited the preceptory. He is currently stationed in Acre, I believe, under Grand Master Bérard?' The Visitor shook his head. 'This is very disappointing. I would have expected better from the son of such a highly respected knight.'

'One moment, brother.' It was Everard who had spoken. He had stepped forward. 'Might I have a word in private?'

'Of course,' said the Visitor, looking mildly perplexed. 'Wait outside,' he told Will.

As Will left the room, he noticed that Everard was looking at him interestedly. He found this somehow far more discomforting than the priest's angry glare.

Garin lay back on his pallet, gingerly touching his split lip. The dormitory was dark and silent. The sergeants had finished their evening meal and would now be completing their chores before the last office. The bed was uncomfortable, the straw digging into Garin's back through his thin undershirt. After a moment, he moved to the window. He didn't want to wait till dawn when the boat would be ready; he wanted to leave Paris now. Garin stared down at the men moving through the torchlit courtyard below.

The door opened. A servant in a brown tunic entered the dormitory, holding a pile of blankets under one arm and a flickering candle in the other. The servant kept his head bowed as he shuffled into the chamber. Garin turned back to the window and chewed hard at his thumbnail, which was already bitten to the quick. The servant's footsteps padded on the stones as he lit the candle on the table with the one he had brought. He moved from pallet to pallet, changing the blankets. Garin heard a rustle of straw then the faint clinking of coins. He spun round. The servant was by his pallet, pulling out his sack.

'No!' cried Garin, springing forwards as the servant reached inside the sack and drew out a small velvet pouch. 'Take your hands off—!' He halted, his words sticking in his throat, as the straggly-haired, lantern-jawed servant looked up at him and grinned, showing brown stubs of teeth.

'Take my hands off what?' enquired Rook, holding up the pouch. 'This?' He gave the pouch a shake.

'What are you . . .?' Garin looked over at the door. It was shut. 'How did . . .?'

'Servants,' said Rook, following his gaze, 'are beneath the regard of knights.' He gestured to his brown tunic. 'Not worth a second look I wasn't. A kindly sergeant told me where to find you.' He lifted his tunic, revealing the curved dagger that was in a sheath at his belt. The ill-fitting garment's voluminous folds had concealed the blade. 'You didn't think you would get away with it, did you?'

Garin watched Rook tie the velvet pouch to his belt beside the blade. 'That's mine,' he said faintly.

'Yours?'

Garin took a step back and bumped into the window ledge as Rook drew the dagger and advanced on him.

'This gold was payment for your service, if you remember.' Rook made a circle in the air with the dagger and brought the tip to rest over Garin's heart. 'But you didn't serve us did you, boy? You served yourself.'

'I did what Prince Edward asked of me! I informed him of the plans for the voyage and met your men in the Golden Fleece at Honfleur to tell them *Endurance* had left.' Garin had been terrified when, two days before the voyage, Rook had brought a message from Edward, demanding that he go to the alehouse at Honfleur when the ship docked to give the mercenaries, who would be in hiding there, the signal to attack. Until that moment, Garin had hoped fervently that the prince wouldn't act on the information he had been given; that Edward would just let the matter drop. 'It wasn't my fault your men died!' he cried, feeling the dagger's tip press into him.

'Our men were well prepared for death. What they weren't prepared for was being attacked by a child. A child who, after so loyally informing them *Endurance* had left, killed the one who had the jewels, giving the knights time to block their escape. Incidentally,' he said, pinching Garin's cheek viciously between his thumb and forefinger, 'they described you most accurately, the four that survived. Yellow-haired, blue-eyed, horse-faced scrap of shit, one of them said.'

'Your man was going to kill a girl!' Anger flooded through Garin, drowning his fear. 'He told me no one would get hurt!'

Rook laughed scornfully. '*He told me no one would get hurt!*'

'You killed my uncle!' yelled Garin, shoving Rook hard in the chest. Rook stumbled back. 'I did what you asked! *And you killed him!*'

Rook recovered and slammed him back against the wall. Garin gasped as the dagger was pushed into his chest, piercing his skin. 'And, now,' hissed Rook, 'you'll join him!'

Garin struggled, but Rook jammed an arm across his throat. Garin felt blood trickle down his chest inside his undershirt.

Rook leaned closer, his sour breath hot on Garin's face. 'You warned the knights, you little shit! You told them about my master!'

'No!' Garin began to choke as his air was cut off by Rook's arm. 'You have . . . my word!'

'Your word means as little as your life to me.'

'I didn't tell anyone!' Garin sagged weakly against the wall.

'Stand up straight, you snivelling little wretch! You warned the knights, didn't you?'

'*No!*'

'You lost us the jewels!'

'I . . . I can't *breathe!*' Garin was panicking, clutching wildly at Rook's arm. His vision was clouding. The world was turning grey. 'God, please! *Don't kill me!*'

'Why shouldn't I?'

'I know things . . . secrets! There's a book that was stolen . . . important to the Temple . . . a . . . a group in the Temple . . . and King Richard was involved . . . and . . .'

'What are you gibbering about?' demanded Rook disgustedly. But he loosened his hold a little.

'There's a secret group in the Temple,' breathed Garin, taking great gulps of air. 'They had a book stolen from them, from this preceptory. It could ruin the Temple.' He shook his head. 'I don't know why.'

'Horse shit.' Rook drew back the dagger. 'I know you told the knights.'

Garin met Rook's gaze. 'Do it then!' he gasped. 'Just do it! But I didn't tell the knights. I swear!' He closed his eyes, tensing for the strike, the bright shock of pain. His eyes snapped open as he heard a snorting sound. Rook had stepped back, a crooked grin splitting his face. He was laughing.

'I didn't come here to kill you, boy.' Rook laughter subsided. 'But I needed to know if you had informed on us and terror makes all men honest.' He sheathed the dagger. 'The loss of the jewels has aggrieved my master greatly, but he believes your continued service will, one day, repay the debt you now owe him. Before your blunder at Honfleur, he thought you most useful.'

'No,' said Garin, swiping at his wet cheeks with a shaking hand, 'I cannot do it. I will not leave the Order.'

Rook's eyes narrowed. 'He doesn't want you to leave the Temple. You are of much greater use to him inside than out. Your status, even as a sergeant, gives you power, power you can wield over others.'

'No,' repeated Garin forcefully. 'It was on his orders that my uncle died. I won't serve him again.'

'You will serve him, boy!' growled Rook. 'And what's more be glad to!' His tone softened. 'What awaits you in London now your uncle is dead?'

Garin flinched at Rook's words. 'I . . . I don't know.'

'Oh, I think you do.' Rook smiled sagely. 'Sir Jacques was a powerful man, a man of influence. There's few in his position, few who could offer you the same great future as he could have and you are as much to blame for his death as the one who ordered the attack.'

'The mercenaries killed him! It wasn't my fault!'

'Their swords delivered the blow, but your tongue delivered the information that made it possible.' Rook sighed. 'By your own deed, you've forfeited your greatest opportunity to raise up that once noble name of yours. Wasn't that what you wanted? Didn't my master say he could do that for you?' Rook lifted his tunic and pulled the velvet pouch from his belt. 'Here.' He tossed it at Garin, who caught it. 'My master is a fair man. Keep the gold. Agree to his request and he'll see you right, refuse and I cannot say what will happen. He, too, is a man of influence. He can make your life easy. And he can make it unbearable.'

Garin stared at the pouch for a moment, then threw it back to Rook. 'It was my uncle who wanted to return our household to its rightful place. I did all this for him. Now he is dead. It doesn't matter to me anymore.'

Rook was silent for a time. 'And your mother?' he enquired softly. 'Does it matter to her?'

Garin stiffened. 'You know nothing of my mother.'

Rook looked thoughtfully at the ceiling. 'The Lady Cecilia is tall, a little thin for my tastes, and she has blonde hair.' He looked back at Garin. 'Beautiful, isn't it? She wears it in a cap. But she's a pretty vision when it's hanging all down her back.'

'You've never seen her.'

Rook placed a hand over his heart. 'I saw her only a few days back. My master likes to know who he has in his service.' His expression hardened. 'And that which is precious to them. He sent me to find your home in Rochester the day after you agreed to aid us.'

'You're lying,' whispered Garin.

'Like I said, your mother is a pretty vision, but I didn't think much of her charity when I knocked on her door, a poor beggar seeking alms. She had one of her servants send me away.' He leaned in close to Garin. 'If I have to knock on her door again, she'll find herself obliged to treat me more liberally. In fact, more liberally than any true lady should ever have to.' He grabbed Garin's hand and thrust the pouch of gold into it. 'So, you see, you will serve us.'

Garin, white faced and trembling, looked up at him.

'Won't you?' demanded Rook.

Garin gave a small nod.

'Say it, boy.'

'Yes,' spat Garin.

'That's better. Now, I'll send word to you at New Temple within the month. I believe my master has a few little tasks for you to be getting on with. And you can tell him all about that book you was talking about just now.' Rook chuckled as he headed for the door. 'I think he'll be very interested in that.'

'I will kill you if you hurt her,' murmured Garin, watching him go.

Rook didn't look back.

Garin threw the pouch onto his pallet when the door had closed. He turned away, his eyes falling on the table that held the night candle. With a sweep of his arm, he sent the table flying. The candle was extinguished, plunging the room into darkness.

Will looked round as the black-painted double doors swung open and a knight came out of the Visitor's solar. It was Sir John. Will had been standing in the passage for over an hour. He had seen Everard leave shortly after he had been told to wait outside, then return with the knight a little while later. Sir John gave him a disapproving look, then headed off down the passage. Will, his stomach churning, looked back to see Everard standing in the doorway. The priest motioned him inside. As Will entered, shutting the door, Everard moved to the hearth and stood before it, holding out his gnarled hands to the leaping flames.

'Sit,' ordered the Visitor, motioning Will to the stools before the table.

Will crossed the room, his footsteps muffled as he walked across a rug. He perched on one of the stools, his hands resting on his knees. 'I'm sorry I drank the Communion, sir,' he began, having practised this speech outside. 'I missed supper and I was thirsty. But I really am sorry and . . .' Will trailed off and pressed his lips together at the Visitor's unresponsive stare.

'I am glad you are repentant, sergeant, but I'm afraid that is not enough.

This is a serious offence. Under different circumstances you would be brought before the weekly chapter, stripped of your tunic and expelled.'

'Different circumstances?' said Will hoarsely.

The Visitor sat back and smoothed his beard with his fingers, running them down either side of his mouth. 'You apparently showed courage and initiative at Honfleur. From what I've been told, you are a sergeant of high calibre, a talented young man of great potential. You won the tournament at New Temple, I believe?'

Will nodded.

'I do not wish to deprive the Temple of someone with your capabilities,' said the Visitor. 'And it would appear that God is watching over you.' He glanced at Everard, only briefly, but Will caught the look.

'Sir?'

'Taking these circumstances into account,' said the Visitor, ignoring him, 'your punishment, we have decided, shall be thus. When you come of age in five years, you will not take the vows of knighthood as other sergeants of your status. You will forfeit the mantle for a year and a day after the appointed time of your inception.'

Will gripped the edge of the stool. Six years? Six years to wait until he took the mantle?

'You will also be whipped. If you behave like a dog you'll be treated like one. I'll not tolerate those who are to take the habit of the warriors of Christ behaving in a manner that is more befitting the habit of the heathen. Brother Everard has agreed to deliver the thrashing.' He nodded to Everard. 'You may take him, brother.'

Will thought he saw a flicker of what might have been triumph pass across the priest's wizened face, before Everard bowed to the Visitor and opened the doors. Will walked in a daze as Everard led him back down the passage and out into the courtyard. They walked in silence to the chapel, every step compounding Will's dread. He had never been beaten.

After shutting the doors, Everard motioned Will towards the altar. 'Quick, boy. I do not have all night.'

Will went slowly.

When they reached the dais, Everard pointed to the floor. 'On your knees.'

Will knelt, his eyes catching the figure of Christ that hung from the crucifix on the altar.

'Now,' said Everard, frowning, 'where is it?' He patted his black robe, then moved to the door in the side wall and disappeared into the sacristy.

The silence seemed to ring in Will's ears. When Everard returned he was holding something in his hands. Will stiffened as he saw the whip.

'Pull up your tunic and put your face to the floor.'

Will lifted his tunic and undershirt, feeling the cool air prickling his skin. He bent forward, pressing his forehead to the stone, and planted his palms on the floor. 'Why didn't the visitor expel me, sir?' he questioned, the interruption delaying the moment when the whip would fall, however inevitable. 'He could have.'

'It was agreed that your expulsion would serve no one,' said Everard calmly, 'and this way, you and I both get something we want.'

'What is that?' Will tried to sit up, but Everard put a foot on his back, pressing him down.

'You get to stay as a sergeant in the Temple, and I,' said Everard, removing his foot from Will's back, 'get an apprentice.'

'An apprentice?' Will flinched as he heard the whip crack above him. When no pain followed he realised that Everard had merely snapped it taut in his hands. He drew in a breath. 'What do you mean?'

'I mean,' said Everard slowly, deliberately, 'that you are now a sergeant of the Paris Temple. And *I* your new master.'

The whip cracked again. A searing agony struck Will's spine like lightning, wrenching a cry from his lips. As it swept through him he dug his fingers into the stone, as if in an attempt to ground the pain, and dimly heard another crack. Will forced in a breath and tried to speak, but the next stroke came before he could form any words. This time the pain was different, worse somehow because it was anticipated. The whip cut down, again and again, the pain making him retch. Will closed his eyes, tears burning from them.

When he had finished, Everard folded the whip in his hands and crossed himself before the altar. Will put his cheek to the stone, where his tears and saliva had pooled.

'On your feet.'

Will's back was on fire and his legs felt like water. He stood, stifling a gasp as his tunic brushed against his torn skin. He wanted to curl up and cry, but he wouldn't give the priest the satisfaction: the loss of pride would be somehow worse than the pain.

There were two high spots of colour on the priest's pale cheeks. 'Why do . . .?' Will closed his eyes and gritted his teeth against the throbbing in his back. 'Why do you, a priest, have need of a sergeant?'

'I am a collector and translator of manuscripts in the fields of medicine, mathematics, geometry, astronomy and the like,' said Everard, carelessly tossing the whip onto one of the benches. 'But although seventy years in this accursed world may have brought wisdom to this mind, they haven't been so gracious to this body.' Everard tapped his temple. 'My eyesight is failing me. I have need of a scribe.'

'A scribe,' echoed Will, trying to keep his voice steady.

'I have been petitioning the Visitor for months, but so far he has been unable to spare me a sergeant for the task.' Everard smiled at Will. 'It's fortunate for me that you are here.' His smile widened. 'And that you chose to defile my Sacrament.'

Will stared at the priest in horrified disbelief. 'A scribe?' he repeated.

'Unlike many of your age and rank you can read and write, can you not?'

'I'm training to be a *knight*, not a clerk!'

'Do you believe that a Templar needs only his sword, boy?' Everard shook his head. 'Your former master taught you to use your arm. I shall train you to use your wits.' He peered at Will through narrowed eyes. 'If you possess any.' He turned away. 'Return to your quarters. After Matins tomorrow, come to my chamber. You can begin your duties by cleaning my floor. By the smell of it one of the cats got in again.'

'No.'

'No?'

'I won't do this!'

'Then walk out of those doors.'

Will opened his mouth, then shut it. He stared at the priest. 'What?'

'Walk away, I cannot stop you.'

Will glanced at the doors. 'Is this a jest?'

'No.'

'Very well,' said Will after a moment. He took a step towards the doors. 'I shall.'

'Walk through those doors, boy,' said the priest behind him, 'and keep on walking until you have left this preceptory. You are no longer a sergeant of the Order of the Temple. I release you from your bond.'

'That isn't what . . .'

'If you cannot obey your master, you shouldn't be here.'

Will stood in the aisle between the doors and the altar. He had never had the same desire to be a knight as other sergeants he knew; to fight for Christendom against the infidel and win glory in arms; to better serve God and receive the power and privileges knighthood brought. But Owein had said that when a man puts on the mantle he is reborn, cleansed of all past sins. Will had understood that. It wasn't the mantle that was important – it was the absolution. He needed his father to see him in that cloth; to see he had been reborn; that he was no longer the boy who had killed his sister. 'No,' he whispered. 'I will not walk away.'

'Then, Sergeant Campbell, I will see you at dawn.'

Everard watched the boy trudge from the chapel. After Will had gone, the priest tutted to himself, then began readying the altar for Compline.

A short time later, the chapel doors opened and a tall man in a grey cloak entered.

'Ah, there you are,' said Everard, peering down the aisle. 'I take it you have given your testimony of the battle?'

'Yes, brother,' said Hasan, coming forward. 'I told the Visitor that I was in London to meet a contact of yours, a bookseller.'

'He didn't question you further? Good.' Everard placed the breviary he was holding on the altar and stepped down the dais to Hasan. 'We can ill afford any further difficulties. Jacques' death has dealt us a heavy enough blow as it is. However, we must continue the search for the book as soon as possible. If Rulli had already handed it over by the time you caught him, whoever may have the book now might still be in the city. Did Jacques speak to you of his thoughts whilst you were in New Temple?'

'He worried, as you, that whoever forced Rulli to steal the Book of the Grail wants it to use as proof with which to expose the Anima Templi and its plans.' Hasan went to sit on the bench, then saw the whip that was lying there. He picked it up. 'Someone has been in trouble?'

Everard grunted and took the whip. 'James Campbell's son, would you believe.'

'James's son?'

'William. A sergeant at New Temple. He came here on the boat from London. I've just taken him on as my apprentice as a matter of fact.'

Hasan raised an eyebrow. 'William? Then he is the one I told you about; the one I caught following me at Honfleur. Do you think he knows?'

Everard shook his head after a moment. 'James knew what was at stake. He wouldn't have told him. And the boy certainly showed no sign that he knew who I was. He was probably just being inquisitive. It's not as if you've never had anyone curious, or concerned about you before, Hasan.' Everard shuffled over to the side room. 'At least I'll get some use out of him whilst he's here.'

Hasan watched Everard stow the whip on a shelf. 'I know you have been looking for a servant, brother. But if you do not mind me saying, I am not certain that was what James had in mind when he asked you to take care of his son.'

'What better way is there for me to keep an eye on him?' responded Everard curtly. 'He is without a master. What do you think James would have me do? Send him back to England alone, or keep him here under me?'

Hasan nodded after a pause, knowing not to push. 'Perhaps we should think again about contacting the rest of the Brethren to inform them that the book has been stolen,' he said, as Everard crossed to him.

'Our brothers in the East have their own work to attend to. War is brewing between the Mamluks and our forces. They will need all their attention focused there if we are to succeed in the trials that I fear will soon be upon us.'

'But without their support it will prove a hard task to find it. Perhaps impossible. If the Book of the Grail is brought to light and the Anima Templi exposed, everything we have worked for could perish. This is surely the greater threat?'

'The book is my responsibility, Hasan,' said Everard firmly. 'I will take care of it.' He rubbed irritably at his forehead. 'Damn Armand!' he snapped suddenly. 'The Grand Master had to have his pomp and ceremony, didn't he!' He sighed and looked at Hasan. 'That book has been a stone around my neck since its creation. When Armand died at Herbiya I should have destroyed it, not brought it back to Paris. Because of me everything all of us have worked so hard to achieve has been put at risk. Our work is too important to this world to be lost, Hasan.'

'It is not your fault, brother.'

'No? I wrote the damn thing. If it isn't my fault I don't know whose fault it is. It was vanity that made me keep it, Hasan.' Everard shook his head. 'Vanity.'

Hasan was silent for a few moments, unsure of what to say. Eventually, he reached into his sack bag and pulled out a cracked, yellowed parchment that he handed to Everard. 'I took this from Jacques' after he died. I did not want anyone finding it.'

Everard took the parchment wearily. 'Did he read it?'

'Yes. He was pleased that James had managed to achieve so much in such a short time within the Mamluk camp.' Hasan paused. 'Will you tell your new apprentice about his father's involvement?'

'No,' said Everard shortly. Tearing up the parchment, he stowed the pieces in his robes. 'That one has much to learn.'

PART TWO

16

Safed, the Kingdom of Jerusalem

19 July 1266 AD

James Campbell rose and crossed himself before the altar. The chapel was cool and silent. It was not yet dawn and most of the fortress's inhabitants were either asleep, or manning the walls. James had risen early for the peace the chapel's emptiness offered, a peace that, just for a few moments, could help him forget where he was. When the Matins bell rang, the benches would fill with people, so many that those who came last would have to kneel outside. Every morning for almost three weeks it had been the same. Before then, only the fifty knights and thirty sergeants who garrisoned Safed would rise at dawn to attend the first office in the privacy of their chapel. But, now, everyone had a reason to pray and the priests didn't have the heart to turn them away. 'In these coming days we will need every prayer,' Brother Joseph had said.

Turning from the altar, James walked down the aisle. He paused before a statue that stood guard at the door. The eyes of St George were directed to the vaulted ceiling, so too was his sword, raised in triumph. On his chest was a carved cross and under his left foot was a serpent, jaws splayed in death. James touched the saint's foot. 'Protect us.'

The doors swung open and a large figure in a white mantle entered the chapel. In the candlelight the knight's hair and beard, thick and dry as straw and bleached white by the sun, took on a golden tinge. 'I thought I might find you here,' he said with a smile. His skin, burnt from recent long watches on the walls, crinkled at the corners of his eyes. 'Do you think God listened to you today, brother?'

James looked up at the knight, who was a good foot taller than he was. James was, himself, neither short nor slender of build, but he always felt rather diminutive when in the presence of this huge man. 'God always listens to us, Mattius.'

'I wonder sometimes, when so many call out to Him at once how can He hear us all?' Mattius half shrugged. 'I hope you're right. They are preparing for another assault. The commander believes it will come at dawn, we're needed on the walls.'

James forced a determined smile and motioned to the door. 'Then I'll show you He hears us when we beat them back again.'

The two men headed out of the chapel and into the night-gloom of the inner enceinte. The chapel, storerooms and cisterns that occupied the central space were dwarfed by the featureless heights of stone that surrounded them. At one end of the enclosure rose the massive keep which housed the quarters and hall of the knights, priests and sergeants. Ranked along the rest of the walls were the towers that held the infirmary, armoury, wardrobe and kitchens.

The two knights walked quickly, heading for a postern at the base of the wall. In the distance, the clinking of hammers echoed from the outer enceinte. Closer were the cries of a man as they passed beneath the infirmary. Once through the postern, they entered a dank passage that cut through the thirteen-foot-thick wall. A faint shimmer of torchlight shone through a grated opening in the passage roof, down which burning oil could be poured from a gallery above. Mattius opened the door at the end and stepped out. The guards manning the postern turned, reaching for their weapons, then relaxed as they saw the two knights.

'Glad to see you're still awake,' said Mattius, shutting the door which was reinforced on the outside with iron plates. He clapped one of the guards on the back, causing the man to gasp and step forward with the force of it. 'Only, I don't think trouble will come from the *inside*.'

'You may have to eat your words, Mattius,' said James, moving off. 'From the inside is how most fortresses fall.'

Mattius grunted and followed him through the outer enceinte, along narrow passages between the buildings and into open areas filled with people huddled around fires, curled up in the doorways of towers. The smell of dung from the animal pens and stables was strong and sickly-sweet. Above the calls of guards on the dawn watch, the murmuring of the waking inhabitants and the whinnying of horses rang the ever-present clinking of hammers as the masons continued the repairs on the barbican. From the curtain walls jutted corner and flanking towers, interconnected by covered walkways that bristled with mangonels and archers. The yellow tongues of torches flickered over the shadows of men moving on the battlements. In peacetime and during sieges the outer enceinte served as a barracks for the soldiers and servants. If an enemy breached the outer walls it would become a killing ground into which the defenders could pour oil, stones and arrows. Should the outer enceinte fall, the garrison would withdraw to the inner, making Safed a fortress within a fortress, one of the most impregnable of all the Crusader strongholds in Outremer. It was the pride of the Temple.

As he walked, James's gaze flitted over the groups of people, some of whom looked up at him, their expressions a mixture of hope and fear. Other than the knights, sergeants and servants, Safed housed a garrison of sixteen hundred Syrian Christian soldiers – lightly armed mercenaries paid to man the fortress. But, in recent weeks, the population had swelled as farmers and their families and herds had fled their homes for the safety of the stronghold. James assessed their numbers. He had set down his quill in London, but his years of bookkeeping at Balantrodoch had never left him and he still viewed everything in the black and white simplicity of a ledger. It was all a question of figures and whether they balanced. So much grain could feed so many people for so long: the more mouths to feed the shorter the time. True, there was no shortage of food or water as yet. But no one knew how long they would be imprisoned here, unable to leave, unable to send word to request more forces. Sieges could last for months.

'They could have at least brought something useful,' muttered Mattius, looking over at a man and woman with three skinny children who were sharing a blanket near one of the fires.

James followed his gaze. He saw a small collection of pots and pans stacked on the ground beside the family. The man kept one protective hand on the stack as if he feared someone might steal them. James imagined them in some mud-brick farm out in the pastures, hearing the distant hoofbeats, or seeing the beacons, snatching the pots and pans from a shelf and running for the door. Out across the fields, the mother carrying the youngest in her arms, the father looking over his shoulder.

'After the Battle of Mansurah, when the Egyptian forces stormed Louis' camp, the king's brother was saved by cooks wielding skillets. Almost anything can be used as a weapon,' said James.

Mattius pursed his lips and looked to the sky for inspiration. 'A feather?'

James grinned. The expression lit up his eyes and smoothed the lines of his brow, making him look years younger. 'A feather can be turned into a quill. With a quill you could sign a man's death warrant, draw up laws or edicts, declare war.'

They ascended a set of narrow steps leading up to the battlements. 'I was thinking of something a little more suited to our current predicament,' said Mattius, as they passed a row of archers kneeling at the loopholes in the wall.

'I suppose,' replied James, enjoying the game, 'that the tip of a feather would be sharp enough to blind a man.'

'A flower then?'

James opened his mouth to retort when his gaze fell on a group of young men standing on the walkway ahead. The five Templar sergeants had been garrisoned in the fortress two months ago, fresh from training at Acre. He saw them stand a little straighter as he and Mattius passed by. The torchlight shone on their pale, beardless faces. 'Dear God, Mattius, they are younger than my son.'

Mattius noticed James's temple pulse as he clenched his jaw, his humour spent. 'And how is your boy?' he asked in a jovial tone. 'I believe, in his last letter, he said he had taken the vows?' Mattius already knew the answers to his questions for James had read him the letter as soon as it had arrived.

James knew that Mattius knew, but accepted his comrade's attempt to lift his spirits. 'William is well, brother, and, yes, he's now a knight. I was concerned when I received word from him whilst I was stationed in Acre. The death of his master, Owein, was a sore blow and he sounded lost, unhappy in Paris. But he seems settled now and his master, Everard, obviously taught him much. His lettering is better than mine.'

'Always the scholar,' said Mattius with a grin.

'I wish I could have been there for his inception, Mattius. It feels like a lifetime since I saw him last.'

'You'll see him again soon enough. Once word reaches the West of what has happened, your son will come with an army to fight at our side.'

James looked back at the sergeants. 'And we will have much to speak of.' He lapsed into silence as they headed along the ramparts to a corner tower.

James had, at first, been overjoyed when he had received the letter from Will, speaking of the inception, but that joy had soon become tainted by feelings of regret and envy. In one sense, he was incredibly grateful that Everard had taken care of his son. After Jacques de Lyons had recruited him into the Anima Templi back in London, impressed by his diplomatic manner and knowledge of Arabic, James had met Everard only once before the priest had asked him to undertake an assignment in the East. The assignment had excited James: it was fundamental to the Anima Templi's aims, aims he had come firmly to believe in, and he'd thought he had a chance to succeed. He had agreed on the condition that Everard keep an eye on Will and, should anything happen to him, make sure that his son was cared for. But although he was glad that the priest had taken the boy on after Owein's death, he was envious that Everard, not him, had raised Will, had been there at his inception.

More and more these past few weeks, Will had been in James's thoughts. Perhaps because there was now the fear that he would never see the boy again, never hold his son, or say he was sorry for leaving the way he had. Standing on the docks at New Temple, James had longed to take Will in his arms and tell the distraught boy that he no longer blamed him for Mary's death; that he had to leave because he was going to do something important, something that could change the world. But all he had been able to do was squeeze his son's hand.

As they approached the corner tower, James glanced at the huge man beside him. Mattius had been a good friend to him over the past few years, but knew nothing of the real reason he was in the Holy Land, or what he did in between his obligations to the Temple and his various postings at garrisons like Safed. Sometimes, James felt so lonely he thought the pain of it would bury him. He missed his daughters, the smell of their hair and the sound of their laughter. He missed the feel of his wife's warm skin against his. He missed his son. At those times, James had to remind himself that the mission, not his family, or friends, or his duty to the Temple was the most important thing. He was doing it, he told himself, for them.

James pushed open the postern at the tower's base and, together, he and Mattius ascended the spiral steps. A cold wind whistled down towards them, blowing specks of dust into their eyes. The wind grew stronger as they neared the top, as did the glare of torchlight. They came out through a hole in the round tower's crenellated roof. The sky was beginning to lighten, the stars fading to turquoise blue. A short, thick-set man with a tanned, leathery face turned to them as they appeared. With him on the tower were eight other Templars, two sergeants and the captain of the Syrian soldiers.

'Good morning, brothers.'

James inclined his head. 'Commander.'

'I hope you slept well, this looks to be a long day.'

'Mattius has informed me of the possibility of an assault, sir.'

The commander motioned to the parapet. 'Come see for yourself.'

James followed him and looked out. Safed was built on a wide, high hill of craggy rock, offering a clear vantage point from all sides over the surrounding lands. One of several Crusader castles ranked along the Jordan Valley, it guarded the road from Damascus to Acre, looking out across Jacob's Ford, the most northerly crossing over the River Jordan. In daylight the view would be of hills and pastures, scattered with the villages that lay under Safed's dominion. Five miles to the south, the Jordan flowed into the Sea of Galilee and the fields stretched up into dusty, pink mountains. In the darkness, James could see nothing but the vast Mamluk army stretched out below the fortress. Thousands of torches were burning, throwing a hellish glow over the encampment of tents, wagons, horses, camels and fluttering banners. Men in coloured cloaks and turbans moved in the pools of light between the skeletal frames of siege engines that rose like monsters from the plain.

'It looks even larger than it did yesterday,' muttered James. 'Have reinforcements joined them?'

'Not reinforcements,' answered the commander. 'Last night, after you retired, they sent heralds to inform us that they had captured another two hundred Christians from the outlying villages. We saw them being brought in cages.'

'Dear God.'

'They should have fled when they had the chance. We can do nothing for them.'

James felt that he should protest. But he didn't. Harsh as the commander's words were, James knew he was right.

The commander pointed to a shadowy area not far from the base of the hill, where a steep, winding path led up to the barbican that guarded the fortress's gate. 'Take a look.'

James and Mattius, who had joined them, followed his finger. Squinting into the shadows, James saw the figures of men moving around a long, rectangular shape that was only visible because it was blacker and more solid than the weakening darkness.

'They've built a cat.'

The commander nodded. 'It could prove a problem. We have only just completed the repairs on the barbican after the last two assaults.' He laughed bitterly. 'And they weren't even aiming for it. If that stone hadn't gone so wide of their mark . . .' He shook his head. 'They know it's a weak spot now.'

James realised that he could no longer hear the hammers: the masons had been pulled back, their job done. He frowned as he studied the cat. A stout frame set on wheels with a sloping timber roof, it would have to be brought right up to the base of the walls to be used. From under its shelter men would go to work on the gate with pickaxes, or else there would be a ram strung from chains attached to the roof, its head iron-plated. The weapon could, indeed, prove a problem. But there were ways of dealing with it.

'Fire?' offered James.

'They would have prepared for that. I expect its roof will be protected with green hides.'

James agreed: green hides – raw skins soaked in vinegar – were difficult to set alight. 'A grappling unit, then?'

'I have already sent them down there. Late last night we noticed an increase of activity in the camp, which gave us the initial warning of a dawn attack. We sent a group of Syrians through one of the tunnels. The concealed exit comes out not far from the enemy's siege engines. The Syrians couldn't get close enough to hear what the soldiers were saying without compromising their position, but they did see them loading the engines.'

The commander pointed to the far left of the encampment.

James looked to where twenty-seven mangonels, which the Mamluks called mandjaniks, were spaced out in a row. The siege engines' long movable beams, were presently motionless. Each beam was suspended diagonally across a frame. The raised end was thrust into a complex system of ropes and the other end, hollowed out to form a bowl-shaped cavity, rested on the ground. In the cavity could be placed a stone weighing up to three hundred pounds. In an attack, the raised end of the beam would be pulled back on the ropes at speed. The end that held the stone would hit a crossbar above the frame and catapult its load towards Safed's walls.

James tore his gaze from the engines as the commander continued.

'For the main assault the enemy will rely on their mangonels again, hoping to breach the walls. We'll concentrate our archers and our own engines on their positions. They are presently out of range, but they will have to come closer when the battle commences.'

'Are you certain, Commander, that the fortress can withstand a prolonged attack?'

James, Mattius and the Templar commander turned. It was the captain of the Syrian Christian soldiers who had spoken.

His brown eyes studied them. 'Is it not better to offer terms of surrender, whilst we still have the chance?'

'Surrender?' scoffed the commander. 'At this early stage? We have already beaten them back twice, with little loss of life on our own side.'

'In these past few years, Commander, I have studied our enemy. I know his tactics. I was at Acre, three years ago, when the sultan attacked the city.'

'I, too, was at Acre then,' said James, seeing the commander's expression hardening. 'The fighting was fierce, yes, but the sultan didn't take the city, nor did he take it last month when he tried and failed again.'

The Syrian captain stared out across the army below them. 'His soldiers call him the Crossbow. They say he will not stop until every Christian in these lands is dead, but I was born here. My men and I have more right to be in this land than he does.'

'All the more reason to stand and fight,' said the commander sharply. 'It is pure cowardice to fold so quickly in the face of an enemy we have so far withstood so well.'

'I'm no coward, Commander, but this fortress was taken before by Saladin, and this sultan has none of his honour.'

The commander folded his arms across his chest. 'In the twenty-six years since Safed was returned to us we have spent a fortune on its fortification. It is far stronger now than it was when Saladin's forces besieged it and we can hold off the enemy for months, years, if we have to. The sultan doesn't want a long campaign: it will be too costly, and I'll not give him the satisfaction of a swift victory.' He patted the edge of the parapet and smiled coldly. 'There is not just mortar in these walls, there is also the will of God.'

As the chapel bell rang out for Matins, James glanced down over the compound. Safed's smooth walls stretched away, guarded by faceless towers and soldiers standing ready. The sight filled him with hope. But then he looked back at Sultan Baybars' formidable force, with all its wall-crushing machines and archers and armaments. The scout he had sent out in secret had seen no sign of his contact within the camp. Hope seemed futile.

17

Saint-Denis's Gate, Paris

19 July 1266 AD

'Do you trust me?'
'Of course.'
'Then close your eyes.'

With a sigh, Will complied. He leaned back on his elbows, the grass tickling his neck. 'Can we not just eat?' He opened one eye a crack and watched as Elwen reached into the sack she had brought. She was kneeling beside him, her white gown, delicately laced at the sides and sleeves, spread out around her. She had removed her cap and her hair fell in tawny tresses down her back. It was a glorious day. The fields sloped down to the city walls where the purple heads of thistles, some as tall as a man, nodded in the breeze. Beyond the city walls, Paris was a white gem glinting in the noonday sun. From this distance, far from the grime and noise, the city was beautiful. Will smiled, his eye winking shut, as Elwen turned back to him.

'What are you smiling at?'

'Your strange notions.'

'If you don't like my game . . .'

'Oh, I'll play,' he said quickly, recognising the tone that told him she was chafed. 'I'm going to win.'

'Would you care to lay a wager on that?'

'What would I gamble? Unlike you, I don't get paid for my services.' A shadow passed across him, darkening the red glow of the sun behind his eyelids. Will felt Elwen's sleeve skim his cheek.

'You could wager your heart.'

He smiled, although her tone caused discomfort to edge in on his contentment. Something hard was pressed against his lips and he opened his mouth to receive it. He chewed slowly, a pleasant sharpness making his tongue tingle. 'Apple. That was easy.'

'The next will be harder.'

Will waited, listening to the thrum of bees in the tall grass as Elwen rifled through the sack. 'Is the queen not expecting you back?'

'No,' she told him brightly. 'I have the whole afternoon to myself.'

Will shook his head, envious of Elwen's freedom. Most women of nineteen would be in their fifth or sixth year of marriage, having forfeited their rights and land in dowries to their husbands. Elwen, unwed and a handmaiden to Queen Marguerite, was granted much greater privileges and could even, should she wish, invest the money she earned in property. This, coupled with the close bond she had formed with her mistress over the past six years, meant that she had a great deal more liberty than Will ever would, bound as he was to the Temple, and Everard.

'I work hard for small favours,' added Elwen, seeing his look. 'Now keep your eyes closed.' She put something crumbly and sweet-smelling to his lips.

The game went on for some time. Will guessed the almond cake, the egg and cheese, and screwed up his face at the lemon, sending Elwen into a fit of giggles.

'Enough,' he said finally, spitting out a mouthful of salt. Will opened his eyes and sat up, blinking at the brightness. 'I've won, surely?'

'No!' insisted Elwen. She pushed him back down. 'One last thing.'

'Elwen,' he groaned.

'One more.'

'Very well.' Will shot her a look of suspicion. 'But not the lemon again.'

She smiled.

He closed his eyes. 'Where did you get all this food from anyway? Are we eating the king's supper?'

Elwen didn't answer. Will sensed her leaning over him. Behind his eyes, the darkness grew solid with her closeness. His heart began to quicken as her hand brushed against his. A moment later, he felt something soft touch his lips. His lips parted, even though he knew that it wasn't pastry, or fruit they opened to receive, but something much sweeter. Will shuddered as Elwen's mouth closed over his own, her tongue darting against his. He had known this would happen, ever since he had received her message asking him to meet her at Saint-Denis's Gate. Passion overcame reason and, reaching up, Will pulled Elwen to him, feeling the heat of her flow across his chest. Her hair spilled like water over his hands and face. His fingers trapped in her curls. He was drowning in her. And if this was sin it tasted of honey and light.

A kestrel, circling the field in search of prey, swooped towards the grass with a cry. The sound tore Will from his oblivion. He grasped Elwen's arms and pushed her gently away. 'Elwen.'

'What's wrong?' she asked, sitting up with a frown.

Will sat up beside her, avoiding her eyes. 'You know what's wrong. We promised we wouldn't do this anymore. For the sake of our friendship, that's what we agreed.'

'*You* agreed,' Elwen corrected, standing. She looked down over the city. 'And I believe you said it for the sake of your mantle, not our friendship.'

Will rose. 'What mantle?'

Elwen was used to his quick temper, but it still managed to startle her, like thunder out of a blue sky.

Will grabbed a fistful of his black tunic. 'Does this look like a knight's cloak to you?'

Elwen sighed. 'Will,' she murmured, shaking her head, 'I'm sorry, I didn't mean to say that.'

But Will wouldn't let her placate him. He held out his palms to her. 'Do these look like hands that wield a sword?' The tips of his fingers were black. He had scrubbed them morning and night for the past six years, trying every conceivable concoction of herbs, getting Elwen to buy him foul-smelling soaps from quacks in the markets. But no amount of scouring had made the ink fade. Elwen had once told him that the stains made him look like one of the university professors. To him, his fingers were a brand, a constant reminder of his thwarted ambitions. 'Do they?'

Elwen bit the corner of her lip. 'Perhaps not, but that isn't important.'

'Not important? You know how hard it has been for me, waiting and watching whilst my friends take their vows and are led from the chapter house as knights. As men. I lied to my father, Elwen. I wrote and told him I had been knighted because I couldn't bear to reveal my disgrace to him.' Will turned away. 'He thinks poorly enough of me as it is.'

Elwen went to him, the dry grass pricking her bare feet. 'It doesn't matter whether you wear black or white, or whether you wield a sword or a quill. It's what's inside you, your heart and spirit, that counts.'

Will snorted derisively, but he let her take hold of his hand. He watched as she uncurled his clenched fingers and kissed the inky tips. He felt some of his anger dissolve.

'Forgive me,' she said. 'I know we agreed we couldn't be together like this, it is just hard to return to how it was before.'

'There's nothing to forgive.' Will withdrew his hand carefully from hers. 'It's hard for me also, but it is best this way.' He paused. 'For both of us.'

'Yes,' Elwen agreed, avoiding his gaze. 'This is best.'

'We should go.' Will fastened his belt around his waist, from which hung his falchion. Sergeants usually only bore arms for specific duties, but Will had started wearing the falchion several months ago. By doing so, he had felt he was saying to Everard that he wouldn't be a priest's servant forever. The challenge had proved ineffectual: Everard hadn't even seemed to notice. But other than a couple of letters that had come from the East, in which James had mostly just spoken of a comrade, Mattius, the sword was the one tenuous link Will had left with his father. He continued to wear it now out of attachment.

He bent to pick up the sack which was heavy with the food they hadn't eaten. 'I have to get to the parchmenter's. If I'm to be back at the preceptory for Vespers, I need to hurry.'

'Well, it wouldn't hurt if I returned early.' Elwen forced a smile. 'The palace has been in a state since the king invited Pierre de Pont-Evêque to perform for him on All Hallows. The servants have been far busier gossiping than working since he announced it. The queen hasn't been in the best of moods.'

'Pierre who?'

Elwen arched an eyebrow. 'Honestly, Will, I know you live in a monastery, but it wouldn't hurt for you have some contact with the outside world now and then.' She sighed at his nonplussed expression. 'Pierre is a troubadour. A very famous one.'

'Oh,' said Will, unenthusiastically; he didn't share Elwen's obsession with Romances.

'He has already caused quite a stir in the south. His material is a little . . . unconventional.' Elwen brushed the grass from her skirts. 'I think it will be an interesting evening.'

They walked down through the fields in silence. As they neared the city, the road became busy with carts and riders, the wheels and hoofs churning up clouds of dust. The road wound northwards to the Abbey of Saint-Denis, the royal necropolis where kings since the time of Dagobert I were interred. Will guided Elwen onto the verge as a cart pulled by oxen came rumbling up the hill towards them. They walked on, passing several farms, sweet-smelling vineyards, a grand estate, two small chapels and a hospital.

The city walls had been built over seventy years ago during the reign of Philippe-Auguste, but Paris had since outgrown its belt and expanded into the surrounding countryside. Outside Saint-Denis's Gate, a group of vagrants had gathered. The guards on the gate kept a close eye on the tattered figures who were dodging the carts and horses to thrust their bowls at the people who queued to pass in and out of the barrier. Will and Elwen moved into the line.

'Damn beggars.'

Will glanced round to see a corpulent man in a velvet cloak glaring at the ragged group. The man spoke the *langue d'oïl*, the tongue of the north. Will had learnt enough of it during his time in Paris to understand what was being said and, as the man continued, he wished he hadn't.

'You cannot move an inch these days without being pestered by outlaws and vagabonds,' said the fat man, jowls wobbling. 'A curse on them all!' Several people in the queue looked over. Roused by the captive audience, the man launched into a diatribe against robbers, whores and idlers and their ruination of his once proud and shining city.

Will looked away. If he were a knight he wouldn't have to wait, he could go to the front and pass straight through, unhindered, unquestioned. He chewed his lip and brooded. Just recently everything seemed to serve as a reminder of his low status.

Will's eighteenth birthday, the day he came of age, had passed like an exasperating milestone informing him that he still had a long way to go. The following January, a year and a day later, he had thought his waiting was over. Now, six months on, he was still an old priest's scribe. He had served his punishment for defiling the Sacrament all those years ago and he had performed, with fewer and fewer complaints, every mean, arduous, or tedious task that Everard had meted out to him. But asking Everard to explain why he hadn't been put forward for knighthood had been like trying to get an answer out of a rock and, eventually, he had given up trying. Will's frustration pricked him a little deeper every day; when he bedded down with the other sergeants whilst his companions retired to the knights' quarters; when he knelt on the floor in the chapel and his friends sat apart from him on the benches. And when he went for his meals, knowing it was their scraps he was eating.

Once through the gate, they moved with the crowds on the Rue Saint-Denis. The street was packed with traders and street entertainers vying for the attention of passers-by. It was cattle market day and the smell of the dung that caked the streets was nauseating. Residing outside the walls in the relative isolation afforded by the preceptory, Will tended to forget how much the city stank. The reminder was always an assault on his senses: sweat; the acrid stench of a tannery; night soil and refuse spread across the market gardens for the hemp and flax; contents of waste buckets thrown from windows. 'Will you wait for a bronette?' he asked Elwen.

Elwen looked up at the sky, shielding her eyes from the sun. 'It's too beautiful a day to be cramped inside a stuffy carriage. I shall walk.' She tucked her hair into her cap. Several unruly strands floated around her cheeks.

Will reached out to brush them aside, then stopped. The gesture, once so natural, seemed inappropriate. His hand hung suspended for a moment, before he let it fall to his side. 'I'd better go.'

'We can go together,' said Elwen, pretending not to notice his awkwardness. 'You said you are going to the parchmenter's? I can walk with you as far as the Cité.'

'I'm not going to the Latin Quarter today,' said Will quickly. 'Everard's usual supplier has run out, I'll go to the one near Temple Gate.'

'Oh.' Elwen straightened her cap to hide her disappointment. 'When will we next meet?'

'When I can next escape the dragon.'

'Everard can't be that bad.'

'You don't have to work for him.'

'He cannot ignore your right to the mantle forever.'

'Oh, I think he probably can,' murmured Will, as Elwen slipped off through the crowds and was gone. After a moment, he headed onto one of the streets that ran parallel to the main thoroughfare. Everard had given him money for a bronette, but the route was so clogged with people and animals that he knew it would be quicker to walk to the Latin Quarter. He felt guilty having lied to Elwen and more than a little foolish to be walking in the same direction a street along from her. But he couldn't be near her after that kiss; it was too tormenting. Skirting the crowds around the cattle market, Will walked down to the Seine, his thoughts as heavy as the afternoon heat.

There had been few changes in his and Elwen's daily routines since they had come to Paris. Elwen had settled easily into her position at the palace and he had submitted, far less smoothly, to his apprenticeship under Everard. Physically, they had both altered: Will had grown taller, his short black beard softening the sharp angles of his cheekbones and jaw; and Elwen had turned into a striking, willowy young woman. But it was between them that the most dramatic changes had occurred.

The shift in their relationship had been gradual, almost unnoticeable. But as the months had become years it had begun to dawn on Will that what had started as a friendship, born out of a shared loss following Owein's death, had become something else. Something thrilling. Terrifying. For his part, he had kept his feelings hidden, stealing furtive glances at Elwen when she wasn't looking, pretending to be interested in what she was saying when all the while he was drinking in her presence like nectar. Elwen had been more forthright. She had shown him a book once that she had found in the palace. Will had thought it one of the Romances she enthused about, until she had opened the creased leather covering. The pages had been filled with illustrations of men and women in various states of undress and licentious abandon. They had laughed over that book, but Will had seen the way Elwen's cheeks flushed as she looked from the pictures to him and had known, in that moment, that she shared his feelings. After that they had begun to meet in secret places, snatching private moments for fleeting kisses that left Will reeling.

Passing the grand houses of the Lombardy merchants and Jews that looked out over the river, he struggled to recall how it was to look at Elwen without a shiver running through him. It seemed impossible; like trying to forget his own name. But he couldn't allow himself to feel this way. By engaging in this sin, outside wedlock, he risked his knighthood, and if they married, as she had once suggested, he would never gain the white mantle, but would remain forever garbed in the black of human sin.

Forcibly banishing thoughts of Elwen from his mind, he crossed the wide bridge to the Île de la Cité; the king's seat of power. On the streets around Notre Dame, dusty footprints marked the passage of the masons who had retired from their work on the cathedral to seek shelter from the midday sun. Will followed the footprints for a time, before crossing another, smaller bridge to the left bank.

The Latin Quarter, which housed the many colleges of the university, was bustling as usual. The colleges, established from pious donations, had sprung up over the last one and a half centuries, and men came from across the kingdoms of France, England, Germany and the Low Countries to study medicine, law, the arts and divinity under some of the West's most eminent masters. Negotiating his way through the crowds of professors, priests and students, Will turned onto the Rue Saint-Jacques that led to the Dominican college, near the parchmenter's. Ahead, two men were blocking his path, one of whom, barefoot, clad in a ragged black robe and wearing a wooden cross around his neck, was recognisable as a Dominican. The stocky young man with the friar was speaking crossly. Will went to go around them.

'I weren't being rude, sir,' the stocky man was saying. 'I want to get to the preceptory. The Temple, the . . .' He waved his hand, frustrated, and said something in broken Latin.

The Dominican gave a terse reply that the young man obviously didn't understand, then swept off down the street.

'Hell's fire!' muttered the young man, glaring after the friar. 'You'll never get a straight answer out of a priest!'

As he passed, Will noticed that the man was wearing the tunic of a Templar sergeant. He walked over, thinking to offer directions, then stopped in amazement. The young man was taller than he remembered, although still short in comparison to himself. His face was full and broad, as was his beard, and his chest was even more barrelled. The sparkling brown eyes and scruffy thatch of hair were the same, however. 'Simon!'

Simon turned. After a few moments, recognition dawned across his face. 'My God! *Will?*'

Will laughed and embraced him, ignoring the grumbles of a passing student who had to go around them. 'What are you doing here?' he said, stepping back and looking his old friend up and down.

Simon hoisted the sack he was carrying higher on his shoulder. 'I just arrived with a company of knights from London. I was following them to the preceptory, but I stopped to look in a shop and when I came out they'd gone.'

'You are definitely lost then. You reach the preceptory via the right bank. This is the left.'

Simon scratched his head, further dishevelling his hair. 'I was asking for directions, but no one seemed to understand me.'

Will grinned. 'It may have helped if you hadn't just asked one of the inquisitors the way to his wife's cowshed.'

'He was an inquisitor?' Simon blew out his cheeks as he stared down the street. 'Trust me.' He turned back, shaking his head in happy wonderment. 'It's so good to see you, Will. Though I'm surprised you're not off waving your sword at Saracens.' He gestured at Will's tunic, black like his own. 'Brocart told me you hadn't been knighted when he came back from Paris last year, but he didn't say why.'

Some of Will's gladness at seeing his old comrade faded. He had purposefully avoided Brocart, whom he had known as a sergeant in New Temple, when the youth had visited the preceptory. 'It's a long story.'

'You'll have a willing ear if you'll show me to the preceptory.'

'I have a better idea,' said Will suddenly, tucking his hand into the pouch that hung from his belt beside his falchion. He brought out the coins Everard had given him for the bronette. 'Let's find an alehouse.'

'Lead the way,' said Simon, grinning.

Will scanned the signs above the doors of the buildings. In a matter of moments, he found what he was looking for. The two youths entered a gloomy doorway that smelt of sweat and mutton, Will feeling satisfactorily rebellious.

After ordering the cheapest bottle of wine and a slab of bread from the surly proprietor, they seated themselves on a bench beside the half-open shutters. Flies drifted over the sticky surfaces of the trestles around which huddled groups of priests nursing jars of ale and arguing in slurred tones over the correct administration of the Eucharist and the wingspan of angels. Some of these establishments, Will had heard, were fronts for a darker indulgence, places where the price of a woman was less than a tankard of ale.

'You first then,' said Simon, tearing the hunk of bread in half. 'What's happened since you came to Paris?'

'Little.' Will took a drink of wine, the taste of which made him wince. 'I've done nothing much for the last six years that didn't involve a quill and a bad-tempered priest.'

'Brocart said you was working for a priest. I was sorry to hear about Sir Owein,' Simon added solemnly. 'He was a decent man.'

'Yes,' agreed Will quietly, 'yes he was.' Over time, his sense of loss had diminished, but the memory of his former master still haunted him. Perhaps more so than it would have had his new master not been quite so disagreeable.

Simon handed him some bread. 'I remember King Henry coming to the preceptory soon after the knights returned from escorting the jewels. He was livid. No sooner had he jumped off his horse and he was bellowing at Master Humbert, red as a fox, saying how we shouldn't have taken the jewels in the first place and how we'd put them and his wife in danger.' Simon whistled through his teeth. 'We was all taking wagers who would throw the first punch – Master Humbert or the king. They investigated him, you know.'

Will nodded. 'No one could find any proof that Henry was involved.'

'They didn't have much chance to. When the civil war came all that was stopped.' Simon shook his head. 'It's been a strange few years. We've been secure enough in the preceptory; no one's really bothered us much. But London's been a mess and the kingdom . . .? We didn't know who was in charge half the time. One day it was the king, the next, Simon de Montfort and the barons. It wasn't long before the barons openly rebelled, saying they wanted to give more power to the people. They seized Gloucester and the Cinque Ports and part of Kent, then met the king and his army head on at Lewes.'

'We heard about that battle.'

'I'm not surprised. People were talking about it for months in England. They said Prince Edward fought like a legend, charging the rebels' ranks at the head of his men.'

'I thought that was what lost them the battle?' said Will, biting into the hard bread. 'Edward's rashness in that charge?'

Simon shrugged. 'I'm only saying what I heard. But anyway, after he was captured at Lewes, Edward escaped from de Montfort's custody and fought the rebels at Evesham. He killed de Montfort himself and then freed his father. After that most of the rebels fled, or surrendered.'

'The war's over now though?'

'De Montfort's loyal supporters are still holding out at Kenilworth, but King Henry's army has been at them for months. I reckon it'll fall soon.' Simon drained his wine and poured himself another goblet.

The two of them lapsed into an uncomfortable silence, unused to one another's company.

'So,' said Simon, sitting up. 'Is Sir Owein's niece still here?' He chuckled. 'We all heard about her.'

Will coughed around a mouthful of wine. 'Heard what?'

'That she stowed away on the ship.'

'Oh,' said Will, nodding and clearing his throat.

'Is she still in Paris?'

'Yes.' Will felt a slow flush spread across his cheeks. He sat back, sweeping his hands through his hair in what he hoped was a suitably nonchalant gesture. 'Elwen is working as a handmaiden to Queen Marguerite. I see her sometimes when our duties permit. But you still haven't told me why you're here?'

'I've been promoted. The Marshal of the Paris preceptory requested me.' Simon looked embarrassed. 'He was in London a few months back and his horse took sick. I managed to save it.' He shrugged. 'It wasn't hard; just had to give it the right herbs to quell its fever and keep it on its feet for a night. But I reckon I must've impressed him because he wrote to Master Humbert and said he wanted me as head groom in Paris.'

'All praise to you.' Will had to force his smile: Simon, son of a tanner from Cheapside, was now in a position of higher regard than his own.

'Thanks,' said Simon modestly.

Will finished his wine and stood, his head spinning a little. 'I should tell you how to get to the preceptory.'

'Aren't you coming with me?'

'I've an errand to run. I'll be a while yet and you need to report to the Marshal. You said you came with a company of knights? I expect they'll have reported to him already.'

'Yes, the—' Simon stopped. 'I haven't told you, have I? Someone else you know was on the ship from London. Garin de Lyons.'

'Garin?'

'Yes,' said Simon, rising and gripping the trestle to steady himself. 'Mother of God, I'm drunk. Of course, he's too stuck up his own mantle to wait for the likes of me. I reckon I'd have been walking about this place for days if I hadn't met you.'

'Garin is a knight?' asked Will, already knowing the answer.

Simon nodded. 'Well.' He clapped Will's shoulder. 'Tomorrow we can nurse our aching heads and you can tell me why you're still a sergeant. Not that I'm disappointed,' he added cheerfully. 'Who wants to be a knight?'

'Who indeed.'

After giving Simon directions to the preceptory, Will trudged down the Rue Saint-Jacques, his stomach soured by the wine and his mood soured by Simon's news. However glad he was to see his old friend, that two of his former comrades were here in Paris and established in the proper, commendable positions for men of their age and status was merely one more thing to heighten his own frustration. He tried to imagine Garin as a knight, but could only see a thin, golden-haired boy with bruises on his face. Elwen's words came back to him. *He cannot ignore your right to the mantle forever.* A month or so back, after Everard had last refused to speak of his initiation, Will had made a promise to himself: that before the year was out he would go the Holy Land. He knew his father was stationed at Safed. If he could only get initiated within the next few months he could request a transfer. Will touched the disc-shaped pommel of his falchion. He had been quiet for too long.

Near the Dominicans' college, he entered the narrow alley that led to the parchmenter's. A large man came stumbling out of an inn in front of Will and they collided, upsetting the stranger's flagon of ale, the contents of which sloshed up and spilled over his front.

'God damn it!' exclaimed the man.

'Sorry,' said Will, stepping back and seeing, by the white cross on the man's black surcoat, that he was a Knight of St John: a Hospitaller. 'I didn't see you.'

'Didn't see me?' demanded the knight, swiping ineffectually at the ale soaking into his surcoat. 'Are you blind?'

'As I said, I'm sorry.'

As Will went to move off, the Hospitaller grabbed his arm. 'That's not good enough!' His eyes focused slowly on Will's tunic and he sneered. 'A Templar, eh?' By his pungent breath and heavy-lidded gaze, Will guessed that the ale wasn't the knight's first of the day. 'What are you going to do about this?' He waved the flagon.

Will pulled his arm from the knight's grip. 'I've apologised. I see no need to do more.'

'What's this, Rasequin?'

Will turned at the voice to see four knights coming out of the inn, carrying flagons and looking almost as worse for wear as their companion.

The Hospitaller staggered round to face them and gestured at Will. 'This Temple scum is spilling my ale and thinking to get away without paying.'

'Apologise to our man!' demanded one of the knights, a pimple-faced youth who looked only a year or so older than Will.

'I already have,' said Will, gritting his teeth. 'And if your comrade wasn't such a mule he would have accepted it.'

'You whelp!' slurred Rasequin, tossing the flagon aside and reaching for his sword.

His companions came forward as he tried to draw the sword with fumbling fingers.

'Leave the boy alone, Rasequin,' said one, who looked older than the rest. 'He's only a sergeant.'

Will flushed and put his hand on the hilt of his sword.

'Come on, Rasequin,' insisted the older knight placidly. 'I'll buy you another.'

'After,' said Rasequin, his sword finally swinging free and causing him to lurch back a few paces, 'I've taught this runt a lesson!'

Will drew his falchion as Rasequin staggered towards him.

'Stand down,' said the older knight to Will, 'I'll deal with this.' He grabbed Rasequin's shoulder. 'Cease, brother!'

The pimple-faced knight pointed at Will's sword. 'Look at that blade!' He sniggered. 'It must be an antique!'

The knight's laughter ceased abruptly as Will raised the sword and lunged forward. Three of the Hospitallers stepped back. The tip of Will's sword was pointed at their comrade's throat. Will was oblivious to everything except the face of the man in front of him. The release of anger intoxicated him: it was much more pleasant vented than dammed.

'Come on,' he goaded Rasequin, his lips pulled back in a half-grin, half-snarl. 'Fight me!'

Rasequin, too drunk to be cautioned by the ferocity of Will's gaze, lifted his blade.

'Stand down!' repeated the older knight. 'Stop, God damn you!' he said to Will, who took another step forward and drew back the falchion as if to strike.

Will was halted by a tight grip on his wrist. He turned to confront his assailant, but was silenced when he saw it was a Templar who had hold of him.

'In a moment, sergeant,' said the knight calmly, 'I'm going to let go and you are going to sheathe your sword.'

Will, trembling with the anticipation of battle, hesitated. Then he nodded.

The Templar dropped his hold and watched Will slide the falchion through the loop in the belt. He then looked at the five Hospitallers. 'What is the cause of this disturbance?'

Rasequin had lowered his blade at the appearance of the Templar, although his baleful gaze was still fixed on Will.

The older knight inclined his head politely. 'It was a misunderstanding. The lad here,' he gestured at Will, 'spilled our comrade's ale.'

The Templar looked back at Will. His eyes were a cool, lucid blue and seemed all the paler in comparison to his long black hair and beard. He looked to be in his mid-forties. His face was strong and handsome and there was an olive tone to his skin that suggested he had spent some time in warmer climes. 'Well?'

Will met his stare. He had seen the knight in the preceptory, but they had never been introduced and he didn't know the man's name. 'It was an accident, sir.'

'Would an apology not have served instead of a duel?'

Will opened his mouth to defend himself, then thought better of it. 'Yes, sir.'

The Templar put his hand into a leather pouch hanging from his belt and drew out a gold coin. He went to Rasequin and handed it to him. 'I believe this will compensate for any inconvenience caused.'

Rasequin grunted something inaudible, but accepted the coin.

'It more than suffices, brother,' said the older knight. He gave another nod and gestured to his comrades. 'Let's go.' They moved off down the alley, Rasequin staggering between them.

Will, watching them go, was taken aback at how easily the situation had been resolved; the Hospitallers could have made a formal complaint against him, or demanded an official duel to settle the matter. He wouldn't have been surprised if they had. The Hospitallers weren't known for their clemency when it came to the Templars. Every chance they had, they would impede Temple business, or argue against the Order; complaining to city officials that a watermill belonging to the Temple had flooded one of their fields; arguing that Templars were taking up more space than they in the marketplace with the wool stalls; alleging that the Temple had bribed church officials and taken possession of an abandoned church, from which to collect alms, which the Hospital had already secured. And yet, for all their complaints, they still adopted many of the Temple's practices. The Order of St John, established prior to the First Crusade over twenty years before the Temple was founded, had been created with the sole aim of providing care for sick pilgrims in the East. But soon after the Temple's establishment, the Hospitallers had begun to emulate the Order in military functions, castle building and economic drive. Their initiations were based on Templar inceptions and even their mantles, with the splayed white cross, were, according to the Templars, just another imitation.

'What did you think you were doing, sergeant?'

Will looked at the knight. 'I'm sorry, sir, I was wrong and I was rash and . . .' He kicked at a stone on the ground, then swung his gaze back to the knight. 'I'm lying, I'm not sorry. I apologised and he wouldn't accept it. The Hospitaller drew his blade before I did.'

'So you drew yours in self-defence?'

'No,' admitted Will after a pause. 'In anger. I wasn't going to wound him,' he added. 'I just . . .' He trailed off. It had felt good to draw his sword. Training on his own wasn't the same as facing someone in a fight and he missed that pure, uncomplicated thrill. But now it was over, he just felt foolish.

'It wouldn't have been much of a fight,' said the knight. 'Your opponent could scarcely stand.'

'I know. I suppose I wanted to humiliate him.'

'*Aquila non captat muscas.*'

'An eagle doesn't hawk at flies?'

'Indeed.' The knight held out his hand. 'My name is Nicolas de Navarre.'

'William Campbell,' said Will, accepting the man's hand which was ridged along the palm with calluses, caused by the frequent handling of a sword.

Nicolas nodded. 'I've seen you in the preceptory. You are a sergeant under the priest, Everard de Troyes?'

'You know Sir Everard?'

'I know his work. I'm a collector of rare books, or I was before I joined the Temple. I've tried speaking with Brother Everard on several occasions, but he seems somewhat . . .'

'Rancorous?' offered Will.

'Reclusive,' said Nicolas with a smile. He glanced around the alley. 'What were you doing down here?'

'Getting fresh skins. We're working on some new translations.'

'Anything interesting?'

'Only if you're fascinated by the medicinal properties of olive trees.'

Nicolas laughed. 'Well, I shan't keep you from your work. Good day to you.' He paused. 'A word of advice, Sergeant Campbell. Be careful about who you draw your sword against in future. The next man might not be so easily dissuaded from spilling your blood.'

'Can I ask, sir,' called Will, as the knight turned to leave, 'whether you plan on speaking of this incident to my master?'

'What incident?' Nicolas smiled, then headed down the alley.

18

Outside the Walls of Safed, the Kingdom of Jerusalem

19 July 1266 AD

♊

O mar looked up at the towering white-grey fortress that loomed from its promontory of rock. The soldiers on Safed's battlements were no bigger than ants from this distance, though these ants had teeth and in one charge alone the Mamluks had lost over fifty men to their arrows. Omar studied the sheer, indomitable walls. If there was one thing that could be said for the Franks, it was that they knew how to build a castle. Their architecture was neither as beautiful nor as elaborate as the Mamluks', but, like the Franks themselves, it was dour and tough. Omar turned and headed for the pavilion at the centre of the camp.

As Omar entered, Baybars looked up. Two of the sultan's eunuchs were pulling on his polished chainmail coat, another was standing by with his sword belt and sabres. Except for the attendants, the pavilion appeared deserted. Behind Baybars, the throne stood empty, the heads of the lions that capped its arms gleaming in the lantern light. Omar heard a grunt come from the shadows. He made out the form of Khadir curled up on a blanket. The soothsayer muttered in his sleep, rolled over and began to snore.

'My Lord Sultan,' said Omar, approaching Baybars and bowing.

Baybars dismissed the attendants and fastened the coat's clasp at his neck. 'Omar,' he greeted, frowning. 'I'm pleased you could join me. Finally.'

Omar bowed his head. 'I was sleeping, my lord. I'm sorry.'

Baybars laughed, his blue eyes glittering. He embraced Omar. 'It's still so easy to bait you to my hooks.' He stepped back, leaving Omar with a taste of the oil that perfumed his skin, and walked over to a perch where his gold cloak, brocaded with inscriptions from the Koran, was hanging.

Omar watched him pull the cloak over his muscular frame. Baybars' appearance had altered little in the six years since he was enthroned as Sultan of Egypt. Other than the few streaks of grey in his hair and beard and the deeper lines on his cheeks, he looked the same. It was on the inside, Omar knew, where most of the changes had taken place.

Omar had hoped, once Baybars' ambition to rule was realised, that the weight of responsibility that came with the position of sultan would temper him. But, as sultan, Baybars had become more determined, violent and unpredictable than ever. Even the birth of his son had done nothing to calm him. Baraka Khan, five years old and heir to the throne, had been born in the year after Baybars' accession. Since then, his father had all but ignored him, saying that he belonged with his mother until he was old enough to be trained to fight the Franks.

Omar knew that his friend was still there, but it was as if Baybars had been split in two. One half of him was still capable of good will; appreciative of beauty and deeply religious, he had restored both Cairo and the caliphate, appointing a Bedouin as leader of Islam. But, more and more, this half was overshadowed by the other, which was ruthless, cunning and utterly merciless.

In the year after his enthronement, Baybars had executed Aqtai and the rest of Kutuz's old supporters and had wrested Aleppo from the governor Kutuz had appointed, under the pretence that the governor had been planning a rebellion. He had gone on to take Damascus, Kerak and Homs from their respective rulers and had made an alliance with one of the Mongol generals, clearing his path to war against the Christians. Since then, he had set out from Cairo at the head of his army, three times, to fall like a hammer upon the Franks.

Omar had no love of the Franks; he wanted them gone as much as anybody and, in war, death was inevitable. But it was the pleasure Baybars had taken in the pain of his victims that troubled Omar. He had feared, more than once, for his friend's soul.

'You have the look of a man weighed down with worries, Omar,' said Baybars, buckling his sword belt at his waist.

'No, sadeek. I'm just tired.'

'If all goes well you should sleep better tonight. I have met with the governors. The regiments are in position. We will focus our attack on the gate, which we damaged during our last strike, and on the outer walls at the other end of the fortress. The simultaneous assaults will stretch and divide their forces, allowing us to get close enough to make a third strike on the central section. If we succeed in breaching the walls a regiment will be standing by to enter the outer enclosure. They will thin the herd before the knights have time to fall back to their keep. I also have another surprise in store for them. It won't kill them, but it will serve to suck their spirit.' Baybars paused, studying Omar's expression. 'You have doubts?'

Omar avoided Baybars' gaze. 'They have repelled us twice already. Can we accomplish this plan without losing a great many more of our men? I wonder whether we should concentrate on a less formidable target? Then, when Amir Kalawun's forces rejoin us from Cilicia we can return at full strength and . . .'

'Kalawun's campaign against the Armenian Christians will take too long for us to wait. Our aim when we set out was to destroy the Franks' seat of power at Acre. We failed in this and the men need a victory. I specifically chose to attack Safed because it is so formidable. Our triumphs over the Franks these past years have been answered with defiance and arrogance. Our enemies are concerned, but they do not truly fear us yet.'

'No?' questioned Omar, remembering the terror on the face of every Christian he had helped to massacre.

'Do you recall, Omar, when I agreed to an exchange of prisoners with the Western barons? The Templars and those they call the Hospitallers refused, saying that the Muslims they held captive were too valuable to them as slaves to be released.' Baybars paced the pavilion, his belligerence rising. 'They haven't taken me seriously yet. But they will. When we have sacked their towns and villages it has been a blow to them, yes, but the fall of one of their greatest fortresses will crush them.' He closed his fist around the air. 'I will prove to them that no fortress and no knight is untouchable.'

Omar went to him and placed a hand on his shoulder. 'I know you will, my lord.'

After a moment, Baybars put his hand over Omar's and nodded. 'Come. It is time.'

The two of them left the pavilion as dawn broke over the Jordan Valley. Joining the rest of the Bahri regiment, they mounted their horses and rode down to the front lines. All the men's eyes were turned to Baybars, the Crossbow, as he rose up in his saddle and lifted his sabre to the sky, his gold cloak flying out in the breeze.

Safed, the Kingdom of Jerusalem, 19 July 1266 AD

James was with a company on the outer walls when he saw the sultan ride down to the front lines.

'Stand ready!' he shouted to the men around him.

The archers fixed their combined gaze on the troops below them, bows taut, and the Syrian soldiers at the mangonel tightened their hold on the ropes that would release the beam. The first rays of sun appeared in the east and heat came washing like a wave across them. James looked southwards to see the mountains flushing pink, then red. These sunrises usually filled him with an immense sense of joy: a feeling that he was standing in God's land, watching a miracle unfurling beneath him. But, now, the distant mountains were a bad omen. There, over seventy years ago, beneath two towers of rock called the Horns of Hattin, the Muslim forces had destroyed a Christian army. Still further south, was the site of the Battle of Herbiya and another Christian defeat. In every direction lay fields and towns, rivers and fords where their forces had been cut down by the defenders of Islam.

James caught the gaze of Mattius, who was standing some distance along the walkway with another company. Mattius raised his sword. James returned the salute, then forced his eyes back to the army.

'God be with us,' he murmured.

The thunderous roar of the Mamluks drowned out his words as the warriors answered their sultan's battle cry. And the first assault crashed like a storm upon Safed.

The mandjaniks were drawn forward, their positions covered by Mamluk archers, who returned volleys of arrows at the soldiers who fired down at them. The missiles hissed through the air from both sides, striking stone, shields, grass and flesh. James ducked as one sailed over the parapet to clatter on the walkway behind him. After the arrows came stones. The beams of the mandjaniks rose and fell, whipping up to strike the crossbars and flinging their loads towards the fortress. Several of the missiles bounced off the walls and crashed, or shattered on the rocks below. One, however, hit the far corner tower at tremendous height and speed and James, some distance away, felt the wall beneath him tremble. The stone fell back to earth, taking a small section of the tower with it. James watched as soldiers, who must have been on the inner staircase, dropped through the fissure. Rock and men smashed on the ground below. James clenched his fists as he saw a sergeant, barely more than a boy, tumbling over and over into the void. He closed his eyes before the boy connected with the rocks beneath. He wanted to shout down over the ramparts and command them all to stop. But gone, for the moment, was any hope of negotiation. They were all in this now. Every man here was fighting for his life.

The cat was rumbling up the path towards the gate, the Mamluks hauling on the ropes. An arrow caught one of the rope-pullers in the neck. He fell back with a shriek, his body falling down the steep hillside, but another was there to take his place. The cat disappeared from James's view as it cleared the distance from the path to the walls. Some moments later, he heard a deep thudding echoing from the barbican. It sounded like a giant pounding a fist upon the gate.

'Sir!'

One of the Syrians was pointing over the parapet. Following the man's gaze, James saw seven mandjaniks being moved across the ground towards the central section, the section he was manning. James's company was one of only three in the immediate vicinity. Most of their forces had been diverted to the gate and the far corner, on which the twenty remaining Mamluk engines were being concentrated. He cursed, then turned to the soldiers, who were looking to him for orders. 'Archers ready,' he said calmly. He nodded to the soldiers at the mangonel beside him. 'Fire when I give the order.' He turned to Mattius to shout a warning, but his comrade had already seen the danger and the company were ready. James looked back at the approaching engines and raised his hand. 'Wait,' he murmured to his men, whilst the mandjaniks were set down and the Mamluk soldiers moved in behind them. 'Wait.' The Mamluks took up the ropes and James dropped his hand. *'Fire!'*

The beam of the engine beside him flew up at almost the same time as the two other mangonels along the wall. Arrows whizzed down in the wake of the three huge stones that went sailing over the parapet. Some of the Mamluks saw them coming and tried to run, but it was too late. One of the stones missed its mark, but the others were direct hits. There was a bright flash of light as a burst of fire erupted across the other mandjaniks and the soldiers manning them. The mandjaniks had been loaded with clay pots filled with Greek fire: a flaming mixture of naphtha, pitch and powdered black sulphur. The fiery matter clung to the other engines, setting them and the men who were manning them alight. The Syrian soldiers on the wall with James roared in jubilation as the Mamluks fell screaming to the ground, clothes, hair and flesh burning.

'*Deus vult!*' they yelled as one. God wills it.

'Dear God,' murmured James. He looked over at Mattius's company, all of whom were revelling in the victory. His friend was yelling the war cry, teeth bared in an ugly grimace. James understood how they felt; it was impossible not to feel triumphant when your life had been spared, even when bought at the price of another's death, but however glad he was to be alive, James could not bring himself to celebrate. Mattius was grinning at him, opening his mouth to call out. James watched his friend's expression change. Mattius's grin vanished. His mouth and eyes opened wider. At the

same time, James heard a soft whistling coming closer. The sound
reminded him, in the second it took for him to turn, of the sudden gusts
of wind that would cascade across the moors near his home in Scotland. His
eyes locked on the large, dark shape flying towards him. They had not
destroyed all of the mandjaniks; one, loaded with a huge stone, was still
operational. James called to the soldiers around him, who were cheering
and punching their fists to the sky, as he turned and ran. His feet moving
nightmarishly slowly, he made it only a few yards when the strike came. He
didn't even have time to cry out as a wave of stone and blood struck his
back, sending him flying. He crashed on his stomach with a winded gasp.
After the thunder of falling masonry, a grisly rain pattered down around
him. Torn limbs with shreds of clothing still attached, a hand, shards of
bone and gristle; it was all that was left of the Syrian soldiers. James turned
his head to one side, the stone grazing his cheek. He tried to lift himself up
on his hands, then collapsed.

He didn't know how long he lay there. Later he was told it was only
moments, but it felt like a lifetime before strong hands grasped his arms and
lifted him to his feet. 'Am I dead?' he asked of the man whose white-
bearded face swum into his vision.

'Not yet, praise be to God.'

James's head began to clear. He turned to the man whose arm was tight
around him, leading him, half dragging him, along the walkway. He
swallowed with difficulty. His mouth and throat were coated with dust.
'Mattius,' he groaned. 'What happened?'

Mattius continued pulling him. 'Not here. We have to get you to the
infirmary.'

'No.' James came to a stumbling halt. 'No,' he said again more firmly.
He removed Mattius's arm from his shoulders and leaned against the
parapet. 'I'm fine.'

Below him, the arrows and stones were still flying up from the field at
the other end of the fortress, but with six of the seven mandjaniks now
smouldering, the Mamluks were unable to mount an effective assault on the
central section.

'I'm no physician,' replied Mattius, putting a hand on his shoulder, 'but
fine isn't a diagnosis I would offer a man drenched in blood.'

James looked down and saw that his mantle was no longer white, but red
and torn. 'The blood isn't mine,' he said, turning to where he had been
standing with the soldiers. He murmured a prayer as he realised how lucky
he was to be alive.

There was a gaping hole in the side of the parapet. Around it the edges of the stones were jagged, as if some huge beast had taken a bite out of the wall. Masonry and corpses were scattered across the walkway, some of it having fallen outwards, some into the compound below. The Mamluks had breached the wall, but not in any place that was of use to them. James winced as Mattius let go of his shoulder and saw, through a tear in his mantle, that a shard of stone was embedded in his upper arm.

Mattius followed his gaze. 'That looks bad, James. Come on. I'll take you to the infirmary.' A cry rose from the walls above the gate. Mattius leaned out over the parapet. 'We've caught the cat!'

They peered over the walls to see a company of Mamluks running down the path. The grappling team had succeeded in attaching their hooks to the ram. They would have yanked it up to make it unusable and then, from the black plume of smoke, it appeared that they had smoked out the Mamluks under the cat's roof by lowering burning bales of tow coated in sulphur. Mattius and James watched as most of the fleeing Mamluk soldiers dropped to the ground, pierced by Frankish arrows.

Another cry rose, this time from the Mamluk camp. The front lines of archers began to withdraw.

'They are retreating,' said Mattius. 'Go on, you *bastards*!'

'Wait,' said James, putting a hand on his arm. 'Look.'

The mandjaniks at the far side of the fortress were being reloaded. James and Mattius watched on in silence as the Mamluks let fire their last barrage of the morning. This time it wasn't stones that came flying over the walls, but bodies. Thirty corpses of the Christians they had captured from the outlying villages rained down into the compound. Beneath the outer walls, screams sounded from the peasants who were barracked in the outer enceinte as the bodies smashed down around them. Each had been painted with a red cross, in mockery of the Christians inside.

Outside the Walls of Safed, the Kingdom of Jerusalem, 19 July 1266 AD

Baybars ripped off his sword belt as he entered the pavilion. His gaze fell on the eunuchs who came forward to remove his cloak. '*Get out!*' he roared.

The attendants fled.

'My lord,' said Omar, watching as Baybars strode onto the platform and sat in his throne, hands curling around the lions' heads. 'All is not lost. It's only our third assault.'

'I wanted it done today.'

'Their hides are thick.'

'If our engines hadn't been hit, Safed would have fallen.' Baybars tapped the lions' heads with his fingers. 'They used their forces well.' He shook his head. 'Like a boar uses its tusks.'

'We could send in the nakkabun? The hill is bound to be riddled with tunnels. We could sabotage them from beneath.'

'No. It will take too long to mine under their walls.' Baybars continued tapping the lions' heads, but slower now. 'We must come at this boar from behind, rather than risk being mauled again. We will find its soft spot and strike.' He rose and jumped down from the platform. 'And I have an idea of where that soft spot might be.' Baybars headed for the pavilion entrance. 'Summon the governors,' he barked at one of the Bahri, who was standing guard outside. 'And bring me the heralds.'

Safed, the Kingdom of Jerusalem, 19 July 1266 AD

James flinched as the Syrian physician drew the stone shard from his skin. The wound had already begun to close and the blood flowed thickly down his arm as the thin scab was torn away. The physician handed him a wad of linen and moved off. The courtyard outside the infirmary was noisy with soldiers, most of whose wounds were minor: abrasions; the odd burn; arrow scratches. Those who were badly injured were in the infirmary proper. James clamped the linen over his arm to stem the blood. He sat back against the wall and picked up the shard the physician had dropped.

'You should save it,' said Mattius, handing him a jar of wine. 'Take it home and show it to your grandchildren.'

James smiled and stuck the stone in the pouch at his belt. 'I will give it to my son.' He leaned his head on the wall and stared up into the sky, which was turning a deep, perfect shade of blue. The afternoon had been spent clearing the debris, carrying the wounded through to the inner enceinte, assessing the damage and overseeing repairs. He would have stayed on the walls for longer, but Mattius had threatened to pick him up and carry him to the infirmary if he didn't go of his own accord. The only signs of life that had come from the Mamluk camp since the battle were the singsong chanting of prayers.

The blood on James's mantle was sticky. He longed to retire to his quarters, but their duties weren't over yet. After Vespers, he and Mattius would take first watch on the walls.

'Do you think they will attack again tonight?'

James saw a Syrian soldier staring at them, the fear apparent in his eyes. 'No,' he told the man, 'it will take them a few days to regroup and plan their next move.' He looked up as he was hailed and saw the commander heading over with six knights. James rose as he saw the look on the commander's face.

'We have trouble,' murmured the commander, coming to a halt.

'What is it, sir?' asked Mattius, standing beside James.

The commander glanced round at the Syrian soldiers who were talking amongst themselves. When he spoke his voice was low. 'Baybars has sent a herald. He has offered unconditional amnesty to all native soldiers who surrender to him. He has given them two nights to decide whether to leave and go free, or stay here with us and die.'

'Christ and the Saints,' muttered Mattius.

'Within the hour,' continued the commander, 'everyone here will have heard what he has promised. Unless we can maintain order, we may be facing an insurrection come morning.'

19

The Temple, Paris

20 July 1266 AD

T he solar was hot and airless. The small group of knights seated around the room sweated inside their woollen cloaks and tried not to fidget. Only Everard, perched on his stool like a hooded buzzard in black cloak and cowl, seemed unaffected by the heat. He was, however, impatient to know the reason for the summons to the Visitor's chambers, which had come whilst he was on the verge of translating a complex section of a Greek text which had been perplexing him for several weeks.

General day-to-day business was discussed in the weekly chapter with all brothers present. A private meeting between a few selected knights called without warning or explanation was, so far as Everard could remember, unheard of. He had tried to guess the nature of it by who else was in attendance, but the five knights, although high-ranking, were otherwise quite ordinary. If he had to put a finger on the anomaly in the company it would fall on himself.

Everard and the knights looked round as the door opened and a servant carrying a tray of goblets and a jug of wine entered. Behind came the Visitor, tall and dignified, his trident-shaped beard flecked with white. With the Visitor was a young man, not much past twenty, the sight of whom caused Everard to sit up with a frown. The young man had a plain, lean face and solemn, dog-like eyes. His black robe was soiled and patched, his feet were bare and dusty and from his neck hung a large wooden cross. He looked like a common beggar, but held the authority of a lord. He was a Dominican: a Hound of God, and an inquisitor.

'Good afternoon, brothers,' greeted the Visitor, closing the door once the servant had left. He motioned the Dominican to an empty stool near the table. 'Please sit, Friar Gilles.'

The young man smiled soberly. 'I will stand.'

The Visitor's expression didn't change. 'As you wish.' He walked around the large table and seated himself in the throne-like chair behind, leaving the Dominican standing erect and at ease in the centre of the gathered knights. 'I apologise for the lack of warning for this council,' said the Visitor, addressing the knights, 'but Friar Gilles cannot stay for long. He came to inform me of this matter in private, but agreed to continue our discussion in your presence, as your services may be required.' The Visitor looked at Everard. 'I wanted you here in an advisory capacity, Brother Everard, considering your field of expertise.'

Everard said nothing, but his frown deepened.

'If you please, Friar Gilles,' said the Visitor, motioning to the Dominican.

Gilles moved slightly so that he could be seen by all of the knights. He swept them with his intent gaze and Everard scowled. Gilles was obviously well practised in oration, no doubt fresh, thought the priest contemptuously, from theology classes at the University of Paris. With their high rhetoric and aggressive stance, the Dominican Friars were more like lawyers than priests.

'For the last few months,' began Gilles, 'my Order has been investigating a troubadour, who has been travelling through the south of the kingdom, making a name for himself with performances of a so-called Grail Romance based on the story of Perceval.'

'Do you mean Pierre de Pont-Evêque?'

It was Nicolas de Navarre who had spoken.

'You have heard of him, brother?' inquired the Visitor, looking to Nicolas.

'In passing,' replied Nicolas. 'The Romances are an interest of mine,' he explained.

Gilles fixed his dog-eyes on the black-haired knight. 'Then you might be interested to know that we plan to arrest him for heresy.'

'Heresy?'

'When one of our houses in the south learnt of the profanities the troubadour had been expressing during his performance, they contacted the head of our Order here in Paris. We petitioned the Court of Aquitaine, where the troubadour had been invited to perform, and managed to have him banned. Some of my brothers were hoping to apprehend him there, but he must have been warned away for he never arrived. We have recently learnt that King Louis has invited him to perform at the royal court in the autumn.' Gilles' smooth brow puckered. 'On a holy day no less. We have petitioned the king to retract that invitation, but he has declined to heed our advice. Word has been sent to our brothers throughout the kingdom that de Pont-Evêque is to be seized, but it is a large country and we are still few for the extent of our assignment. If we do not manage to arrest the troubadour beforehand we will do so when he arrives at the palace. And that,' Gilles said to the knights, 'is when we will call on your assistance. If the Temple supports us in this matter, the king will be forced to yield to our joint authority.'

Everard stirred. 'Grail Romances can occasionally seem, to the sensitive ear, overly ribald, but the code of conduct prevents troubadours from overstepping the bounds of decency. I am frankly amazed that this is a matter for the inquisitors. Do the Hounds of God have nothing better to do than chase a common mummer?'

'Brother Everard,' reproved the Visitor.

Gilles held up his hand. 'No, Brother Everard is right. Usually we would not concern ourselves with such a seemingly petty affair. But this case falls entirely within our remit. Pierre de Pont-Evêque's performance is more than ribald, as I said it is heretical. Within it he speaks of men beating, spitting and urinating on the cross and drinking one another's blood from the Communion chalice. There are whole sections of his performance that describe heathen rites: sorcery; idolatry; animal and human sacrifices and other hideous practices too ungodly to mention.' His eyes swept the room. 'You may remember that we found thousands of Cathars to be guilty of such depravities during our purification of their sect. Pierre de Pont-Evêque has attracted quite a following in the southern regions, regions, I might add, where the Cathar heresies first flourished. He doesn't observe the code of conduct and yet his flouting of the rules hasn't made him unpopular, on the contrary, he has become famed and admired for it. Peasants, in our experience, tend to be drawn to vulgar material like flies to dung and it is our duty, as men of God, to ensure the safety of their souls by not allowing them to be polluted by such malfeasance. I should not have to remind you that before we suppressed their sect, the Cathars had begun to rival the Church in popularity. If we had not acted as decisively as we had, God alone knows how many of the flock would have been lost to their Gnosticism.

'We were established by our founder, St Dominic, specifically to root out the Cathars. Since his death, our numbers and mandate have grown considerably. Our Order is now the front line in the war against heresy. We are responsible for keeping Christendom free from harmful practices and ideas, however innocuous,' said Gilles, his cold gaze flicking to

Everard, 'they may seem to others. It is in the Temple's best interests that this man be stopped.'

Another of the knights spoke up. 'I'm sure no one in this room would dispute whether or not this troubadour, if what you've said is correct, should be stopped. But why in the Temple's best interests?'

'That is simply answered,' replied Gilles, looking down at the knight. 'He has based his performance on an Order of knights who lead Perceval through a series of progressively iniquitous initiations. These knights are described as wearing white mantles adorned with red crosses.'

A few of the Templars stirred uneasily. Everard wiped a hand across his brow. He was sweating.

'So you plan to arrest him when he arrives in Paris?' asked Nicolas.

'Yes.'

'Is there any evidence to charge him with?'

Gilles arched an eyebrow. 'Apart from the thousands of people who have witnessed him uttering these profanities?' He paused. 'Actually, yes. It is something we have only recently discovered. We do not believe Pierre de Pont-Evêque wrote this Romance himself. Ten years ago, he held a position at the royal court, but he wasn't a popular performer and the king dismissed him. Our sources say it is doubtful he has the skill to have written such an . . .' Gilles gritted his teeth '. . . articulate piece. We do know, however, that he is in possession of a book, which he reads from during part of his performance. He claims to have been given it by an angel who took it from a sealed vault beneath the Church of the Holy Sepulchre in Jerusalem. Blasphemy, of course, but we suspect that this book is where he has gleaned much of his material from. The book will be the evidence with which we will prosecute. It may even be a vestige of the Cathars.'

'Do you have a description for this book?' asked the Visitor.

'It is well made, bound in vellum. The words inside have apparently been written in red lead, whilst its title is in gold leaf.'

'Title?' enquired Everard queasily.

Gilles looked at him. 'Yes. It is called the Book of the Grail.'

'Have you heard of it, brother?' the Visitor asked Everard.

Everard cleared his throat. 'No. No, I haven't.'

'Well, this is deeply disturbing,' said the Visitor, sitting back. 'The Temple relies on donations from kings and nobles from many countries. We wouldn't want to lose those endorsements by having our reputation tarnished in any way, particularly with the East so unsettled at present.'

He turned to Gilles. 'In this matter, Friar, you have the Temple's full support.'

Two hours later, Everard, who had given up any attempt at working on his translation and had resorted to stalking about his chamber, huffed with relief as there was a knock at his door. A moment later, the door opened and a figure dressed in grey entered.

'I was beginning to think you weren't coming,' said Everard irritably, crossing to a small table by the window. He picked up a goblet and gave it a quick wipe with the hem of his robe.

'I came as fast as I could,' said Hasan, closing the door. 'What is it, brother?' he asked, watching Everard pour a goblet of wine, spilling some, the priest's hand, with its missing fingers, clumsy.

'It looks like you were right,' said Everard abruptly.

Hasan looked nonplussed.

'About the troubadour. Hang it all!' Everard sat heavily on the window seat. 'Sit, Hasan, you've known me too long to stand on ceremony.'

'Far too long,' said Hasan with a slight smile as he sat beside the priest. 'Tell me what this is about.'

Everard told Hasan about the meeting with the Dominican. 'I should have sent you after the troubadour weeks ago when you came to tell me about him.'

'There was no proof that his Romance had anything to do with your code then. There were only similarities, according to what my sources told me. It made sense that you wanted to wait for further confirmation.'

'And now,' said Everard, 'the inquisitors will be after him.'

'From what you said, it sounds as if they will be focused on seizing de Pont-Evêque when he arrives in Paris, not trying to find him beforehand.'

Everard grunted, but looked a little eased.

'How do you think the troubadour came to possess the Book of the Grail?' asked Hasan.

'I can only assume he must be the one who coerced the clerk to steal it from our vaults.'

Hasan looked unconvinced. 'We thought at the time that whoever stole it must have known of the Anima Templi and our plans. That was the fear; that whoever had taken it would use it as evidence against us. If the inquisitors are correct, then the troubadour has just adapted parts of the code for use in a Grail Romance. That does not seem like the actions of someone who wants to expose, or undermine us, particularly if he is not trying to tie it to the Temple; stating, according to what I have been told, that an angel gave it to him.'

'I don't understand it any better than you, Hasan, but if this troubadour was responsible for its theft and does have knowledge of us he could provide the Dominicans with fatal information if caught. They have some very persuasive methods for inducing confession.' Everard rose and paced the chamber agitatedly. 'You should have heard Friar Gilles.' His face twisted in anger. 'Anything they don't agree with and they call it heresy! You would have thought it was the Dominicans, not God, who wrote the Bible. All those burnt at the stake for having a different opinion to that of the Church? It is they who should burn!' Everard's cheeks were flushed, his scar a hectic red. His voice was rising. 'How many more fathers and sons must be sent into battle for their arrogance? How many wives must be widowed, children orphaned, in the service of our God?' He shook his head. 'The service of *their* pockets.'

'Brother,' said Hasan, trying to calm him.

Everard turned on him. 'Who else would have done what the Anima Templi has done, Hasan? No one, I tell you. They are all too wrapped up in their own desires and politics and opinions. Even our own Order.' Everard's voice quietened a little. 'If the Dominicans seize our book and find out about our plans they will destroy us. What we hope to achieve goes against everything the Church and, indeed, everyone in Christendom believes in. They wouldn't understand, Hasan. As well you know.'

'We have a few months before de Pont-Evêque is due in the city. It is plenty of time.'

'This troubadour must be found. For all its strength, I'm not certain even the Temple would be able to stand against the inquisitors and expect to remain unscathed. The pope might be the only power on this Earth the Order answers to, but the Dominicans have his ear.' Everard went to a large chest, from which he took a pouch of coins. 'If this de Pont-Evêque has the Book of the Grail, then take it from him.' He handed Hasan the pouch. 'And if he was responsible for its theft . . .'

'I understand, brother,' Hasan cut across him. 'The troubadour will not reach Paris.' He paused at the door. 'There is something I have been wanting to mention. It now seems pertinent.'

'What is it?'

Hasan hesitated.

Everard frowned. 'If you have something to say, Hasan, then say it.'

'Your sergeant. I have been thinking that you should involve him. We could certainly use more help and now I am back in Paris, I will no doubt cross paths with him. When I came here last, he still treated me with suspicion.'

Everard waved his hand. 'He is just curious. I'm sure he doesn't suspect anything. I told him the same as I've told anyone who has asked. You're a converted Christian who helps me track down Arabic manuscripts for translation. And why should anyone question that? It is a common enough sight in Acre. The preceptory there employs Arab secretaries.'

'Forgive me if I speak out of turn, but Campbell has served you faithfully for six years, even though you have kept him from his inception, without cause.'

'The initiation isn't something to be rushed, much as all young men seem to think it is these days.'

'You told me how invaluable he has become to you.'

'Campbell's training isn't finished,' said Everard shortly. 'And until I have decided he is ready, he is to have no part in this.'

'He will never be able to prove himself unless you give him a chance. You are holding him back. He could be useful to you. To us. I know James would be pleased for him to be invited into the circle. And, brother,' continued Hasan gently, 'you are not as young as you think you are. Who will continue the work here when you are gone? I cannot. Not in the West. Our work – the gathering and dissemination of knowledge – is important, but you must soon return to the East. The others need their master, especially now the conflict grows there. More must be chosen and elected.'

'You do not need to remind me of this, Hasan,' said Everard tiredly. 'Had the book not been stolen I would have gone back to Acre years ago. I know I am needed there and that others must be found to replace those we have lost. But it is for my sergeant's own good that I've kept silent. Once a man becomes one of the Brethren, he can never live completely in this world. He will always feel apart from it.'

'Or is it that you have kept our secrets for so long you fear to let them go? Be careful that you do not hold our ideals so close that you smother them.' Hasan pulled his cowl over his head. 'You got burned by Grand Master Armand. I understand that, brother. But it is time to forget the past and look to the future. The Brethren's aims will only be realised if there are men to uphold them. If no new members are recruited, the Anima Templi will die with this generation.'

The sun was almost down by the time Will finished the translation. He had been closeted in the dormitory all day and his hand was cramped, aching. Setting down his quill, he gathered up the two bound sheaves of parchment, the pages of one covered with a neat, flowing text, the other crowded with dark-brown lines written in his own blunt hand, and left the dormitory. Will had been working on the Arabic treatise for weeks, labouring long into the night by the light of a single candle, the scratching of his quill out of time with the snores of his fellows. Because of his haste today, the ink on the last few pages was smudged and some of the lines a little askew. He had been planning to decorate it with one of the intricate borders Everard favoured, but after meeting Simon yesterday, he had been filled with a sense of urgency. The finished treatise provided a good excuse with which to confront the priest.

Will made his way from the sergeants' buildings. The sky was blood red and the air was humid, stagnant. Approaching the main yard, he saw a figure in grey walking towards the donjon. Will slowed his pace, his gaze on Hasan, who was striding along the passage that led past the donjon to the preceptory's entrance. After a few moments, Hasan disappeared from view. With a frown, Will continued. Reaching the knights' quarters, he went to push open the door, but it swung inwards before he touched it. A knight came out, almost knocking into him. It was Garin de Lyons.

Garin stepped back. 'William.' He said nothing further and the two of them studied one another in silence.

Garin looked older than his nineteen years, older and handsome. His beard was a darker blond than his hair, which was as golden as ever. Reflected in Garin's dark-blue eyes, Will saw himself: black tunic stained and crumpled; scuffed boots; hair hanging in his eyes. When the silence became unbearable, he forced himself to smile and extend his hand. 'Simon told me you had come. It's been a while.'

Garin took his hand after a pause. 'It has. Are you well?'

'Yes. You?'

'Yes.'

There was another long pause.

'How's London?' asked Will, unable to think of anything else to say.

'Dirty, smelly, crowded.' The corner of Garin's mouth twitched in a smile. 'The same as ever.'

'What are you doing here?' Will realised that the words had come out more forcefully than he'd intended.

'I requested a transfer. There are very few opportunities for advancement in London. I have more chance of becoming a commander here under the Visitor.' Garin's eyes flicked briefly to Will's tunic. 'Now that I'm a knight. I hear you are working as a scribe?'

Will managed to keep any sign of shame from his face. 'Yes, my master, Everard, is a priest here.'

'Everard?' Garin frowned. There was a look of recognition and something else, perhaps resentment, on his face.

'Do you know him?'

Garin shook his head and the look vanished. 'No. I was thinking of someone else. Well.' He moved past. 'I have a meeting with the Visitor. I'd better go.'

'Listen, Garin,' said Will quickly. 'I know it was years ago, but I never did tell you that I was sorry for hitting you that day. That day in the graveyard.'

'It is forgotten.' Garin paused. 'We both did things back then we regret.' He nodded to Will, then swept off, the hems of his white mantle sweeping the ground.

Will watched Garin go. He rolled his shoulders, surprised by how tense he felt. It was a shock to see his former friend looking so much older. It didn't seem so long ago that they were climbing trees and stealing fruit in New Temple.

When he reached Everard's room, Will rapped on the door three times and waited for the summons. Everard had given him his own knock a long time ago. It was, he had decided, just another of the priest's methods for keeping him in his place.

After a pause, came a rasping voice from within, 'Enter.'

Everard was one of only a handful of men who had their own private solar and Will had never been able to discover why the priest had been afforded the luxury. On the back wall, above a narrow bed, was painted a map of the Holy Land, with Jerusalem at the centre and above it, the cities of Acre and Antioch. Whenever Will looked at the painting he was reminded of a knight in New Temple speaking of Antioch; one of the five most holy sees of Christendom, where the first Christians had worshipped in secret services led by St Peter himself. The knight had spoken of a vast city, overflowing with riches and encircled by walls eighteen miles long, with a citadel raised so high on a mountaintop that it touched the clouds. Will hadn't believed that something could be so high as to touch clouds but the first time he had seen the painting, with the castle rising from a mountain, he had thought that it might have been true after all.

Everard was sitting at the table where he worked at his translations, hunched over a book, his threads of white hair drifting like broken cobwebs about his face. A single candle spluttered in the faint breeze that came in around the edges of the tapestry covering the window. The priest glanced up as Will shut the door, scowled, then returned to his study of the pages. 'What do you want, sergeant?'

Will held out the parchments. 'My translation of Ibn Ismail's treatise. I've finished it.'

Everard continued reading for several moments longer, then put the book down and beckoned to Will. 'Give it to me.'

'Why is Hasan here, sir?'

'He is running an errand for me.' Everard snapped his fingers. 'Come on, come on!'

Will was curious as to why Hasan was in Paris: he hadn't seen the man for over a year, but he could tell that he wasn't going to get an answer out of Everard tonight. The priest seemed in a fouler mood than usual. Will lingered by the door, thinking that perhaps this wasn't the best moment to talk to the priest about his initiation. But Everard was waiting. Will walked over and handed him the parchments.

Everard placed the original copy carefully on the table, then flicked brusquely through Will's translation. He glanced at the original.

'I was wanting to speak with you about something, sir,' began Will.

'Tell me what the Arabic word *asal* means, sergeant.'

'What?'

Everard looked up at him.

'Honey,' answered Will, after a pause.

'Then why is it that instead of *honey* mixed with oil of olives and cloves, your work states that oil of olives mixed with wing of buzzard is a suitable cure for fever?' Everard raised an eyebrow. 'I may not be an expert in such remedies, but I would be most sceptical of the abatement of any fever should I be plied with such a broth.'

'I did tell you the text was barely readable.'

'Perhaps by the light of day the words might have been clearer. I do not doubt it will be riddled with such errors, knowing, as I do, that you hastened through this translation when it was probably too dark for you to see past the end of your nose.' Everard tossed the parchment at Will's feet. 'Do it again.'

In that moment, Will wanted to strike the priest down. He forced himself to speak calmly. 'I spent hours on this transl—'

'Were you in an alehouse yesterday, sergeant?'

'What? No.'

'How odd. I was speaking with the Visitor when a young man, a groom, came to report his arrival from London. I overheard him talking to the Marshal. He seemed most excited about meeting his old comrade, Will Campbell, in the city and, one might say, rather drunk. And we both know, sergeant, how fond you are of a potation.' Everard flicked his hand towards the door. 'Go. Leave me.'

'Why can you *never* finish a conversation!'

Everard looked startled at Will's shout, then he slammed his hand down, making the small table rock. 'You seem to have forgotten who is the master and who the apprentice!' He rose to his feet and took a few stuttering steps towards Will. 'I whipped you once, boy. I'm quite prepared to do so again.'

Will stood his ground. 'Do you think that one instance of agony could compare to six years in your service?'

Everard's eyes widened, then he gave a harsh bark of laughter that caused him to succumb to a coughing fit. 'Well,' he spat through the spasms, 'if . . . whipping be too lenient a . . . punishment perhaps you should be . . .' He took a long rattling breath. '. . . sent to some Godforsaken desert garrison on the front line of war!'

'Do you mean the front line my father is fighting on? If so, then please send me there. It wouldn't be a punishment. It would be a blessing.'

Everard grasped the edge of the table. Beads of sweat glistened on his forehead, making his skin look like melting tallow. 'Foolish boy,' he whispered. 'You haven't seen war. Haven't stood on a battlefield with your arms on fire from the weight of your sword, drenched in the blood of your comrades, not knowing when that final strike will deliver you to the Kingdom.'

'I was thirteen when I killed a man,' murmured Will.

'Nothing you have seen, or done in your short life could *possibly* prepare you.' Everard slumped in his chair.

'Then teach me,' said Will, going to the priest. He planted his hands on the table, the divide between them seeming so much greater than the two feet of wood. 'Tell me how to prepare. I *want* to know.'

'No,' muttered Everard, turning the page of his book with a trembling hand. His missing fingers ended in their withered stumps. 'You aren't ready to know.'

'What is it that I have done to deserve your scorn? Have I wronged you in some way? If I have then please tell me how I can make it right. All I've ever wanted is to stand at my father's side as a Knight of the Temple. Why would you keep me from this? I don't understand. What have you got to gain by it?'

Everard didn't reply.

'I've done everything you've asked of me,' continued Will hoarsely. He was horrified to feel tears prickling in his eyes, but he pushed on. 'I've swept your floor and cleaned your chamber when you could have had the servants do it for you. I've sent messages, fetched and carried for you. I've translated God knows how many badly written, indecipherable, boring treatises on . . .' Will snatched up the book Everard was reading. '*Understanding the Curious Nature of Rain*. Christ!' He tossed the book onto the table.

'And how,' spat Everard, 'have you performed these duties? In good grace? Without complaint?'

'If I complained it was because I was supposed to be training for knighthood. You gave me no choice but to be your scribe. It was either that, or leave the Temple. It didn't mean I had to like it!'

'Ha!' Everard jabbed a finger at him. 'So it's all down to your position under me is it? What about your former master? Did you obey and respect Sir Owein? Never utter any objection of his demands on you?'

Will looked away. 'I was young then. I've changed.' He looked back at Everard. 'You know I have.'

'Your trouble,' growled Everard, 'is that you think yourself better than anyone else. Too good to clean a floor, that's what you think you are. I knew it the moment I laid eyes on you. Here is a haughty little lord who is used to getting his own way, I said to myself!'

'That isn't true! I'm the son of a merchant's daughter and knight whose father paid for his admittance to the Temple and I'm proud of it. When I lived with my family, I did every chore I was given gladly.'

'And you are still proud!' shouted Everard. 'That's why you're angry at being kept from your inception. Wounded pride!'

'No! That isn't . . .'

'You look to knighthood as a source of elevation. You hate that you are beneath your friends.'

'It is hard, yes, but it isn't the reason I want to take the vows. I told you, my father—'

'Your father! *Your father!*' Everard threw up his hands. 'He isn't here, boy! Why do you want to be a knight? If not for your father, if not to be in the same position as your friends? Why do *you* want to be a knight?' When Will didn't reply, Everard shook his head. 'Then why,' he said quietly, 'should I put you forward for initiation?'

Will stood there staring at Everard's wizened face, the silence loud in his ears. All he wanted was to see his father, to beg for forgiveness and be a son again. Since the death of his sister he had felt severed – from his family, from his position in the Temple. For the past seven years, the one thing that had kept him going was the thought of re-establishing that connection, if he did that then everything else would, he believed, fall into place. He would be a knight, like his father had wanted, he could move on from the past, begin again with a clean slate, stainless, sinless. The only thing standing in his way was this frail, unrelenting old man in front of him.

Slowly, Will bent to pick up his translation from the floor. Rising, he met Everard's gaze. 'Because if you don't put me forward, I will go to the Visitor and petition him to send me to Safed.' Will was surprised at the composed determination in his own voice. 'I'll say I want to fight the Saracens, that I want to take the Cross for God and for Christendom. Men are always needed out there. If you refuse to allow me to go there as a knight, I will go there as a sergeant.'

'Don't be ridiculous!' scoffed Everard.

But Will was walking away. He left the chamber, slamming the door so hard the frame splintered.

20

Safed, the Kingdom of Jerusalem

21 July 1266 AD

J ames watched the soldiers filing into the Great Hall. As his eyes fixed on
the Syrian captain at the front of the line of men he knew that they were
in trouble. The captain's expression was one of grave resolution. He
didn't look at any of the thirty knights who were seated on a row of benches
on the hall's dais, but strode stiffly to the seats that had been placed on the
floor opposite where he sat with his officers. Fifty Templar sergeants and
four priests were sitting in rows at the side of the chamber. The Syrian
soldiers who had been called to the meeting filled the empty seats around
them. James turned to Mattius who was sitting beside him. The large knight
raised an eyebrow as if to say, this will be interesting. On his other side
James heard the commander sigh.

As the commander had predicted, Baybars' promise of amnesty for the
Syrian soldiers had caused an almost immediate upheaval within the ranks.
The commander had called a council yesterday morning, after word had
spread, to pacify the situation. But the meeting had not gone well and
they'd had to adjourn when tempers began to fray and the discussion turned
into a shouting match. James knew that they needed more time; the soldiers
were still too stirred up from the Mamluks' last assault to think calmly
about this. But by first light tomorrow Baybars would demand an answer to
his offer and the knights only had today to convince the Syrians to stay and
fight.

When the last man was seated the commander rose to his feet. His face
was marked with weariness, his eyes sunken, his cheeks showing pale
through his sun-browned skin, but he held himself erect and his gaze was
stern as he turned his attention to the Syrian captain.

'Captain, let us hope that sleep has served to sweeten our tongues.' He
raked the rest of the company with his stare. 'I suggest we talk with our
heads, rather than our hearts.'

'None of us desires a quarrel, Commander,' said the captain. 'I only wish to do right by my men.'

'And I by mine.'

There was silence.

The commander sat down. 'Perhaps you should begin, Captain, by explaining why you believe you should accept Baybars' proposal.'

'Very well,' said the captain after a pause. He rose. 'As I said yesterday, accepting Baybars' terms of surrender will be our best chance for survival. If Safed falls we face death, or imprisonment. I have sixteen hundred men here. I will not see them butchered when they can be saved by this opportunity.'

The commander raised his hand to silence the murmurs from the knights and the scattered calls of consent from the Syrian troops. 'What makes you think Baybars will keep his word? You said yourself, he has none of Saladin's honour. What makes you so certain he won't kill you all as soon as you leave the fortress?'

'I also told you, Commander, that I have studied the sultan's tactics. He only destroys those who pose a threat to him, or those who challenge him. We are no great threat without a stronghold and when others have surrendered to him he has kept his word. If we do not accept his first offer he will be enraged by our defiance. I do not believe we will get a second chance.'

'It was not so at Arsuf,' said the commander. 'Baybars broke his promise then. He butchered two hundred Hospitallers, who all believed, as you, that they would be saved by surrendering.'

The captain looked at the floor, then back up at the commander. 'They were Franks,' he said quietly. 'Baybars had more of a quarrel with them than he does with us.'

One of the knights on the dais stood. 'Now we see your true face, *Captain*! You and your men might fight for the same God as us, but I think it fair to say that when He was giving out courage He had reached the bottom of the barrel by the time He got to the Syrians!'

'Peace, brother!' ordered the commander, as the captain's face twisted in a scowl and several of his officers leapt to their feet. 'Sit!' he barked at the knight, who did so grudgingly, eyes fixed on the captain. 'Insults afford us nothing but delay. We don't have time to sit and squabble like children!' He turned to the captain. 'If we stay here without your forces, we cannot hope to withstand another assault. Safed is too large to be garrisoned effectively by a handful of men, however stalwart. Together we are strong, but divide us and we will fall. We are well provisioned and we can fend off this siege for many months to come. If we have faith, God will see us victorious.' His eyes bored into the captain's. 'As one soldier to another, Captain, and as a warrior of Christ, I implore you to stand with us against the infidel.'

The Syrian captain glanced at his men, whose eyes all reflected the same fear, the same doubt he felt inside himself. They were good men, but they didn't have the zeal of the Western knights. And neither did he. The knights were on their blind Crusade, stamping righteously across the lands in their quest to annihilate the infidel. Like giants they came, stepping on everything in their path without even noticing what they destroyed, for they and their cause were too lofty for them to see what was crushed beneath their feet. They saw it as God's land. But, to him, it was his peoples' land, their only land, and every village that was ruined, every man, woman and child who was killed for this cause was a loss to them all. They were not backward peasants with no will, or wit of their own who needed to be taught a better way of serving God or themselves by these cavalier foreigners. They could make their own decisions. The captain raised his head. 'I cannot accept your request, Commander. It is suicide.'

The commander hung his head as around him the hall erupted.

'Your heart hasn't been in this from the start!' one of the knights shouted at the Syrians. 'Even before Baybars' offer you were cowering before the prospect of battle.'

'The captain has made his decision,' one of the Syrian officers responded. 'You have no right to challenge him! Did you summon us here to parley, or to beat us down until we submitted to your will?'

'Baybars is not invincible, I tell you!'

'We do not have to stay and listen to this, Captain.'

'Leave then,' yelled one of the Templar sergeants, forgetting his place. 'We don't need half-breeds like you!'

Some of the Syrians on the benches stood, drawing their swords. A Templar priest was trying to make himself heard above the din, but he was being shouted down by both the Syrians and the Templar sergeants, a few of whom had drawn their own weapons and were advancing on the native soldiers. The commander was bellowing at them to stand down, but no one was listening anymore. A brawl began near the back of the hall as one sergeant turned and punched a Syrian who was trying to get away from the youths with the blades. The soldier sprawled on the floor, his nose bloodied. Three of his comrades leapt over him and tackled the sergeant, who had delivered the blow, to the ground.

James rose. 'We're doing exactly what Baybars wants! This is what he intended by . . .!' He trailed off, his words drowned in the clamour.

'*Silence!*'

The roar was followed by a resounding crash that echoed around the hall. The shouters and brawlers halted, mid-sentence and mid-punch. All eyes turned to Mattius, who was on his feet beside James. The knight's face was scarlet and his eyes were blazing. The crashing sound had been made by his fist hitting the board. He turned to James. 'Please continue, brother,' he said calmly into the hush.

James gave a half-smile. 'Thank you, Mattius.' He addressed the Syrian captain. 'Baybars has sent this offer because he knows that he cannot take Safed swiftly by force of arms. Captain, I appreciate your obligation to your men, but you will be playing right into Baybars' hands if you accept his terms. The sultan seeks the quickest, easiest and cheapest route to victory. It's the hottest part of the year and his men are already weary. The longer he remains here the harder it will become for him to maintain his army. If we force him to draw out the siege and stretch his resources he will turn aside in search of a weaker target.' He glanced at the commander. 'With the commander's permission, I propose that we bring this council to a close.' When the commander gave a tired nod, James turned back to the captain. 'I suggest you and your officers retire to discuss this matter in private, Captain. Then, in a few hours, meet with the commander alone to continue this parley. Make your decision, but make it when tempers are less heated.'

There were a few calls of disagreement from the Syrians, but the captain inclined his head. 'I will meet with you alone, Commander, as your man asks. But I don't believe that time will change my mind.'

James sat as the meeting began to disperse, the sergeants shooting black looks at the backs of the departing Syrians and muttering amongst themselves. 'I hope you don't think me presumptuous, sir,' he said to the commander.

The commander gave him a brief smile. 'You spoke well, brother. We may still have an opportunity to salvage this. If I meet with the captain alone, I believe I have a chance to persuade him to see sense.' He rose. 'I want those brawlers disciplined,' he said, motioning to the sergeants who had fought the Syrian soldiers. 'I won't tolerate such behaviour, no matter the circumstances. We are God's men,' he added stiffly, 'not common mercenaries.'

It was with exhausted relief that James shrugged off his mantle and chainmail and collapsed on his pallet that evening. He had bathed and his hair, still wet, was a cold halo around his head. A shaft of orange light slanted in through the slit-window, affording the otherwise plain, grey dormitory a measure of brightness. Outside, the sky was mandarin-gold. James could hear the chanting of a prayer, faint and far off, rising from the Mamluk encampment. He lay outside the blanket, grateful for the slight breeze that played across his bare chest. Usually the heat was dry and solid, but this evening it had turned humid, a clinging heat that wears a man down, making every movement one of deep weariness. James wondered if it might storm. He hadn't seen rain for a long time. Closing his eyes, he thought of the fast-flowing rivers of Scotland; clear water bubbling over brown stones, soft green moors and dark, misty lochs. He saw Isabel wading into a stream, skirts held high, the water flowing around her bare legs, her face laughing. The sunlight gleamed in his wife's hair as she turned to him and beckoned.

'James!'

James woke to find the room in semi-darkness and Mattius leaning over him. He came awake quickly as he saw the knight's troubled face, half lit by the moonlight that had replaced the sun's orange glow.

'What is it?' he asked, swinging his legs over the pallet.

'They are leaving,' growled Mattius, handing James his undershirt.

'Who?' James tugged the shirt over his head.

Mattius paced as James went to the perch for his chainmail coat. 'The Syrians. They're deserting.'

'But the captain agreed to ask Baybars for more time? Heralds were sent. We agreed to wait a few more days before giving our answer.'

'It looks as if the captain only needed a few more hours. He didn't even wait for Baybars' deadline. The Syrians began to leave after dark when most of us were in our quarters, or on the outer walls. They are going out through one of the posterns in the southern wall, white flags raised.'

'Have we tried talking to them?' James drew his mantle around his shoulders.

'The commander had a few choice words with the captain, but he was adamant. It hardened his resolve when he saw that his men were being well received by Baybars' forces. The Mamluks disarm the Syrians as they enter the camp, but let them go without so much as a poke of their swords. Some of them, it is rumoured, have even converted to the Saracens' side.'

'How many have we lost?'

'By the commander's reckoning, at this rate, we'll be down a thousand men by morning.'

'Dear God. And the captain?'

Mattius gave a snort. 'Picked up his hems and fled with the rest of them.' He nodded to the door. 'Come on,' he said, looking suddenly weary, 'the commander needs us.'

When they reached the outer walls, James and Mattius found the commander spitting curses at the straggling line of Syrian soldiers, who were lit up by the moonlight as they stumbled down the steep hillside.

'*Bastards!*' he hissed, spinning round as James appeared on the walkway.

'Commander,' greeted James gravely.

'Look at them!' shouted the commander, throwing his hand across the parapet. 'Faithless cowards!'

A large group of knights and sergeants were with the commander on the walkway, some talking amongst themselves, others watching the Syrians' exodus. Their faces were grim in the silver-blue light. James felt despair creep through him. They didn't stand a chance against Baybars' forces. They were so few and the fortress so very large.

'Sir,' said Mattius, addressing the commander, 'what about the farmers and their families? It isn't so hard to train a novice to prime a mangonel.'

The commander, in mid-curse, glared at him, then sighed. 'They aren't warriors, brother. It would divide us further if we had to keep an eye on them during battle. Besides,' he muttered, 'a good many of them left with the soldiers, although a mass evacuation was halted when they realised that the women and children were being taken captive by the Mamluks. Baybars is not as magnanimous as they were all starting to think. Craven fools,' he added bitterly.

'Commander, sir,' said a timid-looking youth. He was one of the younger sergeants and had been watching the commander's outburst open-mouthed. He dropped his eyes as the commander turned to him, frowning.

'What is it, sergeant?'

'We could, well, I was thinking that maybe, if of course you . . .'

'Spit it out, boy!'

The sergeant took a breath. 'Couldn't we dress like the Syrians and leave with them? I mean, if we cannot defend the fortress without them, sir?'

A few of the other sergeants glanced up at his words, a look of hope spreading across their faces.

'Leave?' bellowed the commander. 'Give Safed to our enemy? *Never!*' The sergeant blinked owlishly, then bowed his head. The commander stared at him. With effort, he checked his rage. 'The Mamluks would see through it. We cannot speak the infidel's language.'

'Some of us can,' said a knight, stepping forwards. 'James can speak their tongue almost as well as they can.'

'I will not sanction any departure from our stations!' repeated the commander, glaring at the knight.

'But if one or two could escape unnoticed,' continued the knight, 'they could retreat to Acre, send word to Grand Master Bérard, request more forces.'

'Bérard couldn't assemble a thousand men in a matter of weeks,' said the commander. 'And if even he could, they would have to fight their way through the Saracens to get to us.'

Everyone fell silent, each lost to his own thoughts.

'It looks to me,' said James finally, his voice loud in the oppressive night air, 'that we only have two options.' The commander and the knights and sergeants looked at him. 'We can either stay here and fight a battle we cannot hope to win, or we can negotiate our own surrender.' James looked at the Mamluk camp spread out below Safed, lit by torches and fires. 'I do not fear death, Commander, but neither do I feel ready to languish in Paradise when there is still so much to be done in this world.'

Safed, the Kingdom of Jerusalem, 22 July 1266 AD

For a time, the commander refused to listen to any talk of surrender. The Syrians' betrayal had cut him deep and his stubbornness to forfeit Safed was his reaction to the wound. But the majority of the knights agreed with James and, when dawn came, and they counted the loss of over twelve hundred Syrians, he relented. James volunteered to enter the camp to negotiate the terms of the Templars' capitulation. The commander didn't like the proposition, but unable to think of any better way to parley with the Mamluks, he agreed.

After Prime, James made his way along the wide passage which led to a postern that came out on the hillside. His horse had been saddled and was being led through the dark, uneven tunnel by a groom. The commander and two other knights were with him.

'Are you sure about this, brother?' said the commander. 'They may kill you on sight.'

'I just hope I can remember the Arabic for surrender,' James replied lightly, ignoring the edge of apprehension that had crept into his voice.

'You won't have to, brother.'

James and the commander turned to see Mattius hastening down the passage. With him was a short, bony-limbed Syrian, with a hooked nose and a thin moustache and beard.

'This is Leo,' panted Mattius, motioning to the Syrian. 'He will go in your place.'

James shook his head as he studied the soldier. He wondered if Mattius had paid the soldier to do this task, or if the man had volunteered. 'I've made my decision, Mattius.'

'And I've made mine,' Mattius replied resolutely. 'I don't want to spend the next few days viewing your head on a pike. It is safer this way. He may be a native, but he's loyal to us. Aren't you, Leo?' he said, clapping the man on the back.

'Yes, sir,' stated the Syrian, in a deep voice that was surprising from such a small, fragile-looking man. 'I disagree with the actions of my comrades and captain and I am grateful for this chance to make amends on their behalf.'

James opened his mouth to protest, but the commander cut him off. 'So be it. I don't want to lose one of my best men if it can be helped.'

With that settled, Leo mounted James's horse and rode out of Safed with the scroll the commander had given him that detailed the knights' offer. James, Mattius and the commander left the passage to watch his progress. But, by the time they arrived on the walls, the knights keeping watch told them that Leo had been received and taken to the sultan's pavilion. After that, there was nothing to do but wait.

James watched the empty hillside as the minutes dragged by. The commander was pacing about the walkway and Mattius was drumming his fingers on the parapet. Almost an hour had passed since Leo had been ushered inside the sultan's pavilion. James looked down over the compound. 'Do you think he will agree to let them go?' he murmured to Mattius, as his gaze swept the smoke-wreathed encampment of men, women and children in the outer enceinte.

'The women and children are the most valuable spoils Safed has to offer. I would, in truth, be surprised if he did.'

'I too,' James admitted soberly.

'There!' called one of the knights.

James and Mattius looked over the parapet to see Leo riding up the hill towards the fortress.

'At least he's still alive,' said another of the knights. 'That has to be a good sign, surely?'

Not long later, Leo arrived on the walls.

'Well?' said the commander, as the Syrian hastened across the walkway flanked by two Templar sergeants. James noted that the soldier looked rather pale and shaken.

'It is done, Commander,' said Leo, bowing. 'Sultan Baybars has agreed to your terms. If you give up Safed without further resistance, he will let you go free. You will be allowed to retreat to Acre unharmed. The remaining soldiers and the peasants are permitted to return to their homes. He's given you the rest of the day to prepare the evacuation. You are to come out this evening. The soldiers and farmers are to wait inside, until Baybars' troops give them the word that they can leave.'

The commander frowned. 'That was simpler than I thought.'

'This is madness,' argued one of the knights. 'Are we to trust, so readily, the word of our enemy?'

'Of course not,' interjected Mattius, 'but, as James said, better a prisoner than a corpse. Out there we have a chance. If we stay here we just delay the inevitable.'

'The sultan wants a swift victory, Commander,' offered Leo. 'He said he doesn't care about a handful of Western savages.' He shrugged apologetically. 'He only cares that the fortress is emptied of your presence, so that it may be razed to the ground and bring an end to your taint of these lands.'

The commander's frown deepened. 'Savages indeed.' He ran his hand along the smooth stones of the parapet. 'Years to build and only weeks to destroy. I cannot believe it is to fall.'

'Do you wish me to return to the sultan with your answer, Commander?' questioned Leo.

The commander looked up. He glanced at James and Mattius and drew in a breath. 'Do it,' he said harshly. 'Take him my agreement and be done with it.'

The priests paced before the company, murmuring prayers and passing their hands in the sign of the cross. Safed towered above the barbican, its walls and towers dusky pink in the evening sun. It had been a testimony to the strength of God and those who served Him, but the tide of war had reached its walls and it could no longer hold back the flood. St George had failed. It was Baybars' fortress now, although the knights had made sure that there would be little of use to him inside. The corpses of the Christians, which the Mamluks had tossed over the walls, had been dumped into the cisterns to poison the water. The stores of food and grain had been spoiled, or consigned to fires that had burned high throughout the day. The blacksmiths and masons had been given the task of destroying weapons: tearing down mangonels, hammering at swords until the blades buckled, snapping bows. All that was left was stone. And a fearful congregation of soldiers and farmers.

James turned at the sound of hushed voices beside him. The garrison's five youngest sergeants were watching the priests nervously.

James guessed the cause of their alarm. 'Don't worry,' he assured them quietly. 'The prayers are only a precaution.'

'Sir Knight,' whispered one of them, 'my comrades and I were wondering how we will make it to Acre without horses, or provisions.'

'It's only thirty or so miles.' James patted the skin that was strung around his belt and smiled. 'We have water. Anything else, we can make do without.'

The sergeant nodded, relaxing a little.

'Amen,' said James with the rest of the men, as the priests finished their prayers.

The commander stood before the knights and sergeants. 'Be strong, men, and hold your heads high in the company of our enemy. Show them that the warriors of Christ will not be bowed. Look all those who seek to destroy our property and hope in the eye with dignity, and in the knowledge that we shall one day return with the full force of our Order to avenge our loss. Look to your faith for solace and your training for courage.' His eyes lingered on the fortress for a moment. 'Let's go.'

Together, the knights, sergeants and priests passed under the barbican's arch and headed out through the gate, the Syrian guards winching up the portcullis. James and Mattius walked behind the commander. At the bottom of the hillside an army was waiting for them.

As the knights walked through the enemy encampment, the gazes of the Mamluk soldiers followed them. Some of the soldiers jeered, others remained silent, arms folded across their chests. James felt his skin prickle under the fierceness of their combined stare, each and everyone's eyes filled with contempt. After being led between a line of tents and wagons, the knights came to a halt in a cleared area, surrounded by soldiers in gold cloaks. James recognised them as Bahri warriors: the Mamluk Royal Guard. In their midst stood a tall, powerfully built man, with short brown hair streaked with silver at his temples and the most chilling blue eyes James had ever seen. A cold fist closed around his heart as Baybars met his gaze. Crouching by the feet of the sultan and watching the knights eagerly was an old man in a shabby robe.

Baybars murmured something to a soldier at his side.

The soldier stepped forward. 'Down your weapons,' he barked in precise Latin.

The commander looked surprised, then scowled. 'Our terms didn't stipulate that we should be disarmed.'

The soldier repeated the command.

James glanced at the commander. 'Perhaps we should do as they ask. The sooner we are released the better.'

The commander looked as if he was about to argue, then he nodded. 'Very well.' He unsheathed his sword and placed it carefully on the ground.

The knights and sergeants followed his example. Several Mamluk guards came forward to collect the weapons. Baybars waited, then beckoned to another of his soldiers. This time, when he spoke, it was loud enough for James to hear.

'Send in the men. I expect the knights have destroyed anything of value, but search the castle anyway. Once you have secured it, kill the Syrians who refused to leave on my request. Take the women and children.'

James stared at him, aghast. 'You gave your word!' he cried in Arabic.

Baybars looked round. His eyes fell on James as the soldiers marched away to do his bidding. 'The tongue of my people sounds ill on your lips, Christian,' he said, after a pause. 'You aren't fit to speak it.'

The commander looked from Baybars to James. 'What does he say?'

James answered him. 'We've been tricked, sir.'

From behind the Bahri warriors came soldiers bearing chains and manacles. Some of the knights shouted as they saw them, reaching instinctively for weapons that weren't there. One of the younger sergeants tried to run. James yelled at him. 'Stay where you are!'

But the boy, in his terror, didn't heed the warning. He only got a few paces before the Mamluks caught him. His cries continued for several moments longer as they beat him to the ground with their swords and he disappeared in their midst. The cries ceased. As the Mamluks moved away, James's jaw tightened at the sight of the bloodied corpse. The sergeant's hands were shredded where he'd tried to ward off their blows. His face was a mess of wide red slashes and his body was punctured. James intoned a prayer as the soldiers approached the company, which had fallen silent.

The knights' mantles were removed, as were their chainmail coats and undershirts. James, forced to his knees beside the commander, watched as his white mantle was tossed onto a fire and his armour was taken away to be given to a Mamluk warrior as a trophy. Heavy chains were looped around him, the iron cold on his bare chest.

When the knights, sergeants and priests were bound, Baybars stepped forward. He looked down at James. 'I may not have kept my word, Christian, but I'm not an unreasonable man.' He paused, then nodded, satisfied by the look on James's face that the knight understood him. 'I shall offer you a choice. Translate my words to your commander.'

As Baybars spoke, James listened, a sick feeling rising in him. When Baybars had finished, James hung his head.

'James?' pressed the commander, who had been watching the exchange intently. 'What is happening? Is it as I feared? Are we to be taken to Cairo as slaves?'

For a moment, James couldn't reply. He forced himself to raise his head and addressed the commander, but kept his eyes on Baybars. 'No, we are not to be taken prisoner. The sultan has given us a choice.' James's voice was clear enough for the whole company to hear. 'We can choose to deny Christ and convert to the faith of Islam, or we can choose to be martyred as Christians. He will give us the night to decide whether to save ourselves, or face execution by decapitation.'

Outside the Walls of Safed, the Kingdom of Jerusalem, 23 July 1266 AD

The night pressed in, warm and airless, around the knights and sergeants as they knelt together on the ground. During the first few hours they had remained, for the most part, silent, each lost to his own thoughts. They had listened to the sounds of the camp, the murmurs of the guards keeping watch on them, and the faint screams that came from Safed as the men were slaughtered and the women and children rounded up. It was gone midnight when the commander's voice broke the stillness.

'It is time.'

The company stirred, all eyes turning to him. The commander's rage had gone. His voice now was calm, if a little husky.

'We must make our choice. I, for one, am set on my decision, but, as brothers, we must speak as one.'

No one said anything. The younger sergeants watched him intently, but the older ones and the knights, those who had served the Temple for years, looked away, knowing what the decision would be.

'Twenty years ago, I knelt before the chapter in Paris and was received as a Knight of the Temple, but although the years since that day have tested my flesh, they have not tested my faith. The vows I took then are as clear to me now as they ever were. I knew what I was being asked to do. We all did, brothers, even those of us who have never worn the mantle.' Some of the older sergeants nodded. 'We made a pledge that we would give our lives in service to the Order.' The commander's voice shook with emotion. 'I shall not renege on that pledge! Were the Devil himself and all the hordes of hell to command it of me, I would not deny Christ!' He paused as some of the knights and sergeants murmured their approval.

'We stand with you, Commander,' said one of the priests. He looked kindly on the terrified young sergeants. 'In death we are born to a new life. Our sacrifice is a small price to pay for the reward we shall receive in Heaven.'

One of the sergeants, his lip trembling, spoke up. 'Can we not pretend, s . . . sir?' He looked around for support from his fellows, but found only downcast eyes. 'Can't we say that we convert to the Saracens' faith, but turn from it when we are safe in Acre? Can't we say that we deny Christ, but not mean it in our hearts?'

'To deny Christ, whether in falsehood or truth, would be blasphemy of the highest order,' said the commander quietly. 'Those who do will find the gates of Heaven barred to them forever. We will not crumble before our enemy. We will stand proud to accept our fate and show the infidel the power of the one true God. The flesh is transitory, but the spirit lives on.'

The sergeant stared at the ground.

After the choice was made even those who were horrified by it were stunned into silence in the face of the resolute knights. The company passed the rest of the night talking quietly of their families and saying prayers. James was disconsolate, hearing the men speaking of their wives and children. He stared at the gradually lightening sky. 'I'm sorry.'

Mattius touched his shoulder. 'Sorry for what, brother?'

James realised he had spoken out loud. His placed his hand over Mattius's. 'Do you have any idea how it is to hate your own child? I hated my son for what happened to my daughter and I hated myself for doing so. My heart was torn, one half broken, the other beating with grief.

It was as if I lost two children that day.' James gripped Mattius's hand. 'But I hadn't.'

'I don't understand, James. You told me your daughter drowned.'

'I have been so selfish. I told myself that I came here for duty's sake, that I was doing it for him and that, in the end, he would thank me for it. But I was fooling myself, wasn't I? I was here to escape my duty. I never should have left him.' A tear welled in James's eye and he knuckled it away. 'Dear God. Who will take care of my family?'

Mattius put an arm around his shoulder, seeing that James needed comfort, not answers. 'The Temple will take care of them.' He gave his friend a rough hug. 'Do not fear.'

James leaned against the large knight, feeling like a child, and drifted into a fitful half-sleep. He dreamed of his father taking his hand and leading him to the loch to fish. When he woke, his cheeks were wet.

Just before dawn, Brother Joseph, the oldest priest, shambled awkwardly on his knees around the group, pausing at each man in turn. As there was no oil available, he used the last drops of water from a skin to anoint them as he delivered the last rites.

When the first rays of sun touched the peaks of the distant mountains, Baybars came to the company. James thought he saw surprise and, possibly, a flicker of respect in Baybars' eyes when he told the sultan they had chosen death. One by one, the eighty-four knights, priests and sergeants were forced to their feet and marched in a line from the encampment, the soldiers encouraging the slower ones with the tips of their swords. When they reached a patch of bald earth that looked out across the valley, they were ordered to their knees.

James knelt beside Mattius. He scanned the men in the gold cloaks who stood close to Baybars. He had never met his contact face to face, but knew, by the soldiers' dress, that the one man who might be able to save him wasn't among their number. But he hadn't failed. He had come to the Holy Land to do something he believed in and he had done it, the price with which he paid for it his family, his life. He would never see the result of his achievement, but maybe, one day, others would. One day, the blood that would be spilt on this bare earth would dry. Flowers would grow here and generations would remember, would not forget. The world he had tried to build was not meant for him. It belonged to the future. It belonged to his son. A strange calm settled over him as he realised this. This calm was shattered by Mattius.

'By God, you Judas!' bellowed the knight, struggling to stand.

James looked for the cause of his comrade's fury. Standing with Baybars, watching as the Mamluks drew their blades, was Leo, the Syrian soldier they had sent with their terms of surrender.

Leo stared at Mattius as three Mamluks grappled the huge knight to the ground. 'I didn't betray you. I gave the sultan's words to you as they were given to me. I didn't know that he would break his promise.'

'Are we to believe that when you stand free beside our executioners?'

'I have converted to the faith of Islam,' admitted Leo. 'But you, too, were given the chance of life. It was your decision to choose death.'

Mattius roared like a caged bear, helpless, under the weight of the soldiers pinning him down, to do anything but watch as Leo bowed to Baybars, then walked away.

'Stop, brother!' begged James, more troubled by his friend's frustration than by the soldiers who were lining up behind them, swords in hands. He leaned over and grabbed Mattius's wrist. 'Please, Mattius! You cannot die with such rage inside you. You must prepare your soul for the journey. Save your strength!'

Mattius's fury subsided, his body relaxing. The soldiers released him and backed away, but kept their swords trained on him. He sat up on his knees, and lifted his bound hands to wipe a smear of dust from his cheek.

James locked eyes with Mattius as Baybars gave the order to begin the executions. 'I regret we never made it to Jerusalem as we planned, brother.'

Mattius gave a bark of laughter. 'What is the Holy City in comparison to Paradise?'

'God be with you, my friend.'

'And with you.'

James turned away and stared straight ahead as the swords began to fall. Below him, the River Jordan was a gold ribbon along the valley floor and the mountains to the south were red in the soft light of morning. He drank in the sight like a man taking his last drop of water before crossing a desert. The dull thuds and cracks of steel meeting flesh and bone echoed out above the grunts of exertion from the executioners. The stench of blood and urine turned the air sour. James closed his eyes as the commander was cut down. He thought of Isabel and his three daughters in Scotland, trying to ingrain their images in his mind so that he might take some small part of them with him. *God keep them safe.* Two more knights fell, then Mattius. James thought of his son in Paris, clad in the white mantle. A gust of wind that smelt of hibiscus flowers lifted his hair, cooling his damp skin. He opened his eyes and smiled. 'I am proud of you, William,' he murmured, as the sword's shadow fell across him.

21

The Seven Stars, Paris

20 October 1266 AD

G arin watched the woman's long fingers pluck at the laces of his undershirt. Candlelight played across Adela's lithe, naked body, making her white skin glow. He kept his eyes on her as she pulled open his shirt and her cool hands drifted across his chest. The sounds of loud conversation and a fiddle being played badly floated up through cracks in the floorboards. From the adjacent room there came a man's low, deep groan, followed by a girl's laughter. A heady smell of incense hung thickly in the chamber, but the sickly-sweet scent couldn't disguise the malodour of ale and sweat and overcooked meat that pervaded the whole building. Adela leaned forward in slow, serpentine movements to kiss his neck, her thick black hair tumbling across her shoulder. Her tongue travelled feather-light towards his ear.

'Why do you keep your eyes open?' she whispered when she reached it, her warm breath sending a tiny shiver down Garin's spine.

He had noticed that she always spoke softly when she was in the room, perhaps to disguise the almost manly huskiness he had heard in her voice when it was raised.

When he didn't answer, she sat back slowly and studied his impassive face. 'You're a strange one.'

'I don't pay you to talk,' said Garin, reaching up and brushing her hair away from her face. He found her eyes mesmerising. They were large, bright and such a dark shade of blue-grey as to be almost violet.

'What do you pay me to do?' murmured Adela, sinking onto him until her breasts touched his chest.

'You know.'

'Yes,' said Adela, sliding down his stomach and tugging open the laces of his hose, 'I do.'

As Adela bent forward, her hair fanning out across his stomach, Garin looked past her into the corner of the room, which was bigger than the other chambers he had seen in the building. A wicker screen partially hid a trestle and a wooden stool – Adela's work area. On the shelves that lined the wall, he made out the globe shapes of bowls and jars beside tall clay bottles. He knew, having studied them on his first visit to the room two months ago, that the containers were filled with herbs. Among her other talents, Adela was a healer. His jaw clenched as her movements quickened and he gripped the mattress, which was split, exposing straw.

Adela, nineteen years old and the proprietor of the once reputable guesthouse in the Latin Quarter, was the first woman Garin had been with and he was constantly amazed by how simple everything was when he was in her bed. He had been in Paris for three months and the only things he had managed to achieve were a brief meeting with the Visitor, during which he had been told that the way to a commandership lay in the Holy Land, and, subsequently, the breaking of his vow of chastity. He had thought, by escaping London, that he could begin a new life, away from the memories of his uncle that had dogged him there and the ties that had bound him.

After Jacques' death, Garin had been assigned to an aged knight who rarely left the preceptory. He had thrown himself into his training, winning every tournament at New Temple. But it hadn't been enough. The life he had resented, the life his uncle and mother had wanted him to live in place of his father and brothers, had worked their way into Garin's being until he had come to realise that he wanted all the same things for himself. At first, when civil war erupted, it had been a blessing; he did not doubt, had it not occurred, that he would have been forced to undertake far more assign-ments than the few simple tasks, mostly sending messages, that Edward had ordered him to carry out. But although Edward's incarceration had prevented Garin's employment, it had also prevented the prince from rewarding him. Edward had promised to make him a lord. Even through his guilt following Jacques' death, Garin had dreamed of this. He had imagined himself in a grand estate, with servants and stables and a whole tower for his mother. But the prince had had more pressing concerns and Garin had discovered that if he wanted these things, he would have to find them for himself.

The move to Paris had not been the solution he had been hoping for. After the Visitor had told him he would have to prove himself in war before he could hope for a commandership, Garin had spent several weeks musing on the idea of Crusading. He had heard tales of knights becoming lords in

Palestine with towns and slaves and harems. But Outremer felt too far and he was scared to go all that way alone.

Feeling spasms of desire building with Adela's adept movements, Garin reached down and grabbed the back of her neck. Catching a fistful of her jasmine-scented hair, he pulled her to him and kissed her mouth roughly, tasting himself on her lips. Sometimes he liked to tease her: to watch the way she arched her back to meet his touch, mouth parted, eyes closed. He liked to make her lose her control whilst he kept his own, every movement slow, deliberate. Not tonight. Garin rolled over on top of her and pulled her legs up over his hips, pressing himself impatiently upon her. Adela flinched at the force with which he entered her. As he drove into her, seeking oblivion, his fears and worries left him. The world outside fell away until only one single moment existed; blissful, careless.

Afterwards, Garin collapsed on top of her, his breaths erratic and his mind empty for a few seconds, until Adela pushed his shoulders up and slid herself out from under him. She winced as she sat up.

Garin saw it and touched her shoulder. 'Did I hurt you?' he asked, knowing that he had, but now the pleasure had gone, feeling regretful and wanting her to pardon him.

Adela looked round. 'A little.'

'I'm sorry.'

'It is fine.'

'No it isn't,' he said, frowning. 'Forgive me.'

'I am fine, Garin. I've had worse, believe me.'

Garin grasped Adela's wrist as she went to stand. 'Stay with me.'

'I have others to see tonight.'

He kept hold of her. 'Just for a little while.'

Adela hesitated, then lay back. Garin rested his head on her chest, feeling it rise and fall with each breath she took. The motion soothed him. Outside the window coverings, it was growing dark. He would have to return to the preceptory soon.

Adela stroked her hand gently across his shoulders. She turned her face closer to his hair. He smelt warm and clean.

'I wish you wouldn't,' murmured Garin.

'Wouldn't what?'

'See other men.'

Adela made no reply.

The Tower, London, 21 October 1266 AD

'You saw him just the once?'

'Yes, my lord. In Carcassonne, about eight months ago. There was as large a crowd there as you would imagine for a royal coronation.' Philippe, a young nobleman from Provence, watched Prince Edward stroke the tawny-gold breast of the hawk on his wrist. The prince was poised on the edge of a table in a wide fan of sunlight that slanted through a narrow window. Philippe was seated on a low stool and felt uncomfortably diminutive in the presence of the tall, erect prince. At twenty-seven, Edward had reached his full, imposing height, and his frame, although lean, was corded with muscle from years of jousting, hunting and, more recently, battle. 'That's a beautiful bird,' the nobleman said nervously into the silence.

Edward glanced at him. 'She belonged to my uncle, Simon de Montfort. I took her after he was killed at Evesham.' He lifted his hand, which was protected by a padded leather glove. The hawk screeched and beat her wings, pulling on the silk jess tethered to her leg that Edward held. She screeched again, shook her plumage, then settled herself, amber eyes unblinking. 'She is still a little skittish.'

Philippe's gaze flicked to the doors. The man who had summoned him to this gloomy, draughty chamber at the top of the Tower, was still standing there. His ugly, pockmarked face was devoid of anything resembling emotion. 'Is there a particular reason you want to know about Pierre de Pont-Evêque's performance, my lord?' Philippe asked tentatively, looking back at the prince.

'I heard you talking about it the other evening at my father's table. I was interested.'

Philippe nodded, relaxing a little. 'It would seem the troubadour's fame is spreading. Several people have asked me about him and his work since I've been here, but I'm afraid I could not do it justice. I said they would have to see his performance for themselves, although he isn't to everyone's taste. I was hoping to see him again when he reads for King Louis at the royal court in Paris, but, alas, I fear my extended visit here will prevent me.'

'Tell me of this book,' pressed Edward. 'You mentioned that it is called the Book of the Grail?'

'Yes,' replied Philippe, 'he reads from it during his performance. That's where the more irreverent content comes from.' The young noble shrugged dismissively. 'But I don't see any real harm in it. He doesn't mean anything he says literally, I'm sure.'

'And the Templars are mentioned in this book?'

'Not directly. But anyone would know who he is referring to when he speaks of men dressed in white mantles with red crosses emblazoned across their hearts. Some think he may have once been a Templar himself, expelled, but with the secret knowledge of their initiations.' Philippe chuckled. 'Not that anyone much minds about the way the knights are portrayed in his reading. A lot of people believe it long past time the Templars be taught a lesson in humility. They are so proud and think themselves better than everyone else, yet I've heard many a man, after too much wine, exclaim he is as drunk as a Templar. And their vows of chastity? Rumour says they wench as well and as often as the rest of us. They call themselves the Poor Knights of Christ, but everyone knows they keep the wealth of kings buried beneath their churches.'

Edward scowled at this last comment and Philippe fell silent, feeling increasingly discomfited. On arriving in London, Philippe had found King Henry much older and weaker than he remembered from earlier visits, worn down by illness and hardships endured through the long imprisonment during Simon de Montfort's rebellion and by the assault on Kenilworth, recently ended. The heads of the fallen rebels were now decorating London Bridge. Philippe had heard people in the palace whisper that Edward, not Henry, was effectively ruling the country he had been instrumental in liberating from the hands of the dissenters. He could quite see why those rumours would be circulating now he was in close proximity with the prince.

'Do you know when, exactly, the troubadour is due to perform at King Louis' court?' Edward asked him.

'In just under two weeks. Are you planning on attending, my Lord Prince?'

Edward glanced at Rook, standing by the doors. He smiled slightly. 'I have a friend who will be present.' He looked back at the noble. 'You may go, Philippe. Thank you for your time.'

Philippe rose hastily and bowed. 'It was my pleasure, my lord.' He bowed again, then hurried for the doors.

'Do you think it's what we've been after?' asked Rook, when the doors were shut. 'This book?'

'The name is the same and there are, as he said, the obvious references to the Templars. It is too close to ignore.' Edward moved off the table and went to the window. He closed his eyes, feeling his face bathed in sunlight. His hair, which had been fair when he was younger, had grown gradually darker over the past few years. In places, it was streaked with black.

Six years ago, when he had learnt, first from Rook, then from a tearful, terrified Garin, of a covert group within the Temple, Edward had immediately ordered Rook to investigate the truth of it. From what Jacques de Lyons had told his nephew, this group, the Anima Templi, had had a book stolen from them, a book that detailed secret plans that could prove fatal to them and to the Temple if disclosed. Rook had been able to discover nothing of either the book's origins or whereabouts, although he had managed to verify that there was a man called Everard, the name, according to Garin, of the head of the circle, residing in the Paris Temple. The prince had been able to confirm his great-uncle, Richard the Lionheart's involvement from an obscure reference in a document, written by Richard, that he had found whilst searching the archives in Westminster. *The Soul of the Temple*, the line had read: *which I have pledged to guard with my life*. Edward had planned to recruit more men to help Rook delve into the Anima Templi and its workings, but the civil war and his subsequent imprisonment had put a stop to that.

'When do you want me to leave for Paris?'

Edward turned from the window. 'Within the next few days.' He studied Rook's doubtful expression. 'What is it?'

'With all due respect, I think we're putting an awful lot of hope on one little book that may or may not have anything to do with a group that may or may not exist according to some snot-nosed whelp.'

'We have confirmed too much of what Garin told us to think it all a lie.' Rook went to speak, but Edward raised a hand. 'What would you have me do? Mount a raid into the Paris preceptory to steal back my jewels? The mercenaries I sent failed to take them when they were sitting on a dockside, let alone in an iron locker thirty feet beneath ground.' Edward's voice was calm, but his grey eyes glittered with anger. 'My father grows weaker all the time. It will not be long before I am crowned. I must exert my authority now over those who would seek to dilute it when I am king. I would not let my uncle, a man I loved and admired for many years, take that power from me. Before he could, I had him killed, his limbs and head severed from his body and his bloodied torso fed to the dogs on the battlefield at Evesham. What makes you think I will let the Templars control me? I want my jewels back, Rook, and if the only way to do that is to take something precious from them for bartering, then that is how it shall be done.'

Rook nodded. 'How do you want me to proceed?'

'I think it is time you paid our young friend a visit.'

'Garin?' said Rook sourly. 'He went to Paris in the summer.'

'Then he will be in a good position to aid you in this task. You will need him, Rook. Besides, we have left that bird unfettered for too long.' Edward stroked the hawk's breast. 'We do not want him to forget who his master is.'

The Temple, Paris, 21 October 1266 AD

'You're locking your wrist again.'

Simon frowned and loosened his grip. He swung the sword, trying to roll it fluidly in his hand like Will had shown him. The sword whirled out of Simon's grasp and Will just managed to duck as it came sailing towards him.

'Holy Mary!' Simon's hands flew to his head. 'Will! I'm sorry!'

'No harm done,' said Will, straightening and looking at the falchion, the point of which had embedded itself in a hay bale. He let out a breath as he went to retrieve it.

'It's no use, I can't do it.'

'You just need more practice.'

Simon managed to cover up his dismay as Will handed him the falchion.

'Sir!' called a young stableboy, peering timidly from around a stall. 'I can't find the grooming brush.'

'In the storeroom,' said Simon, 'second shelf, where you left it last.'

'Thank you, sir,' said the boy, dipping his head and blushing.

'Sir?' said Will, grinning at Simon. 'You seem to be settling well into your new role.'

'Yes,' responded Simon, sweeping a hand grandly across the stables. 'Lord of all I muck out.' He motioned to the hay bales stacked in a corner. 'Why don't we take a rest?' He made a show of studying his wrist. 'I reckon I've sprained something.'

Will laughed. 'You aren't enjoying this, are you?'

Simon sat heavily on one of the bales and laid Will's sword across his lap. 'I just don't reckon I'll ever get good enough to be a half-decent partner for you.'

Will sat beside Simon. 'I cannot ask Robert, or Hugues to train with me. Now they are knights they don't have the time and Everard won't let me attend the training sessions. Not,' he added irritably, 'that I would want to.

The sergeants in the groups are all younger than me. I'm old enough to be an instructor!' Will cupped his hands and breathed into them. They were chapped and sore, bitten by the recent icy winds.

For the last few months, everyone in the preceptory had been busy with the harvest and the preparations for winter. The cote and barns had been cleaned out for the doves, hens and goats, ready for the colder days. The orchard trees had been stripped of their fruit which was then stored, ready to be made into wines and jams. Fish had been taken from the ponds, dried and salted, and honey collected from the hives. When the stores had been filled there had existed, for a short time, an air of contentment in the breath's pause between autumn and winter.

Will had been occupied with several new treatises that Everard had bought for the preceptory and the priest had made him re-bind a stack of books. Will had sat in the orchard to do his work, balancing the tattered books on his knee, threading the needle carefully through the skin along the spine. Often, Simon sat with him and, occasionally, Robert had managed to take a moment between prayers and meetings to talk with him. Robert, who saw Will's frustrations at being kept from knighthood, would make Will laugh by lamenting over the chapter meeting he had just attended at which Brother so-and-so had argued for three hours over what stitch the tailor should be using to darn holes in their hose. Will had spoken to Garin very little. There was an awkwardness between them that made him uncomfortable and he tended to avoid the knight. It wasn't difficult; Garin was often out of the preceptory.

'Don't fret about your training,' Simon told him. 'I'll get good enough if it kills me.' He scratched his head. 'Or you.'

They both looked round as a figure darted into the stables. Will rose, shocked, as Elwen grinned at him. She was wearing a black cloak, fastened with a red pin in the shape of a rose. Her hair hung loose around her shoulders.

'What are you doing here?'

Elwen frowned at Will's abrupt tone. 'I wanted to see you.'

Simon was looking at both of them, his expression uncertain.

Will took Elwen's arm and led her away from the entrance, out of sight of anyone who might be in the yard. 'How did you get in?'

Her grin was back. 'I came in through the servants' passage. Don't worry,' she added, seeing his look, 'no one saw me.' She pulled the hood of her cloak up, hiding her hair and most of her face. 'I asked a sergeant where I might find you,' she said, putting on a deep, manly tone. Laughing, Elwen flicked back the hood and looked around the stables. She wrinkled her nose. 'How can you stand the smell in here?'

'That's how all horses smell,' said Simon, rising from the hay bale. His voice was stiff, awkward.

Elwen smiled at him. 'You're Simon, aren't you? I saw you once in London, when I was staying at New Temple. Will told me you had come.'

'Did he?' said Simon, glancing at Will.

'I'm Elwen.'

Simon looked back at her. 'I reckoned you might be.'

Elwen found Simon's lingering gaze uncomfortable. She felt like he was sizing her up and finding her lacking. 'Aren't you pleased to see me then?' she asked Will, to break the silence and the groom's stare.

As Elwen gave him a sly, sidelong look, Will felt his stomach muscles tense. He couldn't understand how she only had to look at him a certain way and his insides would liquefy. 'Of course I'm pleased,' he murmured. 'But if you're caught, it will be me who will take the blame for it, not you.' He watched as Simon picked up a broom and began sweeping out a stall. 'You cannot come in here like this. It's too risky.'

Elwen sighed. 'I wouldn't have come if you hadn't kept avoiding me. You rarely reply to my messages, or visit me at the palace.' Her expression grew solemn. 'I thought we were friends, Will?'

'We are.' Will leaned against a bench and folded his arms across his chest.

Her brow furrowed at his insouciant posture. 'And anyway, if anyone saw me I would just say I was here to visit my uncle's grave.'

'In the stables?'

Elwen rolled her eyes. 'I'd say I was asking you for directions to the cemetery.'

'I cannot give Everard any more excuses to keep me back, Elwen. You know that. It isn't that I don't want to see you, just that I can't. Not now. Just give me time to work this out.'

'Time? You've had years. You said you were planning on speaking to the Visitor about your inception? That's what you told me when we last met. Will, I can't bear to see you give up like this.' Elwen tossed her hair back impatiently. 'Surely doing something is better than doing nothing?'

Will traced a circle in the dust with his foot. 'He wouldn't see me,' he said flatly.

It was a lie. After the argument with Everard, in which he had given the priest the ultimatum, Will had never gone to the Visitor. His father thought he was a knight. How would it look if he turned up as a sergeant and had to confess he had lied? How could his father welcome him with open arms and forgive him then?

'Listen,' said Elwen, crossing to him. 'I've saved most of the money I've earned in the queen's employ. I want to go to the Holy Land too, I always have. In the next year or so I'll have enough to buy us *both* passage. We can go together if Everard won't initiate you.'

Simon was still sweeping the stall, but he stopped and looked round at this.

Will glanced at her. It was a touching suggestion, but it made him irritated. He didn't want to go to the Holy Land as a peasant on a pilgrim ship. He wanted to go there as a knight and the only place he was interested in seeing was the place where his father was stationed. 'Thank you,' he told her, 'but I need to do this on my own. I just have to find a way to get Everard to agree my inception. I haven't been able to think of it yet.' He forced a smile. 'But I will.'

The Temple, Paris, 24 October 1266 AD

'This doesn't leave us much time.'

'I know, brother. I failed you. Forgive me.'

'I do not blame you, Hasan,' said Everard, turning from his pacing of the chamber. 'It wasn't an easy task.'

'I have accomplished more difficult tasks than this. And in far less time than three months.' Hasan pushed a hand through his black hair. 'The troubadour gave his true name in some inns he stayed in, but must have given false names in others. I believe he kept to the tracks and forests rather than the roads. I do not understand. I doubt he knew I was on his trail. I was careful.'

'I am sure you were.'

'I would have searched for him for longer, only I worried that he would arrive here before me if I left it much later.'

'You were right to return when you did. It may have been simple bad luck that you didn't find him, but Pierre de Pont-Evêque certainly does have reason to be cautious.' Everard sat beside Hasan on the window seat. 'Friar Gilles was here the other day, making sure everything is ready. Nicolas de Navarre will lead the group that goes to the palace. They plan to arrest the troubadour just before the reading to be certain he has the Book of the Grail on him. We have to get it before then, or we'll lose it for good.' Everard shook his head. 'I asked the Visitor if I could be allowed to study it, but both the book and de Pont-Evêque are under the Dominicans' jurisdiction. Our knights are just going along to dissuade the king from interfering.'

'I could keep watch on the southern gates, snare de Pont-Evêque in the city when he enters?'

'The troubadour could arrive at any time in the next five days and a man of your appearance lingering around the walls would rouse the suspicion of the watch. Besides, the gates are barred after nightfall. He will only be allowed entrance during daylight and the streets would be too busy for an ambush then. No. We need to do this quickly and silently.'

'I could attempt to seek an audience with him when he is in the palace?'

'The king has never been fond of foreigners, Hasan.' Everard paused. 'But I may be more affably received. I have certain works that Louis would be keen to lay his hands on for his collection. I could gain entrance to the palace under the pretence of offering the king a manuscript I was looking to trade. Whilst there I could . . .'

'No.'

Everard frowned. 'No?'

'I will not allow you to walk into danger when my failure is the cause of our predicament.' Everard opened his mouth to speak, but Hasan cut him off. 'How will you take the book from the troubadour? By stealth? A known Templar priest stealing through the palace corridors would not go unnoticed. By force? You have not wielded a sword in over twenty years.'

'There is still strength in this body,' snapped Everard, 'frail though it might appear to you, my young Khorezmian soldier.'

Hasan was silent for a long moment. 'I gave up that title when I met you, Everard. I am no soldier.'

'No,' said Everard roughly, 'you are my bloodhound and hounds should look up to their masters, not talk down to them.'

Hasan looked away, his dark eyes glittering.

Everard huffed and went to the table where a jug of wine stood. He poured the dregs into a goblet. 'My life, your life, they do not matter. One day we shall both die. But our cause, Hasan, must live.' Everard shivered as a gust of wind blew in, scattering the embers of a low-burning torch. 'We must do whatever it takes to safeguard that.'

'What about your sergeant?' offered Hasan in a low voice. 'Perhaps if we sent Campbell to the palace on an errand he might be able to—?'

'I haven't spoken to Campbell of this,' interrupted Everard, setting the goblet on the table.

'You agreed, brother.'

'No,' corrected Everard, 'I agreed to think on it. I have thought on it and I don't believe he is ready yet.'

'Whatever it takes,' murmured Hasan.

'I have need of fresh wine.'

'I will fetch it for you.'

'No,' said Everard, heading for the door. 'I also have need of air.'

Hasan walked slowly to the armoire when the door was shut and ran his fingertips lightly over the wood, tracing the whorls in the grain. The chamber seemed darker now that Everard had gone. Hasan felt like a trespasser. The room and everything in it were part of the old priest; every sheaf of parchment covered with his delicate script; every piece of furniture marked with his fingerprints; every flagstone with his footsteps. Hasan had never had a home. The year before he was born, Genghis Khan's forces had destroyed Khorezm, the homeland of his family and the most powerful Muslim state in the East. Khorezm was swallowed by the Mongol empire and the survivors had scattered. As a child, Hasan had lived a nomadic existence with what remained of the Khorezmian army. In the wastes of northern Syria, his father, a commander, had raised him as a warrior and they had eked out a life for themselves, living off the land, hiring themselves as mercenaries, planning their revenge. But Hasan had never felt bitterness for the loss of a country he had never known, and had been a reluctant soldier.

Twenty-two years ago, Ayyub, Sultan of Egypt, had asked the Khorezmians for their aid in overthrowing the Franks in Palestine. Hasan, aged nineteen, had gone with the ten thousand-strong force to Jerusalem. On the journey, his father and the warriors had been heady with ambition. Their lust for retribution had grown indiscriminate and they had believed that the payment for their aid would be great enough to sustain a new campaign, if not against the Mongols then against Egypt itself. The Khorezmian army had stormed through Jerusalem like a black wind, leaving a trail of corpses in its wake. Thousands of Christians had evacuated the city, making for the coast, but Hasan's father had ordered the banners of the Frankish knights lifted on the battlements and many of the fleeing Christians returned, believing they had been saved. Hasan had watched them come, like herds of confused sheep to the slaughter. And slaughtered they were, down to the last man, woman and child. To celebrate their victory and the city's emancipation from Christian hands, the Khorezmians sacked the Church of the Holy Sepulchre and massacred the priests left inside, all but one, who had hidden under the bodies after killing two of the warriors.

Hasan had done things on that day he believed he could never atone for, though he had asked Allah for forgiveness in his prayers each day since. Leaving the city in flames, the triumphant warriors had headed for Herbiya. There they would meet the Mamluk commander, Baybars, and the rest of the Mamluk army to destroy the Frankish forces which had set out against them. Hasan, hiding on the ramparts, had watched them go; his father at the van, yelling the victory. That evening, trailing numbly through the ravaged city, Hasan had found Everard. And in the priest, the deserter had found his purpose.

When Everard returned to the West, Hasan had gone with him. The priest had filled him with the belief that there was something he could do in this life that could change everything. In Christendom, he had spent his time on the road, collecting information, documents and secrets. Always on the move, keeping to the shadows, a stable here to sleep in, a field there. Hasan believed with all his being in the Anima Templi's dream, but lately he had found himself imagining how it would be to have a place, just a room, filled with his memories, his silence. There had been a woman once in Syria. He sometimes wondered what life he had abandoned. What his children looked like.

The door opened and Everard entered, holding a jug. 'Damned servants tried to pass off some local piss water as Gascony wine.'

Hasan noticed that the priest seemed brighter, his movements more brisk.

'What is it?'

Everard turned, lip curled in a smile. 'I've had an idea.'

22

The Royal Palace, Paris

27 October 1266 AD

E lwen moved across the room and sat on the edge of the bed that she shared with one of the other handmaidens. She glanced around the empty chamber, then reached inside the pocket at the front of her apron and withdrew her find. Holding it between thumb and forefinger, she studied the pearl's creamy, glossy surface in the strip of light that slanted through the window. She had found the pearl that morning whilst attending the queen. It had been lodged in a crack in the flagstones of the queen's bedchamber, having fallen from one of her mistress's gowns. While the queen was standing before her silver mirror, examining the complex braids and coils Elwen had made of her hair, it had been the easiest thing for Elwen to pluck it, unnoticed, from the ground. She didn't think of it as stealing. She knew the gown the jewel had dropped from; there must have been a hundred pearls strung from it, like little eyes peeking out from the folds of samite. This one wouldn't be missed.

Reaching under the bed, Elwen pulled out a long wooden box, stained black and decorated with silver flowers. She had seen the box in the market a year ago and had saved her earnings for two months to buy it, going back to the merchant's stall whenever she could, worried that it had been bought by another. It was the only luxury she had ever bought; every other penny she had earned had gone into the fund that would one day take her to the Holy Land. Her desire to travel there, which had formed in her as a girl, had never left her. She was enraptured by stories of it told by visiting nobles, stories she would occasionally overhear whilst sewing one of the queen's gowns, or putting fresh goose feathers in the silk pillows in the solar. No one else, handmaidens or servants, seemed to understand her desire. If not for a pilgrimage, they asked her, then why would she go there? Elwen couldn't explain it in words. She felt it as a pull, as if someone had tied a piece of string to her insides and was drawing her inexorably eastwards. She always felt the pull to be strongest at this time of year, with the fog and the cold closing around the palace towers like a sheet, pinning her within.

She crouched before the box, removing the chain she wore around her neck from which hung a tiny key. There was a soft click as the lock disengaged and she lifted the lid. Inside, the box was divided into rows of small compartments. The merchant had said it was a spice box, but Elwen didn't use it for that purpose. In each of the compartments were treasures: a crimson ribbon from a handmaiden who had left to be married; a frost-white dove feather from the palace gardens; a dented gold coin rescued from the riverbank where it had been half buried in mud. Inside another was a strip of blue linen folded in a square which contained the dried head of a jasmine flower. Delicate and brittle; a keepsake from Will. Elwen never took anything that would be missed, nothing of real value to anyone else. The pearl was an exception, but too precious a find to abandon.

As a child in Powys, she had kept a similar collection, though her hoard then had been more earthy in nature. She had invested these tokens with their own unique histories: a blue-speckled stone was a gift to a knight from a sultan's daughter; a misshapen twig was part of a ship that was wrecked off the coast of Arabia. They had served as talismans against the long nights when the only sounds were her mother's fitful sleep-talk and the wind roaring through the valley to beat its fists against the walls of their hut. In the years since she had left Powys, Elwen's life had changed, but her need for things to treasure remained.

Elwen placed the pearl in the compartment with the gold coin, then closed the lid. After locking the box, she pushed it beneath the bed. She was pulling the chain with the key over her head, when the door opened and one of the handmaidens she shared the chamber with rushed in.

'There you are! I've been looking everywhere for you.' The maid's cheeks were flushed as if she had been running.

'What's wrong, Maria?' asked Elwen, slipping the chain inside the front of her gown.

'There's someone here to see you at the servants' gate.' Maria, a short, fair-haired girl of about sixteen, grinned as she shut the door. 'He has come from the Temple so I was told by the messenger boy.'

'From the Temple?' Elwen untied her apron. 'Are you sure?'

'Yes.' Maria giggled at Elwen's secretive smile. Taking the apron from her, she laid it neatly on the bed. 'When will you tell me who he is? This man you see.'

Elwen smoothed down her ivory-coloured gown. 'Not yet.'

'But we are close as sisters! You cannot keep such things from me.' Maria clasped Elwen's hands eagerly. 'Do you plan to marry? If you do you'll have to do it before he's knighted, won't you? Or he'll have taken his vows.'

'I won't say,' insisted Elwen.

Maria let go of her hands and feigned a pout. 'I'll not tell you my secret.'

Elwen smiled, but remained silent.

Maria sighed and sat on the bed. 'Well, I'll tell you, even though you don't deserve to know.' Her eyes shone with excitement. 'The troubadour is here.'

'You've seen him?' Elwen was intrigued. Along with most of the royal household – and many in the city – she had been awaiting the arrival of the famous Pierre de Pont-Evêque with great curiosity.

'I have,' replied Maria importantly. 'And he doesn't look like the devil some have claimed him to be. I thought him most comely.'

'You think all men most comely.'

'Yes,' admitted Maria candidly, 'but although my eyes appreciate variety, my heart desires one man alone.'

Elwen returned the smile, knowing that the handmaiden spoke of Ramon, a coal-eyed kitchenhand from Galicia, whom Maria held so close to her heart that not even he knew of his place there.

'I cannot wait for the performance,' said Maria, leaning back on the bed. 'We are fortunate.'

Elwen nodded. The queen had permitted four of her handmaidens, including Elwen and Maria, to attend the performance held in five days. They would watch and listen from behind a heavy drape that covered the servants' entrance in the side of the Great Hall. She straightened her cap. 'How do I look?'

'Pretty as a dove.'

Elwen wrinkled her nose. 'A dove?'

'Sorry,' said Maria, rolling her eyes, 'I forgot that you hate all things dainty and sweet.'

'I don't hate sweet things,' corrected Elwen. 'I would just rather be compared to a . . .' She shrugged. 'A raven, or an owl, something more . . .'

'Manly,' said Maria, shaking her head.

Elwen shot her a reproachful look. 'Courageous.'

'I'm jesting,' said Maria with a giggle. She leaned back on her elbows.

'You look like one of those women in the Romances you read. Beautiful and courageous and nothing like a dove.'

Elwen smiled as she headed for the door. 'I will see you later.'

'Give your sweetheart a kiss for me,' Maria called softly.

Passing a cook with a basket of vegetables and two palace guards in their scarlet liveries, Elwen headed through the servants' gate and came out in the paved alley that ringed the palace wall. One way led to the main streets, the other to the riverbank. Wondering why Will had come to see her without any warning, but hoping that he had finally come to his senses and would admit how he felt about her, she made her way along the passage, then passed through an arch in the low wall that led onto the banks. A line of oak trees flanked the water's edge. Leaves, ripped from branches by recent winds, covered the muddy banks in a whispering, russet-gold mantle. Elwen halted. There was only an old man dressed in black standing beneath an oak and staring out across the river. Wrapping her arms around her, Elwen looked about. There was no sign of Will.

'Elwen.'

She turned at the thin, breathless voice and saw the old man walking towards her. Her heart gave a shocked little flutter as she recognised him. It was Will's master, Everard de Troyes.

The Seven Stars, Paris, 27 October 1266 AD

Adela opened her herbal and carefully turned the tattered skins. She found the page she was looking for and ran her finger down the list of ingredients. A fire was glowing dully in the small hearth, but something had blocked the chimney and most of the smoke was curling back into the room in a grey, eye-stinging fog. A dirty light came in through the gap in the sacking that was placed across the window. From the street below came the sounds of carts and horses, men calling to one another, a dog barking, a baby squalling. Adela didn't look round as Garin moved up behind her.

'Come back to bed,' he murmured, pressing himself against her and running his hands over the cool crescents of her breasts and down her stomach.

Adela caught his hands. 'I have to have these potions finished for the market tomorrow, or I'll have nothing to sell.'

Garin looked over her shoulder at the herbal. One of the pages described how to make decayed teeth fall out by pressing a frog to them and how to make an infant who refuses the nipple, suckle by smearing honey on the mother's breasts. 'Why do you do this?' he asked irritably.

'Do what?' she said absently, her eyes on her herb shelves.

'Make these medicines.' He lowered his mouth to her neck and nuzzled it. 'Don't I pay you enough?'

'As it happens, no,' she replied, sliding out from between him and the trestle and going to the shelves where she took down two tall clay bottles. She caught Garin's scowl. 'What me and my girls earn barely covers what it costs us to live. Look at this place. You can see the state of it. If I don't pay for repairs on the building soon, I won't have a workplace, or a home left. When I first opened this house it was the most popular in the Quarter. Now, newer houses are starting to take my custom.' Adela put the bottles on the trestle by her pestle and mortar with a heavy sigh.

How disappointed her father would be to see what she had made of the place. When he had run the guesthouse, they had been wealthy enough. The trouble was most of his customers had been priests and scholars, visiting the Sorbonne and neighbouring colleges. When she had taken over the business, the numbers of guests had rapidly dwindled. She had guessed because the priests and scholars thought it unseemly to stay in a woman's household. When she could no longer afford to pay the tax to the provosts, she had been given the choice to sell up, or change it. Not bearing to part with her childhood home, she had chosen the latter and having no trade and no time to learn one, she had opted, aged sixteen, to sell the only commodity she possessed.

'I don't have a choice but to make these medicines,' she told Garin. 'And if I did, I would gladly choose it over this.'

'This? You mean me?'

'No,' she said quietly, cradling his cheek with her hand. 'Everyone but you.'

Garin put his hand over hers. After a moment, Adela gently disengaged herself and sat down at her bench. Garin went to where his hose lay in a rumpled pile by the pallet. As he picked them up, he dislodged the small velvet pouch which had been lying on them. It clinked on the floor. Garin lifted it by the string. It was worryingly light. Once, he had anxiously hoarded every penny Prince Edward had doled out to him. Now his fortune was almost spent; one coin after another pressed into Adela's palm each time she opened her door to him. He looked at her, shaking poppy seeds into her mortar bowl. His eyes travelled over her smooth white skin, the supple arch and curve of her back, the gap between her thighs that always made his stomach tighten. Her breasts pressed against the trestle edge as she leaned over and took up her pestle. Stone grated against stone as she pounded and ground the mixture. She looked so studious; violet eyes intent; mouth turned down at the corners; brow creased. Garin realised that this was how Adela looked when she was doing something she truly enjoyed. When she was in bed with him, or seeing clients downstairs she seemed happy enough. But watching her now, he realised how much of that was an act. He found himself smiling a little secretive smile, thinking how he was the only one she showed this face to. He wondered if this was what married couples felt. Had his father ever observed his mother perform some familiar task of an evening, content to watch and not to touch? He didn't know. But, for a moment, he caught a glimpse of a possible future where two people could sit and be, safe in the silence of years.

As she rose to take another bottle from the shelf, Garin dropped his hose and the pouch to the boards and crossed to her.

'Garin . . .!' Adela started to say, as he turned her to face him. Her fist was full of lavender buds, their scent cloying.

'I can't help wanting you.' Garin bent to kiss her neck, his mouth hot, hungry on her skin. 'It's not my fault.'

'Stop,' she breathed.

'No,' he murmured in her ear.

The door flew inwards with a bang.

Garin whipped round, naked and startled, as a man strode into the chamber.

Rook took in the scene with a mocking leer. 'So this is what knights spend their days doing? I was wondering why no one had recaptured Jerusalem from the Saracens yet.'

Garin crossed to Rook and shoved him towards the door. 'Get out!'

Rook's smirk vanished. He knocked Garin's fists aside and one of his hands flew to Garin's throat which he gripped with crushing force. 'I've told you before, you little shit. Don't ever get above yourself with me!'

'Get off him.'

Rook glanced round at the cold, husky voice, to see Adela staring at him. She was still naked, but made no effort to cover herself. 'Begone, whore,' he growled, flicking his head towards the door.

Garin was gagging from the pressure around his windpipe. He grabbed Rook's hand and tried to prize it off him.

Adela walked calmly over to Rook, violet eyes glinting. 'I will go nowhere. This is my property and you, sir, are trespassing.'

'Your property?' jeered Rook.

Adela didn't answer, but craned her head and looked past him to the door. 'Fabien!' she yelled.

'Let him stay, Adela,' croaked Garin, keeping his eyes on Rook.

After a moment, there came the sound of pounding footsteps in the passage. The door burst open. Rook was mildly surprised to see a colossus of a man with thick black eyebrows and a grim expression enter the room. He looked from Rook to Garin, then to Adela.

'Are you sure?' Adela asked Garin.

Rook slowly relinquished his hold on Garin's throat, his eyes on the Herculean manservant.

Garin drew a breath and nodded. 'Can you let us alone for a moment?'

After a pause, she waved the manservant away. He left without a word and Adela went unhurriedly to the wicker screen that partitioned her work area and pulled down a red silk robe. She drew it around her shoulders, ignoring Rook's poisonous gaze. She had seen plenty like him in her profession; sly, brutish men who only knew how to communicate with forked tongues and fists. As she crossed to the door, she caught Garin's gaze. 'I won't be far.'

When she had gone, Rook looked to Garin, who swept his hose from the floor and stepped into them, yanking the laces tight. 'Slut's got a mouth on her. But I guess you'd know all about that.' He sneered. 'Well, you've broken every other oath you took in the Temple. Poverty and obedience went a while ago, didn't they? I suppose it's long past time your chastity went. She's a tasty bit too. When she's not talking.' He looked at the closed door. 'Might try her out myself.'

'You can't.'

Rook's eyes narrowed at Garin's rapid response. After a moment, he began to laugh. It was a harsh, hateful sound. 'You're sweet on her, aren't you? You, a high and mighty Templar, in love with a whore? A warrior of Christ tender on some cheap slut? Oh, this'll keep me in humour for days this will!'

Rook's words stung Garin's ears. 'How did you find me?' he said through gritted teeth.

Rook's laughter subsided. 'You want to be careful. I followed you from the preceptory. I take it they don't know what you've been up to?'

'What are you doing here?' said Garin quickly, before Rook could start sniggering again.

Rook sat on the pallet and slid off one of his mud-spattered boots. He massaged a bony, black-soled foot. Time had not been kind to him and although he was only ten years Garin's senior, he looked much older. He inspected a ridge of hard, yellow skin on his heel, then picked at it. 'We've got business, you and I. Business for our master.' He glanced up at Garin and grinned. More of his teeth had succumbed to the rot that infested them since Garin had seen him last. His brown and yellow gums were warped, raw-looking. 'You didn't think we'd forgotten about you, did you?'

Garin didn't respond. Just looking at Rook made him feel physically sick with loathing.

'Remember that book you told our master about? The one what was stolen?'

Garin decided that it was better to play along rather than resist. The sooner he answered, the sooner Rook would leave. 'What of it?'

'We reckon we know where it is,' said Rook, easing a worm of black dirt out from between his toes. 'There's a troubadour who's going to perform for the king. He's got it, so we think. I've had myself a little ask about and I've heard he's already here and is going to do his recital on All Hallows.' Rook wiped the dirt from his toes on the pallet. 'What do you know of Everard de Troyes?'

'He's a priest at the preceptory. Possibly the man my uncle said was head of the Brethren. He's also the master of a former comrade of mine from London, Will Campbell.'

Rook frowned. 'Do you think this Campbell knows about the Anima Templi?'

Garin shrugged moodily. 'How should I know?'

Rook scowled. 'You'll keep a civil tongue with me, boy, or your whore will miss her pleasures when I rip it out. I've heard the Dominicans have been trying to stop the troubadour's performance. They've enlisted the help of the Temple, so my source told me. Have you noticed any unusual visitors to the preceptory these past few weeks?'

Garin kept silent for a few moments. 'Yes,' he answered finally. 'I've seen a Dominican and an old comrade of my uncle's, Hasan.'

Rook looked pleased. 'That fits with what we suspect. Hasan has been associated with both your uncle and the priest. We believe he's some sort of mercenary for their secret group.' Rook slid his boot on with a grunt and stood up. 'Our master reckons the priest will try to get the book from the troubadour. We'll let him do the hard work, then we'll take it from him.'

'How do you know the priest will take it?'

'Well, I guess that all depends on whether or not what you told us was the truth, doesn't it?' Rook took a few steps towards Garin. 'If it's as precious as you said it was, then we've no doubt they'll want it back. Just as they'll want it back when we have it.'

'I told you what my uncle told me. If there was a lie uttered, it was his.' Garin paused. 'What happens if the Dominicans get the book?'

'It would be better if they did. It would be easier to take it from their college than from the Temple's vaults.' Rook grunted. 'We'll deal with that if it happens. Until the performance, you'll be our ears and eyes in the preceptory. You'll keep close watch on the priest and his Saracen friend for the next few days. If they take the book from the troubadour, you'll be waiting to steal it from them.'

'What are you going to do while I'm doing all this?' protested Garin.

Rook glanced at the door. 'I'll be keeping your sweetheart company,' he said, looking back at Garin with a sly grin, 'and making sure you do it right. There'll be that lordship in it for you if you do, our master said. And this.' He reached into his russet cloak and pulled out a pouch. He held it up so Garin could see it. 'Get the book and you'll be swiving that bitch for a year.' He stuffed the pouch back into his cloak and crossed to the door. 'Get dressed. I'm going to have one of those pretty little girls downstairs make me something to eat. We'll talk about our plan some more when I'm done.' Rook headed into the passage, pushing past Adela who was standing outside.

She entered after he had gone. 'Who was that?'

Garin, his cheeks flushed and his breaths shallow, didn't answer. He chewed viciously at a fingernail, then pulled his undershirt from the screen. He paused, his hands tightening around the thin material. He wanted to rip it, feel it break and imagine that it was Rook's neck. He gave a short cry of frustrated rage.

'Hush.' Adela crossed the chamber and eased the shirt from his grip. She let it drop to the floor and laced her hands around his neck. She stood on the tips of her toes to kiss his mouth.

Garin didn't respond at first, then, slowly, he wrapped his arms around her and buried his face in her neck, taking deep breaths of her hair, which smelt of oranges and a spice he couldn't place. It was a warm, exotic smell that reminded him of his mother.

On the death of her husband, after she had been forced to relinquish the estate in Lyons, Lady Cecilia had become very protective of the few valuable belongings she had been able to take to Rochester with her. One of these possessions was a box of spices that she had kept by her bedside. She used to play a game with Garin when he had been especially good, or done his lessons well. She would sit him beside her on the bed and make him close his eyes, then she would take small pinches of the different spices in the box and hold them to his nose for him to guess their names. If he got them right, he would get a taste, just a lick mind, of the residue on his mother's finger. That most of the spices had lost their flavour from being taken out so often didn't bother him, it was the soft, playful tone of his mother's voice and her gentle touch that he had relished. Those rare, intimate moments were the only times he had ever truly felt her love.

Garin relinquished his hold on Adela abruptly. 'I have to get dressed.' He went to the trestle and took up his leather sack that was lying there.

'Who is he, Garin?' repeated Adela behind him.

Garin didn't answer.

'Tell me.'

'Mind your own business, God damn it!'

Adela's violet eyes glittered. 'I can quite easily have you *both* thrown out of here.'

'I'm sorry. I just . . . Can you let me alone for a moment?' Garin looked round. 'Please, Adela.'

She nodded after a moment, then left, closing the door quietly behind her.

Garin pulled on his undershirt and opened his sack. At the bottom of the bag was his stained and crumpled mantle. He touched a finger to the white cloth: symbol of a knight's purity. Rook's words sounded in his mind, searing him. *You, a high and mighty Templar, in love with a whore?* They were so close to the words his own mind had taunted him with. But when he was here, in Adela's bed, his status did not matter, nothing mattered except the smell and taste and feel of her. Sometimes he wondered if she had drugged him with some potion that kept him coming back to her, always hungry, never sated. As he shook out his mantle, something fell out of the folds. It was his uncle's eye patch. He picked it up and ran his thumb in a circle over its centre, where the leather was cracked with time and use. Holding it up to his eye, Garin stared at himself in the dusty, silver mirror hanging on Adela's wall.

23

The Royal Palace, Paris

1 November 1266 AD

E lwen lifted her skirts and stepped lightly through the mud. It had begun raining in the night and the area around the chapel was sodden. In the damp morning the majestic structure seemed rather grey and forlorn, the many stone faces that peered from its walls darkened by rain. Opposite the porch was an old yew. Elwen stooped under its low, brushy branches and waited, her eyes on the closed doors of the chapel.

In her service to the queen, Elwen had been inside Sainte-Chapelle on several occasions. But the first time had been the most memorable. She had discovered the two-storey structure, hidden by a wall and surrounded by trees, two days after her arrival in Paris. She had entered the porch to peek through the doors, and it was there that King Louis had found her. Terrified that she would be reprimanded, Elwen had been astonished when the king, smiling down at her, had ushered her inside. She had tried to look everywhere at once as the king had led her through the ground floor. Her gaze was saturated by the magnificence of the interior: the monumental stained glass, the vivid colours of the murals, the lifelike statues bowing from the walls. On the first floor, the king's private chambers, was a marble stand before an altar on which was placed a small, crooked piece of wood. Elwen had been amazed to discover that this seemingly worthless object, conveyed from Constantinople, had compelled the king to build the chapel which enclosed it. But when Louis had told her in deep, reverent tones that it was a piece of Christ's crown of thorns, Elwen had understood completely. It was like the treasures she collected: the stick wasn't really a stick, but the external manifestation of all that the king held dear – his faith, his dreams. They had knelt together before that fragment of ancient wood for almost an hour. Elwen had never felt so safe, so warm as she had when kneeling on the icy stones beside the King of France. She in her plain white apron and gown, hardly daring to breathe in that stillness, him in his vermilion cloak trimmed with ermine, eyes closed in prayer. Since that day, the king had rarely acknowledged her presence in his household, but, for Elwen, that single moment had been enough.

She wrapped her arms tighter about her, worried that the enchantments of Sainte-Chapelle might delay the troubadour for some time yet. She had been waiting for an opportunity to meet with Pierre de Pont-Evêque for four days, but a persistent following of twittering ladies and inquisitive lords had been continually clustered around him. Everard had said that she had to take the Book of the Grail from Pierre before the reading.

The Great Hall was now being readied for the performance: trestles set with jugs and goblets; walls decked with banners; torches lit. There was an added air of excitement and festivity as today was All Hallows. That evening, the royal court and the visiting nobles would be joining the king and his family for a special Vespers service in Sainte-Chapelle, after which would be the recital and the banquet.

In the city, the mood surrounding the troubadour's arrival had been mixed. Many people, who had been waiting to see him, had been disappointed to learn that Pierre would only be performing for the king. Others, mostly priests from the local colleges, led by the Dominicans, had continued campaigning to have him banned. Louis had spent a great deal of money on the evening's celebrations and wasn't willing to let the performance be ruined and his guests disappointed, but Elwen had gleaned from the queen that he secretly felt he'd got more than he had bargained for by inviting Pierre to his court. He had, however, soothed some of the local colleges by saying that if he felt the code of conduct was being broken he would stop the reading immediately.

Just go to his room and take it whilst he's gone.

But Elwen stayed where she was. Other than the immediate nerves the thought provoked, there was another reason why she wanted to delay her retrieval of the book. Everard had not told her everything and those missing details and the priest's obvious desperation in coming to her intrigued her greatly. In return for undertaking this assignment, Elwen had made Everard promise to initiate Will. The priest had had little choice but to accede to her demand; she would have refused if he hadn't. But despite the fact that she would gain something from this dangerous task, namely in Will's gratitude and the realisation of his dream, there was also a part of her that was excited by what she was about to do. She felt like one of the heroines in the stories she read. *The troubadour probably has it on him anyhow,* she told herself, stamping her feet in an effort to ward off the chill that was seeping into her bones.

A short time later, the chapel doors swung open and two men came out. Elwen felt a rush of anticipation. She watched them through lowered eyes as they stood in the porch talking, acutely aware of how ridiculous a figure she must look, bedraggled and half hidden by the branches of the yew. Pierre de Pont-Evêque was, as Maria had said, a comely man. Although short and slender of build, what he lacked in height and girth he made up for in the way he held himself – erect and self-assured like a man of rank. He had fine brown hair and bright blue eyes that shone with an inner intensity. Elwen averted her gaze as those eyes turned towards her.

'I look forward to entertaining you tonight, my lord,' she heard Pierre say. The troubadour's voice was rich and resonant. 'I ask that you pass on my thanks to his majesty for allowing me to view his private chapel. It is, as people say, a wonder of this world.'

His companion left the porch, cursing as the rain pelted him. Elwen, breath held, watched Pierre stroll towards her, his hide boots sloshing through the mud. His blue hose and velvet tunic were beaded with rain.

'And there, by the mist-wreathed lake, she stood. Guinevere beneath her bower, waiting for Lord Lancelot.' Pierre smiled as he parted the branches of the yew. 'Tell me, lady, is it any drier in there? And, if so, might I join you?'

'No,' said Elwen, with a laugh, ducking out from under the tree. 'It isn't drier at all.'

Pierre studied her. He was shorter than she was, but Elwen felt herself shrink beneath his potent gaze.

'Then why do you stand beneath it, half frozen, when a roof of stone would offer better shelter?'

Elwen didn't answer.

'You are one of the queen's handmaidens?'

Elwen was surprised. She thought, if he knew her position, he might also know her purpose in speaking with him. Perhaps he was a sorcerer? 'I am.' She felt her confidence ebb further. 'How did you know?'

'I enquired who she was, my pretty shadow, lingering behind me these past few days. Everywhere I turned you were there.'

'Oh.' Elwen was crestfallen; she thought she had been careful.

'What is your name?'

'Grace.'

'How apt,' said Pierre, his blue eyes shimmering. 'And you, Grace, do you wish to know if the tales about me are true? Was my Romance written by the Devil? Am I an evil mage, come to tempt the king from the arms of God by my sorcerer's guile?'

'No.' Elwen stood a little straighter and made herself look him in the eye. 'I seek answers from a poet of his art.'

Pierre looked slightly surprised. 'Do you?' He smiled and seemed to think. 'Well, I have a little time left before I must prepare for my reading. You may ask your questions, Lady Grace, but in a drier place. Perhaps we might adjourn to my chamber?' He gestured for her to walk on ahead of him. 'And speak of poetry?'

On the walk through the palace, Elwen kept her head low, hoping that no one would hail her. The passages were busy with servants, clerks and courtiers, some aiding in the preparations for the performance, others going about their daily duties. Every step she took, Elwen heard the troubadour's footfalls a little way behind her, felt his gaze on her back. When they reached the room where he had been lodged in a tower that looked down on the river, her heart was beating so hard against her chest she thought it might break free and fly off like a bird. Pierre glanced quickly up and down the empty passage, then opened the door of his chamber, ushering her inside. As he closed the door, Elwen scanned the small chamber. There were a few chests stacked against one wall and a small sack bag on a pallet, half covered by a blanket.

'The view compensates for the lack of comfort.'

Elwen turned as Pierre moved up behind her.

'Please,' he said, motioning to the window seat.

Elwen glanced out of the window as she sat. The Seine flowed far beneath her, as grey as the sky. Beyond the banks, the city was obscured by mist. She shivered as Pierre sat beside her.

'You are cold,' he murmured, clinching one of her hands between his palms and rubbing it gently.

'I was pleased when I heard you were going to perform here,' said Elwen, watching his hands making slow circles around hers. 'I have always enjoyed the Romances. I've read some works of Chrétien de Troyes and the poems of Arnaut de Mareuil, but I've never had the opportunity to ask a poet where he draws his inspiration from.'

'And is that your question of me, lady?' asked Pierre, lifting her hand to his lips and blowing. 'From where do I draw my inspiration?'

She nodded, feeling his breath hot on her icy skin.

'My inspiration takes many forms.' Pierre lowered her hand and took up the other. 'A whispered conversation, the smell of rain on fallen leaves.' He breathed across her skin again.

'What about the works of others?' said Elwen, delicately removing her hand from his and folding it in her lap. 'I have heard that many poets take inspiration from their fellows.'

'For some works.' Pierre leaned back against the curve of the window, his eyes half lidded by the upward tilt of his head. 'Ancient tales, for example, that draw upon the great men and women of history. Such works are divined, of course, in the first instance from sources other than our own. But I do not need another man's words to tell me how it is to love.' He smiled. 'Therefore, most of my work comes from my heart and mind alone.' Pierre studied her, his head cocked to one side. 'Have you had your fill of questions, lady?'

Elwen pushed on. 'I only ask because I heard a rumour that the Romance isn't your own work.'

'What?' Pierre's eyes focused sharply on her. 'Where did you hear this rumour?'

'Someone in the palace,' said Elwen, surprised by the change in his manner. Gone was his indolent posture. He was as alert as a deer sensing a hunter. 'A servant.'

'And what did this servant say, exactly?'

'That you might have stolen the book you read from,' she replied tentatively. Elwen gasped as Pierre grabbed her arm.

'I am no *thief*!'

'No,' she said quickly, shaking her head. 'I'm sure you're not. It was only what I heard.'

He released her slowly, as if fearing she might bolt. 'I am no thief,' he repeated. 'Neither am I a sorcerer, nor a Devil worshipper.'

Pierre slumped forward, resting his arms on his knees. He seemed suddenly smaller, withered somehow, as if all the air had been sucked from him. The fire was gone from his eyes and his gaze was now dull, downcast.

'When one achieves status, those without it seek to destroy you. Envy is a most effective poison. It seeps inside men's hearts and turns them into wretches. I have spent half my life seeking fame. Now that I have it, I'm no longer sure I want it.' He looked at Elwen. 'No, I didn't write the Book of the Grail,' he said, his tone hard again, 'but neither did I steal it. The rumour you heard is, as with all the rest, false and I ask that you do not repeat it.'

'I promise I won't,' said Elwen. Pierre's sudden change had unnerved her. She didn't feel excited anymore. 'I'm sorry,' she said, rising. 'It was wrong of me to take up your time. I will let you prepare yourself for your performance.'

'Wait!' called Pierre as she made for the door.

Elwen turned nervously.

'Don't go.' Pierre gave her a sad smile. 'Many in the palace have sought my company since I arrived: ladies wishing to be immortalised in poetry, lords looking to entice me into their households where I will be a mark of their status. I've found myself uncommonly nervous at the prospect of entertaining such a rapacious throng in a place where I was once scorned and rejected. But your presence and your interest in my art are welcome in equal measure. I apologise for being short with you when you questioned my ownership of the Romance, but since I have been travelling I have been beset by rumour and evil accusation and, I am fairly certain, pursued.'

'Pursued?' said Elwen, pretending shock. Everard had told her that he had sent someone after the troubadour.

'In several inns I visited on my journey from the south I learnt that a man had been asking questions about me, where I had stayed and when I had left and the like. A foreigner, I was told.'

'Perhaps he just wanted to see you perform?'

'Perhaps,' said Pierre, sounding unconvinced. 'I stayed with a friend for several weeks in Blois and must have evaded him.' He patted the window seat. 'Will you sit, lady?'

Elwen hesitated, then returned to the window seat, feeling a little surer. An idea came to her. 'Might I have the loan of a blanket? I'm wet through.'

'Of course,' replied Pierre gallantly. He went to the pallet and whipped off the blanket, which he wrapped carefully around her shoulders.

Elwen held the blanket to her with one hand and took off her damp cap. She shook her hair loose, noting the way Pierre's eyes were drawn to her tumbling curls. She had often noticed men looking at her in this way: merchants in the markets; guards in the palace corridors; Will before he checked himself, all with that same hunger in their eyes. She liked it. It made her feel unconquerable, yet, at the same time, desiring to be conquered. Whenever she saw that look, she knew, in a world dominated by men, that she, a woman, held all the power.

With a smile she sat, closer to Pierre this time, her body turned towards his. 'You were speaking before of where you found inspiration for your work? I would like to hear more about that.'

'Yes,' said Pierre. 'My work.' His eyes were alight again. He went to the pallet and picked up the sack bag that the blanket had partially covered. Reaching inside, he drew out a vellum-bound book and a sheaf of parchments. As he returned to the window seat, Elwen recognised the book in his hands from Everard's description. 'This is my work,' Pierre said, placing the Book of the Grail between them and handing her the sheaf of parchments. 'My true work.'

Elwen forced her eyes from the book and took the parchments. She read the words on the first skin, written in a delicate hand. It was a poem dedicated to a woman named Catherine. It was deeply sensual. 'Your work is very . . . passionate,' she said, returning the skins to him. Her cheeks felt warm.

'It is passion without a voice.' Pierre looked despondently at the parchments. 'In an age before ours the poets, whose works you've read, wrote with such passion as this. They wrote of the slow, painful delight of a man's attainment of love; the anguish of waiting; the pleasures of the heart and flesh. But courtly love isn't what it was. Now the poets write of the man who denies these pleasures and abstains from his desires. He has become the noble of the piece, not the man who would cast aside all thought of sin for the achievement of his lady's love.' He shook his head. 'But love cannot be caged. It doesn't know reason or sin. It is the wild, ravenous beast that craves without restraint.'

Elwen said nothing, but she nodded. Pierre picked up the Book of the Grail and she watched him turn it over in his hands. The gold-leaf words on the cover glinted brightly in the dull daylight.

'This book was my brother's. I took it when he died of a sickness two winters ago. I used some of its contents to recreate the story of Perceval: a new Romance for a new age. I knew, if I could only make a name for myself, I could give my true poems a voice. This book has given me that name. That power.' He opened it and flicked through the pages. 'The people have flocked to see me.'

'Did your brother write it?'

'No,' said Pierre with a tired laugh. 'Antoine couldn't write his name. My brother's business was wine.'

'How did he come to be in possession of it?'

Pierre glanced at her. 'I must ask for your discretion.'

'You have it,' murmured Elwen. When Pierre hesitated, she placed a conspiratorial hand on his knee. 'I promise.'

Pierre smiled, studying her. 'He found it on his doorstep.' He nodded at Elwen's expression and gave a short laugh. 'I think my version of the angel bringing it to me sounds less absurd, doesn't it? Don't ask me how it got there. One morning, years ago, he opened his door and found it there. He showed it to me once when I visited him. I had a look through it, but I wasn't interested in writing anything at that time. After I was dismissed from this court, I returned to my family home in Pont-Evêque where my father attempted to persuade me into what he deemed more suitable employment. He didn't understand poetry, called it a fool's occupation. I was so disheartened by the king's rejection of my work that, I confess, I had started to believe him. But when Antoine died, the muse had begun to speak to me again and when my father and I came to Paris to deal with his possessions, I took the book and used it as my inspiration.' Pierre looked down at his hands. 'It seemed like the best opportunity I would ever have. I was right. More right than I could have guessed.'

'But are you not concerned? You were, I heard, banned from the court of Aquitaine. Haven't the colleges here been trying to have you stopped from performing? Excommunicated even?'

'My performance has been, I admit, a little strong for delicate palates. I have diluted it since then.' Pierre rose briskly and gathered up the sheaves of parchment and the Book of the Grail. 'Besides, the courtiers here have been awaiting my recital with great eagerness, so I'm told. The Dominicans will not turn the king to their side.'

Elwen, cursing inwardly, watched as he returned the book and his poems to the sack bag. It had been right beside her.

'And it isn't as bad as some say. At least, the Devil hasn't appeared. So far.'

There was a rap at the door.

For a moment, after the knock came, Pierre just stared at the door, then, shaking his head, he went over and opened it a crack. 'Yes? What is it?'

'You wanted to be informed when the Great Hall was ready, sir,' Elwen heard a man's voice say. She guessed it was a servant.

Pierre glanced over his shoulder at Elwen. 'Excuse me, lady,' he said, and slipped out of the door, pulling it to behind him. 'The space has been left clear as I requested?'

'Yes, sir, you'll be performing in front of the royal seat.'

Elwen, listening to their muffled voices, left the window seat and padded to the pallet, straining to hear any creak of the door.

'And the rest of the hall? Has it been arranged as I asked?'

'Yes, sir.'

'Because I performed once near Cluny where someone had set out the benches facing the wrong way. I had to sing to the backs of my audience's heads!'

'It is laid out exactly as you asked, sir.'

'Very well. I will be there shortly.' Pierre opened the door. He looked a little startled to see Elwen standing before him, then smiled. 'Alas, I must depart from your company, lady. I have matters to attend to.'

'I too must go,' said Elwen, returning the smile. 'If I don't complete my chores, I will miss your performance. But thank you for speaking to me. I feel honoured,' she said, feeling utterly wicked, 'that you would take me into your trust.'

'Then perhaps, Grace, you would do me the honour of a second meeting once my recital is ended?'

'If my duties permit.'

Pierre picked up his sack, slung it over his shoulder and opened the door for her. 'I hope they do.' He set off down the passage. 'Oh! One moment!' He pivoted. 'You have something of mine.'

The skin tightened on Elwen's face. 'I have?'

'My blanket,' said Pierre, walking towards her. 'I expect I'll be cold in that tomb of a room without it.'

'It's sodden!' she blurted. 'And the only thing keeping me from freezing where I stand. I'll have a servant fetch another for you, two in fact.'

Pierre bowed. 'Then you may keep it with my blessing.'

Elwen waited for a moment, then set off in the opposite direction to the troubadour, surprised, now that her nerves had begun to calm, by the feeling of triumph that rose in her. Beneath the blanket, the Book of the Grail was a solid shape against her chest.

When she reached her chamber, she found a flustered Maria waiting for her.

'Where have you been?' cried the handmaiden, springing up from her pallet. 'The queen is most displeased. You were expected to dress her after her bathe!'

Elwen's face fell. 'I thought I had no duties.'

Maria flung up her hands in exasperation. 'How can you be so forgetful?'

'Does she plan to punish me?'

Maria gave Elwen a stern look. 'I told the queen that you had taken to your bed with a pain in your stomach. I did your duties for you. And don't worry, you won't miss the performance, I said your affliction would no doubt pass, it being mild and most likely caused by something you ate this morning.'

'I'm fortunate to have a friend like you.'

'You are at that,' agreed Maria. She pointed to the blanket. 'What is that old thing? And where is your cap?' She frowned. 'Elwen, you're soaked through!'

'I need to ask something of you.'

Maria arched an eyebrow. 'Is it your sweetheart you've been meeting out in the rain, whilst I was doing your duties?' She grinned. 'Now you'll have to tell me who he is.'

'This is important, Maria.'

Maria's smile vanished. 'What is it?' she murmured, crossing the room.

'I don't want to involve you in this, but I have little choice. You've helped me already today and I promise I'll repay you for that, but I need you to do something else for me and I cannot tell you my reasons for asking.'

Maria nodded slowly. 'What?'

'I have to send a message to the Temple as quickly as possible. I need you to go to Ramon. I believe he can be trusted and I think he would be able to leave the palace without too much trouble. I know he would take this message if you asked him.'

Maria flushed self-consciously. 'I wouldn't be so certain of that. I don't think he even notices me.'

'But he is your friend, nonetheless.'

'Perhaps. Yes.'

'I don't want to write this message down. Ramon must deliver it in person.'

'Who is the message for?'

'A priest. Everard de Troyes.'

'A priest! Do not tell me you're in love with a man of God!'

'No,' said Elwen, quickly, 'this has nothing to do with that.'

The handmaiden sighed. 'What shall I say to Ramon?'

'Have Ramon tell the priest that I have what he wants. He must send his man to meet me half an hour before Vespers. He'll know where.'

'That's the message?'

'Yes.'

Maria paused, studying Elwen intently. 'Are you in trouble?'

Elwen's laugh was a little high-pitched. 'When am I not?' She grew solemn again. 'Will you do this for me?'

'I will.'

'Then I owe you a second debt.'

'That you do,' said Maria, half seriously, both concerned for her friend and thrilled by the excuse to see Ramon.

When Maria had gone, Elwen pulled out her black box. There was just enough room for the book if she laid it flat across the compartments. Locking the box, she pushed it under the pallet with her foot and went to the clothes-perch for a dry gown.

Pierre poured himself another goblet of wine and strolled to the dais that spanned the far end of the Great Hall. He sat on the boards and leaned back on his elbow, surveying the grand chamber. On his way to the hall, he had been met by a lord who had insisted he come for a sip of wine and a discussion of his prospects in Paris and because of the delay, he had little time left in which to prepare. But the Great Hall was certainly fit for the occasion.

On the dais were placed the thrones of the king and queen, each covered with a feather-filled silk cushion. King Louis' blue banner hung on the wall behind, the gold fleur-de-lys shimmering in the blaze of a hundred candles. Other banners were strung around the hall, decorated with the crests of the noble houses whose dukes and princes would be in attendance. The area before the dais, where Pierre would give the recital, was scattered with dried, scented rose petals. Trestles were placed in rows, decorated with sprays of autumn leaves – amber, crimson, gold – and jewelled basins filled with wine were set at intervals along the centre of the boards. Following the performance, the All Hallows banquet would be served in Pierre's honour. Or, at least, the king's honour, but it felt like his nonetheless.

Pierre finished his wine and jumped nimbly up. His sack bag, containing the Book of the Grail and his poetry, was lying on one of the trestles. He addressed the servants who were arranging the leaves on the trestles. 'My lords and ladies,' he called with a flourish. 'If I may be so bold as to grace you with a verse from the Chanson de Roland?' He cleared his throat, pleased by the hall's acoustics, and closed his eyes.

Most of the servants stopped what they were doing and listened as Pierre sang, the words lifting clear and strong from his mouth to fill the cavernous chamber.

'*The day goes down, dark follows on the day. The Emperor sleeps, the mighty Charlemayn . . .*

'Pierre de Pont-Evêque.'

Pierre opened his eyes and frowned down at the source of the interruption. Two men dressed in ragged black robes were moving through the hall towards the dais. They were barefoot and wore large wooden crosses around their necks. Pierre knew who they were for their appearance was famed. Behind the two Dominican friars came five other men, whose appearance was even more legendary. Pierre's eyes fixed on the swords in the hands of the Templar Knights and a cold dread rose in him. The servants were backing away from the company, whispering.

'I am Pierre. What do you want with me, my good brothers?'

'We are not your brothers,' said one of the Dominicans, stepping forward as the company came to a halt.

The young man had solemn, dark eyes that Pierre felt looked right through him. Pierre tried to pull himself up to his full height, the lack compensated by the level of the dais. 'Whatever this is about, you had best make it quick. I'm afraid I do not have much time for conversation.'

'Pierre de Pont-Evêque,' said the Dominican as if Pierre hadn't spoken at all. 'By order of the House of the Jacobins of Paris, disciples of the Holy Dominican Order, authorised for the elimination of heresy by blessed instrument of God, Pope Gregory IX, you are hereby arrested.'

'Arrested? On what charge?'

'The charge of heresy.'

'Listen,' said Pierre quickly, 'I don't know what you've heard, but I can assure you it is all false. I'm no heretic!'

'You will immediately hand over the book you are in possession of, this . . . *Devil's* work and come with us.'

'You cannot do this!' shouted Pierre, fear taking him over. 'I'm the guest of his majesty! He invited me to perform here tonight!'

'Where is the Book of the Grail?'

'Leave that alone!' Pierre's gaze had been caught by a tall, black-haired Templar who had moved over to the trestles and was reaching for his sack bag.

The Dominican turned. 'Sir de Navarre!' he barked. 'Step away. I will deal with that.'

Nicolas de Navarre paused, his hand hovering over the sack. 'Be my guest, Friar Gilles,' he said after a moment, moving back and motioning to the bag.

As Gilles removed the wooden cross from around his neck and laid it over the sack bag, intoning a prayer, Pierre jumped down from the dais.

'Seize him!' called the second Dominican.

'Get the king!' Pierre shouted to the bewildered-looking servants. He was silenced by a vicious cuff round the back of his head by the chainmailed fist of one of the knights.

'That will teach you to spread filth about us!' hissed the Templar in his ear.

Pierre hung limply in their grasp as Gilles finished his prayer and slid his hand carefully into the sack bag. 'You cannot do this,' groaned the troubadour.

'You have sinned against God and polluted Christendom,' said the second Dominican, his tone as adamant as his gaze. 'But in our house you will be given the chance to redeem yourself. We will endeavour to save you from the darkness that compelled you to go against the Lord and will attempt to exorcise the evil within you. Those who stray from the path of God must pay the price for their actions. If you ally yourself with Satan . . .'

'It isn't here.'

The Dominican turned.

Pierre lifted his head groggily as Gilles shook the empty sack over the trestle. His poetry was scattered across the board, but of the Book of the Grail there was no sign. Nicolas de Navarre began to rifle through the parchments as Gilles strode over to Pierre.

'Where is it?'

'What?' said Pierre, dazed.

Gilles snatched out his hand and took hold of Pierre's chin. He forced Pierre's head up roughly. 'Where is the book?'

Pierre made a few choking noises, his Adam's apple bobbing wildly in his throat.

'Friar Gilles.'

The Dominican glanced round distractedly. Nicolas de Navarre had finished going through the parchments and had come over to where the knights were holding Pierre.

'Perhaps I should have a go,' offered the knight.

Gilles looked as if he were about to argue, then stepped away.

Pierre's breaths were rapid as Nicolas moved forward. The knight had a crossbow and a dagger hanging from his belt, along with his sword. 'It's in my bag!' blurted Pierre, before Nicolas had even spoken.

'I'm afraid it's not,' said Nicolas mildly.

Tears began to well in Pierre's eyes. 'Please! I didn't even write it! I swear!'

'I believe you,' said Nicolas. He lowered his voice to a whisper. 'If you co-operate with the Dominicans you have a chance to escape with your life, but you must tell them where the book is. If you do not, they will be forced to kill you for being a heretic and will hunt down the book without your assistance. They will no doubt start by visiting your family in Pont-Evêque.'

'My family?' murmured Pierre.

Nicolas dropped his voice further until it was little more than a breath on Pierre's cheek. 'If they do not find the book there, the Dominicans will strip them and tie them to stakes in the town square. Your father, Jean, your mother, Eleanor, your sisters, Aude and Kateline. They will each be daubed in oil and roasted over a charcoal fire, so slowly that they will be able to watch their flesh char and split and their own bones blacken and drop out of their feet and their legs and their . . .'

'No! *My God!* I put the thing in my bag earlier! I was in my room. I put it in my bag. *I swear!*'

Gilles, who hadn't been able to hear what Nicolas had said, looked impressed at the outburst. 'Then where is it now?' he demanded as Nicolas straightened.

'I don't know! I haven't taken it out! It should be there, I don't understand why . . .' Pierre stopped.

'What?' said Nicolas quickly.

Pierre raised his head. 'There was a girl, a servant. She came to my room wanting to talk about poetry.'

'She could have taken it? Is that what you're saying?'

'I left the room, not for long, but . . .' Pierre nodded. 'Yes. She could have taken it.'

'Who is she?' snapped Gilles.

'Grace.'

'One moment, friar,' called Nicolas as Gilles made for the doors. 'What does she look like?' he asked Pierre.

'Tall. Slim. Long gold hair. Pretty.'

Nicolas went over to Gilles. 'There must be hundreds of servants here, friar,' he said quietly. 'I will find the head steward and ask him where this girl is. I suggest you take the troubadour to his rooms and search them to make sure he hasn't left the book there by mistake, or is lying about this girl and has hidden it. Also, I expect the king will have been told of our arrival by now. He will want answers.'

Gilles frowned at Nicolas's forthrightness, but acceded with a stiff nod. 'Very well. But you will bring the girl here if you find her. I will want to question her myself.'

'As you wish.'

Nicolas waited for the other knights and the two Dominicans to escort
Pierre forcibly out of the hall, then left himself. After asking one of the
servants still lingering at the back of the hall where the steward's quarters
were, he moved quickly through the wide passages, past courtiers and
officials, ignoring the curious glances his white mantle drew. But when he
reached the steward's room – a small but well appointed chamber on the
lower floors – he found it empty. Nicolas paused in the corridor outside,
wondering whether to wait, or to search for the man elsewhere. A breeze
was coming through the windows that flanked the long, gloomy passage. It
smelled of the river. It was approaching dusk and the sky was overcast. The
windows looked down over a narrow, walled alley that spanned the palace
compound, separating it from the river at one end and the streets of the
Cité at the other. There were arched openings set into the wall. One of
these openings led onto the riverbank. Nicolas, who had a clear view over
the wall to the banks beyond, caught sight of a man in a grey cloak striding
quickly away from the palace towards a long line of oaks that bordered the
water's edge. The man glanced round briefly, then disappeared in the tree
cover. Even in the fading light, his dark skin was apparent.

24

The Streets of the Ville, Paris

1 November 1266 AD

A fter taking a shortcut along the banks of the Seine to the bridge, Hasan crossed the river and entered the twisting streets of the Ville. In the gathering dark, he moved swiftly past the knots of people heading home after a day's labour, his cloak snatched at and buffeted by the wind which had picked up over the course of the afternoon. The ground was slick with mud, pocked with footprints and hoofprints and lined with the deep runnels of wagon tracks. Low, rolling clouds threatened rain. Moving steadily northwards towards the city walls, Hasan entered the labyrinthine back alleys that cut a warren through the Merchants' Quarter. The Book of the Grail sat flush against his spine between his hose and his belt, concealed by his cloak. He had seen Templar horses hobbled outside the palace gates and had decided to avoid the main routes.

Most of the workshops in the quarter were closed for the evening, the owners having retired to their dwellings above to ready themselves for the All Hallows service, dedicated to the saints, but a few labourers were working late. Passing a blacksmith's, a ropemaker's and a tannery, Hasan caught snatches of firelight behind closed shutters and heard sounds of a hammer clanking on iron, the rustle of a broom across a floor, the scrape and swish of metal on leather. He stopped at a junction. The quickest way lay ahead, down a long, winding alley that passed alongside a church, but the entrance was partially blocked by a pile of large stones, and scaffolding had been erected against the side of the church. After a brief pause, Hasan skirted the stones and entered the alley, weaving between the poles, dust from new-chiselled masonry stinging his eyes. The towering lattice of struts and poles quivered in the gusts of wind. Up ahead, the writhing flames of torches made huge shadows on the alley walls. Hasan heard voices, laughter and the squawking of a bird. He moved out from between the last of the scaffold poles and saw a group of youths blocking the way. Some were standing, others were crouched down forming a tight circle outside the open doorway of a masons' lodge. They all wore white aprons. The squawking sound was coming from two cocks. Approaching, Hasan saw the birds being thrown into the centre of the circle. The screeching reached a feverish pitch as the birds danced and pecked and clawed one another bloody. A short distance beyond the youths, the alley opened out into a square and, beyond that, lay Temple Gate.

Hasan moved close to the wall and inched his way past the group to the screams of a bird in its death throes. A few of the youths cheered, or booed as the bird was silenced and coins were tossed onto a barrel. One, who looked to be about eighteen, cursed and slouched back against the wall. He was lean and lupine with a patchy black beard and droopy, sunken eyes.

Hasan felt a few drops of rain. There was a hiss as the water hit the torch flames. 'Excuse me,' he murmured, squeezing between the lean, black-haired youth and the rest of the group. A few of them glanced at him.

'Hey.'

Hasan looked back.

The youth by the wall was studying him. The youth's gaze was hooded, his expression suspicious. 'You shouldn't have come that way. You might have knocked one of the joists out of place.'

'I will go the other way next time.'

There was a pause.

'Where are you from?' asked the youth.

Hasan didn't respond, but kept on moving, pushing carefully through the last of the masons who were collecting and distributing their wagers.

'Hey!'

Hasan glanced round to see the lean youth push himself from the wall and move after him. More of the masons were looking round.

'I asked you where you are from.'

'Lisbon,' said Hasan. He gave the youth a polite nod. 'Good evening to you.'

'If you're from Lisbon, I'm from Paradise.'

Hasan kept on walking. He heard an incoherent murmur of voices behind him and a few sniggers.

'I've seen your like before, Dark-skin.' The youth's voice was louder now, more confrontational than curious. His footsteps made squelching noises in the mud. 'And they weren't from this side of the sea.'

Just before Hasan reached the end of the alley, he glanced briefly over his shoulder. The youth was still following, slowly, yet purposefully, along

with several of his companions, the group staging the cockfight having
thinned out. Hasan quickened his pace, but before he could step into the
square, three youths wearing masons' aprons appeared in his path. They
seemed slightly out of breath. Hasan recognised them as part of the group.
They must, he realised, have gone through the front of the lodge and come
at the square from a parallel alley to cut him off. His apprehension turned
slowly to fear. One of the youths appeared nervous and was hanging back,
but the expressions on the faces of the other two were grim.

Hasan halted. 'What is it that you want from me?' he asked them,
speaking calmly. 'I am in a hurry.'

'Doesn't sound like he's from Lisbon either, Gui,' said one of the youths
in front of him, obviously addressing the lean man.

Gui came forwards until he and the rest of the masons had penned Hasan
in a circle. There were nine of them in total. Two held torches. The rain
was falling harder now. Beyond, in the square, a little girl was sitting on the
step of a poky, ramshackle building. She had a wooden doll in her hand that
she was walking across her knees. Other than her, the area was empty.

'I've known people who've been to the Holy Land,' said Gui, addressing
Hasan in a low voice filled with hostile contempt. 'I've been told what
things your kind does to Christian women and children. And you think to
come here and walk through our streets, our places of work, our homes?
The king makes Jews wear a mark so we all know who they are. Where's
your mark, Saracen?'

'I am a Christian,' said Hasan. He was still speaking calmly, but he could
feel the menace coming off Gui like a cold wind. It made him shudder
inwardly.

Gui spat on the ground. 'You think our God wants you? A black sheep in
His flock?' He took a step closer. 'Last month, a messenger came to my
mother's house from the preceptory of the Hospitallers. The messenger
told her that her son,' Gui jabbed at his chest with his finger, '*my* brother,
had died when their fortress of Arsuf in the Kingdom of Jerusalem had fallen
to the Saracens. He was an apprentice mason there.' Gui's sunken eyes
were bright in the torchlight. 'I'd never seen him to happy as when he left
on one of their ships. After your sultan, the one the knights call Crossbow,
had finished with the Hospitallers, he killed the rest of those inside. My
brother's head was hacked from his shoulders, his body left to rot. He was
fourteen. My mother cannot *speak* for the grief of it. And yet here you are,
one of his murderers, making yourself at home in our city.'

'I am sorry,' said Hasan quietly. 'I truly am. I too know people, good people, who have died in this war. But, I promise you, Baybars Bundukdari is not my sultan. I have never fought for him, nor sworn allegiance to him. My home is here and has been for many years.'

'He's lying, Gui,' said a voice behind him.

'I swear it,' said Hasan quickly, turning to the grim-faced youth who had spoken, 'I am . . .' His words ended in a grunt as someone shoved him roughly from behind. Hasan lost his balance and stumbled to his knees. The mud seeped icily through his hose. He pushed himself up, then collapsed with a winded gasp as a boot came crashing into his side. He curled around the pain and felt another pain in his head, his other side, then his back, which was cushioned slightly by the wedge of the book. His nose filled with the reek of putrid mud and human waste, his face and hands were coated in black slime. Gui was hovering above him. Hasan caught sight of his face, twisted with rage and grief, as the boot came in again. As it sailed into his face, he felt his nose break. Blood flooded his throat. He gagged. Someone was shouting.

'Gui, don't! You said you just wanted to scare him!'

Hasan twisted away. His eyes were streaming. The blurred shape of Gui loomed over him. He reached inside his cloak, his fingers curling around the hilt of his dagger. He pulled it free, blinking blood from his eye and swept it round towards Gui's legs.

'He's got a knife!' one of the masons shouted.

Gui sidestepped the strike, just in time, and leapt backwards. The other youths had backed away. Hasan, blood pouring from his forehead, his nose and mouth, stumbled to his feet, dagger poised. Half blind, his body singing with pain, he turned and staggered towards the cluster of youths blocking the alley mouth. They parted, steering away from his blade. But as Hasan ran for the opening his foot skidded in the mud and he went down, dropping the dagger. One of the masons shouted and grabbed him, hauling him up by the arms before he could reach for it.

'No!' yelled another, as Gui lunged for the fallen blade.

Snatching it from the mud, Gui ran at Hasan, who was pinned against the chest of the youth who held him.

Hasan felt a fierce pain in his side as Gui thrust the dagger into him. He saw Gui's eyes, filled with hatred, widen, then flood with fear. Gui stepped back, leaving the blade in Hasan's side.

'Jesus, Gui!' cried one of the youths. 'What have you done?'

'Come away!' shouted another, pulling Gui by the arm. '*Come!*'

Hasan sank to the ground as the youth holding him turned and fled with the rest of the group. He tried to push himself up, fighting against waves of sickening, crushing pain, but only managed to crawl a few paces into the square. His fingers clutched at the hilt of the dagger, but he didn't have the strength to remove it. Blood gushed hotly over his freezing hands. His cowl was again whipped back by the wind. The little girl on the step of the building opposite was staring at him.

'Help me!' he croaked.

Her mouth formed a wide, shocked oval, which became a scream, then she dashed inside, clutching her wooden doll. Hasan groaned and sank forward into the mud as the door to the house slammed shut. He thought of Everard waiting in the preceptory and the Book of the Grail felt like a stone on his back, pressing down on him. He felt his consciousness slipping away, draining from him like blood, like breath. The rain drenched his bared head and trickled down his cheeks, mingling with the blood and the tears. The distant bells of Notre Dame began to toll the call to Vespers, shortly followed by the bells of all the other churches in the city, summoning the citizens of Paris to their feast day prayers.

'It should be around here somewhere, if the report was right.' The speaker, a brawny man called Baudouin with thick sandy-coloured hair and a square-shaped face, jumped down from his horse and passed the reins to one of his two mounted companions. His scarlet cloak, the livery of a royal guard, was soaked through. 'Give us that, Lucas,' he said, gesturing to the torch his comrade held.

'We should have had the provosts look into this,' said Lucas, the youngest of the three, irritably as he offered the torch. 'God damn this wet!'

'It isn't the provosts' duty to look into murder,' replied Baudouin, scouring the area, which, save for the erratic sphere of light cast by the sputtering torch flames, was pitch-black. The square was eerily quiet, except for the wind and the hammering rain. The windows of the mean, ramshackle tenement buildings that surrounded it were dark; most of the inhabitants were still in church for the evening service. Baudouin moved forwards, holding the torch aloft and blinking the rain from his eyes. 'That unhappy duty falls, unfortunately, to us.' He turned and grimaced at his comrades. 'The good old captain's men.'

'I'd like to see him out here,' growled the third man. 'Instead of sat on his fat arse by his fire in the palace.'

'Oh, I think he's got enough things to worry about, Aimery, with the uproar caused by that troubadour. He's earning his keep tonight for sure.'

'Yes,' Lucas piped up eagerly, 'what was that about? I saw a company of Templars with the king just before we left. They were arguing.'

Baudouin shrugged uninterestedly. 'Something about the troubadour being a heretic, so I heard. The inquisitors took him away for questioning.'

Lucas shuddered. 'Suddenly our situation doesn't seem so bad.'

'What's that?'

Baudouin looked round to see Aimery pointing to the mouth of an alley. He could just make out a humped shape on the ground. He went closer, the torch flames flickering madly in the wind. It was a body. Baudouin bent down and shook the man's shoulder. He didn't move. 'Hold this,' he said, passing the torch to Aimery, who had dismounted and was coming over. As Aimery took the torch, Baudouin turned the body over.

'Christ!' exclaimed Aimery, crossing himself as the man's face was revealed. 'It's a Saracen!'

Baudouin saw the hilt of a dagger protruding from the man's side. His eyes were open, staring into the rain. Between the smears of mud, his face was greyish blue in colour, livid with bruises, his beard matted with congealed blood. 'Poor soul.' Baudouin opened the man's cloak and gave him a cursory pat down, but could see nothing on him apart from an empty scabbard which looked as if it might fit the dagger. 'Killed with his own weapon by the looks of it. We should ask around. Maybe someone saw who did this.'

'They're all in church,' responded Aimery grudgingly. 'The woman who reported it just said she heard shouting, then saw him lying in the alley. She didn't see who did it. We'll tell the captain and he can decide whether we investigate further. But I doubt he'll want to waste time or men on this.' He shrugged, looking at the body. 'I doubt anyone will miss him much.'

Baudouin sighed, then nodded. He wiped the wet from his face with his sleeve. 'Help me with him then. I'll have to tie him to my horse. We'll take him for burial.'

'Where though?' said Aimery, not getting any closer to the body.

'Not in a churchyard that's for certain,' said Lucas, moving up behind them. He had tethered the horses to a post outside a tannery.

'We've got to put him somewhere,' said Baudouin.

They all thought for a moment.

'The lepers' graveyard,' said Aimery finally.

Lucas shook his head. 'The lazar hospital won't want him.'

'We'll say he's a leper. They'll have to take him then.'

Aimery and Lucas looked to Baudouin. Unable to see any better solution
to the problem, Baudouin nodded. 'All right then. Help me get him up.'

The Temple, Paris, 2 November 1266 AD

When the office of Prime had finished, Will headed out of the chapel,
yawning deeply. The service had been especially long as today was All
Souls', the day of the dead, and during each office special prayers were to be
said for the faithful departed. It was a sombre festival in comparison to the
joyous All Hallows, although the weather was anything but. After days of
wind and rain, the morning had dawned stunningly clear, the sky turning
from black to turquoise to a dazzling, radiant blue. But they paid the price
for it with the sudden drop in temperature. At dawn, the stableboys had
had to hack through a layer of ice that had formed over the horse troughs
during the night. Frost had hardened the mud and dusted the grass silvery-
white.

The knights were moving from the chapel in a line towards the Great
Hall. Will, along with the other sergeants, would have to wait until they
had finished before he broke his own fast and so he headed for the wardrobe
to collect Everard's robe, which he had put in to be mended by the
preceptory's tailor.

'Sergeant Campbell.'

Will looked round to see a servant in a brown tunic hurrying over. He
looked rather furtive and kept glancing over at the knights. 'Yes?'

'There's someone to see you at the gate,' murmured the man.

'Who?'

The servant didn't reply, but, after a quick look over his shoulder, held
out his hand to Will. On his palm was a crushed square of blue linen.

Will frowned as he took it. 'What is it?' he asked, opening up the cloth.
He stared at the dried head of a jasmine flower crumpled within the folds of
material.

'She wouldn't say her name,' whispered the servant. 'Just told me to
give you that. She's waiting out by the road.' He bobbed his head and
scurried off.

Will closed his fist around the square of material and felt his heart begin
to pound. But his mind was not so excited as his body and he felt a tremor of
irritation that Elwen hadn't heeded what he had said only last week; that
she couldn't come here like this. After a pause, he crossed the yard and
moved towards the passage that led past the donjon to the main gate. He

had not gone far when he saw a knight approaching him. It was Garin. The rest of the men had dispersed from the yard, the last of the knights disappearing into the hall.

Garin smiled in greeting. The expression didn't quite reach his eyes, however, and when he spoke his jovial tone seemed forced. 'I was hoping to catch you.'

'What is it?' asked Will, stuffing the square of linen into his tunic pocket.

'I wasn't sure, but I thought I saw an old comrade of my uncle's here the other day. A man called Hasan?'

Will nodded. 'Yes, he's here.'

'Robert told me that he is also a comrade of your master?'

'I'm not sure if comrade is the right word. My master sometimes uses Hasan to track down texts he wants to purchase. Why do you ask?'

'It's nothing really.' Garin shrugged and gave an awkward laugh, although again, Will sensed a tension beneath his apparent humour. 'I just wanted to thank him for trying to save my uncle's life at Honfleur. I didn't have a chance to after the battle, but I've never forgotten how he fought side by side with us.' He paused. 'Do you know where he is?'

'I saw him yesterday evening briefly, but I don't know where he is now. I think he has lodgings in the city. That's about all I can tell you.' Will took a step towards the passage that led to the entrance. 'I'm sorry, I have to go.'

'Are you leaving the preceptory?'

'I'm running an errand for my master. I'll tell Hasan you are looking for him if I see him.'

After passing out of the long shadow of the donjon, Will made his way down the Rue du Temple, which was overhung with a creaking canopy of windswept chestnut trees. Elwen was standing beneath one of the trees, ankle-deep in a rippling sea of crimson leaves. She was wearing a white gown and a blue woollen shawl was wrapped tightly around her shoulders. Will called her name. The sound was snatched from his lips by a gust of wind that rattled the branches above him. Elwen looked round. Her face registered relief. She ran towards him, then halted uncertainly short of him. Will saw she had tears in her eyes and his irritation left him like breath.

'What's wrong?' he asked, going to her.

She put her face in her hands.

'Elwen, what is it?' Will grasped her shoulders gently. 'Talk to me.'

After a moment, she took her hands away. Her cheeks were wet. 'I don't know where to begin. Will, I've done something terrible.' She shook her head fiercely. 'It wasn't supposed to happen like this. I didn't think that anyone would get hurt.'

'What are you talking about?'

Elwen took a breath, then disengaged herself from Will's grasp. 'And the worst of it is, I feel like I've betrayed you.'

Will was silent as Elwen spoke of how Everard had come to her at the palace, asking her to take a book from the troubadour, Pierre de Pont-Evêque, a book, the priest had told her, that had been stolen from the preceptory six years ago. Then she told him how she had made a deal with the priest; that in return, Everard would initiate Will.

Will remained quiet for some time after she had finished. 'Everard asked you to steal this book?'

'I'm sorry I went behind your back with your master, Will, but I know how much you long to be a knight and I thought I would be helping you by doing this. It wasn't as if the book really belonged to the troubadour.' She bit her lip and looked at the ground. 'Then the Dominicans arrived and I was so scared they would discover what I had done that all I could think about was getting rid of it. They arrested the troubadour last night before the performance.'

'Arrested him for what?'

'The Dominicans think the Book of the Grail and his performance are heretical.'

Will's jaw tightened. 'Well, all that matters is that you are safe.'

'It's my fault, isn't it? What happened to the troubadour? I heard that when the Dominicans couldn't find the book they accused him of lying about a serving girl taking it. But he was telling the truth. I gave him a false name.'

'It's a good thing you did. Elwen, none of this is your fault.' Will shook his head. 'I cannot believe he has done this,' he murmured.

'Pierre isn't a bad man. He took the book when his brother died. He just wanted to perform his poetry. They'll kill him, won't they?'

'His brother?'

Elwen recounted what Pierre had said about Antoine. 'Everard thought Pierre might have been the one who had stolen the book from the vaults, but he wasn't. His brother, Antoine, found it on his doorstep. Neither of them even knew that it had anything to do with the Temple.'

'Where is the book now?'

'I met Everard's man yesterday evening, as we arranged, and I handed it to him.'

'Everard's man?'

'Hasan,' she said in a small voice. 'He told me that I had done well and that Everard would be pleased. I asked him where he was from and he said Syria. I mentioned that I wanted to go to the Holy Land. He told me that I should, that it was beautiful.'

'Hasan brought the book here, to Everard?'

'He was supposed to. But, Will, some of the royal guards were out on patrol last night and they found a body, not long after Hasan left me. I overheard Baudouin, one of the guards, reporting it to the captain early this morning when I was fetching water for the queen's bath. I asked him about it and he said it was a Saracen and that he had been beaten and stabbed to death in an alley.' More tears slid down her cheeks. 'He said they left him at the lazar hospital outside Saint-Denis's Gate to be buried. It must be him, mustn't it?'

'The leper hospital?'

'Because he was a Saracen.'

'Everard told me that Hasan was a converted . . .' Will trailed off, pushing his hands through his hair. He'd had suspicions about Hasan in the past, but Everard had bluntly dismissed his distrust. If Everard had concealed all of this from him and had gone behind his back to seek Elwen's aid in retrieving this book, he now wondered whether the priest had lied to him about other things over the years. He brushed a tear from Elwen's cheek with his thumb. 'I have to go,' he told her, taking her hand and placing the jasmine flower, wrapped its cloth, in her palm. 'Return to the palace and don't tell anyone what you have told me.'

'Do you hate me?'

'Of course I don't,' he murmured, drawing her into his arms and holding her tightly. 'I'm grateful that you did this to help me, Elwen, I'm just angry that you were ever put in this position.' Will felt her body relax against his. He stroked her hair for a moment, then drew back and kissed her cheek. 'I'll come and see you soon. I promise.'

Garin stepped back into the doorway that led into the donjon, where he had been hiding, as Will came striding up the road towards the preceptory.

Yesterday evening, he had seen Hasan leave and, knowing the troubadour was due to perform that night, had guessed that the Saracen was going to attempt to retrieve the book. Garin had been about to follow when he had been cornered by the Visitor, who had kept him talking about a position that had become available in a preceptory in Cyprus. It was a high position, that of assistant to the Marshal, and the Visitor had wanted to know whether he would be interested in taking it. But all Garin had been able to think about was Rook back at the Seven Stars with Adela, waiting for the book, and Hasan getting further and further away. He had hurriedly agreed to take the position and the Visitor, pleased, had said he should leave for the port of Marseilles as soon as possible to board a ship before the winter storms set in. By the time the Visitor had left to draft a letter to the Master of Cyprus, Hasan had gone. Garin had thought of heading straight for the palace, but if he missed Hasan coming back, he might lose any chance of retrieving it and, in the end, he'd decided to stay put and wait.

When a company of knights, led by Nicolas de Navarre, had returned to the preceptory, Garin, who had seen them leave earlier that evening with two Dominican friars, had managed to corner one of them outside the stables, a young knight he shared a dormitory with.

'What happened at the palace, Etienne?' he had asked the knight quietly.

'You're not supposed to know about that,' Etienne had murmured in reply, handing his reins to a groom.

'It's hard to keep secrets in this place.'

After glancing over at Nicolas de Navarre, who had been in the yard talking to the Visitor, Etienne had leaned in closer to Garin. 'We caught the troubadour and the Dominicans arrested him.'

'Good,' Garin had said, putting on a smile. 'I'm glad you got the bastard.'

Etienne had nodded, grimly pleased. 'I doubt he will be writing anything about us ever again.'

'What about his book? The one people think was written by the Devil?'

'We didn't find it. The troubadour tried to feed us some nonsense about a serving girl having taken it from him, but Brother Nicolas couldn't confirm it.'

'Why not?'

'He said her name was Grace, but the steward said there was no one by that name working in the palace and the troubadour's description – pretty and gold-haired – didn't give us much to go on.'

'Brother Etienne.'

Etienne had looked round at Nicolas de Navarre's stern call. 'I have to go.'

The rest of the night had passed sleeplessly for Garin, who had begun to worry that maybe Hasan wasn't supposed to return with the book after all, that maybe the priest wanted it taken somewhere else entirely.

After speaking to Will, Garin had followed him along the passage, intrigued to see him turn off the road rather than continuing towards the city. It had been a little while before he had recognised the woman Will had met beneath the trees. Garin had been surprised by Elwen's transformation from the flat-chested scrap of a girl whose life he had saved at Honfleur into such a beautiful young woman. He hadn't been close enough to hear their conversation, but had seen that she was upset and Will agitated. Watching them, Etienne's description of the serving girl had returned to him and Garin had felt a jolt of excitement. Elwen was a handmaiden at the palace. For most of their conversation, Will's back was to him and they were certainly far enough away for her to have passed Will something as small as a book without his seeing it. Again, Garin had felt resentment as he speculated that perhaps Will had taken the place his uncle had wanted him to have in Everard's secret faction.

As Will passed by, face stormy, Garin pressed himself further into the doorway. He had to get that book. If he didn't, his life wouldn't be worth living. Rook and Edward would make sure of it.

Will didn't knock as he reached Everard's solar, but pushed open the door and strode inside. In his fist he clutched Everard's robe. After meeting Elwen he had continued to the wardrobe as planned to collect the mended garment, to give himself chance to think and to calm a little before confronting the priest. It hadn't worked. Every step he had taken towards Everard's solar had reinforced his anger, until it was now a hard, coiled knot in the centre of his stomach.

Everard looked up, startled, as the door banged against the wall. Will hadn't seen him at Matins or Prime. The priest, who had been perched on the window seat staring out through the tapestry, was deathly pale; the only colour in his face the dark, bruised-looking circles around his eyes. He looked as if he hadn't slept all night.

Will tossed the black mantle on the floor at Everard's feet. 'How can a man as self-serving as you even wear this cloth?'

'What is the meaning of this?' croaked Everard. He dropped the tapestry into place, throwing the chamber into gloom.

'You tell me.'

'What are you talking a—?'

'I've just seen Elwen,' Will cut across him. 'Do you know what she told me?'

'Elwen?' murmured the priest, rising shakily. 'Where is she?'

Will was slightly taken aback by the urgency in Everard's voice, but he pressed on. 'She told me what you made her do. That you went to her and asked her to steal a book from this troubadour everyone's talking about.'

'Did she say she had taken it? Or anything of Hasan?'

'Hasan's dead.' Will instantly regretted the unfeeling way with which he had said the words and the subsequent pain that filled the priest's face.

'What?'

'Hasan's dead,' Will repeated quietly. 'Or so she thinks. The royal guards found an Arab murdered last night in the city.'

Everard stood stock-still for a long moment, then staggered over to his pallet and collapsed heavily onto it, his breathing laboured. 'No,' he whispered. 'God, no.'

Will felt his rage drain from him as he saw the horror in Everard's face. He crossed to the table where Everard kept a jar of wine and poured out a goblet.

Everard curled his two good fingers around the stem when Will handed it to him. After taking several sips, he leaned his head on the wall and inhaled slowly, each breath accompanied by a high whistling sound. He gestured weakly to a stool by the window. 'Sit.'

'I'd rather stand.'

Silence descended, broken only by the wind surging in through the window, lifting the tapestry, then falling back like a wave.

Everard looked at Will. 'And the book?' he said finally. 'Did she pass it to Hasan?'

'What is this book anyway?' said Will, some of his anger returning at the subject. 'What in hell made you go behind my back and order the woman I . . .' Will caught himself. '. . . order Elwen to take it for you?'

'I had no other choice.'

'Yes, you did. You could have asked me. I would have done it gladly rather than put her in danger. All for the sake of one of your precious texts?'

'You wouldn't have been able to take it,' responded Everard, his exhausted, lined face showing signs of irritation. 'She was the only one who could get close enough to de Pont-Evêque without arousing anyone's suspicions. I need to hear the rest, sergeant. Tell me everything she told you.'

'I should go to the Visitor and report you. You had no right to ask her to do this.'

Everard's eyes narrowed. 'You'll remember that I'm not moved by idle threats.'

'It isn't an idle threat.'

'You have no idea what is at stake!' shouted the priest, his voice strained and rasping.

Will went to speak, then shook his head. 'What am I even doing here? It's not as if you're going to apologise, or explain anything to me, is it?' He crossed to the door.

'William.'

Will halted, his hand on the latch. Everard's face was shadowed, his brow a craggy ridge over his pale eyes, his upper lip curled in its usual scowl where the scar began. Will searched that face, but found no clue as to why Everard, for the first time in all his years of service, had just called him by his Christian name.

'Stay,' said Everard. 'Please. I'll tell you everything.'

25
Aleppo, Syria
2 November 1266 AD

♟

Baybars stood before the wide, arched window, the desert wind warm on his bare skin. His hair, wet from his bath, clung in dark strands to his scalp. The breeze carried the smells of smoke, spices and the faint odour of dung from the horse market. Below him, stretching out from the massive walls that surrounded the citadel, lay the city of Aleppo, the jewel in his Syrian crown. The evening sun had turned the white domes of mosques and madrasahs gold, and the jewelled pinnacles of the minarets shone like beacons. In a dusty square within the citadel a game of polo was underway. The figures on horseback were tiny at this distance. Baybars loved the game: its swiftness and ferocity. He was one of the best on the field.

He watched the game for a little while, before moving into the pleasant cool of his private chambers. The spacious rooms held little in the way of furniture; their grandeur manifest in their construction rather than their contents. Red and black marble columns rose from mosaic floor to gilded ceiling and wood panelling lined the walls, inlaid with mother-of-pearl. Each archway was patterned with stucco carvings and rugs covered the tiles.

Baybars went to a marble stand on which stood a gem-encrusted goblet and jug. He poured some kumiz and sat down on his cushioned couch, but as soon as he had drained the goblet he was on his feet again.

Since his victory at Safed, Baybars had felt his campaign against the Franks to be moving frustratingly slowly. The Christians, Kalawun had pointed out, would doubtless disagree. Following Safed, Baybars had taken a second Templar fortress, which had fallen in a matter of days. A week later, he had destroyed a village where, he had learnt, some of the native Christians had been reporting his army's movements to the Franks in Acre. After that, he had marched his troops down the coast in a massive show of strength. They had killed every Christian they found. And this was nothing when compared to what had been achieved in Cilicia. Whilst Baybars had been attacking the Templars at Safed, Kalawun, whom he had made commander of the Syrian troops, had led half the army north against the Armenian Christians. Kalawun had gone over the mountains, coming in behind the enemy, and had stormed their kingdom. Leaving its cities smoking ruins, he had returned to Aleppo a month ago, with wagons of gold and forty thousand new slaves.

But since then, nothing.

Baybars' impatience gnawed at him. Whilst his officers and soldiers rested, he held talks with the governors of the regiments, meetings with his allies and spent hours drawing up plans for his next campaign against the Franks. But his governors had stuffed themselves so full of victory over the summer they didn't have the appetite for more. Baybars was entirely unsatisfied. And had called a council that evening to tell them so.

He looked round hearing footsteps. Through an archway that bore the inscription, *There is no God but God. Muhammad is His Prophet*, a throng of attendants entered. The eunuchs kept their heads bowed as they moved into the chamber, carrying trays of combs, knives and oils. One of them held Baybars' yellow-gold cloak and turban.

'My Lord Sultan, we have come to dress you.'

'Your purpose is apparent.'

Baybars stood, closing his eyes, as the attendants fussed over him. After six years, he was still unaccustomed to such close attention. He had always preferred to dress himself, but as sultan it was beneath him to do so. The attendants' hands were light and quick as butterflies on his body and scalp as they combed his hair, shaped his beard and massaged oil into his skin. After dressing him in a white silk tunic, hose and soft-skin boots they drew on his cloak. Two embroidered bands on the upper arms bore his name and title. A mirror was held up. Baybars studied himself in the polished metal. A tall, powerful man stared back at him; face sun-darkened, its lines hard and deep; eyes that had seen defeat and triumph; hands supple, veined and ridged with calluses. Beneath all the gold and finery, he was still a warrior. The knowledge relaxed him.

'My lord.'

Baybars turned from the mirror as Omar entered, dressed in a gold cloak, his hair and beard oiled. Omar bowed. 'The throne room is ready. Shall I summon the governors?'

'No,' said Baybars after a pause. He went to Omar and put a hand on his comrade's shoulder. 'Walk with me a while.'

'Of course,' said Omar, surprised and pleased.

Baybars led them along the wide passages, past the chambers of advisors and officials and through marbled reception halls where governors, soldiers and slaves stopped what they were doing and bowed. Before long, they came to an arcade that opened out onto a courtyard overlooked by shaded balconies. Water flowed through channels in the floor from a fountain at the courtyard's centre. It was a cool, green haven of slender trees, feathery plants and fragrant flowers. Above the splashing of water came the chattering of birds from an aviary. Baybars stopped by the aviary and picked up a handful of grain from a feeder. He tossed it inside. 'This citadel is impressive, don't you think, Omar?' he said, watching the birds fly down from their perches.

'I have always thought so, my Lord Sultan.'

Baybars smiled. 'I think I prefer it when you call me friend, at least when we're alone. My Lord Sultan sounds so formal from one who has known me so long.'

Omar returned the smile. 'Yes, sadeek.'

'But,' continued Baybars, 'it isn't nearly as magnificent as the citadel Saladin had built for himself at Cairo. It wasn't just a seat of his power; it was a symbol of it. I too want to build something powerful.' Baybars' eyes, Omar noticed, had a faraway look. 'Something that will endure until the last age of man.'

'You have already built much. You have fortified Cairo and created hospitals and schools and . . .'

'Not a thing of stone,' Baybars cut across him. 'That isn't what I mean.' He moved away from the aviary and climbed a set of steps leading up past the balconies to a high walkway that looked out over Aleppo. Omar followed him. When they reached the top, Baybars rested his arms on the parapet. 'I went out into the city this morning.'

'Alone? You must be careful.'

'Do you know what I saw there?' Baybars turned to him. 'I saw soldiers drunk on Western wine, merchants trading in wool and salt, and books filled with Latin thought. Western women in the alleys were selling themselves to our men. Saladin was a ruler of supreme ability, this I cannot deny. He knew how to win battles and how to unite and lead his people. But Saladin failed. Our lands are still infested.'

'Death brings an end to all men's plans.'

'Death is not the reason Saladin didn't rid us of our enemies. He was willing to parley, to accept surrender and to kill only when necessary. It's because of his mercy that we are not free. Saladin was the sword, Omar, but I am the Crossbow. My reach will be longer. What I want to build is a future free of the West's influence.'

'Fighting the armies of Christendom is a trial in itself. But their influence? How do you propose to fight something so tenuous?'

'It's quite simple. Tomorrow, I will give the order to close every tavern in Aleppo. Then, I will banish the whores. Let them be forced out and left to the mercy of the desert. I shall show them none.' Baybars headed back down the steps to the balcony above the courtyard.

'But our men,' said Omar, hurrying to keep up with his long strides, 'have grown accustomed to such things.'

'They will grow unaccustomed to them. Allah doesn't permit us to drink.'

'The women then. The men need such . . . release as they offer. Better the Westerners as objects of their baser desires than our own women.'

'The labourers should concentrate on their work and their wives, and soldiers and governors have slaves for such purposes.'

'Many of the slaves are Western women. Is it not the same thing?'

Baybars stopped. 'Slaves aren't free to walk our streets and ply their trade among our people. They are under our command, our control. There is a great difference.' Baybars' tone was unyielding. 'And besides, our soldiers will have more important things to turn their attention to after the council tonight.'

'You still plan to tell the governors your next move? I strongly counsel you against this, sadeek. The men have just come from one campaign. They need time to recover, to savour their victory. *You* need time.'

'Time is one thing we do not have, Omar. The Franks will retaliate for Safed, of that I have no doubt. I propose to strike again before they are able to muster any effective force. I want them worn down and defeated before they even get a chance to fight. I want to stun them.'

'But your proposed target is . . .' Omar spread his hands, '. . . considerable.'

Before Baybars could reply, the sound of running footsteps filled the passage. Sprinting towards them was a young woman, her dark hair flying loose around her shoulders. There was a small boy at her side, holding her hand and desperately trying to keep up. Chasing them both were two Bahri warriors. The woman came to a stop before Baybars and Omar. The boy was panting hard and staring fearfully over his shoulder at the warriors, who had halted a respectful distance from Baybars. The boy sniffed and wiped his nose on the wide sleeve of the yellow-gold tunic he wore. Baybars stared at it. It looked suspiciously like the material his own cloak was made of.

'Call off your dogs,' the woman snapped at him. 'I wish to speak with you.'

'Apologies, my lord,' puffed one of the guards. 'We know you aren't to be disturbed, but we couldn't stop her.'

Baybars dismissed them with a nod, then turned on his wife. 'What do you want with me, Nizam?'

'I want you to start paying more attention to your son.'

Baybars stepped back as Nizam thrust the boy towards him. Baraka Khan, his six-year-old son, had a red, runny nose and his narrow-set eyes, dark like his mother's, were watery. His brown, wavy hair was curling in damp rings around his brow and his bottom lip was jutting in a mulish pout. Baybars, shooting his wife a black look, put on a smile and ruffled his son's hair. Baraka Khan pouted even more and tried to cling to his mother's leg. Baybars, laughing good-naturedly, snatched the boy up and swung him upside-down in the playful way he had seen plenty of his soldiers treating their sons. The children usually screamed with delight and begged for more, but his own child, he was disappointed to see, just started wailing. Baybars set the boy upright and patted his behind. 'Go to your mother then.' He straightened, fixing his gaze on Nizam. 'What is he wearing?' he said, gesturing to the yellow-gold tunic, so similar to his own. It made him feel embarrassed, but he wasn't sure why.

'I had him dressed as you,' Nizam replied, flicking Baybars' hand aside and picking up the boy. She rocked him in her arms, making shushing noises to quiet him, then glared at Baybars, her sensuously curved lips flattened in a thin line. 'As befits the heir to the throne.'

Baybars felt his temper rise. Taking his son from her, he set the boy down, whereupon the child began to cry lustily. Omar was intently studying one of the tapestries on the passage wall. Baybars grasped Nizam's arm and propelled her to a large window that looked down over the courtyard. As his wife stopped in a patch of sunlight, he noticed that her white gown was almost transparent. He could see the soft contours of her hips, her lithe, brown legs, the outlines of her breasts. He looked away. 'When Baraka Khan is old enough he will stand at my side as a warrior and as my heir. But until that day comes, as I've told you, he belongs with you.'

'I want another son, Baybars,' murmured Nizam. 'You aren't just a soldier and a sultan, you are a husband and a father. Do not forget your duties to me.'

Baybars looked back at her. 'I have given you the time I've had to give. I could have a thousand slave girls, but I do not.'

'And would you treat them as you treat me?'

'You have palaces, beautiful gowns, servants. I do not treat you ill, Nizam.'

'Any treatment would be better than none. A sultan should have more than one successor, Baybars. Do your duty to me and I will deliver you another heir.'

Baybars leaned against the passage wall and half closed his eyes. Waging wars was much easier than pleasing a woman: they were cunning as serpents and complex as the stars. He dreaded meetings with his wife for the inevitable exhaustion that such encounters brought him. His first wife, who had died giving birth to a daughter, had been just as demanding, but not quite so shrewd as this one. His third wife, Fatima, hadn't borne him any children yet and Nizam was well aware of the strength of her own position. But Baybars, while grateful to her for bearing him a son, could not love her, a fact that never troubled him until he was in her presence. 'I will come to you soon,' he muttered. 'Now, go. Leave me.'

Nizam's eyes narrowed. She opened her mouth as if to say something further, then paused. Drawing a breath, she nodded. 'Soon,' she echoed, turning and moving off down the passage, clutching the hand of their whimpering son.

Baybars, watching them go, realised that it wasn't Baraka Khan's garments that made him feel embarrassed. It was the boy himself.

The sons of his governors, even some of the daughters, would race about climbing trees and sword fighting. They would also sit attentively at lessons in the madrasah, and were able to recite whole passages from the Koran. His own son, by contrast, seemed to have no aptitude, or interest in anything athletic; even less in art and schooling. Baybars guessed, ruefully, that it was his own fault. He had left the boy in the harem too long. Nizam was right. What he needed was the company of men, of warriors. But Baybars had no time to teach a child.

'Omar, I want you to arrange a tutor for Baraka.'

26

The Temple, Paris

2 November 1266 AD

♊

'Have you heard,' began Everard, 'of Gérard de Ridefort?'

Will sighed roughly and turned back, but didn't close the solar door. 'He was a Templar Grand Master, almost a century ago. What of him?'

'Sit,' ordered Everard, snapping his fingers at the stool. He scowled when Will remained in the doorway. 'Do you want to hear this, or not?'

Will closed the door and sat.

'If you speak of this to anyone,' said Everard, draining his wine and fixing Will with a bloodshot glare, 'I swear by God, by Jesus and by all that is holy in this world, I will kill you.' He shivered and snatched up his blanket. 'Gérard de Ridefort was admitted as a Templar after spending some years in the Holy Land as a knight to Raymond III, the Count of Tripoli. I first heard of him when I joined the Order, over fifty years ago. According to those who had known him, de Ridefort had come to the Temple harbouring a grudge against Count Raymond, who had reneged on a promise to award him land. De Ridefort was, I heard, an aggressive, petulant man with an elevated sense of his own importance both in the Temple and the wider world. It was this arrogance perhaps and the appearance of authority that often masks such a temperament that aided his rise through the Order. Either way, the chapter general convened in Jerusalem, still in Christian hands at the time, chose to appoint him Grand Master on the death of his predecessor.

'A year later, the King of Jerusalem died. The successor, his nephew, was a mere child and to protect the interests of the young king a regent was appointed in the form of Raymond III, Count of Tripoli and de Ridefort's former lord. A short time later, the count's control of the throne was thwarted when the new king died, leaving no heir, with the dubious exception of his mother, Sibylla, a princess married to a French knight. She at once rallied support for her claim and quickly crowned herself and her husband, Guy de Lusignan, in Jerusalem, the highest seat of power in all four Christian states of Outremer. Her primary supporter was Gérard de Ridefort, who was delighted to help prise Raymond's fingers from the crown.

'At this time, our forces had a truce with the Muslim ruler, Saladin. But when the truce was violated in an attack by one of the new queen's supporters on an Arab trade caravan, the peace wavered.' Everard coughed mightily and spat into his hand. He held out his empty goblet.

Will obliged with another drink.

After he had moistened his throat, Everard continued. 'Count Raymond, who, unlike de Ridefort, was a learned man, wise in the customs of the Arabs, looked to make a truce with Saladin. Saladin, still furious over the attack on his trade line, entered into negotiations with the agreement that the count allow his son and a battalion of Egyptian soldiers to pass through territory Raymond owned in Galilee. Raymond agreed and sent word to his people not to attack the Muslim company. But a party travelling through the region, led by de Ridefort and the Grand Master of the Hospitallers, learnt of this agreement and, at de Ridefort's behest, set out to surprise the Egyptians, in defiance of Raymond's order.

'The Egyptian force was said to have numbered almost seven thousand. De Ridefort and the Hospitaller Grand Master had one hundred and fifty knights between them. According to one of the survivors, the Hospitallers wanted to withdraw, but de Ridefort mocked their Master for a coward and instigated the assault by charging his men into the Muslim troops. De Ridefort was one of only three to make it out alive. The Grand Master of the Knights of St John fell. The nail in the day's coffin for both our Orders.'

'Both?' questioned Will, when Everard paused to drink. 'Not to sound mercenary, but the Hospitallers aren't exactly our closest allies.'

'Then you know neither your history, nor your Rule. Whose banner would you rally to in battle if ours was to fall?' Everard didn't wait for an answer. 'The banner of St John. No, sergeant, we were allies for many years despite our differences, or, more accurately, our similarities. And we would be still if not for . . .' He stopped, frowning. 'Do you want to hear this? Then don't interrupt me again!'

Will kept silent.

'After de Ridefort's attack, the fragile peace between our forces and Saladin was severed. Count Raymond had no choice but to forgo any agreement with the Muslim leader and Saladin set out to war. Guy, the

King of Jerusalem, declared a call to arms throughout Outremer and the combined force of the empire set out to meet Saladin's army that had assembled at the town of Tiberias. Count Raymond, whose wife and children were being held captive in the town by Saladin, advised the King of Jerusalem to wait and let the summer heat disperse the Muslim force, even though he knew the lives of his family would be at risk. De Ridefort scorned the count, accused him of treachery and told the king to press on and attack. King Guy, a weak-willed man, had been supported in his and his wife's claim to the throne by the Grand Master and was easily manipulated to agree with his patron's instruction.

'The army marched out the next day across barren hills with no watering holes. They were easy targets for the Muslim archers who attacked their lines persistently. When the vanguard came near to Tiberias in the late afternoon, worn down by the archers and parched by the heat, they began to assemble on a high plain between the Horns of Hattin, above the Sea of Galilee. On the shores of that lake, Saladin was waiting with forty thousand men.' Everard drained the goblet. 'After a night without water, our forces woke to find the grasses on the plain burning. In the confusion and smoke, Saladin's men attacked and continued to do so in waves through the first day and into the next.

'Finally, we fell, many from thirst rather than from the swords. Count Raymond and his men escaped, but the rest were killed, or taken prisoner. Countless soldiers from both sides met death needlessly that day.'

'Needlessly? We were defending our lands, our people. The Saracens kill our men, rape our women and make slaves of our children.'

'And we do not?' snapped Everard. 'Who started this war, boy?' he demanded. 'The Muslims? No. We started it. We went to their shores and plundered their cities, driving families from homes and livelihoods, slaughtering men, women and children until streets ran red with the blood of the innocent. We set our churches up in place of their mosques because we thought ourselves worthier than they to worship there, thought our God the one true God.'

'So do the Muslims,' countered Will, 'so do the Jews. We all think our God the true God. Which of us is right?'

'Maybe all of us,' said Everard shortly. He sighed. 'I do not know. But what I do know is that in war we are all the same. We rape, we plunder, we murder, we defile. It doesn't matter in whose name we do these things, we are all destroyers. At Hattin we weren't defending our lands or our people. We were defending Gérard de Ridefort's personal Crusade against Count

Raymond. That is what led our forces to that plain. They never should have been there! And wouldn't have if not for the warmongering of our Grand Master. He survived, incidentally, as Saladin's captive, whilst over two hundred of our men were beheaded. Because so many of our soldiers died that day, Saladin and the Muslims were able to retake Jerusalem. I'm only glad,' said Everard vehemently, 'that de Ridefort lived long enough to see the Holy City ripped from his avaricious grasp.'

Will was shocked to hear the priest talk this way about a former Grand Master. He had never met a head of the Temple, but Thomas Bérard, the current Grand Master, who was stationed in the city of Acre, had always been a distant, godlike figure spoken of, without exception, with the deepest of respect. It seemed, to Will, blasphemy to criticise a man, even a dead one, who had held that position.

'De Ridefort's rule over the Temple,' continued Everard, 'brought us nothing but slaughter, but his death, when it came, heralded the birth of something extraordinary.

'A man named Robert de Sablé was chosen to succeed de Ridefort, four years after the Battle of Hattin, around the time that I was born. De Sablé was a comrade of the English King, Richard Lionheart, and he shared many of Richard's qualities, particularly a genuine respect for Saladin, who, after Hattin, claimed possession of Jerusalem with far less bloodshed than our own forces had managed when entering its gates almost a century before. War profits only the victor, but peace can profit all. Robert de Sablé understood this. He also understood the weight of his position.

'The Temple was then, as it is today, the most powerful brotherhood on Earth. In the one and a half centuries since our founder, Hugues de Payns, first put on the mantle, we have made and deposed kings, waged and won wars, helped establish kingdoms and built ourselves an empire. The Temple answers to the pope alone and as warriors of Christ, ordained by Holy Mother Church, we have, effectively, harnessed the power of God on Earth. We are Heaven's sword and the Grand Master is the hand that wields that sword. That is a grave responsibility.

'De Ridefort used this power for himself, for his own vendetta against another man, a vendetta that led to the deaths of thousands and the destabilisation of Outremer. De Sablé wanted to make certain that Hattin would never happen again: that a master could not use the power of the Temple for personal or political gain. He wanted to put us back into the hand of God. And so, to protect the Order's integrity, de Sablé established, in secret, a company of brothers. He called them the Anima Templi: the

Soul of the Temple. De Sablé handpicked the Brethren from the upper ranks of the Order; officials and men of learning who would be able to use their positions to carry out the Anima Templi's wishes without the knowledge of their Templar brothers. They were formed of nine knights, two priests and one sergeant: twelve for the Disciples of Christ, and like those whose responsibility it was to preserve and continue the faith, it was these men's duty to safeguard and guide the Order. There was a thirteenth position: that of Guardian. The Guardian, a trusted man chosen from outside the Temple, could be used to mediate in disputes between the Brethren and offer advice, or aid, either financial, or military. De Sablé chose his good friend, Richard Lionheart, to fill this office. De Sablé's initial intent was to protect the Temple from those who would use its power to fulfil their own desires. Later, he began to use it to promote peace.

'As I said, he understood that war only profits the victor, but that peace can profit all. He was keen to advance trade between East and West and to share knowledge, and the Arabs, particularly, were far more advanced than ourselves in fields such as medicine, geometry and mathematics. So the Brethren fostered friendships with influential men from many cultures and gathered knowledge with which to educate our own. The Temple became the guise behind which they hid and its coffers, resources and authority their tools. They whispered in the right ears when truces wavered, gave money from the Temple's coffers to recompense one side for the misdemeanours of the other, made bargains and offered compromises. Yes, battles were still fought, but many more were averted by the combined efforts of the Brethren. After Gérard de Ridefort, they brought a measure of stability to a kingdom torn apart by the vainglory of our Grand Master. Three years later, de Sablé died, but his legacy continued. After him, no other Grand Master knew of our existence, until Armand de Périgord took control, thirty-four years ago.'

'Why did the Anima Templi work in secret?' asked Will, wanting the priest to continue, but unable to contain the question. 'It sounds like a good thing, so why keep it from everyone else?'

'Without that secrecy we would be open to corruption from others within the Temple, power-hungry men like de Ridefort, and so to retain our sovereignty and to safeguard our work from enemies both within and without, we needed to remain hidden. When our aims began to evolve and change, this secrecy was necessary to preserve us. We knew that many within our Order and in the wider world would not understand what we were trying to achieve. To them, our aims would be anathema. If our ultimate plan were revealed we would be destroyed, and most likely, because of our connection to it, the Temple also. And the Brethren cannot exist without the Temple, without the power it gives us.'

'Anathema?' said Will. 'I don't understand. What do you mean? What plans?'

'Patience,' said Everard, finishing his wine. 'When Armand was elected to power, he was already one of the Brethren and he remained so as Grand Master. At the time, the Brethren were pleased with his elevation. With the Grand Master on their side, working with them, they believed they could accomplish even more. Armand was . . .' Everard frowned. '. . . an *energetic* leader. I found his enthusiasm quite intoxicating.' He smiled wryly. 'Though I was twice the age you are now and should have known better. It was my first time in Outremer and I was ensnared. By God, but it was Paradise. Acre, where I was stationed, was a city of marvels, with feasts for the eye at every twist and turn of its streets. The blue of those seas . . .' He shook his head with feeling. 'When God made this Earth, He started with Palestine and all the colours on His brush were warm and radiant, not watery and dull as they were by the time He came to paint the West.

'I had gone to Acre in search of a rare treatise on astrology written by a notable Arab scholar. During my schooling at the University of Paris, I developed an interest in the compilation of knowledge in a variety of areas and this interest I was fortunate enough to pursue when I was ordained and admitted into the Temple. I had conceived to compose a book that would give details of every subject known to man from every kingdom on Earth. Far more comprehensive than Celsus's attempt, of course.'

'Who?' said Will.

'Exactly,' said Everard pointedly. His lip curled. 'Alas for the ambitions of youth. I soon discovered the hopeless enormity of the task and instead set about collecting, preserving and translating manuscripts for the sole benefit of the Order. It was during that time that I first heard of the Anima Templi. Despite their best efforts to maintain their secrecy, both in the Temple and the wider world, the Brethren hadn't been able to fully conceal their activities and, over time, rumours had begun to spread. People spoke of a group of knights, connected to the Temple, who were controlling the battlefield of the Crusades. Men who, with a word, could stop a war, or start one. This cabal, it was said, was loyal to no one but its own members, and was working to an ultimate, unknown mandate. Templar officials rigorously dismissed these claims, maintaining that no such group existed and that its knights were loyal to God and to the Order alone. There was even an investigation launched. But there was no proof and, mostly thanks to Armand, the inquiry was dismissed as lunacy.

'Armand de Périgord had been impressed by my work and after six months in Outremer, on the death of a member, he brought me into the Anima Templi of which he was head. He had dispensed with the position of Guardian, preferring to keep our business within the confines of the Temple. There were several members, including a priest who was older than I am now, who had formed the original twelve sworn in by de Sablé. They remembered Hattin and they remembered de Ridefort. Armand made them uneasy. He confused the lines between the Temple and the Anima Templi, which, until then, were two very separate organisations. For me, though, he was a man with the ambition and energy to drive us into a new age of enlightenment. He shared my interest in the collation of knowledge and was keen to advance my work, granting me liberties and favours beyond those enjoyed by the other members. I did not see it then, but he was already grooming me for a task he had planned for some time.

'Armand had an obsession, not uncommon in men of a more extravagant disposition, with the tales of Arthur. He envisaged a kingdom, created solely for the Temple, where the Order would reign autonomous. He wanted to build Camelot in Palestine with himself as Arthur and the Anima Templi as some kind of Round Table which would uphold the ideals of the Temple through all the future ages of mankind. Until that point, potential members were pinpointed and assessed by the Brethren, then approached cautiously and invited in. Armand, however, wanted a formal initiation.

'Some years after my own inception into the Brethren, he charged me to write a code that would set out our ideals and serve as our guide for generations to come. Within it would also be an initiation for new members. This initiation was to be based upon the story of Perceval, and the allegory, similar to many such Grail Romances, would hide the aims and intentions of the Anima Templi. A postulant, when initiated, would now undergo a ritual re-enactment of these aims: unwitting and relying on faith, like Perceval on his Grail quest. And, like Perceval, he would be subjected to certain trials, all of which related to what we, as a group, were working towards.' Everard sighed at Will's nonplussed expression. 'He would, for example, be given the Communion chalice and be told that it was filled with the blood of his brothers: men he would call equal under God. He would then be told to drink it.'

'He drank blood?'

Everard tutted. 'It was wine. As I said, the initiation in the Book of the

Grail was an allegory. We did not mean these things literally. But the postulant didn't know that. He had to have faith in what we were asking him to do.' Everard shook his head. 'I didn't agree with Armand. I thought it was, at best, cabalistic nonsense and, at worst, a risk to our secrecy. But I could not refuse him. And so I wrote it.' He smiled slightly. 'The Book of the Grail was my finest work. I smoothed the calfskin with pumice until it was almost translucent and cut each skin to the exact same length and width. I used red lead for the text and scored each heading in gold and silver. Every page was bordered by intricate illustrations. It took me four years.

'During that time, Armand began to change. It was gradual and few of us noticed it initially. But after a while, we couldn't fail to see what was happening. Armand's drive and ambition to preserve our higher ideals was growing into a ruthless desire for supremacy, over the Brethren, the Temple and Outremer itself. He began to focus on victory rather than peace, favouring power over friendship. This culminated in a vicious attack on our former allies, the Knights of St John.

'A dispute had arisen within Acre's government, the body formed of nobles, merchants and knight-masters from various Western kingdoms that collectively controls the city, with the claim of the German emperor, Frederick II, that he was entitled to imperial authority. The Hospitallers, led by their Grand Master, Guillaume de Châteauneuf, supported Frederick's claim. The Temple, led by Armand, opposed him. The quarrel turned ugly and ended with Armand, in a show of power, ordering a siege of the Hospitaller compound in Acre. This siege lasted six months, during which time we prevented food and medical supplies from entering the stronghold and any knights from leaving.' Everard frowned and looked away. 'I remember our knights laughing about how men in the compound had come to the gates, begging, *crying* for food, and how our forces had thrown rotting fruit at them. Many died, from starvation, or sickness and still we refused them aid. They have never forgiven us.' He looked back at Will. 'Some of us protested against this action, but others of our circle supported it. Armand ejected two members for speaking out against him and the rest of us who opposed him could do nothing but watch. With no Guardian to mediate, the schism between us grew wider, even after the siege on the Hospitallers had ended. Until, in 1244, came the battle that almost destroyed us.

'It may have been prevented, had the Brethren been allowed to negotiate with the then ruler of Egypt, Sultan Ayyub. But Armand had already made an alliance with the Prince of Damascus, an enemy of Ayyub, in exchange for several of our strongholds being returned to us, and forbade any communication. I wasn't in Acre at the time. Had I been I think I would have disobeyed that order. I was in Jerusalem, which we had retaken some years earlier from the Muslims. Whilst I was in the city the Khorezmian army, under order of Sultan Ayyub, attacked. God, that I hadn't been there to see it.' Everard's eyes drifted to the stumps of his missing fingers. 'It was more luck than skill that saved me. That night I met Hasan. He had deserted the Khorezmian army and agreed to escort me safe to Acre.' A look of sorrow crossed Everard's face and it was some moments before he continued. When he did, his voice was hoarse.

'When I reached Acre, I found Armand gone with the rest of the army to Herbiya. The sands outside that village saw the largest Christian force mustered since Hattin and they saw a similarly catastrophic defeat. More than five thousand of our soldiers died. Armand never returned. He was captured by the then Mamluk commander, Baybars. After Herbiya, myself and others tried to restore the Anima Templi. But the rift caused by Armand was too wide to be bridged. It was the end of us and we disbanded. Or so the others thought. I, however, wasn't willing to let de Sablé's cause die. I knew that there were five of the twelve whom I could trust implicitly and who had remained true to the cause. One of these you knew. Jacques de Lyons.'

Will was stunned. 'Jacques? Garin's uncle?'

'These five men agreed to help me continue our work. I was elected head of the Brethren and returned here with Hasan to concentrate on gathering manuscripts for our continued collation of knowledge, followed by Jacques some years later. The others remained in Acre.

'Hasan has kept me in touch with them, sending and receiving messages. But with Jacques dead and myself isolated, we are too few to make the sort of difference we once could. Over these past years I've seen the bridges we managed to build slowly crumble under the wheels of Baybars' war and the egoism of our own leaders who refuse to negotiate with him. I would have returned to Acre long ago, to try to rebuild what was lost, recruit more members and appoint another Guardian, but then the Book of the Grail was stolen.

'I don't know why I kept it. I never even used it. I think some fatuous part of me felt that by destroying it, I would be destroying the Anima Templi. I stored it in the vaults. I assumed it would be safe there. But someone, I do not know whom, forced a cleric to steal it and it has been missing ever since. Until the troubadour emerged with it.' Everard shook his head. He looked exhausted. 'Last night the Visitor told me that the Dominicans had arrested Pierre de Pont-Evêque. If he had anything to do with the book's theft the Brethren may still be in danger now that the Dominicans have him.'

'His brother found it.'

Everard looked up. 'What? Whose brother?'

Will told Everard what Elwen had told him.

'It was lying in a wine shop gathering dust for six years?' said Everard, incredulously. 'De Pont-Evêque had nothing to do with its theft? And the book?' he asked after a moment. 'Did Hasan have it on him when he died? Do you know where it is now?'

'Elwen gave it to Hasan. If he was the man who was murdered last night . . .'

'He was,' Everard cut across him. 'There would be no other reason why he did not return to me.'

'The guards took his body to the lazar hospital outside Saint-Denis's Gate. If he still had the book then I expect he would have been buried with it, or will be soon.' Will shrugged. 'Unless the guards found it.'

'Then we had better hurry,' said Everard after a long pause.

Will felt as if he had been holding his breath since the priest had started speaking. Realising that he wouldn't be able to properly digest the significance of this all at once, he pushed the many questions he had to the back of his mind and focused on one. 'If the book is just an extension of the Anima Templi – your code set within an allegory – why would anyone else want it? Why would someone have had the cleric steal it?'

'As I told you, it contains the aims and ideals of the Anima Templi. It could, along with the testimony of someone involved, act as proof of our existence and of what we are working towards.'

'And what is that?'

Everard threw off the blanket and rose from the bed. He brushed away Will's attempt to help him and shuffled across the room to his bucket. 'I have told you what I can.' He loosened his hose and voided a dark yellow trickle of urine into the bucket. 'Will you help me, sergeant?' he asked curtly.

'How can you ask me to get involved in this?' said Will, standing. 'After you used Elwen like you did without any thought of her safety? You've told me everything and nothing. Anathema, that's what you said the world would think of the Anima Templi's aims. Why would I want to help you to save something abhorrent?'

Everard turned, tying up his hose. 'Your father did.'

Will stared at him. 'What?'

'I said I never used the Book of the Grail, that was true, but I did initiate one new member.'

Will started to shake his head, but Everard continued before he could speak. 'That is why James went to the Holy Land. He went for me, for the Anima Templi. And that is why I took you on as my apprentice. You've been helping me with my work for the Brethren for the last six years. All those translations you have done have been for us.'

'I don't believe you,' murmured Will, feeling his world turn over, tipping him out into a dizzying void. He wanted to tell Everard that his father would have told him this, that James wouldn't have kept such a secret from him. But he thought of how close his father had been with Jacques de Lyons in New Temple, the trips to France and the sudden departure to Palestine, and he couldn't.

'I sent him there on an assignment,' Everard continued, watching the emotions change on Will's face. 'He went there to help stop this war. He made great headway in negotiations with the Mamluks and formed an important contact within Baybars' circle. A contact which will perhaps serve to help end the current crisis that threatens everyone in Outremer. We must make peace with the Mamluks, or it will be the end of us.'

'My God.' Will sat heavily on the stool, his mind filled with the memory of the letter he had found in the solar at New Temple. It all came back to him: *the Brethren, our circle*. 'That was him?' he whispered faintly.

'If we do not recover the book, if we do not make sure that it cannot fall into anyone else's hands, then what your father has worked so hard to achieve could all be undone. Without the Brethren, this war will continue. That, for the moment, is all you need to know. I will tell you the rest in time, but until then please trust me in this, we mustn't let that book go astray again.'

Will looked up suddenly. 'Did you tell him that I hadn't been knighted? Did you write and tell him that?'

'I didn't see any need to. We keep contact between us to a minimum, to limit the risk of anyone discovering us.'

Will leaned forward, elbows on his knees, and put his head in his hands. He felt as if he had been living in a mirror image of the world that had just been smashed to reveal the real one behind it. Nothing he thought was true was. Everything had just been a reflection of reality, not reality itself. But welling up through his confusion, his shock and anger, rose a glimmer of hope. If this was true and his father had left on an assignment for the Anima Templi, then his father hadn't left because of him. The glimmer became a beacon. If his father hadn't left because of him then there was a chance, a *real* chance, that he would be able to make amends, that he could be James Campbell's son again. Will took his head from his hands and looked up at Everard. 'I will help you. But in return, you will initiate me. After that, I will go to Outremer to see my father.'

'We will go together, William,' replied Everard. 'You have my word.'

Garin was in the yard opposite the knights' quarters when he saw Will and Everard leave. He had been waiting there, impatient and restless, since he had seen Will enter. Heart quickening, he watched them head across to the stables, the priest leaning on Will for support. When they disappeared inside, he rose and moved closer to the long timber building. He could hear voices, Will's and another he recognised, Simon's. Through gaps in the wood he saw them moving through the stables. Garin walked up to the entrance and stepped cautiously inside. Simon was leading Will and Everard to the stalls further down, where the palfreys were kept. They had their backs to him. Garin heard footsteps outside, coming closer. He slipped into an empty stall and pressed himself against the wall. The area was shadowy and concealed him well. He heard, but didn't see someone enter the stables. Somewhere close by, a stall door creaked as it was opened.

A few minutes passed, then Garin heard the slow clopping of hooves and Will and Simon's voices again. He risked a look around the stall door. Simon was leading two saddled palfreys into the yard. This had to be something to do with the book, Garin thought excitedly. Perhaps Elwen had given it to Will and now Will and his master were taking it somewhere. Everard looked far too frail to be leaving the preceptory unless for something important. This might be his best chance to take it. Will was unarmed and the old man posed no threat whatsoever.

As Will mounted one of the palfreys, Garin left the empty stall, careful to keep out of sight, and, picking up a saddle from a bench, opened the door of another. This stall had a destrier inside, a huge, black beast of a horse. Garin clicked his tongue soothingly as he hefted the saddle onto the horse's back. He peered over the top of the stall door. Simon had crouched down and cupped his hands to allow Everard a step-up by which to mount the second palfrey. Garin bent to fasten the girth around the horse's stomach.

He heard a rustle of straw behind him, followed by a faint inhalation of breath. He was rising, about to turn, when something solid connected with the back of his head. Garin's vision went black and he crumpled to the ground.

27
The Lazar Hospital, Paris
2 November 1266 AD

Will and Everard took the track that led north-west from the preceptory, the morning sun blinding their eyes and the wind whipping their faces raw. The fields were bare and brown and the trees, stripped of foliage, were gaunt, splayed silhouettes against the blue sky. They rode in silence, the hoofs of their horses loud on the frosty path. Will's thoughts were crowded with his father and with Everard's revelations, and the priest was pensive and sombre.

After about half a mile, the sound of bells echoed hollowly across the fields from the preceptory behind them and the city below for the office of Terce. Everard slowed his palfrey from a trot to a standstill. Will reined in his mount as the priest slid awkwardly from the saddle.

'Why are you stopping?'

'To pray,' said Everard, frowning at him as if it were a ridiculous question.

Will, shaking his head at Everard's fastidiousness after the priest's former insistence on speed, jumped down from his own horse and looped the reins over a hawthorn bush. He picked up the reins of the other palfrey, which Everard had let fall to the ground, and tethered the beast as the priest knelt on the verge, hands clasped. When away from the preceptory and unable to hear a service, knights, priests and sergeants were still expected to pray. Instead of hearing the office, they would now recite seven Paternosters.

As Will was kneeling, he caught sight of a rider some distance behind, where the track rose up before dipping down into the valley he and Everard were now in. The rider was mounted on a black horse, a destrier Will guessed by the size of it. The rider slowed as Will watched, then stopped and dismounted, disappearing from view. Will knelt down and murmured the Paternoster into his clasped hands, the words a stream of meaningless sounds that meant nothing to his troubled mind.

'There,' said Everard, when they were done, rising and shaking the dirt from his robe. He seemed a little brighter, as if the prayers had rejuvenated him. 'You are quiet, sergeant,' he said, after Will had helped him into the saddle.

Will didn't speak as he mounted. The comment had baffled him. What, he wondered, did Everard expect? 'You lied to me,' he said suddenly, after they had been going for a few minutes. 'All these years you knew why my father went away and you never told me why. All this time I thought he left because . . .' Will faltered. Everard, so far as he knew, knew nothing of his sister and, although he couldn't be certain of anything anymore, he didn't want to divulge this to the priest unnecessarily. 'You know how much I have missed him,' he finished.

'If I had told you that,' replied Everard brusquely, 'I would have had to tell you the rest and you weren't ready to hear it.'

'And now? If Hasan had brought you the book and Elwen had never told me what you made her do, I never would have found out, would I? You've told me because you need me. Perhaps it was you who wasn't ready.'

Everard glanced at him, but didn't answer.

'And my initiation?' continued Will. He managed to keep his voice calm, but he could feel anger squirming through his confusion, wanting to leap out and lash at the priest for all the years of humiliation and criticism and deception. A large portion of that anger, however, was directed towards his father for making him believe that the departure to the Holy Land was because of him and he wasn't ready to confront that feeling yet, so he pressed it down and continued. 'When would you have knighted me if Elwen hadn't made you agree to that deal? You're not going to initiate me now because you think I'm ready either. You're going to do it because you have to.' Will looked at the priest. 'That's if you have any intention of keeping your promise.'

'I won't go back on my word,' said Everard shortly. He met Will's stony gaze. 'I've seen many young men go off to war as soon as they are knighted. I've seen very few of them return. Do not be so eager to make that journey. More often than not that path leads to death. *That* is why I kept you from your initiation, because I knew, as soon as you put on the mantle, you would make that journey.'

'Of course,' muttered Will, 'because you care so much for me.'

'No, William, I didn't want to lose such an excellent scribe.'

Will's eyes narrowed as he stared at the priest, looking for a lie, but finding none.

'You must understand,' continued Everard, quieter now, 'I have guarded these secrets for many years. It is hard to let go of something I have held so closely. Hard to trust. I trusted Armand and almost lost everything.'

'Does this mean you trust me?'

Everard flicked the reins of his palfrey. 'We should pick up the pace.'

They came upon the lazar hospital shortly after crossing the Rue Saint-Denis. It was partially shrouded by a copse of large oaks and they almost missed the tiny track that led up to its walls beneath the arched canopy of trees, through which sunlight made dappled patterns of the path. Three large stone buildings were set within a low-walled enclosure, with a chapel off to the right beside neat gardens. It looked like a much smaller, far less grand version of the preceptory, but appeared well kept and homely. This surprised Will. The lepers he had seen begging at the city gates had always been a hideous sight, dressed in their distinguishing rags and gloves, hair loose and matted, faces often grotesquely scarred and distorted, and he would have never imagined them living in such a tranquil, orderly-looking community.

As they dismounted at the gate, Will saw a man heading towards them from one of the buildings. The gloves that he wore marked him as a leper, but, as yet, there were no signs of the disease on his face.

'Can I help you?' the man enquired, a little suspiciously, as he approached. His gaze flicked to the red crosses on their clothes. 'I'm the porter here.'

Everard handed Will the reins of his palfrey. 'I am looking for a friend of mine. He died last night and I believe he was brought here for burial. I've come to pay my respects.'

The porter's gaze moved to Will.

'This is my squire,' added Everard, gesturing offhand to Will, who bit his tongue and turned away to hobble the horses.

'Well, there was someone brought in late last night,' replied the porter. 'Although I'd say it was the dagger in his gut killed him rather than the sickness. The royal guards who brought him said he was afflicted, but I saw no evidence of it.'

'He was in the early stages,' responded Everard.

'Come in then.' The porter paused. 'But be mindful that you enter our domain here. If a path is too narrow for two to walk on, then it is you who will step aside to let one of our number pass without contact. Here, we do not abide by the same laws that govern us beyond these gates.'

'Very well,' said Everard, unconcerned.

Will resisted the urge to place his hand over his mouth as they entered. Leprosy, it was said, was caused by indulging in sin, particularly lust, but it was also thought that you could catch it through physical contact, by sharing food or water with a leper, or even air. For these reasons, lepers were forbidden from touching others, congregating in crowded places such as churches and were supposed to cover their mouths in public. But as the porter showed no sign of doing that, Will breathed thinly through his nostrils, careful to stay upwind of the man as they were led through the yard, past the hospital buildings.

There were a few figures in the gardens, tending a neat row of young apple trees beside what looked to be recently harvested vegetable plots. Many of them wore strips of linen over exposed areas of their bodies and faces and all wore gloves. Some, Will noticed, were barely affected, with just the odd sore, or slight distortion to their hands. Others were in the advanced stages of the disease, after many years of infection. These men were hard to look upon. The bandages covered most of the open sores that had bubbled up on their skin, but couldn't disguise their warped forms. Noses, the bones of which had rotted away, were squashed and distorted; teeth were gone, making mouths saggy and formless; hands were clawed like talons. Some of the men had fingers missing, others, from their stutter-steps, were obviously missing toes, and, beneath the sour tang of unripe apples, Will could smell the sickeningly sweet stench of rotting flesh.

When diagnosed with the disease, a leper would be forced to stand in an open grave whilst the Requiem Mass was said over them. Will now saw, in these men's faces, evidence of that living death. There were no women among their number; those of the female sex were denied hospitalisation and were reduced to begging on roads outside the cities.

'We had a grave opened as luck would have it,' said the porter, leading them towards the chapel. 'Bertrand, we know, will pass on soon. He was still holding on last night, though, so we used his grave for your friend. From Genoa, was he then?'

Everard looked at him. 'Genoa?'

'Your friend,' said the porter, passing through a gap in the low flint wall that ringed the chapel and cemetery. 'He was from Genoa, the guards said.'

Will didn't think the priest was going to answer.

After an awkward silence, Everard did. 'Yes,' he muttered, 'Genoa.'

Under a holly tree in the far corner of the cemetery, which lay in the chilly shadow cast by the chapel, was a freshly turned grave. 'This is where

we put him,' said the porter, as they came closer. 'Wasn't much of a
ceremony. One of the gravediggers and myself put him in and said a quick
prayer. It was dark and raining,' he added, seeing Everard's expression.

'I will say a prayer myself,' Everard murmured, crouching down. He
looked round at the porter. 'Can I have a moment to myself.'

'Take as long as you want,' said the porter. 'You can find your own way
out?'

Everard nodded. He waited until the porter had disappeared around the
side of the chapel, then turned back to the grave. He plucked the small
wooden cross from the head of the mound and tossed it aside, before rising.
'I can see a spade over there, sergeant.'

Will took his eyes from the cross, which had landed in a patch of nettles,
and headed to where Everard was pointing. A moment later, he returned
with the spade, which had been propped against a crumbled-down, mossy
gravestone and was coated thickly in mud. Everard stepped back, keeping
watch, as Will began to dig, turning out the wet, heavy soil. The work
made him sweat despite the cold and his back ached as the pile of earth
beside the grave grew higher. Finally, the spade struck something soft. Will
bent down and scraped the loose soil from around the body that was
revealed, wrapped in a linen shroud. He sat back on his heels when it was
done, the smell of earth strong in his nostrils.

Everard hesitated for a few moments, then came forwards and knelt.
Slowly, he reached out his hands and carefully, tenderly unwrapped the
shroud from Hasan's head. Will looked away as Hasan's face was unveiled,
black with congealed blood and bruises, contorted and rigid, frozen in the
agony he must have been in at the point of death. Everard didn't turn his
face away, but leaned forward, placed his hand on Hasan's brow and began
to whisper.

'Ashadu an la ilaha illa-llah. Wa ashhadu anna Muhammadan rasul-
Ullah.'

Will looked back, hearing the musical chant come from the priest's lips.
It was Arabic. He knew what it meant for he had come across it in several
translations he had worked on over the years.

There is no God but God. Muhammad is His Prophet.

It was the Shahada — the statement of faith that was to be said into a
Muslim's ear upon death, just as the last rites were said to a Christian. It
confirmed Will's suspicion that Everard had lied to him about Hasan's
conversion. But, with Hasan's broken, bloodied face staring up at him, Will
didn't feel shocked or angry, instead he felt ashamed to be a fellow

countryman of those who had done this to the man who had once saved his life.

'Who do you think did this to him?'

'Someone without a soul,' said Everard in reply, still holding Hasan's brow. 'Someone consumed by hatred and fear, who sees only the enemy external to themselves, not the enemy within.'

'It seems so senseless,' murmured Will.

Everard glanced at him. His pale, red-rimmed eyes were wet. 'Hasan died in the service of something he believed in. How many men can say that?'

Will didn't argue. The hopeful look in Everard's eyes pleaded for confirmation, comfort. 'Not many,' he agreed.

Finally, Everard wiped his eyes. 'Help me,' he said, drawing aside the rest of the shroud.

Will bent down on the other side of the grave. The shroud caught on something sticking up from the body. After unravelling it, Will saw that it was the hilt of a dagger, still buried in Hasan's side. Sickened, he reached out to remove it, but Everard put a hand over his.

'Leave it. It doesn't bother him where he is now.'

They opened Hasan's grey cloak and Everard patted him down. He began to look worried, but then slid his hand in under the dead Arab's back and a look of triumph passed across his face. 'It's here.'

Will struggled to roll Hasan over as the priest reached in under him and pulled out a dirty, vellum-bound book. The parchment was damp, the cover smudged with mud, but a few of the gold-leaf words were still visible and glittered in the light. Everard closed his eyes as he held it and whispered something beneath his breath. A prayer, Will guessed, by the look of utter relief on his face.

'It is done,' said Everard, as he opened his eyes. 'Finally, I can return to Acre to finish my life's work.' He looked sadly, fondly upon Hasan. 'Before I join him.'

'Give me the book, Everard,' came a glacial voice from behind them. 'Or you will join him sooner than you think.'

They both turned, startled. Nicolas de Navarre was standing there. In his hand he held a loaded crossbow. It was pointed at Everard. He wore a black cloak over his white mantle and his long, dark hair was tied back in a tail.

'Brother Nicolas?' voiced Everard, clutching the book. He looked beyond the knight, expecting to see Gilles and the Dominicans, but the graveyard was empty.

'I knew you would send your bloodhound to fetch the book from the troubadour. But I have to say I wasn't expecting you to use a serving girl to execute the theft. You must have been truly desperate.' Nicolas looked past the priest to Hasan's body. 'I heard that a Saracen was found murdered last night and when he didn't return to the preceptory, I guessed it would be him. It is a shame. I wanted to use him as further evidence of your corruption. He isn't a Christian, is he, Everard?'

'What is the meaning of this, brother?' asked Everard, trying to sound incensed but only managing to sound fearful.

'I am not your brother. Give me the book.' Nicolas aimed the crossbow at Everard's throat. 'I will not ask you again.'

Everard's eyes moved slowly to the weapon. 'My God, it was you, wasn't it?' he breathed. 'You forced Rulli to steal the book from the vaults and killed him in the alley? That is why you are alone. You aren't here for the Visitor, or the Dominicans. You are here for yourself.'

Will glanced down at the dagger that was protruding from Hasan's side. Whilst Nicolas's eyes were fixed on Everard, he took a step closer to the grave.

'I might have let the clerk live,' said Nicolas, 'if Hasan hadn't interfered. But I couldn't allow him to reveal my identity.'

'How did you learn of the book?' demanded Everard.

'I have spoken to some of those who broke your circle after Armand's term in power. I know all about you, Everard; your secrets, what you've done.'

'You have been here all this time? A snake in my midst.' Everard's voice was low, but his eyes did not stray from the crossbow.

'I have been waiting for this moment for more than seven years. Seven years since I left my home to come to this country; was forced to don this false mantle, pretend to be one of you, your brother.' Nicolas's eyes were filled with enmity. 'Justice has been long in coming. But we will have it now. Too long have the Temple and its leaders hidden behind the pope's robes. When he sees what it is that you do at your initiations, when he sees what filth you have written as your secret code, he will have no choice but to destroy you. Every last one.' Nicolas's olive skin was flushed with triumph and open fury. 'You are a man of words, Everard. You have, I am sure, heard the tale of David and Goliath?'

Everard didn't respond.

'And as with just one tiny stone, David slew the beast before him, I will bring down the mighty Temple with nothing but a book.'

Will took another step towards the grave.

'Why would you do this?' murmured Everard. 'Who are you?'

'I am one of the men your Order betrayed at Acre. One of the men you and others under that bastard, Armand, had barricaded in our stronghold, refusing to let food or medicines enter and any, even the sick and the dying leave. I am a Knight of the Order of St John. And the man who will bring about your end.'

Will stared at the knight, remembering how Nicolas had so easily resolved the situation he had found himself in with the drunken Hospitaller several months ago.

'I and others in my group petitioned Armand to stop that madness,' Everard was saying. 'We tried, believe me. What Armand did was inexcusable, yes, but it was not our doing.'

'You tried? Whilst you were trying, Everard, I was watching friends and brothers die from wounds, or sicknesses that could have been treated. We begged the Templars to allow medicine and food through the blockade for the sick. They refused and when those same men died they wouldn't even open their lines to let us take out the corpses for burial. For months, we choked on the stink of our comrades' rotting flesh. Inexcusable?' Nicolas's tone was implacable. 'I cannot think of a strong enough word to describe it.'

'Will destroying the lives of so many more rebalance those scales?'

'It will be a start.' Nicolas held out his free hand.

'You cannot know what this truly is!' said Everard, clinging desperately to the Book of the Grail. 'If you did you would not seek to destroy me and my Brethren. We are not the ones who wronged you, I tell you! Armand is dead and buried. He was served his justice in a Cairo jail.'

'You and the other leaders of the Temple and your secret group defended his treachery. All of you must pay for what you did. If the laws of courts and kings will not serve to punish you for your sins, then we will.'

'By destroying the Temple, you destroy us all!'

As the priest shouted these last words, Will dove for the dagger and wrenched it from Hasan's side. It stuck fast for one awful second, then came free with a sucking sound. He turned the blade on Nicolas.

Nicolas swept the crossbow round to point it at Will. The two of them stared at one another. In Nicolas's eyes, Will saw none of the humour or friendliness he had seen that day outside the parchmenter's. It was as if he were looking at a different man.

'I warned you once about drawing a weapon so readily, Campbell.' When Will didn't move, Nicolas addressed Everard. 'Tell your sergeant to stand down, Everard, or I will kill him.'

Will felt a hand on his shoulder.

'Do as he says,' murmured Everard. He sounded defeated.

Will hesitated, but Everard gripped his shoulder tighter and he lowered the weapon.

As he did so, Everard tossed the Book of the Grail at Nicolas's feet. 'You do not know what you are doing.'

Nicolas reached down and picked up the book. 'I have never been clearer.' He backed away, still training the crossbow on Will. When he had reached the chapel, he turned and sprinted off. Within a moment, he was out of sight.

Will went to go after him.

'Wait, sergeant,' said Everard.

Will looked back. 'He's going to get away.'

'And we will let him. For now.' Everard took the dagger from Will's hand and laid it on Hasan's chest. 'I'm sorry, my friend,' he whispered, snatching the shroud over the Arab. 'Come,' he said to Will. 'We shall return to the preceptory. We need help.'

But when Will and Everard got to the gate, they found their palfreys gone.

The Seven Stars, Paris, 2 November 1266 AD

Garin took the rickety stairs two at a time. His head was pounding and a large bruise had swollen on his scalp, which was tender to the touch. He felt sick. Seven doors lined the gloomy passage at the top, with an eighth at the end. Light issued out from beneath some, along with faint noises: cries and groans that hinted at pleasure, or pain, or both. The floorboards were rotten in places and creaked ominously beneath Garin's boots as he walked down the passage, his eyes on the door at the end. He paused before opening it, afraid of what lay beyond. Steeling his nerves, he entered. Rook was sitting at Adela's workbench, devouring a chicken leg. Grease had dribbled down his chin and tiny scraps of flesh clung to his stubbly cheeks. He was alone.

Garin closed the door. 'Where's Adela?' he asked nervously, glancing around the chamber.

'In the yard,' said Rook through a mouthful of meat. 'Do you have it?'

Garin didn't reply for a moment. Through the window he heard a scraping sound, followed by Adela's voice. He guessed she was having fresh barrels brought in for the evening. The sound of her voice reassured him. 'No,' he told Rook. 'I don't have it.'

Rook dropped the chicken leg to the platter. 'Where is it then?' he growled, rising and wiping his greasy mouth with the back of his hand. 'My source tells me the troubadour was arrested last night, but no book was found. So, if you don't have it, you better damn well know who has.'

'I saw Will Campbell, Everard's sergeant,' replied Garin, not coming any closer into the chamber, which was filled with smoke from the hearth that swirled in the shafts of sunlight coming through the window coverings. 'He was talking with Elwen outside the preceptory this morning.'

'Who?'

'They knew one another at New Temple. She is a handmaiden at the palace.' Garin paused. 'I don't think Hasan took the book. I think she did.' Garin told him what Etienne had said about the serving girl with the false name who fitted Elwen's description; the serving girl de Pont-Evêque had accused of stealing the Book of the Grail. 'I think she might have given it to Will,' he finished.

'And?' demanded Rook impatiently.

'I saw Will and Everard leaving the preceptory about two hours ago. I was going to follow them, but . . .' Garin faltered, pressing his lips together. 'But I was hit over the head by someone and I . . . I didn't see who it was,' he finished into Rook's unnerving silence.

'I see.' Rook came around the workbench and walked towards Garin. 'So our one chance of getting this book is gone, is it? All because you were stupid enough to let yourself get seen.' He rushed at Garin, slamming the youth into the door.

Garin cried out as his bruised head connected solidly with the wood. 'Don't, Rook! My *head*!'

'Hurts, does it?' said Rook. He grabbed a fistful of Garin's blond hair and smashed the knight's head against the door. '*Does it?*'

The pain almost blinded Garin with its intensity. 'I don't think they went far! They didn't have any supplies and Will was unarmed. Wherever they went it must be within the city! We can still find it!'

'How?'

'I'll think of a way!'

'You'd better hope you do, or I swear by my life, I'll make you sorry. You and that bitch downstairs.'

Garin, fighting off waves of nausea from the pain in his head, stared at Rook, hatred rising in him like bile, bitter, stinging.

He was a Knight of the Temple, a nobleman of a grand lineage stretching back, his uncle had said, to the time of Charlemagne. Rook was a glorified thief, a bastard born on Cheapside's streets, one of a notorious pack who had terrorised London for years until one of their own mothers had informed on them and they had been caught and sentenced to hang. Rook had been spared the gallows by Edward and lifted from the gutter. But he was still nothing but a dog.

Garin forced himself to concentrate on the rewards he would reap for completing this task, not least, Rook's departure from the city. 'We'll have to be careful whatever we do,' he said, touching his scalp gingerly. His fingers came back dotted with blood. 'I don't know who attacked me in the stables. Either they were after the book too, or they saw me watching the priest and wanted to stop me from following.' He shook his head. 'Perhaps it was Hasan? I haven't seen him since yesterday evening.' An idea of what he would have to do came into Garin's mind, but he hesitated before voicing it. If he went down this road, it might be hard for him to return. 'I think we should turn our attention to Will,' he said finally, unable to think of any other solution and unable to bear any more pain. 'He knows, I'm sure, where the book is now.' Garin took a deep breath. He thought of his dreamed-of estate, his title and riches. He thought of his mother's pride and happiness and he thought of Adela, sharing his bed only, of having her every night he wanted her. He exhaled decisively. 'We'll bring him here and you can ask him where it is.'

'How do we get him to come here?' said Rook, after a pause.

Garin met his gaze. 'You use Elwen.'

28

The Ville, Paris

2 November 1266 AD

'Are you going to tell me any more of what this is about?' panted Simon, as he jogged along the road beside Will, skirting the groups of people who thronged the streets. It was market day and the Ville was bustling with traders and shoppers. 'It's plain you haven't told me everything.'

'I've told you all I can,' said Will, glancing at him. He felt guilty, having dragged Simon into this without a proper explanation, but Everard had insisted he take someone with him to watch his back and Simon was the only one he trusted with that responsibility. Having the brawny groom alongside did make him feel a little surer.

'Don't confront de Navarre alone,' the priest had warned, as Will had strapped his falchion to his hip back at the preceptory. He had planted a bony hand on Will's shoulder. 'I'm relying on you. Get me the book and, I swear, I will see you knighted.'

'Nicolas de Navarre a traitor?' breathed Simon, his face red and sweaty with the exertion. 'I can hardly believe it. And what was this book he stole?'

'A valuable text belonging to Everard. We think he plans to sell it, as I said, so we must hurry.'

'And he's sent us to get it back for him?' Simon shook his head. 'I don't understand it. Why didn't he send armed knights?' He glanced worriedly at the falchion on Will's hip. 'Are we expecting trouble? Because, Will, you know I can't fight.'

'I wouldn't ask you to. But if Nicolas sees two of us, he'll be less willing to confront us.' Will hoped this was true. He knew he was good with a sword, but he had no idea of Nicolas's capabilities and didn't much fancy his chances against a crossbow. That was if Nicolas had even gone to the Hospitallers' preceptory. If he hadn't, Will had no clue of where they might find him.

'We would have been quicker on horses,' Simon told him.

Will didn't answer. Simon hadn't been in the stables when he and Everard had returned from the lazar hospital without the two palfreys they had taken. Everard had had to explain to the stable master that their mounts had been stolen. The master had subsequently refused to allow the priest to take any more horses from the stables without a proper report being filed with the Visitor, which was why he and Simon were now running to the preceptory of St John instead of riding.

Will hated that he was putting his friend in danger. But above and beyond his guilt he felt clear, determined. His initiation was in sight and, for the first time in years, perhaps ever, he had purpose. His promise to himself, that he would go to the Holy Land and see his father, was no longer a fantasy. It was real. What was more, he was finally doing something that he knew his father would be proud of. Absolution wasn't just achievable; it seemed inevitable. What better way to atone for his sins than by saving the Anima Templi and bringing peace to Outremer? Whatever happened, he would get that book. He would not let Nicolas ruin this for him, however understandable or justified the man's anger seemed. He too had been waiting for this moment for many years.

They picked up the pace as they left the crowds around the cattle market. Ahead, above the rooftops, Will could see the grey towers of the preceptory rising from its walled enclosure. Pulling his black cloak tighter to cover the red cross on his tunic, he led them down a tight alleyway that opened out onto the street the preceptory bordered, Simon struggling to keep up behind him. Through the narrow opening ahead, Will could see the gates. They were open. He slowed to a walk, breathing hard, but as he reached the opening, four knights rode out of the gates on war-chargers. They were clad in plain riding cloaks, but Will, coming to a halt in the alley mouth, saw that they wore long black surcoats beneath, upon which was embroidered the white cross of the Hospitallers. He recognised two of them. One was Rasequin, the man he had challenged outside the parchmenter's. Rasequin didn't look drunk now; he looked watchful. One of his hands was on the pommel of his sword as he swept out of the gate, the hooves of his destrier kicking up great clods of mud from the street. Beside him rode Nicolas de Navarre. He too was wearing the uniform of a Knight of St John.

Will shouted as they passed him, but the thunder of their hooves was too loud for any of the knights to hear as they galloped off down the street, people scattering out of their way. On the backs of their saddles were tied sacks and blankets. They were set for a journey. Will cursed as he watched them disappear around a corner and the street filled slowly with people again. The gates of the preceptory clanged shut.

Simon leaned forwards, hands on knees, panting. 'That was Nicolas, weren't it? Why was he dressed as a Hospitaller?'

'He was sent in by their Order to take the book,' admitted Will after a pause. Before Simon could ask any more questions, he gestured to a side street that bordered the preceptory's wall. 'We'll go inside. Find out where they're going.'

'Aren't we going the wrong way?' said Simon, as Will led him down the side street. 'The gates are back there.'

'I don't know who else in there knows about Nicolas. They might all be in on it.' Will came to a stop, looking up at the flint wall, beyond which was a line of trees and the spire of the preceptory's chapel. 'We can't just walk in.'

'I can't get up there,' said Simon adamantly, as Will began to climb, his fingertips clutching for purchase on the jagged, protruding stones.

Will reached the top and pulled himself up onto his arms, muscles straining. He peered over the wall. Beyond the trees was a large area of open ground dotted with stone crosses – the knight's cemetery. Will could see a yard and several tall buildings behind the chapel. There were men moving about in the yard, but the wall he had hoisted himself onto, covered by the trees, was out of plain sight and he and Simon could only be seen if someone was looking directly at them. 'Come on,' he urged Simon, who was peering anxiously up at him.

'Christ,' muttered the groom, clumsily scrabbling up the wall after a moment's hesitation. 'You'll be the death of me,' he panted, wincing as he skinned his knuckles on the sharp stones. He dug his foot into a tiny hollow as he neared the top, but it was too small for his booted foot and he slipped.

Will grabbed his wrist and held on. Gripping the top of the wall with his thighs and gasping at Simon's weight, Will hauled the groom up the last few inches, until Simon managed to seize the top. For several moments afterwards, Simon was too shaken to do anything but sit astride the wall. Finally, Will coaxing him on, the two of them dropped down into the cemetery and, using the tree cover, made their way along the wall.

'I don't know who you think is going to tell you where Nicolas has gone,' murmured Simon, rubbing his grazed knuckles. 'If they're all involved in stealing this book, I doubt the Hospitallers will tell you anything.' He looked up at the towers of the main building. 'Most likely they'll just throw us in their dungeon.'

'I'm not going to ask a knight,' replied Will, heading for a long timber building bordering the yard, outside which were stacked several bales of straw: the stables. As he and Simon came out of the cemetery, they saw a group of knights standing in the porch of a building opposite the stable's entrance. Will checked that the crosses on his and Simon's tunics were covered, then struck out across the yard. 'Act normally,' he said beneath his breath to Simon, who was looking surreptitiously over at the men. The knights paid the two youths no heed as they crossed the yard and disappeared inside.

Will looked around as they entered, his eyes adjusting to the gloom. A boy of about twelve was standing at a bench further down, polishing a row of saddles. 'Check the rest of the stables,' Will murmured to Simon, as he approached the boy.

'Check them?' said Simon, looking baffled. 'For what?'

'To make sure they're empty.'

Will smiled. The boy had stopped polishing the saddles and was looking at him.

'Can I help you, sir?' he asked, his voice high-pitched, childish.

'I hope so,' replied Will, still smiling. 'You saddled four horses for a company of knights just now, didn't you?'

The boy nodded. 'I did, sir.'

'Can you tell me where they were going?'

The boy glanced at Simon who was moving down through the stables, peering over the stall doors. 'Who are you?' he asked, frowning. 'I've not seen either of you before.'

'We're new,' said Will. 'These knights. Tell me where they went.'

The boy put down his cloth uncertainly. 'I think you better ask the Marshal.' He went to move past Will. 'I'll go and fetch him for you.'

Will caught his arm in a strong grip. 'There's no need to bother him.'

'Let go of me!' said the boy, looking panicky. 'You're hurting!'

'Jesus, Will!' hissed Simon, as Will forcibly dragged the struggling boy further into the stables and pinned him against one of the stall doors.

'I'm not going to hurt you,' murmured Will, 'but I need to know where the knights were going. It's very important that you tell me this.'

'Please let me go,' said the boy in a small voice. His lip began to quiver.

'Will . . .' began Simon, watching the exchange in shock.

Will glanced at him and Simon fell silent at the look in Will's green eyes. It scared him.

'Tell me,' insisted Will, drawing aside his cloak slightly, so that the boy could see the falchion.

'La Rochelle,' blurted the boy, his gaze transfixed by the blade. 'They were going to La Rochelle. I heard them talking about Acre and the Grand Master.'

'Acre?'

'That's all I know,' sobbed the boy. 'Honest it is!'

Will searched his face, then nodded. 'Get in,' he ordered, unbolting the stall door he had pushed the boy against and opening it.

The boy did as he was told. They could still hear him sobbing as they left the stables.

'I can't believe you did that,' muttered Simon as they made their way back through the cemetery towards the wall.

'He'll be fine,' replied Will, distractedly.

Simon stopped. 'You didn't need to scare him like that!'

Will turned back to him. 'Simon, come on. We have to get back to the preceptory.' He went and grasped Simon's shoulder. 'I didn't want to do it, but I had to. He would have run off and got the Marshal and where would we be now? None the wiser and probably in a cell, like you said.'

Simon said nothing, but followed him.

Morning had turned into early afternoon by the time they passed through Temple Gate and hastened up the Rue du Temple. The wind had picked up and huge white clouds were rearing in the east, scudding fast across the sky and casting shadows across the hillsides. As they were nearing the preceptory, the chapel bell began to toll.

It wasn't the slow, sonorous call to prayer. It was fast and frantic: a call of alarm. The sound filled Will with foreboding.

When he and Simon reached the main courtyard, they saw a large company of knights filing into the chapter house. Others were joining them, hurrying across the yard. The bell was still clanging.

'Campbell!'

Will turned to see Robert de Paris jogging towards him.

Robert swept his fine blond hair back and nodded to the chapter house. 'Do you know what's happening?'

Will shook his head. 'No, I've been out in the city.' He saw a group of knights, including the Visitor, Everard and Hugues de Pairaud, coming towards them. With the company were several knights in travel-soiled mantles. Will took a step forward, thinking to call to Everard, but something in the men's faces stopped him. The group passed him and headed into the chapter house, but Hugues hung back at a questioning signal from Robert.

Robert went over to him. 'What's going on?' Will heard him ask.

Through the open chapter house doors came the sound of shocked, raised voices. Above the clamour, Will heard Hugues say something to Robert that made him forget all about Nicolas de Navarre and the Book of the Grail. He hastened over.

Robert's face was troubled. 'Will . . .' he began.

'Did you say something about Safed?' Will cut across him.

'Yes,' said Hugues, answering for Robert. Years of training had stripped most of the fat from Hugues' body, but there was still something unfortunately pig-like about his small dark eyes and blunt nose. 'It has fallen.'

Will opened his mouth to speak, then shook his head and looked at Hugues as if he hadn't heard the knight correctly.

'Brother Marcel has come from our base at La Rochelle,' continued Hugues, gesturing to a darkly-tanned man who was standing inside the chapter house porch. 'He's the captain of one of our warships, which arrived at the port last week. Grand Master Thomas Bérard sent him from Acre as soon as it was known. Safed was taken in July by the Mamluk sultan, Baybars. There were no survivors.'

'How do you know it has fallen then?' asked Simon.

'Baybars sent a message to Grand Master Bérard, detailing the fate of our brothers. He beheaded the entire garrison and put their heads on pikes around the fortress.' Hugues scowled bitterly. 'Apparently to warn us all of what to expect. Captain Marcel has brought only a small crew from Acre. The rest of our forces in Outremer have been sent to reinforce our garrisons and towns throughout the Kingdom of Jerusalem. As many men as can be spared will be sent East.'

'Hugues,' murmured Robert, touching his shoulder.

Hugues glanced at him, but continued speaking gravely to Will and Simon. 'Baybars and his army have retired to their base at Aleppo, but that they will attack again is certain. Baybars has declared the Jihad against us. We are at war.'

'Hugues,' said Robert, firmly now.

'What?' said Hugues.

'Shut up.'

They watched as Will suddenly staggered away and vomited into the mud.

29

Aleppo, Syria

2 November 1266 AD

B aybars sat, subdued and silent, watching the men moving about the throne room. The governors lounged on cushions, or shifted from group to group, pausing to take fruit cordials from the trays held aloft by the servants. Above the sounds of laughter and conversation drifted the musicians' plaintive melodies. Girls in floating gowns danced in the centre of the hall, bodies writhing. Men, mesmerised, watched their spiralling forms. The dancers suddenly scattered as a hunched figure in tattered grey robes darted into their midst. Some of the younger officers laughed as Khadir, mimicking the girls' high-pitched screams, chased them around the pillars. The remnants of the evening's feast lay scattered across the boards: crumbs of honey cakes; slabs of kid congealed in their own grease; woody stumps of asparagus; sugared almonds.

Nearby, Omar was talking with Kalawun and several other governors. Baybars caught his eye and beckoned.

Omar left the group and ascended the steps to the throne. 'My lord?'

'Let us dispense with the festivities.'

'Wait a little longer?' suggested Omar. 'Let the men have their . . .'

'Now, Omar.'

'Yes, my lord.'

The governors and commanders of the regiments fell silent as one of the servants rang a golden bell, signalling the start of the meeting. The musicians ceased their playing and the dancing girls flitted from the hall. All eyes turned to Baybars, who rose from the throne. 'I hope you enjoyed the feast.' His words were answered with a polite smattering of applause. 'We shall have many more in the coming year.' There was more applause. 'For we shall have even greater victories to celebrate than those we have gained so far.' He nodded to Kalawun. 'I have spoken with some of you over the past weeks, regarding the next stages of our campaign. I have since decided upon our main objective.' He paused, scanning their expectant faces. 'We will take the city of Antioch.'

There were a few murmurs of surprise, more of concern.

'My Lord Sultan,' said one of the governors, an ambitious man and always one of the first to speak. 'This would require a massive assault. Antioch is the most fortified city in Syria.'

'The sheer extent of those fortifications,' replied Baybars, 'also makes it one of the hardest to defend. I have studied the plans we have of the city. I believe that a small force could take it in less than a week. Three regiments at most.'

'When do you propose this attack should be executed, my lord?' said another of the governors.

'The harvests are in. The troops could leave, fully supplied, by the end of the week. Khadir's predictions for that time are favourable.'

A few of the governors glanced dubiously at the soothsayer, who was sitting under a table gnawing on a bone.

Baybars, seeing their unresponsive expressions, grew annoyed. 'Did I not promise you victories?'

'And none of us doubts your ability to provide them, my Lord Sultan,' said Kalawun, his voice rising above the murmurs. 'But many of the men have only just returned from Cilicia. Perhaps, for the rest of the winter, it would be better to concentrate on smaller military strongholds, before tackling a target such as Antioch?'

Baybars, shooting Kalawun a dark look, seated himself in his throne and raked the rest of the company with his stare. Most of them chose not to meet his gaze. 'You do not see what I am proposing?' His voice was hard. 'Then let me explain. If we capture Antioch it isn't just a city the Christians will lose: it is their whole principality.' He fell silent for a moment, letting them digest his words. 'Without Antioch, the few scattered settlements and fortresses the Franks have left in the region would become islands in a sea ruled by us. I doubt they would even fight.'

'It is true,' agreed one of the generals, after a pause. 'It would be a massive blow to the Franks. The Principality of Antioch was the first state they established in our territory.'

'And,' said another, 'it's their richest city, after Acre anyway.'

'It is also a holy city,' Baybars reminded them. 'With Edessa gone, and if we take Antioch, the Franks will rule only two states: the County of Tripoli and the Kingdom of Jerusalem, and, of those, few of their former towns and strongholds remain in their hands. In time, we will drive them back into the seas they came from.'

Some of the governors had been stirred by the mention of plunder, but there was still not the enthusiasm Baybars wanted. By the end of the council, however, he had accepted their grudging agreement and had picked out three commanders to lead the attack. After the meeting was over, he left the throne room, avoiding his secretaries, who had various things for him to sign, and Omar, who tried to catch his eye.

Donning a dark robe and turban, Baybars headed out of the citadel by a small side exit and walked down into the city, feeling the tension uncoiling like springs in his body the further he went. The air was balmy. After a time, he came to a dusty street lined with rows of mud-brick houses. At the end of this street was a whitewashed house, larger and grander than the others. There was lantern light coming through the windows and a child's laughter. Baybars turned aside at the entrance and walked around the back of the house, an indistinct figure striding through the shadows. Behind the house was an old barn that had crumbled into disrepair, no one having claimed ownership of, or responsibility for it. Half the roof was missing and fallen timbers littered the ground inside. Baybars often wondered why no one had used it for fuel. Every time he came here he half expected to find it gone. He plucked a hibiscus flower from the bush that grew beside the entrance and stepped inside the place that no one, not his wives, governors, Omar or Kalawun, knew about. In the darkness, he knelt and put the flower to his lips, drawing in its bright scent, remembering how it had smelled in her hair. The light from the stars and from the house beyond filtered into the gloom, illuminating the floor at Baybars' knees. It was strewn with the pink husks of dead hibiscus flowers.

30

The Temple, Paris

2 November 1266 AD

W ill watched the spider enlarge the web it had built inside a crack in the stone. Every once in a while, a cold breeze would flow in through the window, causing the spider to quiver on its line. Each time the wind came, it would scuttle back up its thread and creep into the safety of the crack before darting out and starting again. Will found the spider's industrious activity absorbing. Up, down, round and round. It seemed so simple. Unlike the half-started letter on the window ledge beside him.

Writing the first few lines of the letter to his mother, Will had been numb and it had been easy. But as he'd continued, images of his parents had started to form in his mind. Memories so seemingly insignificant that he had forgotten about them had welled to the surface and brimmed over, flooding him. Most were before Mary died. One had been especially clear: an image of his mother sitting on the edge of the table in the estate's kitchen, her lips pressed together. She had been in the garden picking herbs for dinner when she had stood on a wasp. His father had sat down on a stool and had taken her small white foot gently in his hands. Will, sitting at the table, had watched his father, eyes narrowed in concentration, remove the sting. James had then closed his mouth over the tiny puncture to draw out any poison that might have remained. When he had finished, Isabel had wrapped her arms around his neck, her springy red hair tumbling over his shoulder. 'What would I do without you?' Will had heard her murmur.

That memory had been abruptly replaced by an image of his father's severed head, stuck on a pike, eyes plucked out by birds, mouth filled with maggots. And the quill had snapped in Will's hand. He hadn't bothered to fetch another and the letter had lain there unfinished, fluttering now and then in the breeze.

After running from the yard, Will had gone straight to the empty dormitory, where he had sat on the window ledge, knees squeezed to his chest, taking huge gulps of air. Some time later, he had left the ledge to fetch a quill and parchment from the chest by his pallet, before taking up his seat once more, the same place he'd sat six years ago on the day of Owein's funeral.

The spider slipped down its thread and began to spool out another line. Will touched his throat. For an hour or so, he had been plagued by a subtle yet persistent burning sensation whenever he swallowed. He leaned his head on the stone and gazed out of the window. The clouds that had rolled in over the afternoon had turned the sky white, streaked with wide bands of grey. Will could hear the distant cries of gulls down near the river flats. They would be circling the fishermen bringing in the nets and eel traps. Every day he heard them. But now, the familiar sound was heavy with new significance. Will pressed his hands to his eyes.

He was sitting on warm rocks beside his father, legs dangling above the water. His father had the line submerged and would tug it every so often to re-check the weight. Sunlight, reflected by the water, played on the undersides of the rocks and glinted in James's eyes. Beside them was a bucket filled with three silver-skinned fish. The gulls that wheeled above them would cry and swoop closer every so often, their shadows passing across the rocks.

James's cheeks were sun browned and there was a graze of yellow sand just above his beard. Will wanted to brush it away, but didn't want to disturb his father, who was watching the line placidly with a faraway smile.

'We should build a boat,' James said after a while.

'A boat?'

James looked out over the wide green loch, that smile still playing about his lips. 'Do you think, William, that the fish would be bigger the deeper we were?'

Will thought hard, then nodded.

'With another baby on the way, we'll want bigger fish, won't we?'

'Mother's going to have a baby?'

'A girl, she thinks.'

'What will you call her?' asked Will, trying to sound nonchalant, but feeling his bliss tainted by the news. Another sister? Three was more than enough.

'Ysenda.' James studied Will for a moment. 'You would have to help me, William. I don't think I could build it alone.'

'Of course, father!' Will sat up straight, his disappointment replaced by a weighty sense of responsibility. He frowned in contemplation. How he would build it, he wasn't yet sure, but he did know that it would be the best boat his father had ever seen.

After Mary died, Will had been back to the loch only once before he had left Scotland. The boat was where he had left it, on the high ground above the waterline. He had never made the oars, or waterproofed it with oakum. Grass had begun to sprout up through the cracks in the boards. Will had thought about pushing it out into the loch on that final visit, but even then he'd hoped he would return with his father to sail it. His mother had been nearing the end of her pregnancy and he was certain, however much his father hated him, that they would still need to find those bigger fish.

When he had thought of the boat in later years it was as a rotted carcass for weeds and hermit crabs, but he wondered, now, whether someone might have found and saved it. He knew, from the few letters he had received from his mother, that his older sisters, Alycie and Ede, had left the nunnery some years ago to live with their husbands in Edinburgh, where they had had families of their own. But perhaps Ysenda, who would be eight now, might one day go back to the estate where she was born and find the boat. She might not be able to sail it, but Will fancied she could use it as a place to play and think of the brother and father she never knew.

Will took his hands from his eyes, hearing the sound of hooves in the yard outside the stables. Other than that and the faint cries of the gulls everything was still and silent. Most of the knights, priests and sergeants were in the chapel where they had been called following the news of Safed. They had spent the early part of the afternoon in mourning.

Soon, the silence would end. Soon, the call to arms would sound.

Will didn't look round when the door opened. He heard someone shuffle across the room towards him. When he did glance round, he saw Everard's bloodshot eyes peering down at him, then the inviting numbness closed in around him again and he looked away.

'I've been looking for you, sergeant.'

Will didn't say anything.

'How long were you planning on hiding in here for?'

'I have to finish my letter.'

Everard frowned. His eyes fell on the parchment. 'This?' he asked, picking it up. He read, eyes squinting in the gloom. 'This can wait,' he said quietly, putting it down. 'There are matters we must discuss.'

'I have to write to my mother, sir, and tell her that her husband and the father of her children is dead.'

'Your mother and sisters will be taken care of by the Temple,' said Everard brusquely. 'They will not want for anything. I promise you.' He sighed when Will didn't respond. 'I understand that you are upset.'

'Understand?' Will looked round. 'You understand? Then perhaps you can explain it to me, to my mother. Perhaps *you* should write and tell her why he died. You sent him there, after all.'

'That is unfair,' said Everard shortly. 'James didn't die whilst in service to the Anima Templi. He died in service to the Temple, doing something he would not have chosen to do.' His expression softened. 'When your father went to the Holy Land, he did so of his own free will. He went because he believed, because he wanted to make a difference in this life. A different world, he told me once, for the sake of his children. For you, William.'

Will glanced at him, but remained silent.

'I need to hear what happened at the Hospitallers' preceptory,' said Everard quietly, but insistently.

'Nicolas has gone to La Rochelle with three of his brothers,' Will said eventually. 'A stableboy said they were talking about Acre and the Grand Master.'

'Acre?' said Everard worriedly. 'So Hugues de Revel is behind this?'

'De Revel?' said Will listlessly.

'The Grand Master of the Hospital. I've not met him, but I knew his predecessor, Guillaume de Châteauneuf – the man who was in charge of their Order when Armand laid siege to their stronghold.' Everard rubbed at his chin. 'I expect Nicolas plans to take the book straight to him. If the Grand Master believes it evidence enough of the Anima Templi's existence and, as Nicolas so wrongly surmises, corruption, he will no doubt involve the pope in Rome.' He inhaled sharply. 'We cannot let them leave these shores with it. We ride for La Rochelle at dawn.'

Will looked at him. 'We?'

'I cannot do this alone.'

'And I cannot do this at all,' responded Will, swinging his legs over the ledge and jumping down to face the priest. 'Even had I strength to, I could not. I'm just a sergeant. I have no authority over any knight, whether from the Temple, the Hospital, the Teutonics, or the king's own army!'

'Well, that is about to change,' said Everard after a pause. 'I spoke to the Visitor and he has agreed your inception.'

'What?'

'He felt it fitting, to have lost the father that we should gain the son. A symbol,' muttered Everard, 'that we shall prevail and not be cowed by our enemy. The Visitor wants to do it soon, before the council he has called to discuss what shall be done. I'm afraid your inception will take place in amongst all the warmongering, but that cannot be helped.'

'Is this some kind of jest? You have chosen the worst day possible to do this!'

Everard's scarred face mellowed. 'Grief is one of the purest emotions we are capable of. In experiencing true sorrow all the . . .' He waved his hand impatiently, searching for a word. 'All the *noise* inside us falls away. In that silence we find ourselves. Those are the moments that shape us. So, on the contrary, I believe today is the best day to do this.'

Will rested his palms on the window ledge and hung his head. 'I'm no longer sure I want to be a knight.'

'I thought it was your father's wish?' said Everard in a tone of suggestive enquiry.

'My father is dead.'

'Then does everything he did and wished for in life cease to have meaning? Does what he believed in, what he worked and bled to achieve become unimportant?' Everard shook his head. 'James Campbell began something. It is up to us to finish it. Only if we ignore that does his life, his *death* become meaningless.'

Will raised his head and stared out of the window, his tears cold on his cheeks. The world outside was flat and grey. For years, he had been running towards one place: a place at his father's side. Now that place had ceased to exist, where would he go? However aware he was of the dangers facing fighting men in Outremer, it had never entered his head that he might not see his father again. 'I have no purpose,' he whispered, not realising that he was speaking out loud.

'You have purpose to me.' Everard reached out and placed his disfigured hand on Will's shoulder. 'Great purpose.'

Two iron braziers filled with charcoals had burned in the chapter house throughout the morning, taking the bite out of the November chill. But no one had thought to replace them for the ceremony and they had mostly turned to ash. Heavy tapestries covered the windows, blocking out the grey afternoon.

Will's skin prickled as he removed his black tunic and handed it to the cleric who was waiting beside him. He took off his boots, then unfastened his belt and sword. As he pulled his undershirt over his head, he became acutely aware of the large company of men seated behind him. The vaulted chamber was dimly lit, but he felt they could all clearly see the thin, white lines that crisscrossed his back where Everard had once whipped him. Will looked to Everard standing on the dais, but the stooped, gaunt-faced man arranging the holy vessels on the tabernacle showed none of the sour asperity he had on that day six years ago. Behind Everard, in a throne-like seat made out of pale white stone, sat the Visitor. He looked fatigued. There were two other knights on the dais.

As Will handed the cleric his shirt and stood in the empty space between the seated knights and the raised altar, clad in nothing but his hose and illuminated in a tiny pool of torchlight, he felt more alone than he ever had in his life.

When the cleric moved off with his old garments, Will looked around, seeking a friendly face in the crowd. He saw Robert. The knight, who was sitting beside Hugues in one of the front benches, caught his eye and smiled. Will turned back to the altar feeling his sense of isolation dissipate fractionally as Everard lit the incense in the censer and called for silence. The low murmur of conversation coming from the company, which seemed impatient to begin the war council, died away. Everard, wreathed in smoke, prompted Will to kneel. He did so, aware that he hadn't learnt, as other initiates would have during the night-long vigil, what he was supposed to say, or do. There was no time to worry about it now though, as the Visitor had risen and was addressing him.

'You have spent time in vigil, that you might reflect upon the sacred office that has been offered to you.' The Visitor's deep voice filled the chamber. 'William Campbell, son of James, do you now wish to accept the mantle, knowing that in doing so you shall cast away your worldly duties and become a true and humble servant of Almighty God?'

'I do,' answered Will.

And so his vows began.

Will spoke when he was supposed to, prompted by Everard on occasion and remembering, with surprising clarity, the words of the postulant he had seen initiated when he and Simon had been hidden in the grain store at New Temple. He said he believed in the Catholic faith and that he had been conceived in legitimate wedlock. He denied offering anyone a gift so that he might join, or having any debt, or belonging to any other Order. And, although his throat was starting to burn and his chest felt as tight as a drum, he confirmed that he was fit in body.

One of the two knights descended to him and held out a copy of the Rule, opened at the first page. 'Read these words. If you cannot, speak, and they shall be translated for you.'

Will could barely see the Latin text in the gloom, but after staring hard at the faded ink, he managed to recite what it said. 'Lord God, I come here before you and before these good brothers here present, to ask for companionship of the Order and participation in the spiritual and temporal goods herein. I wish for the duration of my life to be a serving slave in the Order of the Temple and to put aside my will for that of God's.' Will swore to uphold the laws of the Temple; to preserve his chastity; remain in poverty; be obedient. Once he had prostrated himself before the altar to ask for the blessings of God, the Virgin and all the saints, the second knight stepped from the dais, sword drawn. The blade gleamed dully as it was held, point-down, towards Will.

'Kiss this blade and accept the burden of protection placed upon you. Against all enemies shall you defend the one true faith and, in direst need, shall you offer your life in this defence.'

Will leaned forward to touch his lips to the shaft, his breath misting the blade. And the vow he was making felt all too real. As the knight sheathed the blade and ascended the dais, Everard hobbled over to where one of the clerics was waiting with a sword and a folded white mantle. In the pause, Will realised that he didn't understand why his father and the other men at Safed had chosen martyrdom. To him, their deaths seemed senseless. Had fulfilling this vow meant more to them than their families? How many sons and daughters had they abandoned to secure a place in Paradise? James had written to Will only twice in the past six years and although the letters hadn't been full of blame for Mary, neither had they contained any words of love. From them, Will had learnt far more about Outremer than he had about his father's heart. He now longed to know why his father had chosen death; longed to scream up to Heaven and *demand* to know.

And that was when the anger he had been holding back since that morning finally overflowed.

He was angry at the Temple for demanding his father's life in its service, angry at Everard for deceiving him, angry at the Saracen who had killed his father and the sultan, Baybars, who had commanded it. But most of all he was angry at his father for leaving, for lying to him, for not forgiving him, for dying. Now his father was gone and he would never know absolution and his head was pounding and Everard was coming towards him and his father's words were ringing in his ears.

One day, William, you will be admitted as a Knight of the Temple and when you are, in God's name, I will be at your side.

In God's name, his father had broken one vow and fulfilled another. So, had he served God's will, or his own? And had he died defending the Order, or the Anima Templi, or to punish a son for the death of a daughter?

'With this sword, may you defend Christendom from the enemies of God.'

Will rose to his feet, dazedly, and raised his hands as Everard held out the sword. His eyes focused on the polished length of iron, the blade of which was unmarked. He dropped his hands to his sides. Everard frowned, then seemed to understand. He snapped his fingers at a cleric who was waiting with the mantle. The cleric looked uncertainly up at the Visitor, then crossed the floor to Everard, who spoke quickly and quietly to him. Will heard a couple of curious murmurs come from the crowd at the interruption to the ceremony as the cleric hurried through a small side door. When he returned, he was carrying Will's falchion. Everard passed him back the new sword, then took the short, scarred blade with the loose wire around the hilt and handed it to Will. Will frowned away the tears that threatened, more touched by the priest's display of empathy than by anything else. He fastened the belt around his waist.

Everard held out the mantle. 'With this cloth are you reborn.'

Will took it and opened up the folded material. The splayed cross on the back and above the heart was as red as wine and blood and Elwen's lips. He drew the mantle around his bare shoulders, his nose filled with the astringent smell of freshly felted cloth. It was, he realised, a bit short. Usually, the tailor would measure the intended wearer before the ceremony, but, of course, there hadn't been time. Will told himself that it didn't matter; he would have the tailor alter it. But, even so, the mantle didn't feel like the pair of wings he had once imagined it would. It hung heavily from his shoulders and itched.

Everard fastened it at the neck for him with a simple silver pin. 'I absolve you,' murmured the priest, passing his hand in the sign of the cross, 'of all your sins. In the name of the Father, the Son and the Holy Spirit. Amen.'

The Visitor rose from the throne. '*Ecce quam bonum et quam jocundum habitare fratres in unum.*'

After the visitor had finished intoning the psalm, Everard placed his hands on Will's shoulders. 'In the words of the blessed Bernard de Clairvaux, I tell you that a man of the Temple is a fearless knight, safe from all sides, who, as the body is covered by iron, so is the soul by the defence of the faith. Without doubt, fortified by both arms, he fears neither demon nor man. Nor indeed,' said the priest, gazing intently into Will's eyes, 'is he afraid of death. We behold you, Sir William Campbell, Knight of the Temple. May God make you a worthy man.' He stood on tiptoe to kiss Will's mouth, then every man in the chapter house rose and, one by one, came forward to do the same.

The Royal Palace, Paris, 2 November 1266 AD

'How can this have happened?' Louis IX, the King of France, sat forward in his throne, addressing the company of knights who were standing before him in the Great Hall. The chamber was empty and echoing, the trestles and decorations that had been set out for the troubadour's performance the evening before having been hastily cleared away. The servants had missed a few dried rose petals, which were scattered at the feet of the knights. 'How can Safed have fallen so swiftly?'

It was the Visitor who answered the king. 'Reports say that Baybars promised unconditional amnesty to the native forces within if they surrendered, my liege. Our fortress was strong, yes, but without enough men to garrison its walls it would have been indefensible.'

Will, standing at the back of the company of six knights who had escorted the Visitor to the palace, watched Louis bow his leonine head, which was framed by a mane of dark hair, streaked white at his temples. His vermilion cloak, trimmed with ermine swathed his frame, which had been muscular in youth but had tended towards fat in his middle years. Blemishes on his face were the pockmarks of diseases he had survived in the East and his hands were thick and liver-spotted. Only sixteen years ago, this king had headed the Seventh Crusade to the Holy Land, leading thirty-five thousand men to an initial victory, then, ultimately, death in Egypt. After the Battle of Mansurah, Louis and his remaining, beleaguered forces had been rounded up and imprisoned by the Muslims. The ransom for his release had been paid by his wife, Queen Marguerite.

Will's vision clouded as he stared at the king and he shook his head, trying to shake off the sluggish feeling that had come over him during the war council that had taken place after his inception. When the Visitor had told him in a solemn tone that he would join the company going to the palace, it had been an effort to hide his reluctance. He felt dazed, numb.

Louis raised his head after several moments, during which he appeared to be praying. 'This is a black day. A black day indeed.'

'I have sent word to our principal preceptories throughout the West, informing our brothers what has happened,' said the Visitor.

The king was quiet for a time. 'Baybars whittles us away as a carpenter would a block of wood. Last month, the Hospitallers told me that Arsuf had fallen to him, and before that Caesarea and Haifa. His reach has become longer than any of us could have imagined.'

'Yes, my liege,' agreed the Visitor gravely. 'If we do not act soon, I fear our territories will shrink to nothing. The fortifications you made during your time in Palestine will only hold for so long without men to defend them. Safed was one of our greatest fortresses and we let Baybars take it.' The Visitor's eyes were bright with sorrow, but his tone was uncompromising. 'We, in the West, have done nothing to halt his war against us, leaving it to our brothers in the East to fight and defend our dream. We now pay the dear cost of our inaction.'

'What do you propose?'

The Visitor was silent for a pause. When he spoke, his tone was resolute. 'The Temple is ready and willing to apportion funds and men for a move eastwards to counter the threat posed by Baybars. But it will take many months to build ships for the journey, then more to make it. We must act now and we will need your support, and the support of every willing man, be he peasant or monarch, on this side of the sea. A new Crusade led by you to Palestine, my liege. That is what I propose.'

Louis clasped his hands under his chin. 'This is not an unexpected proposition. I have recently been in contact with my brother, Charles, Count of Anjou. He has already spoken to me, extolling such an endeavour.'

The Visitor met the king's thoughtful gaze. 'Will you do this, my liege?'

Louis sat back in his throne, his vermilion cloak settling around him. 'Yes, Master Visitor, I will launch a new Crusade. And the Saracens will pay dear themselves for the lives of the Christians they have taken. As soon as I am able, I will take the Cross.'

As the king spoke these last words, Will felt a wave of dizziness wash over him. His vision went black and he stumbled, just managing to catch the arm of the knight beside him to keep himself from falling.

'What is wrong?' murmured the knight, staring at him. 'You're as white as a lily.'

'I . . . I need air,' breathed Will, staggering away towards the doors at the far end of the chamber.

'Is your man sick?' Will heard the king's voice echo behind him.

'His father was one of those butchered at Safed, my liege,' replied the Visitor as Will pushed open the doors and reeled out into the passage beyond.

Torches, freshly lit, were burning along the corridor. The light hurt his eyes. Passing two servants who looked curiously at him, Will fled to the end of the passage, where a tall, arched window looked down over the Seine. He grasped the ledge, fighting off the vertiginous sensation that engulfed him in great waves, drawing in deep draughts of briny-smelling air. Since that morning, his world had been turned upside-down and he now felt that revolution in every fibre of his being. Only hours before, he had been digging up the body of a man who had been murdered by his countrymen, and, even as he had been feeling shame for such a brutal act, his own father's body lay rotting in Palestine, slain by Muslims like Hasan. But he didn't want Hasan to be lying in that grave; he didn't want his father to have died alone, one man striving for peace in a land torn apart by the hatred of those on both sides; he didn't want his friends sent to that place, swords in hands. The king and the Visitor wanted retribution, but Will could not see how killing more men would make any of this right.

Will tugged at the collar of his mantle. He could feel sweat trickling down his back, even though the air was freezing. Was this what it meant to be a knight? To fight and die for another man's cause? Because a king willed it? Because God willed it? Will couldn't believe that. To him those words were hollow, lifeless. His father hadn't believed that; he would have known that even had he never been told the reason his father had gone to the Holy Land. Tall and dignified, James had been to him; noble in spirit; honourable in battle; generous in heart. But it wasn't the mantle that had made him that way, or the vows he had taken. It was the man inside who had embodied those things. Other men had abandoned their families for the sake of war, for God and for country. His father had abandoned him, his mother and sisters for the sake of peace. The world outside blurred as Will's eyes filled with tears. The anger he had felt towards his father was vanquished by an all-consuming feeling of love and, with it, an utterly desolate sense of loss.

'Will?' came a woman's voice.

Will turned to see Elwen. The flames of the torches highlighted the copper tones of her hair, which was bound up with spirals of silver wire. Her wide, green eyes were luminous in the shifting flames. Her plain gown and mantle were the colour of a canary's wing and girdled with a silver chain. She looked like a queen.

Elwen's eyes were fixed in shock on his mantle. 'When did this happen?'

'Elwen,' he began, his voice hoarse. But he couldn't find any more words and so instead he went to her, grasping her as tightly as if he were a drowning man and she the one piece of timber left after a shipwreck.

'I heard that knights from the Temple had come to see the king,' she said, her voice muffled against his chest. 'But I didn't imagine it would be you. What is happening? The queen told me that the king was called to an urgent council.'

'Safed has fallen,' Will said into her hair. 'My father is dead.'

Elwen drew back and looked up at him. 'Will,' she breathed, cradling his wet cheek with her hand. 'My God.' Her own eyes filled with tears at the sight of his distress.

'The king will launch a new Crusade.'

Elwen touched her fingertips to the cross on Will's mantle. 'Then you will be . . . ?' Her voice cracked. 'You will be going to war?'

'No,' said Will determinedly. 'I will not leave you.' He looked down into her fear-filled face and realised what a fool he had been. All this time he had been chasing a ghost. Forgiveness was no longer achievable; could never be fulfilled. He would never know his father's love again except in memory. But Elwen was here, tangible and solid, wanting him, loving him, and he had spurned her for the sake of the mantle he now wore that meant no more to him than the soiled black tunic he had been wearing for years. He hesitated, just for a second, before he said the words. 'I love you.'

Elwen's eyes searched his face.

'And I want to marry you,' finished Will.

'You don't mean that,' she said with a short, astonished laugh.

'I've never meant anything more.'

'But you can't, you're a knight! You've taken your vows.' Her tears spilled over. 'Now we'll never . . .' Her words vanished as he bent to kiss her. Slowly, she kissed him back. Will's hold on her tightened as she opened her mouth to explore his with her tongue. She felt a flush of desire bloom on her cheeks. She reached out, took his hand in hers and tentatively placed it on her breast. She felt him tense, then relax.

Will wasn't even aware that he was breaking his first vow as he ran his hand across her and heard a tiny sigh rush from her lips.

There was a snigger behind them.

They broke away from one another to see a servant passing by with a tray of goblets. He was still chuckling as he moved off down the corridor.

Will took her hands. 'We can marry in secret. No one has to know.' Everard's words filled his mind. *James Campbell began something. It is up to us to finish it.* 'But there is one thing I must do first.'

The Seven Stars, Paris

2 November 1266 AD

A dela fastened the red and gold necklace at her throat and stared at herself in her silver mirror. The glass beads were cold against her bare skin. She touched the necklace, remembering Garin saying she looked pretty in it. He had been gone for almost three hours and Rook was still downstairs, drinking her ale for free.

Earlier, Garin had come to her, pale and agitated. 'I have to go to the preceptory,' he had told her. 'But I'll return as soon as I can. If all goes well, Rook will be gone tomorrow. Whatever happens, keep out of his way until then.'

'Why won't you tell me what he's doing here?' she had asked him. 'Why does he have this hold over you? I can have Fabien make him leave. Just ask me to and I will.'

'No! Don't anger him. Let me help him do what he came here for. He'll leave when he's got what he wants.'

'You are a Templar, Garin, why are you letting a snake like that treat you this way?'

He hadn't answered.

Adela rose and went to her workbench to fetch a bottle of jasmine oil to scent her hair. A group of merchants from Flanders had arrived just after Vespers and it looked to be a busy night. Her eyes fell on her herbal, which was open at a page with a recipe for a contraceptive solution. In the margin were a few notes she had made on the best method for aborting a baby if the solution failed. A travelling physician who had stayed for a night had shown her how to do it on one of her girls who had fallen pregnant. But Adela didn't want to abort babies: she wanted to make them. She wanted a little house with land enough for a herb garden and happy, cherubic children laughing in her kitchen whilst she made lavender cakes and solutions for grazed knees and nettle-stings. She closed the book. Could Garin really give her that? Sometimes, in the months he had been coming to her, she had thought he might be able to, then something would upset him and he would become childish and withdrawn. Adela had never met a man who could be so selfish in one moment and so tender in the next. She wouldn't have put up with it, only she knew that curled up beneath that irascible veneer was a tired, frightened boy with no real sense of himself, or his place in life. Some nights, he had just lain in her arms spilling hot, silent tears across her breasts. She had found herself wanting to mother and love him at the same time. She had even found herself believing the promises he had made in his euphoria – that he would take her away from this place, that she could come and live with him when he was rich and owned an estate. Time and time again she had instructed her girls over the necessity for detachment. Her weakness for the handsome, volatile knight had made her doubt herself, her life.

The door opened and Rook entered. His face was flushed with drink, his eyes heavy-lidded.

Adela reached for her robe and pulled it around her, covering her nakedness. 'Is Garin back?'

'No,' said Rook, scowling. His expression changed as he watched her tie the robe at her waist, a malignant grin splitting his face. 'But don't worry, he'll return soon enough. He knows what'll happen if he doesn't.'

Adela flinched at the threat within his words and the way he looked at her as he said them. But she stood her ground as he came into the room, closing the door behind him. She tensed as he walked towards her. 'What are you doing?'

Rook didn't answer, but moved past her to the stool that was placed before her mirror. He picked it up, seemed to test its weight in his hands, then frowned and dropped it carelessly to the floor. His gaze roved around the room and alighted on the bed, his frown replaced by a nasty grin. 'Have you got any rope?'

'Rope?'

'Yes, rope,' he said gruffly. 'With luck we'll have a guest this evening.' He chuckled. 'And we'll want to make him comfortable, won't we? I need rope, or strips of cloth, or . . .' Rook stopped, noticing the girdle on her robe. 'That'll do.'

Adela gasped as he snatched at the length of plaited material. She pushed at him. 'Get your hands off me!'

Rook backhanded her viciously across her face. She staggered back and sprawled to the floor with the force of the blow, her silk robe riding up to her thighs. Adela cried out as Rook bent down over her and yanked the girdle through the loops on the robe.

'Your place is on your back, whore,' he growled, standing. 'Know it.'

Adela sat up, her hand pressed to her cheek which stung as hotly as if she had been burnt. She tasted blood and realised that the slap had split her lip. 'Get out.' She rose, clutching her robe shut. 'I don't care who you think you are, or what you think you are doing here with me, with Garin. It stops now.'

Rook tossed the girdle onto the bed and looked back at her. 'Garin should have warned you what would happen if you interfered. You'll do as you're told or I'll hurt you some more.'

'And I'll have Fabien break your legs, you bastard!' she snapped back at him, heading for the door.

Rook was on her in two strides. Wrenching her round by the arm he pinned her against the door, pressing himself on her so that she couldn't move. Adela fought him like a cat, flinging her long-nailed hands at his face and neck, but although he wasn't a large man, Rook had a surprising, wiry strength. He pushed his arm up under her throat, forcing her head back and crushing her windpipe so she couldn't call out. With his free hand, he drew his dagger and held it to her eye.

Adela stopped fighting immediately. Her breaths came short and sharp from the pressure on her throat and from terror. The dagger tip glinted in her vision.

'Now,' murmured Rook, his voice low, almost soothing. 'Are you going to keep quiet and find me another cord for our guest, or are you going to make me take out one of these pretty eyes?'

'Yes,' she breathed quickly.

'Yes what?' he asked, placing the dagger's cold tip ever so lightly into the corner of her eye.

She didn't dare move, or even blink. 'I'll help you.'

'Good,' he said, nodding his approval, 'because if you kick up a fuss again, I'll make sure there's not enough left of you, your whores or this stinking hole to fill a tankard.' He held her for a moment longer, finding himself aroused by the little gasps she was making and the feel of her trembling body against his, then released his grip on her slowly, in case she tried to bolt.

She didn't. Holding her robe shut with a shaking hand, Adela rooted through her gowns until she found another girdle.

Rook smiled as she passed it to him without a word. 'That weren't too hard, was it?' he said, expertly tying the lengths of plaited cord to the short, squat legs of the bed. He tugged hard on each of the tethers to check that they were secure, then straightened. 'Now we just have to keep ourselves busy till that wretch returns.' He turned to her. 'Get on the bed.'

'What?' she said, startled by the emotionless way in which he spoke the words.

'You're here to service men, aren't you?' Rook nodded to the pallet. 'So, service me.'

'You'll have to pay,' she told him, trying to sound defiant, but feeling tears welling in her eyes.

'Garin will see to my bill.' Rook watched her twist her head away, the sight of her distress pleasing him. 'I didn't think it would take much to break you.' He went to her and pulled apart her arms so that her robe fell open. He stepped back, appraising her until he felt his arousal build again, then grasped her wrist and led her to the pallet.

Adela told herself that he was just another customer, that he wasn't much worse than some of the brutes she'd had to service over the years. But she couldn't stop the tears falling as Rook climbed on top of her, his foetid breath hot on her face.

The Temple, Paris, 2 November 1266 AD

'How long will you be gone for?' asked Simon, placing a second saddle on the bench.

'I don't know,' said Will. 'A few weeks maybe.' He shivered and wiped his brow, which felt cold and clammy. His hand came back wet.

'I don't like this,' said Simon adamantly. 'What will you do if you catch up with Nicolas? There's four of them and, I don't mean to be rude, but Everard's hardly up to a fight and you . . . ?' Simon sucked on his lip as he looked at Will. 'You look as if you couldn't pick up a sword at the moment, let alone wield one.' He went to Will and put a hand awkwardly on his friend's shoulder. 'You haven't said a word about your father, Will, not since we heard about Safed.'

'We're not going to confront Nicolas,' said Will, moving away and taking down two sets of reins from one of the hooks on the stable wall. He passed them to Simon. 'If he's planning on going to Acre, he'll have to wait for a ship. Everard will enlist the help of knights from our base at La Rochelle. We'll arrest and detain Nicolas and his brothers there.'

'But why do you have to go? Can't Everard have the Visitor send knights after them from here?'

'There would be too many questions asked that Everard doesn't want to answer just yet. The knights at La Rochelle won't know Nicolas.'

'Well, I'm surprised the stable master's even letting you take these horses,' said Simon, irritated at Will's lack of regard for his concerns. 'He told me you lost the other ones.'

'We got them back,' said Will, picking up the sacks Everard had given him that were to be filled with supplies from the kitchens. That afternoon, a knight riding in from one of the preceptory's farmsteads near Saint-Denis had come across the two missing palfreys wandering loose in a field and, seeing that they bore the Temple's brand, had brought them in. The stable master had had no choice but to agree when Everard had come to the stables an hour ago ordering two mounts to be shod and readied for dawn.

'Sir Campbell?' A sergeant appeared in the stable's entrance. He bowed to Will. 'I've a message for you. I was given it some time ago, but I haven't been able to find you.'

'I've been out. What is the message?'

'A boy delivered it to the gate when I was on duty. He said a woman called Elwen had told him to pass it on to you. He said she wants you to meet her in an alehouse in the Latin Quarter called the Seven Stars. It's on the street which leads up the hill to the Abbey of Saint Geneviève, he said.'

'Did he say anything else?'

'No, sir,' replied the sergeant. 'That was it.' He bowed again, then headed off.

Frowning, Will slung the sacks onto the bench.

'What are you doing?' asked Simon, watching as Will picked up his mantle, which he had taken off and placed on a hay bale. 'You're not going, are you?'

Will didn't answer.

'You've got to get ready, get your supplies,' said Simon. 'And what's she doing in an alehouse anyway?'

'I don't know,' replied Will, wearily slinging his mantle around his shoulders. 'But I asked Elwen to be my wife this evening. I have to go.'

'You did what?' said Simon, staring at Will as he opened the stall door and led out a sprightly tan gelding. 'How could you? You're a knight! Will, you can't!'

'I won't be long,' insisted Will, 'just pass me one of those saddles.'

The Seven Stars, Paris, 2 November 1266 AD

Garin entered the tavern by the back door and, slipping through the crowded downstairs room, hastened up the stairs. He pushed open the door to Adela's room. Rook was standing by the pallet, tying up his hose. Adela was sitting hunched on the bed, knees pressed to her chest. There was a red imprint shaped like a hand on her cheek and her lip looked swollen. She was naked.

Garin looked at Rook as Adela turned away and picked up her robe, unable to meet his gaze. 'What did you do?'

'You took your time,' said Rook shortly. He took in Garin's expression, savoured it, then grinned. 'You shouldn't have been so long, should you.' He finished tying up his hose. 'Well? Is it done? Did you get the message to him?'

Garin took one last look at Adela, then turned and sprinted down the passage, ignoring Rook's shouts for him to stop. Pounding downstairs, he threw open the alehouse door and fled into the cold darkness, tears of rage burning his eyes.

32

The Seven Stars, Paris

2 November 1266 AD

T he alehouse door was barred. Will pushed against it with his shoulder, but it didn't budge and so he pounded on the sturdy wood with his fist. The sounds of voices and laughter from within didn't dissipate. In the square outside the building were several horses and wagons and a few men, possibly drivers or squires, standing around a small fire, their conversation made visible by their white plumes of breath. It was fully dark now and a half-moon had risen, high and bright, turning the rooftops silver. Will was about to knock again when a bolt rattled and the door swung open. The noise became instantly louder and washed out over him, along with hot air that smelled of perfumed oils and beer. A mountain of a man with black hair and thick, shaggy eyebrows was framed in the doorway.

'Yes?'

'I'm meeting someone here,' said Will.

The man didn't answer, but stepped aside.

Will stopped just inside the chamber as the huge man shut the door behind him. It took once glance around the room for him to realise that, although he had never visited one, this was a certain type of alehouse that he and Robert had sometimes joked, nebulously, about. There were twenty or thirty men in various states of dress and inebriation: sitting at benches where the remnants of an evening meal were scattered; dancing to the energetic sawing of a half-cut fiddle player; standing about talking and laughing raucously. But it was the room's other occupants that so arrested Will's attention. For every two men there was a woman, bejewelled and red-lipped. Many of them wore revealing silk gowns, others just long skirts and some nothing at all. Will's eyes refused to look away as his gaze fell on one woman, who was sitting at a bench in front of him on the lap of a well-dressed man. The man, a merchant by the cut of his clothes, had a hand curled around one of her breasts and was sucking greedily at her large, brown nipple. The woman, meanwhile, was chatting animatedly over his shoulder to a plump brunette. Will tore his gaze away to look round at the large man. 'I think I might have got the wrong place.'

'Is it Elwen you are meeting?' asked the man, his eyes on Will's white mantle.

Will couldn't answer. His mind, already dazed, refused to make any connection between the orgiastic scene before him and his future wife.

'I was told to look out for a Templar,' explained the man into Will's silence. 'She's waiting upstairs.' The man pointed to a set of stairs. 'Last door at the end of the passage.' He moved off, leaving Will standing alone.

Seeing a blonde woman with scarlet lips wearing nothing but a large gold torque weaving her way purposefully through the crowd towards him, Will headed for the stairs. He took them slowly, his limbs heavy and his mind filled with trepidation. As he climbed, he tried to think of the reasons Elwen might have for bringing him to this place, but only one remained as he reached the top and was faced with a long passage. He remembered the lewd book she had shown him, the way she had pressed him down and kissed him in the field outside Saint-Denis's Gate, how she had placed his hand on her breast in the palace and all their fumbling, nervous trysts. He paused as he reached the door at the end. He didn't want this, not tonight, nor in this squalid building with his head thumping and his throat raw. But neither was he willing to leave her in this place and so he opened the door, hoping she would understand. The room was dimly lit and smoky. Standing in front of a bench lined with bottles and jars, her back to him, was a woman. She wore a red silk robe and a lacy cap over her hair.

'Elwen?' said Will cautiously into the gloom. He moved into the room. As he did so, the door slammed shut behind him and a curved dagger flashed up to his throat. The man holding it had been pressed against the wall next to the door.

'Take off your sword,' said the man, moving in behind him, still holding the dagger to his neck.

Will hesitated, then felt a sharp pain when the dagger cut into his skin. 'Do it!'

Will slowly unbuckled the sword belt. The man with the dagger took it from him and tossed it onto the pallet. The woman standing at the bench turned. It wasn't Elwen. Her expression was fearful and she looked as if she had been beaten.

'You can go now,' said the man.

Will realised after a pause that he was addressing the woman.

'Make sure we're not disturbed. And if that wretch comes back you tell him to come up here.'

As the woman slipped past, she looked at Will, her violet eyes full of remorse. 'I'm sorry,' she murmured.

After she had gone, the man kicked the door shut. 'The bed. Go and sit on the floor in front of it.'

Will walked slowly towards the large pallet. The man was right behind him, walking with him. Will could smell his rancid breath. The dagger was still pressed against his throat. His heart was thudding in his chest, but fear had sharpened his mind, clearing the daze he had been in. He was almost at the bed. Suddenly, he grabbed the man's wrist with his left hand, forcing the dagger from his throat, and pivoted round, ducking away from the blade as he pulled the man's arm wide. Will caught sight of his face, which was concealed by a triangle of black cloth so that only the eyes were visible, dark and glittery, as he slammed a fist into the man's stomach. The man doubled over with a winded gasp and Will brought a knee up into his face. The man's wheezy exhalation became a sharp, whistling intake of breath. He dropped the dagger. Will let go of the man's wrist and ran for the door, but the man barrelled into him on his way past. It was a clumsy movement; he was still fighting for breath and half bent over, but this awkwardness aided him and as he staggered heavily into Will, the knight stumbled sideways and went down. As Will pushed himself up on his knees, a wave of dizziness came over him, causing his vision to cloud. He swayed forwards, throwing his hands out to stop himself falling. His vision cleared in seconds, but the pause was all the man needed to recover his own balance.

The man threw himself on Will, forcing him back down to the floor, punching him in the kidneys, the side, the back, hissing curses and threats in a vicious, breathless stream. Will tried to twist away, but the man was on top of him, pressing him into the floor and each blow knocked the last of the breath and the strength from him, until finally he crumpled under the torrent, the room darkening around him. He felt the man's weight leave him, then hands grabbing his shoulders, hauling him roughly back. Dimly he felt something, rope, or cord, being looped around his wrists, securing him painfully tight.

The Temple, Paris, 2 November 1266 AD

'Where is he then?' asked Everard irritably. 'He should have collected our supplies by now. I wanted to go over the plans for our journey.'

Simon continued brushing at the horse's flanks with his grooming brush. 'He went out, sir,' he muttered uncomfortably, after a moment.

Everard's eyes alighted on the two leather sacks that he had given Will that were lying on a hay bale by the stable's entrance. They were empty. 'Out? Where?'

Simon sighed heavily and turned to the priest. 'He went to see Elwen. She sent him a message asking him to meet her.'

Everard's eyes narrowed. 'Meet her where? Answer me!' demanded the priest when Simon went quiet.

'An alehouse in the city.'

Everard's face was thunderous. 'Do you know where? Good,' he snapped, as Simon nodded. 'Then you'll take that horse and fetch him back this instant!'

'Sir . . .!' began Simon.

But Everard would not let him argue and, an hour later, Simon was riding across the bridge to the Île de la Cité, making for the Latin Quarter.

In a market square some distance from the palace, a group of traders had set up a late pitch for people coming home from feast day prayers and celebrations. There were less than two hours to go before Compline, but they were doing a roaring trade and the little square was packed. The smell of smoke and burnt meat made Simon's stomach growl as he manoeuvred his horse at a walk through the people who had spilled into the road. There were stalls selling pastries and beer and spices and one selling silk, lengths of which floated ethereally like butterfly wings. Beside the silk stall, standing stationary on the road, was a wagon. It was covered with a scarlet cloth on which was embroidered a gold fleur-de-lys. Two richly caparisoned mares were haltered to the front where there was a small bench on which sat a driver, dressed in a black cape and cap. Standing by the horses, stamping his feet and looking cold and bored, was a royal guard. Simon frowned as he saw a woman approaching the wagon, her arms draped with several folded lengths of silk. He brought his horse to a standstill. It was Elwen.

Dismounting, Simon threw the reins over a hobbling post where several other mounts were tethered. Elwen looked up as he jogged towards her, passing the wagon.

'Simon?' she called out in surprise.

Before he could reach her, Simon felt a heavy hand clamp down on his shoulder, forcing him to halt.

'What are you doing?' said the royal guard, frowning down at him.

'It's all right, Baudouin,' said Elwen, coming over. 'I know him.'

Baudouin let go of Simon's shoulder. After a moment, he went back to the wagon, but kept a firm eye on the groom.

Simon turned back to Elwen. 'Where's Will? Has he left?'

'What do you mean?' she asked, disconcerted by the abruptness of his tone. 'He went back to the preceptory with the others.'

'Others?'

'The knights. After they finished their parley with the king.'

'No, I don't mean that,' said Simon flatly. He glanced at the guard and dropped his voice slightly. 'I know about the Seven Stars.' Simon, studying Elwen's perplexed expression, realised that she didn't know what he was talking about. His annoyance turned to confusion, then concern. 'You didn't meet him there?'

'No,' she replied, becoming annoyed. 'I've been in the palace all evening, then I came here. The queen sent me to buy material for a new gown she wants made before the assembly tomorrow evening.'

'Assembly?'

'Where the king will announce to the court his decision to take the Cross. Simon, what is this about? Who told you I was meeting Will? The last thing I knew was that he was going away for a few weeks with Everard.' She lowered her voice. 'Something to do with the book.'

'He told you about that?'

'We should get back, miss,' called Baudouin. 'The queen might want her carriage.'

'She won't be going anywhere this late,' said Elwen quickly. She heard Baudouin mutter to the driver and the stamp of hooves as the mares grew restless. Simon was staring uncertainly at her, but she could see that he wanted to share his concerns with someone. 'Please tell me what this is about,' she encouraged.

Simon sucked on his bottom lip, then shook his head. 'It's nothing. I've got to go.'

'Go where?' she demanded, following him. 'Simon, talk to me! What is the Seven Stars?'

'Seven Stars?' said Baudouin, glancing round. 'What do you want with that place?'

'You know it?' asked Elwen, stepping between Simon and the guard.

'I know *of* it,' said Baudouin, looking embarrassed. 'It's in the Latin Quarter, near the Sorbonne.' He ruffled his sandy hair uncomfortably. 'It's a . . . well, it's a whorehouse to be frank, miss.'

'Why do you think Will would be meeting me there?' asked Elwen, staring at Simon. 'Is he there now?'

Simon nodded after a moment. 'I think so.'

Elwen turned to Baudouin. 'Do you know where it is?'

'Yes, but . . .'

'We're going there,' Elwen said to the driver of the wagon, before Baudouin could finish. The driver looked nonplussed, but nodded. 'And you're coming with me,' she told Simon. Her voice was stern, but she looked upset. 'Then you can both explain to me what is going on.'

Elwen was about to make her way round to the back of the wagon, when the guard stepped in front of her. Baudouin was a big man, filling his scarlet uniform to the seams, and he seemed to grow even larger as he spoke. 'I'm sorry, miss, but I can't allow you to do that. We're going back to the palace.' He shot Simon a warning look. 'Alone.'

Elwen went to protest, but she could already see that it wouldn't be of any use. Baudouin could be as placid as an ass and as stubborn as a mule and, right now, his mulish side was quite apparent. She fell silent, feeling beaten, when she thought of something Maria had told her a few months ago. 'If you don't allow me to go where I will, Baudouin, I shall feel forced to tell the captain of the guard that you have been seeing his daughter.'

Baudouin stared at Elwen's defiant expression, then turned to the driver. 'Do as the lady says.'

As Elwen climbed into the wagon with Simon and settled herself on the cushioned seat, she sent up a quick prayer for Maria and the handmaiden's inability to keep a secret.

The Seven Stars, Paris, 2 November 1266 AD

Adela surveyed the room. There were men dancing on the tables and she had lost count of how many jars of wine had been dropped and smashed on the flagstones. Fabien had thrown one customer out for hitting a girl and two others were unconscious in a corner, but everyone else looked as if they would be up for some time. It was the busiest night she had had in a long while. A man nearby was watching two girls dancing together. Adela felt sickened by the way his gaze lingered on them. She looked away, unable to shake the memory of Rook's hands on her, his sour breath. She wanted to have Fabien go up there, drag him out and beat him senseless in the yard outside. But she knew Rook's threats were real.

'Adela.'

She turned at the voice to see Garin standing behind her. His face was flushed and despite the evening chill there was a sheen of sweat on his brow. 'You came back.' Her voice was lost in the room's din.

Garin touched her bruised cheek. 'I know you're not to blame for what he did.'

'No,' she said suddenly, drawing away from his touch. 'I'm not the one who brought him here.'

'Don't say that,' Garin pleaded, 'it's not my fault. I didn't ask him to come. I'm sorry,' he repeated, taking hold of her shoulder as she turned away. 'Listen to me, Adela.' Garin had to raise his voice over a burst of boisterous laughter that filled the room as one of the merchants fell off the table. 'If Rook gets what he wants, he will pay me and we can be together. I always meant what I said.'

'What about the Temple?' she said accusingly. 'Will they let you marry a whore?'

'I'll leave the Temple,' said Garin carelessly. 'I've been promised a lordship and if all goes well tonight I should be granted it. I'll buy an estate back in England.' He shook his head. 'Or anywhere you want, if you'll only come with me.'

'What if they won't let you leave?'

'I told the Visitor yesterday that I would go to Cyprus, he's expecting me to leave as soon as possible. When I don't return he will think I've gone. It will be a long time before anyone misses me.'

'Why did you run? Why did you leave me with him?'

'I was angry.' Garin frowned as he tried to touch her face again and she brushed his hand aside. 'But I came back for you, didn't I?' He took her cool hands in his hot, nail-bitten fingers. 'I don't want to share you anymore, not with that bastard, not with anyone! Leave this place. I can take care of you.'

'You had better go upstairs,' said Adela quietly, gently removing her hands from his. 'Rook has the Templar up there and the last thing I need tonight is a murder on my hands.'

Garin looked fearfully up the stairs. 'Will's here?' He looked back at her. 'First, just say you'll come with me. I can't do this without knowing that.'

'I'll think about it.'

After a pause, Garin acceded with a nod and a feeble smile, then headed for the stairs.

As he reached Adela's room, he heard Rook's voice on the other side, muted through the wood, followed by a muffled cry of pain. Taking a deep breath, Garin knocked. The door opened after several moments.

Rook's eyes narrowed as he saw Garin standing there. 'You ever run off like that again and I'll unmake you,' he growled through his black mask, opening the door wider.

Garin could just make out Will. He was sitting upright on the floor, strapped to the legs of the bed by his wrists, his arms pinioned wide apart as if he were opening them to receive an embrace. His ankles were bound together with a belt. He looked like a broken crucifix. Garin saw him try to turn his head, then cough violently and spit a mouthful of blood onto the floor. He realised, with shock, that Will was wearing the white mantle of a knight.

'The whelp's not talking. You'll have to help me.'

'I can't!' hissed Garin. 'He knows me!'

'And you him,' snapped Rook. 'You know better than me what'll pluck his strings.'

'No,' said Garin. 'I don't want any part in this.' He nodded to Will. 'He's been knighted, for God's sake! If we're found out, you'll be strung up and I'll be sent to Merlan!'

'Help me,' came a breathless groan from Will.

'Shut your hole,' growled Rook over his shoulder. He grabbed Garin by the arm. 'Stop your whining and get in here.' Garin stumbled into the room as Rook yanked him forwards. 'I've had enough of this shit!' he spat, slamming the door shut. 'You make that bastard speak, or I'll kill both of you!'

Garin went slowly around the bed. Will's head was lolling to one side, his eyes half closed. His lip and nose were bloodied and there was a large, purple bruise showing on his forehead above his right eye. His face was deathly pale and covered in a film of sweat. 'No wonder he's not talking,' murmured Garin, looking at Rook. 'What have you done to him?'

'Garin?'

Garin glanced back to see Will staring faintly at him.

'Garin?' Will repeated, more coherently now. He tried to sit up. 'Has he gone? Get me out of here!'

Garin was unable to meet his gaze. 'I can't. Not until you tell him what he wants to know.'

Will shook his head slowly. 'I don't understand. What are you . . .?' He stopped as Rook came into view. 'What is this?'

'He wants to know where the Book of the Grail is. You have to tell him.'

Will just stared blankly at the knight.

'*Tell me!*' roared Rook, stepping forwards and drawing back his fist.

Will twisted away, but couldn't avoid Rook's fist as it smashed into his face, mashing his lip against his teeth. Will rocked sideways with the blow, his mouth filling with fresh blood. Rook grabbed his hair and wrenched back his head. Will was wheezing desperately with each breath.

'Will, just tell him!' urged Garin. 'Do it and he'll let you go!'

Rook straightened, waiting for Will to catch his breath.

'Garin,' gasped Will, his eyes swivelling to the knight. 'He said he has Elwen. But I didn't believe him. Tell me it's not true.'

Garin glanced at Rook, then back at Will. 'It's true.'

'And can you imagine what I'll do to her if I don't get what I want?' said Rook, crouching before Will and leaning in close. 'You'll get off light compared to your sweetheart.'

Will looked past him to Garin. 'How could you do this? How could you *let* him do this?'

'Tell me!' hissed Rook in Will's face. 'Or I'll bring her in here and slit her throat. After I've had my fun with her.' He rose when Will didn't speak. 'Go and get her,' he ordered Garin. He turned when Garin didn't move. '*Now!*'

'*No!*' shouted Will, as Garin moved towards the door. 'Wait, I'll tell you! Just let her go!'

'He will,' promised Garin, 'if you tell him where the book is.' He went over to Will. 'I swear I won't let anything happen to her, Will. I *swear* it. If you believe nothing else, believe that.'

'Nicolas de Navarre has it,' said Will, swallowing thickly. 'He took it from us and went to La Rochelle.'

'Who?' demanded Rook.

'He's a Hospitaller. He's taking the book to Acre for his master.'

'Why does a Hospitaller have it?'

'He wants to use it to bring down the Temple,' coughed Will weakly. He looked at Garin. 'Let her go, I've told you all I know.'

Rook stepped back. The mask lifted at the corners as he smiled. 'Well, isn't that interesting.' He looked at Garin. 'I'll go and secure us horses. We'll leave tonight, try to catch up with this knight on the road.' He headed for the door, then turned back. 'Kill him.'

Garin stared at him open-mouthed. 'What?'

Rook opened the door. 'You said he'd inform on you if he saw you. The wretch won't be able to if he's dead now, will he?'

33
The Seven Stars, Paris

2 November 1266 AD

W ill strained against his bonds, but they held tight and he only succeeded in exhausting himself further. Garin had left the room several minutes after the man with the dagger, but he guessed that he didn't have much time. The only things he could think of were getting free and getting to Elwen, wherever she was. He couldn't think yet about Garin's treachery and the reasons behind it; that could come later. Trying to ignore the pain that was coursing through him, Will stopped struggling and craned his head awkwardly to look at the bed behind him. The pallet was large and appeared fairly sturdy, but if he could gather enough strength, he might be able to shift it enough to reach the wall or even the door. If he banged on the wall with his feet, someone in one of the other rooms might hear him. It was a desperate plan, but the only one he could think of. He had to try something. After taking a breath, he pulled his arms and upper body forward, gasping with the effort. The bed shunted a few inches and came to rest, nestled snugly against his back. Will shuffled along the floor, then pulled again, the cords biting his wrists. The bed squeaked and moved along behind him another few inches. He did this three times, managing to move the bed only a couple of feet, before the door opened.

'You have to help me,' he heard Garin say urgently, followed by two sets of footsteps and the bang of the door as it was closed.

Will barely managed to raise his head as Garin appeared in front of him, leading the woman he had thought was Elwen.

The woman pressed her hand to her mouth as she saw him. 'Where's Rook?'

'Getting horses,' Garin replied, heading to the trestle. Picking up one of the jars, he inspected it.

'Horses?' asked the woman. 'Where are you going?'

'Elwen,' said Will thickly.

They both looked round.

Will struggled to focus on Garin. 'Do what you want with me. But let her go.'

'We don't have her,' Garin told him. 'He was lying.'

'She's not here?' said Will, with a small sob of relief.

'No,' said Garin quietly. He went to say something further, then turned back to the trestle and picked up another jar.

'You're leaving?'

Garin glanced round at the woman's accusing tone. 'Not for long. I promise you, Adela,' he said, earnestly, 'help me do this one last thing and I will do everything I said.'

'That's henbane,' murmured Adela, as Garin turned the jar over in his hands. 'It's poisonous.'

'I need you to make up a potion for me.'

Adela stepped forward. 'Put it down, Garin. I'm not going to help you kill him.'

Will watched them in silence, his mind growing foggier by the minute.

'Not kill,' Garin said quickly. 'Not that.'

She gestured to the pot in his hands. 'Then why . . .?'

'I want you to make me a sleeping draught. That's right, isn't it?' He lifted the jar. 'Henbane? My mother used it.'

'A sedative? Well, certain parts of the plant. Get it wrong and it wouldn't be something you would wake up from.'

'Can you do it? I'll try to keep Rook away until we leave, but we need to make it look like Will's dead, just in case.'

'And what do I do when he wakes up and charges me with abducting and drugging him?' said Adela angrily.

'He won't do that,' said Garin, looking at Will.

'How do you know?'

'Because he'll be too busy coming after me.'

Adela looked from Will to Garin. Finally, she took the jar from Garin's hands and placed it on her trestle. 'There's no need for me to make up a potion,' she said quietly, crossing to her shelves and bringing down a tall, black bottle. 'This will do it.' She handed it to Garin.

'How much?' Garin pulled the cork stopper from the top, sniffed inside and grimaced.

'A quarter will keep him sedated for about ten hours.'

'At least it will slow his pursuit.' Garin crossed to Will. 'Open your mouth.'

'You're right,' murmured Will. 'I will come after you.'

Garin's jaw tightened. 'I'm saving your life, Will. Just remember that.' He took hold of Will's chin and tilted his head back, firmly, but not roughly.

Will tried to turn his head away, but Garin kept a tight hold on him and pressed the bottle to his lips. Will felt a gritty, thick liquid fill his mouth. He tried not to swallow, but more kept coming, and now Garin was holding his nose shut and he couldn't breathe. He swallowed, half choking on the foul-tasting sludge.

Garin stepped back when it was done and placed the bottle on the trestle. 'How long?' he asked Adela.

Will coughed, dribbling black liquid down his chin and onto his mantle, staining it.

'Not long.'

Will watched Garin pace the chamber as the minutes passed. 'Why did you do this? Why are you after the book?'

'I'm not,' said Garin shortly. 'He is.'

'Who is he?'

Garin didn't answer.

After a while, Will started to feel queasy. He went to speak, then a violent rush came up through his stomach and he doubled over and vomited on the floor. When he had finished, he slumped back against the bed. His tongue felt swollen and tingly. Shivers were running playfully up and down his spine. The tingling in his tongue spread to his cheeks, scalp, the back of his neck. He felt an irresistible urge to laugh. He did so. The laughter was as violent as the vomiting and his eyes watered until he was crying and laughing at once. He sagged sideways, then tried to sit up, but his limbs weren't working. He slid lower, his euphoria fading. His arms and legs felt like they belonged to someone else; someone who had decided not to move, but to lay down. Garin was speaking, but the words made no sense and grated in his ears. He tried to push them away, but only succeeded in flapping one hand uselessly. The room was lurching. Garin's face was distorted and the woman, Adela, had a wide, red slash for a mouth. All the colours and shapes were bleeding into one another. 'Why?' he tried to say to Garin. Will heard the knight's reply as if it was coming down a hole, elongated, echoing.

'For what it is worth, Will, I'm sorry. But you don't know what I've been through.'

Will felt himself falling.

Adela walked over to Will's prone body. Lifting one of his eyelids, she nodded. 'It is done.'

'Good. I'll go and tell Rook we poisoned him.'

'Help me get him untied first.'

'Why?'

'I'll not take the chance of someone coming in here and seeing him tied
and beaten like this. At least if he's on the bed they'll just think he's drunk.'

Garin helped Adela untie Will's bonds.

'Won't he tell the rest of your Order that you did this to him?' asked
Adela, struggling to bear Will's weight as Garin hauled him onto the pallet.
'Won't they arrest you?'

Garin felt his already frayed nerves giving at the thought of Merlan. There
was a pit there especially reserved for traitors. It was, he remembered
someone saying, barely big enough for a man to crouch in. He would be left
there, bent double in total darkness and solitude without food or water until he
died. 'I told you, I'm not going back to the Temple.' He went to the trestle
where his leather bag, filled with his few belongings, including the letter from
the Visitor, was lying and shrugged off his mantle. 'When I come back, we'll
go somewhere where they can't find us. I'll come for you when I return. You
can sell this place, or leave it behind. It doesn't matter, either way we'll be
gone.' Garin paused as he put the white mantle into his sack. *So that is it?* a voice
in his mind said mockingly. It sounded like his uncle's. *You are going to give up
everything, your place in the Temple, your duty as your mother's son, as a de Lyons, for a
whore?* Garin shook the voice away and stuffed the mantle into the sack.

'Is it done?' demanded Rook, as Garin stepped out into the yard at the
back of the alehouse a short time later, his pack slung over his shoulder. The
moon was concealed by a stipple of cloud and the area was dark. The yard
filled with the squat shadows of barrels.

'Yes,' said Garin. He looked round, hearing a whinny, and saw two
horses tethered outside one of the alleys that led off between the buildings
which bordered the yard.

Rook crossed to the beasts and tied a sack he was carrying to the back of
one of the saddles.

'Where did you get those?' Garin asked.

'Why did it take you so long?' questioned Rook, looking round, his eyes
glinting in the pale light that washed out, along with the sounds of singing
and laughter, from the alehouse's back door.

'I poisoned him. I had to wait to make sure he was dead.'

Rook continued to stare at him, then picked up another pack that was sat
on one of the barrels and slung it at him. 'Poisoned, you say?'

'That's right,' said Garin, catching the pack.

'A tricky business that. Sometimes it doesn't work. I'd better check for myself.'

'There's no need!' said Garin quickly. But Rook was already stepping through the door.

Adela wrapped her arms about her as she stood in the crowded chamber. She couldn't imagine how she had once thought herself happy here. It was as if a veil had been lifted from her eyes. Things that had only niggled at her before: the cracks in the walls which the rot bubbled up through; the blood- and vomit-stained floor; the tears in her girls' gowns, all looked so much worse now.

'You said to tell you when Dalmau had gone upstairs, Adela.'

Adela turned at the voice to see one of her girls, a buxom redhead called Blanche, looking expectantly at her.

'Send Jaqueline,' Adela told her, sounding sharper than she meant to. She sighed and motioned to the boisterous merchants. 'I have to deal with this lot.' It was a lie: Fabien was more than capable of handling the merry crowd. But Garin hadn't left yet and she wanted to say a last goodbye and, besides, she didn't think she could bear to be touched by another man tonight, especially not the bull-shouldered butcher.

'Jaqueline?' said Blanche doubtfully. 'I thought Dalmau liked his women experienced?'

'Dalmau will no doubt be too drunk to notice,' responded Adela curtly. 'Tell him he can have this one for free. I'll pay Jaqueline myself. Double.'

'As you say.'

Adela moved away, heading for the opening at the back of the room that led down a short passage past the kitchen to the back door. She halted in the opening as she saw a figure moving up it. 'Where's Garin?' she asked, as Rook came striding out of the shadows towards her.

Blanche stood on tiptoe to scan the crowd and saw Jaqueline sitting with a small group in a quieter corner. She went over. 'You're seeing mistress's customer tonight.'

Jaqueline, a wide-eyed girl of fourteen with a thin, pale face and a mass of curls that tumbled in a cascade of gold down her back, looked up fearfully. 'Mistress's?'

'Don't worry,' Blanche reassured her. 'He'll be drunk as a fiddler. Just do what I showed you. It'll be over in no time.' She shrieked as one of the merchants grabbed her from behind and spun her round. 'He'll be in her room!' she shouted to Jaqueline, as the man whirled her away across the floor.

Taking a sharp breath, Jaqueline rose and headed over to the stairs. She ascended into darkness, leaving the shrieks and roars of laughter to fade behind her.

After trundling past the Sorbonne, the distinguished college of theology established by King Louis' chaplain, the wagon turned down the street where the Seven Stars was.

'This is it,' Elwen heard Baudouin say from the driver's seat.

Before the wagon had come to a stop, she was at the back, sweeping aside the cloth. She leapt lightly down and stared at the large alehouse. Torchlight shone behind the window coverings. She could hear the high-pitched tones of women between louder male voices. A few men outside the alehouse, standing near a group of hobbled horses and two wagons looked over at her. One made a lewd gesture and the others laughed. Elwen's heart beat faster, but she ignored them and walked towards the door.

'Hey!' shouted Baudouin. He vaulted from the driver's seat and ran after her. 'I don't know where you think you're going,' he said, moving to block her path.

'To look for my soon-to-be husband,' replied Elwen, stepping past him.

'I'll go in and see if he's there,' said Baudouin, taking hold of her arm. 'A woman in this area is only here for one thing. And you can tell the captain whatever you want about me and his daughter. The king himself would have me strung up if I let you go wandering off to get . . . Well, begging your pardon, miss, but all men have desires.' He glanced over at the drivers by the wagons. 'When a man sees a pretty girl like you, there'll be only one thing on his mind. It is the Devil in us.' He turned to Simon who was jogging over. 'Wouldn't you agree, sergeant?'

Elwen didn't give Simon a chance to reply. She shrugged her arm from Baudouin's grip. 'Then you had better come with me.'

Simon looked vaguely impressed by Elwen's forthrightness, but Baudouin was clearly not amused. Unwilling to stop her by force, however, he had no choice but to follow as she strode up to the alehouse door, the hems of her yellow mantle whispering across the frosty ground. Simon came after them, leaving the royal wagon sitting incongruously in the middle of the street. Up close, the music and singing was much louder. Elwen paused at the door, feeling a little intimidated by the thought of so many people on the other side, then pushed it. It didn't open. She rapped on it cautiously.

'They're not likely to hear that,' said Simon, moving past her to bang his fist against it.

There was no response, although Elwen thought she saw one of the downstairs window coverings move. Simon hammered on the door again and Baudouin huffed loudly to show his displeasure. Elwen bit her lip as the door remained closed.

'You poisoned the knight?' said Rook, as he approached Adela.

'Yes,' she said, trying to keep the fear from her voice. 'I helped Garin do it.' She looked past him to the back door, which was closed. 'Is he out there? I wanted to say goodbye.'

'You can do that when I've seen the knight's dead for myself,' answered Rook. 'Get out of my way.'

Adela hesitated, then steeled herself. 'I have to dispose of the knight's body before anyone sees. It is time you left.'

'I'll not tell you again.'

As she stared at Rook – his mean, pockmarked face lined with cruelty and contempt, the sly malice in his black eyes – loathing and anger rose within her, quelling her fear. 'Just go,' she snapped huskily. 'Or I'll bring the royal guards in here myself and show them what you've done.'

'Are you threatening me?' he said in a low voice.

'It's finished. You've got what you came for. Go now and I'll not say a word of it to anyone.'

Rook's face was unreadable. He said nothing for what seemed, to Adela, several minutes, but was probably only a few seconds. Her breaths sounded loud in the dim passage, the music and laughter in the room behind her a long way away. Finally, Rook took a step back.

'You'd better get on with it then. It wouldn't be good for either of us if he was found now would it?'

'No,' she said after a moment, the surprise she felt at his submission almost making her smile at the bastard. She watched him walk towards the back door, then, trembling with relief, she turned and headed for the main chamber, the sawing of the fiddle player growing louder with each step. She had almost reached the end of the passage, when a hand was pressed hard over her mouth. She gave a muffled cry as she was dragged away from the light and the noise, and shoved against the wall by the kitchen door.

'You think to threaten me?' hissed Rook in her ear. 'Think to tell me what to do?' Adela twisted like an eel, but his grip was too strong. 'You'd inform on me, would you? Tell the guards what I'd done, you worthless slut?' With his free hand he yanked his dagger from its sheath. 'You'll tell them nothing!' His hand still clamped over her mouth, Rook pulled back her head, exposing her long, white neck to the indomitable edge of his dagger. One quick movement of his wrist drew a spray of blood across the wall. Adela's body bucked and convulsed against him. Tears slipped from her violet eyes as she slowly crumpled, her red robe darkening, the stain spreading as the blood kept coming.

Kicking open the kitchen door and seeing it was empty beyond, Rook hauled her limp body inside. Her blood had left a dark smear across the floor. He shoved his dagger, still wet, into its sheath, shut the door and moved out into the passage. Rook entered the bright chamber, and was making his way towards the stairs when he saw Fabien heading towards him through the crowd.

'Where's Adela?' asked the large man, looking at Rook with undisguised hostility.

'I don't know,' responded Rook. 'I was looking for her myself.' Glancing down, he saw he had blood on his hand. He moved it slowly behind his back.

'There's a royal guard and a sergeant from the Temple outside. She'll need to speak to them.'

'From the Temple?' asked Rook worriedly.

'Yes,' replied Fabien coldly. 'They are no doubt here for their friend.' He lowered his voice and took a step towards Rook. 'My mistress has told me to afford you every courtesy whilst you're here, but if you've brought trouble down on her, I'll be forced to disobey her.'

'Why don't you keep them busy,' responded Rook swiftly, 'and I'll go and find her.'

Fabien frowned, studying Rook intently. 'Be quick. I won't be able to bar entry to a royal guard for long.'

As Fabien turned away, Rook moved quickly for the opening at the back of the room. Passing the kitchen, he hastened out of the back door.

Garin turned as Rook dashed out.

'We're leaving,' said Rook, grabbing the reins of one of the horses.

'But Adela . . . ?' Garin started to say, wondering if Rook had been foiled by his ruse after all.

'Can wait,' snapped Rook. 'We ride now.' He climbed into the saddle. 'Or you can stay behind and explain to a Templar and a royal guard why there's a knight dead upstairs.'

Garin looked to the back door, fearfully, wistfully, then mounted his horse. Together, he and Rook cantered out down the alley, the hooves of their horses clattering in the night.

'It's no use,' muttered Simon, stepping back from the door and craning his neck to look at the upstairs windows. 'They aren't going to open up.'

'Let me try again,' said Elwen determinedly. She curled her hand into a fist and banged on the door until it hurt. 'Let me in!' she shouted, causing Baudouin to wince and look around worriedly. As she went to hit the door again, it swung open. She just managed to catch herself from falling into the huge man who was revealed.

'Yes?' he said, frowning down at her.

Elwen recovered her poise. 'We're looking for a friend of ours.'

'You'll have to wait outside for him. This is a private guesthouse.'

'Just let the lady find her friend and we'll be on our way,' said Baudouin, stepping up to the door.

'You're not here on official business?'

'No!' said Baudouin quickly. 'Nothing official.'

'Then, like I said, you'll have to wait out here.'

'Please!' called Elwen, as the man went to close the door.

Simon pushed past her, wedged his foot against the door and shouldered it open. He punched the huge man in the stomach. As he dropped to his knees with a groan, Simon rushed into the chamber, heart thumping. Ignoring the naked women, he searched for Will. He couldn't see him, but his gaze fell on a little staircase winding upwards and he started towards it, not waiting for Elwen and Baudouin, who had sidestepped the groaning man and entered.

Elwen halted in shock at the scene in the ale room, but the guard steered her towards the stairs.

'Come on. The sooner we're gone the better.'

Simon took the stairs two at a time, using the walls as leverage. At the top, he was faced with a long, narrow passage lit by a single torch, with eight doors leading off. Faint light issued from under several of them. The first couple Simon burst in on sat up, startled. Ignoring their indignant calls, Simon moved on to the next. Hearing footsteps behind him, he spun round, then relaxed as he saw Elwen and Baudouin. 'We must check each room,' he said to the royal guard.

Baudouin headed down to aid the search. Elwen watched the royal guard disappear into one room, heard a few alarmed shouts, then pressed herself against the wall as a naked girl darted out and dashed past her down the passage.

'Fabien!' she was yelling as she pounded down the stairs.

Simon was almost at the end of the passage, opening another door, when a half-naked, bull-shouldered man charged out. He barrelled into the groom so hard that the two of them crashed through the door on the opposite side. From the room came the sounds of a fierce struggle.

'Baudouin!' Elwen shouted.

The royal guard appeared in one of the doorways and rushed into the room to help the groom, as more people exited their rooms and ran past her down the stairs. She heard grunts and splintering sounds coming from the chamber Simon, the bull-shouldered man and Baudouin had entered. She stood there helpless, not knowing what to do. Her eyes fixed on the last door at the end of the passage. It was still closed. Elwen headed for it, running past the open doors, anticipating more people to come flying out of them at any moment. She pushed it open. And halted in the doorway of the smoky chamber, where embers had turned white in the hearth.

Her eyes went first to the silver mirror on the far wall, where she saw herself reflected: cheeks flushed; copper hair coming free of its pinioning wires. Her gaze flickered quickly over a wicker screen, trestle, shelves lined with pots, the pallet against the wall nearest to her. She locked eyes momentarily with the pale-faced girl with the cascade of golden curls who was on the pallet. The girl was sitting astride a man, her skirts bunched up to her waist. Elwen felt her world turn upside-down as her gaze came to rest on the man recumbent beneath the girl. His face was turned away from her, but she recognised the ragged cut of his black hair and the line of his neck and jaw. She vaguely felt hands gripping her shoulders and moving her aside.

Jaqueline, who had frozen on hearing the commotion in the passage, rolled off Will and scrabbled back against the wall, her face a mask of fear, as Simon rushed into the chamber. He too halted, just for a moment. Then he was at the pallet, drawing down Will's undershirt to cover what was displayed.

As he laced up Will's hose, his fingers shaking, Simon heard Elwen cry out behind him. Will's skin was ashen, his face badly bruised. Simon gently lifted one of his eyelids. His eye was rolled up to the white. Will uttered a breathless groan. In it, Simon thought he heard a name. Garin.

'Will!' Elwen's cry became a sob and she tried to go towards the pallet, but Baudouin, who had dispatched the bull-shouldered attacker, held her back. 'What's wrong with him? Why won't he wake? *Will!*'

Simon looked back at Will. He recognised those rolled-back eyes; he had seen the same with horses when they had been sedated with opiates for surgery. He felt a rush of fury.

'What's wrong with him, Simon? *Tell me!*'

Simon met Elwen's gaze. He gave a slight shrug. 'He must have got drunk, or something. I don't know.'

'No! He wouldn't have done this! He *wouldn't*!' Elwen collapsed against Baudouin's chest.

The guard lifted her into his arms. 'That's it. I'm taking you back to the palace.'

Elwen was crying too hard to protest as Baudouin carried her out of the room, leaving Simon kneeling beside Will.

When they had gone, Simon, feeling shaken, carefully pulled Will's boots on. The girl, who was still quivering against the wall, suddenly rushed out of the door. Simon let her go. Once he had dressed Will, he looped the sword belt around his waist and hefted his unconscious friend over his shoulder. He wondered why the man he had punched hadn't come after them and why he could now hear screaming as he descended into the ale room. It looked much emptier and the music had ceased. There was a knot of people clustered around an opening at the back of the room. The screams were coming from several women. With all the occupants' attention focused elsewhere, none of them noticed Simon carrying Will out of the front door.

34
The Temple, Paris
3rd November 1266 AD

Will dreamed he was in a boat. He was with his father out on the loch, fishing. The motion of the water was soothing. His father kept hooking enormous, silver-skinned fish. But he didn't keep them.

'This is a beauty!' he would exclaim, unhooking the fish and tossing it back into the water.

Will wasn't catching any. He could see them weaving around the boat in vast glimmering shoals just below the surface, but none were biting his line.

'Rotten bait,' said his father knowingly.

Will started to feel queasy. The rocking motion became more intense as the shoals of fish swam faster and faster, spinning the boat round and round with their momentum. His father was laughing and pulling them up by the fistful.

Will came awake, grabbing hold of the pallet he was lying on to stop himself from falling. He lay there, thinking he was going to be sick and blinking at the ceiling until, gradually, the sensation passed. His tongue felt swollen and there was a foul taste in his mouth. He had no spit when he tried to swallow and his throat hurt with the action. Everything felt wrong: the light; the odd shapes of furniture around him; the softness of the blanket he was wrapped in. Even the smell of his own sweat was unfamiliar. Will sat up slowly, the daylight coming through the gap in the tapestry making his eyes ache. His muscles were sore and although he was drenched in sweat, he was freezing. Teeth chattering, he pushed off the blanket and swung his legs over the pallet. As he stared at the room, he realised that he did know it. He was in Everard's solar.

The door swung open. 'Good,' said Everard, seeing Will sitting up. 'You're awake.' He closed the door and crossed to the window seat, on which he placed two large leather bags. One was empty and the other was crammed with stuff. Will could smell fresh-baked bread. Everard went to his writing table and picked up a jar. He paused to pull a length of white cloth from a stool with his free hand. As he dropped the cloth onto the pallet, Will saw that it was a surcoat: the sleeveless white tunic that went under his mantle. 'I got it from the tailor this morning,' said Everard. 'It should fit.' He held out the jar to Will. 'Drink this and get dressed.'

As Will took the goblet, which was filled with a dark liquid, the memory of the night before came to him in a series of confused images. 'What happened to me?'

'What do you remember?'

'Garin,' said Will suddenly. He tried to rise, but his limbs were too weak and he collapsed.

'Simon said you mentioned his name several times,' said Everard intently. 'Was he at this tavern?'

'I went there to see Elwen,' said Will slowly, trying to make sense of the confusion of images. He glanced at the priest, but Everard made no comment. 'She sent me a message. At least, I was told it was from her. But when I got there, I was . . .' He frowned. 'I was attacked by someone . . . a man in a mask. He knew about the Book of the Grail.' Will felt his face carefully with his fingertips. His lip felt twice its normal size and there was a lump on his brow above his eye. He winced as it stung. 'He beat me. I think I must have told him about Nicolas de Navarre because I didn't see him again. Then Garin came in with a woman.' Will nodded, his memory gradually becoming clearer. 'They were together, Garin and this man.' He looked up at Everard. 'How could Garin have found out? Would Jacques have told him about the Anima Templi?'

Everard sighed. 'I would not have thought so, but I do not see how else he would know. This man. Do you remember anything about him?'

'No. As I said, he was wearing a mask.' Will paused. 'Rook,' he said, finally. 'I think the woman called him Rook. Garin forced me to drink something. I don't remember much after that, just a door opening and light.' Will frowned. 'A woman's voice.' An image of a girl with golden curls, pale face taut in the firelight, came into his mind. The goblet slipped from his grasp and clanged on the floor. 'The woman,' he breathed. 'She . . .' But he felt sick and couldn't finish.

Everard, however, seemed to understand. He bent and picked up the goblet. 'I will absolve you. You need not worry about breaking your vow of chastity. I will not tell anyone.'

'Elwen!' said Will, his head snapping up. 'She was there! I heard her voice!'

'Simon told me, yes.'

Will rose, queasily. He looked around for his clothes and spotted his undershirt on a stool, under which were placed his boots.

'What are you doing?' said Everard, watching him.

Will tugged his shirt over his head. 'Where is my sword?'

'William . . .'

'*Where's my pissing sword?*'

Everard took a step back as Will spun to face him, eyes blazing. 'Over there,' he said, motioning to one of the chests.

Will snatched it up. After putting on the new surcoat, which did fit, he fastened the sword belt around his waist.

'What are you going to do? William?'

'I have to see Elwen.' Will's teeth were chattering. He clenched his jaw to stop them. 'I have to explain.'

'You don't have time.' Everard's voice was calm, but firm. 'Nicolas already has a day on us and if you are correct, it sounds as if de Lyons and the man who tortured you will be going after him also. Simon carried you here from the alehouse. He has our horses saddled and is waiting for us outside. He will be coming with us. I have requisitioned him as our squire.'

'You've told Simon about the Anima Templi?'

'No. But he has proved his use and already knows about de Navarre. The Visitor thinks we are going to Blois to view a seminal treatise on seafaring. I've told him that de Navarre had to leave urgently on personal business. The last thing we need is an investigation into his disappearance.'

'I cannot go.' Will looked around for his mantle. He found it balled up on the foot of the pallet and swung it around his shoulders. He made for the door.

Everard stepped in front of him. 'If Elwen feels as much for you as you do her, she will forgive you. Whether you explain it to her today, tomorrow, or next week.'

'Get out of my way, Everard,' said Will flatly. 'You don't command me anymore.'

Everard grabbed his arm. 'De Lyons drugged you and put you in bed with a filthy, no doubt pox-riddled slut! Are you going to let him get away with it?'

Will tried to push Everard away, but he didn't have the strength. Everard's words stung his ears and made him feel sick to his core. 'Stop!' His voice cracked. 'Don't say it! I don't want to hear!'

'He had a woman violate you,' hissed Everard, his bloodshot eyes narrowed to fierce slits. 'That worthless shit *violated* you!'

'Shut up!'

'He made you break your vow, the vow you made to the Temple in honour of your dead father!' He grabbed Will's other arm and shook him. 'What are you going to do about it?'

'*I'm going to kill him!*' Will collapsed against the priest, shaking. Images of the girl and Garin and his father and Elwen crowded and clamoured in his mind.

Everard stumbled, then caught him. 'We will find him together,' he murmured in Will's ear. 'I will get my book and you will see de Lyons hang. I promise you that.'

Caesar's Road, just outside Orléans, 5 November 1266 AD

For two days, they had pursued Garin and Rook, heading gradually west along Caesar's Road towards La Rochelle. On the first, they had made good progress and had been rewarded when they had rested for the night in Etampes, a prosperous town that had built up around several cloth mills, to find that people had seen a Templar and another man pass through that afternoon. Everard hoped, if they impeded Garin and Rook's pursuit of Nicolas de Navarre, or got ahead of them, they could continue unhindered to La Rochelle and execute their plan to arrest the Hospitallers.

In Etampes, Will, Everard and Simon had shared a room in a guesthouse, the owner of which, on seeing their mantles, had invited them to dine with him and his wife on wild boar. The rich meat had sat badly on Will's stomach, however, and, much to Everard's frustration, he had been slower in the saddle the next day. His sore throat had grown steadily worse throughout that morning until he could hardly bear to swallow, and his nose and eyes streamed continuously, causing him to ride almost blind. Even though it was bitterly cold, he had been soaked in sweat and last night, when they had sheltered in a farmer's stable, he had kept the others awake with his fitful tossing and talking. Simon had been watching him worriedly. But Everard had been too focused on retrieving the book to pay Will's rapidly declining health much heed.

'He'll be fine in a day, or two,' said the priest testily, when they dismounted at around Nones and Simon pointed out Will's feverish colour.

They had stopped a short distance from the road by a copse of stunted trees, alongside which ran a narrow river, swollen by recent rains. The banks were shallow enough for them to water their horses. A light drizzle misted the air and clouds hung low in the sky. The land around them was brown and bleak with winter.

Will had gone down to the water's edge to fill their skins. Simon took Everard's reins, as the old priest unpacked some bread and cheese from his bag and set them on a tree stump. The groom watched Will drag the skins in the rushing river, desperate to go to him, yet unable to move. He had tried several times to speak to Will since they had left Paris, but his tongue kept cleaving to the roof of his mouth and no words would come. He had endeavoured to rid his mind of the sight of Elwen's distraught face when he had told her that Will must have got drunk, but it kept returning. The lie had slipped from his mouth so readily. Once out, it had been too late to put back in. Now, when he looked at Will, his betrayal was all he could think of.

'Water the beasts then,' said Everard crossly, rousing Simon from his helpless inertia.

Whilst Everard went off to find a suitable bush to take his toilet, Simon walked the horses down to a low bit of bank, where they hung their heads to drink. He patted the flanks of his tan pack-horse, a young mare they had laden with most of the supplies, and glanced at Will out of the corner of his eye. He called out, startled. Will had removed his mantle and surcoat and had tossed them carelessly on the muddy bank. He was now pulling off his undershirt. Will didn't look round at Simon's call. Leaving the horses, Simon ran along the bank as Will kicked off his boots and staggered down the muddy slope, into the brown, foaming water. It was only waist deep, but the current was strong and Simon knew it would be freezing.

'Will! Come out!'

Will didn't turn. Instead, he started splashing water up his arms and chest, rubbing at his bare skin.

Simon swore, yanked off his own boots, then waded, with a torrent of curses and grunts of pain, into the river.

Will's lean body was starkly white against the dark water, but there were hectic spots of colour on his cheeks. He turned as Simon clutched his shoulder. His green eyes were wide and unfocused. 'I have to get clean.'

'Come back in and I'll wet a rag for you then,' gasped Simon, the cold slicing through him like a scythe. As Will tried to wade further in, Simon held him back. Despite his weakened condition, he was surprisingly strong and it took all of Simon's might to stop him. 'Please, Will! We'll catch our deaths!'

'All I see when I close my eyes is her!'

'Elwen?' said Simon, now clinging to Will, no longer able to feel his feet, or legs.

Will's gaze seemed to focus. 'I thought it was her, Simon. I thought that girl was her. It felt like a dream. And I wanted her. I . . . I *touched* her . . . and . . .' He shook his head deliriously. 'Then when I saw her face, her *real* face, I tried to tell her to stop. I tried, Simon, you have to believe me. But I couldn't speak. I couldn't move! I can still . . . *smell* her on me. And I can't *stand* it!'

'It's going to be all right,' Simon told him. The rush of the river was loud in his ears.

'Elwen saw me.'

'Once we get the book and go back to Paris you can explain. Tell her what you just told me.'

'Tell her what, Simon? That I bedded a whore thinking it was her?' Will let out a fierce sob. 'Why did she go? I don't understand. She must have known I wouldn't do that? I don't understand!'

'Elwen will forgive you.' Simon faltered, churned up in a maelstrom of emotions. He wanted that to be true: he was desperate to make amends and to alleviate his own guilt. But his words stuck in his throat, choking him. 'And if not, maybe it's for the best,' he stammered.

'How could it be best?' cried Will, his voice hoarse.

'Sometimes bad things happen for a reason, don't they? Maybe it was too soon, you asking her to be your wife? Maybe you should wait a bit to be sure it's what you really want?'

'I cannot wait!' Will struck out towards the bank, but he slipped and went under. Simon grabbed him and pulled him up, choking and coughing. 'You don't see, do you?' Will shouted at him. 'I waited all those years for my father to forgive me and he died!' He grasped Simon's shoulders. 'I cannot wait for her!' As Will crumpled, Simon just managed to catch him. 'Let me go,' Will whispered, his voice fading.

'Not on your life,' said Simon, able to haul Will to the bank now that he had stopped resisting.

'What have you done!' cried Everard, coming out of the bushes to find Will and Simon collapsed in the mud, soaked and shivering.

Whilst they built a small fire to warm Will by, Simon bore the brunt of Everard's wrath in silence. The priest was fuming at both of them for the needless delay, but Will, in delirium, was oblivious to his rage. As Everard ranted and packed up their supplies, Simon tried to persuade Will to eat some bread, but with little success. Will hadn't opened his mouth since he had come out of the water, except to cough. Simon hated the chesty, whooping sound immediately. His father would have called it a graveyard cough.

Finally, Everard stamped out the mean little fire and they set off again, hoping to reach Orléans by nightfall. As Will was too weak to ride, Simon sat behind him, one arm firmly around his waist to hold him in the saddle. Everard led Simon's pack-horse alongside his own, muttering to himself every now and then. Their pace was dreadfully slow, but they did, as hoped, reach the city that evening.

They entered Orléans behind a small trade caravan, whereupon the gates were closed at their backs for the night, the guards waving them along. Everard led them through the streets. The sky above the maze of rooftops, towers and spires was grey-green in the fading light and it had begun to rain by the time the priest brought them, after several wrong turns, to the city's Templar preceptory. It was a small compound overlooking the Loire, but it had its own chapel and stables and was well appointed inside. The Master came out personally to greet them when their arrival was announced. Will was taken immediately to the infirmary with Everard, and Simon was shown to quarters.

He waited anxiously in the tiny room, staring out through a slit window, through which came a cold wind and the brackish smell of the river. Other than a stool, there was only a narrow pallet and a toilet bucket in the chamber. Simon realised that he would be bedding on the floor tonight.

When Everard entered a short while later, Simon rose. 'How is Will, sir?' he asked tentatively.

'What?' said Everard, sitting heavily on the stool. 'Oh. Not good.'

'Was . . . was it the whore, sir?' Simon managed to ask.

'No, I do not think so. He has a bad fever. The infirmarer thinks it will abate in a few days. The moon is in the appropriate phase and they have begun the bloodletting.'

Simon nodded, some of his fear subsiding.

'You will have to follow the book alone.'

Simon's mouth fell open. 'Sir . . . !'

'We have to get it from the Hospitallers,' Everard cut across him. 'If de Navarre leaves these shores with it, I'll never see it again!' He opened one of the leather bags he had brought up to the chamber and pulled out a fat pouch and a long hunting knife. 'Take these,' he said, thrusting the pouch and the knife into Simon's hands. 'There is money enough in that purse to see you to La Rochelle and back five times. Go straight to our base there and tell the knights that Hospitallers have stolen an important book from the Temple in Paris. Tell them you had to ride on ahead of your party and that they must arrest Nicolas and his brothers, and also de Lyons and this companion of his if they are there. Will and I will follow as soon as we can.'

Simon stared at the pouch and the knife, then back at the priest. He couldn't speak the native tongue and his Latin was dreadful. He could hardly write his own name, or count to ten and he had only ever wielded a weapon in the Paris preceptory's stables when Will had been teaching him. Now, this wild-eyed priest wanted him to take more gold than he had seen in his life and go chasing after two groups of armed men? Simon thought of all the distance that lay between him and the coast and although he didn't know how many miles it was, Everard might just as well have asked him to walk to Jerusalem for all the despair he felt. 'I . . . I don't think I can do it, sir,' he stammered. 'You could go, sir? I could stay with Will and then ride with him when . . .'

'Don't be ridiculous!' snapped Everard. 'You would be far quicker than I would. We've already been delayed. You must get to La Rochelle before Nicolas leaves. Will and I will not be far behind.' His voice quietened, became insidious. 'There is no one else, Simon. If you do not do this de Lyons will never be punished for the injustice he has done to Will. And if that happens, Will shall never find peace.'

35
The Temple, Orléans

2 February 1267 AD

W ill watched the line of women passing down the hill towards the cathedral. With cupped hands they sheltered the lighted candles that they held against the raw wind that ruffled the dark waters of the Loire. It was the Festival of the Purification of the Virgin and all those who had given birth in the previous year would take their candles to church to ask the Holy Mother for good health to attend their babies. Priests, monks and clerics throughout Christendom would tonight purify all the candles that would be used during Mass over the coming year.

As he turned from the window, Will caught a glimpse of himself in the basin of water that was placed on the table beside his pallet. His cheeks were gaunt, his eyes sunken and his ribs were craggy ridges over the cave of his stomach. Over the past three months, he had lost almost a third of his body weight. What had started as a fever had become a sickness of the lungs that had almost taken his life. Alongside the scars on his back where Everard had whipped him were a series of fresh cuts, made by the infirmarer's knife to release the bad humours from his chest. The tiny room stank of the rue and laurel oil that had been used to dress the wounds. For weeks, Will had lain in a sweat-drenched stupor, whilst pints of blood were drawn from his veins and as all that warm life-liquid had drained from him, so too had his rage, his grief and his guilt, leaving him an ashen-skinned husk who could neither feed, nor dress himself, let alone feel.

But, gradually, over the past fortnight, his cough had started to decrease. The bloodletting had been halted because of the new moon and the colour had started to return to his cheeks. With it had come memories. And the stirrings of anger. It was a colder, more intense anger than he had ever experienced. It had kept him awake for the past few nights; overwhelming even the deep pangs of sorrow he had felt when he had started to think of Elwen.

The door opened.

'Have you seen the procession?'

Will didn't look round at Simon's voice. 'Yes.'

Simon, ignoring Will's flat tone, kept smiling. He was carrying a bowl of steaming broth and a cup of lamb's wool: a drink made of roasted apples, ale, sugar and nutmeg. 'Here,' he said, pushing the door shut with his foot. 'Why don't you sit. I'll help you with your dinner.'

The only outward sign of Will's irritation was the twitch in his jaw. 'I can manage.' He was finding the groom's coddling increasingly annoying and the claustrophobically small room he had been confined to wasn't helping matters. He was sick of his own smell that had saturated the blankets he slept in and the air he breathed, sick of the square of grey sky in his window. Taking the bowl, Will sat on his pallet and sipped at the broth. The heat ran down the back of his throat and spread through his chest, easing the tightness.

'Brother Jean thinks you will be well enough to travel by the end of the month,' said Simon after a long silence, which was filled by the singing of the women in the streets.

Will nodded. Brother Jean, the infirmarer, had told him as much that morning. Everard, who had come to hear the diagnosis, had been delighted. The priest, Simon had said, had been like a man possessed and had spent the last few weeks in his room, pacing like a caged tiger and consulting all the maps he could find that showed the different routes to the Holy Land – by land and sea.

Will had been tightly enfolded in the fever's tenacious arms by the time Simon had returned from La Rochelle just before midwinter. The groom's journey to the port had begun well and he had made good speed, following the Loire down to Blois. But late one evening, just before he reached Tours, his horse had stumbled on a rock. He had walked the lame beast to the city, where he had been forced to spend Everard's money on a new one. The delay, combined with several days of bad weather, had meant that he had arrived in La Rochelle much later than planned. He had seen nothing of Garin, but had had less difficulty tracking Nicolas's whereabouts.

When Simon had informed the Templars that a Hospitaller had stolen a valuable book from the preceptory in Paris, the Marshal had sent two knights to the Hospital to demand that Nicolas be handed over. The Hospitallers, who had denied any knowledge of a book, had coolly informed the Templars that four knights had recently arrived from Paris, but that they were no longer there. Three of them had returned to Paris and one, a man named Nicolas de Acre, had left on one of their ships, bound for Acre, six days before. The Templar Marshal, unwilling to further sour relations with the Hospitallers, had told Simon that there was nothing he could do and that it would be up to the Visitor in Paris to pursue the matter further.

When Simon had returned to Orléans, Everard had wanted to leave for the port immediately. But Will had been far too ill to travel and Simon had informed the frustrated priest that no more vessels would be heading that far east until the spring. One of these would be a Templar warship, the *Falcon*; one of the first of the fleet due to leave in the wake of Baybars' attack on Safed. Everard had sent a message to the Visitor in Paris to inform him that they would be travelling to Acre, himself to make a pilgrimage and Will and Simon to aid in the city's re-fortification.

Simon watched Will drain the lamb's wool. 'I've been thinking. Maybe we shouldn't go to Acre. What about the war? I can't even hold a sword right, you know that.'

'I've made up my mind,' replied Will, wiping his mouth with the back of his hand. He glanced at Simon. 'You don't have to come.'

'Yes I do. Everard won't take care of you.'

'I don't need taking care of.'

Simon sighed heavily. 'You can barely walk. It will take weeks to get to La Rochelle, then months and months on a ship. And if we get to the Holy Land, how will we find Nicolas, or Garin, if he's even there?'

Will rose and went to the window. He put his hands on the ledge and closed his eyes, taking in thin breaths of icy air. For several days he had been thinking of Outremer: his father's burial place. His pale, chapped skin craved the imagined heat of that Eastern sun. His mind craved revenge. The Saracens had taken away his father and Nicolas de Navarre had taken away his one opportunity to redeem himself, to do the one thing he knew his father would have wanted. If Nicolas succeeded in bringing down the Anima Templi and the Temple with it, his father's death would truly mean nothing and the war would continue unchecked. And Garin? His old friend? The boy who had once made the shadow disappear? He had taken away the one thing Will had left. Elwen. He opened his eyes. 'I will find them,' he said, as much to himself as to Simon.

PART THREE

36

The Hospital of the Order of St John, Acre

18 January 1268 AD

I t was a cool day in the city of Acre, although warm in comparison to a day of the same month in France or England. In the distance, south of the city, the foothills below Mount Carmel were crowned with indigo clouds, dark against the bleached whites and yellows of the coastal plain. Ethereal bands of rain hung like veils from the sky. In a light, airy chamber in a tower of the Hospital of the Order of St John of Jerusalem, Nicolas de Acre watched the rain drift steadily westwards. Through the windows came the clamour and stench from the cattle market that lay outside the compound's walls. The compound itself was busy. Nicolas spotted two men, pilgrims he guessed, being led across the courtyard to the hospice, one leaning on the other for support. Growing up in Acre, he remembered the hospice, founded, like their Order, for the care of Christian travellers, had always been busy. Now, most of the beds lay empty. A blessing in one sense, Nicolas supposed, but a sign that fewer Christians were here to be treated.

Turning from the view, Nicolas glanced again at the mahogany desk upon which lay the product of ten years of his life. The vellum-bound book had been pushed to one side to accommodate the parchments and inkwell of the clerk who was diligently transcribing a letter that the Grand Master of the Order of St John, Hugues de Revel, was dictating. The Grand Master, a tall, slender man of middle years with a neat moustache and beard, was sitting upright in a high-backed chair. The clerk was perched awkwardly on the edge of a cushioned couch, as if concerned not to look too at ease on the comfortable furniture. Nicolas, hiding his impatience behind a cool, self-possessed expression, turned back to the window.

He had been waiting for this meeting for almost five months, since his arrival in Acre the summer before. As soon as his ship had docked, he had gone to the Hospital to hand the Book of the Grail to the Grand Master, who, when Nicolas had assumed the name de Navarre and left for Paris, had been a knight like himself. But a few weeks after his arrival a dispute over control of the city's harbour between the rival Venetian and Genoese merchants had erupted into a civil war that had run on into the autumn. De Revel, one of the many rulers, both assigned and self-appointed, of Acre, had been too busy with negotiations, parleys and the aftermath to see him until now.

'And so, in conclusion, I am sending you twenty knights to bolster the garrison at our preceptory in the noble city of Antioch.' The Grand Master paused and patted his neat beard with his forefinger. 'I wish to God that I could send more, dear brother, but these past few years have left us diminished.'

The clerk raised his head at these last words, the point of his quill hovering over the parchment, then wrote, the quill scratching at the skin.

'End it with my regards and send it with the company,' finished de Revel.

'Yes, my lord,' said the clerk. He gathered up his parchments, quill and inkwell, and left the chamber, his feet silent over the rose and jade silk rugs that carpeted the white stones.

De Revel's eyes flicked to Nicolas. He motioned to the couch. 'Sit, Brother de Acre.'

Nicolas did so, not sitting quite as stiffly as the clerk, but not relaxing either. He met the Grand Master's gaze. Hugues de Revel, although slight of build, was a man of rigidity, like a willow with a rod of iron running through it. Nicolas had seen that steel in the man's eyes when he had first come to these chambers five months ago and he saw it again now. 'I couldn't help but overhear, sir; we are sending troops to Antioch?'

The Grand Master clasped his long-fingered hands in his lap. His black mantle, with the white cross on the chest, fell expansively around him. 'We are sending troops everywhere. I've received word from one of our spies in Cairo. Baybars plans to begin his new campaign against us this month, only the sultan, it would seem, has drawn in his net and we cannot get any reliable information as to where he proposes to strike first. For the last few years, Acre has been his primary target, but each time we beat him back from our walls, he turns aside and wreaks bloody vengeance upon our less defensible settlements, although these are becoming fewer with every year that passes. Antioch is of particular concern to me, though. It is one of the more desirable targets left and I doubt, with Baybars leading this campaign, that Prince Bohemond would be able to pay for his preservation a second time.'

Nicolas agreed. A fellow knight had told him of the Mamluks' attempt on Antioch, fourteen months ago. When Baybars' commanders had appeared beyond its walls, its ruler, Prince Bohemond, had sacrificed ten wagons filled with gold, jewels and young girls to save his city. Placated by the offering, the commanders had retreated to Aleppo, leaving Antioch untouched. Baybars, it was rumoured, had been incensed.

'The sooner King Louis' Crusade arrives, the better,' muttered the Grand Master. 'Although there is still no firm word on when that will be. He took the Cross last year, but the last tidings I received from the West said that the king has been in discussion with his brother, Charles, Count of Anjou, who was recently appointed King of Sicily. De Anjou has apparently been attempting to persuade Louis that Tunis should be taken before any advance on Egypt can be made effectively.'

'Tunis?' said Nicolas with a doubtful frown. 'Louis and his men are needed here, in Palestine.'

'I do not disagree, brother. There are those in Acre who believe de Anjou desires to broaden his newly established kingdom. His ambitions for an empire of his own in the East may affect Louis' plans. We may find ourselves alone in this still come the king's arrival. I do not think we can count on him to aid us. However,' said the Grand Master, leaning forward to pick up the Book of the Grail, 'these are troubles for another hour and not why you are here.' He opened the book and flicked through the first few pages. 'I read it some weeks ago,' he explained. After a moment, he returned it to the table. 'You have done well, brother. You have sacrificed much in pursuit of this and undertook this action selflessly in the interests of our Order.'

Nicolas inclined his head respectfully. 'It was my duty, sir. I undertook the task gladly. I admit, for a time, I worried that my quest might prove fruitless; that the book might not be able to do the irreparable damage to the Temple that Grand Master de Châteauneuf had hoped when we first learnt of it. But, having read it myself, I see that this hope was not unfounded.'

De Revel's expression was grave. 'Yes. It is without doubt the work of heretics and blasphemers. I was sickened reading it. The pope would be outraged were he to discover what the Templars are involved in. But I do not believe that the book would be enough, alone, to compel him to dissolve the Order.'

To Nicolas, the words were a blow, but one he recovered from quickly. 'If I may explain, sir, it is not simply its heretical nature that could be levelled at the Order. I was told by my informants that the book also contains the plans of the Anima Templi hidden within the allegory. Plans, they assured me, that could bring down the Temple were they exposed. Grand Master de Châteauneuf hoped, by sending me to retrieve it, that we could use the book to do just that.'

'Even if that is so, brother, any strategies hidden within the narrative would only be clear to those who already know explicitly what they are. The Temple itself launched an investigation into this group years ago and found nothing. We will need more proof if we are to make firm accusations. Do you have any idea as to the exact nature of the Anima Templi's plans?'

'I have suspicions.' Nicolas sat forward, his gaze intent. 'I know that the Anima Templi exists, sir. After the Temple's attack on our Order, they disbanded, but the priest, Everard de Troyes, is continuing with the aims Armand and the rest were working towards originally. I know this for a fact.'

'I am not disputing what you say. But we will have only one chance to do this and we must make sure that our strike is targeted accurately. Our enmity towards the Temple is well known. We might be chastised for causing trouble needlessly when Outremer is so unstable. The pope is counting on the Temple, just as he is counting on us, to hold back the Saracens. I believe that we should gather more information on this group and their plans before we take any action. The testimonies of those formerly involved, your informants, would greatly strengthen our case.'

'The man who told me about the book died several years ago. He was the only one willing to testify against the Anima Templi and only then when we had possession of it. The others I have had contact with are too scared of the consequences of their betrayal to come forward.'

'Could you persuade them?'

Nicolas was silent for a few moments. 'It may be possible using the right means, yes.'

'Good.' De Revel sat back. 'Then this may well be of great use to us in the future.'

'The future, sir?' Nicolas frowned. 'Shouldn't we move on this as soon as possible? The sooner we act, the sooner the Temple falls.'

De Revel didn't speak for several moments. 'When Grand Master de Châteauneuf told me of his plan, I admit I thought it a hopeless cause. He was, I believed, chasing rumours. After he died and you wrote and told me of the book's disappearance, my own interest in your infiltration of the

Temple lay more in the possibility of discovering more about their assets: funds; properties; holy relics. When you came to see me a few months ago, you gave me a fairly comprehensive list of what they own in the Kingdom of France, but I had hoped to be able to make reasonable calculations of their financial worth in its entirety.'

'And I still don't know the reason for that, sir. Can I ask why you wanted to know this?'

The Grand Master pursed his lips, as if deciding whether to answer. 'My interest in their worth is due to a proposition that I, and others in our Order, have been considering for some time now.'

'Proposition, sir?'

'We have been discussing whether to attempt to ally ourselves with the Temple.'

Nicolas stared at the Grand Master. 'That surely cannot be a possibility, sir?'

'I have no love of the Temple, brother. What Armand and his knights did to us was unforgivable. But Baybars' Jihad has left us little choice. If we pool our resources, we may be able to withstand his army long enough to regain some of our territories. If not, both our Orders, *all* of us stand to lose everything.'

'With all due respect, sir, you weren't here when Armand and his knights lay siege to this compound. You have no idea what we went through during those months.'

'You will keep a civil tongue in my presence, brother.'

Nicolas didn't speak. To have the products of his efforts so brusquely abandoned by another man was upsetting; to have them used for the opposite of the original purpose was nothing short of devastating.

'If the Temple falls now, brother,' said de Revel, 'so do we all. Only by allying with them can we hope to continue our dream for a Christian Holy Land. As I said, you have already sacrificed much, but we must now make an even greater sacrifice and work with our enemy for the greater good, or face the very real possibility that we may not live to see another winter in these lands.' Nicolas went to protest, but de Revel continued before he could speak. 'I must to do what is in the best interests of our Order and, for the moment, any attempt at undermining or destroying the Temple would run counter to this. If we survive this war and reclaim enough territory, we may find ourselves in a strong enough position to move against the Templars without damaging ourselves. But until such time arises, I will not jeopardise our Order by continuing with de Châteauneuf's plan, however damning this book may prove. For now, we must concentrate on winning this war. Then, when we are in a position of strength, we can strike.' De Revel picked up the Book of the Grail and rose from his chair. 'Until that time, you are finished with this business.' He went to a large iron locker that was set into the wall behind his chair. Taking a key, which hung on a chain from his belt, he unlocked it and put the book inside. 'In the coming months, the citizens of Outremer will be relying heavily upon us all.' De Revel nodded to Nicolas. 'You are dismissed, brother.'

Nicolas rose and bowed. 'Sir.' He turned on his heel and left. In the passage outside, the tall arched windows provided a magnificent view of the city. Nicolas's gaze skimmed the vista of towers, churches and market-places, and came to rest out on the bay where six Templar warships, surrounded by a cavalcade of smaller vessels, were drawing steadily towards the harbour.

The Falcon, *the Bay of Acre, 18 January 1268* AD

The decks of the thirteen ships were crowded with people: sergeants, knights, pilgrims, merchants, all trying to catch their first glimpse of the city that was slowly taking shape on the horizon. To the north and south lay mountains and dark, clouded skies. In the foreground, stretching from the high city walls to the distant hills, was a sweep of yellow-white emptiness. As the ships drew closer and the detail in the land became clearer, the people on board began to discern pockets of green that marked the barren plain: fields, orchards and hills watered by blue rivers. Some fell to their knees at the sight. This was Palestine: the Holy Land and birthplace of Christ.

On board the *Falcon*, at forty-five yards the longest in the fleet, Will stood on the rembata, leaning against the parapet. Below him, the sides plunged dizzyingly to the water and before him, the iron-tipped ram extended from the bowsprit like a fist. The two-level platform that was built onto the bow also housed the ship's trebuchet: a similar weapon to the mangonel, only more accurate and using a sling to toss stones rather than a scooped-out beam. Now that they were in friendly waters the catapult was unloaded, its sling swinging loose. When they had passed through the Straits of Gibraltar it had been primed and ready, a comfort when they had seen the first Saracen ships off the coast near Granada. But, in the end, it hadn't fired a single stone. The six Templar warships, recognisable by the red crosses on their mainsails, had been deterrent enough.

As a bell clanged, summoning the rest of the oarsmen to the benches, Will turned from the emerging strip of land to look down over the crowded ship; his home for the last eight months.

The *Falcon*, with its five sister vessels, had set out from La Rochelle in early June of the previous year. With the slender warships were four uscieres – stocky, unwieldy vessels carrying horses, wagons and siege engines – and a Templar roundship loaded with bales of wool and cloth for trade in Outremer. The sea and sky had grown gradually darker as they had headed into the Bay of Biscay and the ships had lurched like drunken men over great, green waves, until, caught in the teeth of two storms, one of the horse-carrier ships had foundered. Will, being flung about on his pallet below deck, had been woken by a loud splintering sound. He had raced up on deck, along with Simon and a score of other drowsy men, to find that the usciere's mainmast had snapped in half and smashed through the decks. Clinging to the side of the rolling, creaking warship, rain and salt spray lashing their faces, they had watched, helpless, as the usciere had pitched forwards, plunging men and horses into the mountainous waters.

There had been little respite from the violent storms until the fleet had reached the Kingdom of Portugal, where they had limped into Lisbon, four of the ten ships damaged, two severely. Here, they were forced to remain for three months to carry out repairs and most of the knights and sergeants had gone by boat down the River Tomar to a town of the same name that was owned by the Temple.

For Will, it was the best thing that could have happened.

Earlier in the year, whilst Will lay sick in Orléans, Robert de Paris had been journeying to one of the Temple's preceptories in the Kingdom of Castile, on business for the Visitor. When word had come that the Templar fleet had put in at Lisbon for repairs, Robert and several others had petitioned the Master to allow them to join the ships. Their request granted, they had ridden across country to Tomar. Robert had been billeted in the castle with Will.

In the mornings, they had trained together on the field outside the Templar castle that dominated the town. Will, whose muscles had grown languid and whose lungs burned when he climbed a few steps, had hardly been able to mount a horse, let alone hold a lance. But, gradually, the exercise and the Portuguese sun had breathed new life into him and as his muscles had strengthened and his skin darkened, his mind had begun to settle. One evening, as he and Robert had sat on the castle ramparts, looking out over the sun-drenched hills, lizards scurrying over the walls,

Will had told him about the prostitute. He had spoken too of Garin's part in
it, although little of the reasons behind the treachery, just a mention of a
manuscript Everard had had stolen. Robert had listened silently, then had
passed Will a skin of Burgundy wine that he had confiscated from a
sergeant.

After this confession, things had changed for Will. His desire for revenge
for what Garin had done to him hadn't left him, but he had managed to
press it into a place inside himself where it wouldn't plague him so
persistently.

He had another place for Elwen.

During the day, training with Robert, fishing in the river, or talking
with Everard and Simon, he had managed to keep her at bay. But at
night, with nothing to occupy his mind, she had slipped often into his
thoughts. Many dawns he had woken with a fading image of her face and
a hollow space inside. At those moments, he had wondered about
returning home, but the fear that she would not forgive him had
prevented him, whilst, compelling him eastwards, was a growing desire
to see his father's burial place.

When they had set out once more from Lisbon, two merchant galleys
and a pilgrim ship had gone with them, the captains paying a tax for the
armed escort to Acre. The seas had changed colour the further south they
travelled, from the slate grey of the coast of France and the deep navy of the
Spanish seas, to the emerald Portuguese waters and, finally, the azure
Mediterranean.

'Is it what you expected?' asked Robert, climbing up the side of the
rembata from the outrigger. He handed Will a skin, then clambered nimbly
over the parapet. 'Drink up. Last of the Burgundy.'

'What I expected?'

'Acre,' said Robert, gesturing to the city, which was now much closer.
The oarsmen had begun to slow their pace as the ship drew near to a long
breakwater that led into the biggest and busiest harbour Will had ever seen.

Will took a swig of wine, then handed the skin back to Robert. 'It looks
like Paris. Only yellower.'

'I think that lot are going to be disappointed,' said Robert, draining the
wine and tipping his head towards a knot of sergeants clustered together on
the quarterdeck. They were polishing swords and looking towards the city,
their faces grim. 'One of the crew was just telling me about some knights a
few years back who refused to leave the ship because they thought they
could see Saracens waiting for them on the beach. They started arguing

about how they could get close enough to fire the trebuchet at the enemy without coming into range.'

'Were they Saracens?' asked Will, already smiling.

'No. A group of Templar sergeants waiting to help them unload the ship's cargo. He said he sees it every time he comes. Half the men think they are stepping off the boat into a war.'

An hour later, Will, Robert and the other knights and officers from the *Falcon* were in one of the ship's two pinnaces, being rowed ashore. Simon and Everard were in the other. The warships, the uscieres and the roundship had been anchored off the breakwater alongside the other galleys that were too large to enter the city's inner harbour, which was crowded with merchant vessels. Will sat beside Robert at the pinnace's stern and watched as one of the oldest cities on Earth was slowly revealed.

It was late afternoon and the light was golden. Acre's walls, doubled and ranked by a series of towers, seemed to soak up the sun and glow. Timber, stone and mud-brick buildings lined the harbour and behind a packed marketplace beyond the city gates, the noise of which Will could already hear, rose domed churches, imposing towers and elegant spires. The rest of the city he couldn't see because of the walls that encircled it, but he had an impression of opulence and strength. 'What is that?' he asked one of the *Falcon*'s officers, an old veteran who had been born in the city. He pointed to a huge wall that spanned the sea's edge before turning sharply and continuing into the city beyond. Great towers jutted from it. One of these, on the city side, was topped with four turrets, the pinnacles of which seemed to be made of gold. Within the vast walls, he could see the spire of a church and the rooftops of many grand, white stone structures.

'That,' said the veteran, following Will's gaze, 'is our preceptory.'

Will fell silent. Their preceptory looked like a miniature version of the city itself: immaculate, imperious and magnificent.

The pinnace reached the shore, the oarsmen jumping into the shallows to haul the boat onto the sands. The market Will had seen from the bay was, indeed, packed and noisy. This one, the veteran told him, belonged to the Pisans. There were others, run by the Venetians, the Lombards and the Germans, all of whom had their own quarters in the city which were like separate states with their own laws, churches and government. It was as if, the knight said, they had each carved a piece out of their homelands to stick on this strip of sand. There were twenty-seven quarters in total: Montmusart beyond the walls to the north, which was where the general population lived and worked; St Andrew's, which was where the local Frankish nobility lived, many of whom had fled to Acre after the fall of Jerusalem; the Jewish quarter; the Patriarch's quarter and so on.

Will tried to listen to everything the veteran was saying as they made their way up the beach behind the captain, but his eyes were telling him their own story and he found it hard to concentrate.

'Will!' Simon was hastening up the sands, his cheeks flushed. He was followed by the sergeants and crewmen from the second pinnace. 'Have you seen them? Look!'

Will followed Simon's finger to the marketplace and saw a line of the oddest-looking beasts he had ever seen. They were larger than horses and beige in colour, with long necks and knobbly-looking mounds on their backs. A small crowd was gathering on the wall, people idling from the market to watch the knights disembark. Some lounged there, watching the knights with mild curiosity, then turned back to the stalls, more interested in the merchandise.

The first thing about these people that captivated Will were their clothes. Not only were they far more elegant in design than Western garments; clinging gowns and richly embroidered tunics for women; well-fitted hose and brocaded surcoats for men, the fabrics were also extraordinarily luxurious. There wasn't a woollen cape, or a wooden clog between them, just silk, damask, soft linen and samite. Each and everyone, even the children, looked like kings and queens at a coronation.

Will found himself unable to take his eyes off the crowd as he drew closer and further peculiarities started to become apparent. Initially, he had thought they must all be foreign by their sun-browned faces, the strange cut of their rich garments, the turbans they wore over their hair and their unfamiliar accents. But now he realised that some of them were speaking Latin, others English and French. They were Westerners. But they were mingling freely, and indeed laughing and joking, with tall, graceful-looking men with ebony skin, whose teeth showed incredibly white when they smiled, other men with olive skin, almond-shaped eyes and round faces, and men who looked like Hasan.

'Saracens!' Will heard one knight hiss.

A few of the others reached for their swords and looked to their captain, but he was striding through the crowd, unconcerned. Will caught sight of Everard, hobbling a little way behind. The priest was smiling.

The knights followed their captain in a daze, past stalls where black-eyed Venetians bartered with Muslim traders over timber and iron, and Bedouin, swathed in their keffiyehs, hawked casks of mare's milk for fistfuls of bezants. There were sweet lemons and dates piled high on wagons beside stalls stacked with rubies, dyes, swords, silks, porcelain and soap. A Jew wearing spectacles laughed with a Greek merchant as he weighed a glut of sapphires in his scales. Dung and sweat, spices and balm suffused the air. The crowds jostled one another, calling out in so many different tongues and accents that Latin became indistinguishable from Hebrew, French from Arabic. Even as the knights turned aside from the market and walked the narrow, winding streets to the preceptory, every corner delivered a new vision. Glass in the round windows of a church captured the afternoon sun and dazzled them. Women wearing the barest of gowns lounged in darkened alleys and beckoned to them. Old men sat in doorways, wreathed in incense smoke and others sat at tables, playing chess on boards made of ivory and Egyptian glass.

By the time they reached the preceptory, the knights were so over-whelmed they hardly noticed the four lions made of gold which capped the turrets of the tower straddling the Temple's massive gates. The knights guarding the entrance greeted them and ushered them through a smaller door that was cut into the gates. They stepped through into a busy quadrant bordered by large stone buildings. Will stopped just inside. His eyes darted over the men in the quadrant, seeking out the knights. But none that he saw had golden hair.

Robert tapped Will's shoulder. 'One of the officers has asked me to draw up a list of our names to give to the bailiff. I'll come and find you when I'm done.'

Robert was led to a building where the Temple's banner fluttered from a pole on the roof. Behind Will, the men who had been on the other warships poured in through the gate, most wearing the same bewildered expressions. Simon came to stand at his side as clerks appeared from the building Robert had entered and began to divide the swelling group.

'My father will never believe this. I'm not sure I believe it. Did we really see Saracens in the market?'

Before Will could answer, Everard came over.

'William, I want you to find out if Nicolas de Navarre is at the Hospitaller compound in the city.' Everard's voice was more rasping than ever. His persistent cough, which had worsened after Hasan's death, had been exacerbated by the long voyage and some days, he struggled to speak at all.

'Now?' Even Will, who knew how much the priest had been fixated on this moment since leaving La Rochelle, was taken aback by his single-mindedness.

Everard glanced round as a clerk approached them. 'There are people I must see. I'm relying on you, William.'

'This way, brothers,' said the clerk, motioning for them to follow.

'I know the way,' said Everard, shuffling off ahead of the clerk.

'What are you going to do when you find Nicolas?' murmured Simon as they fell into line.

Will shook his head, distracted by the towering walls where knights patrolled the battlements, which were riddled with arrow slits and lined with mangonels and trebuchets. This preceptory was nothing like those in London, or Paris, or La Rochelle. He realised why. It wasn't a preceptory: it was a fortress. 'I don't know,' he said, as they passed an armoury where men worked at benches, sharpening swords.

Simon, throwing worried glances over his shoulder at Will, was led away with the sergeants to a row of buildings beyond the main quadrant. Will was taken with the knights past stables, workshops, a magnificent church that made the chapel at Paris look like a barn and a palatial structure that the clerk told them formed Grand Master Bérard's quarters. They came eventually to a set of buildings surrounding a courtyard with a cistern at the centre. Will was shown to a room with seven other knights. Comfortable-looking pallets lined the walls and each man had a wooden chest for his belongings. There was a perch for their mantles and braces for their swords. The blankets on the pallets were made of lamb's wool and pillows had been placed at the head of each bed; not straw-filled sacking, but feather-stuffed linen. The stone floor was clean and covered with a woven mat. After months on the deck of the *Falcon*, it looked like a palace, but rather than take the opportunity to relax in the princely surroundings, Will, after depositing his sack on a pallet, headed out.

Sergeants and servants nodded respectfully to him as he walked through the preceptory. Knights, older than himself with tanned faces and a hardness to their eyes, ignored him. Will guessed that they would know Garin if he had indeed come here following Nicolas, but something stopped him from asking. Now the moment had come, he had no desire to see the man who had betrayed and dishonoured him. Neither had he any desire to head out alone into the unfamiliar city to search for Nicolas.

After a time, Will found himself on the battlements looking out across the city. The sight was arresting. Beyond Acre's main walls was a packed settlement that was bordered by another wall and a moat. Beyond this lay orchards, gardens and olive groves, stretching off into a gold-amber haze.

'Beautiful, isn't it?'

Will looked round to see a white-haired knight on the battlements beside him.

'I come here every evening before Vespers. It never fails to move me.' The knight smiled. 'You have come from France, brother?'

Will nodded. He thought the knight might be able to answer a question he had. He looked out over the city and asked it. 'Where is Safed from here?'

The knight pointed east. 'Thirty or so miles across the plain.'

'Could I find it easily?'

The knight looked surprised. 'There's a road that leads there from the city, but Baybars' men command most of the route now. You know Safed is in Saracen hands?'

'Yes. My father died there.'

'I'm sorry. But I would advise against visiting his grave, for it would become yours. The barons of Acre sent an envoy there to treat with the sultan last year. They found the fortress surrounded by the heads of murdered Christians.'

Will thought of his father's body, once a pillar of strength and dignity, defiled and unburied. He wanted to gather the bones in his arms and bring them to a place of peace. The thought of his father's spirit, blown and scattered by the gritty winds, haunting these foreign plains, anguished him. It wasn't Scotland. It wasn't home.

'I will leave you,' said the knight gently.

'Do you know a knight called Garin de Lyons?'

The white-haired knight shook his head slowly. 'I don't think so.'

'He would have arrived in the past year. He's my age.' Will described Garin.

The knight spread his hands. 'Many come through here.'

'He might have been alone. Not on board a Templar ship.'

'Alone? A young man did arrive on his own just before the Christ Mass. De Lyons?' The knight gave an apologetic shrug. 'That might have been his name. I cannot say for sure. He came by land from Tyre. The harbour was closed, so whatever ship he came on would have been re-routed there. The merchant states were at war at that time,' the knight explained.

'He isn't here anymore?'

'If I remember rightly, he was posted with a company of knights heading for Jaffa.'

'Jaffa?'

'A city on the coast near Jerusalem, about eighty miles from here.' The knight pointed south to the distant mountains. 'We have a garrison there.'

'Thank you.' Leaving the knight to his sunset, Will returned to the quadrant. He found himself back at the gates. He was about to head to his quarters when he heard his name being shouted. Will saw Simon running towards him.

'I've been looking for you everywhere!' panted the groom. 'You have to find Everard.'

'Why?'

'We've been posted,' said Simon in an anguished tone. '*Both* of us.'

'Posted? We aren't here for . . .'

'A knight came into our dormitory with a list,' Simon cut across him. 'Just after we'd settled in. He told me I was being posted with a company. I found out you and Robert were in it too.'

'Posted to where?'

'Somewhere called Antioch,' said Simon despairingly.

37

The Temple, Antioch

1 May 1268 AD

T he city of Antioch, although diminished in its former importance as a
    centre of trade, was still considered one of the wonders of the world.
Three miles long and one mile wide, people seeing it for the first time were
rendered speechless, unable to believe that man, not God had built it. The
walls that encircled it, erected by the Roman Emperor Justinian, ran for
eighteen miles and were set with four hundred and fifty towers. On one
side they bordered the River Orontes, known by the Arabs as the Rebel,
and on the other they marched up to encompass the steep slopes of Mount
Silpius, atop which, towering one thousand feet above the city, was a
colossal citadel. The city within this girdle of stone was equally impressive.
There were villas and palaces where palm trees and crumbling Roman
arches rose from tiled courtyards, there were bustling markets, lush market
gardens, numerous churches and monasteries. It was, according to the
native Christians who formed the majority of the population, a city unlike
any other.

Will, standing on the battlements of the Temple's preceptory, had a
clear view down the plunging Orontes Valley, where the river flowed
through limestone chasms into fertile plains. To the north marched the
Amanus Mountains, the highest peaks of which were capped with snow.
The Temple owned two fortresses perched on those rocky heights, one of
which guarded the Syrian Gates – the high pass that led into the Kingdom of
Cilicia. South, beyond the plains, lay the Jabal Bahra Mountains. Those
peaks hid the stronghold of the Order of Assassins.

'Seen anything?'

Will looked round as Robert stepped out onto the battlements. 'Sheep,
rocks, grass, more sheep.'

Robert arched an eyebrow and passed Will a skin of water. 'You know
what I mean.'

'Thanks,' said Will, taking the skin. It was a warm morning, although not nearly as warm as it would be by midsummer, the relentless heat of which Will, Robert and the other men who had been arriving in Outremer since the beginning of the year had yet to experience. 'No, I haven't seen any sign of the scouts.' He drank thirstily, then handed the skin back to Robert. 'But it could take them a week or more to gather any useful information.' Will leaned against the parapet, Mount Silpius filling his view. Shepherds were leading their flocks down from the rough pastures. Two days ago, Will, Robert and several other knights had ridden along the walls to those slopes, their orders: to make sure that the escape tunnels there were still passable. They had found the mountain riddled with passages and caves, some of which, their Armenian guide had told them, the first Christians had used for their services. Now, they mostly seemed to be used by children as hideouts.

'A knight I knew in London used to talk about this city,' said Will with a smile. 'We all used to laugh behind his back when he said the citadel touched the clouds. We thought he was brainsick.'

Robert shielded his eyes against the glare. 'Everything here does seem too big, doesn't it?' He shrugged. 'Well, just as long as the Mamluks aren't giants.'

'I think that depends on which stories you listen to.' Will bent to adjust his coat of chainmail, the rings of which were catching on his sword belt. The coat had been given to him back in Acre, along with a new mantle that fitted him properly. 'But unless you believe they can breathe fire, or curdle a man's blood by looking at him, then I'd guess them to be of a normal size.'

'Good. I had visions of standing on a box to fight them.'

'Fight who?'

They looked round as Simon appeared behind them, his face troubled. 'No one,' said Will.

Simon came tentatively to the parapet, avoiding the vertiginous view to the courtyard below. 'Those scouts haven't come back then?'

'No,' replied Will and Robert together. They both laughed.

Simon looked disgruntled.

'We don't know anything yet,' said Will, trying to reassure him. 'Just rumours. That's why we sent the scouts.'

'What if it's true? What if Baybars' army is headed our way?'

Will sighed. What was he supposed to say, he wondered? He knew as much as anyone, which wasn't a great deal. In the past week, reports had reached Antioch of fighting in the south, but they had differed greatly in detail. A merchant from Damascus had said he had heard that Baybars' army was marching on Acre; a farmer that the Mamluks were coming for Antioch; three Coptic priests that the Mamluks had been turned back by the Franks. After hearing these rumours, the constable of the city, Simon Mansel, had called a council between the military leaders. With Antioch's ruler, Prince Bohemond, visiting the city of Tripoli, Mansel had been left in charge. He had ordered a patrol to be sent out to verify the claims and the Master of the Temple's garrison had offered five knights for the task. They had left four days ago. 'If Baybars' army comes, we'll deal with it when it gets here.'

'How can you be so calm?'

'Because I don't know anything yet. I know it's hard, but the only thing any of us can do is wait and try to remain calm.'

Robert nodded as Simon looked to him. 'He's right.'

'It's all well and good for you two,' muttered the groom. 'You have swords and you know how to use them.'

'It took the first Crusaders seven months to capture Antioch from the Turks.' As soon as the words were out, Will realised it was the wrong thing to say.

'But they *did* capture it!' exclaimed Simon. 'Besides, I heard you and Robert talking after the council. You were saying how you didn't reckon the city could be defended properly with so few men.'

Robert and Will shared a look. 'We were only talking,' said Will.

'Don't cosset me,' said Simon testily.

Will threw up his hands. 'Then don't act like you want cosseting!' He glanced at Robert, then took Simon by the elbow and steered him along the battlements. 'What's wrong?' he murmured.

'The same as everyone. I'm worried about getting a sword in the gullet.'

'It isn't just this. You've been on edge since we left Acre.'

'What do you expect, Will? I thought we would find Nicolas and you would do whatever it was you were going to do, Everard would get the book and we would all go home.'

'Everard tried to get our posts changed.'

'He should have tried harder,' responded Simon obstinately.

'He did all he could,' said Will, thinking of Everard's frustrated defeat in the face of the adamant Marshal.

Back in Acre, on learning of their posting, Will had gone straight to the priest, who had immediately requested that the Marshal change the assignment.

'I need him here,' the priest had insisted. 'He was my sergeant in Paris.'

'He is a knight now,' the Marshal had responded, looking at Will. 'And in Paris we aren't at war. King Louis' Crusade is unlikely to reach us anytime soon. We must rely on ourselves to defend the little we have left from Baybars' forces.'

'I have come here specifically to secure a rare and extremely important work on medicine for study. I must track down this text.' Everard had drawn himself up and had fixed the Marshal with a stern look. 'The Visitor of the Kingdom of France sent me on this assignment, Sir Marshal. William is my escort and the groom our squire.'

The Marshal had been unimpressed. 'When this war is won, brother, you may have a battalion escort you to find your precious work, but until that time I will use every man at my disposal in any way I see fit. It is not manuscripts that will save us.' The Marshal had crossed his chamber to the door and had opened it. 'Only swords will do that. Now, if you will excuse me I have important matters to attend to.'

'I will appeal against this decision, Sir Marshal,' Everard had said in a restrained voice as he had left the chamber.

'You may do so at the next chapter meeting.'

Everard, seething with impotent anger, had stalked from the building, out into the yard.

'What will you do about the book?' Will had asked him.

'Leave that to me. There may only be three of us left here, but we still have resources.' Slowing his stride, Everard had turned to Will. 'I'll get you and Simon out of Antioch as soon as I can.'

As yet, Will had received no word from Acre.

'Did you really do all you could to convince Everard?'

Will frowned at Simon. 'What do you mean by that?'

'You just don't seem bothered by the prospect of Baybars' army being just over that hill.' Simon's brow creased. 'It's like you want them to be. Like you want to fight?'

Will looked out over the valley to avoid Simon's probing gaze. He didn't *want* the Mamluks to be coming, but then neither was he disappointed by the prospect. He hadn't wanted to come to Antioch, to defend a foreign city, or fight the Saracens. But being here had altered his perspective. He was still a Templar, a warrior. The ideals of the Anima Templi had been known to him for eighteen months, the Temple's ideals had been instilled in him his whole life. He had tried to remember Everard's words; that peace was beneficial to all. But when he thought of the agony his father must have felt when that Mamluk sword had hacked down into his neck, there was no white flag in Will's mind, just the thought of the blood to be spilt, just the cold of the steel in his hands.

'Riders!' called Robert.

Leaving Simon, Will crossed to Robert. 'Where?'

'Down there.' Robert was staring intently into the valley. 'They're too far for me to see who they are.'

Will followed his finger and saw movement on the valley floor: horsemen moving fast along the road to St George's Gate, the north-west entrance to the city. A rocky slope that rose up to the right was currently shadowing them, but as the shelf tumbled away and became fields they passed into sunlight and their white mantles shone. Will glimpsed a tiny flash of red on the back of one of the riders, who slowed to lean forward in his saddle momentarily.

'Templars.'

'Must be the scouts.'

Will shook his head. 'We only sent five. I count nine.'

Garin fell back behind the other riders, pausing to tighten his stirrup strap, then kicked his spurs into his horse's flanks and urged the beast on. For the last few miles, Antioch had been growing in the distance and the nearer he came to those vast, sheer walls the smaller he felt himself becoming. Antioch was like the hand of God stuck on the plain, palm upraised, commanding all those who came before it to halt. For a moment, Garin couldn't imagine how any army could hope to take it. But then he thought of Baybars and he wasn't so sure.

Baybars.

Garin had heard that name often in the past few months, but few people, he had come to realise, knew what they were talking about when it came to the Mamluk sultan. Some believed that Baybars was Satan and God had sent him to punish the Christians in Outremer for their love of fine clothes and harems, and forgetfulness of the path of humility and poverty extolled by Christ. Those people said that the only way to defeat Baybars was through prayer and penance. Others thought him a savage whose faculty lay in brute strength rather than intelligence or bravery and that he would only be placated by plunder so they should seek to bribe him into submission. Garin, however, had seen Baybars fight and knew that the sultan lacked neither courage, nor cunning. Baybars was a force of nature: a raw, raging power, terrible and extraordinary. He had changed Garin's life.

Garin had boarded a Genoese ship at La Rochelle, intending to follow the Hospitaller, as Rook, who had returned to England to tell Edward what had happened, had ordered. But almost as soon as he had stepped off the ship in Tyre, he had felt that he had been wearing an invisible chain that had just snapped in half. For the first time in his life he had felt free. It was with a surprisingly light heart that, forsaking any attempt to track down the book, which Rook had demanded he retrieve on pain of death, he had received his posting at Jaffa. It was here that he'd had his first encounter with the blue-eyed sultan.

In Jaffa, the only things required of Garin had been that he fight and stay alive. He did not have to lie, or sneak about, or live in fear of displeasing or angering Rook. It was brutally, refreshingly simple. It was against Baybars that Garin had got his first taste of praise and pride. Against Baybars, he had become a hero.

As Antioch's guards opened the gates for the company, Garin, who knew all too well what was coming behind him, couldn't help but smile at the thought that he might be the man to save this godlike city.

Will and Robert remained on the battlements when the nine rode in and it wasn't until they were summoned to an urgent chapter, a short time later, that they saw who had come.

'This doesn't look good,' murmured Robert to Will, as they filed with the fifty other knights of the garrison into the chapter house. He motioned discreetly to a grim-faced officer who was talking with a knight in the porch of the building.

'No,' agreed Will. 'But at least we might get some news.'

They crossed to a bench at the back of the chamber, the front rows having already filled up. On the dais, the Master of the garrison and two officers were standing in a close circle with five knights. They finished speaking as Will, Robert and the last few men were seated. The Master gestured for the doors to be shut and the knights behind him broke their circle. Will's breath caught in his throat as Garin turned to face the assembly. Will went to stand, but something stayed him. Glancing down, he realised that Robert had gripped his forearm. The knight shook his head. Will, his whole body trembling, sat on the edge of the bench as the Master began to speak.

'I apologise for the abruptness of this council, but haste is of the essence. The scouts we sent out met with four of our brothers on the road, who have come with grave news from our fortress of Beaufort. I invite one of them, Sir Garin de Lyons, to address you.' The Master moved aside.

Will's eyes were fixed on Garin who stepped up to the front of the dais. He looked tired, dirty and tanned. There were bloodstains on his mantle and his hair was tousled and more blond than golden. He looked uncomfortable, clenching and unclenching his hands as if he didn't know what to do with them. 'As the Master says, we've just come from Beaufort, which has been besieged by Sultan Baybars' army.'

A few murmurs rose from the knights.

'The fortress had been under heavy attack for almost eight days when we left it. I expect it has fallen by now. The Mamluks are on their way here, taking out any strongholds that could threaten their rear on the way.'

The low buzz of voices rose into exclamations and questions.

'How do you know this?' asked one knight.

'When will they be here?' voiced another.

The Master stirred as Garin looked uncertainly to him. He raised his hands for silence. 'Please. Let Brother de Lyons finish. Perhaps if you start from the beginning, brother.'

'Of course.' Garin faced the company. And caught Will's rigid gaze. His mouth remained open, but no words came out. After a moment, he shut it and looked away. 'I was in Jaffa in March. The Mamluks attacked us and the city fell to them in a day.' Garin pushed on through the murmurs, avoiding Will's gaze. His hands were making fists again. 'It has been impossible to guess the sultan's plans for individual battles, as well as for his general campaign because he's so unpredictable. Sometimes he promises freedom to surrendering garrisons, then goes back on his word as at Arsuf and Safed.' Garin's eyes darted to Will, then flicked away again. 'Sometimes he lets the women and children go and makes slaves of the men and at other times he does the opposite. In Jaffa, he killed most of the citizens, but let the garrison go free. As we left, we saw slaves dismantling our castle. It's rumoured the sultan is building a new mosque in Cairo. They say he wants to build it out of all the Frankish strongholds left in Palestine. We retreated to Acre.

'A few weeks later, I was in a company sent to reinforce Beaufort, after we received reports that Baybars was headed that way. The Mamluks arrived at our walls in April. On the seventh night, I was on watch when I saw a man crawling through a ditch to a postern in the wall below me. I went down to the postern thinking to capture him to discover what he had been sent to do. He was a deserter. When he had tried to abandon his post, he had been caught and sentenced to death. He had escaped and had fled to our fortress, hoping we would disguise him as one of our servants in exchange for information. We were able to discover through him that Baybars' primary target in this campaign is Antioch.' Garin gestured to the three knights behind him. 'Beaufort's commander helped the four of us to flee so that we could warn you.' He looked to the Master. 'That's it.'

'Thank you, Brother de Lyons,' said the Master, stepping forward. 'Your quick thinking and selfless actions have no doubt greatly enhanced our chances for survival.'

Many of the knights voiced their agreement, or nodded, although their praise was muted by the gravity of the news. Robert yawned loudly and Will gripped the edge of the bench until his knuckles turned white.

'May I ask, brother,' called one knight, 'has Grand Master Bérard been informed of this?'

The Master looked to Garin, who shook his head.

'There wasn't time. We came straight here.'

'Then we should send word to Acre at once.'

'Any message we sent now would arrive too late,' said the Master. 'Baybars would be ahead of any reinforcements that could come to our aid. We cannot look to outside help, but we can muster all that we have here in our defence. A city expecting a fight is a far more formidable target than one that waits, hoping there won't be one. I will inform Constable Mansel immediately. No doubt, he'll want to convene a council.'

A few knights spoke up, asking about the general preparations and offering suggestions. But aside from this, and a prayer for the knights at Beaufort, the chapter was done. The Master gathered his officers around him as a clerk was brought in to send a message to Antioch's constable.

Will rose as Garin descended the dais. The knight glanced briefly at him, then hastened for the doors. Will strode after him.

'Will!' shouted Robert, sprinting out of the doors behind him into the sunlit yard.

Garin, who was halfway across the yard, turned at the call. He looked fearful as Will came at him, but stood his ground. Will didn't break his stride, but grabbed Garin and propelled the knight into the wall of the armoury. Garin gave a winded gasp as he was slammed against the rough stone. Will's hands pressed into his shoulders, pinning him.

'Will!'

'Stay out of this, Robert,' snapped Will, turning on him.

'All right,' said Robert, holding up his hands and coming to a halt. Two knights came out of the chapter house. They stopped as they saw Will holding Garin against the wall. Robert smiled at them. 'Brothers,' he explained, cocking his head towards Will and Garin. 'Haven't seen one another in a while. Emotional reunion.'

The knights walked on after a pause.

'I don't have the book if that's what you're after,' Garin told Will quickly. 'I never tried to get it from the Hospitaller. I don't know where it is.'

'The book?' Will's voice was low, hardly more than a whisper, but his eyes were blazing. 'You think I give a shit about that?'

Garin cried out as Will's hands dug into his flesh.

'The whorehouse,' said Will, forcing the words through his teeth. 'The poison you gave me.'

'I'm sorry for that!' exclaimed Garin, trying to push Will away. 'But I had to do something. Rook wanted to kill you! He would have if I hadn't drugged you.'

Will grabbed two fistfuls of Garin's mantle. 'The girl,' he snarled in the knight's face. 'What about her? Are you going to tell me you're sorry for leaving me in bed with a whore?'

Garin stopped struggling. 'What?'

'Don't even try to deny it!'

'I don't know what you're talking about!'

As Will went for his sword, Robert sprang forwards and grabbed his arm. Will twisted away, but Robert held him fast.

'*I'm going to kill you!*' Will yelled at Garin.

Garin slid out from between Will and the wall and backed away. 'I didn't leave you in bed with anyone, I swear!'

'You expect me to believe that when you had me meet you in a whorehouse?'

Garin faltered. 'Adela,' he said finally. 'That was why we had you meet us there. I had been going to her for a few months. Rook just wanted to get you out of the preceptory.'

'You were bedding her?'

Garin was still. 'I loved her.'

Will began to laugh. It was a harsh sound that made Garin flinch as if struck. The laughter became a choked cry. 'Don't you *dare* talk to me about love!'

Robert had to use all his strength to restrain Will from drawing the falchion.

'Elwen saw me with that girl. I lost her because of you, you *bastard!*'

'I don't know anything about any girl, I promise you.' Garin held up his hands. 'Will, none of this was my fault. I didn't want to do it. Rook made me.' He spoke in a rush. 'Rook wanted the book, not me. I don't know how he knew of it, but he somehow found out that my uncle had been involved with Everard. He came to me in Paris and made me tell him everything I knew, everything my uncle had told me. He said he was going to use it against the Temple. Will, he threatened to rape and kill my mother if I didn't do as he said.' Garin's face crumpled and his eyes filled with tears. 'You have no idea what he's capable of. But I've left him now. He can't threaten me anymore. I'll do anything you want to make this right! Tell me and I'll do it!'

Will stared at Garin: the bloodstains on his mantle; his raised hands; his tear-filled eyes. He stared at the man who had filled him with such hatred and saw only the scared little boy who used to lie about the bruises on his face. All the tension in his body drained, leaving him weak and shaking. 'I want nothing from you.' Brushing Robert's hands aside, Will walked away.

38

The Walls, Antioch

14 May 1268 AD

They couldn't take their eyes off it. For the last two hours they had watched it come; an incredible, awful sight, like a wave rearing far out to sea that the people on the shore can only stand and wait for as it washes in to flood houses, overwhelm fields, drown children. Their hope lay behind them in the castles and armouries of the knights, where men donned helmets, fastened chainmail, strapped on swords. Their doom lay ahead, marching through the valley in a wide golden line, making a new river beside the Orontes. For the citizens of Antioch, one of the five most holy sees of Christendom, the approach of the Mamluk army was by far the more arresting view.

'What the hell are they doing up there?'

Will, helping to guide a mangonel into place, glanced round to see Lambert, the young officer in charge of their company, pointing to a group of people on the tower next to theirs. Will could tell by their dress that they weren't soldiers. Bishops, or nobles, he guessed, by the cut of their silks. 'Praying probably,' he said, going over to Lambert as the sergeants manoeuvred the siege engine into position.

Lambert turned to Will. 'I've seen children on the walls this morning, throwing stones into the valley, trying to hit the enemy. They'll wind up dead, or in our way. Someone should be marshalling them, getting them inside their houses, or up to the citadel.'

'I agree,' said Will, 'but there aren't enough soldiers for the walls, let alone for keeping order.' He looked down into the valley where the Mamluk army was steadily approaching, then back at the nobles clustered on the tower. 'It might work in our favour, you know. The Mamluks will think we have more troops than we do.'

'It will just give them more targets to aim at.' Lambert cupped his hands around his mouth. 'Hey!' he yelled at the nobles. A few of them looked in

his direction. 'Get down, you fools!' He swore when they turned their
backs on him.

'They'll soon move when the arrows start flying,' said Robert, coming
over.

'Where's Simon?' asked Will.

'Settling the horses. They're getting skittish now they can hear the
drums.'

'I know how they feel,' muttered Lambert.

They all did. The sound, which had begun as a faint throbbing like a
tremor in the earth then had risen with the Mamluk's approach to a
rhythmic, maddening thudding, was viscerally disturbing. The Mamluk
army had thirty bands, each of which was ruled over by an officer called the
Lord of the Drums. The knights on the walls could just about make out
these companies now: tiny men beating tiny drums that made an enormous
noise.

'How is Simon?' Will asked Robert.

'Don't ask. Every time I try and say something to comfort him, he runs
off to piss. I'm thinking, if he goes much more, we can open a sluice-gate
and drown the bastards.' Robert rested his hands on the parapet. 'Can't say
I blame him though.'

The three of them watched as the head of the army funnelled through the
valley mouth and swelled into the plain. At the vanguard came the heavy
cavalry – armoured men on armoured horses, bearing spears and swords.
Each regiment was marked by the different colours of their surcoats: blue,
jade, crimson, purple, and, at the head, the yellow-gold of the Bahri, whose
cloaks glittered in the morning sun.

Companies of mounted archers flanked the cavalry and behind them
marched a solid mass of infantry: men carrying shields slung over their
shoulders; nakkabun with their mining tools; soldiers with barrels of deadly
naphtha. In the midst of the infantry lines, camels loaded with medical
supplies, weapons, food and water were herded alongside siege engines that
were being hauled up the valley by the companies who would prime and fire
them in the battle. The Mamluks, an older knight had told Will and the
others, gave these weapons names like the Victorious, the Leveller, the
Bull. On hearing this, the company of ten knights and seven sergeants under
Lambert, had christened their two engines – a mangonel and an espringale,
which was smaller and fired javelins rather than stones. One they called the
Undefeated and the other, Sultan-Killer.

'I reckon they'll set up their main camp down there,' said Lambert, pointing to a flat strip of land the gold-clad Bahri were moving towards, like a pride of lions. 'Well out of range,' he added.

Will glanced round as the nobles on the opposite tower began to leave, heading along the walkway towards the ramparts that curled steeply around Mount Silpius to the citadel. For several hours, since the alarm had been raised, little streams of people had been winding their way up the mountain towards the fortress. But many citizens, as Lambert had complained, had been milling about in the city; gathering on corners to chatter fearfully with their neighbours; going to the walls to watch the soldiers come; staying home to nail timber over doors and bury coins and land-deeds in holes in their gardens. The only ones with any apparent sense of purpose or urgency were the companies of men heading for their posts.

All along the walls, mounted on the towers, were little groups like theirs: Hospitallers, Teutonic Knights from the Kingdom of Germany, Syrian and Armenian soldiers, city guard under Simon Mansel. But only half the towers were occupied and the eighteen-mile-long perimeter seemed conspicuously empty. The walls, for the most part, were in good repair and any weaker sections had been more heavily manned where possible.

At the last war council, called yesterday, the Templar and Hospitaller Masters, in a rare show of unity, had expressed concerns over an area near the Tower of the Two Sisters, where the wall began its steep march up the slopes of the mountain. Constable Mansel, however, had already allocated all of his men and had refused to spare anyone for the task.

Mansel had been confident that Baybars would be persuaded to listen to reason. After all, he had reminded the sceptical commanders, the Mamluks had been turned away once before with just a few wagons of treasure. Whilst the constable had drawn up settlements for negotiation, it had been left to the Templar Master to redirect Lambert's company from St George's Gate to the area concerned. Will, on seeing the section that ran from the Tower of the Two Sisters up the spine of Mount Silpius, hadn't been able to see how the Mamluks could easily storm the walls from the treacherous terrain below. But, then, he had never been involved in a siege.

It had been a shock to discover, when the army had appeared, that all his years of training apparently counted for nothing. He and the others of his company had been breaking their fast in one of the tower's bare, cobwebbed chambers that was littered with bat droppings when the alarm had sounded. They had raced up the spiralled stairs to the battlements, hands on swords. And there they had stopped. Hand to hand, face to face, they could fight, but from the tower top they had only been able to watch and wait as the Mamluks advanced.

The older knights, those who had fought most of their lives in campaigns in Outremer, were calm, preparing themselves and their weapons. The younger men were restless; joking nervously one moment, snapping at the slightest annoyance the next, skittish like their horses, which were stabled in a potter's workshop Lambert had commandeered outside the tower that was to be their home for the next few days, weeks, or possibly months.

Will took a drink from his water skin and adjusted his sword belt. He felt the need to have the weapon in his hand, to strike out at something tangible. His anticipation was reverberating inside him like the Mamluks' drums, setting him on edge. Four knights came out onto the battlements, carrying javelins for the espringale. Among them was Garin. As they locked gazes, Garin lingered for a moment on the battlements, then moved off across the walkway to the other tower where they had set the espringale.

Robert shook his head. 'Eighteen miles of wall and they put him here?'

Gripping the hilt of his falchion, Will turned to Lambert. 'Is there anything I can do?'

Lambert nodded. 'Same as the rest of us. You can wait.'

The Mamluk Camp, Antioch, 14 May 1268 AD

The sun was going down in the west as the eunuchs finished washing Baybars' feet and patted his skin dry with fresh linen cloths. When they were done, he rose and descended the throne platform that had been erected inside the royal pavilion. The wings of the pavilion had been pinned back and a space cleared outside it. His governors were waiting, barefoot, on a strip of springy turf where prayer mats had been laid out.

Baybars faced Mecca. The walls of Antioch occupied his vision, but as he stood with his men and began to chant the words of the first sura of the Koran they seemed to fade into the vista and become nothing more than rock and sand.

In the name of God, most Gracious, most Merciful. All praise is for God, the Lord and Sustainer of all the worlds!

When their prayers were done, the Mamluks rose and continued with their tasks; unloading supplies from the camels; erecting tents; priming the engines; lighting fires; preparing for the evening's feast. Tomorrow was the first day of the holy month of Ramadan and for the next four weeks they would fast during daylight hours.

'My lord.'

Baybars turned as Omar came towards him, moving around the servants who were rolling up the prayer mats. 'Have you relayed my orders to the governors?'

'I have, my lord. Everyone knows their positions.' Omar paused. 'Except for me.'

'I want you at the rear with the engines.'

'The rear?'

'You heard me,' said Baybars, ignoring his hurt look. Over the last few campaigns he had been placing Omar further and further back from the front lines. Whereas he feared little for his own safety, he had, during these past years, become increasingly concerned with the welfare of his friends. Perhaps because he had so few of them.

'Sadeek,' protested Omar in a low voice, 'if you insist on leading this battle, I want to be at your side. Didn't you listen to what Khadir said?'

Baybars raised an eyebrow. 'I thought it was you who never listened to Khadir.'

'I do when he says he fears a threat on your life. A threat within the city.'

'Khadir could not be specific about the nature of it and so I'm inclined to believe it is nothing more than the general desire of the Franks to be rid of me. He was, however, certain that the signs for the battle itself are auspicious. I will take the more confident prediction. Khadir is always unsettled so near his home,' Baybars added, referring to the Assassins' stronghold of Masyaf in the Jabal Bahra Mountains – the place and Order Khadir had been exiled from.

'Do you have to lead the battle though, my lord?'

Baybars' jaw tightened. 'When I let others lead a force against this city, they were turned around by a petty offering. We do not accept gifts from the Franks, Omar.'

'My Lord Sultan.'

Baybars looked round to see Kalawun approaching. With him was a commander of one of the regiments.

Kalawun bowed to Baybars. 'Can I speak with you?'

'Yes,' said Baybars. 'We were finished, weren't we, Omar?'

After a pause, Omar inclined his head. 'We were, my lord.'

Baybars waited until he had gone, then turned to the two men. 'Are you set?'

'Yes, my lord,' replied Kalawun.

'Good. I want you both in position by morning.'

'Then with your permission, we will go now, my lord,' said the commander.

'You have it.' As they went to leave, Baybars called Kalawun to wait. 'Allah be with you,' he said quietly.

Kalawun's strong-boned face creased in a faint smile. 'I fear it is you who will need God's protection, my lord. My task, I expect, will be simple by comparison.'

'That will depend on whether you meet resistance and the longer you remain, the more likely that will become, either from the Templars at Baghras and La Roche Guillaume, or from Cilicia.'

'We hit the Armenians hard last year,' said Kalawun quietly. 'I doubt they could muster any great force.'

'Do not doubt anything, Kalawun. When we left Tripoli unscathed, Prince Bohemond would have certainly entertained the concern that we would come here. He may be able to marshal an effective army from the remnants of the kingdom in time, although I don't intend to spend enough of it here to allow him the opportunity.'

There was the sound of a commotion and a small dark shape came rushing towards them out of the shadows. Kalawun went to step in front of Baybars, then saw that it was the sultan's son. Hastening after Baraka Khan, puffing and panting, was his tutor, a retired commander called Sinjar whom Kalawun had suggested as a suitable mentor for the boy. There was a large red stain on the front of Sinjar's white tunic. For a moment, Baybars thought he had been wounded, then realised that it was too pale for blood. Baraka skidded to a halt, breathing hard.

'Why aren't you studying?' Baybars demanded of the seven-year-old. He looked questioningly at Sinjar, who bowed, trying to catch his breath.

'Apologies, my lord, we were embarking on a simple algebraic problem. When Baraka couldn't solve it, he became angry and threw a jug of cordial over me.' Sinjar gestured to his stained tunic. 'I went to punish him and he ran from me.'

Baraka glared at his tutor. 'Sinjar was going to beat me, father.'

'As well he should,' said Baybars, swinging his son roughly into his arms. 'I don't want to hear of any more trouble from you, do you understand?'

Baraka pouted. 'Yes, father,' he muttered.

Baybars nodded to Sinjar. 'Leave him with me.'

'My lord.'

'If you refuse to attend to your studies,' said Baybars to his son, as Sinjar left, 'then you can help me instead.' He half smiled at Kalawun. 'Perhaps we should put him to work on one of the mandjaniks?'

Kalawun returned the smile. 'Perhaps.' He ruffled Baraka's hair. 'Although I'm not sure that is fitting work for the heir to the throne and my future son-in-law.'

Baraka pouted even more. Baybars had told him that he would be marrying Kalawun's daughter in a few years, when he was old enough. Baraka hoped his father would put *her* to work on one of the mandjaniks. She might have an accident and end up tossed over the wall into the city. He grinned at the thought as Kalawun bowed to Baybars and headed off across the camp to where a battalion was waiting. 'Where is Amir Kalawun going, father?'

'Into the mountains,' replied Baybars, carrying his son into the pavilion. Since Baraka had left the harem and the clutches of his wives, he had begun to find the child an oddly pleasant distraction from the strains of leadership.

'Why?'

Baybars, ignoring the eunuchs, bodyguards and advisors in the pavilion, set his son down on a rug and picked up a silver dish of figs. 'I'll show you,' he said, crouching down and putting a fig into Baraka's little fist. He placed three of the fruits in a triangle on the rug. 'This is Antioch,' he told his son, pointing to the fig at the bottom right-hand point of the triangle. 'The one above is the Syrian Gates, where Kalawun is going.' He pointed to the apex of the triangle. 'Kalawun will prevent any aid coming to the Christians from the north.' He moved his finger to the fig at the bottom left. 'This is the port of St Symeon. I've sent a second battalion to capture it. They will prevent any reinforcements coming from the coast.'

'What will you do, father?'

Baybars smiled. Taking the fig that was Antioch, he popped it into his mouth. Baraka laughed.

'My Lord Sultan!'

Baybars rose as a Bahri warrior entered the pavilion.

The warrior bowed. 'Someone is coming from the city.'

'Who?' said Baybars, glancing down at Baraka, who was squashing the remaining figs into the rug with his fist.

'A company, led by their constable. They came out of the north-west gate.'

Baybars and his advisors followed the warrior out of the pavilion. A tiny snake of torchlight was making its way down from the walls where other fires were now flickering. 'Go and meet them,' said Baybars to the warrior. 'Disarm them and bring them to me. I expect they think to negotiate.'

'I have come to parley!' insisted Simon Mansel as he was marched forcibly into the royal pavilion by two Mamluk warriors, his troop of guards having been rounded up, their weapons taken. 'You will free me at once if you wish to hear my terms!' He repeated this last demand in broken Arabic.

'Your terms?' questioned Baybars, his deep voice causing Mansel to fall silent and look warily up at the throne. Baybars studied the corpulent constable as he was brought before the dais. The man was clad in a sumptuous silk robe and turban and was dripping with jewels. 'I do not believe you are in a position to offer any.' When Mansel looked uncertainly at him, Baybars gestured to one of his staff. 'Translate my words to the constable.'

The translator came forward and spoke.

'Now tell him to kneel,' added Baybars.

Mansel looked affronted by the request, but had no choice but to comply as the two Mamluk warriors holding his arms pushed him to the ground. Out of the corner of his eye, he noticed a small boy crouching behind a mesh screen to one side of the tent. As he turned, the boy stuck out his tongue and giggled. Ignoring the boy, Mansel looked to the translator.

'Tell your sultan that I have arranged for wagons of gold and jewels to be delivered to him if he stands down and leads his army from our walls. He has until tomorrow to accept these terms. It will be my only offer.'

Baybars' expression didn't change as the translator spoke. 'Gold? You think to placate me with such a worthless offering?'

'Worthless?' scoffed Mansel, when the question was relayed. 'I can assure you that . . .'

'Gold means nothing to me,' said Baybars, not waiting for the constable's words to be translated. 'There is only one thing that will turn my army aside and will secure your life and the lives of every man, woman and child in your city. Surrender. Tell your knights to open the gates of the city, the city the Franks took for themselves one hundred and seventy years ago. Tell them to lay down arms and let us in. Once we have taken the city, you will leave, all of you, and never return. Antioch is lost to you; to all Christians.'

'I will not accept those terms!' Mansel began in an outraged tone. 'There are thousands within the city. Where will they go? I cannot simply ask them all to leave their homes, their livestock! What about the sick? The young and infirm? Take what I have offered and be satisfied with . . .'

He trailed off as Baybars rose from the throne and motioned to one of the Bahri standing by the entrance. Mansel didn't understand what was said, but he flinched with fear as Baybars drew one of his sabres and came down the steps of the dais towards him.

'If you hurt me you will get nothing! Nothing, tell him!' he cried to the translator. '*Tell him!*'

There was a noise behind him. Mansel looked round to see his guards being forced into the tent by seven Bahri warriors.

'Take my son out of here,' Baybars ordered one of his eunuchs.

Baraka cried out and kicked at the attendant as he was picked up and carried from the tent.

Mansel's six guards looked fearful as they were lined up in front of the dais, glancing uncertainly to the constable. The Bahri forced the troop to their knees.

'What are you doing?' said Mansel to Baybars.

The blue-eyed sultan didn't reply, but walked up to the first of the guards, a young man with wide brown eyes and a freckled face. Grabbing a fistful of the man's hair, Baybars wrenched back his head and sliced the edge of his sabre across the man's throat. Blood spurted in a wide arc, splattering the steps of the dais.

'Dear God!' cried Mansel as the young man slumped sideways, blood pumping from his neck.

He hadn't even had a chance to scream. The remaining guards were shouting at the sultan and at the Bahri. Two, in terror, tried to run, but they were soon pushed back into their places by the soldiers who came forward, blades drawn.

Baybars turned to Mansel, his sabre streaked with blood. Some of it had sprayed onto his yellow-gold cloak, obscuring the inscriptions from the Koran. 'Do you concede to my demands? Or will you let more of your men die? It is up to you. The lives of your men for your city. That is what I offer you.'

Mansel didn't need a translator to know what was said. 'You heartless bastard,' he said in a low, bitter voice.

The translator went to speak, then looked at Baybars and thought better of it.

Baybars went to another of Mansel's guards. This one did scream as the sultan pulled back his head, exposing his throat to the blade. He struggled, trying to twist away, but two Bahri came forward to hold him still.

'Your man or your city?' demanded Baybars, looking to Mansel. 'Which is more important to you? Decide!'

The translator spoke quickly.

'I will not be threatened like this!' insisted Mansel.

'*Captain!*' shouted the guard.

Baybars' eyes narrowed as the translator told him the constable's response. His jaw tightened as he slashed the blade across the guard's throat. This one took longer to die, writhing around on the floor beside his fallen comrade, gurgling spouts of blood and pressing his hands vainly to his cut throat.

Mansel averted his gaze.

'Finish it,' said Baybars gruffly, gesturing to the agonised guard.

One of the Bahri stepped forward and stabbed down.

'I'll see you burn in hell for this!' said Mansel hoarsely to Baybars.

'Do you accept my terms?'

'*I do not!*' roared the constable.

His response resulted in a third dead guard.

'Enough!' snapped Baybars. He strode to Mansel, his sabre dripping blood.

Mansel tried to scrabble to his feet, but the Bahri were on him in seconds. '*No!*' he cried as Baybars towered over him, grabbing his hair. 'My wife is a cousin of Prince Bohemond's princess!' he shouted in Arabic. 'My ransom is worth more than my death to you!'

'Only your city is worth anything to me. Surrender it now, or I will cut your head from your body and have it tossed over Antioch's walls to show your citizens the price of refusal.' Baybars pressed the blade to the squirming, roaring man's throat. '*Surrender!*'

'*I accept!*' shrieked Mansel, as the blade cut into him. A hot trickle of blood dribbled down his neck. 'I accept your demands! I surrender the city!'

'Take him to the walls,' growled Baybars, stepping back from the constable and addressing the Bahri. 'Have him relay this command to his garrison. Ready the men. We will go in tonight.'

With that, Simon Mansel, Constable of Antioch, was marched up to St George's Gate where, in a tremulous voice, he ordered the garrison of the city, and all the garrisons of the military Orders, to stand down.

A short time later, whilst Baybars was cleaning his hands in a basin, one of the Bahri warriors he had sent to escort Mansel entered. The bodies of the guards had been removed and the eunuchs were on their knees, cleaning blood from the dais steps.

'My Lord Sultan.'

Baybars reached for a cloth to dry his hands. 'Is it done?'

'Mansel gave the order, as requested.'

'Have they opened the gates?'

'No, my lord,' replied the Bahri warrior. 'The garrison of Antioch refused Mansel's order. They will not surrender the city.'

39

The Walls, Antioch

18 May 1268 AD

S imon picked up a brown, wrinkled orange from the rations that had been laid out. 'How long is this going to go on for?' he said suddenly, turning to Will.

Will was surprised by the abruptness of his tone. 'If Mansel manages to persuade the commanders to surrender it might be over soon.' He seated himself on a barrel. His watch had just finished and he was exhausted. Outside, dawn was breaking. A pale light was starting to fill the doorway, but the circular, windowless chamber at the base of the tower would remain gloomy for the rest of the day. 'I'm not sure he will though,' he added, yawning.

Twice, Constable Mansel had been led up to the gates and twice the city's garrison had refused his demand to surrender. Yesterday, the men on the walls had watched, warily, as the Mamluk army had started to spread out around the city, some battalions moving north towards the river, others south to the slopes of the mountain. One regiment had set up their engines facing the two towers occupied by Lambert's company.

Simon dropped the orange onto the table. 'I'm not talking about the battle,' he said roughly. 'I'm talking about you and me.'

Will frowned. 'What do you mean?'

'Nothing,' muttered Simon. 'Forget I said anything.'

'No,' said Will, crossing to Simon. 'If you have something to say, then say it.'

Simon lowered his eyes. 'Really. It's nothing.'

'Yes, it is,' said Will harshly. 'You haven't spoken to me in days. Every time I come near you, you make some excuse to leave. You're still blaming me, aren't you? For us being here?'

'Don't,' said Simon, shaking his head. 'I don't want to fight.'

'I never asked you to come, Simon.'

'No, I got posted, remember?'

'Not to Antioch, to Outremer. Back in Orléans I told you to stay if you didn't want to come, but that I'd made up my mind.'

'To get Nicolas,' said Simon, nodding his head vigorously, 'to get Everard's book. That's what you'd made up your mind to do. You didn't come here to fight a war!'

'Well, I'm in one. And so are you.' Will thrust his finger towards the wall, beyond which was the Mamluk camp. 'Those men killed my father. Perhaps even the one who hacked his head from his shoulders is out there.'

'You've been so cold,' said Simon quietly. 'We don't talk, or laugh like we used to.'

'I'm not exactly in a laughing mood.'

'You do with Robert and the others! I feel like I'm here on my own. You don't know how frightening it is to know what's out there and know you can't fight it. You don't know what it's like to not be able to defend the people you . . .' Simon hung his head. '. . . people you care about.'

'Why avoid me if you feel so alone?'

Simon looked away, then back at him again. 'I want to go back to the way things were.' He gave Will a tentative smile. 'Like when you was teaching me to sword-fight in Paris.'

'I can't go back.'

'Why?'

'Because I no longer have what I had then.'

'What you had then?' echoed Simon in a small voice.

'I had my father, or, at least, the chance of seeing him again. I had Elwen. I had no hatred inside me, either towards a man who was once my closest friend, or towards men I've never met. I didn't know anything of war, or the . . .' Will trailed off, slumping on the barrel. 'I didn't know any of it,' he finished, looking up at Simon. 'I had hope.'

'You can still have hope,' Simon insisted, going to him.

'Hope of what? I failed as a brother, as a son. I cannot go back to what I was before. There is nothing left for me there.'

'But what will you do? Stay here and fight and die?'

Will didn't answer. Following Simon's question was a long, wailing cry. Others joined it, swelling into a strident, relentless sound that pierced the dawn and their ears.

'What is it?' said Simon, turning pale.

'I don't know.' Will ran for the stairs as he heard running footsteps and shouts from above. 'The trumpets of the watch?'

His words were answered by a series of incoherent yells. Then something hit the walls. The whole tower shuddered with the impact and a shower of masonry came down in the street outside. Will started up the stairs.

'What do I do?' Simon shouted after him.

'Go to the horses.'

'Will!'

Will paused on the stairs and looked back. 'What?'

Simon stared at him, then swallowed thickly and shook his head. 'Nothing.' He stood there for a moment after Will had disappeared, until there was another violent thud against the walls and he hurried out into the street to the potter's workshop as more dust and loose rock pattered down.

Will was racing up the stairs. 'What's happening?' he demanded of a sergeant coming down. 'Are they attacking our section?'

'All sections, sir,' stammered the sergeant, hurrying past him. 'They're attacking all sections!'

Will hastened onto the battlements, where Robert, half dressed, was helping Lambert and two other knights prime the mangonel with one of the stones they had hauled up the side of the tower in slings. They were straining with the weight of it. Will ran to help, but was halted by the sight beyond the battlements. The Mamluks, who had moved into their assault positions under the cover of night, blanketed the plain and the mountain slopes in a seething mass of bright cloaks and turbans, horses, spears, ladders, rams and catapults.

As Will watched, the three mandjaniks closest to their section were fired, the beams whipping up to strike the crossbars, slinging three huge stones towards the wall between the two towers. They smashed into the stone, shaking the towers to their foundations and sending razor shards of rock flying. There was a cry from the adjacent tower and Will saw one of the knights go down, hit by this lethal debris. Garin was there, priming the espringale. Will came out of his shock and rushed to Robert and Lambert's aid as Garin fired the engine, sending a javelin shooting into the heart of the Mamluk forces. Will didn't wait to see if it hit anything, but grabbed one of the mangonel's ropes and yanked the beam free.

All along the walls, with the exception of the precipitous mountain summit and the boggy borders of the Orontes where the terrain was impassable, the assault had begun. The thumps and crashes of stones were as steady and resonant as the drumbeats, echoing through the valley, one after another, like giant rolls of thunder. Pots of fiery naphtha were hurled onto the walls, setting men and siege engines alight. Other Mamluk companies catapulted flaming barrels of pitch from their engines that flew up from the ground like comets to explode on tower tops in blossoms of fire that lit up the dawn sky. Hollow arrowheads filled with naphtha and black sulphur burst into flame as they sailed through the air. Men crumpled to their knees, struck by these missiles, others fell screaming from the walls, hair and flesh burning, and, on one section, a whole company of Hospitallers were crushed by a stone.

Antioch's forces kept up a valiant defence: cutting down the ladders the Mamluks set against the walls; firing volleys of arrows into the infantry who answered with clay bullets shot from slings; hurling boulders into the cavalry to break horses and men.

But Justinian's walls, although godlike in their proportions, were not enough, alone, to hold back a determined force. Over the centuries they had yielded to the Persians, the Arabs, the Byzantines, the Turks and the Franks. That they would yield again was inevitable. It was simply a question of when.

'We need some men up there!' yelled Lambert, pointing up the mountain slopes to a section half a mile or so away, which was empty of soldiers. The Mamluks were concentrating seven mandjaniks on it and already a sizeable hole had appeared in the wall's centre, although too high to allow the waiting infantry through. More Mamluks, seeing the opportunity, were heading in that direction, led by a group of cavalry, wearing yellow-gold cloaks.

'Bahri!' shouted one of the older knights on the adjacent tower, pointing at the riders.

'Dear God, it's him,' murmured Lambert, going to the parapet. His gaze was on a large man clad in gold robes and gleaming armour, riding a black charger at the head of the Royal Guard.

'Who?' panted Will, hauling another stone into the mangonel's cavity and jumping back as two knights fired it.

'The Crossbow,' answered Lambert. 'Where's our damned troops?' he roared over the city-side of the battlements, where people were watching fearfully from the windows of their houses. Down below, he caught sight of Simon in the doorway of the potter's workshop.

'Saddle the horses!' he shouted to the groom.

Simon disappeared at once.

Will went to the edge and watched Baybars ride up the slope towards the breach. He felt a strange thrill looking at the Mamluk sultan; he couldn't tell whether it was fear, or anticipation. Some citizens on the ramparts that led up to the citadel had seen the danger and were jumping up and down, waving their arms and shouting down to Lambert's company.

Lambert muttered beneath his breath.

Another hole appeared in the wall as a stone went sailing through and landed in the pasture beyond.

'What do we do?' shouted Will, ducking as a hail of arrows came whizzing over his head.

Lambert was looking around helplessly. 'Shit!'

Will grabbed him by the shoulders. 'Lambert! What do we do?'

'We go up there,' said a voice behind them.

Will turned to see Garin. His hair was plastered to his head with sweat and his face and mantle were filthy. His sword was in his hand.

'We get the horses,' Garin told Will and Lambert, 'and we go up there and fight them back until more men get here.'

'It's too late!' said Robert. 'Look!'

The three of them turned to see the wall crumbling. There was a distant roaring sound as it fell, taking two towers with it in a soaring pall of dust and rubble.

'Mother of God,' said Lambert in a faint voice, as the Mamluks, led by Baybars Bundukdari, surged forward into the billowing clouds.

'They're through! They're through!' one of the knights starting shouting over the battlements. A trumpet was blown from a Hospitaller company who had also seen the towers crumble. Others took up the sound and led it around the walls. The Mamluks were coming. The city had fallen.

Lambert came to his senses. 'Down!' he shouted to the knights and sergeants. 'To the horses!'

Leaving the engines, the company raced through the tower, pausing to grab helmets and shields from one of the chambers. They ran out into the rubble-strewn street where Simon was leading three of the horses he had managed to saddle. He was pale, but talking softly to the animals who were tossing their heads and snorting. Four of the sergeants ran into the large workshop to help saddle the others. The potter was there, his wife and three daughters huddled behind him.

'What is happening?' he demanded.

Lambert whirled on him. 'Get to safety, you fool!'

'They're coming!' warned one of the knights, pointing up the mountain.

Looking up to where the knight was pointing, the group of Templars and the potter and his family saw the Mamluk heavy cavalry fanning out across the slopes. They would hit the city from different points. In their gold, scarlet and purple cloaks they looked like streams of lava pouring from a volcano. Some carried torches and bows, but most their long, gleaming swords that were inlaid with gold and covered with Arabic inscriptions.

The potter grabbed his terrified wife and daughters and bundled them up the stairs through a trapdoor at the back of the workshop, which he slammed shut behind him. Other people, who had come out into the streets, began to run. Cries of terror rose as those clustered at the windows of houses saw the Mamluks thundering towards the city, scattering sheep and cutting down families who had been making their way up the slopes to the citadel.

Will realised that his hands were shaking. He wrapped one of them around the hilt of his falchion and the quakes ceased. 'Come on!' he shouted, as much to himself as anyone else. Running to a horse, he hauled himself into the saddle. A knight passed him a shield. Garin and Lambert followed suit, as did two others, taking two more mounts from the sergeants.

'Where do we go?' shouted one knight to Lambert. 'Where's the front line?'

The young officer, white and tight-lipped, turned in his saddle. 'We are the front line!' He raised his sword as the first Mamluks reached the streets ahead. '*Deus vult!*' He kicked his heels into the horse and charged forth to meet them, sword whirling.

Will heard Simon shout his name as he followed with Garin and the other two knights. He realised that he wasn't wearing a helmet, but it was too late to do anything about that now. He raised his sword and the first light of the rising sun was caught in the blade. It was a Scottish blade, born to lochs and moors and rain, far from these dusty, sun-bleached mountains. It was a clan blade, wielded by his father and grandfather. Tears were snatched from his eyes as he urged his horse on and he found himself crying out as one of the Bahri, gold cloak flying, came rushing to meet him. '*For the Campbells! For the Campbells!*'

The impact was brutal. All those practice runs on the jousting field were nothing when compared to it. A controlled blow designed to unhorse an opponent could never feel the same as one intended to kill. Thrown backwards, Will would have been tossed from his saddle if his knees hadn't gripped the horse's flanks with all his strength. As he pulled himself upright, dazed and bruised, the Mamluk had gone, there was a splintered gash through his shield and another Bahri warrior was almost upon him. He swung his sword round, leaned forward and struck. The falchion, with its rusted crossguard and frayed wire bands, caught the Mamluk on the upper arm, between his hauberk and vambrace. The man screamed as blood spurted from the wound and, losing control of his horse, he was carried off into the current of men who were flowing around Will, Garin and the other Templars and pressing into the city.

Among them was a large man on a black charger. Will caught a flash of blue eyes and bared teeth as Baybars swept past only yards to his left, then another blade came swinging towards him. It glanced off his shield and cut into the neck of his horse. As the animal reared, an armoured Mamluk horse collided with it, knocking it sideways and throwing Will from the saddle. His stirrup snagged his foot and he cried out as his horse crashed down on top of him. Somewhere above him, Lambert screamed.

Simon was in the doorway of the potter's workshop when he saw Will and Lambert go down. Robert and the other knights and sergeants, who hadn't had time to saddle more horses, had rushed to the shelter of the buildings when the first Mamluks came cantering through the streets. They had shouted at the people who were trying to flee the area to do the same. Some had listened and piled into towers, or pressed themselves against walls. Others, in blind panic, had kept on running. They had been cut down by the first soldiers, skulls and backs cleaved by the swords, and trampled by those who followed. Robert had drawn his sword and was standing in front of Simon. One Mamluk rider had taken a swipe at them, but most were ignoring the scattered knights and citizens to push further into the city. Cries of *Allahu akbar* rose above the din of hooves and screams of inhabitants.

Simon, watching dumbstruck as the way ahead filled with Mamluks, shouted when he saw Will thrown from the saddle. He pushed past Robert and ran out into the street. Robert yelled a warning as two riders bore down on the groom. Simon dropped to his knees and covered his head with his hands and the swords of the riders lashed the air where he had been, missing his head by inches. Robert darted out when they had passed and dragged him back into the doorway. Simon fought against him, shouting Will's name.

'You can't help him!' Robert was startled by the groom's violence. He slammed Simon against the doorframe. 'You'll be cut down like a sapling, you idiot!'

'He can't die!' cried Simon, trying to shove Robert away. His brown eyes were wide and wild. Tears were coursing down his cheeks. 'It's my fault he's here! *It's my fault!*'

The Mamluks were still thundering past them. Screams, near and distant, rose on the air, along with the first plumes of smoke as soldiers tossed torches onto rooftops.

'What the hell are you talking about?' shouted Robert to Simon.

'Elwen wouldn't have left if she'd known about the drug. I lied so she would leave him. I lied to end them. He'd have lost his mantle if he'd married her! But I never meant for us to come here!' Simon choked the words through his sobs. 'I knew he'd never . . . But I . . .!' He struck Robert's chest with his fists, but he had no more strength. 'I loved him longer than *she* did!'

Robert stared at Simon, bewildered, as behind them there came a shout from the street.

Simon lifted his head, recognising the voice. Through his tears, he saw a blurred white rider coming towards them. His vision cleared and he realised that there were two knights astride the horse. Garin, his sword bloodied, was at the front and Will was seated behind. Robert shouted in surprise and joy. With them was one of the two knights who had ridden out from their company and ten Teutonic Knights in their white tunics with black crosses, several of whom were wounded. The street was now empty of Mamluk riders, except for a few lying dead amongst the bodies of the citizens who had tried to flee.

'Lambert?' asked Robert, taking the reins as Garin drew the horse to a stop.

'Dead,' replied Garin, vaulting from the saddle.

The Teutonics were dismounting, some helping their injured comrades. A few of the Templars in Lambert's company, who had remained with Robert, joined them.

'They came to our aid,' said Garin, nodding over his shoulder to the German knights.

'Where are the Mamluks?' said Robert, staring down the now eerily quiet street.

'The cavalry have gone on into the main city,' replied one of the Teutonics, coming over. 'We don't have much time. They will soon take the gates and the rest of the army will enter. We can do nothing.'

'What are you saying?' said Will, slipping down from the saddle. 'That we surrender?'

'I don't believe the Saracens would accept it if we did. We were on the hillside a little way from here. It's not a battle; it's a massacre. They are butchering everyone they find.' The Teutonic wiped blood from a cut on his head that was dripping into his eye. His hand, Will noticed, was trembling.

'We should try and get to the preceptory,' suggested Robert, 'or the citadel.'

'It's too late for that,' replied the Teutonic. He pointed up the street towards the fields where the Mamluks had first come through; the only way left to the citadel from their side of the city. Hundreds of Mamluk infantry were now pushing through the hole in the wall and streaming down the hillside. 'We'll never make it.'

'What do we do?' said one of the sergeants, terrified.

'We run,' replied the Teutonic.

'He's right,' agreed Garin, 'we have no chance if we stay. We'll take one of the tunnels.'

'That's where we're headed,' replied the Teutonic. 'There's one not far from here. It leads under the walls and comes out in a cave below the slopes of Silpius. We can make it if we take the battlements. We'll wait inside the tunnel until nightfall, then escape through the valley.'

'Or we could go north,' said another sergeant, 'to Baghras, or . . .'

'Baybars sent troops that way,' Robert cut across him.

'Let's go!' called one of the Teutonics, slapping the horses away with the flat of his sword.

'Come if you're coming,' said the knight to Will, Garin and Robert. Joining his brothers, he sprinted for the walls.

'If we leave, there'll be no one to help these people,' said Will to Robert. 'We can't run.'

'What else can we do?' responded Robert sharply. 'Wake up,' he said, prodding Simon who was standing stunned against the doorframe. 'Come on!' he called to the others.

Swords drawn, they moved into the street behind the Teutonics who had disappeared inside the tower opposite. A sergeant handed Simon a hammer, which he took numbly.

'Do you want to live, Will?' shouted Robert. He pointed his sword in the direction of the fast-approaching mob of Mamluk soldiers. 'Time to decide!'

Will looked from Robert to the bloodied sword in his hand. At Safed, his father and the knights had chosen death. But Will knew he would find no rest in a grave. He felt unfinished. Everard, Owein, his father, the Temple, the Anima Templi – all of them had pushed him in one direction or another. But he was tired of being told what to fight for, what rule to live by, when he had seen how those rules changed from one man, or group to another and how oaths and promises could be broken without consequence. Peace or war, forgiveness or revenge, whichever he chose would mean nothing unless he chose it for himself. And he wanted to choose. He wanted to live.

'Come on!' Robert shouted to him.

Will began to run.

The city, which had taken the first Crusaders seven months to capture from the Turks, had fallen to Baybars after just four days. Citizens barricaded themselves in their homes, hiding children in cellars and under beds. Others, seeing the plumes of smoke as buildings began to burn, fled their houses for the citadel. Only a handful made it through the lines of troops. A few managed to reach St Peter's Grotto, a cave in the mountainside where the first Christians had worshipped in secret and, later, hidden from persecution. Inside, they huddled together: priests, soldiers, farmers, merchants, prostitutes and infants, breath and sweat filling the darkness, as the city gates fell, one by one, and the Mamluks poured in. Baybars had ordered the gates to be closed behind them to prevent anyone from escaping.

Knights and city guard abandoned their posts as hope and courage left them. Some tried to surrender, but the Mamluks had their orders and everyone found outside was put to the sword. Children, orphaned or forgotten, cried on doorsteps as cavalry came thundering up the street, blades dripping. Muslims who had lived alongside their Christian neighbours for generations begged in Arabic to be spared, but the marauding soldiers were deaf to any pleas. Maddened by battle, stained in the blood of friends and enemies, ears ringing with war cries, the Mamluks took hold of Antioch. And they broke it.

After the initial slaughter and the streets had been emptied of the living, the soldiers stormed the churches and palaces, butchering priests and servants, ransacking rooms for treasures, pissing on altars, tearing down crucifixes, burning the Gospels. And amidst the fire and the killing there was rape and there was torture. In St Peter's Cathedral the tombs of the Patriarchs were opened and the bodies tossed out. Heavy gold rings and jewels clattered to the floor with bones that crumbled, or were crushed to dust beneath the heels of soldiers. An archdeacon, sheltering in the catacombs, was cuffed to the floor as Mamluks pushed past him to get to another tomb. He clung to the leg of one of the warriors, pleading for the bones of his father to be spared the defilement. The soldiers laughed as they dragged the decayed corpse from the tomb and scattered it about the chamber. One soldier then beat the archdeacon to death with his father's rotted skull.

In the centre of the dying city, Baybars had taken over a large Roman villa as his base. As he was bending over a fountain in the courtyard, which was littered with bodies that his men were dragging into a pile, one of his governors came to him. Baybars' sword arm was aching and his thigh was stinging where a Templar had grazed him with a sword point. The air was filled with smoke, his throat was parched.

The governor waited for Baybars to finish washing before he spoke. 'The Christians in the citadel have surrendered, my lord.'

'Tell them we accept. They are to lay down arms and let us in.'

The governor bowed. 'Do we let them go free, my lord?'

'No,' said Baybars, cupping his hand in the fountain and drinking. 'All those left alive in the city will be enslaved. Tomorrow the men can take their pick of them and the rest we will sell.' He looked down as his foot stepped on something. It was a small doll made of cloth. Baybars bent to pick it up, wondering if Baraka might like it. 'And the treasure?' he asked the governor.

'We have taken so much I expect it will have to be handed out by the cartload,' replied the governor.

Baybars turned the doll over in his large hand. He supposed it was more of a girl's toy. As he thought this, he caught sight of a child's body among the pile of corpses. Her black hair was matted with blood. She looked a little younger than his son. Baybars saw that the governor was staring at him. 'What?'

'I just said, my lord,' began the governor cautiously, 'that the treasure will be almost too much to carry, but that I'm sure we will manage.'

'Good.' Baybars seemed to shake himself. 'We'll distribute it and the slaves among the men tomorrow.'

As the governor bowed and left, Khadir came scurrying over. The soothsayer had blood on his grey robes. 'Master,' he said, sinking to the dust and touching Baybars' knee. 'I want a slave.'

Baybars took hold of the soothsayer's chin and lifted his face. 'Where is this threat you foresaw?' He gestured to the burning city. 'It seems you were wrong.'

Khadir's milky eyes glinted in the sunlight that appeared through the tatters of smoke. 'The future gives itself up unwilling, master,' he said sullenly.

Baybars paused, then tossed him the doll. 'Here then. Have yourself a slave.'

Khadir pounced on the doll like a cat with a mouse. He sat back, cradling it in his hands, and made cooing noises as he lifted it to his face to sniff.

Baybars beckoned to one of the Bahri who was standing guard outside the villa's main entrance. 'Bring me a scribe and bring me Mansel. The constable can deliver a message for us. I think Prince Bohemond will want to know the fate of his city.' The warrior disappeared into the villa and Baybars gestured to the men by the pile of corpses. 'Burn those bodies,' he snapped, 'before the flies come.'

40

The Temple, Acre

15 June 1268 AD

Simon was in the stable yard, refilling the horse troughs with fresh water, when he saw Will. The groom set down his pail and wiped his hands on his tunic. His heart was thudding painfully fast and all he wanted to do was slip inside the stables until Will had gone. But he couldn't do that today.

Will looked round as Simon called to him. He smiled and half raised his hand, but not before Simon had seen a fleeting look of irritation cross his face. Simon felt a stabbing sensation in his stomach. The feeling was familiar; he had been getting it each time he saw Will since they were boys in New Temple, but it wasn't so pleasant now, tinged, as it was, with fear.

'What is it?' said Will, as Simon crossed the yard to him.

'How are you?' Simon kept his smile going. 'I haven't seen you for a few days. Not since we got back.'

'I'm fine.' Will glanced up at the sun, which was low in the sky. It had been another hot day and the air was close. The smell of dung and hay from the stables was warm, pungent. 'Did you want something?'

His tone wasn't unfriendly, but the words – so formal – caused another pang to shoot through Simon. 'Everard passed by here earlier, looking for you. He asked me to tell you to go and see him.'

'I will.' Will turned to leave.

'He said it was important,' said Simon despairingly at Will's back.

'I'm sure it can wait a few hours.'

Simon bit his lip. 'Why? Where are you going? It's almost Vespers.'

'I've got things to do.'

'Anything I can help with?'

'No.'

Simon watched Will head off.

Things hadn't been right between them for a while, but it was worse since Antioch. He had a fear of why that might be, but Robert had assured him otherwise.

They had all been affected by the battle and by the journey that followed, but whereas most of the men who had fled Antioch had become more uplifted the closer they came to Acre, Will had grown more and more subdued. Their ragged company had stumbled south through the rocky plains, the sky behind them still tinged with smoke during the day and the darkness creeping thick around them after dusk. On several nights, between the cries of the wounded and the murmurs of men trying to comfort their comrades, Simon had heard Will talking in his sleep. Elwen, he could have sworn he heard Will saying, softly like a sigh.

Elwen.

That name was a stone around Simon's neck, heavy with guilt and fear and envy. He went to pick up his pail, then straightened. 'You know what you have to do,' he muttered to himself. 'Just do it and be done with it!'

Asking one of his fellow sergeants to finish his chores for him, Simon went to see Robert, after stopping by the officials' building.

Robert was in his quarters, washing his hands for Vespers. He frowned as he opened the door and saw Simon holding a quill and parchment. 'What is it?' he asked, as the groom moved past him into the chamber.

'Have you spoken to Will?' questioned Simon, looking about to check that the room was empty.

'I saw him earlier,' said Robert, closing the door.

'No,' said Simon, turning to face him, 'I mean about . . .' He hung his head, then forced himself to raise it. There was no use pretending now; the thing he had kept hidden all these years had already been loosed from its cage. He would just have to hope that his near-death confession to Robert didn't come back and bite him. 'About what I said in Antioch.'

'Oh!' said Robert, looking uncomfortable. 'I gave you my word that I wouldn't.'

'He's been so short with me.'

'It's to be expected. Will has lost a lot over the past few years. His father, Elwen, then Garin's betrayal. He needs time to come to terms with it.'

'I reckon he needs more than that.' Simon hesitated, then held out the parchment and quill to Robert. 'Which is why I need you to do something for me.'

St Mary's Church, Acre, 15 June 1268 AD

Will headed through the Pisan Quarter, along the Street of the Three Magi. Birds spiralled into the rose-pink sky, flying up from the spire of the church of St Andrew where the bells had begun to chime for Vespers. Other churches swiftly took up the call until the whole city echoed with the hollow peals, which, Will had been told, could be heard for a mile out to sea. The buildings that lined the narrow streets glowed in the evening light and any glass in the windows blazed gold, too bright to look at. Will continued walking as the bells faded away. The marketplace was empty, the ground littered with dung, fruit peelings, a lost silk shawl fluttering limply in the hot, salt wind from the harbour.

It was almost midsummer. Back in Paris, the summer fair would soon begin. Already the jousting lists would be set up in the tournament ground. The girls would wear ribbons in their hair.

Will crossed an open square, shaded by a canopy of blue and green cloth, and entered the Venetian Quarter. As a Templar, he had no trouble passing through the gates that separated each of the walled suburbs. When the guards, nodding nonchalantly, had waved him through, he made his way quickly to the church of St Mary. By the time he arrived, the service was almost over and the Eucharist was being administered. He slipped in, recited the Paternoster with the congregation, then waited for them to file out. A few people lingered, kneeling in prayer, as the priest began to clear the tabernacle of the Communion chalice and a dish of crumbs that had been the Host. Will's gaze came to rest on one bowed head in the front benches. He moved down the side aisle, passing an altar dedicated to the Holy Mother, which was encircled by dozens of candles. These votive offerings had been lit all over Acre since Prince Bohemond had sent tidings of Antioch's fall. The news had reached Acre just before Will and the other knights, and they had entered a city already in mourning. Will took a fresh candle from the stack on the floor and lit it with the flame of another. After placing it before the marble statue of the Madonna, who was looking tenderly down at him, he went to the front bench and sat next to the bowed figure.

'Who did you pray for?' asked Garin, raising his head.

Will ignored the question. 'Is everything ready?'

Garin paused, then nodded. 'It's in the vestibule. The priest will let us through.'

'We can trust him?'

'I met him for the first time this evening. It was my informant who wanted to use him.' Garin lowered his voice and watched the priest head through a door off the choir aisle. 'But he seems willing enough to help. The Temple supported Venice during the civil war with the Genoese, who were aided by the Hospital. We apparently saved a brother of his during a street battle.'

'You really think this can work?'

Garin frowned. 'You're not backing out?'

'No, I've lost too much for the sake of this damn book. I want it finished. I just want to make sure you know what you're doing. What about this servant? How do you know he isn't going to lead us into a trap?'

'He willingly offered his help. He told me how he'd asked to become a sergeant in the Hospital, but had been turned down and how upset he was because he had been working for the Grand Master for twenty years. He was old and bitter and poor. I simply offered him an outlet for his frustrations.' Garin shrugged. 'That and some gold. Everyone has desires, Will. You just need to know which strings to pluck to make people sound them.'

'Is that some trick you learnt whilst working with Rook?'

Garin sighed heavily. 'What you're really wondering is if you can trust me, isn't it?'

'No, Garin,' said Will, meeting his gaze easily. 'I'll never trust you. But I want to be certain that this is going to go smoothly. If the servant is right and the book will soon be moved to a more secure location, we'll only have this one chance to take it.'

Garin looked down at his hands. 'You don't believe I've changed?'

Will sat back with an impatient sigh.

Garin leaned closer. 'Remember, I'm the one who came to you with this.'

'Everard has his own plan to retrieve the book.'

'Well, from what you said, his first plan didn't work all that well.'

Will said nothing. He had returned from Antioch to discover that, in his absence, the Anima Templi had sent two mercenaries into the Hospital compound to take back the Book of the Grail. The mercenaries hadn't returned and a week later, during a meeting of Acre's rulers, Hugues de Revel had warned the other leaders that thieves had tried to break into his safe. These men, he had told the assembled leaders, had been apprehended for questioning, but had tried to escape and had been killed. Desperate to retrieve the book, but knowing that he couldn't send more men inside the Hospital so soon after the failed attempt, Everard had been forced to wait.

'My plan at least has a chance of working,' added Garin. He glanced at Will. 'And, anyway, if I was trying to get the book for myself, do you think I would have told you about any of this? I would have done it alone, wouldn't I?'

'What about Rook? Won't he be annoyed when he finds out that you helped me get the book for Everard instead of him?'

Garin avoided Will's accusatory glare. 'I told you I had no choice but to work for him.'

'If he was threatening you, you could have spoken to someone in the Order. They would have put a stop to it.'

'Not before he killed my mother!' Garin lowered his voice. 'Listen, Will, I've told you I'm finished with him. I don't know what else I can say.'

'You could start by telling me the truth. I don't believe you know nothing about him. How did he find out about the book in the first place?'

'I don't know!' insisted Garin. He reached into a pouch that was hanging from his belt. 'Look,' he said, producing a small brass disc, 'do you remember this?'

Will took it grudgingly as Garin handed it to him. He looked at it in some surprise. It was the seal of the Order; a brass badge displaying two knights astride a single horse.

'You gave it to me after the tournament. You won and I lost, but you gave your prize to me.' Garin watched Will nervously, hoping he wouldn't notice that it was the wrong badge. He had tossed the one Will had given to him in the Thames years ago. 'I wanted to give it back to you. To prove I have changed.'

Will paused for a moment, then returned the badge to him. 'You saved my life at Antioch and I'm grateful for that, but we'll never be friends, Garin, and I cannot forgive you for . . .' His jaw tightened and he looked away. 'For what happened in Paris.'

Garin pressed his lips together, then stuffed the badge back into his pouch. 'I understand,' he said quietly, as the vestibule door opened and the priest beckoned to them.

Inside the chamber, which was fogged with incense smoke, the priest showed them to a large chest. 'Here,' he said, waving them closer. His accent was strong. 'The man came this morning and left them with me. He said all you will need is here.'

'Thank you,' said Garin.

The priest nodded. 'I will leave you to change. You can keep your garments here. I will leave this unlocked tonight.' He pointed to a small door. 'You may go out by this way too. Follow the street to the wall. There you enter the Quarter of the Jews and after that you will pass the public baths. You will see the wall of the Hospital.'

The priest headed out of the chamber and Garin opened the chest. He pulled out two neatly folded black surcoats with white crosses on the chests and backs. Handing one to Will, he took the other. Will removed his white mantle and Garin pulled a rolled piece of parchment from the bottom of the chest. As he unravelled the skin, a small object slipped out and clinked on the floor. Garin bent to pick it up. It was a key. Putting it into his pouch, he scanned the badly drawn, yet simple plan of the Hospital, with Grand Master de Revel's room and its iron locker clearly marked.

Stowing their mantles in the chest, Will and Garin headed into the dark streets. The priest's directions were easy to follow and it didn't take them long to reach the Hospital compound. Will held his breath as they were challenged at the gate, but the guards, holding up lanterns, let them through when they saw their surcoats.

Supper had just finished and the compound was busy. Will and Garin moved purposefully through the crowds of servants, messenger boys and sergeants. They nodded politely to any knights they passed, who nodded in return. The Hospital, as the Temple, was a major base and with so many people coming and going all the time, the men didn't always know their fellows that well.

On entering the main buildings, they had to pause surreptitiously in a lighted passage to check the skin, but it wasn't too hard to discover which stairs led up through the tallest tower, at the top of which was the Grand Master's chamber. On the way from the church, they had agreed that if they found the chamber occupied they would say they had come to make an appointment with the Grand Master to discuss a personal matter. They moved up the stairs without hesitation, so as not to arouse suspicion from anyone they might meet. So far, their plan seemed to be working remarkably well. The only thing concerning Will was what they would do if they met Nicolas de Navarre.

At the top of the stairs, they came out in a vaulted passage that led left or right to a set of double doors at either end. After consulting the skin, they went right. In the curved wall were set high arched windows that gave a stunning view across the city which was lit by torch fires and a pale half-moon.

From beneath the closed doors came the faint glow of candles. Garin nodded to Will, who rapped his knuckles on the dark wood. They waited. After a few moments, Will knocked again. Still, there was no reply. He pushed carefully at one of the doors, which creaked open. The chamber was lit by a couple of candles on a large table in the centre, in the wall behind which, Will immediately saw the locker. There were marble pillars supporting the chamber's ceiling at the edges and, beyond these, arched windows like those in the passage. The area outside the pool of candlelight was gloomy.

Will entered, and Garin followed, but stopped when Will halted. 'What's wrong?'

Will pointed to the desk. It was chaotic with papers and quills, some of which were littering the floor around it.

'Perhaps it's always like this,' murmured Garin, over his shoulder. 'They are Hospitallers. Come on.' Moving past Will, he crossed quickly to the locker, taking the key from his pouch.

Will frowned as his eyes grew accustomed to the gloom. There were a number of chests and an armoire. These had all been opened and their contents disturbed. There was an odour of dampness and stale sweat in the room. 'Garin,' warned Will.

Garin reached for the locker, the key in his hand, then stopped, his hand hovering over the lock. 'It's open,' he said, frowning. Putting the key into the pouch at his belt, he pulled open the door, which creaked on its hinges. 'Damn it!' He looked back at Will. 'It's not here.'

To his right, a shadow sprang out from behind one of the pillars. Garin shouted in terror as a hunched figure lunged at him, russet cloak flying, rotten teeth bared in a snarl, dagger drawn.

Before Garin could even move, Rook had grabbed him, twisted him round and pressed the curved dagger to his throat. 'That's because I've got it, you stupid little shit!'

Will glimpsed a vellum-bound book, its title embossed in gold-leaf, stuffed in the belt of the man who had tortured him in the whorehouse. He knew it was Rook by the eyes and voice. He went to draw his sword.

'You can put that down,' said Rook, looking at Will, 'unless you want his throat slit.'

Will hesitated and Garin cried out as Rook sliced the blade across his skin, drawing blood.

'You know I'll do it.'

'All right,' said Will. He went to place the sword on the floor.

'Not there,' growled Rook. 'Over by those chests. I don't want you going for it.'

Will did so.

'Get back where you were.'

Will went to his place, keeping his gaze on Rook. He watched Rook draw Garin's sword and toss it onto the rug behind.

'Well, this is a pretty picture,' said Rook to Garin. 'I knew you'd betray me.'

'I haven't betrayed you!' Garin, breathing hard with fear, looked to Will. 'I was using Campbell to get the book, then I was going to take it back to London like we agreed.'

Will's eyes narrowed. He stepped forward.

'Stay there!' snapped Rook, dragging Garin back. 'He's lying anyway. You was never any good at it, was you, de Lyons? You don't have the nerve.'

Will stood still, noticing that Garin's hand was inching slowly towards the pouch at his belt.

'I, on the other hand,' Rook continued softly, unaware of what Garin was doing, 'am very good at it. You might say it's one of my talents.' He chuckled. 'Like picking locks.'

'What are you talking about?' said Garin in a low voice.

'Oh, I'm going to enjoy this! You can call it payment for my having to come all this way to sort out your mess. And after I've told you, you and your friend here is going to get into that locker and I'll be on my way.' He laughed louder. 'I wish I could see the face of the Grand Master when he finds you cuddled up together in his safe! I expect you'll be seeing the inside of one of their cells for a good long while.' His tone hardened. 'Just be thankful I'm leaving you alive. At least for now,' he whispered to Garin. 'What was I saying? Oh, yes. Remember the night we left Paris? I had blood on me and when you asked me where it was from I said I'd got cut.'

In the periphery of his vision, Will saw Garin reach into the pouch.

Rook pressed his stubbly cheek against Garin's. 'I lied. It wasn't my blood. It was that bitch, Adela's.'

'What?' said Garin, going still.

'I stuck her like a pig.' Rook sniggered. 'Only that time with my blade.'

'I don't believe you,' whispered Garin, but his expression said otherwise.

Rook put his mouth over Garin's ear. 'And whilst you're thinking on that, just imagine what I'm going to do to your mother when I return to

England.' His hot breath moistened Garin's cheek. 'I reckon I'll have myself a lot of fun with her.'

Garin wrenched his hand from the pouch.

Will caught a flash of metal as Garin's hand flew up. He realised that it was the tournament badge, as Garin plunged the pin of it into Rook's eye.

There was a sudden spurt of blood. Rook began to scream.

Dropping the dagger, he staggered back, clutching his face. Garin let the badge fall to the rug, then snatched up the curved blade. He fell on Rook in a frenzy, stabbing indiscriminately at any part of flesh he could find. Rook collapsed, howling, to writhe on the floor, one hand pressed to his eye, the other trying to fend off the stinging blows. Blood spattered in long lines across the silk rug and up the whitewashed wall as Garin straddled him, plunging and withdrawing the dagger again and again. 'You bastard!' he was shrieking. '*You filthy bastard!*'

Their combined screams echoed around the chamber.

'Garin!' called Will, running across to him.

Garin jerked round, dagger poised in the air at Will. His gaze focused and his shoulders slumped. 'I have to finish it.'

Will hesitated, then nodded. Garin raised the dagger and stabbed down, once.

Rook, almost unconscious, hardly felt the blade enter his heart.

Will pulled the bloodstained Book of the Grail from Rook's belt, then hauled Garin up.

'Get your sword.'

He snatched up his falchion and ran for the door, but halted when Garin didn't follow. The knight was staring at Rook's body. Will sprinted to him, gripped his arm and dragged him away, out of the door, along the passage and down the stairs. As they reached the bottom, they heard running footsteps coming towards them. Will bundled them through a door into an empty room. He opened it a crack as the footsteps receded and saw the back of a knight disappearing up the stairs. 'Come on!' he urged Garin, who followed him numbly into the balmy night.

Nicolas de Acre had been in the main quadrant when he had heard the faint screams coming from the tower. Calling two knights to his side, he raced into the main building and up the stairs to the Grand Master's chambers. As they entered, one of the knights cried out on seeing the body with the dagger protruding from the chest, thinking it was the Grand Master.

Nicolas, sword drawn, searched the chamber whilst the other two inspected the corpse. 'Who is it?' he said, sheathing his sword and going over to them when he found no one.

'Not one of ours,' said one of the knights.

Nicolas frowned and bent closer to the body. The face and upper torso were covered in blood and horribly mutilated. 'Raise the alarm,' Nicolas told one of his comrades, crossing to the locker. 'Whoever killed him might still be here.' He opened the locker and cursed when he saw it was empty. Nicolas was searching the body when the Grand Master arrived.

'What has happened?' demanded de Revel, sweeping into the room, where he was halted by the sight of the bloody corpse.

Nicolas rose. 'Sir, the Book of the Grail has been taken.'

'Leave us,' said the Grand Master to the remaining knight. 'By whom?' he demanded of Nicolas as the man disappeared. 'And who is that?' He pointed to the corpse.

Nicolas turned to the Grand Master. 'He could be another mercenary, sent by the Temple.'

'We do not know for certain that the Temple sent anyone, brother.'

'Who else would it be, sir?' said Nicolas insistently. 'Everard is in the city. I've seen him. He knows we have his book. It makes sense that he would try to take it back.' He crossed to the door.

'Where are you going?'

'If I go now I might be able to catch whoever was with this man. They cannot have gone far.'

'No.'

'Sir?'

'I cannot allow you to pursue this any further. If our intruders were Templars, or working for the Temple, then they came to reclaim property that rightfully belongs to their Order; property we stole.' De Revel went to his desk and bent to pick up some of the fallen papers. 'We cannot risk a feud with the Temple. Not when our situation is so precarious, not after what happened at Antioch. Baybars will not stop until either he is dead, or we are gone.' He rose and placed the papers on the table. 'I kept my oath to de Châteauneuf. We failed. The only thing we can do now is to concentrate on what needs to be done.'

De Revel turned to Nicolas, who was watching him in silence. 'The rift between our Orders has to end. We must try to put the past behind us for the good of the future.'

41

The Temple, Acre

15 June 1268 AD

'We have to keep moving,' insisted Will, jogging back to Garin, who had been stumbling along behind him.

'Stop!' begged Garin, bending over, hands on thighs. 'I'm going to be sick.' He retched, but nothing came up. After a moment, he straightened, eyes and nose streaming. He looked truly pitiful.

'They'll have raised the alarm by now. We have to get to the church and change our clothes. We're too noticeable in these.' Will gestured at their stolen surcoats. Garin's was sticky with blood and gleamed wetly in the moonlight.

Garin bent forward. He retched again, then began to sob, great heaving sobs that wracked his body.

Will looked round as two men came out of a nearby building. He turned back to Garin as the men looked curiously at them. 'Come on!' he hissed, grabbing the knight by the shoulders.

Garin raised his head. His blood-spattered face was taut with anguish. 'It's my fault Adela died! *My* fault!'

'We don't have time for this.'

'Time? What's that? Nothing, Will, that's what time is! It's all just empty moments unless you fill it with things that mean something. My mother, my uncle, everyone in the Temple, you all wanted me to be someone I wasn't. Adela was the only one who wanted me to be me!'

'And you'll mourn her and it will pass,' said Will roughly, wiping a clot of blood from Garin's cheek with his thumb.

'Like it has passed for you?' snapped Garin. His brow creased. 'I didn't mean that. I'm sorry. God, I'm sorry.'

'Don't be sorry. Be faster.'

Garin finally responded to his urging and the two of them sprinted through the night from quarter to quarter, zigzagging between houses, shops, churches and mosques.

After depositing the soiled surcoats and collecting their mantles from the Venetian church, they made their way back to the Temple, entering the compound by the underground tunnel that ran from the harbour, rather than by the main gates.

'You should wash before anyone sees you,' said Will to Garin.

Garin nodded dumbly, then turned and sloped away across the yard. Will watched the knight go, his emotions confused, then headed for Everard's chambers. As in Paris, the priest had his own room in the preceptory, provided by the Seneschal, one of the three remaining members of the Anima Templi. There was light coming out from under the door. Will looked at the book in his hands. The gold words on the cover glimmered beneath his fingers. For some reason, he felt like crying. He rapped on the door, waited for Everard's rasping voice, then entered.

The priest was sitting at a table, holding a quill poised over a skin. He had a blanket wrapped around his shoulders despite the warm night and a brazier filled with charcoals was smoking in the corner. His cheeks were webbed with age and his few remaining threads of hair drifted aimlessly about his cheeks. He seemed to have aged ten years in the space of a few months.

'William,' croaked Everard wearily, 'you finally deign to grace me with your presence.' He turned his attention to the skin he was writing on. 'I spoke to Simon hours ago. I take it he passed on my message?'

'He said you wanted to see me, yes.'

Everard scowled. 'Then why did it take you so long to——?' He stopped as his eyes moved to the book in Will's hands. 'What is that?'

Will went to him and placed the Book of the Grail on top of the skin.

Everard stared down at it. His hands began to shake, causing him to drop the quill, which struck the table and twisted down to the flagstones. He placed his hands, palms down, to either side of the book, where they trembled like two pale leaves. Looking up at Will, he said one word in a hoarse voice. 'How?'

Will sat and told the priest what had happened.

'De Lyons helped you do this?' said Everard, when Will had finished.

'Yes, he wanted to make amends.'

'He had a lot to make,' said Everard sharply. 'You say the man who wanted the book – Rook – is dead?'

Will nodded.

'Do you believe he was working alone?'

'Garin said he was, but we cannot be sure either way and even if he was working with someone else, Garin might not have known about it. Garin did, however, tell me Rook had threatened to hurt his mother if he didn't comply and, from what I saw tonight, I don't think he was lying about that.'

The priest sighed, then rose slowly, picking up the book. 'Perhaps,' he mused, going over to the brazier, 'it was all part of God's grand, indecipherable plan. At least I am now here, where I am needed most.'

'What are you doing?' cried Will, leaping up as Everard held the book over the hot coals.

Everard didn't look round. 'It should never have been written in the first place. I told you that.'

'Then it was all for nothing?' said Will, watching the flames begin to lick around the thick pages, blackening the vellum and obscuring the gold writing.

'Nothing?' Everard let the book drop into the brazier. The fire caught hold and he stepped back as the dry parchment burned brightly. 'We have protected the Soul of the Temple from those who would seek to destroy it. I would not call that nothing.' He held out his hands to the flames. 'The Book of the Grail was Armand's obsession. Our aims live on without it.'

Will sat back down as Everard shuffled over. 'So it's over?'

Everard chuckled. 'On the contrary, William, we've only just started.' He sat and leaned forward, resting his gnarled hands on the table. He looked suddenly awake; wide awake and impatient, like a man who has just found out he has been given the wrong diagnosis after having been told he has only a few days left to live. 'Now I can concentrate on restoring the Anima Templi. I think, over the past months, whilst trying to build it up, I was really just waiting for it to be pulled down. My heart wasn't in it.' His brow creased. 'I would have liked Hasan to be here for this.'

'Getting rid of Baybars has to be our most pressing priority.'

'Baybars?' Everard shook his head. 'Certainly not.'

'Someone has to.'

'We must make sure they don't,' replied Everard sharply.

'What do you mean?'

'Getting rid of Baybars, as you so eloquently put it, goes against everything that the Anima Templi has been working towards since its creation.' Everard sighed at Will's nonplussed expression. 'Robert de Sablé's initial intent was to protect the Temple from those who would use its power to fulfil their own desires and to promote peace with the aim of fostering trade and knowledge between the races. The second aim, our ultimate aim, is an extension of this. What is the Grail, William?'

'The Grail?' Will shrugged. 'The cup that caught Christ's blood at the Crucifixion, or possibly a chalice used at the Last Supper. The stories differ on its origins.'

'A cup, or a chalice?'

'So it is written. But what does this have to do with . . .?'

'In earlier versions of the story, yes, but in later works the Grail is a sword, a book, a stone, even a child. In my book it appears in three different guises: a golden cross, a silver candlestick and a crescent made from lead. Which, do you suppose, is its true form?'

Will shook his head. 'I don't believe the Grail exists. I think it is a symbol, not an object.'

'Then if the story tells of Perceval's search for the Grail what is it, exactly, that he is seeking, if not an object?'

Will shrugged.

'Salvation! Perceval's search is his search for salvation. The Grail, the object of his quest, isn't something that can be held in the hand. It cannot be bought or sold and it will not be found by looking, but only by opening the heart to its essence. That is where it exists.' Everard touched his breastbone. 'In the vessel of the heart. Those who see the Grail as a sword believe salvation can only be found in war. Those who see it as a book believe wisdom will bring their search to fruition.'

Will had never seen the priest so impassioned; Everard's pupils were wide, his pale cheeks blotchy with colour.

'At the end of the initiation ritual, the postulant, playing the part of Perceval, is guided by one of the Brethren to a cauldron filled with burning oil, symbolised in the story by a lake of fire. Here he is given three treasures: the three Grails. He is told that the cross contains the soul of Christianity, the crescent the spirit of Islam and the candlestick, the Menorah, the essence of the Jewish faith. He is then told to throw the treasures into the cauldron where they will melt and become one. Thus, in order for Perceval to achieve salvation, or, in the case of a postulant, initiation, he must bring about a ritual reconciliation of the three faiths. And, in reality, this is what we, as an Order, must do.'

'My God!' Will's mouth fell open. 'How could that *possibly* be your intent? You're a priest! How could you, or any Christian, sanction this? Forget heresies in some book. *This* is sacrilege!'

'I'm disappointed,' said Everard reproachfully. 'I thought that you, more than most, understood that we aren't so different from Jews or Muslims. You've read enough of their texts after all.'

'I know our races have similarities, Everard, but what you are proposing violates everything our society is built upon! And not just ours, theirs too. Do you honestly think Muslims or Jews would be interested in reconciliation? It goes against the laws of all our faiths. How would it work when Jews and Muslims see Christ as no more than a prophet and deny His divinity? I can imagine how hard Baybars would laugh if he knew what you are proposing. He's a fanatic.'

'Yes, he is,' agreed Everard, 'but then so is King Louis.'

Will almost laughed. 'Louis? The most pious king who ever lived?'

Everard pounced. 'Pious to us, yes. No doubt to the Muslims, Baybars is just as devout and Louis a savage fanatic. This circle of hatred will only ever stop when one side steps out, sees the whole and shows it to the rest of the world. Our three religions are inextricably linked in faith, tradition and birthplace. We are siblings, each with our own identities and personalities, but who have all come from the same womb and grown up in the same cradle.' Everard spread his hands. 'We are like brothers, squabbling for our father's affections.' His voice softened. 'It is not such a strange notion, William. You need only walk the streets of Acre to see that we can live together quite well when given the opportunity. The Anima Templi isn't proposing to change our faiths to suit one another. What it proposes is a mutual truce in which all children of God benefit from the knowledge and experiences of one another. And this,' he said, gesturing to the window, beyond which the city lay sleeping, 'is where we will begin. Our Camelot.'

'I never knew you were such an idealist.'

Everard's eyes narrowed. 'Your father believed in this aim. And if we had realised our dream, he might still be alive. Should we ignore the ideal solution because it is too good to aim for? Or is it because we are scared of having to work to achieve it?'

'You don't see the world as it really is, Everard,' said Will, piqued by the mention of his father. 'You sit locked away in your private little room and imagine things that could never be. Acre might be peaceful, but look beyond its walls and you'll find only death and hatred. If the Anima Templi's aims were possible, people would have stopped warring long ago. Our faiths can never be reconciled. They are too different.'

'Faith generally has nothing to do with war. When men invade another country for better land, or resources, or greater power, faith is an excuse they hide behind to mask their mundane cause. To say that God wills it gives their actions justification. We'd all be rather more culpable if we said *I will it*, wouldn't we? Then we would cease to be seen as men of reason and become avaricious brutes. It is rare that men wage wars because they believe. Men like Baybars and Louis believe. It makes them dangerous.'

'So, you agree? Baybars should be stopped.'

'Kill the man and make a martyr. Baybars is doing what he believes in. He is protecting his people from who he sees as the enemy. And he has a point.' Everard held up his hand as Will went to speak. 'Our aims go beyond Baybars. I doubt that they will be realised in my lifetime, but maybe in yours.' He sighed. 'Maybe they will never be realised. But we have to hope, William. We have to believe we can all be better than we are.'

'So, you plan to rebuild the Anima Templi and continue with this plan?'

'Yes. I had been planning to elect new members, both here and in the West, and appoint a Guardian.' Everard pursed his lips. 'That is, in fact, why I wanted to see you tonight. I wanted to tell you that I have chosen you for initiation into the Anima Templi. That is, if you don't think it all too foolish for you.'

'Me?'

'Why not? You already know about it and I believe we have learnt to work together relatively well. I haven't whipped you for a long time.'

'I don't know,' said Will quietly. 'I just don't know.'

'What don't you know?'

'If I agree with you for a start.'

'I'm glad to hear it. If all of us in the Anima Templi always agreed with one another, we would go along with whatever silly idea came along. Dissension isn't always a bad thing. Hasan was right; I have been holding our ideals too close. We need young men like you to put some fire back into us.'

Will was silent for a time. Finally, he nodded.

Everard smiled. 'Your father would have been proud.'

Will said nothing. He felt cheated. He had gone through all of this, lost his father, Elwen, just to have Everard destroy the thing he had been trying to save. He felt no relief, or pride for helping to save the Anima Templi. He thought their aim, which he had been helping to fulfil for the last eight years, six of those unwittingly, was impossible. In the face of the blue-eyed sultan, reconciliation seemed ridiculous; more than that, it seemed wrong. When Will thought of Baybars, all he could see was his father's rotted skull, one of a hundred or more stuck on a pike around Safed's walls. How could peace be made with that?

Everard, not seeming to notice Will's disaffection, rose. 'I must speak with the Seneschal briefly. There is one thing I must do to conclude this matter.' The priest shuffled across to the door. 'Then we can have ourselves a drink.'

Garin was standing before a table in his quarters, on which was a dish of water. Behind him, the knights he shared the room with lay snoring on their pallets. Garin trailed his hand through the water, watching it eddy and swirl in the candlelight. The movement was soothing, but it wasn't doing much to clean the blood off. He didn't know how much time had passed since he had entered the room. It felt like only minutes, but he thought it was probably longer. As he cupped his hands in the water and bent forward to splash his face, the door opened. Garin straightened and looked round. A few of the men turned over in their sleep as three knights entered.

'Garin de Lyons?' said one of them.

Garin nodded, feeling the water trickling away between his fingers.

'By order of the Seneschal, you are hereby charged with the crime of desertion.'

The knights were stirring and waking now.

'Desertion?' murmured Garin.

'It has come to the Seneschal's attention that you deserted your designated post in the Paris preceptory and came here without the permission of the Visitor of the Kingdom of France. This crime is punishable by life imprisonment.'

Garin went to defend himself, but the words failed to come. He had no doubt that the charge was really being levelled at him because of his part in Rook's attempted theft of the book. But what could he say? The charge itself was true enough.

'You will be taken now to the cells beneath this preceptory. You will not be granted the opportunity to appeal against this decision until you have served no less than five years.' The knight came forward. He was, Garin saw, holding a pair of manacles. The other two had swords drawn and were poised to spring if Garin tried to resist.

They needn't have worried.

Garin watched listlessly as the irons were fastened around his wrists. It felt like it was happening to someone else. When he stumbled as he was led out of the room, his captor caught him.

'Thank you,' said Garin.

42

The Pisan Quarter, Acre

4 June 1271 AD

W ill looked round as the tavern door opened. He watched a tall, thin man dressed in a garish cerulean robe enter. The man caught Will's eye briefly, without any show of recognition, then headed to a table where a group of merchants were gathered. Pulling out a stool, the man said something that made the others laugh as he sat and helped himself to wine from a jug. Will turned back to his drink. The sun slanted in through the gaps in the shutters, drawing white lines across his table. A wasp tilted fretfully at the light. It was hot and Will was tired of waiting. Often these days he felt impatient. He slept badly, more so since the weather had turned humid, and, just recently, he had begun to feel that he couldn't get enough air into his lungs no matter how deeply he breathed.

The door opened again some time later and a stocky, olive-skinned man in brown hose and a homespun cape entered. He looked around, saw Will sitting alone and walked over. 'A beautiful day,' he remarked in an unplaceable accent.

'The good Lord graces us,' replied Will, in Arabic.

'That He does,' agreed the man, chuckling. 'Will Campbell, I trust?'

Will nodded and held out his hand. The man looked at it, then seemed to recognise the gesture. He took Will's hand and pumped it vigorously. His grip was strong. 'Can I offer you a drink?' asked Will.

'Water,' said the man, sitting. He swatted the wasp away with a quick flick of his hand.

Will beckoned to the serving girl, who was sitting at one of the tables fanning her damp face with a large, dry leaf. 'We'll have two jars of water,' he told her, when she traipsed over.

She frowned. 'I'll have to charge you.'

'Fine.'

'You can't sit in here and drink Adam's ale all day for nothing,' she grumbled.

'I said I'll pay,' said Will sharply.

'No need to take that tone,' she snapped back, turning on her heel and heading for the kitchen.

The olive-skinned man leaned across the table. 'A wise man might advise against rudeness with one who is about to bring you food or drink.' He sat back. 'I will make sure not to take the one she offers you. I expect she will have spat in it.'

'I'll take my chances.'

Whilst they waited for the drinks, Will appraised the man. There was nothing special about him. With his stout frame and large hands he looked like a tradesman of some physical, earthy craft – a smith, or a tanner, or maybe a lower-class merchant, a trader from the iron mines at Beirut perhaps. He didn't look at all how Will had imagined. The Pisan merchant who had arranged the meeting hadn't told him what to expect.

The serving girl returned with the waters. She placed one jar before the olive-skinned man and the other she plonked in front of Will, spilling some. Will grudgingly handed her some pennies. He studied his drink when she had gone. The man chuckled.

'Let's get on with it, shall we?' said Will irritably, pushing the jar to one side.

'Of course, of course. You have the money?'

Will showed the man the bag that was hanging from his belt, which girdled the plain linen shirt he wore over his hose.

The olive-skinned man sat back and sipped at his water. 'Then let us discuss, exactly, what it is that my Order can do for you.'

The Temple, Acre, 4 June 1271 AD

His business concluded, Will returned to the preceptory. The mood in the fortress, as in the rest of the city, was black; almost as black as it had been the autumn before when they had received news of King Louis' death. The king, having taken the advice of his brother, Charles de Anjou, had made for Tunis, but following his successful capture of Carthage, a pestilence had ravaged his army. Louis had eventually succumbed to the fever and his great Crusade, the eighth since Pope Urban II had called men to arms almost two hundred years earlier, had ended before it had begun. His body was taken back to France to be buried in the Abbey at Saint-Denis.

Now, the collective despondency of Acre's citizens was caused by tidings of the fall of Krak des Chevaliers to Baybars' forces. Krak, considered to be the most indomitable fortress in Eastern Christendom, had been the largest stronghold of the Hospitallers. The garrison had capitulated after five weeks of intense fighting and with its destruction the last game-piece of the Franks had been swept from the Palestinian hinterland. In the past three years, Baybars had pushed them gradually, yet inexorably back, until they controlled just a few scattered towns and cities along the coast.

Will studied the faces of the men as he walked through the compound. He saw exhaustion and fear. At one time, the Temple had owned nearly forty major bases in Outremer. By the time Baybars came to power that number had dropped to twenty-two and now they held only ten.

In the last few weeks, doubts over what he had been planning for so long had begun to gnaw at Will, but it helped to see the defeat in the eyes of his fellows. It affirmed that he was doing the right thing. The only thing. A few of the knights greeted him in passing as he made his way to the seaward tower in the north-west corner. The tower, which had been built by Saladin, formed the oldest part of the preceptory. The sand-dashed stones were cracked and tufts of spiky grass had sprouted up through the fissures. There were two sergeants standing to either side of the entrance. They both had swords.

'Morning, sir,' said one cheerily, as Will approached. 'Haven't seen you for a while.'

'I've been busy, Thomas.' Will went to duck through the low archway.

'Just to warn you,' cautioned Thomas, 'he's not a pretty sight.'

Will paused.

'It's the leonardie,' explained Thomas. 'He came down with it last week.'

'Leonardie? How bad?'

'Wouldn't like to say. Don't look good though.'

Will entered the tower, stepping from warm June into damp November. A short passage curved round to a set of steps that led to the upper levels of the tower, which housed the treasury. Three armed sergeants guarded the stairwell. Will turned right before he reached the steps into a draughty, circular room, which was occupied by two knights: one sitting at a table studying a ledger; the other standing sentry beside a trapdoor that was covered with an iron grate.

The knight at the bench looked up as Will walked in. 'Brother Campbell,' he said unenthusiastically. 'Here to see the prisoner, I take it?'

'One of the guards told me he is sick. Is he comfortable?'

The knight raised an eyebrow. 'It isn't our job to make prisoners comfortable. We just hold them here until their sentence is served. But,' he added dryly, as he rose, 'I'm sure your visit will be comfort enough.' He nodded to his companion, who slid back the bolt that kept the trapdoor's grate in place, then lifted it. Stairs fell away into darkness.

The steps were uneven and Will brushed his fingertips along the walls to keep his balance. A faint draught that smelt of brine and mildew and decay lifted his hair. The walls were soft and crumbly in places like stale biscuits. A rhythmic booming sound that vibrated in the stone grew louder the further Will descended. The treasury tower was so close to the sea that the waves would lash it with each white surge. As Will neared the bottom, he saw torchlight. Moving down the last few steps, he came out in a narrow passage that had been hewn out of the bedrock. Puddles on the floor gleamed blackly. The area was below sea level and the rough walls cried moisture that slowly pooled, then equally slowly drained through a gutter cut through the floor. Along one side of the passage were ten doors, each reinforced with iron strips and barred with timber beams. Along the other side was a trestle and bench where three sergeants were playing draughts.

'Morning,' said Will.

'Is it?' asked one of the guards. He shook his head as he rose. 'I swear time moves different down here.' Leaving his fellows to continue the game, he went to a door at the end of the passage. The guard raised the timber beam that was resting on two brackets to either side of the door. He kicked the door twice, then opened it. 'You can take that torch there, sir.'

Will took the brand from its holder and entered the cell. Immediately he was struck by a thick wave of the sickly odour of decay he had noticed on his way down. The guard shut the door behind him and there was a heavy *thump* as the timber was dropped back into place. After three years of coming here, Will was still unnerved by that sound and the rush of claustrophobia that followed it. The torch flared in the draught from the door, then settled into a pale glow that struggled to push back the shadows of the dank cell. On the floor was a bowl filled with an oleaginous-looking stew, over which had formed a wrinkled skin. Beyond the bowl, sitting with his back against the wall, one arm held up over his face against the light, the other chained by the wrist to an iron ring set into the wall, was Garin.

At first, Will couldn't see anything wrong. Garin looked the same as he usually did. His once golden hair was grey with dirt and lack of sunlight, and fell in tangled hanks to his chest, matting with his beard which was equally long and filthy. His shirt and hose – the only things he had been left with on imprisonment – were threadbare, the cloth rotting in the damp, and his chest was hollow, the bones protruding through pallid skin. The fingernails on his free hand were bitten to the quick, but the nails on the hand bound to the wall, which was set at such a height that he could just crouch over his toilet bucket, were as long as talons. It was only when Garin took his arm away, blinking painfully at the light, that Will saw what the guard had warned him about.

He had heard of the leonardie – the disease Richard the Lionheart had once suffered with on campaign – but he had never seen anyone with it. As well as reducing men to utter weariness, the illness blighted certain areas of the skin. Garin's face had been ravaged. His cheeks and forehead were red raw where his skin had cracked, flaked, then peeled away. His lips were split and bleeding and one of his eyes was crusted shut where the lid had opened, bled, then formed a scab. There were signs of the disease on his hands and arms.

'My God,' murmured Will, setting the torch in the wall bracket and crouching before Garin. He tried to ignore the rancid smell coming from the toilet bucket.

Garin peered at Will accusingly through narrowed, weeping eyes. 'You haven't been for days.'

Will didn't tell the knight that it had been over a fortnight since his last visit. 'I'm sorry.'

'You're the only one who tells me what is going on.' Garin's voice was insubstantial as a breeze and his mouth hardly moved when he spoke, but Will could clearly see his agitation. 'You said Prince Edward had come. What's happening? I need to know, Will. I need to . . .' He gave a high, frustrated cry as his lip cracked where he opened it too wide. Blood welled up.

'I'm here now,' said Will quickly. 'I'll tell you anything you want.' He picked up the bowl of stew. 'But first you should eat something.'

'I'm dying, Will,' said Garin softly.

'Don't be a daff. King Richard had the leonardie and he didn't die.' Will went closer to Garin and tried to put the bowl in the knight's hand. 'You just need food and rest.'

Garin pushed the bowl away. 'It hurts too much.'

Will looked at the open sores around his mouth, then at the wide-rimmed bowl. Sitting cross-legged before the knight, he picked a lump of gristly meat from the stew. Carefully, so as not to touch the corners, he pushed the meat between Garin's desiccated lips.

When Garin had first been imprisoned, Will had visited his cell rarely, and only then because Garin had begged the guards repeatedly to ask him to come. But the part of him that had still blamed Garin for what had been done to him in the whorehouse, had gradually been subdued by the high price the knight was paying for a crime that had not been solely his fault.

Over time, the visits had become more frequent, until they were now part of his weekly routine; a part, despite himself, he often found he looked forward to. He hadn't been able to talk to Everard or any of the Brethren about his feelings and thoughts, nor anyone outside that circle. Garin, who already knew about the Anima Templi, but was not loyal to it, had become the only person Will had been able to share certain things with. He had come to value the knight's opinion more and more over the past months.

Sometimes, too, they talked about ghosts. Jacques, Owein, James, Adela, Elwen: the sum of their collective loss. The latter only rarely. Garin had once suggested that Will contact Elwen, but Will had opposed the idea so vehemently that it had never been mentioned again. Will had long given Elwen up to memory, telling himself that she would be happily married to some rich duke. But she was a wound that had never properly healed and still caused him pain. Now and then, he craved the empty darkness that was Garin's existence, where weeks went by in days.

'There,' said Will gruffly, pushing another piece of meat between Garin's lips, aware of how demeaning it must feel, 'I don't know what you're complaining about.'

Garin chewed the tough meat slowly, then swallowed with effort. He looked sixty, not twenty-four. 'Talk to me,' he whispered, insistent.

'There's not much to tell. Everyone has been shocked by the fall of Krak. Prince Edward has sent ambassadors to the Mongols to ask for their help, but Grand Master Bérard and most of the others in Acre's government aren't expecting to receive any. The prince held a few councils with the nobles and tried to rally them, but so far the only things he has managed to fire up are tempers.'

'What do you mean?' said Garin, chewing another piece of meat Will fed to him.

'It's like everyone who comes here for the first time. Edward doesn't understand it yet,' sighed Will, who had been in the company which had greeted the thirty-two-year-old English prince, who had come with one thousand knights. King Henry, complaining of ill health, had apparently been excused from taking the Cross. The leaders of Acre had welcomed the fresh troops and the prince's enthusiasm. At least, for a few days.

'He thought the war was a simple matter of us against them. He was furious when he found out that the Venetians sell arms to Baybars, the Genoese supply him with slaves and the nobles of Acre endorse it all, whilst quarrelling with each other over who should have the biggest cut. And they have the gall to complain when Baybars takes their lands and properties with his nice new weapons and soldiers?' Will sighed roughly as he fished more meat from the bowl. 'But none of it will matter soon.'

Garin pushed his hand away. 'You went through with it?'

Will set the bowl down and sucked the gravy from his fingers. 'I met him today, yes.'

Garin studied him. 'Well, you have certainly become a friend to danger.'

'I thought you agreed with my plan?'

'You know I do. I always have. But if Grand Master Bérard discovers what you've done in the name of the Order?' Garin shook his head. 'Let's just say I'd expect to see a lot more of you. Not to mention what Everard and the Anima Templi would do if they found out.'

'I've tried doing things their way,' responded Will hotly. 'I've done everything Everard has asked of me: formed alliances with knights in other Orders; curried favour at the High Court; introduced myself to influential Jewish scholars; enticed Muslim informants. On the surface, I agree, the Brethren have made some important advances in the last few years. The Hospitaller Grand Master has even started talking to Grand Master Bérard during formal occasions. But I feel like I'm getting nowhere. The nobles are too wrapped up in their schemes and internal politics to see beyond their own walls. How many more strongholds will we relinquish to Baybars? The Anima Templi will never achieve its aims if there is no Holy Land left to us. Why doesn't Everard understand that?'

'Have you tried asking him?'

'I ask all the time what he plans to do and how he imagines we will survive this war long enough to achieve any kind of peace. But he won't speak his mind. He still keeps things from me. I know he has an important contact high up in the Mamluks, a contact my own *father* made! But he will not tell me who.' Will shook his head, frustrated. 'He's left me no choice!'

'Are you trying to justify what you have done to me, or to yourself?' murmured Garin.

Will glanced at the knight. The plan, which he had formulated almost eighteen months ago, had taken a long time to execute whilst he quietly made contacts and slowly syphoned money from the Anima Templi's secret coffers. He had wrestled with his conscience more than once in that time.

'I've made my decision,' he told Garin finally. 'In my heart, I believe this is the only way. I didn't want to come here and get involved in this war, but I am involved and the only thing I can do now is what I feel is right.'

'For what it's worth, I think you are doing the right thing. I've always said the Anima Templi's aim was hopeless. Since the day you first told me of it.'

'When it's done things will change, I'm certain of it. The nobles will have more enthusiasm for the fight and Prince Edward might be able to rally them. Then,' Will added quietly, 'we can start taking back our lands and holdings.'

For months now, he had been having a dream where he met his father's spirit in Safed's abandoned halls. Will would go in to bury him, but the decapitated bodies were so decomposed that James never knew which was his.

The dream haunted him.

But soon it would be over. Soon, he could bury his father and maybe then there would be a chance for peace.

'I've got to go,' said Will, rising. 'I'll come back tomorrow with a poultice for those sores.'

'Don't trust anyone else to help you change things, Will. Don't trust Edward, or the nobles. Trust only yourself.'

Will nodded. He banged on the door and a few moments later the guard let him out. Will stepped from the tower into the blinding afternoon.

It was there that Everard caught him.

Will was surprised to see the old priest, who rarely left his room, hobbling across the yard. He went to raise his hand, then stopped as he saw the expression on Everard's face. Will almost took a step back at the violence in the priest's eyes.

Everard didn't break his ungainly stride, but stumbled forward to grab Will by the mantle with his withered hands. 'You fool!' he seethed, his spittle striking Will's face. 'What have you done, you damned *fool*?'

Will took hold of Everard's wrists and tried to prise him off. 'What are you talking about?'

'Don't give me that! One of the Seneschal's guards saw you in the tavern!'

'You had me followed?'

'I've been watching you for weeks,' spat Everard. 'You've been very busy, haven't you, with your secret meetings and plans. I know all about it!'

'How?' murmured Will, giving up trying to fend the priest off.

'I had it forced out of that Pisan merchant you went to see. He told me who you were meeting with. You can go back and tell them whatever deal you made is off.'

'No.'

Everard's bloodshot eyes blazed. '*No?*'

'It's too late, unless you caught him.' When Everard didn't answer, Will knew that they hadn't. 'He'll have left the city by now.'

'Then you can get on a damn horse and go after him!'

'No,' repeated Will, pulling roughly from Everard's grasp. 'Even if I knew where to look I wouldn't go. We've done it your way for three years, Everard. It hasn't worked. Baybars isn't interested in peace. We've sent almost a dozen men to treat with him. How many returned?'

Everard's lips were pressed in a flat line. His scar was red, livid. 'We must keep trying.'

'It's too late for that.' Will went to turn away.

'They won't do it,' said Everard, grabbing him by the shoulder. 'They work with him, you fool! He pays them levies. Why would they bite their master's hand?'

'Not all of them trust him. Baybars has started to move his own lieutenants into positions of power in their Order. They fear he will try to take it over.'

Everard's breathing was fast and shallow. 'Where in God's name did you get the money for this contract?' When Will didn't answer, Everard's mouth dropped open. 'From my coffers, was it?' he demanded incredulously. 'Oh, you *serpent!*'

'You wanted my help, Everard. You wanted me to speak my mind and make my own decisions. Well, you've got it. Your way didn't work. We'll do it my way now.'

43
Aleppo, Syria
8 August 1271 AD

'Doesn't she look radiant, my lord?' murmured Kalawun. He smiled as his daughter scooped up a sleek, almond-eyed cat that had wandered in through the throne room's open doors. The air was hot and still and attendants were kept busy trying to cool the assembly of governors, commanders and courtiers with iced sherbets. Slaves worked the large fans that were suspended from the ceiling, hauling on ropes to rotate the blades.

'Fit for a sultan,' agreed Baybars, watching his daughter-in-law weave through the crowds, conveying the cat to the banqueting table where the servants were clearing away the remains of the feast. Women cooed over the pretty child as she placed some leftover kid meat on a silver dish and fed it to her charge. Baybars' wife, Fatima, was among them, holding a squalling infant in her arms – his second heir – Nizam having borne him no further children.

Baraka Khan was lounging at the side of the chamber with some of his friends. In the past three years, the boy had shot up and his face already revealed a trace of the man he would become. He hadn't shown any interest whatsoever in his bride-to-be, but Baybars knew there would be plenty of time for that. The betrothal feast was just for show. The marriage that was to come would yield the real fruits of this union.

Moving through the dancers who were twirling to the musicians' skilful plucking and tapping of zithers, drums and qanuns, Omar ascended the dais and bowed to Baybars. 'The performers are here, my lord. Do you wish them to be brought in?'

'Yes. But stay, Omar,' Baybars called, as the officer went to leave. 'Sit with me.'

Omar smiled. 'It would be a pleasure, my lord.'

Baybars beckoned to a servant. 'Have the entertainers shown in and a space cleared. And bring me some kumiz.'

As the servant hastened off, Kalawun turned to Baybars. 'I'll make sure that our bride and groom are seated together for the performance.'

When Kalawun left Baybars motioned Omar to the cushions placed on the dais' top step – the place reserved for the highest governors. As Omar sat, taking a handful of figs from one of the dishes that had been set on a low board, Baybars chuckled. 'Be careful, my friend. Soon you won't fit into your uniform. I fear we have all spent too much time eating and not enough fighting.'

'You deserve to indulge yourself,' Omar told him. 'Take this opportunity to rest. The Franks can cause us little trouble now and we have the Mongols under control.'

'I will rest in time.'

Omar, looking up at Baybars, noticed an expression of pain cross the sultan's face. From this angle, the lines on his brow and cheeks were more pronounced. The relentless fury with which he had attacked the Franks and forced them back towards the sea was a fire, consuming him from within just as it burned them. Baybars could never truly take pleasure from anything he did whilst his aims remained unfulfilled: inflaming, tormenting him. But, if that was so, then what, Omar wondered, was the point of it all?

'They're here,' said Baybars, leaning forward to take the kumiz the servant brought him.

Two men had entered the throne room, pulling a handcart that was covered in a black velvet cloth embroidered with silver stars and moons. The dancers ceased their spinning and the crowd was ushered to the sides of the chamber, directed to cushions by the servants. Baraka and his young bride-to-be were seated on the couch, facing a section of whitewashed wall near the dais, ready for the performance. The doors to the garden were closed and embroidered drapes were drawn across windows, turning day to night. A servant leapt back as a tattered, hissing figure scuttled out from beneath one of the drapes. People fell back in fear as the soothsayer scurried, wild-eyed, up the dais to crouch, panting, at Baybars' feet. The ancient soothsayer had the tiny cloth doll the sultan had given to him in Antioch clasped in his fist.

Omar inched away, but Baybars placed his hand upon Khadir's sunburnt, liver-spotted head. 'Did he disturb your dreams?'

'Dreams disturbed,' snapped Khadir. He trembled suddenly and offered Baybars the doll.

Baybars smiled and laid the doll on his knee.

Omar frowned. He wished Baybars wouldn't encourage the old man, who seemed to have become even more erratic since Antioch.

'My Lord Sultan.'

Baybars looked down as one of the men, who had entered with the handcart, greeted him, dropping to one knee before the dais. He had brown skin, black eyes and a shock of scarlet hair, dyed – like his beard and moustache – with henna.

'We are honoured to entertain you and your guests on this joyous occasion, my lord.' The man swept his hand towards his companion, a slender youth who, like himself, was dressed in a patchwork cloak made out of silks of many shades of blue: azure, indigo, turquoise, aquamarine. These garments shimmered with every movement they made, like water rippling with invisible currents.

'You may begin,' said Baybars, motioning to the space that had been cleared before the young couple. Baraka was already looking bored and was sitting as far away from Kalawun's daughter as possible on the narrow couch.

The man rose gracefully and returned to his companion who had taken a lantern from the handcart. The air was blue with incense that hung in shifting layers in the arrows of light shooting through the drapes. As the last attendants hurried to the sides of the chamber to melt into the shadows, the man with scarlet hair faced the silent audience. 'We present to you a story of love and betrayal.' He motioned to his comrade who set the lantern on the top of the handcart, where it bathed the whitewashed wall. 'Performed by shadows.'

There was a flurry of applause. The two shadow-puppeteers were renowned for their displays.

'Once in Arabia,' began the scarlet-haired man, 'there lived a woman of such radiant beauty that the moon herself would pale each evening when she went down to the river to bathe.'

Kalawun's daughter laughed and clapped as the slender man played his hands across the lantern and his fingers became the shadow of a woman skipping across the wall. The courtiers mirrored their princess's approval as the story continued and the puppeteer's hands became women that loved, men that battled and beasts that snarled.

Baybars began to feel restless. The performers weren't as enthralling as he had expected them to be; the shapes on the wall not as convincing to a forty-eight-year-old warrior as they might be to a nine-year-old child. Khadir was hunched at his feet, watching the two men through hooded eyes. Every now and then the soothsayer would start when the scarlet-haired man's voice rose, then settle when it fell back to a whisper.

The scarlet-haired puppeteer took a straw and a pot from the handcart. He approached the dais. 'At last,' he murmured into the hush, 'the radiant beauty came to a palace, drawn by the song of the old woman whose voice lingered on the wind like the scent of flowers.' He dipped the straw into the pot, set it to his lips and blew a stream of bubbles. Crouching, he placed the pot and straw on the marble steps as one of the bubbles floated up to land on Omar's hand. Smiling, Omar held it out to Baybars. It burst. A high-pitched shriek blasted the silence. Baybars sat up sharply. The sound was coming from Khadir, who had shrunk back against Baybars' legs, his milky eyes fixed on the puppeteer who was now standing. His shimmering cloak slipped from his shoulders like liquid and in his hand was a gold-handled dagger, its hilt inlaid with a gleaming red ruby. '*Hashishim!*' Khadir was screaming. '*Hashishim!*'

The scarlet-haired Assassin lunged up the marble steps and threw himself at Baybars. The sultan didn't stand a chance. Even as he was rising, the Assassin was upon him, bringing up the weapon to strike. Omar flung himself forwards. The Assassin let out a fierce cry as the blade punched into Omar's chest, sending the officer crashing into Baybars' lap. Screams sounded around the chamber. Seeing that his comrade had failed, the slender puppeteer had drawn a dagger and was running for the throne, but Kalawun, who had rushed to protect Baraka, cut him down.

'Capture them!' roared Baybars, clutching Omar, who was gasping for breath. 'I want to know who sent them!'

The remaining Assassin, weaponless, had fallen back from the throne, but he stood calm and still as several Bahri warriors came towards him. There was a shriek from behind the throne. The soothsayer leapt up and sprang at the Assassin, his own blade drawn.

'No!' shouted Baybars, grappling with Omar as he began to slip to the floor, the dagger sticking out of his chest.

Khadir didn't heed his cry. The exiled Assassin fell on the man, who went down under his frenzied attack shouting a prayer. As the Bahri warriors tried to pull the soothsayer away, Baybars let Omar sink gently onto the cushions. 'Hold on,' he said, stroking Omar's pale cheek. '*Physicians!*' he roared at the crowd, sending servants scurrying.

Omar licked his dry lips and looked up at Baybars, his brown eyes narrowed with pain. He smiled faintly. 'You look tired, sadeek.' He raised his hand to Baybars' face. It fell back before he could touch it.

Baybars gave a harsh cry as Omar slumped against him and went still. He curled over the body, clasping the officer's face. 'Not for me, Omar,' he whispered. 'Not this for me.' He sat up after a moment and shook Omar by the shoulders. 'Get up! I command you!'

But the power of a sultan was really just an illusion when all was said and done.

The physicians arrived, but came no closer, seeing that they were too late. There was only one thing left to do. Baybars bent down and put his mouth to Omar's ear. Into it, he breathed words.

'*Ashadu an la ilaha illa-llah. Wa ashhadu anna Muhammadan rasul-Ullah.*'

There is no God but God. Muhammed is His Prophet.

44

The Temple, Acre

19 September 1271 AD

'**Y**ou failed.'

Will glanced round. Everard was standing on the battlements behind him. The priest's face was sweaty with the climb, his breathing laboured. 'I know,' said Will, turning back to the view. The plains beyond the city walls were golden in the evening. They stretched east towards Galilee where the land rose to meet the sky and became obscured by distance. He had never seen beyond those veiled hills, though they were often in his thoughts.

'Baybars is alive and well,' added Everard.

'I said I know.'

'Although,' the priest continued, 'one of his officers was killed in the attempt. A good friend of his, so I was told. The sultan has sent troops against the Assassins.' He came to the parapet and blew out his papery cheeks. 'I do not envy them. His wrath will be severe.'

'It was their choice to accept the contract.'

'But it was you who approached them with the deal.'

'I know you'll never forgive me for this, Everard,' said Will, facing the priest, 'but someone had to do something. Your aim for peace is all very laudable, but if the other side won't adhere to it, it is mere wishful thinking.'

'*My* aim?' said Everard sharply. 'How you set yourself apart! As a member of the Brethren, you are part of a whole. Yes, we all have different ideas and opinions, but in the end when we speak we do so as one. Your recent behaviour has been that of a vigilante.' His rasping voice hardened further. 'Did you not listen to a word I said about de Ridefort and Armand? This is exactly the kind of action the Soul of the Temple was set up to prevent!'

'You cannot possibly compare me to them.'

'No? They used the power of the Anima Templi for their own ends, for their own personal gain. What were you doing when you signed your private deal with the Assassins and handed over our gold? Who were you serving?'

'Us,' replied Will, defiant, 'the Temple, Christendom.'

Everard jabbed a finger at him. 'Kill the man and make a martyr, that's what I told you on the night you returned the book to me. Best for us? For Christendom? Do not delude yourself! You were doing it for yourself. Retribution for your dead father, wasn't it?' The priest paused, his breathing ragged. He coughed deeply and hawked a plug of mucus over the side of the parapet. 'You didn't give me a chance to tell you my own plans, William,' he said, still angry, but quieter now, fatigued by the outburst. 'But then perhaps I am also to blame for not coming to you when I saw you were growing disillusioned with the slowness of our work.'

Will was surprised by the priest's suggestion of personal culpability. 'What plans?'

Everard sniffed and looked over at the orchards where sweet lemons were thick on the branches. 'It is quite beautiful this time of year, isn't it?' When Will didn't respond, Everard turned to him. 'For some time now, I have been in contact with the man your father was in talks with when he was here; a man amenable, unlike Baybars, to negotiation.'

'My father's contact in the Mamluk army?'

'Yes.'

Will waited for the priest to continue. After a pause, he did.

'Your father's contact was Amir Kalawun.'

'Kalawun?' said Will, shocked. 'But he is Baybars' main lieutenant? He led the invasion of Cilicia, which resulted in the deaths of thousands of Armenians. How could he possibly be working for us?'

'At his heart, Kalawun is a man of peace. He wants what is best for his people and understands that war does not always provide that. Early on, he realised that Baybars would become a man of power. Initially, he manoeuvred himself into Baybars' trust to advance his own position. But in time he came to realise that the sultan was acting out of a personal hatred of us; a hatred that Kalawun saw could damage their own people as much as it could ours. He has no great love of the Franks, but he is sympathetic to the aims of the Anima Templi and knows his people could benefit as much as we could from continuing trade between our nations. Your father made a great impression on him, from what I have been told. In order to retain his position of influence within Baybars' circle Kalawun had to continue to follow the orders he was given, even if those orders had begun to run contrary to his personal beliefs. As a man of peace he couldn't have remained in this position, he had to prove himself as a man of war to do that. Peace sometimes has to be bought with blood.'

'But if this is true, what can Kalawun possibly do against Baybars? He might be in a position of power, but he isn't sultan. How can he change anything?'

'Slowly,' responded Everard. 'That is how it must be done. Kalawun will not move directly against Baybars, but already he is making provisions for a greater hold over the throne on Baybars' death. Baybars' heir, Baraka Khan, has recently become his son-in-law and Kalawun is seeking to influence the boy. If your plan had succeeded and Baybars had been murdered on the orders of a Frank, the Mamluks would have struck back at us with everything they had. It would been another Hattin. In the weak position we are in, we would have most likely lost the little we have left to the fury of the Muslims and any chance at friendship, or peace. This way takes longer, but in the end it is the safer route and the one where less blood may be spilt in the future. If Baybars dies naturally, in battle or of old age, and if Kalawun can exert enough influence over his son, the next sultan could become an ally of ours. Imagine, William, what we can accomplish if we use our tongues, rather than our swords.'

Will stared at the priest. 'Why didn't you tell me this sooner? If I'd known what you were doing, I wouldn't have . . . I didn't know.' He shook his head, his shoulders slumping. 'I didn't want to know.'

'I've seen you up here before, staring into that distance.' Everard gestured to the plains. 'You'll find nothing out there, you once told me, but death and hatred. Is that what you are seeing?'

'I see nothing,' murmured Will. 'What I'm looking for isn't there.'

'Your father,' said Everard, nodding. 'I'm not so blind I can't see that. You look to Safed like a Muslim looks to Mecca. You have to let him go. This grief will eat you up inside.'

'I miss him, Everard,' said Will hoarsely. 'I miss him so much.'

Everard said nothing, as Will put his head in his hands. After a moment, he reached out and gently grasped Will's shoulders. 'Look at me, William. I cannot give you your father back, no one can. But I can tell you that he did not die in vain. Because of what he achieved with Kalawun, we may yet see peace between the peoples of this world.'

'I never had the chance to tell him I was sorry.'

'I do not know what happened between you and your father. But I do know that he loved you. I only met him once, but that, more than anything else, was apparent. He didn't come here to leave you, he came here to do something that very few men on this sorry Earth have ever had the heart, or the courage to do. He didn't come here for himself, for money, power, or God. He came here because he believed in a better world; a world he wanted to help make reality and, for that, I praise him. As should you.'

'He never forgave me.'

'Have you considered that the only person you need forgiveness from is yourself? However you wronged your father, whatever you feel your sins are, even if he had absolved you, would you have truly been free of them?' Everard shook his head. 'I am a priest, William. I can absolve a man in the eyes of God, but if he will not forgive himself he will live with his sins for the rest of his life, even if God, in the next one, will pardon him.'

'I don't know how to forgive myself. I don't know how to change. My friends, the men I speak to, they all know what they want. They fit in here. Simon is happy working in the stables. Robert might act the fool, but, ultimately, he is content to follow the rules and get on with it like everyone else. Even Garin seems more at peace in his cell than he ever was before. You were right in what you once said, about my becoming a knight for my father. I spent so many years waiting for him to see me in the mantle that when he died I realised I had never known what I wanted for myself. Then there was Elwen, but . . . When I look to tomorrow, Everard, I see nothing.'

'You do not need to know what is in tomorrow to live in today,' responded Everard briskly, 'and you don't have to see the future in order to walk towards it.'

'But what do I have today?'

'A chance to change the future.' Everard paused. 'I cannot tell you how to forgive yourself, or to lay your guilt to rest. But I can offer you something to work towards. I didn't just come up here to berate you. I came to offer you a choice. There is a meeting of the Brethren. We are welcoming our new Guardian.'

'Guardian? You found one?'

'Yes, at long last. You can come with me now and join us for the meeting, or I can release you from your bond.'

'From the Brethren you mean?'

'And from the Temple if you wish.' Everard shrugged. 'I know you only helped me to retrieve the Book of the Grail because you wanted to become a knight and, as you've just admitted, you only wanted to become a knight for your father.'

'I didn't help you just for that, Everard.'

Everard brushed his words aside with a wave of his hand. 'And I don't blame you for wanting to escape your apprenticeship. I know I played a great part in your frustrations. But it is long past time that you chose something for yourself. Preferably,' he added dryly, 'something that won't get us all killed. In the Book of the Grail, the knights guide Perceval through his quest, but in the end he alone must decide the final course of action that will bring about a reconciliation of the three faiths, or shatter the peace forever. He chooses reconciliation.' Everard's lip curled. 'But not before he makes a few mistakes. I leave it up to you, William. Work with us for the future, or find your path along some other road. But either way, walk forwards.'

Will looked east towards the hills. Whilst they had been talking, the sun had set and the first star had appeared, far off and bright in the northern sky. The breeze was warm and smelled of olives, salt, hay and leather. Below, in the compound, he heard men calling to one another and the whinnying of horses. Fainter, from the city, he heard cattle in the marketplace, a bell clanging, a child's laughter. All around him life continued. Its patterns were familiar, reassuring.

Everard was right; his father's reasons for coming here were selfless. But he had known that already, back in Paris on the day Louis had agreed to take the Cross. Since then, that clarity and the purity of the love he had felt towards his father had been obscured by bitterness and by revenge. His own reasons for coming here had been ultimately selfish and by following them he had almost destroyed what his father had worked to achieve. But he had a chance to make it right. He *wanted* to make it right. He didn't want more men to die, more sons to lose their fathers. His desire for vengeance, for blood, for war, had been the product of his own guilt and he had shunned the Anima Templi's ideals, not because he didn't believe, but because he hadn't wanted to believe, hadn't wanted to give up that chance for retribution. But the path to absolution, he knew, did not follow such a course. It lay in helping Everard and the Anima Templi achieve what had been his father's wish, a wish, he now realised, looking out over the tranquil city, that was also his own.

'I want to stay.'

'Then we have work to do,' said Everard, not seeming at all surprised by his answer. 'Come.'

Will let Everard lead him from the battlements. The moment of clarity had dissipated by the time he reached the courtyard, but the knowledge remained, like a pearl trapped in the core of his being, formed out of the sand and the grit. This was where he belonged. As he walked beside the priest, Will felt a renewed sense of purpose stir him. He had to live. That was all. He just had to live.

The Brethren rarely held a full council and then always in different places so as not to arouse attention from anyone in the preceptory. Today, they were holding it in the Seneschal's quarters. Everard had managed to elect four new members, but as one of the original members had died last year they were still only six. They were all gathered by the time Will and Everard arrived.

The Seneschal, a powerfully built, prematurely bald man with a hot temper, opened the door. He inclined his head respectfully to Everard and glared at Will. When Everard had informed the Brethren of Will's contract with the Assassins, the Seneschal had pressed for his immediate imprisonment. He was obviously not pleased that the two-month suspension, which he had called sentimental leniency, had ended.

Seated on stools around the sparse chamber were three other figures. There was a young Templar priest from the Kingdom of Portugal whom Everard had handpicked after noticing the youth's keen study of the similarities between the Muslim, Jewish and Christian faiths. A fresh-faced knight, born and bred in Acre's diverse community, and an older knight who, like the Seneschal and Everard, remembered the days of Armand de Périgord.

There was, Will realised as he entered the chamber, one other figure in the room; a tall, dark-haired man dressed in a black cloak that was edged with rabbit fur. He was standing by the hearth, studying a map of the world on the wall, with Jerusalem at its centre.

'William,' said Everard. 'I would like you to meet the new Guardian of the Anima Templi. A man, who, I am certain, will bring as much value to our circle as his great-uncle before him. My liege,' he called, heading over to the hearth. 'This is the young man I told you about.'

The figure turned. It was Prince Edward, son of King Henry III and heir to the throne of England.

Will recovered himself quickly enough to manage a bow. 'My lord.'

Edward held out his hand. 'It is an honour.'

Will shook the prince's hand. Edward's grip was strong, confident. 'It is my honour to meet you again, my lord.'

'Again? I do not remember having met you before.'

'It was eleven years ago, at New Temple. You came with his majesty,

King Henry, to a meeting with Humbert de Pairaud. I was bearing the shield of my master, Owein ap Gwyn.'

'That was you?' Edward smiled. 'I'm afraid I do not recall faces too well, but I suppose I did have other things on my mind that day.' His smile faded a little and Will caught a brief flash of what might have been irritation cross his face.

Up close, the prince was very different to how Will remembered him. He'd had poise then, but the refinement of youth had hardened into a shrewder, self-possessed adulthood. His eyelid still drooped like his father's, but he appeared to be compensating for the defect by opening the eye a little wider than the other. This gave him a permanently arched brow that lent him a slightly mocking expression. Standing there, head held high, his gaze cool and unwavering, he already looked like the king he would be. When he spoke, he addressed them all.

'My father has not had the kind of relationship he would have liked with the Temple these past years. Unlike his uncle, Richard, he hasn't found it so easy to accommodate the Order's autonomy in his lands. I am glad to have been given this opportunity to follow in the footsteps of the first Guardian of this council and I hope that relations between the Order and the English crown can become as civilised as they once were under his reign.'

'Your devotion to our cause is most welcome, my Lord Prince,' said the Seneschal, as Will pulled up a stool and sat beside the Portuguese priest, who gave him a wary smile. The Seneschal looked around at the gathering. 'Shall we bring this meeting to order?'

'Yes, brother,' replied Everard, 'we have much to discuss. Although, I believe our Guardian has an announcement of his own that he wishes to make before we become too embroiled in the details. My liege?'

Edward nodded. 'When Father Everard told me of the aims of your circle, I believed that I could help you achieve your goal. Baybars shows no sign of discontinuing his campaign against our forces and if we continue to lose territory at the rate we have been you will no longer have a base from which to continue your work. Therefore, we must act swiftly.' The prince paused to let his words sink in. 'Peace,' continued Edward intently, 'is not simply an ideal; it is our only hope for survival. I have been in talks this past week with a select number of nobles, including your Grand Master and the Master of the Hospitallers, and I have managed to convince them to support me in my proposal. Of course, they know nothing of my dealings with yourselves. I intend to approach Baybars with the offer of a truce.' He held up his hand. 'Obviously, even if it is agreed, it is doubtful that it will be the end of the fight, but the Anima Templi will have a firmer foundation from which to continue its plans for reconciliation and we will all be able to preserve the lands we still possess.'

'A truce? With Baybars?' questioned the Seneschal. 'I cannot imagine him agreeing to it.'

'One thing that may help to sway him is the Mongol Empire. Upon my arrival I sent ambassadors to the Ilkhan of Persia, Abagha, to ask for his aid in countering the threat posed by Baybars. My ambassadors have since returned from his court with news that the Mongols are interested in an alliance between our nations. The Mongols may be able to bolster the garrisons we still hold and Baybars might be dissuaded from further attacks if we present a united front against him. I now plan to persuade the Ilkhan to send a small force from Anatolia to threaten the Mamluks' northern strongholds. I myself will travel south to attack several holdings there. I know you do not want war, but, in the short term, such an action may be our only hope. Casualties would be few, if any. The attacks would be staged to prove to Baybars that, as a combined force, we could pose a problem to him. This, I believe, would make him more willing to accept any truce we offer.'

Will, watching the prince, couldn't help but be impressed by the man's energy. He had never met anyone so self-assured. When Edward spoke, men listened. He was dynamic. Everard, Will noticed, had a smug smile playing about his thin lips. The priest obviously felt he had made the right choice. The others seemed to think so too, murmuring their approval. So why, Will had to ask himself, did he not trust the prince.

As the meeting continued, other members adding their thoughts and questioning Edward on the details of the proposal, Will watched the prince for any sign that could explain his distrust. He saw none; the prince was civil and attentive, but that flash of irritation he had glimpsed in Edward's face stuck in his mind. It wasn't the look itself; more that he felt Edward had been wearing a mask that had slipped, just for a moment, but long enough to reveal a second face beneath that unruffled exterior.

When the meeting was done, the two younger knights and the priest left. The Seneschal and the older knights remained. Will, too, lingered as the prince crossed to Everard.

'I'm pleased that you came to me with this position, Father Everard,' said Edward.

'As am I,' replied Everard. 'I believe we can do much for one another.'

'There is just one last matter. We discussed it briefly the other day. I wonder, did you come to a conclusion?'

'Ah, of course. My answer is yes.'

Edward smiled. 'Thank you, you have no idea how pleased this will make my father.' He opened his cloak and took a pouch from his belt, which he handed to Everard. 'This covers part of the debt. As I said, I will hand over the rest when I return to England.'

'I will write to the Visitor in Paris. He will arrange it.'

'I would be grateful if I could have a receipt for this transaction.'

'Certainly,' replied Everard. 'I will send someone to fetch one for you.'

'No need, brother,' said the Seneschal, standing. 'I need to make an inspection of the cells this afternoon. I can escort the prince on my way to the treasury tower.'

'Cells?' said Edward. 'Do you have many prisoners here?'

'Just three at present.' The Seneschal opened the door. 'It is unfortunate that we have to punish our brothers, but discipline is the backbone of our Order. Without it we would be crippled.'

The Seneschal shot Will a black look as they left the chamber, the prince pulling a hood over his head to hide his face.

'You made the right decision.'

Will turned at Everard's voice. 'What?'

'To stay. I truly believe we have a chance to change things.' The priest smiled, his eyes shining. 'What do you think of his plan?'

'Effective, if it works. What was that he gave you?' Will pointed to the pouch in Everard's hand.

'Part of the debt King Henry still owes us.' Everard looked at the pouch. 'A small part, granted, but it's a start.' He stuffed the pouch in his robes. 'I will need you to write to Visitor de Pairaud in Paris.'

'Hugues? What do you want me to say?' Will hadn't seen Hugues de Pairaud since he left Paris, although he knew Robert kept up some correspondence with their old comrade, who had been made Visitor of the Kingdom of France upon the death of the predecessor.

'I want you to issue him an order to deliver the English crown jewels to King Henry in London.'

'Under whose authority?' said Will, astonished.

'You'll sign it as Grand Master Bérard,' replied Everard, heading for the door.

Will shook his head. 'Discipline?' he muttered beneath his breath.

'Make sure you do it today, William,' said the priest, before he disappeared, 'we have more important things to be getting on with.'

Garin put the bowl to his lips and drained the dregs of the thin soup, which had a few strands of uncooked rice floating in it; a cook's afterthought. He held it out to the guard.

'Thank you, Thomas.'

Thomas nodded and took it from him. 'I'm sorry it's not too good, sir, but you know them upstairs won't let anything but scraps come down here.'

'I was a sergeant once. I ate scraps then.' Garin gave a shrug. 'It's not so bad.' He smiled. 'But another drop of that wine might help it go down?'

Thomas glanced warily at the cell's open door. 'I'm sorry, sir,' he whispered, shaking his head. 'I can't do that for you today. The Seneschal is coming, you see, for an inspection. If he knew I'd been giving you my rations, he'd—'

'It's all right,' Garin cut across him, 'I won't say anything. I'll drink it quick.'

Thomas rose, still shaking his head. 'Not today, sir.' He left hurriedly and shut the door.

Garin let his head fall back against the wall as the timber beam thudded into place. He swore tiredly. Without the wine, the moments were much longer. He wondered if he might be able to cajole some later when the inspection was over, but that would depend on who was on duty. Some of the guards, like Thomas, were sensitive to his situation, even calling him Sir, although Garin hated that last courtesy. It felt more mocking in some ways than *filth* or *turd*, the appellations favoured by others who revelled in the chance to humiliate a fallen superior, themselves being sergeants of low birth who would never rise to the rank of knight.

Garin had quickly learnt to hide his dignity and pride, not just from those who wanted to strip him of both, but also from himself. If the guards opened the door when he was taking his toilet, he wouldn't flinch, but forced himself to continue. When they slopped his food onto the floor and told him he could eat it like a dog, he would say thank you and eat it all the same. He had told himself that he could cope with it all for so long that he almost believed it himself. But asleep, when he dreamed of things beyond the walls and woke with the memory of colours and places he had forgotten, he came close to the brink and, sometimes, fell into the abyss he teetered over each day.

Garin raised his head as he heard muffled voices outside. He quickly put his chin to his chest and closed his eyes. The Seneschal was fond of sermons and it paid to be asleep for his visits. The door opened.

'Knock when you're done, sir,' Garin heard Thomas say.

The guard sounded shaken. As the door shut, Garin's heart sank; the Seneschal obviously wasn't going to be foiled by sleep today. He could feel a presence in the room; the almost imperceptible softness of breath; the faint odour of something sweet, wine or fruit perhaps that the man had had for lunch. He waited for the Seneschal to wake him with a kick, but the man just seemed to be standing there. Garin opened his eyes a crack and was surprised to see the hems of a set of black robes in front of him. He thought for a moment that they must belong to a priest, but then he saw that they weren't made of rough wool, but black velvet. They were fringed with a delicate trim of rabbit fur. Garin looked up in puzzlement, not bothering to pretend to be stirring from his feigned slumber. His heart gave a violent leap in his chest as he met the cool gaze of Prince Edward.

'God!' he said involuntarily.

'Not quite,' said Edward. He crouched down before the chained and filthy knight, whose face was scarred with lesions from the leonardie and whose eyes were wide with terror. 'Although I have been known to send men to hell when they displease me, as you might remember, Garin.'

'How did you . . .?' Garin's voice broke and he couldn't finish the question.

Edward understood. 'It was easy for my agents to discover where you were. You know how talkative servants can be. I simply waited for an opportunity to be invited here.'

'What do you want?' whispered Garin, looking past Edward to the door, wondering if Thomas would come if he shouted.

Edward followed his gaze. 'We won't be interrupted. The Seneschal was very amenable to my coming down here to inspect his errant charges.' He laughed. 'Perhaps offer them a few words of wisdom, extol the benefits of sincere repentance, that sort of thing.' His laughter faded. 'As for what I want, I did want to know what happened to the book you were sent here to retrieve for me, but since I have discovered that it has been destroyed, I would like to know where my manservant, Rook, is.'

Garin experienced a flare of hatred at that name; a name he had buried so deep inside himself he had almost forgotten it. The strength of his vitriol overwhelmed some of his fear. 'I killed the bastard!' he spat at Edward. 'I riddled him with holes so numerous his own mother wouldn't have recognised him!'

Edward's eyes narrowed in anger, but the emotion vanished quickly as he recovered his poise. 'Yes, I thought something fatal must have had happened to him when he didn't return. He was a very obedient man.'

'He was a malignant little toad,' growled Garin. 'He threatened to kill my mother. He did kill my——' He cut off abruptly and closed his eyes.

'I admit, Rook's methods were occasionally vulgar, but he always got the job done. That's all I ever ask of my servants. You know that, Garin.'

Garin swallowed back his bitterness and the rest of his fear and made himself meet Edward's gaze. 'Yes, I betrayed you and killed your servant. But I was left with nothing when I finished working for you. What is it you want to take from me now?'

'When you were in my service you were well rewarded. It was your choice to leave all that for . . .' Edward swept a hand around the dank cell. '. . . this.'

'No. I was left with nothing *because* I chose to work for you. My uncle, my friends in the Temple, Adela, my freedom. I've lost everything. I have nothing left. So if you've come here to kill me, then do it. If not, get out.'

Edward looked mildly surprised by Garin's bellicosity. 'If you have nothing more to lose,' he said after a pause, 'then I would think you would have everything to gain.'

'What do you mean?' muttered Garin.

'The Anima Templi,' said Edward, his manner now curt, businesslike, 'the group your uncle was involved in; I have just been appointed its Guardian.'

'What?' Garin felt his tiny world, already reeling with Edward's arrival, slip further out from under him.

'Everard de Troyes came to me some weeks ago with the invitation. He felt I could be of some assistance to his cause.' Edward laughed. 'The crown jewels will be returned to my family and I will be crowned with them when I am king. I now have influence in the Temple, influence I can use to ensure that the Order will never attempt to control me like they controlled my weak-minded fool of a father.' Edward's eyes were hard as stones, glittering with contempt. His face was adamant, implacable. Edward had many facades, but this was the prince at his most genuine. And his most terrifying. Naked ambition came off him like heat.

Garin had seen that same focused ruthlessness in the prince's eyes when he had worked for him briefly in London. But now it was sharper, more well defined, like his face. 'Then you have what you wanted?' he murmured. 'They just gave you what you wanted all along?'

'When I take the throne it will be mine, not the Temple's,' Edward continued, hardly hearing Garin. 'I have plans to expand my kingdom in the coming years. Through my position of power within the Anima Templi I will be able to use the Temple's vast resources to help me achieve that. They will not use *me*.' His eyes focused on Garin again. 'Other than that, I have no interest in the plans of the Anima Templi. Their aims are unrealistic and unChristian.' His brow furrowed. 'Indeed, they go against everything our society is founded upon; against God. In time, when I have taken what I want from them, I will see to their demise. But for now I will let them continue with their foolishness for they will not succeed and it will keep them busy and out of my affairs. Once I have secured my proposed truce with Sultan Baybars, I shall leave Everard and his callow minions to struggle futilely for their utopia, whilst I use the men and money they have at their disposal for my own purposes. I doubt that they will complain. I do, after all, now know their secrets. Secrets that, as we both know, they would not want divulged to the wider world.'

'You're making a truce with Baybars?' said Garin, feeling sick to his stomach.

'Of course. It will give our forces a chance to re-group and re-establish the war against the infidel. I did not come here to make peace. I came here to fulfil the dream of Christendom. The truce will only be temporary. When our forces are gathered, we will strike back at the Saracens with all our might.' Edward's handsome face was flushed with triumph. 'We will take back Jerusalem and cleanse its streets like we did the first time we set foot upon these shores. We will, once again, be the guardians of the Holy City in a land that belongs rightfully to us.'

Garin closed his eyes. 'Then you would have only had to wait and it would have all come to you anyway. I needn't have done anything?'

'But none of us knew that,' replied Edward solemnly. 'Not then.' He paused, his voice softening. 'I can always use men like you Garin.'

'No,' murmured Garin, feeling the last of his strength failing and the abyss yawning beneath him. 'Please. Just go.'

'I can get you out of here, get you pardoned. You could go back to England and see your mother again.'

Garin's eyes fluttered open. 'My mother?'

'She hasn't been well these past few years.'

'You . . . you've seen her?'

Edward nodded gravely. 'She's still living in that damp little house in Rochester. You could give her the life she always wanted.'

'Why would you do this?'

'Because I know you better than you know yourself.'

Garin tried to fight back his tears. 'No, you don't. I've changed.'

'You and me, Garin, we are alike. I saw that when I first met you. We both know what we want: power, wealth, land, status. But unlike other men, all of whom crave such things, we go out and we take it for ourselves, rather than dwindle in the dirt and deny our desires. I believe we are the more honest of men for it.'

Garin shook his head. 'The Temple will never let me back in. The Seneschal is one of the Brethren. He would see me dead before I was ever given the mantle again. They know I tried to take the Book of the Grail.'

'You don't have to be a Templar to help me. Like I said, when I take the throne I wish to expand my kingdom. I will need assistance in other areas in future and, quite frankly, your talents are wasted in this cell.' Edward rose, his height even more imposing to Garin, huddled on the floor. 'I can see that you are tired. I'll leave you to think on it. I will remain in Acre until the truce with Baybars is secured, then I will return to the West to gather support for a new Crusade. I'm sure you can get a message to me when you've made up your mind.' He went to the door and knocked. As the beam was raised on the other side, he glanced down at Garin's toilet bucket. 'And you might want to ask them to get rid of that for you, the smell is really quite appalling.'

Garin just managed to wait until the door was shut, before he broke down.

45
Aleppo, Syria
10 February 1272 AD

B aybars sat back in his chair, watching Baraka Khan study the papers that were laid out on the table. His son's brow was puckered in concentration, jaw jutting. The corners of the papers lifted in the breeze that came in through the arched windows. Baybars reached for his goblet of kumiz and drained it. A servant stepped from the shadows to refill the goblet as Baybars set it down, then moved back out of sight. Through the windows drifted the sounds of men working on the citadel's gates, which had been damaged four months ago when the Mongols had attacked the city.

In October, a touman, sent by the Ilkhan of Persia, had descended from Anatolia and had entered the city, defeating the garrison Baybars had left in place when he had travelled with the larger part of his army to Damascus to lead several raids against Frankish strongholds in the south. The Mongols had taken the citadel, causing widespread panic, although the horsemen had done little in the way of damage and had taken very few lives. But when the ten thousand-strong force of horsemen had continued the raid south of Aleppo and panic among the local Muslim population had swelled to fear, Baybars had sent his army north to counter them. The touman, far outnumbered, had retreated to Anatolia.

Whilst the Mongols were attacking from the north, a company of Franks, led by an English prince by the name of Edward, a man Baybars had heard much mention of in recent months, had conducted a raid in the southern regions around the Plain of Sharon. The raid had proved fruitless, but Baybars had been given the distinct impression that the prince was not to be underestimated. King Louis' Crusade may have come to nothing, but the king's brother, Charles de Anjou, was an uncle of Edward's and although Baybars had had relatively cordial contact with the Sicilian king in the past, he had seen, in these two men, the threat of a new Crusade.

Khadir, too, had seen it, and had warned him to tread carefully where the prince was concerned.

'He might be young,' the soothsayer had muttered, 'but he has a lion in him. I see it.'

'Or you hear it in my court,' Baybars had responded dryly.

'He is like you, master,' Khadir had murmured with sly subtlety, 'when you were younger.'

Baybars drained the rest of the kumiz and looked up as Baraka sighed heavily. 'Are you finished?'

'I cannot do it!' snapped Baraka, throwing his quill to the floor, splattering the tiles with ink. 'Sinjar sets me problems he knows I will not be able to solve.'

'He does that so you will learn,' responded Baybars wearily.

'Can I finish it tomorrow, father?' said Baraka, turning in his chair to look at Baybars. 'I wanted to go on the hunt this afternoon. Kalawun said he would take me.'

'You can go when you have finished your lessons.'

'But, father . . .'

'You heard me!' snapped Baybars, slamming his goblet on the table.

Baraka started at the violence in his father's tone, then turned back to the papers that were covered with algebraic problems, his lower lip puffing in a sullen pout.

'Am I disturbing you, my lord?'

Baraka and Baybars both turned at the voice to see Kalawun standing in the doorway. He was almost as tall as the apex of the arch. His dark hair, which was turning silver around his brow, was slicked back in a tail, making his strong features appear even sharper and he wore a cloak of royal blue – the colour of his regiment.

'Amir Kalawun!' exclaimed Baraka, leaping up. He went over and grabbed the commander's large hand. 'Come, sit with me. Help me with my lessons.'

Kalawun smiled down at the boy. 'I am sure you are doing well enough on your own.'

'I'm not,' said Baraka, pouting again, 'but only because Sinjar's lessons are stupid.'

'He is a good teacher,' responded Kalawun gently. 'You should value him. He taught me Arabic when I was first enlisted in the Mamluk army.'

Baraka dropped his hand from Kalawun's and looked moodily at the floor. Suddenly, he brightened. 'You will take me on the hunt like you promised?'

'If,' said Kalawun, glancing at Baybars, 'your father agrees.'

'Please, father,' pleaded Baraka.

'Take your work to Sinjar and finish it with him, I want to speak with Kalawun alone.'

Baraka went to protest, then strode over to the table and picked up his work. He turned on his heel and headed for the doors.

'Your quill,' Kalawun called after him.

'The servants can fetch me another,' said Baraka sourly. 'That is what they are there for.'

Kalawun watched him go, then turned to Baybars. 'You summoned me, my lord?'

Baybars rose wearily from his chair and crossed to a large chest. 'It seems, these days, that my son likes you better than he does me,' he said, glancing at Kalawun as he opened the lid and withdrew a silver scrollcase.

'It is easier for him to like me, my lord. I do not have to be the one to discipline him.'

Baybars handed him the case, then sat.

Opening it, Kalawun pulled out a rolled piece of parchment. 'The Franks wish to make a truce with you,' he murmured, reading the words on the parchment. He looked up from the scroll. 'When did you receive this?'

'Yesterday.'

'Have you told anyone of this?'

Baybars shook his head. 'You are the first.'

'It is signed by the King of Sicily.'

'Yes, as he says in the letter, Charles de Anjou offered to mediate between myself and the Franks when he learnt of Prince Edward's intentions. I presume he believes our former favourable relations will help to sweeten the proposition.'

'They do not want much,' said Kalawun, scanning the letter again. 'Nothing more than to keep what they already have.'

'No doubt because they mean it to be only temporary. If the Franks wanted to end this war they would go home. They would not stay and make bargains with me.'

'The Mongols,' said Kalawun, after a pause, 'pose more of a threat to us than the Franks. We have taken much of what the Franks once owned and they can muster no great force of arms to oppose us in the immediate future. Even if they mean the peace to be temporary, it may be in our best interests to accept.'

'Peace,' said Baybars in a low voice, 'was never my intention with the

Franks. I told Omar that we would never be cleansed of the West's influence if we showed them the kind of mercy Saladin once did, if we were open to negotiation with them.' He rose and crossed to the window.

'Compromise,' said Kalawun carefully, 'is sometimes needed for the good of our people. We shouldn't divide our forces against two allied armies, even when one is so weak; not when we have been offered this reprieve.'

'Good?' murmured Baybars. 'I can no longer see what is good. Not since Omar . . .' He closed his eyes. 'Not since he died.'

It was six months since Baybars had buried the officer. The two Assassins had been unceremoniously burned, along with their handcart. The real puppeteers who had been due to perform at the betrothal feast had been found at a lodging house in the city. Judging by the decomposition of the corpses, they had been dead for some time; long enough for the Assassins to have practised their performance. Baybars had all but annihilated the Order since then, but although revenge had been served, it hadn't filled the space left at his side by Omar's death; a void that had become more engulfing as the months had gone by. Sometimes, he would summon Omar, only to be nervously reminded by the servants that the officer was gone.

'I did not realise how much I valued him. I don't think I ever told him.' Baybars opened his eyes. 'I miss his counsel.'

'What do you believe Omar would have suggested if he were here, my lord?' Kalawun asked him.

Baybars smiled slightly. 'He would have advised me to accept. He was a warrior, but in his heart, he could not abide war. He tried to hide it from me, but it was as plain as his face.' His smile vanished. 'And you, Kalawun? You would suggest the same?'

'I would, my lord.'

Baybars was silent for some time. Finally, he turned from the window. 'So be it,' he said in a hard tone. 'Send the Franks at Acre my agreement. I will give them their peace. For now.'

That evening, Baybars left the citadel and walked into the city, dressed in a dark cloak and turban. Following him at a discreet distance, were two Bahri warriors. Each carried a torch.

When he reached the barn, Baybars ordered the two warriors to remain outside and went in alone. The last few times he had come here, he had found signs of occupation. Children, he had guessed, by the charcoal drawings on the floor. The hibiscus petals that had collected in a dusty pile with each of his visits had been scattered. He did not bring a flower for her this evening, but knelt empty-handed on the dry earth. He closed his eyes and saw her as she had been, thirty years ago. Age and war hadn't touched her. She was still sixteen, as she always would be, her skin smooth and unlined, her hair glossy black. She was laughing, flicking water from a pail to splash his bare chest, marked with recent whip lines, as he chopped wood in the barn. He had been laughing too, until he had seen the shadow in the doorway. He did not know how long their master had been standing there, watching them.

Baybars opened his eyes and the image remained; the red cross on the knight's white mantle imprinted like a brand upon his vision. He touched his fingers to his lips, then pressed them to the earth. 'I must rest a while, love, before I finish what I started. I am tired. So very tired.'

Baybars lingered a while longer, then rose and went outside. 'Burn it down,' he said to the two Bahri who were waiting there. He paused to detach a flower from the hibiscus bush outside, then walked away. Behind him, the flames took hold.

46

The Temple, Acre

15 May 1272 AD

♏

E verard was sitting at his worktable, sharpening the end of a quill with a small knife. His brow was knotted, his impaired eyes straining to focus on the delicate task. He didn't look up as Will entered the solar. 'Did you get them?'

As Will placed the leather pouch he was carrying on the table, the priest made one decisive scrape with the knife, then set down the quill. Everard pulled open the pouch, pushing the soft dark leather down into folds. The sunlight coming through the window glittered richly off the handful of stones inside: cinnabar, agate, malachite, lapis lazuli. 'Beautiful. They'll make inks to last a thousand years.' Everard looked up at Will as he drew the pouch shut. 'I can powder them down tomorrow. Thank you. I would have gone to the market myself, only . . .' He stood stiffly and took the pouch over to his armoire. '. . . I hardly find the strength to rise from my bed these days.'

'I want to go to Caesarea, Everard.'

'What?' Everard turned.

'I want to take the treaty.'

Everard stowed the pouch on a shelf and closed the armoire. 'How did you hear of it? It hasn't been announced yet.'

'Robert de Paris was asked to go.'

Everard shook his head. 'Well, no matter how you heard, it is out of the question.'

'Why?' asked Will, his voice calm, but slightly flat as he tried to keep his need disguised.

Everard arched a brow. 'I think you know why. You hired Assassins to kill the man, for goodness' sake!'

'It's because of that that I want to go.'

'Because you failed the first time?' Everard's tone was sardonic, but worry was plain in his face. He made a flicking movement with his withered hand as if to swat the problem or Will away. 'And anyway, the company who will take the peace treaty to Baybars has already been chosen.'

'I know you can talk to Edward, get him to request me on this mission. You can tell him you want a member of the Anima Templi to go. Besides, I'm one of only a few men here who can speak Arabic.' Will continued quickly as the priest started to shake his head. 'I want to make it right, Everard. I want to prove to you that I meant what I said before, that day on the battlements when you told me about Kalawun. I do want to stay, to be a part of this work, the work my father began.'

'I know, I know,' said Everard, as if it didn't need saying.

'Then why have you had me running around playing the errand boy ever since, rather than working on the tasks you've set the other Brethren?'

Everard glanced at Will, but didn't speak.

'Because you don't trust me,' Will answered for him.

'That isn't true.'

'It is,' countered Will. 'And I don't blame you. But it's been six months, Everard! I want to help but I'm sitting around here wasting time. If you do not want me as one of the Brethren then dismiss me, but if you do then let me prove myself to you. Let me make amends for what I did.'

After a moment Everard gave a small nod.

Will's hope leapt, then sank again as the priest continued.

'You are right. I have kept you from certain tasks because of what you did, but not to punish you. I was merely being cautious. But this mission would not only bring you face to face with a man you wanted dead so desperately that you betrayed everyone and everything to which you had ever sworn an oath of loyalty to achieve it, it will also take you into danger. You know how many men we have sent to treat with Baybars over the years, and how few have returned. He may well use this opportunity to prove how little our peace means to him, slit all your throats and send back your heads in a basket!' Everard sat back down in his chair. 'And as much as you have driven me towards an early grave over the years, I actually like your head where it is, William.'

'I don't believe the sultan would do that,' replied Will. 'It would be petty. And whatever else Baybars is, petty he isn't. But either way, I want to do this.' Will's voice was still calm, but need was creeping into his tone. 'I've never asked you for anything else, Everard, not for myself. But I'm asking you now, let me do this.'

Everard picked up the quill and the knife, then put them back down with an irritated sigh. 'You swear to me you will not do anything foolish?' He shook his head quickly before Will could answer. 'No, not swear to me, swear on your father's name!'

'I swear it, Everard.' Will held his gaze. 'I won't let you down again.'

After a long pause, Everard nodded.

The stables were sweltering, the air clotted with trapped heat and the smell of dung. Simon was heaving sacks of precious oats up to the hayloft. Every so often he would shake off the flies that droned persistently around his head, causing sweat to drip from his nose and brow. His muscles were aching and his cheeks, already ruddy from the sun, were mottled an even deeper red with the exertion. Setting down a sack, he bent to pick up a jar of water from the floor.

'Simon?'

The voice made him straighten so quickly that he banged his head on a manger. With a curse, he dropped the jar, which broke apart, and he spun round, one hand clasped to his head.

In the entrance, silhouetted by the white light outside, was a tall woman with copper-gold hair. Simon had recognised her voice even before he had turned, but it was still a shock to see her standing there, solid and tangible, in her rose-coloured gown. She was a sight he had both longed for and dreaded every day of the last four years.

'I got your letter,' said Elwen. She looked older, calmer.

'I didn't think you would come.'

'Neither did I. Not for a long time. But I always wanted to see the Holy Land.'

Wiping his hands on his tunic, Simon went tentatively over to her. 'How did you get here?'

'On a merchant's ship.'

'The queen let you leave?'

'It was at Queen Marguerite's bidding that I left. After King Louis' body was brought back to Paris and we buried him in Saint-Denis, the palace became a place of mourning. Many of the other servants left because they couldn't bear to live there without him. I decided to stay. When I got your letter I tore it up,' Elwen shrugged, 'but I kept the pieces. I don't know why. The queen found them one day and made me tell her what it meant.'

Simon blushed to think that the queen knew his secret.

'She said I should go,' continued Elwen. 'She said I shouldn't waste an opportunity to find love because there are too few of them in life as it is. I don't know if that is what I have here; Will's a knight and I know he can't . . .' Elwen faltered. 'I just wanted to tell you that I got your message.' Her green eyes studied him for a long moment. 'And that I understand why you did what you did.'

Simon looked away. 'Do you want to see Will?' he said quietly.

'He's here? I didn't know if . . .' Elwen took a breath and nodded. 'I think so. Yes,' she added, with greater conviction. 'Yes, I do.' She glanced over her shoulder towards the main gate, where several sergeants were standing sentry. 'But I had best not draw too much attention to myself. The guards only let me in because I said I was the Grand Master's niece.' She grinned suddenly and Simon caught a glimpse of the mischievous girl who had stowed away on board the *Endurance* all those years ago.

'Right.' He looked around the stables, which were deserted. Most of the sergeants were in the Great Hall for the midday meal, although they would be finished any time now. Simon headed over to the storehold, where the saddles and tack were kept. 'You can hide in here if you like?' He opened the door. 'I can go and find Will for . . .' His voice cracked and he had to cough to clear the thickness in his throat. 'I can bring him to you.'

As Simon spoke, Elwen watched him shuffle awkwardly, his thick, muscled arms hanging stiff by his sides, fists bunched, eyes downward, unable to meet hers. In his face she saw the dispute between his words and his feelings. She felt like a thief. 'Thank you,' she said softly, hoping that was enough.

Will was heading from the knights' quarters when he saw Simon trudging across the yard. The groom glanced in his direction, came to a stop, then half raised his hand. Four young sergeants ran across the gap between them, laughing. When they had passed, Will saw the groom's expression. He crossed the yard, which was gradually filling with men and boys, the midday meal having ended. 'What's wrong?'

'Nothing,' replied Simon quickly, relaxing his face.

Will raised an eyebrow. 'By the look on you I'd say someone had just died.'

Simon made a valiant attempt at a smile. 'No. Everything's fine. It's . . . well I just had a bit of a surprise is all.'

'A surprise?'

'Will.'

They both turned to see Robert heading towards them. His fine blond hair, swept back in a tail, was bleached almost as white as his mantle.

Robert nodded to Simon, then grasped Will's shoulder companionably. 'Did you speak to Everard?'

'I did.'

'And?'

'He agreed to talk to Edward.'

'Good,' said Robert, grinning. 'Then we face the Crossbow together.'

'Will,' murmured Simon. 'We need to go.'

Will glanced at him distractedly. 'Just tell me what it is.'

Simon went to speak, then shook his head. 'I think it's best you see for yourself.'

Turning, he moved back the way he had come.

Will smiled bemusedly at Robert. 'I think he's been working in the sun too long. I'll talk to you in a minute.'

Robert nodded. 'I'll be in the armoury.'

'Wait then,' called Will, following the groom.

Simon didn't slow, but kept on walking towards the stable yard.

As they approached the stables, Will came to a stop. 'Simon,' he said, lightly, but firmly, when the groom went to head inside.

Simon turned.

'I don't have time for games. Tell me what this is about. I've got things to do.'

'Just come in here a moment,' insisted Simon, disappearing inside.

Will sighed irritably, but followed him in. Simon was standing by the storehold, his face, shadowed in the oppressive gloom, unreadable. He opened the door, then stepped away. Will, frowning now, made uneasy by his friend's odd manner, walked forwards. He stopped dead in the doorway, as the woman inside turned to face him. Thin shafts of sun slanted through cracks in the back wall, catching her in a fragile web of gold. Will's mouth dried up and with it the thousand words that burst into his mind demanding to be shouted out at once. After the initial flood of exclamations and rushing, tumbling thoughts, just one word remained. He said it in a strange, calm voice that didn't sound like his own.

'Elwen.'

She smiled slightly. 'Hello, Will Campbell.'

Will took a step towards her, not noticing Simon shutting the door quietly behind him.

Silence descended. And with every second that slipped by it stretched out, encompassing them. The confined, sun-shot room, which smelt overpoweringly of leather and dung, seemed to expand and become the whole world. The feeling was so intense, Will started to feel dizzy. He realised he hadn't taken a breath, or taken his eyes off Elwen since he had entered the place. He moved and looked away from her, and his surroundings seemed to diminish and come back into focus.

'How are you?' said Elwen, watching him.

Will shook his head. 'Fine.' He shook his head again, then glanced at her. 'And you?'

'I am well.'

Will suddenly stepped forwards, his eyes fixing on hers. 'Elwen, I never meant to leave like that. I never meant anything to change the way it did, for any of it to happen. Any of it,' he repeated firmly.

'Why did you leave then?' she answered, her tone changing, becoming serious, accusatory. 'Why were you with . . .?' She stopped, looked away, then met his gaze quickly, fiercely. 'Why were you with that girl?'

Will gave a drawn-out sigh. He rubbed at his forehead. 'Do you remember the book Everard asked you to take for him?'

'The one I took from the troubadour? Of course.'

'And do you remember I had to go after someone who had stolen it from us?'

'Yes,' she murmured, 'you told me when we met at the palace. When you asked me to be your wife.'

Will studied the floor. 'That evening, when Everard and I were getting ready to leave, Garin de Lyons sent me a letter, pretending it was from you. In it, he asked me to meet him at that tavern.' Will shrugged helplessly. 'I went there thinking I was going to meet you. I was captured by a man who wanted the book for himself. They made me tell them where it was and Garin drugged me, put me on the bed in that room and left me there.'

'Garin?' said Elwen, her brow furrowed in confusion and anger. Simon had told her very little in the letter, only that he had lied to her, having known Will was drugged. 'Why would he do that?'

'He was forced to do it by the man who captured me.' Will shook his head. 'It doesn't really matter; that man is dead and Garin is in prison, all I need you to know is that I wasn't there willingly.'

'And the girl? How could you have let her do that? You must have been able to stop her. She was only young and you're . . .'

'Let her do it?' Will interrupted. 'I didn't *let* her do anything.' His voice was hard, cold. He paused, checked his anger, and spoke again. 'I was drugged. I didn't know what was happening. I can only recall part of it.' He frowned, as if either trying to remember or to close his mind to the memory. 'I think for a time I thought she was you. The sleeping draught and the fact that I had gone there to meet you, it just made me think that. Then, when I realised it wasn't you, I was paralysed. I couldn't even speak.'

Elwen nodded slowly. 'If all that is true, why did you not explain it to me? Why did you leave and never come back?' Her eyes filled with tears and she turned away abruptly.

Will wanted to go to her, but couldn't. 'The next morning, as soon as I knew what had happened I wanted to see you, but Everard stopped me. I . . . I don't know why I listened to him. I don't really remember. I think I was confused still. He told me about Garin and I . . .'

'You wanted revenge more than you wanted me,' she said, turning back to face him. But her tone was now matter-of-fact, rather than accusatory.

'I can't explain what it was like,' said Will slowly. 'What it felt like to have that choice taken away from me. How it felt to be speechless, helpless. I felt as though I had been tainted by something . . . as though something diseased and wrong had crawled inside me. I couldn't have lived like that, Elwen. When we went after Garin, I fell ill. We were in Orléans for three months. I almost died. By the time I was well again, Garin and the book had gone to the Holy Land, Simon had found us a ship to leave on and I just knew, however much I wanted to return to you, that I had to finish it. I had to take my choice back.'

'Why didn't you write?' she said after a long moment.

'I tried. I started a hundred letters. I couldn't finish any of them. Then time just went and I thought you would be married and have a family, that you would be happy. I didn't want to hurt you, or intrude on a life I knew nothing about. And I was scared,' he finished lamely, and then, quietly, 'I was a fool.'

'Yes, you were.' Elwen pressed her lips together, then smiled. The expression surprised him. 'Do remember how we used to talk about the Holy Land when we were young?'

Will nodded morosely.

Elwen's smile broadened. 'When I was a girl, living in the palace in Paris, I used to dream we would go there together. When the fog came in on winter days, I would close my eyes and imagine us standing on some warm marbled balcony of a golden palace, the walls and floors adorned with jewels, the bluest sea imaginable stretching before us.' Elwen had half closed her eyes. 'You wore the cloak of a knight and polished armour and I wore a white silk gown. You took me in your arms and told me you loved me. I went to sleep on that dream for years.' Elwen spread her arms to encompass the cramped, smelly storehold, with its straw-littered floor and cracked, cobwebbed walls. She laughed. It was a gentle rushing sound, not mocking, nor bitter.

Will looked at her, a smile tugging at his own mouth. He tried to press it back, then it broke across his face and he was laughing with her. Then, without either of them seeming to move, she was in his arms. And they were giggling and sobbing and clutching each other. Finally, they broke away, each embarrassed by the outburst.

'I don't even know how you got here,' said Will.

'It's a long story,' she said, wiping her eyes with the back of her hand, 'and one for another day. In short, I came with a merchant. A Venetian.'

'Do you have somewhere to stay?'

'Yes, with him.' Elwen caught Will's look and smiled. 'He is a supplier to the royal household in Paris. At Queen Marguerite's request he offered me work and lodgings here. He has a cloth factory in the Venetian Quarter. He's a good man, and his wife is a good woman. They have three daughters I get on well with.'

Will smiled. Outside, a bell clanged. He glanced round. 'I wish we could talk for longer, but . . .'

'I know,' she cut across him, 'I've got to go. I understand.'

'No, you don't. Elwen, listen, I might have to go away. It will only be for a few days, I hope. But it is just something I have to do. I'm sorry.'

Elwen nodded.

'After that,' Will continued, 'we can talk some more.' He looked down at his mantle. 'I don't know what we . . . or even if we . . .'

Elwen stopped him with a finger to her lips. 'There's no need to say anything. We don't have to think about any of this yet. It's still so strange to be here. I need time too.' She went to slip past him, then paused, rose onto her toes and kissed his cheek. 'I will see you when you return.'

Will remained alone for some time after she had gone, his cheek seeming to burn where she had touched him.

47

The Temple, Acre

20 May 1272 AD

'**B**e careful with it. My signature is barely dry.'

Will took the leather scrollcase Prince Edward held out to him. He eased it into his saddlebag and pulled the strap tight, feeling a profound sense of weight bearing down on him. Everard had done more than request his presence in the company; he had asked the prince to let Will lead it.

'Are you sure we are sending enough men, my Lord Prince?'

Edward turned to the Grand Master of the Hospital. 'We aren't expecting a fight, Master de Revel.'

'We don't know that, my lord. And even if Baybars plans to honour this agreement, it is a two-day ride to Caesarea. Bedouin use the road. They may think to attack such a small party in the hope of plunder.'

'It is doubtful,' came the deep voice of Thomas Bérard, the Templar Grand Master. Edward and Hugues de Revel turned as he approached. 'Besides, brother,' he added, addressing the Hospitaller Master, 'we don't want to appear too belligerent. This is a peace treaty, after all.'

Hugues de Revel pursed his lips, but gave a curt nod. 'I was merely being cautious, brother. We don't want anything to go wrong with this.'

The three men looked at Will.

Will inclined his head. 'And nothing will, my lords.'

The Templar and Hospitaller Grand Masters looked satisfied and turned away to talk with the other dignitaries from Acre's government who had come to oversee the company's departure.

Edward lingered for a moment. 'Good luck, Campbell,' he said after a pause.

Will watched the prince sweep off to his three royal knights, who were readying their horses.

Edward's plan to secure peace in the Holy Land had so far gone more smoothly than anyone could have expected. He was also, Will knew, responsible for Garin's release from prison. After four years in the cell, the knight had been freed without warning three days ago. He had come to find Will to say goodbye, before leaving by the servants' entrance, pale, subdued and banished from the Temple forever. When Will had asked Everard what had made him change his mind, the priest had replied, our Guardian. It seemed, when Edward had visited Garin in the cell, that he had been moved to pity by his plight. Some months after this visit, he had spoken with Everard and the Seneschal and, when he had discovered the reasons for Garin's imprisonment, had offered to take Garin back to England with him. The knight, the prince had told them, would aid him, in a purely secretarial post, with his work for the Anima Templi. It would be hard work and he would be granted little freedom, but he would, the prince had said, at least have the chance to use his knowledge to benefit the Brethren, rather than rotting uselessly in a cell. Following the prince's plea, Everard, who had, for some time, been implored by Will to reconsider the harsh punishment, had eventually relented.

But although there seemed no reason for Will to doubt the prince's motives, something about Edward still made him uneasy, like the faint hint of smoke in a forest, or an ambiguous shadow on a wall.

'William.'

Will looked round to see Everard shuffling over, his cowl pulled over his head despite the heat of the day.

'Keep it safe,' murmured the priest, nodding to the saddlebag.

'I will.'

'You hold the hope of us all.'

Will was surprised to see tears in Everard's bloodshot eyes. The priest's wizened face was anxious. 'Perhaps I should go with you?' he said, glancing at the knights gathered in the yard, tying water skins to belts, adjusting helmets and swords. Along with Edward's men, there were six Templars, four Hospitallers and three Teutonic Knights going with Will to Caesarea: a show both of strength and unity that demonstrated that with this covenant they spoke for all of Christendom.

'Everard,' said Will firmly, 'I will make sure it gets there. I promise you.'

The priest's lined face creased in a smile. 'I know, William. I know.' He stepped back as Will climbed up into the saddle and trotted the horse over to Robert de Paris and the other Templars. Robert was talking with Simon.

Simon smiled as Will approached. 'I found you one of these,' he said, holding up a water skin.

'I already have one,' said Will patting the skin that was tied to his saddlebag.

'Right,' said Simon, nodding, 'of course you have.'

'But there's no harm in taking two,' said Will, as the groom turned away. 'Here,' he said, offering his hand. 'Pass it up.'

As Will tied the skin beside the other, Simon puffed out his cheeks and hooked his thumbs in his belt. 'Well, good luck then.'

Will laughed and rolled his eyes. 'Why is everyone acting as if we're not coming back?' He looked at Robert. 'It doesn't inspire confidence, does it?'

'I didn't mean it like that,' protested Simon.

Will smiled. 'We'll see you in a few days.'

Caesarea, 22 May 1272 AD

The city of Caesarea was a wasteland. The rubble of broken buildings lay scattered and the tall arches of the cathedral rose into the sky and stopped abruptly, the domed roof they once supported gone. Soot and sand and dust had blown down empty streets, through colonnades and inside houses, covering everything in a layer of powdery grey.

Baybars, looking down from the hillside at the product of one of his campaigns, felt the city's emptiness like a pressure inside him. He turned to Kalawun, who was mounted beside him. 'We'll make camp inside the city. Send in the scouts to make sure we are the first to arrive, then post guards at the entrances. We'll flank them as they come in.'

'Yes, my lord.'

'Kalawun.' Baybars paused, his eyes drawn back to Caesarea.

'My lord?'

Baybars' gaze focused on him. 'When they arrive, you will meet them. Have guards secure the others and bring the leader to me, alone.' His voice roughened. 'We must be careful, Kalawun. The Franks are all but finished in these lands. One more push and they will be gone for good. But a cornered beast is one to be wary of. They may see this as another opportunity to strike at me directly.' His eyes hardened at the reminder of the Assassins' attempt on his life. 'Make certain that does not happen.'

'Of course, my lord.'

It was early evening when Will and the knights approached the ruined city. The sun had turned the jagged rooftops and arches amber and, beyond, the sea broke against the shoreline with constant rushing sighs. Seabirds wheeled overhead, agitated by the trespassing knights. The men were silent as they entered the city's crumbled walls, their horses' hooves loud in the quiet. To Will, it felt like they were entering a tomb or a church, somewhere hallowed where the sound of human voices was irreverent.

'We're signing a treaty of peace here?' murmured Robert.

Will didn't answer. To him, Caesarea seemed like the best place to sign one. This is what was, it said. And the scroll in his saddlebag answered, this is what could be.

'We're not alone,' said one of Edward's men in a low voice.

As the knight spoke, a flash of gold caught Will's eye. Mounted on a war horse, in a gap between two half-disintegrated buildings, was a Mamluk warrior. He wore the uniform of the Bahri, Baybars' royal guard. The knights kept riding cautiously past the warrior, who regarded them dispassionately. After a few moments, Will glanced over his shoulder and saw that the warrior had come out from between the buildings. Will felt a thrill of fear as four more mounted soldiers emerged from a street opposite to join him.

'Up there,' murmured Robert, nodding to a rooftop that looked down on the street ahead.

Standing there, a bow, fixed with an arrow, in his hands, was another Mamluk. The warrior's loaded bow followed the knights as they moved under his shadow. There was a crunching of hooves on shattered stone as two more soldiers moved out of an alley.

'What are they doing?' growled one of the Hospitallers. He had his hand curled tight around the hilt of his sword.

'Herding us,' muttered a Templar, as four Mamluks appeared ahead, blocking their path.

The knights drew closer together, most had now drawn weapons, but the four soldiers in front of them made no move to intercept them, and simply watched as they approached.

'I think they want us to go this way,' said Will, as the company came to a crossroads. To their left a wide, rubble-strewn avenue stretched down towards the cathedral, the severed arches of which were stained red by the sun, which was sinking into the sea's dark horizon. Inside the skeletal frame of the cathedral, the rest of the Mamluks had made camp. Will could make out horses, wagons and many men, maybe a hundred or more, moving around the bright plumes of fire made by torches. 'Come on,' he said quietly to the others, steering his horse down the empty avenue, as the Mamluks followed.

Will had felt tense and restless when Everard had told him he would lead the party, a feeling which had continued up until the company had left the safety of Acre's walls. But, oddly, as they had ridden out into enemy lands, his nerves had dissipated and he had calmed. It had felt good to be on the road, to be moving towards something so definitive, so significant. It had also given him time to think of Elwen, and the private, languid moments he had allowed himself for those thoughts had kept his mind from his destination. But now, caught in the dead city's oppressive hush, with the erratic cries of birds and the silence of the soldiers who followed them, he felt a deepening sense of dread pushing down on their little company from all sides.

He thought of his father's fate at the hands of these men and of Everard's warnings that he had dismissed so assuredly. He thought of Elwen. The image of her face filled his mind and he made the decision that whatever else happened tonight, he would survive. But as the Mamluk soldiers moved in behind them and the distance between their company and the small army of men inside the cathedral closed, his mind mocked him for a fool.

The knights approached the cathedral and a group of seven Mamluks came riding out to meet them. At their head was a tall man, dressed in the robes and armour of a man of rank. The group stopped a short distance away and the tall man dismounted. Will's party came to a halt as he walked towards them.

'Trapped,' said one of the Templars, looking round at the line of Mamluks blocking the street, barely ten, twelve yards behind them.

Will dismounted and opened the saddlebag. Robert jumped down beside him as the tall man came to a stop a little way from them.

'*Assalaamu aleikum*,' Will called, facing the man, hoping his years of translating Arabic treatises made his vocabulary comprehensible. 'My name is William Campbell, I have come to meet with Sultan Baybars on behalf of Prince Edward of England and the government of Acre.'

The tall man smiled at Will's awkward pronunciation, but his amusement seemed benevolent rather than mocking. '*Wa-aleikum assalaam*, William Campbell,' he replied, speaking slowly so that Will could follow him. 'I am Amir Kalawun. You have the treaty?' He frowned when Will didn't answer and repeated the question.

'I do,' replied Will, studying the man keenly.

'Come with me. Your men can wait here.'

'What does he say?' asked one of Edward's guards of Will.

When Will told them, Robert shook his head. 'No. Tell him that's unacceptable. We must come with you.'

Will didn't take his eyes off Kalawun. The Mamluk commander, although imposing in his physique, had a calm about him and a subtle intelligence in his brown eyes. A diplomat, thought Will, in the body of a warrior. He found it an interesting mix. 'It's all right,' he said to Robert. 'I'll go alone. I don't think we have a choice.'

Kalawun raised his palm as Will approached. 'You must leave your sword here.'

Will hesitated, then unfastened his sword belt and placed the falchion in the dust.

'Walk towards me,' said Kalawun calmly. 'Lift your arms.' He patted his hands down Will's sides and around his hips, checking for any concealed weapons.

'You knew my father,' said Will quietly, as Kalawun checked inside his sleeve. 'James Campbell. Everard de Troyes has told me of you.'

Kalawun stopped, his hands around Will's wrist. He glanced at the Bahri guards behind him, but they were well out of earshot. 'I cannot claim to have known him,' he said, checking Will's other sleeve. 'We never met face to face. It would have been too dangerous for me to do so. But I felt as though I knew him.'

'I am continuing with my father's work,' said Will beneath his breath.

'Then perhaps we will meet again, William Campbell.' Kalawun stepped back. 'For now, let us take your treaty to the sultan.' He went to turn away, then paused. 'Be careful,' he murmured. 'Sultan Baybars has no love of your people, especially your Order, and he is wary following a recent attempt by the Assassins on his life, an attempt he believes to have been instigated by the Franks. Make no sudden movements and only speak if spoken to. His guards have orders to kill you if they suspect you mean him harm.'

Will's insides churned uneasily as he walked with Kalawun down the long avenue into the torch-lit camp, passing scores and scores of men, and banners emblazoned with crescent moons and stars. The red cross on his mantle seemed to blaze like a beacon, commanding all their eyes to look upon him, making him feel horribly conspicuous.

Inside the cathedral, on what would have been the choir, now just a raised bed of cracked stone, was set a throne, its arms capped with two gold lions. Crumbled steps led up to it and the remaining two walls that framed it were rent in places with giant fissures, through which Will could see the sea. On the throne, erect and resplendent in brocaded gold robes and glimmering ornate armour, sat Baybars Bundukdari, the Crossbow, Sultan of Egypt and Syria, and the murderer of his father.

There was a hissing sound as Will and Kalawun came towards the steps. Will saw a tattered figure in grey robes hunched by the steps to the side of the choir, watching him with glaring white eyes and bared teeth. Behind the figure were five Bahri warriors, all of whom had crossbows trained on Will.

'You may approach the sultan,' said Kalawun at his side, making him start slightly.

Will did so, cautiously, his eyes respectfully downcast. His heart was drumming rapidly in his chest. When he reached the top step he bowed, then raised his head.

It was with a jolt that Will met the sharp blue eyes of Baybars, one of which had an odd gleam in it, caused by a white, star-shaped defect. As he stared into those eyes, a voice in his mind began chanting: *this man killed your father, you tried to kill this man.* The words sounded so clear and certain that for one terrible second Will thought he had said them out loud.

He was only feet away from the man who had ordered his father's death, from the man the Assassins had tried and failed to kill. Will imagined reaching out, wrapping his hands around Baybars' throat. Squeezing. He knew he would be dead before he touched the sultan, riddled with crossbow bolts. But it wasn't that that stopped him. The image caused distaste to rise in him. Something that, only last year, he had dreamed fervently, constantly of, now seemed inapt, petty even. His need for revenge was truly dead. The realisation surprised him.

All this whirled through Will's mind in a matter of seconds, and then he was leaning forwards, holding out the peace treaty.

Baybars didn't move. Will hesitated, then retracted his arm slightly.

After a lengthy pause, during which he scrutinised Will acutely, Baybars finally spoke, his Arabic deep and rich. 'What is your name, Christian?'

'William Campbell.'

Moments crawled by, filled with the rushing and dragging of the sea, before Baybars spoke again. 'You have a treaty for me, William Campbell?'

Will passed over the scroll, feeling every eye in the cathedral on him. As Baybars took the case, their fingers touched briefly, skin grazing skin. The sultan opened it and unfurled the two scrolls that were rolled inside. He studied each closely, then gestured to a man wearing a green silk robe and a jewelled turban, who was standing to one side with a small group of others, similarly dressed. Will guessed they were advisors. The man walked over, took the scrolls, read them, then passed them back to Baybars with a nod. Another came forward, holding a glass tray upon which were a small phial and a quill. Will waited as the sultan signed the skins, then Baybars handed one scroll and the case back to him.

And there it was, a treaty of peace to last for ten years, ten months, ten days and ten hours, granting the Franks possession of the lands they still held and use of the pilgrim road to Nazareth.

Everyone seemed to relax as Baybars sat back and Will slid the scroll back inside the case.

Will heard a voice behind him. 'Come,' said Kalawun, who had climbed the steps. 'I will escort you back to your men.'

Will didn't move, but remained standing there, staring at the sultan. The crossbowmen tensed. Will felt Kalawun place a warning hand on his shoulder.

Baybars frowned and leaned forwards, his eyes narrowing in suspicion.

Will spoke quickly. 'My Lord Sultan, I wish to be granted permission to travel unhindered to the fortress of Safed. My father was killed there during the siege and I wish to bury him and pay my respects. I know I have no right to ask this of you and that you have no cause to grant it, but . . .' He faltered, his confidence slipping, his tongue awkward around the foreign words. 'But I have to ask.'

Out of the corner of his eye, Will noticed guards and advisors exchanging a mixture of surprised, amused and scornful glances. Beside him, Kalawun seemed to stiffen.

Baybars seemed to study Will with renewed interest for a few moments. Then he nodded. 'I will grant your request,' he said into the quiet. 'But you will go without your men and will be guarded by mine.' Without taking his eyes off Will, he gestured to two of the crossbowmen, who lowered their weapons and came forwards. 'Take him to Safed,' he said. 'Then escort him back to Acre.'

'Thank you,' Will murmured.

'We are finished here,' replied Baybars, leaning back in his throne and grasping the lions' heads. 'You may go.'

Turning, Will walked from the throne, down the steps and out of the cathedral, his whole body humming with the release of tension.

Outside, it was almost fully dark and a yellow silver of moon was hanging above the city.

'That was a foolish thing to do,' said Kalawun quietly, as they neared the waiting company of knights, the two Bahri Baybars had chosen to escort Will following behind.

'I had to do it,' said Will, pausing to collect his falchion from the street where he had left it.

'I understand.' Kalawun inclined his head. 'Peace be with you, William Campbell.'

'And with you.'

Kalawun walked away down the street.

'Did he sign it?'

Will turned as Robert came up behind him. 'He did. I need you to make sure the treaty is taken safe to Acre.'

'What do you mean?' Robert asked, frowning. 'Where are you going?'

Will smiled as he handed Robert the scrollcase. 'To lay a ghost to rest.'

AUTHOR'S NOTE

I was aware from the initial concept for the novel, five years ago, that I wanted to tell the story of the Crusades from both the East and West's points of view. The real men behind the enduring myths attached to the Templars fascinated me, but so too did the extraordinary rise of the Mamluk warrior, Baybars, who remains, in the Middle East, a hero to this day.

In the writing of the novel, I tried to remain as faithful to real events, characters and period detail as I could without sacrificing pace or plot, with the result that, at times, the novel is rooted in fact, at times it is pure imagination and, occasionally, it is a mixture of the two. Events at Ayn Jalut, Safed and Antioch, for instance, probably happened much as I have described them. The Anima Templi is my own invention, although I loosely based Everard's Book of the Grail on a thirteenth-century Grail Romance, the *Perlesvaus*, an anonymous work filled with unorthodox imagery, thought, by some, to have been written by a Templar. Likewise, the attack on the Templar company at Honfleur is fiction, but King Henry III was forced to pawn the English crown jewels to the Order because of debts he was unable to pay.

For period detail I relied on over one hundred sources, most purely factual, some slightly more fantastical, many contradictory, all illuminating. But those I relied most heavily upon deserve a mention as they were invaluable and are certainly worth a read for anyone wishing to know more on this incredible period, the surface of which I have only been able to scratch at. These works are Steven Runciman's stunning trilogy *A History of the Crusades* [Cambridge University Press]; *The Templars*, Piers Paul Read [Weidenfeld & Nicolson]; *The Knights Templar: A New History*, Helen Nicholson [Sutton Publishing]; *The Wars of the Crusades*, Terence Wise [Osprey Publishing Ltd]; *The Cross and the Crescent: A History of the Crusades*,

Malcolm Billings [BBC Publications]; *The Trial of the Templars*, Malcolm
Barber [Cambridge University Press], and *History of Medieval Life: A Guide to
Life from 1000 to 1500AD*, David Nicolle [Chancellor Press].

I am grateful to have been granted permission to reproduce two lines
from *The Song of Roland*, translated by Dorothy L. Sayers, Penguin Books,
1957. I must also credit historian Malcolm Barber, author of *The Trial of the
Templars*, from which I have taken two quotes of Bernard de Clairvaux, and
in which appears a translation of an eyewitness account of a Templar
initiation which proved invaluable when it came to my own portrayal of the
Order's inceptions.

Robyn Young. August 2005.

GLOSSARY

ACRE: a city on the coast of Palestine, conquered by the Arabs in 640 AD. It was captured by the Crusaders in the early twelfth century and became the principal port of the new Latin Kingdom of Jerusalem. Acre was ruled by a king, but by the mid-thirteenth century royal authority was disputed by the local Frankish nobles and from this time the city, with its twenty-seven separate quarters, was largely governed oligarchically.

AMIR: Arabic for commander, also used as a title for some rulers.

ASSASSINS: an extremist sect founded in Persia in the eleventh century. The Assassins were adherents of the Ismaili division of the Shi'ah Muslim faith and, over the following years, spread to several countries including Syria. Here, under their most famous leader, Sinan, 'the Old Man of the Mountain', they formed an independent state, where they retained control until they were eventually subsumed into the Mamluk territories controlled by Baybars.

AYYUBIDS: dynastic rulers of Egypt and Syria during the twelfth and thirteenth centuries, responsible for the creation of the Mamluk (slave) army. Saladin was of this line and during his reign the Ayyubids achieved the height of their power. The last Ayyubid was Turanshah, who was killed by Baybars under the orders of the Mamluk commander Aibek, ending the Ayyubid dynasty and beginning the reign of the Mamluks.

BERNARD DE CLAIRVAUX, St: (1090–1153) Abbot and founder of the Cistercian monastery at Clairvaux in France. An early supporter of the Templars, Bernard aided the Order in the creation of their Rule.

BEZANT: a gold coin of the medieval period, first minted in Byzantium.

CALIPH: title given to the rulers, civil and religious, of the Muslim community, considered to be Muhammad's successors. The Caliphate was abolished in 1924 by the Turks.

CRUSADES: a European movement of the medieval period, spurred by economic, religious and political ideals. The First Crusade was preached in 1095 by Pope Urban II at Clermont in France. The call to Crusade came initially as a response to appeals from the Greek emperor in Byzantium whose domains were being invaded by the Seljuk Turks, who had captured Jerusalem in 1071. The Roman and Greek Orthodox Churches had been divided since 1054 and Urban saw in this plea the chance to reunite the two Churches and, in so doing, gain Catholicism a firmer hold over the Eastern world. Urban's goal was achieved only briefly and imperfectly in the wake of the Fourth Crusade of 1204. Over two centuries more than eleven Crusades to the Holy Land were launched from Europe's shores.

DESTRIER: Old French for war horse.

DOMINICANS: the Order, whose rule was based on that of St Augustine, was founded in 1215 by Dominic de Guzman in France. Guzman, who promoted an austere, evangelical style of Catholicism, used the new Order to aid the Church in eradicating the Cathar heretics. In England they were known as the Black Friars, in France the Jacobins. The Dominicans, who continued to grow rapidly after Guzman's death, eschewed the luxuries enjoyed by many in the priesthood and were highly educated. In 1233 they were chosen by the Pope to root out heretics and official inquisitors were appointed. By 1252, inquisitors were permitted to use torture to obtain confessions and many Dominicans became active members of this newly established institution which would become known as the Inquisition.

ENCEINTE: fortifications enclosing a castle.

FRANKS: in the Middle East the term Franks (*al-Firinjah*) referred to Western Christians. In the West, it was the name of the Germanic tribe that conquered Gaul in the sixth century, which thereafter became known as France.

GRAND MASTER: head of a military Order. The Grand Master of the Templars was elected for life by a council of Templar officials and until the end of the Crusades was based at the Order's headquarters in Palestine.

GRAIL ROMANCE: a popular cycle of romances prevalent during the twelfth and thirteenth centuries, the first of which was *Joseph d' Arimathie* written by Robert de Borron at the end of the twelfth century. From this time, the Grail, the concept of which is thought to be derived from pre-Christian mythology, was Christianised and adopted into the Arthurian legend, made famous by the twelfth-century French poet, Chrétien de Troyes, whose work influenced later writers such as Malory and Tennyson. The following century saw many more takes on the Grail theme, including Wolfram von Eschenbach's *Parzival*, which inspired Wagner's opera. Romances were courtly stories, usually composed in verse in the vernacular, which combined historical, mythical and religious themes.

GREAVES: armour worn to protect the shins.

GREEK FIRE: invented in Byzantium in the seventh century, Greek fire was a mixture of pitch, sulphur and naphtha that was used in warfare to set fire to ships and fortifications.

JIHAD: meaning 'to strive', *Jihad* can be interpreted in both a physical and spiritual sense. In the physical it means holy war in the defence of and for the spread of Islam, in the spiritual it is the inner struggle of individual Muslims against worldly temptations.

KINGDOM OF JERUSALEM: the Latin Kingdom of Jerusalem was founded in 1099, following the capture of Jerusalem by the First Crusade. Its first ruler was Godfrey de Bouillon, a Frankish count. Jerusalem itself became the new Crusader capital, but was lost and regained several times over the following two centuries until it was finally reclaimed by the Muslims in 1244, whereupon the city of Acre became the Crusaders' capital. Three other states were formed by the Western invaders during the early Crusades: the Principality of Antioch, and the Counties of Edessa and Tripoli. Edessa was lost in 1144, captured by the Seljuk leader, Zengi. The Principality of Antioch fell to Baybars in 1268, Tripoli fell in 1289, and Acre, the last principal city held by the Crusaders, fell in 1291, signalling the end of the Kingdom of Jerusalem and of Western power in the Middle East.

KNIGHTS OF ST JOHN: Order founded in the late eleventh century that takes its name from the hospital of St John the Baptist in Jerusalem, where it had its first headquarters. Also known as the Hospitallers, their initial brief was the care of Christian pilgrims, but after the First Crusade their objectives changed dramatically. They retained their hospitals, but their primary preoccupation became the building and the defence of their castles in the Holy Land, recruitment of knights and the acquisition of land and property. They enjoyed similar power and status as the Templars and the Orders were often rivals. After the end of the Crusades, the Knights of St John moved their headquarters to Rhodes, then later to Malta, where they became known as the Knights of Malta.

KNIGHTS TEMPLAR: order of knights formed early in the twelfth century after the First Crusade. Established by Hugues de Payns, who travelled to Jerusalem with eight fellow French knights, the Order was named after the Temple of Solomon where they had their first headquarters. The Templars, who were formally recognised in 1128 at the Council of Troyes, followed both a religious rule and a strict military code. Their initial *raison d'être* was to protect Christian pilgrims in the Holy Land, however, they far exceeded this early brief in their military and mercantile endeavours both in the Middle East and throughout Europe, where they rose to become one of the wealthiest and most powerful organisations of their day. There were three separate classes within the Order: sergeants, priests and knights, but only knights, who took the three monastic vows of chastity, poverty and obedience, were permitted to wear the distinctive white habits which bore a splayed red cross.

LEONARDIE: an unknown disease whose symptoms were similar to those of scurvy, including severe lethargy, the peeling or wasting of the skin and hair loss. Richard the Lionheart is said to have suffered from it.

MADRASAH: a religious school dedicated to the study of Islamic law.

MAMLUKS: from the Arabic, meaning 'slave', the name was given to the royal bodyguard, mainly of Turkish descent, bought and raised by the Ayyubid sultans of Egypt into a standing army of devout Muslim warriors. Known in their day as 'the Templars of Islam', the Mamluks achieved ascendancy in 1250 when they assassinated Sultan Turanshah, a nephew of Saladin, and took control of Egypt. Under Baybars, the Mamluk empire grew to encompass Egypt and Syria, and they were ultimately responsible for removing Frankish influence in the Middle East. After the end of the Crusades in 1291, the Mamluks' reign continued until they were overthrown by the Ottoman Turks in 1517.

MARITIME REPUBLICS: Italian mercantile city-states of Venice, Genoa and Pisa.

MARSHAL: in the Templar hierarchy, the chief military official.

MONGOLS: nomadic tribespeople who lived around the steppes of eastern Asia until the late twelfth century when they were united under Genghis Khan, who established his capital at Karakorum and set out on a series of massive conquests. When Genghis Khan died, his empire extended across Asia, Persia, southern Russia and China. The Mongols' first great defeat came at the hands of Baybars and Kutuz at Ayn Jalut in 1260, and their empire began a gradual decline in the fourteenth century.

OUTREMER: French word meaning 'overseas', referring to the Holy Land.

PALFREY: a light horse used for normal riding.

PARLEY: a discussion to debate points of a dispute, most commonly the terms of a truce.

PRECEPTORY: Latin name for the administrative houses of military Orders, which would have been like manors, with domestic quarters, workshops and usually a chapel.

QUINTAIN: a precision training device used for jousting practice, consisting of a wooden frame mounted on a pole, which the knight would strike at with his lance, or a ring hung from a cord which the knight had to snare on the lance's tip.

RICHARD the LIONHEART: (1157–99) Son of Henry II and Eleanor of Aquitaine, Richard ruled as king of England from 1189 to his death in 1199, but spent very little time in the kingdom. Along with Frederick Barbarossa and Philip II of France, he led the Third Crusade to recapture Jerusalem, which had fallen to Saladin.

RULE, THE: the Rule of the Temple was drawn up in 1129, with the aid of St Bernard de Clairvaux, at the Council of Troyes, where the Temple was formally recognised. It was written as part religious rule, part military code and set out how members of the Order should live and conduct themselves during their daily lives and during combat. The Rule was added to over the years and by the thirteenth century there were over six hundred clauses, some more serious than others, the breaching of which would mean expulsion for the offender.

SADEEK: Arabic, meaning 'friend' (male).

SALADIN: (1138–93) Of Kurdish origin, he became sultan of Egypt and Syria in 1173, after winning several power struggles. Saladin led his army against the Crusaders at Hattin and dealt the Franks a devastating blow. He reclaimed most of the Kingdom of Jerusalem created by the Christians during the First Crusade, leading to the launch of the Third Crusade, which saw him pitted against Richard the Lionheart. Saladin was a hero throughout the Islamic East, but was also admired, and feared, by the Crusaders, for his courage and gallantry.

SARACEN: in the medieval period, a term used by Europeans for all Arabs and Muslims.

SENESCHAL: the steward or chief official of an estate. In the Temple's hierarchy, the Seneschal held one of the highest positions.

SIEGE ENGINE: any machine used to attack fortifications during sieges.

SHI'AH & SUNNI MUSLIMS: two branches of Islam formed in the schism that arose after the death of Muhammad over the question of who should be his successor. The Sunnis, forming the majority, believed that no one could truly succeed Muhammad and appointed a caliph as leader of the Muslim community. Sunnis revere the first four caliphs appointed after Muhammad's death, whose example they follow as the custom (*sunna*) that all Muslims should follow. Shi'ahs hold as their figure of authority the *imam*, whom they consider heir of the Prophet, descended from the bloodline of Ali, Muhammad's son-in-law, the fourth caliph, and the only one they revere, rejecting the first three caliphs and the traditions of Sunni belief.

SURCOAT: a long linen or silk sleeveless garment, usually worn over mail or armour.

TAKE the CROSS: to go on Crusade, a term derived from the cloth crosses that were handed out to those who pledged to become Crusaders.

TEUTONIC KNIGHTS: military Order of knights, similar to the Templars and the Hospitallers, originating in Germany. The Teutonics were founded in 1198 and during their time in the Holy Land were responsible for guarding the area north-east of Acre. By the mid-thirteenth century they had conquered Prussia, which later became their base.

USCIERE: horse-carrier ship usually comprising two decks, one of which was capable of carrying up to 100 horses, the other of which was used for siege engines and wagons.

VAMBRACES: armour worn to protect the forearms.

VELLUM: parchment used for writing, most commonly taken from the skin of a calf.

VISITOR: a post within the Temple's hierarchy created in the thirteenth century. The Visitor, who was second only to the Grand Master, was the overlord of all the Temple's possessions in the West.

Don't miss the second book in the magnificent BRETHREN trilogy.

CRUSADE

After years of bloodshed, peace has finally come to the Holy Land. But, as Baybars retreats to Cairo, and the ambitious Prince Edward returns to England with plans of his own, there are those on both sides who begin to plot in the shadows . . .

. . . for a cause, for vengeance, for power, for profit.

For war.

To be published by Hodder & Stoughton in 2007.